**HARCOURT HORIZONS**

HARCOURT **HORIZONS**

# The Pledge of Allegiance

I pledge allegiance to the Flag

of the United States of America,

and to the Republic

for which it stands,

one Nation under God, indivisible,

with liberty and justice for all.

# ★★★★★★★★★★★★ HARCOURT HORIZONS

# United States History

 **Harcourt**

Orlando   Austin   Chicago   New York   Toronto   London   San Diego

Visit *The Learning Site!*
www.harcourtschool.com

# HARCOURT HORIZONS

## UNITED STATES HISTORY

## General Editor

**Dr. Michael J. Berson**
Associate Professor
Social Science Education
University of South Florida
Tampa, Florida

## Contributing Authors

**Dr. Robert P. Green, Jr.**
Professor
School of Education
Clemson University
Clemson, South Carolina

**Dr. Thomas M. McGowan**
Chairperson and Professor
Center for Curriculum and Instruction
University of Nebraska
Lincoln, Nebraska

**Dr. Linda Kerrigan Salvucci**
Associate Professor
Department of History
Trinity University
San Antonio, Texas

## Series Consultants

**Dr. Robert Bednarz**
Professor
Department of Geography
Texas A&M University
College Station, Texas

**Dr. Barbara Caffee**
Coordinator, K–12 Social Studies
Carrollton–Farmers Branch Independent
    School District
Carrollton, Texas

**Dr. Asa Grant Hilliard III**
Fuller E. Callaway Professor
    of Urban Education
Georgia State University
Atlanta, Georgia

**Dr. Thomas M. McGowan**
Chairperson and Professor
Center for Curriculum and Instruction
University of Nebraska
Lincoln, Nebraska

**Dr. John J. Patrick**
Professor of Education
Indiana University
Bloomington, Indiana

**Dr. Cinthia Salinas**
Assistant Professor
Department of Curriculum and Instruction
University of Texas at Austin
Austin, Texas

**Dr. Philip VanFossen**
Associate Professor,
    Social Studies Education,
    and Associate Director,
    Purdue Center for Economic Education
Purdue University
West Lafayette, Indiana

**Dr. Hallie Kay Yopp**
Professor
Department of Elementary, Bilingual, and
    Reading Education
California State University, Fullerton
Fullerton, California

## Content Reviewers

### United States Geography

**Dr. Phillip Bacon**
Professor Emeritus
Geography and Anthropology
University of Houston
Houston, Texas

### Native Americans and European Exploration

**Dr. Susan Deans-Smith**
Associate Professor
Department of History
University of Texas at Austin
Austin, Texas

**Dr. John Jeffries Martin**
Professor
Department of History
Trinity University
San Antonio, Texas

**Richard Nichols**
President
Richard Nichols and Associates
Fairview, New Mexico

### Early Settlement and the American Revolution

**Dr. John W. Johnson**
Professor and Head
Department of History
University of Northern Iowa
Cedar Falls, Iowa

**Dr. John P. Kaminski**
Director, Center for the Study of
    the American Constitution
Department of History
University of Wisconsin
Madison, Wisconsin

**Dr. Elizabeth Mancke**
Associate Professor of History
Department of History
University of Akron
Akron, Ohio

## The Constitution and United States Government

**Dr. James M. Banner, Jr.**
Historian
Washington, D.C.

**Carol Egbo**
Social Studies Consultant
Waterford Schools
Waterford, Michigan

**Dr. John P. Kaminski**
Director, Center for the Study of
 the American Constitution
Department of History
University of Wisconsin
Madison, Wisconsin

**Dr. John J. Patrick**
Professor of Education
Indiana University
Bloomington, Indiana

## The National Period and Westward Expansion

**Dr. Ross Frank**
Professor
Department of Ethnic Studies
University of California at San Diego
La Jolla, California

## Civil War and Reconstruction

**Dr. Judith Giesburg**
Assistant Professor
Department of History
Northern Arizona University
Flagstaff, Arizona

## The United States in the Twentieth Century

**Dr. Carol McKibben**
Visiting Professor
Monterey Institute of International Studies
Monterey, California

**Dr. Albert Raboteau**
Henry W. Putnam Professor
Department of Religion
Princeton University
Princeton, New Jersey

## Classroom Reviewers

**Kathleen Arseneau**
Teacher
St. Matthew's School
Kalispell, Montana

**Jane Blankenship**
Teacher
Prestonwood Elementary School
Dallas, Texas

**Portia F. Bohannon-Ramsey**
Teacher and Social Studies Chair
James E. McDade Classical School
Chicago, Illinois

**Judy S. Crawford**
Teacher
Settlers Way Elementary School
Sugar Land, Texas

**Lucille Ferragamo**
Teacher
A. C. Whelan Elementary School
Revere, Massachusetts

**Barbara Haack**
Teacher
Perkins Academy
Des Moines, Iowa

**Amy M. Krohn**
Teacher
Tombaugh Elementary School
Las Cruces, New Mexico

**Cindy Merchant**
Teacher
Denver Place School
Wilmington, Ohio

**Barbara Motzer**
Teacher
General Wayne Elementary School
Malvern, Pennsylvania

**Wendy Ogawa**
Schoolwide Coordinator
Wheeler Elementary School
Wahiawa, Hawaii

**Elma Schwartz**
Teacher
Ascarate Elementary School
El Paso, Texas

**Maps**
researched and prepared by

**Readers**
written and designed by

**Take a Field Trip**
video tour segments provided by

Acknowledgments appear in the back of this book.

Printed in the United States of America

ISBN 0-15-320182-7

4 5 6 7 8 9 10  048  10 09 08 07 06 05 04 03

# Contents

· UNIT ·

2

# Time of Encounters

· UNIT ·

# The English Colonies

· UNIT ·

# The American Revolution

## · UNIT · 5

# A New Nation

· UNIT ·

6

# Civil War Times

· UNIT ·

# 7

# The Twentieth Century

## · UNIT ·
## 8

# The United States and the World

# Reference

# Features You Can Use

# Science and Technology

# Charts, Graphs, and Diagrams

# Maps

# Time Lines

# Reading Your Textbook

## Getting Started

Your textbook is divided into eight units.

Each unit has a Unit Preview that gives facts about important events. The Preview also shows where and when those events took place.

Each unit begins with a song, poem, story, or other special reading selection.

Each unit is divided into chapters, and each chapter is divided into lessons.

## The Parts of a Lesson

This statement gives you the lesson's main idea. It tells you what to look for as you read.

This statement tells you why it is important to read the lesson.

These are the new vocabulary terms you will learn in the lesson.

Lesson title

This part of the time line shows the period when the events in the lesson took place.

Each new vocabulary term is highlighted in yellow and defined.

Each lesson is divided into several short sections.

**xvi**

General Braddock (above) and his troops panicked when the French and Indians fired on them from behind rocks and trees.

Each lesson, like each chapter and each unit, ends with a review. There may be a Summary Time Line that shows the order of the events covered in the lesson. Questions and a performance activity help you check your understanding of the lesson.

The British, trained to fight in open fields, had never fought an enemy this way. They "broke and ran," Washington later wrote, "as sheep before the hounds." When the battle ended, two-thirds of the British were dead or wounded. Braddock was one of those killed.

Braddock's loss left the British colonists in the Ohio Valley without protection. For the next two years, the French and their Indian allies carried out attacks against those colonists.

**REVIEW** What was a major cause of General Braddock's loss?

Each short section ends with a **REVIEW** question that will help you check whether you under-stand what you have read. Be sure to answer this question before you continue reading the lesson.

**LESSON 1 REVIEW**

Summary Time Line
1750 — 1755

1754
Fort Necessity is attacked
Albany Congress meets

1755
General Braddock
is defeated

1. **MAIN IDEA** How did conflicts over land lead to a war between Britain and France?

2. **WHY IT MATTERS** How do you think the outcome of the French and Indian War would affect the colonization of North America?

3. **VOCABULARY** Use the words **congress** and **delegate** in a sentence about the Albany Plan of Union.

4. **TIME LINE** Which event took place first, General Braddock's defeat or the attack on Fort Necessity?

5. **READING SKILL—Cause and Effect** What caused the French and Indian War?

6. **GEOGRAPHY** Where was the opening battle fought in the French and Indian War?

7. **HISTORY** What was George Washington's role in the French and Indian War?

8. **CRITICAL THINKING—Analyze** Why is the Albany Plan of Union important in American history?

**PERFORMANCE—Draw a Cartoon** Imagine that you have been asked to draw a cartoon different from the one Franklin published to show support for the Albany Plan of Union. Draw your cartoon and share it with a classmate.

272 ▪ Unit 4

## Skills

Your textbook has lessons that will help you build your reading, citizenship, chart and graph, and map and globe skills.

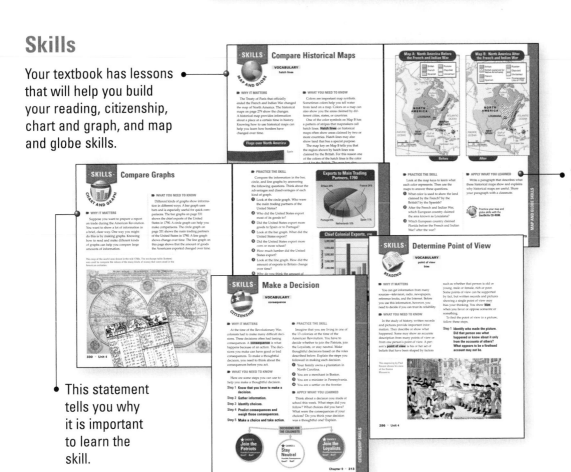

You will be able to practice and apply the skills you learn.

This statement tells you why it is important to learn the skill.

## Special Features

The feature called
Examine Primary
Sources shows
you ways to learn
about different kinds
of objects and
documents.

The Visit feature lets
you "visit" many
interesting places.

## Atlas

The Atlas provides maps
and a list of geography
terms with illustrations.

## For Your Reference

At the back of your textbook, you will find
the reference tools listed below.

- Almanac
- American Documents
- Biographical Dictionary
- Gazetteer
- Glossary
- Index

You can use these tools to look up words
and to find information about people,
places, and other topics.

# Atlas

# Read a Map

## VOCABULARY

| | | |
|---|---|---|
| map title | grid system | compass rose |
| map key | locator | cardinal directions |
| inset map | map scale | intermediate directions |

### ⟹ WHY IT MATTERS

Maps provide many kinds of information about the world around you. Knowing how to read maps is an important social studies skill.

### ⟹ WHAT YOU NEED TO KNOW

A map is a drawing that shows all of or part of the Earth on a flat surface. Mapmakers add certain features to most of the maps they draw.

Mapmakers sometimes need to show places marked on the map in greater detail or places that are beyond the area shown on the map. Find Alaska and Hawaii on the map of the United States on pages A10–A11. This map shows the location of those two states in relation to the rest of the country.

- A **map title** tells the subject of the map. It may also identify the kind of map.
  - Political maps show cities, states, and countries.
  - Physical maps show kinds of land and bodies of water.
  - Historical maps show parts of the world as they were in the past.

- A **map key**, or legend, explains the symbols used on a map. Symbols may be colors, patterns, lines, or other special marks.

- An **inset map** is a small map within a larger map.

**The United States**

Now find Alaska and Hawaii on the map below. To show this much detail for these states and the rest of the country on one map, the map would have to be much larger. Instead, Alaska and Hawaii are each shown in a separate **inset map**, or a small map within a larger map.

To help people find places on a map, mapmakers sometimes add lines that cross each other to form a pattern of squares called a **grid system**. Look at the map of the United States below. Around the grid are letters and numbers. The columns, which run up and down, have numbers. The rows, which run left and right, have letters. Each square on the map can be identified by its letter and number. For example, the

top row of squares in the map includes square A1, square A2, and square A3.

## ▶ PRACTICE THE SKILL

Use the map of the United States to answer the following questions.

**1** What city can be found in square D3?

**2** In which direction would you travel to go from Austin, Texas, to Richmond, Virginia?

**3** About how many miles is it from Richmond, Virginia, to Albany, New York?

**4** Which two oceans border Alaska?

## ▶ APPLY WHAT YOU LEARNED

Choose one of the maps in the Atlas. With a partner, identify the parts of the map and discuss what the map tells you. Ask each other questions that can be answered by reading the map.

• A locator is a small map or picture of a globe that shows where the place on the main map is located.

• A map scale compares a distance on the map to a distance in the real world. It helps you find the real distance between places on a map.

• A compass rose , or direction marker, shows directions.
  • The cardinal directions , or main directions, are north, south, east, and west.
  • The intermediate directions , or directions between the cardinal directions, are northeast, northwest, southeast, and southwest.

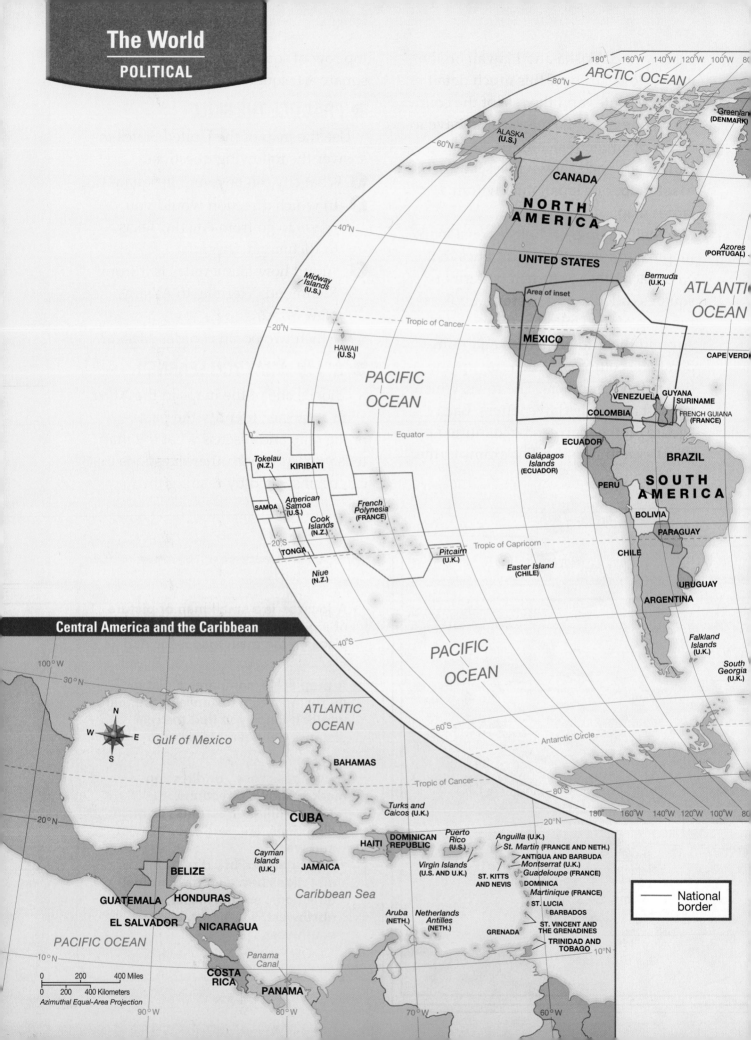

# The World

## POLITICAL

ARCTIC OCEAN

180° 160°W 140°W 120°W 100°W 80°

80°N

60°N

Greenland (DENMARK)

ALASKA (U.S.)

CANADA

NORTH AMERICA

40°N

UNITED STATES

Azores (PORTUGAL)

Bermuda (U.K.)

ATLANTIC

OCEAN

Midway Islands (U.S.)

Area of inset

20°N

Tropic of Cancer

MEXICO

CAPE VERDE

HAWAII (U.S.)

VENEZUELA

GUYANA SURINAME

PACIFIC

OCEAN

COLOMBIA

FRENCH GUIANA (FRANCE)

0°

Equator

ECUADOR

Galápagos Islands (ECUADOR)

BRAZIL

Tokelau (N.Z.)

KIRIBATI

PERU

SOUTH AMERICA

SAMOA

American Samoa (U.S.)

Cook Islands (N.Z.)

French Polynesia (FRANCE)

BOLIVIA

PARAGUAY

20°S

Tropic of Capricorn

CHILE

TONGA

Pitcairn (U.K.)

Easter Island (CHILE)

URUGUAY

Niue (N.Z.)

ARGENTINA

PACIFIC

OCEAN

Falkland Islands (U.K.)

40°S

South Georgia (U.K.)

## Central America and the Caribbean

100°W

30°N

ATLANTIC

OCEAN

60°S

Antarctic Circle

Gulf of Mexico

N
W E
S

180° 160°W 140°W 120°W 100°W 80°

80°S

BAHAMAS

Tropic of Cancer

20°N

20°N

CUBA

Turks and Caicos (U.K.)

Cayman Islands (U.K.)

HAITI

DOMINICAN REPUBLIC

Puerto Rico (U.S.)

Anguilla (U.K.)

St. Martin (FRANCE AND NETH.)

ANTIGUA AND BARBUDA

Montserrat (U.K.)

Guadeloupe (FRANCE)

10°N

BELIZE

JAMAICA

Virgin Islands (U.S. AND U.K.)

ST. KITTS AND NEVIS

DOMINICA

Martinique (FRANCE)

GUATEMALA

HONDURAS

Caribbean Sea

ST. LUCIA

BARBADOS

EL SALVADOR

NICARAGUA

Aruba (NETH.)

Netherlands Antilles (NETH.)

ST. VINCENT AND THE GRENADINES

PACIFIC OCEAN

GRENADA

TRINIDAD AND TOBAGO

10°N

Panama Canal

0 200 400 Miles
0 200 400 Kilometers
Azimuthal Equal-Area Projection

COSTA RICA

PANAMA

90°W

80°W

70°W

60°W

——— National border

ARCTIC OCEAN

40°W 20°W 0° 20°E 40°E 60°E 80°E 100°E 120°E 140°E 160°E 180°

80°N

Arctic Circle

60°N

ICELAND

Area of inset

RUSSIA

ASIA

EUROPE

KAZAKHSTAN

MONGOLIA

40°N

UZBEKISTAN

KYRGYZSTAN

NORTH KOREA

JAPAN

GEORGIA
ARMENIA
TURKEY

AZERBAIJAN

TURKMENISTAN TAJIKISTAN

CHINA

SOUTH KOREA

PACIFIC OCEAN

CYPRUS SYRIA
LEBANON
ISRAEL

IRAQ IRAN AFGHANISTAN

Canary Is.
(SPAIN)

MOROCCO

TUNISIA

JORDAN

KUWAIT

NEPAL

BHUTAN

TAIWAN

20°N

WESTERN SAHARA
(MOROCCO)

ALGERIA

LIBYA

EGYPT

BAHRAIN QATAR

SAUDI ARABIA

U.A.E.

PAKISTAN

BANGLADESH

MYANMAR (BURMA)

Northern Mariana Islands (U.S.)

OMAN

INDIA

LAOS

MARSHALL ISLANDS

MAURITANIA

MALI

NIGER CHAD

SUDAN

ERITREA YEMEN

THAILAND

VIETNAM

PHILIPPINES

Guam (U.S.)

SENEGAL

BURKINA FASO

DJIBOUTI

CAMBODIA

AFRICA

GUINEA
SIERRA LEONE

BENIN
CÔTE
D'IVOIRE

NIGERIA

CENTRAL AFRICAN REPUBLIC

ETHIOPIA

SRI LANKA

BRUNEI

PALAU

FEDERATED STATES OF MICRONESIA

LIBERIA

EQU.
GUINEA

CAMEROON

UGANDA

SOMALIA

MALDIVES

MALAYSIA

GUINEA-
BISSAU

GHANA
TOGO

GABON

REP.
CONGO

KENYA

THE GAMBIA

SÃO TOMÉ
AND PRÍNCIPE

RWANDA

SINGAPORE

INDONESIA

PAPUA NEW GUINEA

NAURU

CABINDA
(ANGOLA)

DEM. REP.
CONGO

BURUNDI

SEYCHELLES

INDIAN

EAST TIMOR

KIRIBATI

TANZANIA

TUVALU

ANGOLA

MALAWI

COMOROS

OCEAN

SOLOMON ISLANDS

ZAMBIA

MOZAMBIQUE

MADAGASCAR

VANUATU

FIJI

NAMIBIA

ZIMBABWE

MAURITIUS

New Caledonia (FRANCE)

20°S

BOTSWANA

ATLANTIC

SWAZILAND

AUSTRALIA

OCEAN

Reunion (FRANCE)

SOUTH AFRICA

LESOTHO

N
W E
S

0   1,000   2,000 Miles
0   1,000   2,000 Kilometers

Scale accurate at equator
Winkel Projection

NEW ZEALAND

40°S

Kerguelen Islands (FRANCE)

60°S

80°S

ANTARCTICA

40°W 20°W 0° 20°E 40°E 60°E 80°E 100°E 120°E 140°E 160°E 180°

## Abbreviations

| | |
|---|---|
| **DEM. REP. CONGO** | DEMOCRATIC REPUBLIC OF THE CONGO |
| **EQU. GUINEA** | EQUATORIAL GUINEA |
| **NETH.** | NETHERLANDS |
| **N.Z.** | NEW ZEALAND |
| **REP. CONGO** | REPUBLIC OF THE CONGO |
| **U.A.E.** | UNITED ARAB EMIRATES |
| **U.K.** | UNITED KINGDOM |
| **U.S.** | UNITED STATES |

Arctic Circle

FINLAND

60°N

NORWAY

ESTONIA

RUSSIA

SWEDEN

LATVIA

North Sea

Baltic Sea

LITHUANIA

UNITED KINGDOM

DENMARK

KALININGRAD (RUSSIA)

BELARUS

IRELAND

50°N

POLAND

NETHERLANDS

GERMANY

BELGIUM

CZECH REPUBLIC

UKRAINE

N
W E
S

ATLANTIC OCEAN

LUXEMBOURG

SLOVAKIA

MOLDOVA

LIECHTENSTEIN

AUSTRIA HUNGARY

ROMANIA

0   200   400 Miles
0   200   400 Kilometers

Azimuthal Equal-Area Projection

FRANCE

SWITZERLAND

SLOVENIA
CROATIA

40°N

SAN MARINO

BOSNIA AND HERZEGOVINA

YUGOSLAVIA

BULGARIA

Black Sea

ANDORRA

MONACO
Corsica
(FRANCE)

ITALY

MACEDONIA

TURKEY

ALBANIA

PORTUGAL

SPAIN

Balearic Islands (SPAIN)

VATICAN CITY

Sardinia (ITALY)

GREECE

40°N

Mediterranean Sea

GIBRALTAR (U.K.)

10°W   0°   10°E

Sicily (ITALY)

MALTA

20°E

Crete (GREECE)

**A5**

# The World
## PHYSICAL

**Legend:**
- Arid
- Evergreen forest
- Grassland
- Mixed forest
- Mountains
- Tundra
- National border
- ▲ Mountain peak

ARCTIC OCEAN

Beaufort Sea

Denali (Mt. McKinley) 20,320 ft. (6,194 m)

Queen Elizabeth Islands

Baffin Island

Great Bear Lake

Great Slave Lake

Hudson Bay

Bering Sea

Yukon R.

Mt. Logan 19,550 ft. (5,959 m)

Mackenzie R.

Aleutian Islands

Gulf of Alaska

Vancouver Island

Columbia R.

NORTH AMERICA

ROCKY MOUNTAINS

Missouri R.

Great Lakes

Newfoundland

Mt. Whitney 14,495 ft. (4,418 m)

Colorado R.

Mississippi R.

Ohio R.

APPALACHIAN MTS.

GREAT PLAINS

Bermuda

ATLANTIC OCEAN

Rio Grande

Gulf of California

Tropic of Cancer

Gulf of Mexico

Bahamas

Hawaiian Islands

Pico de Orizaba 18,855 ft. (5,747 m)

Yucatán Peninsula

Cuba

Hispaniola

West Indies

Caribbean Sea

PACIFIC OCEAN

Equator

Galápagos Islands

Orinoco River

Guiana Highlands

AMAZON BASIN

Amazon R.

SOUTH AMERICA

Polynesia

Brazilian Highlands

ANDES MOUNTAINS

Tropic of Capricorn

Atacama Desert

Gran Chaco

Paraná River

Mt. Aconcagua 22,834 ft. (6,960 m)

Pampa

PACIFIC OCEAN

Patagonia

Falkland Islands

Strait of Magellan

Cape Horn

Tierra del Fuego

Antarctic Circle

Ross Sea

Antarctic Peninsula

## Northern Polar Region

Sea of Okhotsk

ASIA

EUROPE

Kamchatka Peninsula

New Siberian Is.

Severnaya Zemlya

Novaya Zemlya

Barents Sea

Baltic Sea

0   400   800 Miles
0   400   800 Kilometers
Azimuthal Equidistant Projection

ARCTIC OCEAN

Svalbard

North Sea

British Isles

Bering Sea

Wrangel Island

Bering Strait

North Pole

Norwegian Sea

BROOKS RANGE

Beaufort Sea

North Magnetic Pole

Queen Elizabeth Islands

Greenland Sea

Greenland

Iceland

ATLANTIC OCEAN

PACIFIC OCEAN

NORTH AMERICA

Baffin Bay

Arctic Circle

ARCTIC OCEAN

Greenland
Svalbard
Iceland
Barents Sea
Severnaya Zemlya
Novaya Zemlya
New Siberian Islands
80°N
Arctic Circle
60°N
SIBERIA
Lena River
Yenisey River
Ob River
URAL MTS.
North Sea
British Isles
Baltic Sea
North European Plain
EUROPE
Volga R.
Irtysh River
ASIA
Lake Baikal
Amur R.
Kamchatka Peninsula
Sea of Okhotsk
Kuril Is.
Hokkaido
40°N
Mt. Elbrus 18,510 ft. (5,642 m)
Aral Sea
Caspian Sea
TIAN SHAN
GOBI (DESERT)
Huang He
Sea of Japan
Honshu
Shikoku
Kyushu
PACIFIC OCEAN
Mont Blanc 15,771 ft. (4,807 m)
ALPS
Danube R.
Balkan Peninsula
Caucasus Mts.
Black Sea
Azores
Pyrenees
Iberian Peninsula
Asia Minor
Zagros Mts.
Tigris R.
Euphrates R.
Persian Gulf
HINDU KUSH
K2 (Godwin Austen) 28,250 ft. (8,611 m)
HIMALAYAS
Plateau of Tibet
Mt. Everest 29,035 ft. (8,850 m)
Chang Jiang
East China Sea
Madeira Islands
Mediterranean Sea
Atlas Mts.
Nile R.
Indus R.
Thar Desert
Ganges R.
20°N
Taiwan
Canary Islands
SAHARA
Red Sea
Arabian Peninsula
Deccan Plateau
Hainan
South China Sea
Philippine Islands
Micronesia
Cape Verde Islands
SAHEL
Lake Chad
Niger River
AFRICA
Arabian Sea
Bay of Bengal
Sri Lanka
Malay Peninsula
Ethiopian Highlands
Mt. Kenya 17,058 ft. (5,199 m)
Maldives
Sumatra
Borneo
Celebes
New Guinea
0°
Congo River
CONGO BASIN
Lake Victoria
Mt. Kilimanjaro 19,340 ft. (5,895 m)
Seychelles
Java
Melanesia
Lake Tanganyika
INDIAN OCEAN
Lake Malawi
Fiji
Madagascar
20°S
Kalahari Desert
AUSTRALIA
GREAT VICTORIA DESERT
GREAT DIVIDING RANGE
Darling R.
ATLANTIC OCEAN
Cape of Good Hope
Cape Agulhas
Murray R.
Mt. Kosciusko 7,310 ft. (2,228 m)

N
W        E
S

0    1,000    2,000 Miles
0    1,000    2,000 Kilometers
Scale accurate at equator
Winkel Projection

Tasmania
New Zealand
40°S

ANTARCTICA

40°W  20°W  0°  20°E  40°E  60°E  80°E  100°E  120°E  140°E  160°E  180°

60°S
Ross Sea
80°S

**Southern Polar Region**

South Shetland Islands
South Georgia
Bellingshausen Sea
Antarctic Peninsula
Alexander I.
ELLSWORTH LAND
Weddell Sea
MARIE BYRD LAND
Vinson Massif 16,066 ft. (4,897 m)
Ronne Ice Shelf
ATLANTIC OCEAN
PACIFIC OCEAN
Ross Sea
Ross Ice Shelf
TRANSANTARCTIC MOUNTAINS
South Pole
POLAR PLATEAU
QUEEN MAUD LAND
ANTARCTICA
ENDERBY LAND
WILKES LAND
Antarctic Circle

0    400    800 Miles
0    400    800 Kilometers
Azimuthal Equidistant Projection

South Magnetic Pole

A7

# Western Hemisphere
## POLITICAL

ARCTIC OCEAN

Beaufort Sea

*Viscount Melville Sound*

*Baffin Bay*

*Greenland*
(DENMARK)

Bering Strait

*Bering Sea*

ALASKA
(U.S.)
•Fairbanks
•Anchorage
•Whitehorse
Juneau•

*Gulf of Alaska*

*Yukon River*
*Mackenzie River*
*Liard River*
*Peace River*

Great Bear Lake

•Yellowknife
Great Slave Lake

Foxe Basin

Arctic Circle

60°N

*Davis Strait*

*Hudson Strait*

Hudson Bay

*Labrador Sea*

CANADA

•Edmonton
•Calgary
Vancouver•
•Seattle
Portland•

*Athabasca R.*
Lake Athabasca
*Saskatchewan R.*
•Saskatoon
•Regina
•Winnipeg
Lake Winnipeg

James Bay

•Thunder Bay

*Puget Sound*
•Boise
*Columbia R.*
*Snake R.*

UNITED STATES

•Salt Lake City
Great Salt Lake
•Reno

*Colorado R.*
•Denver

*Missouri R.*

Great Lakes
•Ottawa ⊛
Montreal•
•Quebec
St. John•
St. John's•

*St. Lawrence River*
*Gulf of St. Lawrence*

•Chicago
Detroit•
Toronto•
•Albany
•Boston
Halifax•

•San Francisco
•Las Vegas
Los Angeles•
San Diego•
•Phoenix
Tucson•
•El Paso

•Cleveland
•New York City
•Philadelphia
⊛Washington, D.C.
•Indianapolis
•Richmond
•Norfolk

ATLANTIC OCEAN

30°N

Hermosillo•
Chihuahua•

*Mississippi R.*
St. Louis•
•Memphis
•Dallas
Houston•
New Orleans•

•Atlanta
•Raleigh
•Charleston
•Savannah
Jacksonville•

Tropic of Cancer

*Gulf of California*

*Rio Grande*

MEXICO
Durango•
Monterrey•
San Antonio•
Tampa•
•Orlando

Honolulu•
HAWAII
(U.S.)

León•
•Tampico
Guadalajara•
Mexico City•
Acapulco•
Puebla•Veracruz•

•Miami
Gulf of Mexico

BAHAMAS
⊛Nassau
⊛Havana
CUBA HAITI
JAMAICA
⊛Port-au-Prince
•Santo Domingo
Puerto Rico (U.S.)
DOMINICAN REPUBLIC

PACIFIC OCEAN

BELIZE
GUATEMALA⊛Belmopan
Guatemala City⊛
HONDURAS
San Salvador⊛⊛Tegucigalpa
EL SALVADOR ⊛Managua
NICARAGUA
COSTA RICA ⊛San José
PANAMA ⊛Panama City

⊛Kingston

Caribbean Sea

•Maracaibo
•Caracas GUYANA
VENEZUELA ⊛ SURINAME
Georgetown⊛ ⊛Paramaribo
•Cayenne
FRENCH GUIANA (FRANCE)

*Galápagos Islands*
(ECUADOR)

•Medellín
Cali•
COLOMBIA⊛Bogotá

•Quito
Guayaquil•
ECUADOR
•Iquitos

Manaus•

*Rio Negro*
*Amazon R.*
*Tapajós River*
*Xingu R.*

Belém•
•Fortaleza

0° Equator

French Polynesia
(FRANCE)
Papeete•

•Trujillo
PERU
•Lima⊛
•Cuzco

*Lake Titicaca*
•La Paz
•Arequipa
BOLIVIA
•Sucre

•Brasília⊛
Goiânia•
Campo Grande•

*São Francisco R.*
*Tocantins*

BRAZIL

Recife•

•Salvador

•Belo Horizonte
•Rio de Janeiro

Tropic of Capricorn

Antofagasta•

PARAGUAY
•Salta
San Miguel de Tucumán•
•Córdoba

*Paraguay R.*
•Asunción⊛
*Paraná*

•São Paulo
•Curitiba

30°S

Valparaíso•
Santiago•
Concepción•

CHILE

Rosario•
Buenos Aires⊛
La Plata•

URUGUAY
⊛Montevideo
*Rio de la Plata*
•Mar del Plata
Bahía Blanca•

Valdivia•

0    1,000    2,000 Miles
0    1,000    2,000 Kilometers
Miller Cylindrical Projection

ARGENTINA

—— National border
⊛ National capital
• City

A8

N
W    E
S

Punta Arenas•

*Falkland Islands*
(U.K.)

South Georgia
(U.K.)

150°W          120°W          90°W          60°W          30°W

ARCTIC OCEAN

North Magnetic Pole +

Queen Elizabeth Islands

Ellesmere Island

Melville Island

Devon Island

Bering Strait

Point Barrow

Beaufort Sea

Banks Island

Viscount Melville Sound

Baffin Bay

Greenland

B r o o k s   R a n g e

Victoria Island

Baffin Island

Davis Strait

Arctic Circle

Mt. McKinley 20,320 ft. (6,194 m)

Yukon

Yukon River

Mackenzie Mts.

Mackenzie River

Foxe Basin

Cape Farewell

60°N

Alaska Range

Plateau

Llard R.

Peace River

Great Bear Lake

Great Slave Lake

Hudson Strait

C A N A D I A N

Mt. Logan 19,550 ft. (5,959 m)

Coast Mountains

Athabasca R.

Lake Athabasca

Hudson Bay

James Bay

Labrador

Labrador Sea

Gulf of Alaska

Kodiak Island

Saskatchewan River

Lake Winnipeg

S H I E L D

Alaska Peninsula

Bering Sea

Queen Charlotte Islands

R O C K Y

G R E A T

Aleutian Islands

Vancouver Island

Puget Sound

Cascade Range

M O U N T A I N S

NORTH AMERICA

Great Lakes

St. Lawrence R.

Newfoundland

Gulf of St. Lawrence

Nova Scotia

Bay of Fundy

Long Island

Cape Cod

Coast Ranges

Snake R.

Sierra Nevada

P L A I N S

Black Hills

Missouri R.

Mississippi R.

Platte R.

Great Salt Lake

GREAT BASIN

INTERIOR PLAINS

Ohio R.

APPALACHIAN MTS.

Mt. Whitney 14,495 ft. (4,418 m)

Colorado R.

Arkansas R.

Ozark Plateau

River

Cape Hatteras

Death Valley (lowest point in N.A.) -282 ft. (-86 m)

Sonoran Desert

Gila R.

Rio Grande

Sierra Madre Oriental

COASTAL PLAIN

ATLANTIC OCEAN

30°N

Baja California

Gulf of California

Sierra Madre Occidental

Gulf of Mexico

Bahamas

Hawaiian Islands

Tropic of Cancer

Yucatán Peninsula

Cuba

Greater Antilles

Hispaniola

Puerto Rico

Pico de Orizaba 18,855 ft. (5,747 m)

Caribbean Sea

Lesser Antilles

PACIFIC OCEAN

Lake Nicaragua

Isthmus of Panama

Lake Maracaibo

Llanos

Orinoco R.

Guiana Highlands

Chimborazo 20,702 ft. (6,310 m)

Galápagos Islands

Rio Negro

Amazon R.

Cape São Roque

Equator

A N D E S

AMAZON BASIN

Line Islands

Marquesas Islands

Huascarán 22,205 ft. (6,768 m)

Tapajós River

Xingu River

Tocantins R.

São Francisco River

Mato Grosso Plateau

Brazilian

Cook Islands

Tuamotu Archipelago

Society Islands

Lake Titicaca

Altiplano

Paraguay R.

Highlands

SOUTH AMERICA

Tropic of Capricorn

Atacama Desert

M O U N T A I N S

Gran Chaco

Paraná R.

Iguazú Falls

30°S

1,000   2,000 Miles

Mt. Aconcagua 22,834 ft. (6,960 m)

Uruguay R.

Rio de la Plata

1,000   2,000 Kilometers

Pampa

Miller Cylindrical Projection

Patagonia

Valdés Peninsula (lowest point in S.A.) -131 ft. (-40 m)

▲ Mountain peak

▼ Point below sea level

N

— National border

W     E

≈ Waterfall

S

Falkland Islands

A9

South Georgia

150°W          120°W                    90°W                    60°W          30°W

Strait of Magellan

Tierra del Fuego

Cape Horn

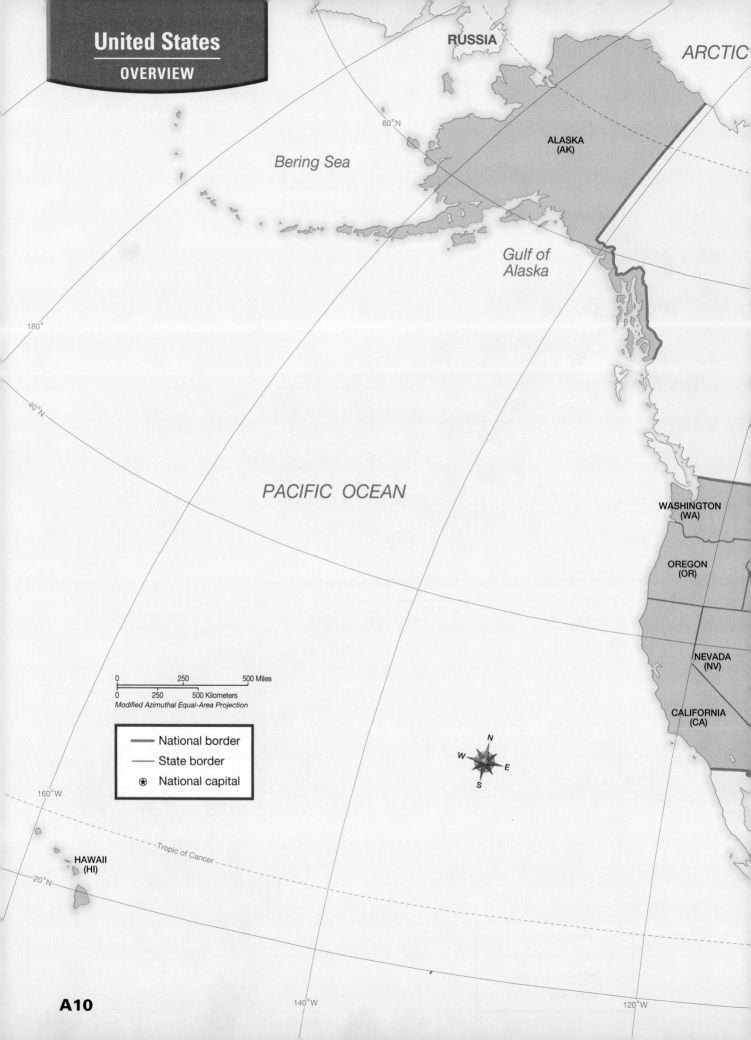

RUSSIA

ARCTIC

60°N

Bering Sea

ALASKA
(AK)

Gulf of
Alaska

180°

40°N

PACIFIC OCEAN

WASHINGTON
(WA)

OREGON
(OR)

NEVADA
(NV)

CALIFORNIA
(CA)

0        250        500 Miles

0    250    500 Kilometers

*Modified Azimuthal Equal-Area Projection*

━━━ National border

─── State border

⊛ National capital

N

W        E

S

160°W

Tropic of Cancer

HAWAII
(HI)

20°N

140°W

120°W

# United States
## POLITICAL

**RUSSIA**

ARCTIC OCEAN

70° N

ALASKA

Arctic Circle

170° E

Yukon River

180°

60° N

Fairbanks

CANADA

Yukon River

60° N

Anchorage

Bering
Sea

Gulf of
Alaska

Juneau

PACIFIC
OCEAN

50° N

170° W    160° W    150° W    140° W    130° W

0    250    500 Miles
0    250    500 Kilometers

**CANADA**

130° W    120° W    110° W

40° N

| | |
|---|---|
| Northeast | ✪ National capital |
| South | ★ State capital |
| Middle West | • Major city |
| West | ⎯ National border |
| | ⎯ State border |

**PACIFIC
OCEAN**

30° N

130° W

Seattle
Tacoma
Olympia
Spokane
WASHINGTON
Portland
Columbia River
Salem
Eugene
OREGON

Great Falls
Helena
MONTANA
Billings
Yellowstone R.

IDAHO
Boise
Snake River
Pocatello

WYOMING
Casper
Cheyenne

Lake
Tahoe
Reno
Sacramento
Carson City
NEVADA
Great
Salt
Lake
Ogden
Salt Lake City
Provo
UTAH
Colorado River

San Francisco
Oakland
San Jose
Fresno
CALIFORNIA
Bakersfield

Las
Vegas

Denver
Colorado
Springs
COLORADO
Puebl

Los Angeles
San Bernardino
San Diego

Flagstaff
ARIZONA
Phoenix
Tucson

Santa Fe
Albuquerque
NEW MEXICO
Roswell
El Paso
Rio Grande

**MEXICO**

N
W    E
S

160° W    PACIFIC    155° W
OCEAN
Honolulu
HAWAII
Hilo    20° N
0    100    200 Miles
0    100    200 Kilometers

20° N

0    250    500 Miles
0    250    500 Kilometers
Albers Equal-Area Projection

A12

120° W    110° W

100°W   90°W   80°W   70°W

50°N

**CANADA**

St. Lawrence River

**MAINE**
Augusta ★

Lake of
the Woods

Lake Champlain

Lake Superior

**VERMONT**
Burlington
• Montpelier

Portland •

**NORTH
DAKOTA**   Grand
Forks •

Duluth •

Sault Sainte Marie •

**NEW
HAMPSHIRE**
Concord ★

Bismarck ★   Fargo •

**MINNESOTA**

**M I C H I G A N**

Lake Huron

**NEW
YORK**

Manchester

Lake Ontario

Syracuse
•

Rochester •

Worcester • Boston
★

**MASSACHUSETTS**

**SOUTH
DAKOTA**   St. Paul
★
Minneapolis •

Green
Bay •

Grand
Rapids
•

Albany ★

Providence
Hartford ★ • **RHODE ISLAND**

Mississippi River

**WISCONSIN**

Madison ★

Milwaukee •

Lansing
★

Flint •

Lake
St. Clair

Buffalo •

**CONNECTICUT**
• Bridgeport

Pierre ★

Detroit •

Lake Erie

Cleveland •

Newark •
★ • **New York City**

**PENNSYLVANIA**

Trenton ★

Rapid
City •

Sioux
Falls •

Rockford •

Toledo •
Akron •

Harrisburg
★

**NEW JERSEY**

Philadelphia
•

40°N

Sioux
City •

Cedar
Rapids
•

Chicago •

Gary
•

South
Bend •

**OHIO**
Columbus
★

Wheeling •

Pittsburgh •

Baltimore
•

Wilmington •
Dover ★

**IOWA**

**NEBRASKA**

Davenport •

Des Moines ★

**ILLINOIS**

Omaha •

Peoria •

Decatur •

**INDIANA**

Indianapolis ★

Dayton •

Cincinnati •

Annapolis
Washington,
D.C. ★

**DELAWARE**

**MARYLAND**

70°W

Missouri River

Springfield ★

**WEST
VIRGINIA**

**VIRGINIA**
Richmond ★

Lincoln ★

Platte River

Charleston •

Newport News •

Louisville •

Frankfort ★

Ohio River

Roanoke •

Norfolk •

Topeka ★

Kansas
City •

St. Louis •

Evansville •
Lexington •

**KENTUCKY**

Missouri River

Jefferson
City ★

**KANSAS**

Wichita •

**MISSOURI**
• Springfield

Knoxville •

Nashville ★

Winston-
Salem •
Charlotte •

Greensboro
•
• Raleigh ★

Arkansas River

**NORTH
CAROLINA**

**OKLAHOMA**

Tulsa •

**ARKANSAS**

Chattanooga •

**TENNESSEE**

Amarillo •

Oklahoma
City ★

Fort
Smith •

Arkansas River

Memphis •

Huntsville •

**SOUTH
CAROLINA**
Columbia ★

Charleston •

Red River

Lake
Texoma

Little
Rock ★

Birmingham •

Atlanta
★

Lubbock •

Mississippi River

**MISSISSIPPI**

**ALABAMA**

**GEORGIA**

Macon •

Columbus •

Savannah •

**ATLANTIC
OCEAN**

30°N

Fort
Worth •

Abilene •

Dallas •

Shreveport •

Meridian
•

Montgomery ★

**LOUISIANA**

Jackson •

Odessa •

**TEXAS**

Austin ★

Beaumont •

Baton Rouge ★

Biloxi •

Mobile •

Tallahassee ★

Jacksonville •

Houston •

New Orleans •

**FLORIDA**

Orlando •

San
Antonio •

Rio Grande

Tampa •
St. Petersburg •

Lake
Okeechobee

West
Palm
Beach •

**B A H A M A S**

Laredo •

Corpus Christi •

Miami •

*Gulf of Mexico*

80°W

**CUBA**

100°W   90°W

**A13**

# United States
## PHYSICAL

CANADA

**RUSSIA**

ARCTIC OCEAN

Brooks Range

Seward Peninsula
ALASKA
Yukon River

Arctic Circle

CANADA

St. Lawrence Island

Bering Strait

Mt. McKinley 20,320 ft. (6,194 m) △

Alaska Range

Yukon River

Bering Sea

Gulf of Alaska

Aleutian Islands

Kodiak Island

0   250   500 Miles
0   250   500 Kilometers

WA
Mt. Rainier 14,410 ft. (4,392 m) ▲
▲ Mt. St. Helens 8,366 ft. (2,550 m)
Columbia River
▲ Mt. Hood 11,237 ft. (3,425 m)

Coast Ranges
Cascade Range

OR

Columbia Plateau

Bitterroot Range

ID
Salmon River Mountains

Snake River

ROCKY

Fort Peck Lake

MT
Yellowstone River

Bighorn Mts.

Teton Range
Wind River Range

WY

Great Divide Basin

MOUNTAINS

Cape Mendocino

Coast Ranges

Pyramid Lake

Donner Pass
Lake Tahoe

Sierra Nevada

Sacramento River

Central Valley

San Joaquin R.

NV

GREAT BASIN

Great Salt Lake

Wasatch Range

Uinta Mts.

UT

Lake Powell

Colorado River

Mt. Elbert 14,433 ft. (4,399 m)

San Juan Mts.

CO

Front

San

## Legend

| | |
|---|---|
| | Arid |
| | Evergreen forest |
| | Grassland |
| | Mixed forest |
| | Mountains |
| | Tundra |
| ▬ | National border |
| ─ | State border |
| ▲ | Mountain peak |
| △ | Highest point |
| ▽ | Lowest point |

PACIFIC OCEAN

Mt. Whitney 14,495 ft. (4,418 m) ▼

CA

Death Valley -282 ft. (-86 m) ▽

Mojave Desert

Lake Mead

Grand Canyon

Colorado Plateau

AZ

Point Conception

Channel Islands

Salton Sea

Imperial Valley

Sonoran Desert

Baldy Peak 11,403 ft. (3,476 m) ▲

NM

Guadalupe Peak 8,749 ft (2,667 m)

Rio Grand

MEXICO

N
W   E
S

**HAWAII**

PACIFIC OCEAN

Kauai
Niihau
Oahu
Molokai
Lanai   Maui
Kahoolawe
Hawaii
Mauna Kea 13,796 ft. (4,205 m) ▲

0   100   200 Miles
0   100   200 Kilometers

0   250   500 Miles
0   250   500 Kilometers
Albers Equal-Area Projection

A14

100°W        90°W        80°W        70°W

**CANADA**

50°N

40°N

70°W

30°N

80°W

100°W        90°W

Lake of the Woods

Upper Red Lake
Lower Red Lake
Leech Lake
Mille Lacs Lake
Mesabi Range

Isle Royale
Keweenaw Peninsula
Lake Superior
Upper Peninsula

Lake Huron

St. Lawrence River

ME
Mt. Katahdin 5,269 ft. (1,606 m)
Moosehead Lake

Lake Sakakawea

**ND**

**MN**

**WI**
Wisconsin River
Lake Winnebago

Lake Michigan
Lower Peninsula

**MI**
Lake St. Clair

Lake Erie

Lake Ontario
Niagara Falls

Lake Champlain
**VT**
Adirondack Mountains
Green Mts.
White Mts.
Mt. Washington 6,288 ft. (1,917 m)
**NH**
Cape Ann
Cape Cod
**MA**
Finger Lakes
Connecticut R.
Hudson R.
**CT**
**RI**

**NY**

Lake Oahe
Missouri River

**SD**

Black Hills

North Platte R.
Sand Hills
**NE**
South Platte R.
Platte River

**IA**

Mississippi River

Illinois River

**IL**

Wabash River

**IN**

**OH**

Allegheny Mts.
**PA**

**MD**
Potomac R.
**DE**
Delaware Bay

**WV**
**VA**
Cape Charles
Chesapeake Bay
Albemarle Sound

**G R E A T**

**P L A I N S**

Smoky Hills
**KS**

Red Hills

**I N T E R I O R**

**P L A I N S**

Missouri River

**MO**

Lake of the Ozarks
Harry S. Truman Reservoir

Ozark Plateau

**C E N T R A L   P L A I N S**

Ohio River

**KY**
Lake Barkley
Cumberland R.
Cumberland Gap

James R.
Roanoke R.

**NC**
Cape Hatteras

Mt. Mitchell 6,684 ft. (2,037 m)

Cape Fear River

**A P P A L A C H I A N   M O U N T A I N S**

**P I E D M O N T**

Llano Estacado

Arkansas River
Canadian River
**OK**
Red River
Ouachita Mountains
Lake Texoma

**AR**

Mississippi River

**TN**
Tennessee R.

Stone Mountain
Clark Hill Lake

**SC**
Cape Fear

Savannah River
Oconee R.
Ocmulgee R.

Pecos River

**TX**
Edwards Plateau

Brazos River
Colorado River
Sabine River

Sam Rayburn Reservoir
Toledo Bend Reservoir

**LA**
Lake Maurepas
Lake Pontchartrain

**MS**

**AL**
Tombigbee R.
Alabama R.
Chattahoochee R.

**GA**
Altamaha R.
Okefenokee Swamp

**C O A S T A L   P L A I N**

**A T L A N T I C**

**O C E A N**

Rio Grande

Galveston Bay

Mobile Bay
Mississippi Delta

**Gulf of Mexico**

Tampa Bay
Lake Okeechobee

**FL**
St. Johns River
Cape Canaveral

Everglades
Cape Sable
Florida Keys

Straits of Florida

**BAHAMAS**

**CUBA**

**A15**

# Canada

ICELAND

Greenland
(DENMARK)

Denmark Strait

Arctic Circle

Davis Strait

Labrador Sea

ARCTIC OCEAN

Beaufort Sea

Baffin Bay

Baffin Island

Foxe Basin

Lancaster Sound

Gulf of Boothia

Ellesmere Island

Axel Heiberg Island

Devon Island

Queen Elizabeth Islands

Somerset Island

Prince of Wales Island

Prince Patrick Island

Melville Island

Banks Island

Victoria Island

Amundsen Gulf

Southampton Island

Hudson Strait

Ungava Bay

Ungava Peninsula

Puvirnituq

Iqaluit

Chesterfield Inlet

Kugluktuk

Coppermine River

NUNAVUT

Back River

Thelon R.

Dubawnt River

Great Bear Lake

Great Slave Lake

Yellowknife

Hay River

NORTHWEST TERRITORIES

Fort Simpson

Fort Liard

Inuvik

Mackenzie R.

Hudson Bay

Churchill

Fort Severn

Belcher Islands

Labrador Peninsula

NEWFOUNDLAND AND LABRADOR

Smallwood Res.

Churchill R.

Happy Valley-Goose Bay

Schefferville

Caniapiscau River

Caniapiscau Reservoir

Leaf River

George R.

La Grande R.

Manicouagan Reservoir

Labrador City

Havre-St. Pierre

Sept-Îles

Grand Falls-Windsor

Corner Brook

Newfoundland Island

St. John's

St. Pierre and Miquelon (FR.)

Gulf of St. Lawrence

QUEBEC

Rimouski

Lac St-Jean

Lac Mistassini

Saguenay R.

Rupert R.

Chicoutimi

Trois-Rivières

Quebec

Sydney

Charlottetown

PRINCE EDWARD ISLAND

NEW BRUNSWICK

Moncton

Fredericton

Saint John

Sherbrooke

Dartmouth

Halifax

NOVA SCOTIA

ATLANTIC OCEAN

Montreal

Hull

Ottawa

St. Lawrence R.

Ottawa R.

Kingston

Lake Ontario

St. Catharines

Toronto

Hamilton

London

Sarnia

Windsor

L. St. Claire

Lake Erie

Lake Huron

Lake Michigan

Lake Superior

Sault Sainte Marie

Sudbury

Nipigon

Thunder Bay

Lake of the Woods

ONTARIO

Fort Albany

Moosonee

Albany R.

Attawapiskat R.

Winisk R.

Severn River

James Bay

Abitibi R.

Mattagami R.

York Factory

Nelson R.

Thompson

The Pas

Flin Flon

MANITOBA

Lake Winnipeg

Lake Manitoba

Lake Winnipegosis

Dauphin

Winnipeg

Brandon

Reindeer Lake

Churchill R.

Lake Athabasca

SASKATCHEWAN

Prince Albert

Saskatoon

Moose Jaw

Regina

N. Saskatchewan River

S. Saskatchewan R.

Peace River

ALBERTA

Grande Prairie

Edmonton

Athabasca R.

Banff

Calgary

Medicine Hat

Lethbridge

UNITED STATES

ROCKY MOUNTAINS

BRITISH COLUMBIA

Prince George

Fraser River

Columbia R.

Williston Lake

Kamloops

Kelowna

Vancouver

Victoria

Vancouver Island

Coast Mountains

Prince Rupert

Queen Charlotte Islands

Queen Charlotte Sound

PACIFIC OCEAN

Stikine R.

Skeena R.

YUKON TERRITORY

Dawson

Whitehorse

Carmacks

Pelly River

Yukon R.

ALASKA (U.S.)

Gulf of Alaska

Bering Strait

A16

## Legend

⊛ National capital

★ Province capital

• Other city

— National border

— Province border

500 Miles

500 Kilometers

250

250

0

Azimuthal Equal-Area Projection

N E S W

# Geography Terms

1. **basin**  bowl-shaped area of land surrounded by higher land
2. **bay**  an inlet of the sea or some other body of water, usually smaller than a gulf
3. **bluff**  high, steep face of rock or earth
4. **canyon**  deep, narrow valley with steep sides
5. **cape**  point of land that extends into water
6. **cataract**  large waterfall
7. **channel**  deepest part of a body of water
8. **cliff**  high, steep face of rock or earth
9. **coast**  land along a sea or ocean
10. **coastal plain**  area of flat land along a sea or ocean
11. **delta**  triangle-shaped area of land at the mouth of a river
12. **desert**  dry land with few plants
13. **dune**  hill of sand piled up by the wind

14. **fall line**  area along which rivers form waterfalls or rapids as the rivers drop to lower land
15. **floodplain**  flat land that is near the edges of a river and is formed by silt deposited by floods
16. **foothills**  hilly area at the base of a mountain
17. **glacier**  large ice mass that moves slowly down a mountain or across land
18. **gulf**  part of a sea or ocean extending into the land, usually larger than a bay
19. **hill**  land that rises above the land around it
20. **inlet**  any area of water extending into the land from a larger body of water
21. **island**  land that has water on all sides
22. **isthmus**  narrow strip of land connecting two larger areas of land
23. **lagoon**  body of shallow water
24. **lake**  body of water with land on all sides

| 26 | **mesa** flat-topped mountain with steep sides |
| 27 | **mountain** highest kind of land |
| 28 | **mountain pass** gap between mountains |
| 29 | **mountain range** row of mountains |
| 30 | **mouth of river** place where a river empties into another body of water |
| 31 | **oasis** area of water and fertile land in a desert |
| 32 | **ocean** body of salt water larger than a sea |
| 33 | **peak** top of a mountain |
| 34 | **peninsula** land that is almost completely surrounded by water |
| 35 | **plain** area of flat or gently rolling low land |
| 36 | **plateau** area of high, mostly flat land |
| 37 | **reef** ridge of sand, rock, or coral that lies at or near the surface of a sea or ocean |
| 38 | **river** large stream of water that flows across the land |
| 39 | **riverbank** land along a river |

| 40 | **savanna** area of grassland and scattered trees |
| 41 | **sea** body of salt water smaller than an ocean |
| 42 | **sea level** the level of the surface of an ocean or a sea |
| 43 | **slope** side of a hill or mountain |
| 44 | **source of river** place where a river begins |
| 45 | **strait** narrow channel of water connecting two larger bodies of water |
| 46 | **swamp** area of low, wet land with trees |
| 47 | **timberline** line on a mountain above which it is too cold for trees to grow |
| 48 | **tributary** stream or river that flows into a larger stream or river |
| 49 | **valley** low land between hills or mountains |
| 50 | **volcano** opening in the earth, often raised, through which lava, rock, ashes, and gases are forced out |
| 51 | **waterfall** steep drop from a high place to a lower place in a stream or river |

**A19**

# Introduction

" The history of every country begins with the heart of a man or a woman "

—Willa Cather, *O Pioneers!*, 1913

## Learning About Our Country

This year in social studies, you will be studying the United States, past and present. You will learn about past events and the places where those events occurred. You will also read about people who helped shape our country. You will see how people have worked together to meet their needs and wants and to govern themselves. You will learn what it means to be a citizen of the United States.

Civics and Government

Culture and Society

What Is Social Studies?

History

Economics

Geography

# Why History Matters

## VOCABULARY

history       oral history       historical empathy       analyze

chronology       point of view       frame of reference

Studying **history**, or what happened in the past, helps you see how the past and the present are linked. Studying history also helps you understand how the events of today may be linked to the future. As you learn to recognize these links, you will begin to think more like a historian, a person who studies the past.

## Measuring Time

One way historians see connections in history is by studying the order in which events happened. The order of events is called their **chronology** (kruh•NAH•luh•jee). By looking at the chronology of events, historians can learn how the past is connected to the present.

## Finding Evidence

Historians study the past by looking for clues in the objects and documents that people have left behind. They read journal entries, newspaper articles, and other writings by people who experienced past events. They also listen to or read records of oral histories. An **oral history** is a story of an event or an experience told aloud by a person who did not have a written language or who did not write down what happened. Historians also look at photographs, films, and artwork. By examining such clues, historians can piece together what took place in the past and can better explain why they think events happened as they did.

In the past and the present, many people from other countries have chosen to immigrate to the United States.

In the past, many immigrants to the United States arrived by boat at Ellis Island in New York. The letters and diaries and oral histories of the immigrants tell much about their adventures.

## Identifying Points of View

Historians examine people's points of view. A person's **point of view** is how he or she sees things. It can depend on whether that person is old or young, a man or a woman, rich or poor. A point of view is also shaped by a person's background and experiences. People with different points of view may see the same event differently.

Historians learn about the times and places in which people lived. They study how scientific discoveries and new ways of doing things affected people's lives. In that way, historians can understand earlier people's actions and feelings. This understanding is called **historical empathy** (EM•puh•thee).

This display at Ellis Island shows a few of the people who arrived there. Immigrants to the United States have many different backgrounds and experiences. This may lead them to have different points of view.

## Understanding Frames of Reference

Historians also work hard to understand people's **frames of reference**. A frame of reference includes where people were when an event took place and what part they took in it. Historians must be careful not to judge the actions of people in the past based on the way people of today would act.

Immigrants wait at Ellis Island. Historians use photographs like this one to draw conclusions about early United States immigration.

## Drawing Conclusions

Many events in history are connected to other events. To **analyze** an event, historians look closely at how the parts of it connect with one another and how the event is connected to other events. Analyzing an event allows historians to draw conclusions about how and why it happened.

**REVIEW** Why is it important to study history?

# · SKILLS · READING

# Compare Primary and Secondary Sources

## ➡ WHY IT MATTERS

To know what really happened in the past, you need to find proof. You can do this by studying and comparing two kinds of sources—primary sources and secondary sources.

## ➡ WHAT YOU NEED TO KNOW

**Primary sources** are the records made by people who saw or took part in an event. These people may have written down their thoughts in a journal, or they may have told their story in a letter or a poem. They may have made a speech, produced a film, taken a photograph, or painted a picture. Primary sources may also be objects or official documents that give information about the time in which they were made or written. A primary source gives people of today a direct link to a past event.

This photograph **A**, letter **B**, and pen and ink bottle **C** are all examples of primary sources from the time of the Civil War.

A **secondary source** is not a direct link to an event. It is a record of the event written by someone who was not there at the time. A magazine article, newspaper story, or book written by someone who only heard about or read about the event is a secondary source. So is an object made at a later time.

Some sources can be either primary or secondary, depending on how the event is reported. A newspaper might print the exact words of a person who saw the event take place. It might also print an article about the event, written by a reporter who was not there. Oral histories, textbooks, and online resources can also be either primary or secondary sources.

## ▶ PRACTICE THE SKILL

Look at the photographs of objects and printed materials that give information about the American Civil War. Then answer these questions.

**1** How are items A and F alike and different?

**2** What kind of information might be found in item B but not in item D?

**3** Why might secondary sources D and E also be considered primary sources?

## ▶ APPLY WHAT YOU LEARNED

Look through your textbook for examples of primary and secondary sources. Explain to a classmate what makes each source you selected a primary source or a secondary source.

This newspaper **D**, Civil War Web site **E**, and recent photograph of people dressed as Civil War soldiers **F** are secondary sources.

# Why Geography Matters

## VOCABULARY

| geography | physical feature | modify | region |
|-----------|------------------|--------|--------|
| location | human feature | adapt | |

Every event you will read about in this book has a setting, and part of the setting is the place where the event happened. Learning about places is an important part of **geography**—the study of Earth's surface and the way people use it. People who study geography are called geographers.

## The Five Themes of Geography

Geographers often speak of five main themes when they study a place. You will find that most of the maps in this book focus on one of these themes. Keeping these themes in mind as you read will help you think like a geographer.

**Human-Environment Interactions**
Humans and their surroundings interact, or affect each other. People's activities may **modify**, or change, the environment. The environment may affect people, causing them to **adapt**, or adjust, to their surroundings.

**Location**
Everything on Earth has its own **location**— the place where it can be found.

**Movement**
Each day, people in different parts of the country and around the world exchange products and ideas.

**Place**
Every location has features that make it different from all other locations. **Physical features** are formed by nature. **Human features** are created by people.

**Regions**
Areas of Earth that share features that make them different from other areas are called **regions**. A region can be described by its physical features or human features.

## Essential Elements of Geography

Geographers also use six other topics when they study a place. These six topics are called the six essential elements of geography. Thinking about them will help you understand the world around you.

### • GEOGRAPHY •

**The World in Spatial Terms**
Geographers use maps and other kinds of information to study relationships among people and places. They want to know why things are located where they are.

**Human Systems**
People's activities include where they settle, how they earn a living, and the laws they make. All of these help shape Earth's surface.

**Places and Regions**
People are linked to the places and regions in which they live. Places and regions have both physical and human features.

**Environment and Society**
People's activities often affect the environment, and the environment affects people's activities.

**Physical Systems**
Physical processes, such as wind and rain, shape Earth's surface. Living things interact with physical features to create and change environments.

**The Uses of Geography**
Knowing how to use maps, globes, and other geography tools helps people in their everyday lives.

**REVIEW** **What is geography?**

# Why Economics Matters

**VOCABULARY**

economy

economics

Have you ever earned money for doing chores? Did you use the money to buy something you needed or wanted? When you do these things, you are taking part in the economy. An **economy** is the way people of a state, a region, or a country use resources to meet their needs. The study of how people do this is called **economics**.

In this book you will read about how people in the past made, bought, sold, and traded goods to meet their needs. You will learn how the economy of the United States changed over time to become one in which businesses are free to sell many kinds of goods and services.

**REVIEW** How are resources important to a country's economy?

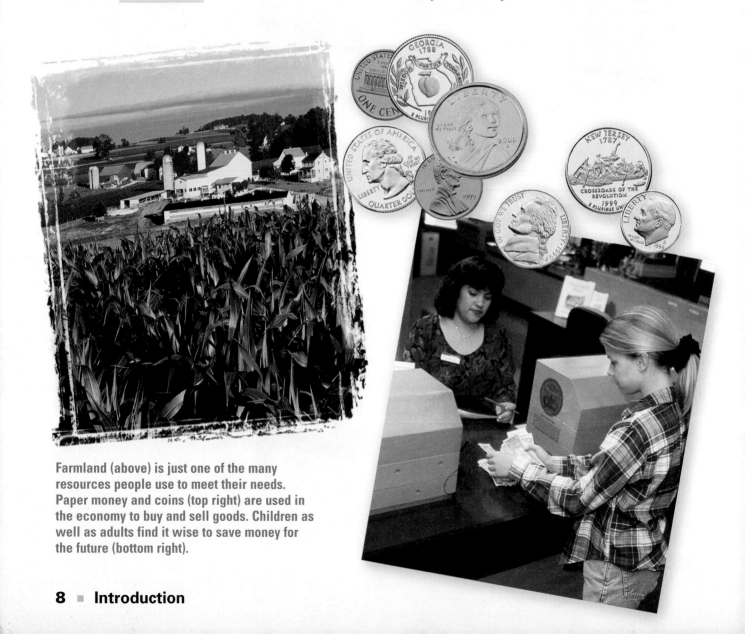

Farmland (above) is just one of the many resources people use to meet their needs. Paper money and coins (top right) are used in the economy to buy and sell goods. Children as well as adults find it wise to save money for the future (bottom right).

# Why Civics and Government Matter

"Ask not what your country can do for you; ask what you can do for your country." When President John F. Kennedy said these words in 1961, he was talking about another key area of social studies—civics. **Civics** is the study of citizenship. In this textbook you will read about the rights and responsibilities of citizens of the United States. You will also learn about the importance of **civic participation**. Civic participation is being concerned with and involved in issues related to your community, state, or country or the entire world.

In the United States, citizens have an important part in making government work. A **government** is a system of leaders and laws that helps people live together in their community, state, or country. It protects citizens and settles disagreements among them. In this book you will read about the people and events that shaped government in the past. You will also find out how government works today.

**REVIEW** How is civics different from government?

The Constitution of the United States (below left) and the United States Capitol building (below right) are both symbols of American government.

# Why Culture and Society Matter

In this book you will read about people of the past who helped shape the present. You will learn about their customs and beliefs, their families and communities, and the ways they made a living. All these things make up a **culture**, or way of life.

Each human group, or **society**, has a culture. This book will help you discover the many cultures of our country, both now and in the past. You will also learn about our country's **heritage**, or culture that has come from the past and continues today.

**REVIEW** How are the terms *culture* and *society* related?

The photograph above gives a glimpse of Mexican culture within the United States. The photograph below shows the many different heritages of the students in a Gary, Indiana, classroom of long ago.

# The Land and Early People

A Cheyenne shield,
1860–1868

Paria Canyon, Vermillion Cliffs National Monument, Arizona

# The Land and Early People

> 66 **And the People came to live in the Northern Mountains and on the Plains, in the Western Hills and on the Seacoasts, in the Southern Deserts and in the Canyons.** 99
>
> —Simon Ortiz, *The People Shall Continue*, 1977

## Preview the Content

Scan the pictures in each chapter and lesson. Use them to create a list of topics you will learn about in Unit 1.

## Preview the Vocabulary

**Word Meanings**   Write what you think each word below means and why. Use the Glossary to check your answers.

| WORD | POSSIBLE MEANING | WHY |
|---|---|---|
| savanna | | |
| tepee | | |
| wampum | | |

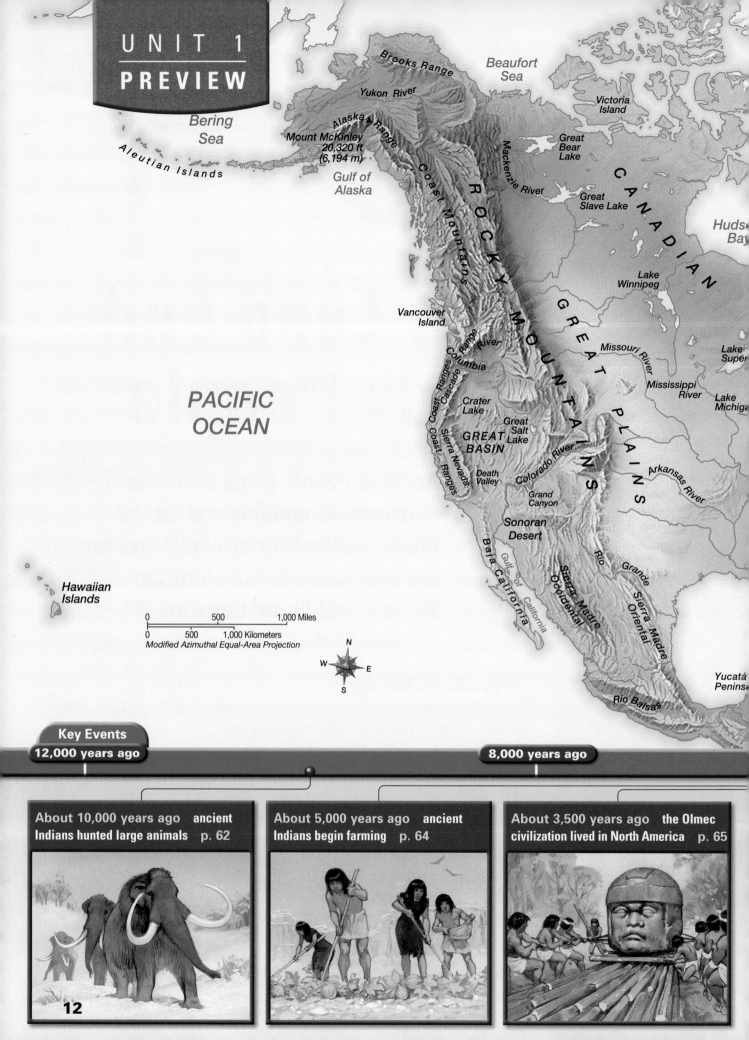

UNIT 1
PREVIEW

Bering
Sea

Aleutian Islands

Brooks Range

Beaufort
Sea

Yukon River

Alaska Range

Mount McKinley
20,320 ft
(6,194 m)

Gulf of
Alaska

Victoria
Island

Great
Bear
Lake

Mackenzie River

Great
Slave Lake

CANADIAN

Hudson
Bay

Lake
Winnipeg

ROCKY MOUNTAINS

GREAT PLAINS

Vancouver
Island

Coast Ranges

Cascade Range

Columbia River

Crater
Lake

Sierra Nevada

Coast Ranges

GREAT
BASIN

Great
Salt
Lake

Missouri River

Lake
Super

Mississippi
River

Lake
Michiga

PACIFIC
OCEAN

Death
Valley

Colorado River

Grand
Canyon

Arkansas River

Sonoran
Desert

Baja California

Gulf of California

Sierra Madre Occidental

Rio Grande

Sierra Madre Oriental

Yucatá
Penins

Hawaiian
Islands

Rio Balsas

0        500        1,000 Miles
0    500    1,000 Kilometers
Modified Azimuthal Equal-Area Projection

N
W    E
S

Key Events
12,000 years ago

8,000 years ago

About 10,000 years ago   ancient
Indians hunted large animals   p. 62

About 5,000 years ago   ancient
Indians begin farming   p. 64

About 3,500 years ago   the Olmec
civilization lived in North America   p. 65

12

**North America**

Labrador Sea

Labrador

SHIELD

Newfoundland

Lake Huron

St. Lawrence River

Lake Ontario

L. Erie

Ohio River

APPALACHIAN MOUNTAINS

Mammoth Cave

COASTAL PLAIN

ATLANTIC OCEAN

Bahamas

Gulf of Mexico

Cuba

Caribbean Sea

Hispaniola

Puerto Rico

Baffin Bay

Baffin Island

Greenland

## Facts About United States Geography

| PHYSICAL FEATURE | LOCATION |
|---|---|
| Largest Gorge | Grand Canyon, Nevada/Arizona |
| Largest Freshwater Lake | Lake Superior |
| Deepest Lake | Crater Lake, Oregon |
| Longest River | Mississippi River |
| Highest Mountain | Mount McKinley, Alaska |
| Lowest Point | Death Valley, California |
| Largest Cave | Mammoth Cave, Kentucky |

## United States Population

Two out of ten people live in rural, or country, areas.

Eight out of ten people live in or near cities.

4,000 years ago

PRESENT

**About 1,000 years ago** the Navajos moved to the Southwest   p. 72

**By 800 years ago** more than 30,000 people lived in Cahokia   p. 66

**About 700 years ago** the Iroquois lived in the Northeast   p. 89

13

Between Earth & Sky

LEGENDS OF NATIVE AMERICAN SACRED PLACES

Joseph Bruchac          Thomas Locker

# IF WE SHOULD

# TRAVEL

## by Joseph Bruchac

Many people use poems, songs, or stories to tell about important events and people in their past. Some of these stories are legends. A legend is a story handed down by a group of people over time. Some legends tell about brave or heroic people. Others try to explain the origins of animals, plants, and physical features found in the world.

If we should travel
far to the South,
there in the land
of mountains and mist,
we might hear the story
of how Earth was first shaped.

Water Beetle came out
to see if it was ready,
but the ground was
still as wet as a swamp,
too soft for anyone to stand.

Great Buzzard said, "I will help dry the land."
He began to fly close above the new Earth.
Where his wings came down,
valleys were formed,
and where his wings lifted,
hills rose up through the mist.

So the many rolling valleys and hills
of that place called the Great Smokies
came into being there.
And so it is that the Cherokee people,
aware of how this land was given,
know that the Earth is a sacred gift
we all must respect and share.

## Analyze the Literature

1 What is the author describing in the poem?

2 Explain why people use poems, songs, and stories to explain the world around them.

## START THE UNIT PROJECT

**A Multimedia Presentation**
Work with your classmates to create a multimedia presentation about the landforms and early people of the United States. As you study the unit, write down the landforms you read about and tell how early people used the natural resources around them.

## USE TECHNOLOGY

Visit The Learning Site at **www.harcourtschool.com/socialstudies** for additional activities, primary sources, and other resources to use in this unit.

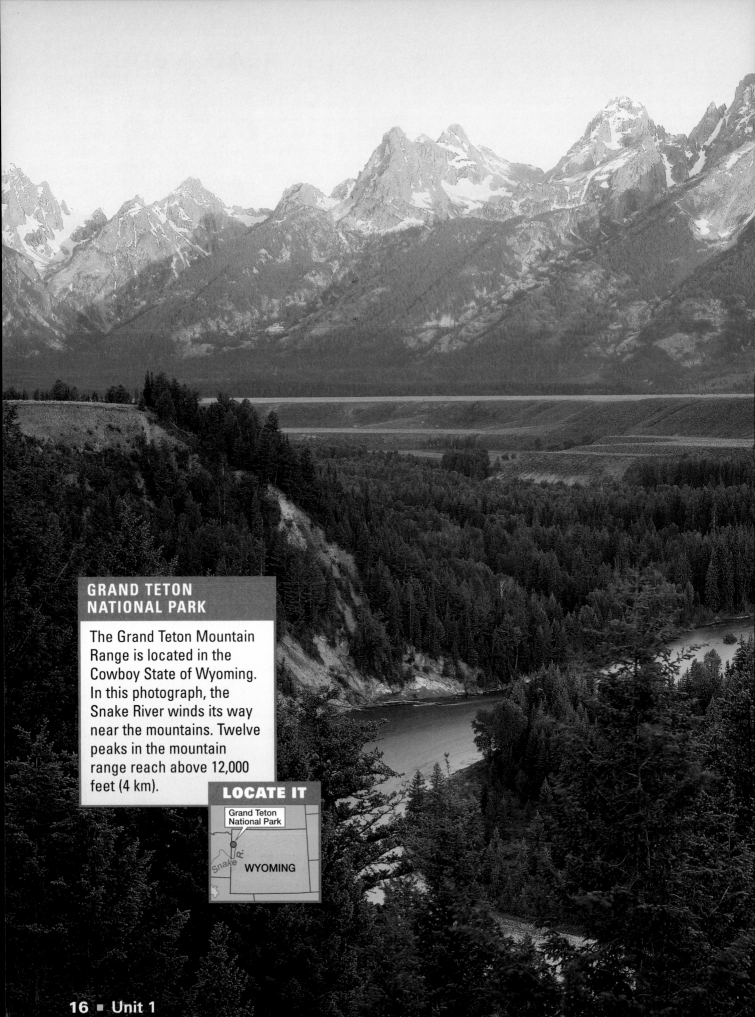

## GRAND TETON NATIONAL PARK

The Grand Teton Mountain Range is located in the Cowboy State of Wyoming. In this photograph, the Snake River winds its way near the mountains. Twelve peaks in the mountain range reach above 12,000 feet (4 km).

**LOCATE IT**

Grand Teton National Park

Snake

WYOMING

# 1

# Our Country's Geography

" O beautiful for spacious skies,
For amber waves of grain,
For purple mountain majesties
Above the fruited plain! "

—from the poem "America the Beautiful"
by Katharine Lee Bates, 1893

## CHAPTER READING SKILL

### Main Idea and Supporting Details

The **main idea** of a paragraph or lesson is what it is mostly about. The main idea may be stated in a sentence, or it may only be suggested. **Supporting details** give more information about the main idea.

**As you read this chapter, list the main ideas and show how those ideas are supported with details.**

```
                    MAIN IDEA
        ↗                           ↖
SUPPORTING              ↑    ↑            SUPPORTING
 DETAIL                                    DETAIL

          SUPPORTING      SUPPORTING
           DETAIL          DETAIL
```

# Land and Regions

**MAIN IDEA**
Read to learn how the United States can be divided into regions based on different kinds of land.

**WHY IT MATTERS**
Learning about kinds of land will help you understand how areas of the country are similar and how they are different.

**VOCABULARY**
landform
mountain range
piedmont
sea level
plateau
basin
volcano

In 1893 the poet Katharine Lee Bates saw the Rocky Mountains for the first time. She was in Colorado on a tour. "One day some of the other teachers and I decided to go on a trip to 14,000-foot (4,267-m) Pikes Peak," she later wrote. "We hired a prairie wagon. Near the top we had to leave the wagon and go the rest of the way on mules. I was very tired. But when I saw the view, I felt great joy. All the wonder of America seemed displayed there, with the sea-like expanse." By the time she left Colorado, Bates had written the opening lines to her poem "America the Beautiful." Her poem later became a well-known song when it was set to music.

## Landform Regions

The United States is more than a land of beauty. It is also a land of many different places. To better study the land of the United States, geographers often divide it into landform regions. A landform region is a region that has similar landforms throughout. **Landforms** are physical features on the Earth's surface, such as plains, mountains, hills, and valleys. Each landform is unique because of its shape and the way it came to be made.

All of the United States, except for the island state of Hawaii, is in North America. North America is one

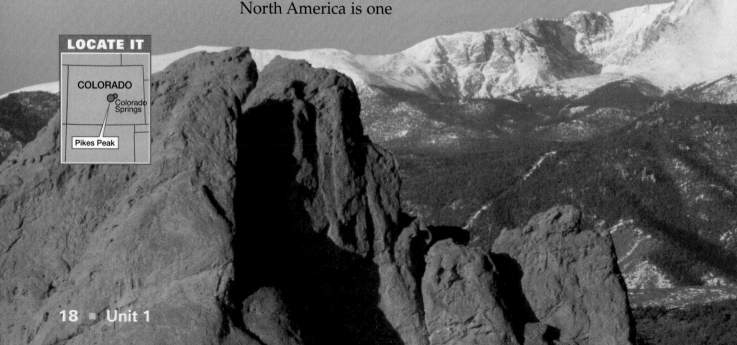

LOCATE IT

COLORADO

Colorado Springs

Pikes Peak

of the Earth's seven continents, or largest areas of land. In addition to sharing the continent of North America, the United States shares landform regions with its neighbors, Canada and Mexico.

**REVIEW** **What are landform regions?**

## America's Largest Mountains

The two largest mountain ranges in the United States are the Appalachian (ap•uh•LAY•chee•uhn) Mountains and the Rocky Mountains. A **mountain range** is a group of connected mountains. The Appalachians cover much of the eastern United States. They stretch all the way from central Alabama to southeastern Canada. The Rocky Mountains cover much of the western United States. They extend north from Mexico through Canada and into Alaska.

Most scientists believe the Appalachian Mountains were formed more than 250 million years ago. Over time the mountains' peaks have been worn down. The highest peaks in the Appalachians are less than 7,000 feet (2,134 m) tall.

Most of the mountain peaks in the Appalachians are less than 3,500 feet (1,067 m) tall.

A large part of the Appalachians is made up of a series of ridges and valleys that run next to each other. Among these ridges are the Blue Ridge, Catskill, Pocono, and White Mountains. The area of high land on the eastern side of the Appalachians is called the Piedmont (PEED•mahnt). A **piedmont** is an area at or near the foot of a mountain. The Piedmont begins in New Jersey and stretches as far south as Alabama.

Pikes Peak (center) is one of many peaks that make up the Rocky Mountains.

FAST FACT

Pikes Peak was named for explorer Zebulon Pike. Because he did not have enough supplies, Pike was unable to climb to the top of the mountain he first saw in 1806. Today people can reach the top by using a highway or a mountain railway.

## Landforms of North America

**Map Legend:**
- Mountains
- Plateaus
- Hills
- Plains

ARCTIC OCEAN

Bering Sea

Aleutian Islands

Greenland

Beaufort Sea

Baffin Bay

Brooks Range

Arctic Coastal Plain

Yukon River

Alaska Range

Mt. McKinley 20,320 ft (6,194 m)

Mt. Logan 19,550 ft (5,959 m)

Gulf of Alaska

Mackenzie River

Great Bear Lake

Labrador Sea

Great Slave Lake

CANADA

Hudson Bay

Coast Mountains

R O C K Y

Lake Winnipeg

Newfoundland

PACIFIC OCEAN

Vancouver Island

CANADIAN SHIELD

LABRADOR

ATLANTIC OCEAN

Cascade Range

Columbia Plateau

Snake R.

GREAT

M O U N T A I N S

P L A I N S

Great Lakes

St. Lawrence River

0    500    1,000 Miles
0    500    1,000 Kilometers
Lambert Azimuthal Equal-Area Projection

Sierra Nevada

GREAT BASIN

Great Salt Lake

Black Hills

Missouri R.

INTERIOR PLAINS

CENTRAL PLAINS

Ohio R.

APPALACHIAN

MOUNTAINS

PIEDMONT

Coast Ranges

Central Valley

Mt. Whitney 14,494 ft (4,418 m)

Death Valley

Colorado Plateau

UNITED STATES

Ozark Plateau

Mississippi R.

COASTAL PLAIN

Baja California

Gulf of California

SIERRA MADRE OCCIDENTAL

Rio Grande

SIERRA MADRE ORIENTAL

Gulf of Mexico

Bahamas

Cuba

Citlaltépetl 18,700 ft (5,700 m)

MEXICO

Yucatán Peninsula

Caribbean Sea

---

**GEOGRAPHY THEME**

**Regions**
North America is made up of several landform regions.

❖ What mountain region lies to the east of the Mississippi River?

---

Many scientists believe that most of the Rocky Mountains were formed more than 30 million years ago. Like the Appalachians, the Rocky Mountain Range is so large that it is made up of smaller ranges. Each range is separated from another by high plains and valleys.

Unlike the peaks of the Appalachians, the peaks of the Rockies appear sharp and jagged. They are also much higher because they are newer and have not been worn down by wind and water for as long a time. More than 50 peaks in Colorado alone are higher than 14,000 feet (4,267 m). Because the Rockies are so high, many of the peaks are covered with snow all year.

**REVIEW** What mountain range covers much of the eastern United States? the western United States?

## Regions of Plains

The two largest landform regions in the United States are plains—the Coastal Plain and the Interior Plains. A coastal plain is low, mostly flat land that lies along an ocean or another large body of water. The Coastal Plain stretches inland from the Atlantic Ocean and the Gulf of Mexico. The Interior Plains, also called the Interior Lowlands, extend across most of the center of the United States. The word *interior* means "the inside or inner part."

The Coastal Plain region begins along the Atlantic Ocean in Massachusetts. There it is only a narrow strip of land no more than 10 miles (16 km) wide. It gets wider—hundreds of miles wider—farther south toward Florida. From Florida the Coastal Plain extends west along the Gulf of Mexico into Texas and eastern Mexico. The land of the Coastal Plain region lies close to sea level and gradually rises inland. **Sea level** is the level of the surface of the oceans. It is used as a starting point in measuring the height and depth of landforms. Another, smaller coastal plain, the Arctic Coastal Plain, lies in northern Canada and Alaska.

The very large Interior Plains region stretches across the middle of North America, from the Appalachian Mountains in the east to the Rocky Mountains in the west. It extends north from Mexico, across the United States, and into Canada. In the eastern part of the Interior Plains, often called the Central Plains, the land is mostly flat to rolling with areas of forests to the east and grasslands to the west. Farther to the west, however, the land becomes much flatter and rises to meet the base of the Rocky Mountains. This western part of the Interior Plains is called the Great Plains. The Great Plains stretch from southern Texas into Canada.

While most of the land between the Appalachians and the Rockies is plains, there are areas with other kinds of landforms. To the north of the Interior Plains is the Canadian Shield. This rocky, horseshoe-shaped region wraps around Hudson Bay. There are hundreds of lakes in this region. In other places, such as the Black Hills of South Dakota and the Ozark Plateau (pla•TOH) in Missouri and Arkansas, the land rises very sharply to an area of hills and small mountains. A **plateau** is a broad area of high, mostly flat land.

**REVIEW** How is the location of the Coastal Plain different from that of the Interior Plains?

This wheat field in Kansas is a part of the miles and miles of flat land that makes up the Great Plains.

## A Region of Basins, Ranges, and Plateaus

Between the Rocky Mountains and other mountain ranges farther west is a large area sometimes called the Intermountain Region. *Intermountain* means "between the mountains." Part of this land is the Great Basin, which includes Nevada and parts of five neighboring states. A **basin** is low, bowl-shaped land with higher ground all around it. At the southwestern edge of the Great Basin lies the lowest point on the continent of North America. Part of Death Valley in California lies more than 280 feet (85 m) below sea level.

Because the Intermountain Region has areas of low and high land, it is often called the Basin and Range Region. Not only basins and mountain ranges but other landforms mark this region. These include plateaus and canyons. The two largest plateaus in the region are the Columbia Plateau to the northwest of the Great Basin and the Colorado Plateau to the southeast.

The Grand Canyon, one of the world's natural wonders, cuts across part of the Colorado Plateau. Carved by the Colorado River over thousands of years, it extends 280 miles (451 km) through Arizona. It is up to 18 miles (29 km) wide and about a mile (1.6 km) deep.

**REVIEW** What kinds of landforms are found in the Intermountain Region?

## More Mountains and Valleys

Lying west of the Intermountain Region and stretching to the Pacific Ocean is the Pacific Mountains and Valleys region. This region extends north from Mexico to Canada and Alaska. It is made up mainly of separate mountain ranges and a series of valleys between those mountain ranges.

On the eastern edge of the Pacific Mountains and Valleys region is the Sierra Nevada (see•AIR•ah neh•VAH•dah). *Sierra Nevada* is Spanish for "Snowy Mountain Range." The Sierra Nevada runs almost the length of California. Other mountains lie north of the Sierra Nevada. These are the Cascade Range in northern California, Oregon, and Washington, and the Coast Mountains in Canada. These ranges include some

Death Valley is about 140 miles (225 km) long and about 5 to 15 miles (8 to 24 km) wide.

**LOCATE IT**

Death Valley National Park

Sacramento

San Francisco

CALIFORNIA

Los Angeles

volcanoes. A **volcano** is an opening in the Earth through which hot lava, gases, ash, and rocks may pour out. When this happens, a volcano is erupting. Sometimes the lava and ash build up to form a mountain.

In Big Sur, California, steep cliffs have formed where the Coast Ranges meet the Pacific Ocean.

Farther north, in Alaska, is the Alaska Range. It has the highest mountain peak in North America, Mount McKinley. The peak, which is sometimes called by its Native American name, Denali (duh•NAH•lee), is 20,320 feet (6,194 m) high. *Denali* means "The Great One" or "The High One." The peak was first climbed in 1913.

Beside the Pacific Ocean in California, Oregon, and Washington are the Coast Ranges. These low mountains give much of the Pacific Coast a rocky, rugged look. At many places these mountains drop sharply into the ocean. Unlike the Atlantic Coast, the Pacific Coast has very little flat land along its coast.

Sandwiched between the Coast Ranges, the Sierra Nevada, and the Cascade Range are three large, fertile valleys. The largest is the more than 400-mile (644-km) long Central Valley in California. The others are the Puget Sound Lowland in Washington and the Willamette (wuh•LA•muht) Valley in Oregon.

**REVIEW** What region extends north from Mexico to Canada and Alaska?

## LESSON 1 REVIEW

1 **MAIN IDEA** What are the major kinds of land that determine the landform regions of the United States?

2 **WHY IT MATTERS** How are the kinds of land in the United States different?

3 **VOCABULARY** Write a paragraph that includes the terms **mountain range**, **piedmont**, and **sea level**.

4 **READING SKILL—Main Idea and Supporting Details** What region extends across most of the center of the United States?

5 **GEOGRAPHY** How do the Appalachian Mountains differ from the Rocky Mountains?

6 **GEOGRAPHY** What are the two largest landform regions in the United States?

7 **CRITICAL THINKING—Analysis** How might the similarities and differences of the land in different parts of the United States affect how people live in various regions?

**PERFORMANCE—Draw a Map** Draw a map of the United States that shows the main landform regions. Describe and label each region, and list some of the region's main physical features. Share your map with a classmate.

# ·SKILLS·

# Use Elevation Maps

**VOCABULARY**

elevation

contour line

## ▶ WHY IT MATTERS

Different maps provide different kinds of information. If you want to know how high or how low the land is, you need to use an elevation (eh•luh•VAY•shuhn) map. **Elevation** is the height of the land in relation to sea level.

## ▶ WHAT YOU NEED TO KNOW

The elevation of land is measured from sea level, usually in feet or meters. The elevation of land at sea level is 0 feet (0 m). Find sea level on Drawing A. The lines on this drawing of a mountain are contour lines. A **contour line** connects all points of equal elevation. Find the contour line for 13,120 feet (4,000 m) on Drawing A.

This line connects all the points on the mountain that are 13,120 feet (4,000 m) above sea level.

Drawing B shows the hill as you look down on it from above. On the steeper side of the hill, the contour lines are closer together. On the sloping side of the hill, the lines are farther apart.

On Drawing C, color is added between the contour lines. A key is used instead of labels. The key for Drawing C shows that every place shown in green is between sea level and 655 feet (200 m). The border between green and yellow on the map is a contour line for 655 feet (200 m). The borders between the other colors are also contour lines.

## Reading Contour Lines

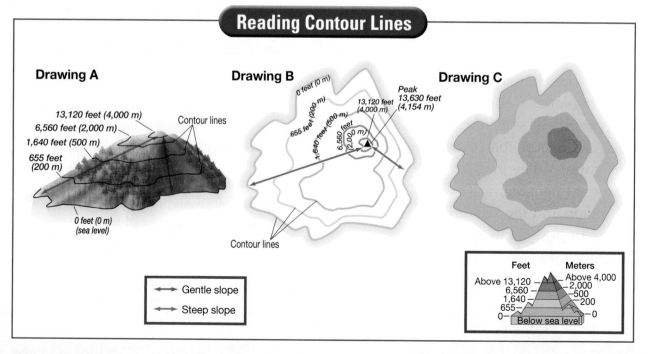

**Drawing A**

13,120 feet (4,000 m)
6,560 feet (2,000 m)
1,640 feet (500 m)
655 feet (200 m)

Contour lines

0 feet (0 m) (sea level)

**Drawing B**

0 feet (0 m)
655 feet (200 m)
1,640 feet (500 m)
6,560 feet (2,000 m)
13,120 feet (4,000 m)
Peak 13,630 feet (4,154 m)

Contour lines

**Drawing C**

←→ Gentle slope
←→ Steep slope

| Feet | | Meters |
|---|---|---|
| Above 13,120 | | Above 4,000 |
| 6,560 | | 2,000 |
| 1,640 | | 500 |
| 655 | | 200 |
| 0 | | 0 |
| | Below sea level | |

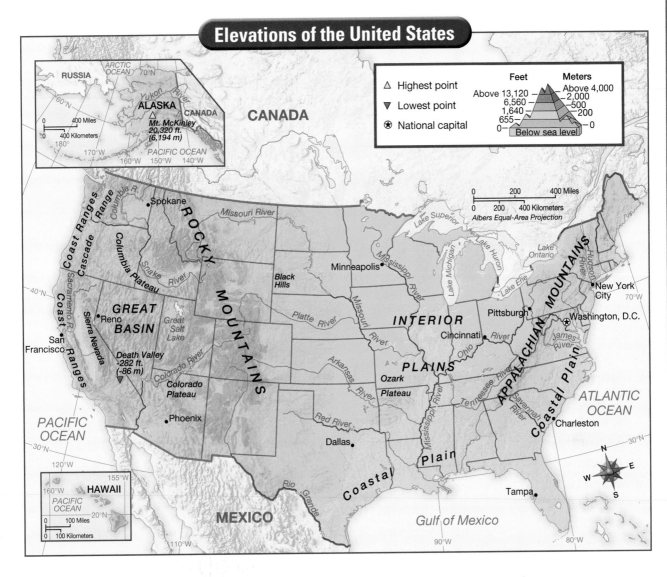

## Elevations of the United States

| | | Feet | Meters |
|---|---|---|---|
| △ Highest point | | Above 13,120 | Above 4,000 |
| ▽ Lowest point | | 6,560 | 2,000 |
| | | 1,640 | 500 |
| ✪ National capital | | 655 | 200 |
| | | 0 | 0 |
| | | Below sea level | |

0    200    400 Miles
0    200    400 Kilometers
Albers Equal-Area Projection

Mt. McKinley
20,320 ft.
(6,194 m)

Death Valley
-282 ft.
(-86 m)

Most elevation maps use only a few important contour lines, with colors added between the lines. Look at the elevation map of the United States on this page. The map does not show exact elevations. Instead, the key shows the range of elevation that each color stands for. On this map, green is used for land in the range between sea level and 655 feet (200 m).

### ▶ PRACTICE THE SKILL

Use the map to answer the following questions.

**1** Find the Coastal Plain on the map. What is the elevation of the land around Dallas, Texas?

**2** What range of elevations is shown by the color red?

**3** Which city has a higher elevation: Reno, Nevada, or Tampa, Florida?

### ▶ APPLY WHAT YOU LEARNED

Lay a ruler across the map on this page to connect any two cities. Describe the elevation of the land you would cross if you were to travel by car from one city to the other. Compare your description with that of a classmate.

Practice your map and globe skills with the **GeoSkills CD-ROM.**

MAP AND GLOBE SKILLS

**MAIN IDEA**
Read to learn about the different kinds of bodies of water.

**WHY IT MATTERS**
People use different bodies of water to meet their needs.

**VOCABULARY**

current
tide
inlet
sound
tributary
drainage basin
fall line

**FAST FACT** Oceans cover almost three-fourths of the entire Earth's surface.

# Bodies of Water

**B**odies of water are important to life in the United States. Oceans help connect the United States to other countries of the world. Lakes and rivers provide fresh water for wildlife and, in many places, for people and their farms, factories, and cities. Large lakes and rivers also provide important transportation routes within the United States. Like landforms, bodies of water have different shapes and sizes.

## Oceans

The largest bodies of water on Earth are the four oceans. From largest to smallest, they are the Pacific Ocean, the Atlantic Ocean, the Indian Ocean, and the Arctic Ocean. The Pacific Ocean alone covers nearly one-third of the Earth's surface, an area larger than all the continents put together.

These four oceans hold most of the Earth's water. They also separate most of the Earth's seven continents. From largest to smallest, these continents are Asia, Africa, North America, South America, Antarctica, Europe, and Australia. Geographers sometimes group Europe and Asia together and call them Eurasia (yu•RAY•zhuh).

Oceans form a natural boundary for a large part of the United States. On the northern coast of Alaska is the Arctic Ocean. On the eastern coast of the United States is the Atlantic Ocean. On the western coast and surrounding Hawaii is the Pacific Ocean.

Oceans move in the form of waves and currents. A **current** is that part of a body of water

# Oceans and Continents

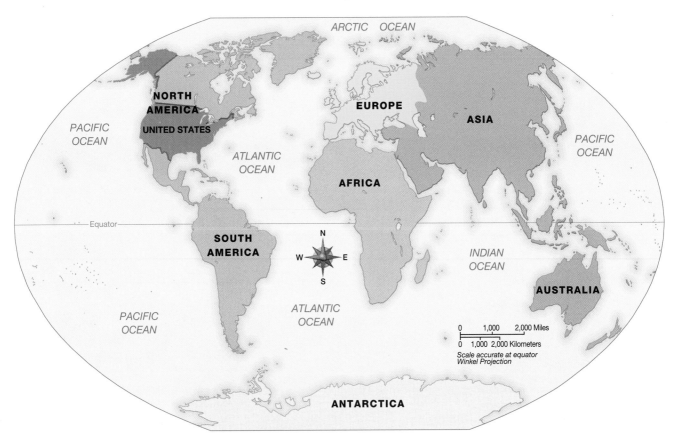

**Movement**   **Oceans separate most of the continents.**

❓ What ocean separates North America and Africa?

flowing in a certain direction. Ocean currents are caused mainly by the Earth's wind patterns.

Ocean water also moves in the form of tides. **Tides** are the regular rise and fall of an ocean and of the bodies of water connected to it. When the tide is high, some of the low-lying land near the ocean is covered with water.

**REVIEW** **What is the main cause of ocean currents?**

## Gulfs, Bays, and Inlets

Hundreds of inlets along the Coastal Plain help define the shape of the United States. An **inlet** is any area of water extending into the land from a larger body of water. The largest of these inlets are called gulfs. The largest gulf bordering the United States is the Gulf of Mexico. Several states in the southeastern United States border this gulf. Another large gulf, the Gulf of Alaska, lies south of Alaska, along the Pacific Coast.

Hundreds of bays also shape the coastline. Many large bays provide harbors where ships can safely dock.

Most of the largest bays and other inlets in the United States are found along the Atlantic and Gulf Coasts. On the Atlantic Coast these include Chesapeake Bay between Maryland and Virginia, Delaware Bay between Delaware and New Jersey, and Albemarle (AL•buh•marl) Sound in North Carolina.

## The Water Cycle

Clouds are formed from water vapor.

Precipitation falls.

Land, animals, and plants lose water to the air.

Some water from precipitation flows along the land.

The warm sun causes water to evaporate, forming water vapor.

Some water from precipitation soaks into the ground, some is absorbed by roots of plants, and some flows into lakes, rivers, or oceans.

**Analyze Diagrams** Water travels to all parts of the environment.

❓ What happens to the water that falls as precipitation?

A **sound** is a long inlet that often separates offshore islands from the mainland.

Other large bays and inlets are found along the Gulf Coast. The largest of these are Tampa Bay in Florida, Mobile Bay in Alabama, and Galveston Bay in Texas. The largest bays and inlets on the Pacific Coast include San Francisco Bay near San Francisco, California, and Puget Sound in Washington State.

**REVIEW** What large bays can be found along the Gulf of Mexico?

## Lakes

North America has more lakes than any other continent. The largest lakes in North America are together known as the Great Lakes. They are located along the border between the United States and Canada. These five lakes—Superior, Michigan, Huron, Erie, and Ontario—are among the world's largest freshwater lakes.

One-fifth of all the fresh water on Earth is found in the Great Lakes, and Lake Superior is the world's largest freshwater lake. It covers about 31,800 square miles (82,362 sq km), an area almost the size of South Carolina. Today the Great Lakes and the rivers connected to them form an important inland waterway for ships. This waterway links the Middle West region of the United States to the Atlantic Ocean. Other large freshwater lakes in the United States include Lake Okeechobee (oh•kuh•CHOH•bee) in Florida and Lake Tahoe on the California–Nevada border.

Most lakes in the United States are made up of fresh water, but the Great Salt Lake in Utah is as salty as any sea or ocean. Some people even consider it to be a sea—an inland body of salt water. Although freshwater streams feed the Great Salt Lake, they carry small amounts of salt. Because the lake lies in the Great Basin, surrounded by higher ground, the water coming into the lake has no way to escape. Over time, as water evaporates, salt is left behind. As a result, the lake is so salty that no fish can live in its water.

**REVIEW** What is the world's largest group of freshwater lakes?

**Location** Lake Michigan is the only Great Lake that is completely in the United States.

♦ What states border Lake Michigan?

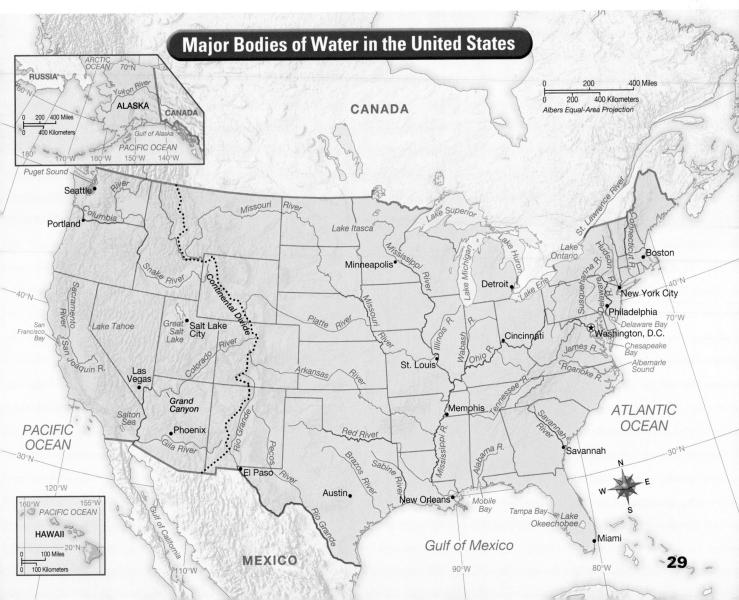

## Major Bodies of Water in the United States

## Samuel Langhorne Clemens
### 1835–1910
#### Character Trait: Individualism

As a young man Samuel Clemens began his career by writing short, humorous stories for his brother's newspaper. At age 21 Clemens stopped writing for a while and took a job aboard a steamboat that traveled the Mississippi River. Clemens learned to guide a steamboat through the winding channels of the river and became a steamboat pilot. He traveled the Mississippi River for almost four years before ending his career as a pilot in 1861.

Clemens used his experiences to write about life along the Mississippi in his novels *The Adventures of Tom Sawyer* and *The Adventures of Huckleberry Finn* and in his autobiography, *Life on the Mississippi*. He wrote these books under his pen name, Mark Twain. The name Mark Twain comes from a term steamboat pilots used on the Mississippi. It meant that the river was at least 12 feet (about 4 m) deep, which was a safe depth for steamboats.

**MULTIMEDIA BIOGRAPHIES**
Visit The Learning Site at
**www.harcourtschool.com/biographies**
to learn about other famous people.

## The Mississippi River System

Rivers are bodies of fresh, moving water. Every river begins at a source and ends at a mouth, where it empties its water into an ocean or another body of water. As a river crosses the land, it may be joined by other streams or rivers. A stream or a river that flows into a larger stream or river is called a **tributary**. Tributaries are also called branches. Together, a river and its tributaries make up a river system.

River systems drain, or carry water away from, the land around them. The land drained by a river system is its

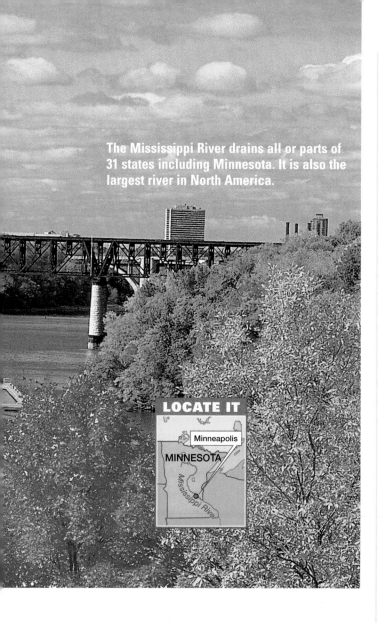

The Mississippi River drains all or parts of 31 states including Minnesota. It is also the largest river in North America.

LOCATE IT

Minneapolis

MINNESOTA

Mississippi River

## Rivers East of the Appalachians

Many rivers cross the Coastal Plain and flow into the Atlantic Ocean. They include the Delaware, Hudson, James, Potomac, Roanoke, Savannah, and Susquehanna (suhs•kwuh•HAN•uh) Rivers. All of these rivers, or their tributaries, begin in the Appalachian Mountains.

Many cities in the United States have grown near where these rivers flow into ocean inlets. Philadelphia, for example, was built along the Delaware River near where it flows into Delaware Bay. New York City was built at the mouth of the Hudson River. Baltimore was built where the Patapsco River empties into Chesapeake Bay.

Cities such as Richmond and Raleigh were built farther inland on rivers where the Coastal Plain meets the Piedmont. These cities lie along the Fall Line. A **fall line** is a place where the elevation of the land drops sharply, causing rivers to form waterfalls or rapids. Cities grew along the Fall Line because people used the fast-moving water there to power machines in factories.

**REVIEW** Where is the source of many rivers in the eastern United States?

The Delaware River passes through the Kittatinny Mountains of Pennsylvania.

**drainage basin**. When a river is long, its drainage basin can be quite large. The Mississippi River, along with its largest tributaries—the Arkansas, Illinois, Missouri, Ohio, and Red Rivers—creates a gigantic drainage basin in the middle of North America. The mighty Mississippi and its tributaries drain most of the land between the Appalachian and Rocky Mountains.

The Mississippi River's source is Lake Itasca (eye•TAS•kuh) in Minnesota. From there the river flows more than 2,300 miles (3,701 km) south to the Gulf of Mexico.

**REVIEW** What is a drainage basin?

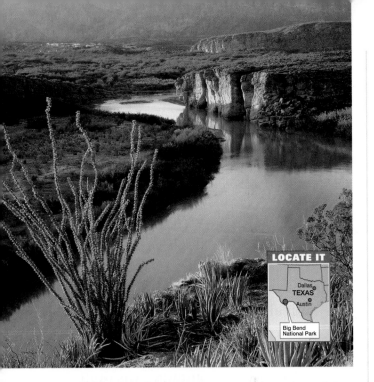

The Pecos, Chama, and Puerco Rivers are some of the tributaries that flow into the Rio Grande.

## Rivers in the West

An imaginary line runs north and south along the highest points of the Rocky Mountains. This line is called the Continental Divide. It divides the major river systems of North America into those that flow into the Gulf of Mexico and the Atlantic Ocean and those that flow into the Pacific Ocean. Western rivers that begin east of the Continental Divide empty into the Mississippi River or the Gulf of Mexico to reach the Atlantic Ocean. Rivers that begin west of the Continental Divide empty into the Pacific Ocean.

Many western rivers flow from sources on the eastern side of the Continental Divide. The largest of these include the Missouri and Arkansas Rivers and the Rio Grande. The Rio Grande forms part of the border between the United States and Mexico. In Mexico the river is known as the Río Bravo.

The major rivers on the western side of the Continental Divide include the Sacramento, San Joaquin (wah•KEEN), and Columbia Rivers. Another important western river is the Colorado. The Colorado River flows from the Rocky Mountains across the Colorado Plateau to Arizona before it empties into the Gulf of California in Mexico. The river passes through three national parks.

**REVIEW** What river forms part of the border between the United States and Mexico?

## LESSON 2 REVIEW

**1** **MAIN IDEA** Identify the major bodies of water in the United States.

**2** **WHY IT MATTERS** Why are bodies of water important to life in the United States?

**3** **VOCABULARY** Write a couple of sentences that explain how the terms **tributary** and **drainage basin** are related.

**4** **READING SKILL—Main Idea and Supporting Details** What are the largest bodies of water on the Earth?

**5** **HISTORY** Why did many cities grow along the Fall Line?

**6** **CRITICAL THINKING—Synthesize** Why do you think it is important to have a waterway that links the states in the Middle West to the Atlantic Ocean?

 **PERFORMANCE—Draw a Poster** Find out what river is located nearest to where you live. Make a poster showing the river and its surrounding landforms. Label nearby cities and any tributaries the river may have. Share your poster with the class.

# Climate and Vegetation Regions

At any time or place on Earth, the weather may change—sometimes quickly or violently. Weather is the day-to-day conditions in a place. **Climate** is the kind of weather a place has most often, year after year. The climate of a place can affect what people wear, what kinds of activities they do, and how they earn their living. Few countries in the world have as many different kinds of climate as the United States.

Climate and **natural vegetation**, or the plant life that grows naturally in a place, are closely related. The different climates in the United States influence the kinds of vegetation found in different parts of our country.

## Factors Affecting Climate

The climate of a place depends partly on its distance from the equator. Usually, the closer a place is to the equator, the warmer it is. For example, average temperatures between Maine and Florida can vary greatly, especially in winter. That is because places closer to the equator, like Florida, receive more direct sunlight than places farther away. This causes higher average temperatures. Generally, the farther a place is from the equator, the cooler it is.

**MAIN IDEA**
The United States can be divided into regions based on different kinds of climate and vegetation.

**WHY IT MATTERS**
Learning about climate and natural vegetation will help you understand why people live differently in different parts of the country.

**VOCABULARY**
climate
natural vegetation
rain shadow
humidity
drought
arid
tundra
prairie
savanna

In places with high elevations, some mountains can have snow year-round.

Distance from oceans and other large bodies of water also affects climate. Water heats and cools more slowly than land does. Near the ocean, temperatures are usually not as hot in summer and not as cold in winter as they would be inland. The ocean often helps warm the land in winter and cool it in summer.

Ocean currents can also affect climate. The currents carry cold water from the North Pole and the South Pole toward the equator, and warm water from the equator toward the poles. The Gulf Stream, which carries warm water northward along the east coast of the United States, helps make winters there less cold than places farther inland. The California Current, which flows along the west coast of the United States, brings cold water southward from the Arctic Ocean. It helps keep places along the west coast cool in the summer.

Elevation affects climate, too. Places in the mountains are usually much cooler than places where the elevation of the land is closer to sea level. Temperatures drop about 3°F (about 2°C) for every 1,000 feet (305 m) above sea level. Because elevation can affect the temperature so greatly, even the tops of high mountains in tropical Hawaii are sometimes covered with snow.

Where a place is located on a continent can affect climate in other ways. In the West, mountain ranges such as the Sierra Nevada and the Rocky Mountains act like huge walls. When streams of air meet the mountains, they are forced to rise. As air rises, it cools. Because cool air cannot hold as much moisture as warm air, rain

## The Rain Shadow

**Analyze Diagrams** Places in the rain shadow of a mountain get little rain or snow.

**What causes rain or snow?**

**2** Winds push clouds up one side of the mountain.

**3** Cooler temperatures cause rain or snow.

**4** Remaining clouds have little moisture.

dry lands or deserts

rain

**1** Air picks up moisture from the ocean. Moist air forms clouds.

winds

ocean

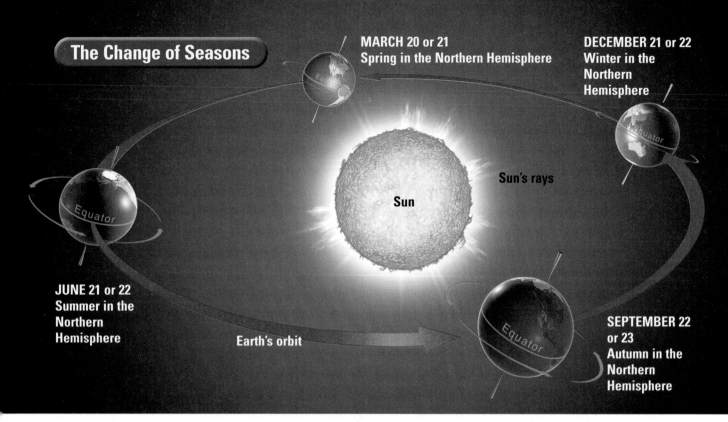

## The Change of Seasons

**MARCH 20 or 21**
**Spring in the Northern Hemisphere**

**DECEMBER 21 or 22**
**Winter in the Northern Hemisphere**

**Sun's rays**

**Sun**

**JUNE 21 or 22**
**Summer in the Northern Hemisphere**

**Earth's orbit**

**SEPTEMBER 22 or 23**
**Autumn in the Northern Hemisphere**

**Analyze Diagrams** As the Earth moves around the sun, the seasons change.

� When does summer start in the Northern Hemisphere?

or snow falls on the mountains' western slopes. As the air begins to slide down the eastern side of the mountains, it gets warmer. The warm air can hold more moisture. As a result, places on the eastern sides of the mountains get little precipitation. They lie in the **rain shadow**, or on the drier side of a mountain.

Not having mountains can affect the climate almost as much as having them, but in a different way. Because there is no large mountain range in the central part of the United States to block the flow of air, bitter-cold air masses can move rapidly out of Canada across the plains. Called northers because they come from the north, these large, cold air masses can bring freezing temperatures to places as far south as the states of Texas and Florida.

**REVIEW** What factors affect the climate of a place?

## Climate Regions

The United States has 11 climate regions. These climate regions vary from the mostly year-round cold in the *polar climate* and *subpolar climate* regions of Alaska to the mostly year-round heat in the *tropical wet climate* region of Hawaii and the *tropical wet and dry climate* region in South Florida. The change of seasons—summer, autumn, winter, and spring—is not very noticeable in those climate regions.

The *continental climate* region covers the northeast quarter of the United States. This region usually has four very different seasons, including a hot, wet summer and a cold winter. Most of the southeast quarter of the United States is in the *humid subtropical climate* region. This region also has four seasons, but its winters are milder and its summers are hotter than in the continental climate region.

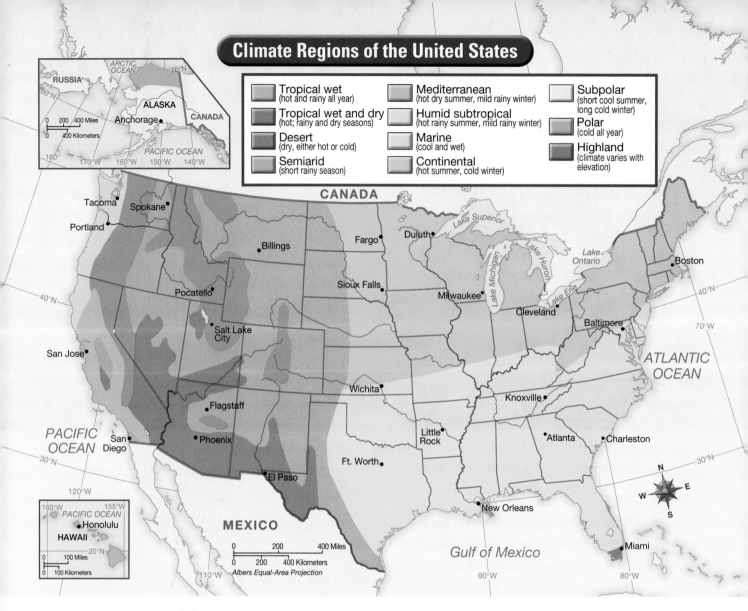

## Climate Regions of the United States

| | |
|---|---|
| Tropical wet (hot and rainy all year) | Mediterranean (hot dry summer, mild rainy winter) |
| Tropical wet and dry (hot; rainy and dry seasons) | Humid subtropical (hot rainy summer, mild rainy winter) |
| Desert (dry, either hot or cold) | Marine (cool and wet) |
| Semiarid (short rainy season) | Continental (hot summer, cold winter) |
| | Subpolar (short cool summer, long cold winter) |
| | Polar (cold all year) |
| | Highland (climate varies with elevation) |

**Regions** There are 11 different climate regions in the United States.

❓ In what climate region is your state located?

For most of the year, places in the humid subtropical region experience plenty of precipitation and high humidity. **Humidity** is the amount of moisture in the air. Like most other climate regions, however, this region does experience droughts (DROWTS). A **drought** is a long period with little or no rain.

Because the western United States is much more mountainous than the eastern part of the country, the climate varies more from place to place. The *semiarid climate* region covers much of the West. In

this region the climate is hot and **arid**, or dry, for most of the year with only a short rainy season. The writer Michael Grant once described the semiarid region with the words "hot, dry, wind, cold, sleet, thunder, puddles, drama." The "drama" was Grant's way to describe the huge thunderstorms that often form in the region during the spring and fall. These storms can drop hail that can damage crops as well as automobiles, roofs, and windows.

Mountainous areas in the western United States have a *highland climate*. In those areas, climate varies with elevation. Places at higher elevations have very cold winters with lots of snow.

The *desert climate* region covers a large part of the southwestern United States. Places with desert climates receive, on average, less than 10 inches (25 cm) of precipitation per year. The desert climate region receives little precipitation because much of it lies in the rain shadow of the western mountains. The land is part of a much larger desert region called the North American Desert, which extends southward into Mexico.

Most of the land near the Pacific Coast has one of two climates, a *marine climate* or a *Mediterranean* (meh•duh•tuh•RAY• nee•uhn) *climate*. A cool and wet marine climate can be found on the northern Pacific Coast west of the Cascade Mountains and is greatly affected by its location near the Pacific Ocean. The Mediterranean climate in central and southern California provides for long, sunny summers and mild, wet winters. This climate is called Mediterranean because it is very similar to the climate of some European countries located on the Mediterranean Sea.

**REVIEW** Why does the climate vary more from place to place in the western United States than in the eastern United States?

## Vegetation Regions

The Earth is covered with different kinds of natural vegetation. The natural vegetation that grows in a place varies depending on whether the soil there is sand, clay, or loam. These are the three main kinds of soil. The natural vegetation also varies because of temperature and precipitation. In fact, the amount of precipitation in a place is the single most important factor affecting where different kinds of natural vegetation will grow.

Most of the United States can be divided into four main vegetation regions. These are forest, grassland, desert, and tundra. Tundra regions are found far to the north and high on mountains. A **tundra** is a cold, dry region where trees cannot grow.

The forest vegetation region is found in much of the eastern United States. Across the northern Coastal Plain, the Appalachian Mountains, and much of the Central Plains, forests have mostly evergreens, such as cedar and pine, and broadleaf trees, such as oak, ash, and birch. While evergreens stay green all year round, broadleaf trees change color in autumn and drop their leaves in winter.

Sequoias are some of the world's tallest trees.

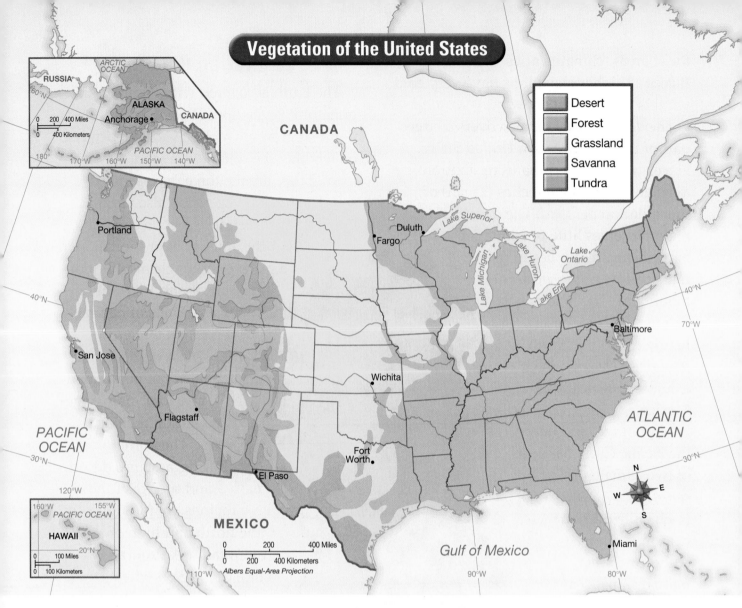

## Vegetation of the United States

**Desert**
**Forest**
**Grassland**
**Savanna**
**Tundra**

RUSSIA
ARCTIC OCEAN
ALASKA
Anchorage
CANADA
PACIFIC OCEAN

CANADA

Portland
Duluth
Fargo
Lake Superior
Lake Michigan
Lake Huron
Lake Ontario
Lake Erie
Baltimore

San Jose
Wichita

Flagstaff
PACIFIC OCEAN
ATLANTIC OCEAN

Fort Worth
El Paso
MEXICO
Gulf of Mexico
Miami

HAWAII
PACIFIC OCEAN

Albers Equal-Area Projection

**Regions** Most of the nation can be divided into five vegetation regions.

❖ What vegetation region can be found on both the east and west coasts of the United States?

Forests of evergreen pines and broadleaf oaks cover much of the southern Coastal Plain and the Gulf Coast.

Forests also cover areas of the western United States. In western Washington and Oregon and in northern California, rainfall amounts are often greater than 80 inches (203 cm) per year. Redwoods and giant sequoias, which are some of the world's oldest trees, grow in the forests there.

Trees need lots of water, but grasses can survive in much drier areas. The largest grassland region in the United States stretches across the middle of the country. It includes the western part of the Central Plains and all of the Great Plains. This part of the Central Plains is sometimes called a tall-grass prairie. A **prairie** is an area of flat or rolling land covered mostly by grasses and wildflowers. Left to grow, the grasses on this prairie would become as tall as people! Mostly short grasses cover the drier Great Plains. The land there has almost no trees and few rivers. As a result, it often looks the same, mile after mile.

Another vegetation region—savanna—is generally found between areas of grasslands and forests. A **savanna** is a kind of grassland that has areas with some trees. These trees are scattered, and the land is mostly covered with shrubs and bushes.

Only plants that can grow in a dry climate can grow in deserts. These plants include short grasses, low bushes, and cactuses. Cactuses store water in their thick stems so that they can survive until rain falls. A shrublike tree known as mesquite (muh•SKEET) sends its long roots 70 feet (21 m) into the ground to find water.

Small, hardy plants such as mosses, lichens (LY•kuhnz), herbs, and low shrubs grow in tundra regions. Tundra regions are covered by snow more than half the year. Yet there is not enough water for trees to grow because the water in the soil is frozen year-round.

There are two kinds of tundra regions. They are arctic and alpine. Arctic tundras lie near the Arctic Ocean. The only arctic tundra region in the United States is in northern Alaska. Alpine tundras can be found on mountains with elevations that make it too cold for trees to grow.

**REVIEW** **What four main vegetation regions cover most of the United States?**

## LESSON 3 REVIEW

1. **MAIN IDEA** What are the main climate and vegetation regions found in the United States?

2. **WHY IT MATTERS** How do climate and natural vegetation affect how people live in different parts of the country?

3. **VOCABULARY** Write a description of a **savanna** region.

4. **READING SKILL—Main Idea and Supporting Details** In which climate region do people experience heavy precipitation, high humidity, and droughts?

5. **GEOGRAPHY** What are some kinds of plants that grow in the desert?

6. **CRITICAL THINKING—Analyze** How are winter weather in the continental climate region and winter weather in the humid subtropical climate region different?

**PERFORMANCE—Write a Poem** Write a poem about the climate and vegetation of the region in which you live. Share your poem with classmates.

Caribou and sheep feed on the plants that grow in the tundra.

# Using the Land

The United States has many important natural resources. A **natural resource** is something found in nature that people can use. Natural resources include such things as soil, water, minerals, and vegetation.

Different physical environments and the natural resources found in them affect the way people live in different parts of the country. At the same time, people and their activities also affect their environment. People clear land to build houses and roads, and they use natural resources to meet their needs.

## People and the Environment

The environment affects the activities of many people. It affects not only the kinds of activities people take part in for recreation, but also how they earn a living. That is because people often do work related to the resources around them.

People throughout time have used the land and its resources to meet their needs. However, not all resources are spread out equally around the Earth. Not every place has enough of every resource it needs. To meet their needs or to do their jobs, people must often **modify**, or change, their environment. People modify their environments based on how they value and use the Earth's resources.

Many people agree that water is one of the most important natural resources. Without it, crops would not grow and people could not live. To make sure they have enough water, people sometimes modify their environment by digging wells in the ground. They also build dams across rivers and streams. These dams form reservoirs (REH•zuh•vwarz) behind them. Both people and industries use the water stored in those reservoirs. Dams help make electricity, too. Water from large reservoirs can be used to turn large machines called generators, which make electricity. This hydroelectric power is an important source of electricity in many parts of the country.

This builder is modifying the environment.

Some natural resources are difficult to find. To reach coal and mineral resources such as copper, gold, and silver, people dig huge mines into the Earth's surface. To reach oil and natural gas resources, they must drill wells deep into the ground or down into the ocean floor.

Soil is another important natural resource. Without fertile soil, the United States could not grow food to feed its people or to sell to other countries. Before people can plant crops, however, they must often plow or disk the land to prepare it for planting. They may also add fertilizers. **Fertilizer** is material added to the soil to make it more fertile.

Many places in the United States have fertile soil, but sometimes the land is too dry for crops to grow well. Farmers in those areas have modified their environment by using irrigation. **Irrigation** is the use of canals, ditches, or pipes to move water to dry areas. With irrigation, many desert regions have been turned into productive farmland.

When people modify the environment for one purpose, they often change it in other ways. For example, if too much water is pumped from the ground for irrigation, then the amount of underground water available for other uses decreases. Once nonrenewable resources, such as minerals and fuels, are used up, there will be none left for future use. **Nonrenewable** means that a resource cannot be made again by nature or people. However, as people use these resources, they often find ways to use them more efficiently. They may also discover new resources to take their place.

Sometimes the results of changes to the environment may not be seen for years. At one time, forests covered almost all of the eastern United States. One early traveler told of spending "day after day among the trees of a hundred feet high, without a glimpse of the surrounding country." Over time, however, people cut down many of those trees and some of the forests disappeared.

People modify the environment when they lay pipes and build highways.

## Land Use and Resources of the United States

**Legend:**
- Manufacturing
- Farming
- Grazing
- Forest
- Little-used land
- Fishing
- Oil or natural gas
- Coal
- Iron
- Copper
- Gold
- Silver
- Limestone
- Uranium
- Zinc

**Human-Environment Interactions** People in the United States use the land in many ways.

❓ Where is most of the land used for grazing?

In the past, many people thought that our supply of natural resources would last forever. However, Americans came to understand that the Earth does not have an endless supply of trees. People began planting new trees to replace the ones they cut down. They understood that trees are a renewable resource. **Renewable** means that a resource can be made again by nature or by people.

When people first plowed the grasslands of the Interior Plains, the topsoil—the fertile top layer of soil—was as deep as 16 inches (41 cm). Now, in many places, only 6 to 8 inches (15 to 20 cm) of topsoil are left. Plowing the land can speed up the process of erosion. **Erosion** is the wearing away of the Earth's surface, usually by wind and rain. Over time, people came to understand that they had to take action to protect soil and other natural resources.

**REVIEW** Why do people modify their environment?

## Patterns of Land Use

People use the Earth's surface in a variety of ways. They divide it into nations, states, and other government units. They build communities, transportation systems, and businesses on it. They also gather natural resources from it. Some of the land is owned by the public, and some of it belongs to private property owners. People buy and sell the land and make laws to decide how it can be used.

In every place on Earth, landforms and climate influence **land use**, or how most of the land in a place is used. In the United States, about half of the land is used as farmland. Most farming takes place on the Coastal Plain, on the Interior Plains, and in the large valleys in the western part of the country. In those regions, the land is fertile and there is enough water for crops to grow. In more arid regions, most of the land is used for grazing cattle, sheep, and horses.

Forests cover about one-third of the land in the United States. The largest forests are found in mountain regions, along the Great Lakes, or on the Coastal Plain. Much of the mining in the United States also takes place in mountain regions, although mining may take place wherever there are ore or fuel deposits.

Cities also occupy large areas of the United States. There, most of the land is used for housing, transportation, and businesses. In cities, most people work in service industries, such as banking, education, or health care. Most manufacturing also takes place on land in or near cities.

**REVIEW** What factors influence land use?

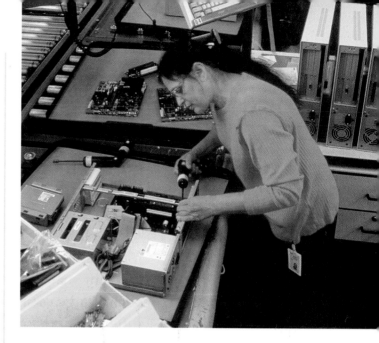

This worker has a job in manufacturing. She is building computers.

## LESSON 4 REVIEW

1. **MAIN IDEA** What are two ways that people use the land in the United States?

2. **WHY IT MATTERS** How can people minimize the effects of the changes they make to the land?

3. **VOCABULARY** Explain why the use of **fertilizers** and **irrigation** are examples of how people modify their environment.

4. **READING SKILL—Main Idea and Supporting Details** What are the two types of natural resources?

5. **GEOGRAPHY** Why do people dig wells or lay pipes that take water to dry places?

6. **GEOGRAPHY** What might people discover as they use resources?

7. **CRITICAL THINKING—Synthesize** How do the natural resources found in your community affect the way you live?

**PERFORMANCE—Write a Paragraph**
Use sources from the Internet and the library to research land use in your state. Then write a paragraph describing the different ways the land is used.

# Where People Live and Work

Regions can be based on physical features, such as landforms, climate, and vegetation. But people can define a region by using just about any feature. Because the United States is such a large country with so many differences, there are many different kinds of regions.

## Regions of the United States

To make it easier to talk about different areas of the country, people often group the 50 states into four large regions—the Northeast, the South, the Middle West, and the West. Each of these regions is based on its relative location in the United States. The **relative location** of a place is where it is, compared to one or more other places on the Earth. For example, the relative location of the Northeast region is in the northeastern part of the country.

The states in each of these regions are alike in many ways. In addition to being in the same part of the country, they often have the same kinds of landforms, climate, and natural resources. Because of that, the people who live there often earn their living in ways that are alike. The states in each region may also share a history and culture.

**REVIEW** What are the four large regions of the United States?

Newfane, Vermont, is typical of the small towns located in the Northeast.

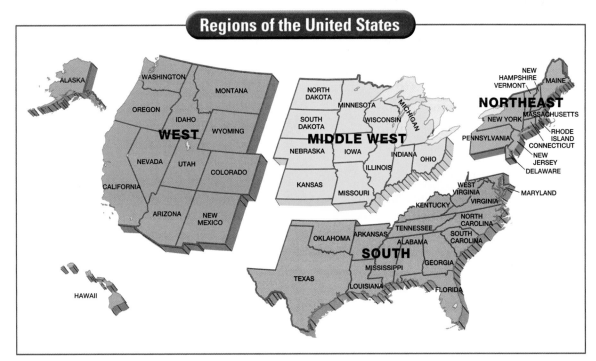

## Regions of the United States

**Regions** People often divide the United States into four regions based on location.

❓ In which region is your state located?

## Regions Based on People's Activities

Regions can also be based on patterns of human activity. Patterns of human activity include such factors as how people move from place to place and make settlements. These patterns also include how people work together to meet their needs and how they divide and share the land. Regions based on people's activities often form and change over time as people move and adopt new ways of living.

One kind of region based on patterns of human activity is a political region. A **political region** is a region in which people share a government and have the same leaders. Nations, states, counties, and cities are all political regions. Each political region has an exact boundary either set by law or agreed upon by the people in the neighboring areas. If people cannot agree on where a boundary is, conflict often results.

Other kinds of regions, known as **economic regions**, are based on the work people do or the products they make. In agricultural regions many people are farmers or ranchers. In manufacturing regions many people work in factories.

Another region based on human activity is a **cultural region**, a region based on culture. In a cultural region the main group of people who live there share customs and beliefs. The region may be based on the religion that most of the people follow or the language they speak.

Still another kind of region that is based on people is a population region. A **population region** is one based on where people live. Today, about three-fourths of the people in the United States live in **urban**, or city, regions. In urban regions many people live close together in cities.

Almost every large city has suburbs, or smaller cities and towns around it.

People who live in these **suburban** regions often work in the larger city nearby. Other people live in **rural**, or country, regions. Homes in rural regions are built farther apart, and people there often have to travel farther to go to school or work or to go shopping.

**REVIEW** What are the four kinds of regions that are based on people's activities?

## Patterns of Settlement

Geographic factors, such as landforms, bodies of water, and climate, usually affect where people settle. Through most of human history, people have tended to settle in areas where the soil is fertile and good for farming. People have also settled where there is enough fresh water to meet their needs. Having waterways and other transportation routes nearby has always been important, too.

Geographic factors have also discouraged people from settling in areas. Most people have avoided settling in deserts, tundras, or high, mountainous areas. That is because building shelters, finding food and water, and meeting other basic human needs are more difficult in those areas. Today, however, people use tools and inventions to modify their environments and make living in some of those areas possible. In fact, some of the fastest-growing cities in the United States are in desert regions of the West.

When more and more people settle in a particular place, they tend to cluster, or group together, near harbors or crossroads. In the past, a **crossroads** was a place where two roads or railroads crossed and people met to buy and sell goods, communicate, and rest. Today, it is any place that connects people, goods, and ideas. A crossroads may be a shopping center or a business park.

Other people may create settlements that are more spread out. These settlements are often found along major rivers, roads, or railroads or along a coast. Wherever people settle, their settlements become part of the physical environment. Settlements change the land on which they are built, and they are in turn changed by the land.

**REVIEW** What are the leading influences on where people settle?

New York Harbor has helped to make New York City a busy crossroads.

LOCATE IT

Lake Ontario
NEW YORK
New York City

## The Center of Population
### Understanding Human Systems

Since the beginning of our nation, the center of population has gradually moved westward. A nation's center of population is the place within that nation where there are an equal number of people living to the north, south, east, and west. The center of population in the United States has shifted westward because over time people have moved farther west to settle the land and seek new opportunities. In 1790 the center of population was near Baltimore, Maryland. Today it is located at a point southwest of St. Louis, Missouri.

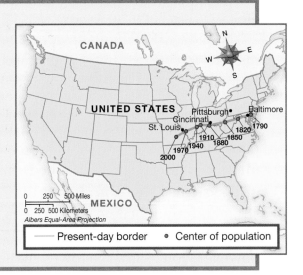

## Types of Settlement

Settlements of many sizes can be found in the United States and around the world. Some are made up of single houses scattered far apart across the landscape. Others are clusters of houses neatly arranged in villages or towns. Still others are crowded cities. About half of all the people in the world live in cities.

Cities are the largest and the most crowded type of settlement. Together, a large city and its surrounding suburbs make up that city's **metropolitan area**.

Some metropolitan areas are so large that they stretch across state borders. The largest metropolitan area in the United States, the New York City metropolitan area, stretches across parts of three states.

Settlements also differ in how they are arranged and how they are used. The way settlements are arranged often depends on the background of the people who settled there or the leaders who planned the community. For example, many communities in the Northeast are built around a town square or common.

Many early settlers there were from England, where they used this kind of area to graze their farm animals.

The ways people organize their settlements reflect not only their past and their economic activities but also their culture and the way they govern themselves. If you flew over the Middle West in an airplane, for example, you could see that many places there were planned using a grid system. The roads are mostly straight, framing large, square plots of land. If you flew over parts of the West, however, you might see towns that are laid out a different way because of the culture of the people who first settled there. Many of the towns in the West were first settled by people from Spain and from Mexico, and other countries in Latin America. Like many towns in Latin America, some of the towns in the southwestern United States have a central plaza with a church surrounded by buildings that are made of stone or a clay-and-straw mixture known as adobe (ah•DOH•bee).

**REVIEW** What are the largest types of settlements?

## The Location of American Cities

In the 1700s most people in our country lived in rural regions. At that time there were only 24 cities in the whole country. The biggest of these were port cities along the Atlantic Ocean.

Over time, new cities developed. Many grew up along the Mississippi River or its tributaries or along the shores of the Great Lakes. Other cities developed along railroad lines that were being built to connect different parts of the country. New cities also developed along the Pacific and Gulf Coasts.

Improvements in farm machinery, new methods of farming, and the growth of manufacturing encouraged people to move to cities. With new tools and new ways of growing food, farmers could produce more. That meant that not as many farmers were needed. Many people also moved to cities to find work in manufacturing and in other businesses.

Other factors have also caused the population to move from one area to another. Sometimes the importance of an industry

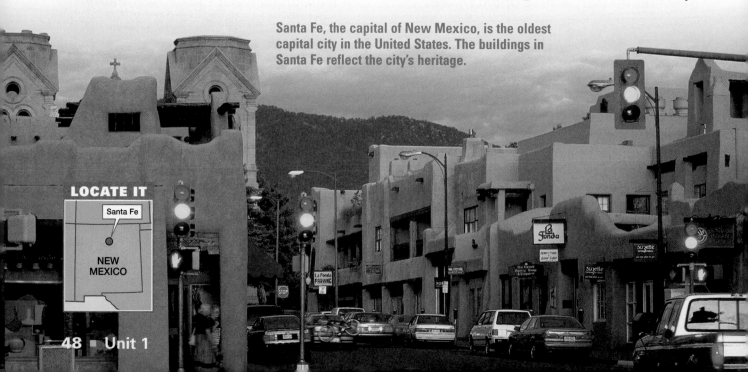

Santa Fe, the capital of New Mexico, is the oldest capital city in the United States. The buildings in Santa Fe reflect the city's heritage.

**LOCATE IT**

Santa Fe

NEW MEXICO

changes, and people may leave a place to get a job with a growing industry. For example, when oil was discovered in Texas, many people from across the country moved there to take jobs in the oil industry. People moving to the United States from other countries have also affected population in different areas of the country. They continue to do so today.

Today, most of the largest cities in the United States continue to be found near a coast, along rivers or the shores of the Great Lakes, or on other major transportation routes. In fact, the five largest cities in the country—New York City, Los Angeles, Chicago, Houston, and Philadelphia—are all located within 50 miles (80 km) of a coast or one of the Great Lakes.

Location also played a role in the selection of some cities as capitals. Often these cities were chosen because they were located near the central part of a state or country. Some state capitals were chosen because they were among the largest cities in their states or were located near the coast or near a major transportation route.

## The Ten Largest Cities in the United States

| CITY | POPULATION |
| --- | --- |
| New York City, NY | 8,008,278 |
| Los Angeles, CA | 3,694,820 |
| Chicago, IL | 2,896,016 |
| Houston, TX | 1,953,631 |
| Philadelphia, PA | 1,517,550 |
| Phoenix, AZ | 1,321,045 |
| San Diego, CA | 1,223,400 |
| Dallas, TX | 1,188,580 |
| San Antonio, TX | 1,144,646 |
| Detroit, MI | 951,270 |

**Analyze Tables** Three of the country's largest cities are in the state of Texas.

◈ Which city has a larger population—Dallas or San Antonio?

At the time the site for our nation's capital was chosen, there were only 13 states. The capital, Washington, D.C., was built about halfway between the northernmost and southernmost states.

**REVIEW** Where are most of the largest cities in the United States?

## LESSON 5 REVIEW

1. **MAIN IDEA** Describe regions in the United States that are based on human activity.

2. **WHY IT MATTERS** How do people's activities help shape a region's identity?

3. **VOCABULARY** Explain in a sentence or two how the terms **urban** and **suburban** are related.

4. **READING SKILL—Main Idea and Supporting Details** What features describe a political region?

5. **ECONOMICS** In what kind of region based on people's activities would a community of farmers live?

6. **CRITICAL THINKING—Analyze** Why do you think that people tend to live near crossroads?

 **PERFORMANCE—Make a Brochure** Work with a partner to make a brochure about your community. Include information about the types of settlements there and the activities people do. Take the brochure home and share it with family members.

# ·SKILLS·
# Use Latitude and Longitude

| VOCABULARY | | |
|---|---|---|
| absolute location | parallel | meridian |
| line of latitude | line of longitude | prime meridian |

## WHY IT MATTERS

Lines of latitude and lines of longitude help you describe the **absolute location**, or exact location, of any place on Earth.

## WHAT YOU NEED TO KNOW

Mapmakers use a system of imaginary lines to form a grid system on maps and globes. The lines that run east and west are the **lines of latitude**. Lines of latitude are also called **parallels** (PAR•uh•lelz). This is because they are parallel, or always the same distance from each other.

Lines of latitude are measured in degrees north and south of the equator, which is labeled 0°, or *zero degrees*. The parallels north of the equator are marked *N* for *north latitude*. This means that they are in the Northern Hemisphere. The parallels south of the equator are marked *S* for *south latitude*. This means they are in the Southern Hemisphere.

The lines that run north and south on a map or globe are the **lines of longitude**, or **meridians**. Each meridian runs from the North Pole to the South Pole. Unlike parallels, which never meet, meridians meet at the poles.

Meridians are numbered in much the same way that parallels are numbered. The meridian marked 0° is called the **prime meridian**. Lines of longitude to the west of the prime meridian are

Latitude and Longitude

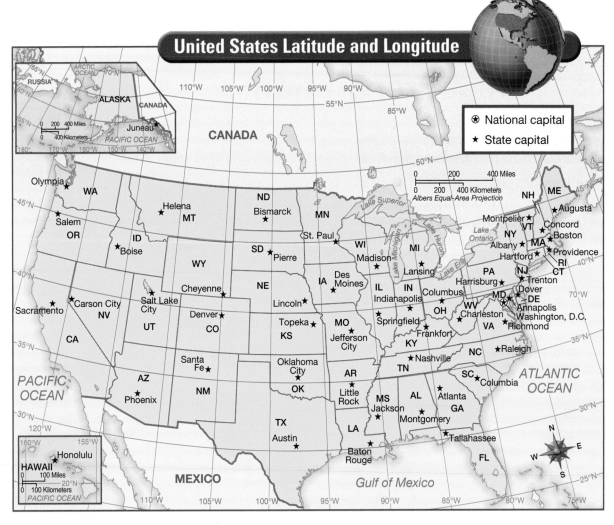

## United States Latitude and Longitude

- ⊛ National capital
- ★ State capital

*Albers Equal-Area Projection*

---

marked *W* for *west longitude*. They are in the Western Hemisphere. The meridians to the east of the prime meridian are marked *E* for *east longitude*. They are in the Eastern Hemisphere.

### ➡ PRACTICE THE SKILL

The map above, which shows the locations of state capitals in the United States, uses crossing lines of latitude and longitude to describe absolute location. On this map every fifth parallel is shown and every fifth meridian is shown.

At the left-hand side of the map, find 40°N. At the bottom, find 90°W. Use your fingers to trace these lines to the point where they cross. Springfield, Illinois, is not far from this point. So you can say that Springfield is near 40°N, 90°W.

Now use the map to answer these questions.

1. What line of latitude is closest to Austin, Texas?

2. What line of longitude is closest to Denver, Colorado?

3. Which location is farther north—50°N, 80°W or 30°N, 90°W?

### ➡ APPLY WHAT YOU LEARNED

Use latitude and longitude to describe the location of your state's capital city. Write a paragraph to descibe how you found the capital's location.

Practice your map and globe skills with the **GeoSkills CD-ROM.**

# 1 Review and Test Preparation

## USE YOUR READING SKILLS

Complete this graphic organizer to show that you have identified the main ideas and supporting details in this chapter. A copy of this graphic organizer appears on page 13 of the Activity Book.

## Regions of the United States

**SUPPORTING DETAILS**

**SUPPORTING DETAILS**

**MAIN IDEA**

The United States can be divided into regions based on people's activities.

**SUPPORTING DETAILS**

**SUPPORTING DETAILS**

## THINK & WRITE

**Write a Letter**   Imagine that you are traveling across the country, from New York City in New York to San Francisco in California. Write a letter to a friend that describes how the climate changes as you travel from east to west.

**Write a Compare and Contrast Report**   Write a report about the mountains in the United States. In your report, compare and contrast the mountains in the eastern United States with those in the western United States.

## USE VOCABULARY

Identify the term that correctly matches each definition.

| |
| landform (p. 18) |
| inlet (p. 27) |
| rain shadow (p. 35) |
| fertilizer (p. 41) |
| relative location (p. 44) |

1 where a place is, compared to other places

2 physical feature on Earth's surface

3 material added to soil to make it more fertile

4 any area of water that extends into the land from a larger body of water

5 the dry side of a mountain

## RECALL FACTS

Answer these questions.

6 What group of lakes makes up the world's largest freshwater lakes?

7 What do river systems do?

8 What is the Continental Divide?

9 How do people today modify their environment?

10 How does erosion change the land?

Write the letter of the best choice.

11 **TEST PREP** Which of the following vegetation regions has low bushes and cactuses?
 A forest
 B grassland
 C desert
 D prairie

12 **TEST PREP** Cultural regions can be based on all of the following except—
 F the religion that people follow.
 G the language people speak.
 H the work that people do.
 J the customs of the people.

## THINK CRITICALLY

13 What types of regions are based on people's activities?

14 What are some ways the land is used in the United States?

## APPLY SKILLS

**Use Elevation Maps**
Use the map of the United States on page 25 to answer these questions.

15 How would you describe the land in the Great Basin?

16 What is the highest elevation in the Interior Plains?

17 Which mountain range has a higher elevation, the Rocky Mountains or the Appalachian Mountains?

**Use Longitude and Latitude**
Use the Latitude and Longitude map on page 51 to answer these questions.

18 What capital cities are located closest to 45°N?

19 Which is farther north, a city at 40°N, 85°W or a city at 35°N, 80°W?

20 What city is located closest to 40°N, 120°W?

21 What is the location of Denver, Colorado?

# The Earliest Americans

66 **It is from this land that we obtained the timber and stone for our homes and kivas.** 99

—Hopi, quoted by Alvin M. Josephy, Jr. in *500 Nations*, 1994

## MESA VERDE NATIONAL PARK

For more than 700 years, from A.D. 600 to A.D. 1300, many Native American peoples made their homes in the area that is today Mesa Verde National Park. These early Americans built sturdy stone villages carved directly into the canyon walls. This photograph shows the Cliff Palace in winter.

### LOCATE IT

COLORADO

Mesa Verde
National Park

## CHAPTER READING SKILL

### Compare and Contrast

When you **compare** information you are showing how things are alike. Words such as *like, both, also,* and *similarly* indicate a **comparison**. When you **contrast** information, you are identifying how things are different. Words such as *instead, but,* and *however* signal a **contrast**.

As you read this chapter, compare and contrast information about the Native American tribes in what is now the United States.

DIFFERENCES    SIMILARITIES    DIFFERENCES

**MAIN IDEA**
Read to find out how people may have first come to live in North and South America.

**WHY IT MATTERS**
Over time, groups of early people spread out across North and South America, becoming the first Americans.

**VOCABULARY**

glacier
migration
theory
archaeologist
artifact
descendant
origin story
ancestor

# The First Americans

The history of the United States of America begins long before there was a United States. It begins with the first people in North America many thousands of years ago. At that time, however, the continent was a far different place from what it is today.

At different times in its past, the Earth has experienced long periods of freezing cold. During these periods, known as the Ice Ages, the Earth's climate became so cold that huge, slow-moving sheets of ice called **glaciers** formed. These glaciers covered large parts of the Earth. So much of the Earth's water was trapped in glaciers that the level of the oceans dropped. At several different times this caused a "bridge" of dry land to appear between the continents of Asia and North America.

## The Land Bridge Story

Scientists gave the name Beringia (buh•RIN•gee•uh) to this land bridge between Asia and North America. It was named for the Bering Strait, a narrow body of water that now separates Siberia, in present-day Russia, from Alaska. Some scientists believe that between 12,000 and 40,000 years ago, hunting groups from Asia began traveling across the Beringia land bridge.

FAST FACT During the Ice Ages so much water was trapped in glaciers that the water level in the oceans dropped as much as 350 feet (107 m).

This **migration**, or movement of people, probably took place very slowly, with groups traveling only a few miles in an entire lifetime. Finally, after thousands of years, Asian hunters reached what is today Alaska. However, they and the animals they hunted could go no farther. Huge glaciers blocked their path.

About 12,000 years ago, the climate began to get warmer. Some of the glaciers started to melt. As a result, the oceans began to rise. Once again water covered Beringia. At the same time, a narrow path opened between two melting glaciers that covered what is now Canada.

The animals followed the path between the glaciers, and the hunters followed the animals. Slowly the hunters made their way farther into the Americas—North America and South America. These people became the first Americans.

**REVIEW** According to the land bridge story, why did the hunters make their way into the Americas?

## New Discoveries

The land bridge story is one **theory**, or possible explanation, for when and how the first Americans arrived in the Americas. Scientists, however, continue to ask if the first Americans could have been here earlier, and if they could have come by some other means.

The scientists who study the cultures of people who lived long ago are known as **archaeologists** (ar•kee•AH•luh•jists). In recent years archaeologists have made discoveries that seem to support an "early arrival" theory. According to this theory, Beringia appeared during an earlier Ice Age.

**GEOGRAPHY THEME**

**Movement** According to the land bridge story, it took thousands of years for people to spread out over North and South America.

❓ **About how many miles is it from Asia to the tip of South America?**

**Land Routes of Early People**

ASIA

ARCTIC OCEAN

Arctic Circle

EUROPE

180°

Bering Strait

NORTH AMERICA

40°N

40°N

20°W

ATLANTIC OCEAN

60°W

Tropic of Cancer

140°W

PACIFIC OCEAN

0°

Equator

0   750   1,500 Miles
0   750 1,500 Kilometers
Azimuthal Equal-Area Projection

N
W   E
S

SOUTH AMERICA

Tropic of Capricorn

40°S

100°W

20°W

Land
Glacier
Sea ice
→ Land route

One of the most important discoveries that supports the early arrival theory was made at a dig, or an archaeological site, located in southwestern Pennsylvania. This site, known as the Meadowcroft Rock Shelter, appears to have been an Ice Age campsite. Archaeologists discovered **artifacts**, or objects made by early people, at the site. Most of the artifacts are 14,000 to 15,000 years old. A few are more than 19,000 years old.

Discoveries in South America also support the early arrival theory. In Monte Verde (MOHN•tay VAIR•day), Chile, archaeologists uncovered artifacts, animal bones, and even a child's footprint. This evidence, or proof, shows that people were there at least 13,000 years ago. In Brazil human-made stone chips were found that may be 30,000 years old.

Other discoveries, in California and Peru, support the theory that the first Americans did not cross the land bridge at all. Instead, they may have traveled to the Americas in boats. Some may have actually crossed the Pacific Ocean. On San Miguel Island, about 25 miles (40 km)

off the coast of California, archaeologists found evidence that people lived there about 13,000 years ago. Archaeologists know that these people used oceangoing boats because they ate fish that could be caught only far from shore. In Peru archaeologists found two 12,000-year-old sites whose residents also ate foods only found in the deep ocean.

**REVIEW** Why do many archaeologists believe that the first Americans arrived earlier than previously thought?

## Origin Stories

There are also people today who believe that the first Americans did not come from Asia or anywhere else. Many present-day Native Americans, or American Indians, the descendants of the first Americans, believe that their people have always lived in the Americas. A **descendant** is a person's child, grandchild, or later relative.

All Native American peoples use stories to tell about important events and people in their past. Some of these stories

Many archaeologists believe that these tools (above) found in Pennsylvania, and the cave paintings (left) at Pedra Furada, Brazil, are proof that people arrived in the Americas earlier than previously thought.

Native American storytellers, like this one, share stories of the past with young people.

tell about the origins, or beginnings, of Native American people. Such stories are called **origin stories**. Like the Creation story in the Bible, some Native American origin stories explain how the world was made. The Blackfoot people, for example, tell a story of Old Man the Creator. According to the story, he made the animals and plants and formed the prairies and mountains.

The Hurons tell an origin story that begins when water covered the Earth. According to the story, land was formed from a tiny bit of soil taken from the claws of a turtle. The turtle had picked up the soil from the bottom of the ocean. Because of this story and others like it, some Native Americans use the name Turtle Island to describe the Americas.

No one knows exactly when the first Americans arrived. However, it was so long ago that the descendants of the first Americans have no stories of distant homelands where their **ancestors**, or early family members, once lived. They tell only stories of the Americas.

**REVIEW** What do Native American origin stories tell?

## LESSON 1
## REVIEW

**1 MAIN IDEA** By what ways may early people have arrived in the Americas?

**2 WHY IT MATTERS** Why do you think the arrival of early people in the Americas caused many different cultures to form?

**3 VOCABULARY** What is a **theory**?

**4 READING SKILL—Compare and Contrast** How do Native Americans' views on how they arrived in the Americas differ from archaeologists' views?

**5 HISTORY** How did the artifacts found at Meadowcroft Rock Shelter change many archaeologists' theories?

**6 CULTURE** Why do many Native Americans believe that their people have always lived in the Americas?

**7 CRITICAL THINKING—Evaluate** Why do people disagree about when and how the first Americans came to the Americas?

 **PERFORMANCE—Make a Chart** With a classmate, make a chart that compares the points of view on how people first came to the Americas.

# ·SKILLS·
### CHART AND GRAPH

# Read Time Lines

## ▶ WHY IT MATTERS

An easy way to see relationships among events in history is to look at a **time line**. A time line is a diagram that shows events that took place during a certain period of time. Knowing how to read a time line can help you understand the order of the events and the amounts of time between events.

## ▶ WHAT YOU NEED TO KNOW

A time line looks like a ruler marked in dates instead of inches. Like inches marked on a ruler, the dates on a time line are equally spaced. However, not all time lines look the same or are read in the same way. Most time lines run horizontally, or across the page. But some run vertically, or down the page. Horizontal time lines, like the one shown below, are read from left to right. The earliest date is on the left end of the time line, and the most recent date is on the right end. The time line on page 61 is a vertical time line. It is read from top to bottom. The earliest date is at the top of the time line, and the most recent date is at the bottom.

Time lines can show events that took place during any period of time. Some time lines show events that took place over a **decade**, or a period of 10 years. Others show events that took place over a **century**, or a period of 100 years. Both a decade and centuries are shown on the horizontal time line below. Some time lines even show events that took place over a **millennium**, or a period of a thousand years. A millennium is shown on the vertical time line on page 61.

### Horizontal Time Line

1201    1301    1401

• 1211

decade

century

13th century    14th century

The vertical time line here shows dates from the ancient past to today. Notice the letters B.C. and A.D. in the middle of the time line. Many people today identify years by whether they took place before or after the birth of Jesus Christ. The years before the birth of Christ are labeled B.C., which stands for "before Christ." Years after the birth of Christ are labeled A.D. This stands for the Latin words *Anno Domini,* which mean "in the year of the Lord."

An event that happened in 100 B.C. took place 100 years before the birth of Christ. An event that happened in A.D. 100 took place 100 years after the birth of Christ. Because every year in modern times is A.D., these letters are often not needed.

You may also see the letters B.C.E. or C.E. with dates. The abbreviation B.C.E. stands for "before the Common Era." It is sometimes used instead of B.C. The abbreviation C.E., which stands for "Common Era," is sometimes used in place of A.D.

### ▶ PRACTICE THE SKILL

Use the horizontal time line on page 60 to answer the following questions.

❶ How many centuries are shown on the time line?

❷ What were the first and last years of the thirteenth century?

Use the vertical time line on this page to answer the following questions.

❸ How many millenniums are shown on this time line?

❹ Which year came earlier, 1000 B.C. or A.D. 500?

### ▶ APPLY WHAT YOU LEARNED

Make a time line that shows the twentieth and twenty-first centuries. Label the first and last years of both centuries and the year you were born. Mark some other important events for you in the past and in the future. Display your time line in the classroom.

**Vertical Time Line**

2000 B.C.

millennium { 1500 B.C.

1000 B.C.

500 B.C.

B.C.
A.D.

A.D. 500

A.D. 1000

A.D. 1500

A.D. 2000

**MAIN IDEA**
Read to learn how changes in the environment caused the ancient Indians' ways of life to change.

**WHY IT MATTERS**
As different cultures developed among the ancient Indians, North America became a place of great diversity.

**VOCABULARY**
nomad
technology
extinct
agriculture
tribe
civilization
class
slavery
pueblo

# Ancient Indians

| 10,000 years ago | 5,000 years ago | Present |
|---|---|---|

**10,000 years ago – 600 years ago**

In many ways, the story of the first Americans, or ancient Indians, is filled with mystery. Just when archaeologists think they have some answers, they find new evidence that creates new questions. One thing, however, is known for certain. For many generations, the ancient Indians and their descendants slowly moved throughout the Americas. They settled in different regions and developed many different ways of life.

## Hunters and Gatherers

After the last Ice Age, the climate of North America remained mostly cool and humid. Rich vegetation provided food for very large animals, including horses and camels. Giant mastodons and mammoths also roamed the vast grasslands and forests. Mastodons and mammoths looked like huge, hairy elephants. They stood 14 feet (4 m) tall, had tusks up to 14 feet (4 m) long, and weighed as much as 10,000 pounds (4,536 kg).

Many of the ancient Indians depended on these giant animals in order to survive. They ate the meat and used the fur, skins, and bones to make clothing, shelter, and tools. Daily life for these ancient Indians was spent mostly tracking and hunting the animals and gathering fruits and nuts for food along the way. These people were mostly **nomads**, or wanderers who had no settled home. They built shelters in caves or in tents made from animal skins. The ancient Indians lived and hunted together in small groups or in families.

Compared to the animals they hunted, the ancient Indians were small and weak. Over time, however, they had learned to sharpen stones into spear points and tie them to wooden poles.

Some hunters also made and used clubs and axes with stone blades. From

A Clovis point

time to time, different groups of ancient Indians invented new tools or weapons. One such important weapon was the atlatl (AHT•lah•tuhl), or spear-thrower.

At about the same time the atlatl was invented, another early inventor had found a way to make a spear point by a process scientists call flaking. Using a bone or a stone, the early inventor knocked off flakes, or small thin chips, from flint or another kind of stone. The inventor continued to flake the stone until a sharp point was formed. The point was then hollowed out and fastened tightly to a spear. These new spear points were razor-sharp, making them the best weapons early hunters had ever had.

These delicate yet deadly spear points are called Clovis points. They are named after the town of Clovis, New Mexico, where archaeologists first found them. Similar points have been found in places ranging from Alaska to the Andes Mountains, in South America.

The atlatl and Clovis points were two improvements in technology by ancient Indians. **Technology** is the use of scientific knowledge or tools to make or do something. These inventions were just as important to the ancient Indians as computers are to many people today.

**REVIEW** Why were Clovis points important to ancient Indians?

The ancient Indians moved from place to place to follow the animals they hunted.

Early farmers may have ground corn into flour by using a grinding stone (left) and may have stored kernels in containers like this one (above).

## A Time of Change

Over thousands of years the environment of North America slowly changed. The climate became warmer and drier. As a result, much of the vegetation the giant animals ate could no longer grow. This may be one reason the giant animals became **extinct** (ik•STINGT), or died out. By about 10,000 years ago, most of them had disappeared from North America.

Life no longer centered around the hunting of giant animals. People began to fish and to hunt more of the smaller animals, such as deer and rabbits. To hunt them, the ancient Indians developed new hunting tools, such as the bow and arrow.

The ancient Indians also began to eat a greater variety of plants. In time they learned where certain plants grew best. They learned at what time of the year nuts, berries, and other plant parts became ripe. Each season the people traveled to places where they could gather food and hunt.

As the ancient Indians gathered more food than they could use at a time, they found ways to store the extra food. They made storage containers from reeds, vines, or strips of wood. Later, people learned to make storage containers out of other materials, such as clay.

Over time some ancient Indians changed their way of life even more. Some took the first steps toward producing their own food. They planted seeds and grew food crops. This was the beginning of **agriculture**, or farming.

Agriculture started at different times in different parts of the world. Ancient Indians in Mexico, however, were among the first to develop agriculture in North America. Some of the earliest farmers lived in the Tehuacán (tay•wah•KAHN) Valley in central Mexico. The early farmers of the valley grew at least 12 kinds of corn, as well as avocados, squash, and beans. Maize (MAYZ), or corn, became the most important crop for many ancient Indians living in North America.

Farming changed the lives of many of the ancient Indian groups. By about 5,000 years ago, some were building stronger homes and had started villages. Some groups also formed what are now called tribes. **Tribe** is a term often used to describe a group of Native Americans who share a language and customs. Over time each tribe came to have its own culture. A tribe's culture set it apart from other tribes.

**REVIEW** How did farming change the lives of many of the ancient Indians?

## Early Civilizations

Having turned to a more settled way of life, some ancient Indian groups began to develop civilizations. A **civilization** is a culture that usually has cities and well-developed forms of government, religion, and learning. Among the most ancient American civilizations were the Olmecs (AHL•meks), the Maya (MY•ah), the Mound Builders, and the Anasazi (ah•nuh•SAH•zee).

From about 1500 B.C. to A.D. 300, the Olmecs lived in what is now southeastern Mexico. They developed their own calendar, number system, and form of writing. Because later groups learned so much from them, the Olmec culture came to be known as the "mother civilization" of the Americas. The Olmecs shared their ideas through trade with other groups.

One of these groups was the Maya, who lived south of the Olmecs. The Maya began to develop around 500 B.C. Building on what the Olmecs had done, the Maya slowly created their own civilization. They built more than 100 stone cities. Each city had its own ruler and government. Tikal, in what is now Guatemala, was the largest.

Like the Olmecs, the Maya were divided into social **classes**. Depending on what the people of a certain class did to make a living, its members were treated with different amounts of respect. At the top were the Mayan priests.

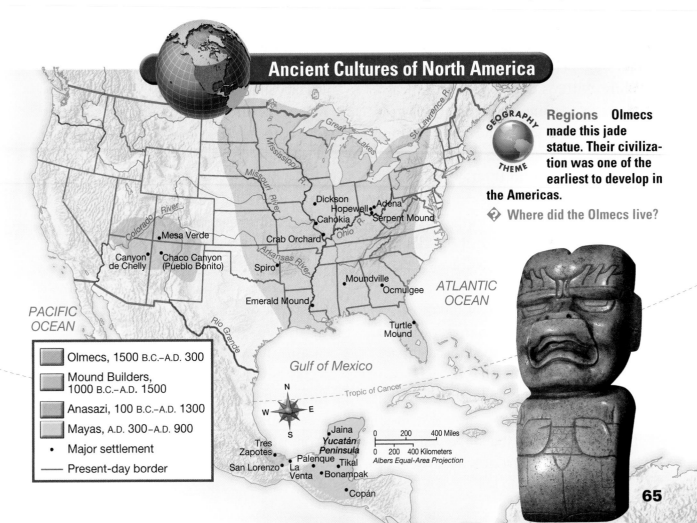

**Ancient Cultures of North America**

GEOGRAPHY THEME

**Regions** Olmecs made this jade statue. Their civilization was one of the earliest to develop in the Americas.

◆ Where did the Olmecs live?

Dickson
Hopewell • Adena
Cahokia
Serpent Mound
Crab Orchard
Mesa Verde
Canyon de Chelly • Chaco Canyon (Pueblo Bonito)
Spiro
Moundville
Ocmulgee
Emerald Mound
*ATLANTIC OCEAN*

*PACIFIC OCEAN*

Turtle Mound

*Gulf of Mexico*

Tropic of Cancer

Olmecs, 1500 B.C.–A.D. 300
Mound Builders, 1000 B.C.–A.D. 1500
Anasazi, 100 B.C.–A.D. 1300
Mayas, A.D. 300–A.D. 900
• Major settlement
— Present-day border

Jaina
*Yucatán Peninsula*
Tres Zapotes
Palenque • Tikal
San Lorenzo • La Venta • Bonampak
• Copán

0    200    400 Miles
0   200  400 Kilometers
*Albers Equal-Area Projection*

**65**

Then came the people from important families. Below them were the traders and craftspeople, the farmers, and finally the slaves. **Slavery** is the practice of holding people against their will and making them carry out orders. In Mayan society most slaves were people accused of crimes.

While cultures developed in Central America, other ancient civilizations grew in what is today the eastern half of the United States. These people became known as the Mound Builders because of the earthen mounds they built as burial sites or as places of worship.

The earliest of the Mound Builders were the Adenas (uh•DEE•nuhz), who lived in the Ohio River valley from about 1000 B.C. to A.D. 200. One of the most famous Adena mounds, Serpent Mound, is about 1,330 feet (405 m) long. When you look at it from the air, you can see that it forms the shape of a snake.

Around 300 B.C. a larger mound-building civilization known as the Hopewells developed in the central part of what is now the

United States. The culture of the Hopewells was the strongest in the region for nearly 500 years. Hopewell goods and ideas spread far and wide through trade.

The greatest mound-building civilization was that of the Mississippian culture. It developed in the Mississippi River valley about A.D. 700. The Mississippians lived in hundreds of towns and several large cities. The largest Mississippian city was near where East St. Louis, Illinois, stands today. By A.D. 1200 more than 30,000 people lived in this city, called Cahokia (kuh•HOH•kee•uh).

From about 100 B.C. to A.D. 1300, the Anasazi, or "Ancient People," built a civilization in what is today the southwestern United States. They lived in groups of houses built next to or on top of one another, like apartment houses today. Spanish explorers later described these homes as pueblos (PWEH•blohz). **Pueblo** is the Spanish word for "village." Most pueblos were built on top of mesas, or high, flat-topped hills. Others were

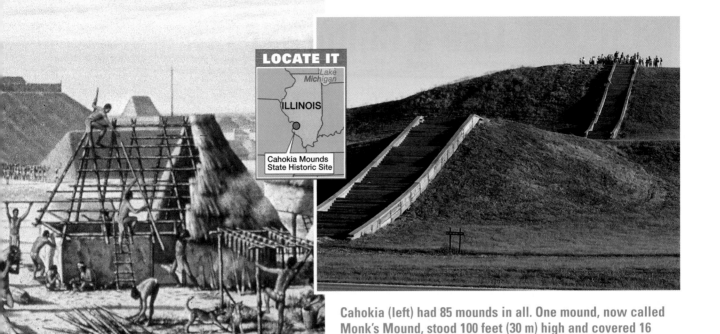

Lake Michigan

ILLINOIS

Cahokia Mounds State Historic Site

Cahokia (left) had 85 mounds in all. One mound, now called Monk's Mound, stood 100 feet (30 m) high and covered 16 acres. People today can climb steps to reach the top of this mound (above).

built into the sides of high cliffs. The largest was Pueblo Bonito (boh•NEE•toh) in present-day New Mexico.

Over hundreds of years, the Anasazi and other early civilizations in North America gave way to new cultures and new civilizations. By about A.D. 1400,

hundreds of different tribes of Native Americans lived throughout North America. North America was a land of great diversity—a land of many different peoples and cultures.

REVIEW **Which early civilization lived in what is now the eastern United States?**

LESSON 2
REVIEW

**Summary Time Line**

10,000 years ago        600 years ago

**10,000 years ago**
Early hunters are using the atlatl

**7,000 years ago**
Farming may have begun in the Tehuacán Valley

**600 years ago**
Hundreds of Native American tribes are living in North America

1. **MAIN IDEA** Why did the ancient Indians have to change their way of life?

2. **WHY IT MATTERS** In what ways is North America still a land of great diversity?

3. **VOCABULARY** Explain how the terms **civilization** and **technology** are related.

4. **TIME LINE** When were early hunters using the atlatl?

5. **READING SKILL—Compare and Contrast** How were the Olmec and the Mayan civilizations similar?

6. **CULTURE** Why is the Olmec culture known as the "mother civilization"?

7. **CRITICAL THINKING—Application** How did the ancient Indians use natural resources?

**PERFORMANCE—Make a Collage** Use photographs from old magazines or your own drawings to make a collage that shows how technology affects people's lives today. Then present your collage to the class.

# ·SKILLS·

MAP AND GLOBE

# Use a Cultural Map

This butterfly was made by a Crow Indian.

## WHY IT MATTERS

Some maps give you a general picture of the cultures of the people living in different regions. Maps showing cultural regions often use colors or symbols for places where most of the people speak a certain language or follow a certain way of life. Knowing about cultural regions can help you understand more about people and where they live.

## WHAT YOU NEED TO KNOW

Learning about the general picture of a place can help you make generalizations. A **generalization** is a statement that summarizes groups of facts and shows relationships among them. A generalization tells what is true most of the time.

The map on page 69 shows the early Native American cultural regions of North America. Each of the 11 regions is based on the unique location, landforms, climate, and vegetation that affected the cultures and traditions of Native Americans.

Within each cultural region are labels giving the names of some of the Native American tribes that lived there. The map also includes present-day state borders so you can better understand where these early cultures were located.

## PRACTICE THE SKILL

Use the following questions as a guide for making generalizations about the early cultures of North America.

1 Identify the color that covers most of the eastern half of what is today the United States. What generalization can you make about the way of life of the people who lived there?

2 Which three cultural regions included parts of present-day Texas?

3 What generalizations can you make about early Native American cultures in the present-day states of Arkansas, New Mexico, and Virginia?

## APPLY WHAT YOU LEARNED

Draw a cultural map of present-day North America based on the main languages spoken. Gather information for your map by using books or Internet sources. Use colors to show where different languages are generally spoken today. Have a classmate use your map to make generalizations about the cultures of North America.

Practice your map and globe skills with the **GeoSkills CD-ROM**.

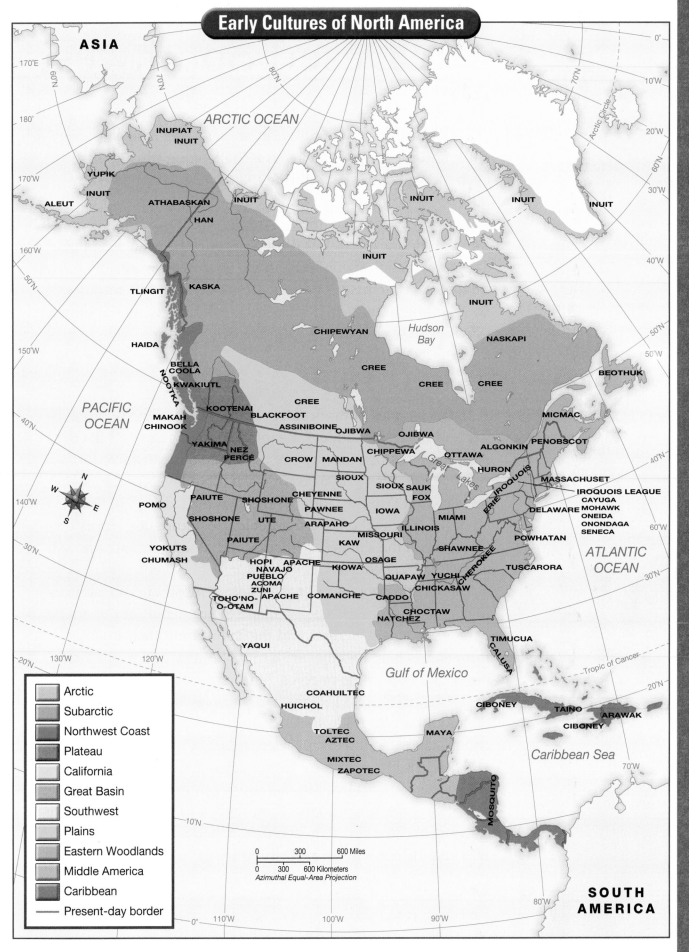

# Early Cultures of North America

ASIA

ARCTIC OCEAN

INUPIAT
INUIT

YUPIK
INUIT
ALEUT
ATHABASKAN
HAN

INUIT

INUIT

INUIT

INUIT

INUIT

TLINGIT
KASKA

HAIDA

INUIT

CHIPEWYAN
Hudson
Bay
NASKAPI

BELLA
COOLA
KWAKIUTL
CREE
CREE
CREE
BEOTHUK

PACIFIC
OCEAN
MAKAH
CHINOOK
KOOTENAI
BLACKFOOT
CREE
MICMAC

NOOTKA
ASSINIBOINE
OJIBWA
OJIBWA
ALGONKIN
PENOBSCOT

YAKIMA
NEZ
PERCÉ
CROW
MANDAN
CHIPPEWA
OTTAWA
HURON
MASSACHUSET

POMO
PAIUTE
SHOSHONE
CHEYENNE
PAWNEE
SIOUX
SIOUX
SAUK
FOX
IOWA
ERIE
IROQUOIS
IROQUOIS LEAGUE
CAYUGA
MOHAWK
ONEIDA
ONONDAGA
SENECA

SHOSHONE
UTE
ARAPAHO
MIAMI
DELAWARE

MISSOURI
ILLINOIS
POWHATAN

YOKUTS
CHUMASH
PAIUTE
KAW
OSAGE
SHAWNEE
TUSCARORA
ATLANTIC
OCEAN

HOPI
NAVAJO
PUEBLO
ACOMA
ZUNI
APACHE
KIOWA
QUAPAW
YUCHI
CHEROKEE
CHICKASAW

TOHO'NO-
O-OTAM
APACHE
COMANCHE
CADDO
CHOCTAW
NATCHEZ

YAQUI

TIMUCUA
CALUSA

Gulf of Mexico
Tropic of Cancer

COAHUILTEC
HUICHOL
CIBONEY
TAÍNO
ARAWAK
CIBONEY

TOLTEC
AZTEC
MAYA
Caribbean Sea

MIXTEC
ZAPOTEC

MOSQUITO

SOUTH
AMERICA

## Legend

- Arctic
- Subarctic
- Northwest Coast
- Plateau
- California
- Great Basin
- Southwest
- Plains
- Eastern Woodlands
- Middle America
- Caribbean
- Present-day border

0    300    600 Miles
0    300    600 Kilometers
Azimuthal Equal-Area Projection

# 3

**MAIN IDEA**
Read to learn how the way of life of Indian peoples of the Southwest was affected by the dry environment.

**WHY IT MATTERS**
People often have to adjust or modify their environment in order to live.

### VOCABULARY

**adapt**
**staple**
**surplus**
**ceremony**
**hogan**

# The Desert Southwest

The Southwest, with its rocky mesas, deep canyons, steep cliffs, and rugged mountains, is a challenging place to live, even today. Intense heat during the day can be followed by bitter cold at night. Weeks can go by without a drop of rain or snow. However, in summer, a sudden storm can bring so much rain that floods occur. It is difficult to survive in such a land. The many peoples who lived in the Southwest were able to **adapt**, or fit their ways of living to the land and its resources. By adapting to their environment, they found ways not only to survive but even to live well in the desert region.

## The Pueblo Peoples

To the peoples of the Southwest, the expression "up the ladder and down the ladder" meant "to enter a house." Like their Anasazi ancestors, many peoples of the Southwest lived in pueblos. To enter a home or to reach other levels of the pueblo, people went "up the ladder and down the ladder." In time all of the tribes who lived in pueblos, including the Hopis (HOH•peez), the Zunis (ZOO•neez), and others, became known as the Pueblo peoples.

The Pueblo peoples built their homes mostly from resources they could find nearby. Some made their pueblos out of adobe. Others, such as the Hopis and the Zunis, built their pueblos from stones held together with mud. Some wood was used to build the roofs of the pueblos, but there are very few trees in the desert. Pueblo Indians had to travel long distances into the mountains to find pine and juniper trees from which they could make wooden beams. Here is how Charlotte and David Yue describe life in an early Hopi pueblo in their book *The Pueblo*.

"Pueblo families lived in one room, but most of the daily activities were out of doors. Their homes were used mainly for sleeping and for being sheltered from bad weather. The terrace was an outdoor kitchen and sitting room. The women went up

Pueblo families helped their children learn the names of the kachinas (kuh•CHEE•nuhz) by giving them kachina figures.

**A CLOSER LOOK**
Pueblo

Some pueblos had as many as five levels. The roof of one level was the floor of the next level above it.

1 kiva
2 pottery making
3 grinding corn
4 cooking
5 weaving
6 preparing food

❓ What activities are shown in this pueblo?

and down ladders to outside ovens on the terrace or down to the ground. The outdoor drying racks had to be tended, and baskets and pottery were often worked on outside."

The land of the Southwest also affected how the Pueblo Indians hunted and grew food. The **staple**, or main, foods of the Pueblos were corn, beans, and squash. As it was for most Native American groups, the most important of these was corn. The Pueblos also grew cotton, from which they made blankets and clothing. To grow these crops in the dry climate, the

Pueblos depended on water from rain and underground springs, which they used to irrigate the land. While the men tended the crops, the women spent hours each day grinding corn into meal, using smooth, flat stones. Part of every home was filled with containers of corn and cornmeal. A food **surplus**, or an amount more than what is needed, meant survival during times of drought.

The Hopis and other Pueblo peoples believed in gods of the sun, rain, and Earth. Spirits called kachinas (kuh•CHEE•nuhz) were an important part of the Hopis' religion.

The Hopis believed that kachinas visit the world of living people once a year and enter the bodies of kachina dancers. The kachina dancers were men who wore painted masks and dressed to look like the kachinas. Kachina dancers took part in many Hopi ceremonies. A **ceremony** is a series of actions performed during a special event, such as a religious service. Some of these ceremonies were held in special underground rooms called kivas (KEE•vuhz), and others were held in large meeting places outside. Today many Hopis continue to perform their traditional dances, some with kachina masks and some without.

**REVIEW** What kinds of natural resources did the Pueblo peoples use to build their homes?

## Desert Newcomers

Not all of the people of the Southwest were Pueblo Indians. Before moving to the Southwest, peoples such as the Navajos (NA•vuh•hohz) lived mainly as nomads. They traveled in groups of families and did not have a formal leader.

The Navajos began moving into the Southwest about A.D. 1025. They settled in an area known today as the Four Corners. This is the place where the corners of the states of Arizona, Colorado, New Mexico, and Utah meet. The Navajo people still live in the Four Corners area today.

Some of this land was also Hopi land. In time the Navajos began learning Hopi ways of life. Soon they, too, were growing crops and making cotton clothing as the Hopis did.

In this land, the Navajos built shelters called hogans (HOH•gahnz). A **hogan** was usually cone-shaped. It was built by covering a log frame with bark and mud. Rather than building their hogans close together, the Navajos built them in small, family-sized groups miles apart from one another.

**REVIEW** What ways of life did the Navajos learn from the Hopis?

## Navajo Beliefs

The Navajos believed in gods they called the Holy People. Some gods, such as the Earth Mother, were kind. Others, such as the sun god, could cause crops to dry up. The Navajos believed that they needed to honor the gods so that the gods would not use their powers against the people.

The Navajos honored their gods in ceremonies. Navajo ceremonies were led by religious leaders and healers called medicine people. Medicine people called upon the gods to protect the Navajos' families, homes, and crops or to cure the sick. In healing ceremonies medicine people made sandpaintings, also called dry paintings, that were believed to help heal people. First, the medicine person created a pattern of symbols on the ground, using colored sand. Then, the sick person sat or lay on the sandpainting while the medicine person held a ceremony that the Navajos believed would help the sick person feel healing powers. The painting was always rubbed away after the ceremony.

**REVIEW** **What is a medicine person?**

Today some sandpaintings are preserved. This one was made by Michael Tsosie.

**LOCATE IT**

The desert lands of Monument Valley are part of the Navajo lands.

---

## LESSON 3 REVIEW

① **MAIN IDEA** How did the dryness of the environment affect the Indian people of the Southwest?

② **WHY IT MATTERS** In what ways do you think the environment affects how people in your community or state live?

③ **VOCABULARY** Use the term **ceremony** in a sentence to describe Hopi customs.

④ **READING SKILL—Compare and Contrast** In what ways were the Navajos different from the Hopis?

⑤ **HISTORY** Why was it important to the Pueblo peoples to store food?

⑥ **CRITICAL THINKING—Evaluate** How do you think the Navajos' way of life affected their need for a formal leader?

**PERFORMANCE—Make a Graphic Organizer** Using the information in the lesson, make a graphic organizer about the way of life of the Hopis. Then use your organizer to write a story about them.

# PRIMARY SOURCES

# Native American Pottery

For hundreds of years, pottery-making has been an important part of Native American cultures. Over time, products such as metal pans, glassware, and imported ceramics have changed the way traditional pottery is made and changed its uses. However, the designs and decoration of pottery continue to reflect themes that are important to Native American cultures.

This present-day potter makes pottery in the Native American tradition.

**FROM THE PHILBROOK ART CENTER, THE MAXWELL MUSEUM OF ANTHROPOLOGY, AND THE NATIONAL MUSEUM OF AMERICAN HISTORY AT THE SMITHSONIAN INSTITUTION**

## 1990

This traditionally styled Pueblo seed pot shows contemporary images of the space shuttle and an astronaut.

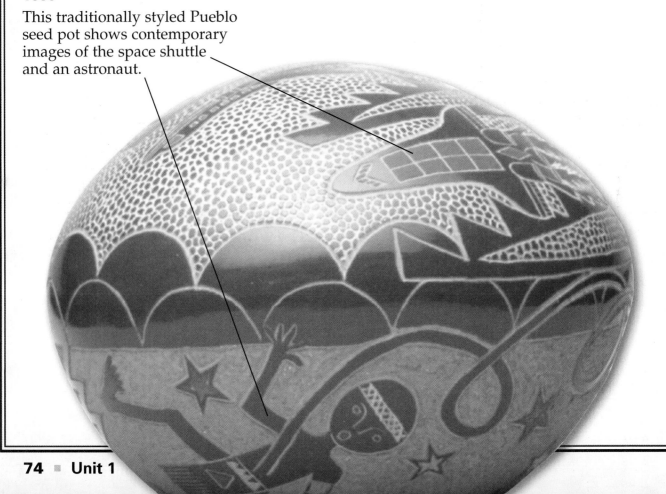

The paints used to decorate pots were made from plants.

## Analyze the Primary Source

❶ How do you think these pots are similarly decorated? How are their decorations different?

❷ What differences do you see in the pottery of different time periods? How do you think each vessel would be used today?

### About 1000

Bowls like this may have been used to store grain.

### Middle 1800s

Jars like this were made for storing food and water. By the late 1800s, however, glass jars were often used instead.

**ACTIVITY**

**Compare and Contrast** Make a list of uses that you might have for a clay pot. Then select designs that you would like to show on your pot. Use your information to draw a picture showing what your pot will look like. Share your drawing with your classmates. How are your pottery designs alike? How are they different?

**RESEARCH**

Visit The Learning Site at **www.harcourtschool.com/primarysources** to research other primary sources.

# 4

**MAIN IDEA**
Read to learn how the environment of the Northwest Coast and Arctic regions made life different for the peoples who lived there.

**WHY IT MATTERS**
The environment continues to affect the unique ways of life of peoples in different parts of the world.

**VOCABULARY**
dugout
barter
potlatch
clan
pit house
harpoon
totem pole

# The Northwest Coast and the Arctic

The Indians of the Northwest Coast and the Arctic lived in a place that was very different from the deserts of the Southwest. The Northwest Coast is a strip of land that stretches along the Pacific Ocean from northern California to Alaska. Nestled between the ocean and rugged mountains, it is a land of rivers and forests filled with fish and game. The Arctic region is much colder, and the land is frozen for most of the year.

## River Traders

Along the Northwest Coast there was little agriculture. But there were plenty of fish, especially salmon. There were also plenty of deer, bears, and other animals. Therefore, instead of growing their own food, the Indians of the Northwest Coast met their need for food by fishing, hunting, and gathering plants. The enormous trees that grew in the forests provided them with wood for boats, houses, and tools.

If the Indians of the Northwest Coast needed items they could not make, they could get them through trade. Although the region's mountains made overland travel difficult, people could travel long distances on its waterways. In fact, the Columbia River became the "highway" of the Northwest. People used it to travel from place to place in wooden dugouts. A **dugout** is a boat made from a large, hollowed-out log.

One of the greatest trading centers located on the Columbia River was called The Dalles (DALZ). People would travel hundreds of miles to trade there. Dozens of tribes, some speaking languages as different from each other as English is from Chinese, took part in the trading through the mild summer months.

**REVIEW** What was one of the greatest trading centers on the Columbia River?

The people of the Northwest Coast traveled from place to place in dugouts.

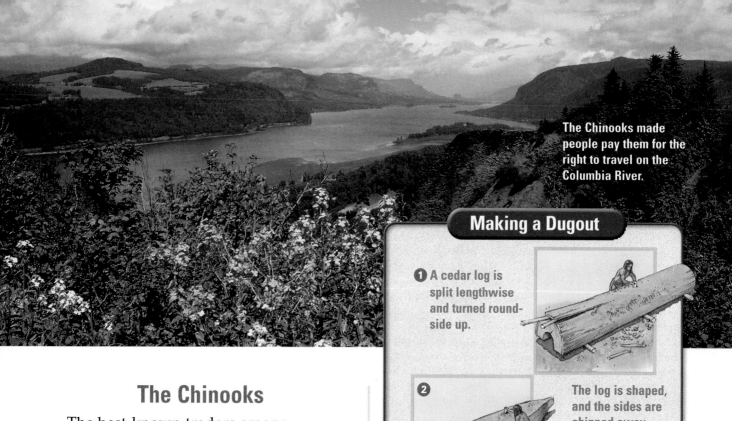
The Chinooks made people pay them for the right to travel on the Columbia River.

## The Chinooks

The best-known traders among the Northwest Coast Indians were the Chinooks (shih•NUKS). The Chinooks, who lived at the mouth of the Columbia River, controlled the river from the coast all the way to The Dalles—about 200 miles (322 km) upstream.

Because many tribes gathered at The Dalles to trade, the different languages they spoke made communication difficult. To help solve the problem, the Chinooks developed a language for trading. It was made up of Chinook words and words borrowed from other languages. This language made it easier for people of different tribes to talk to each other and to **barter**, or exchange goods. People traded dried fish, shells, furs, whale products, seal oil, cedar, dugouts, masks, jewelry, baskets, copper, and even prisoners.

Wealth was important to the people of the Northwest Coast. Tribes often attacked one another to gain wealth and, in turn, respect. Prisoners, a sign of wealth, were frequently taken as slaves during the many wars.

### Making a Dugout

**1** A cedar log is split lengthwise and turned round-side up.

**2** The log is shaped, and the sides are chipped away.

**3** The wood is removed from the interior.

**4** Water that is heated by rocks is put in the dugout to soften the dugout and make it wider.

**5** After the end pieces are attached, the dugout is ready for sanding and painting.

**Analyze Diagrams** Dugouts allowed the Northwest Coast Indians to travel on the many rivers in the region.

◆ How were the dugouts made wider?

**Chapter 2 ▪ 77**

During a whale hunt the chief harpooner showed his respect for the huge animal by singing a special song, promising to give the whale gifts if it allowed itself to be killed.

The Chinooks and other Northwest Coast people held **potlatches** to show their wealth. These were celebrations with feasting and dancing. During a potlatch, the hosts gave away gifts as a sign of their wealth. Members of some clans spent years preparing gifts to be given away. A **clan** is a group of families that are related to one another.

Chinook villages were made up of rows of long wooden houses. The houses were built of boards and had no windows. Each house was built so that part of it was over a hole dug in the earth and some of its rooms were partially underground. Such a house is called a **pit house**.

In each house lived several families belonging to the same clan. Each clan was headed by its oldest member. The Chinooks traced their clans through the mother's family line. The people of the clan had the same mother, grandmother, or great-grandmother.

**REVIEW** What were potlatches?

## The Makahs and the Kwakiutls

Most peoples of the Northwest found plenty of food in rivers and nearby coastal waters. Salmon and other fish and whales were in good supply. The Makahs (mah•KAWZ), who lived in what is now the state of Washington, were one of the many coastal peoples who built dugouts to hunt whales at sea. Some other coastal tribes, such as the Kwakiutls (KWAH•kee•oo•tuhlz), captured whales only if they became stranded on the shore. The Kwakiutls lived north of the Makahs on what is now Vancouver Island and western Canada.

Whale hunts were very important to the Makahs. Makah whale hunters often spent months preparing for a whale hunt. They fasted and prayed to their gods to favor them. They made new wooden **harpoons**—long spears with sharp shell points. They repaired their canoes and paddles. Made of wood, their canoes were 6 feet (about 2 m) wide and carried up to 60 people. They were built to travel over the open ocean. However, they still could be tipped over by an angry whale.

Imagine one group of whale hunters setting out to sea. The chief harpooner leads the hunters. Once they get close enough to the whale, the chief harpooner throws his harpoon. The whale is hit! Sealskin floats tied to the harpoon line make it difficult for the whale to dive down into the water and escape. Harpooners from nearby canoes throw

their weapons, too. When the whale dies, the hunters start towing it to shore.

It takes hours of paddling for the hunters to reach their village. Wooden houses line the narrow beach between the water and the forest. Outside each house stands a tall wooden post called a **totem pole**. Each totem pole is carved with shapes of people and animals.

Some of the best woodcarvers in the Northwest Coast were the Kwakiutls. Like the Makahs, the Kwakiutls lived in wooden houses along the shore. Some houses were huge, up to 60 feet (18 m) long. Like others in the region, the Kwakiutls ate plants, shellfish, salmon, elk, and deer. They also held the most lavish potlatches of all the Northwest Coast Indians.

**REVIEW** How did the Makahs prepare for a whale hunt?

• HERITAGE •

## Family Heritage

In the past the Indian tribes of the Northwest Coast had no written language. Because of this, they passed on their family and tribal histories in other ways. One way was through expertly carved and painted masks and totem poles. Masks were used in elaborate dances and ceremonies to act out stories of important events in the Indians' lives, such as births, deaths, and marriages. Totem poles were used to represent their ancestors and to tell the history of their people.

The carvings on a totem pole show a family's history and importance.

These Inuit sisters are wearing traditional dress.

## The Inuit

The native peoples of the Arctic lived mostly north and east of the Northwest Coast Indians. Among them were the Inuit, who first settled in the harsh environment of the Arctic region of present-day northern Alaska and Canada only about 4,000 years ago. Since much of this land was frozen tundra, it was much too cold for farming. The early Inuit, like the early Northwest Coast Indians, got most of their food and made most of their clothing, shelters, and tools from the animals they hunted. Although resources were scarce in the Arctic, the Inuit developed the skills necessary to survive in a land of ice and snow.

To survive in the harsh environment, the Inuit had to be skilled hunters and fishers. They hunted seal, walrus, and caribou. They used the meat for food, the bones for tools, and the skins for clothing. Like the Makahs, the Inuit along the Alaskan coast hunted whales.

The Inuit made many kinds of shelters. Some built igloos—dwellings made of ice—in which they lived during the winter months. Igloos were made from large blocks of ice stacked into a dome shape. A hole in the top allowed the smoke from cooking fires to escape, and blocks of clear ice served as windows. During the summer the Inuit lived in tents made of animal skins. Other Inuit lived in tents and huts year-round.

**REVIEW** How did the Inuit use the environment to meet their needs?

## LESSON 4
## REVIEW

1 **MAIN IDEA**   How was life in the Northwest Coast region different from life in other regions?

2 **WHY IT MATTERS**   How does the environment cause people today to have a unique way of life?

3 **VOCABULARY**   Use the term **barter** in a paragraph about trade on the Northwest Coast.

4 **READING SKILL—Compare and Contrast**   In what ways were the Makahs and the Kwakiutls similar?

5 **CULTURE**   Who was the head of a Chinook clan?

6 **HISTORY**   Why did the Makahs build canoes that could travel on the open ocean?

7 **CRITICAL THINKING—Synthesize**   What do you think the Northwest Coast Indians learned from each other by trading at The Dalles?

**PERFORMANCE—Write a Description**   Using facts from the lesson, write a paragraph that describes what life was like for the Indians of the Northwest Coast or the Arctic. Then read your paragraph to a classmate.

# The Plains

Millions of buffalo, or American bison, as scientists call them, once roamed the grassy lands of the Interior Plains. These hairy, cowlike beasts moved in huge herds made up of thousands of animals. The herds were so large that they were said to blacken the horizon. To the Plains Indians, who lived on the Interior Plains between the Mississippi River and the Rocky Mountains, the buffalo were second only to water as the region's most important resource.

## Life on the Plains

Imagine a Native American hunting party coming upon a herd of buffalo. Wearing animal skins as disguises, the hunters creep into position around some of the buffalo. At a signal, the hunters all shout together. The frightened buffalo run, and the hunters drive them toward a steep cliff. The buffalo fall over the cliff and are killed.

Most of the women of the tribe were not hunters. Their job was to skin the buffalo and prepare them for many uses. Some of the meat was eaten right away. The rest was dried and saved for winter or a time when there were no buffalo nearby to hunt. Dried meat, which people today call jerky, can be kept for many months.

**MAIN IDEA**
Read to learn how the Plains Indians used natural resources to live in their environment.

**WHY IT MATTERS**
People continue to depend on natural resources to live in their environment.

### VOCABULARY
**lodge**
**sod**
**tepee**
**travois**

This painting by George Catlin shows two hunters hiding under wolf skins.

81

The Plains Indians used every part of the buffalo they hunted. They made clothing, blankets, and moccasins from the skins. They carried water in bags made from the stomachs. They twisted the hair into cord. They made needles and other tools from the bones and horns.

**REVIEW** What did the peoples of the plains make from buffalo skins?

## Farmers and Hunters

Among the many Plains Indians who lived on the tall-grass prairies of the Interior Plains were the Mandans, Pawnees, Wichitas (WICH•ih•tawz), and some bands, or groups, of Sioux (SOO). These groups lived mostly in the eastern part of the Plains cultural region. They were both farmers and hunters. They farmed the rich land in the valleys along rivers such as the Missouri, Mississippi, and Platte. They also hunted deer, elk, and buffalo.

These people lived in villages made up of circular houses called **lodges**. Each lodge was built over a shallow pit. On the northern prairies of the Interior Plains, the lodges were covered with sod. **Sod** is earth cut into blocks or mats and held together by the grass and its roots. Because these houses were covered with earth, they are often called earth lodges. On the southern prairies, the earth lodges were covered with grass or animal skins.

Each earth lodge was home to several families. Sometimes as many as 60 people, plus their dogs, lived in one lodge. Each family had its own bed or beds next to the outer wall. In the center of the earth lodge was a shared fireplace under a hole in the roof for letting out smoke. The earth lodge was warm, and it protected the people during the cold winters.

Buffalo were a very important resource to the Indians of the western Plains. Buffalo hides were used to make much of their clothing, such as dresses and moccasins (right).

This painting by Karl Bodmer shows the Mandan lodges and the boats the Mandans used. To make the boats, they stretched buffalo skins around a wooden frame.

About twice a year the villages on the prairies emptied, as men, women, and children took part in a great buffalo hunt. The people walked for several days from their villages in the river valleys and forests to the grassy hunting areas.

When they were not hunting, the Indians on the prairies farmed. Their farms were small—more like gardens than farms. Their crops were mainly beans, corn, squash, and sunflowers. The farmers often traded their crops for goods that other tribes brought to them. Some of the villages along the Missouri River became trade centers for Native Americans from faraway places. The present-day site of Pierre (PIR), South Dakota, for example, was once the capital of the Arikara (uh•RIK•uh•ruh) Indian nation and a center for trade for more than 400 years.

**REVIEW** In what ways did the Plains Indians get their food?

## The Great Plains Nomads

Many of the people who lived on the Great Plains, the western part of the Plains cultural region, did not farm or live in villages. Groups such as the Crows, the Cheyennes (shy•ANZ), the Kiowas (KY•uh•wuhz), and the Comanches (kuh•MAN•cheez) were nomads. They moved from place to place because they followed herds of buffalo. They did not grow crops because the flat grasslands on which they roamed had no rich river valleys. The roots of the short grass were so tough that it was almost impossible to break the soil with a digging stick.

Although these nomads had no permanent dwellings, they claimed certain areas as their own hunting lands. They followed specific routes within their lands. These routes usually depended on the movement of the herds of buffalo.

## Analyze Primary Sources

Many Plains Indians kept the history of their tribe on what is now called a calendar robe. Each year leaders met to decide what event should be recorded on the robe. The drawings of the events could be read from left to right, right to left, or outward in a spiral from the center. This calendar robe was drawn by a Dakota Indian named Lone Dog. It covers the period 1800–1871.

1 **1837–1838:** A successful elk hunt was held.

2 **1840–1841:** The Dakotas and the Cheyennes made peace.

3 **1845–1846:** Buffalo meat was plentiful.

◆ Why is it important to record historical events?

They depended on the buffalo as one of their most important resources. Houses, clothing, food, and even fuel for fire came from the buffalo. For fuel they used dried buffalo droppings, called chips.

Because the nomads had no permanent home, they built shelters that were easy to move. One kind was a cone-shaped tent called a **tepee** (TEE•pee). The nomads set wooden poles in a circle and tied them together at the top. They covered the poles with buffalo skins, leaving a hole at the top to let out the smoke from their fires.

Wood was hard to find because few trees grew on the Great Plains. The early Native Americans made double use of their wooden tepee poles by turning them into a kind of carrier called a **travois** (truh•VOY). A travois was made up of two poles fastened to a harness on a dog. Goods were carried on a skin tied between the poles.

In the Plains Indian way of life, each person was equal in the group. No one person was born more important than anyone else. Any man could become chief by proving himself a good hunter and a good leader of people. He was chief because his people chose and trusted him.

Women were responsible for sewing buffalo hides together to make tepee coverings. They also set up the tepees. Tepees were usually set up so that the entrance faced east. This kept the strong western winds on the Great Plains from blowing inside.

In some nomadic tribes, members who did not follow the ways of their group were free to live on their own. Sometimes a leader and his followers would start a new group. In this way, one tribe often had many subgroups. Each subgroup was made up of families who worked together.

**REVIEW** How could a man become chief of a Plains Indian tribe?

## LESSON 5 REVIEW

**1 MAIN IDEA** How did the peoples of the Plains use natural resources to live in their environment?

**2 WHY IT MATTERS** In what ways do people today depend on natural resources to live in their environment?

**3 VOCABULARY** Write a sentence that compares and contrasts a **lodge** and a **tepee**.

**4 READING SKILL—Compare and Contrast** How were the Great Plains nomads different from the Indians who lived along the rivers in the eastern part of the Interior Plains?

**5 GEOGRAPHY** What were the two most important resources to the Plains Indians?

**6 CULTURE** How did the Plains Indians divide the work that went into a buffalo hunt?

**7 CRITICAL THINKING—Analyze** How did the way of life of the Plains Indians affect the type of shelters they built?

 **PERFORMANCE—Do Research** Use library resources or the Internet to find more information about the Plains Indians. Then report your findings to the class.

# 6

**MAIN IDEA**
Read to find out how the people of the Eastern Woodlands shared similar ways of life even though they spoke different languages and had different governments.

**WHY IT MATTERS**
Like the peoples of the Eastern Woodlands, the people of the United States today come from different backgrounds, but they share similar ways of life.

**VOCABULARY**

palisade
slash-and-burn
wigwam
wampum
longhouse
confederation
council

# The Eastern Woodlands

The cultural region known as the Eastern Woodlands covers most of the present-day United States east of the Mississippi River. Its name comes from the dense forests that once blanketed the land and that were the region's main natural resource. In some places, it was said, the forests were so thick with trees in the Eastern Woodlands that only a little sunlight could reach the ground.

## Life in the Eastern Woodlands

The people of the Eastern Woodlands had many uses for trees. They used trees and tree bark to make canoes and shelters. Some trees even provided food. Nuts came from trees such as the walnut, the hickory, and the American chestnut. In the northern part of the Eastern Woodlands, maple sugar was made from the sap of maple trees.

Eastern Woodlands people were farmers, gatherers, and hunters. However, the Eastern Woodlands was a huge region of great diversity. In the northeastern part of the Woodlands, where the soil was rocky and there were many mountains, the people did more gathering and hunting than farming. In

**FAST FACT** The sugar maple tree of the northeastern part of North America is one of the most valuable trees on the continent. Its sap is used to make maple syrup, and the wood is used for lumber.

The rich forests of the northeastern United States were home to the Eastern Woodlands people.

The people of the Eastern Woodlands used resources like deer hides and clay to make storage containers, such as this bag (left) and this pot (right).

southern areas, the soil and climate were better for growing crops. In their fields, the Eastern Woodlands people raised corn, beans, squash, and other plants.

Because they farmed and got enough food where they lived, the Eastern Woodlands people settled in villages. The villages often included a community building for meetings and ceremonies. Surrounding many villages was a wall, called a **palisade**, made of sharpened tree trunks. The palisade was built to protect the village from enemies and wild animals. The farm fields were located outside the palisade.

The Eastern Woodlands people made clearings in the forests for their fields. They cleared the land by cutting away a circle of bark on selected trees in the fall. By spring the tree was dead. With the leaves gone, the sun shone through the branches to the ground. Among the dead trees, the Woodlands people planted crops. After a year or two the dead trees were burned. After several more years, a field might be completely cleared. This method of clearing fields and growing crops is called **slash-and-burn** agriculture.

Some people in the Eastern Woodlands used fish as fertilizer. Others did not. Without fertilizer a field wore out in about ten years and no longer grew good crops. As a result some peoples had to move to new places, build new villages, and start clearing new fields.

Although Eastern Woodlands people raised much of their food, they also gathered and hunted. They gathered nuts, berries, wild fruits, greens, and shellfish. They caught fish and hunted beavers, porcupines, deer, and birds. They also hunted to get animal skins for clothing. Furry beaver and bear skins made warm robes, capes, and blankets. Scraped and tanned deer hides made soft buckskin for lighter clothing.

The peoples of the northeastern part of the Eastern Woodlands included two main language groups, the Algonquian (al•GAHN•kwee•uhn) and the Iroquoian (ir•uh•KWOY•uhn). Most of the Native Americans who spoke the Algonquian languages generally lived on the Coastal Plain. Most of the Iroquoian people, or Iroquois (IR•uh•kwoy), lived farther inland.

**REVIEW** How did Eastern Woodlands people get their food?

## The Algonquians

Among the Algonquian tribes were peoples such as the Delawares, Wampanoags (wam•puh•NOH•agz), and Powhatans (pow•uh•TANZ), who lived along the Coastal Plain. Some of the Algonquian tribes lived farther inland, around the Great Lakes. These tribes included peoples such as the Algonkins (al•GAHN•kuhnz), the Chippewas (CHIP•uh•wahz), and the Miamis.

Each Algonquian tribe had anywhere from 1 to 20 villages. In most villages, 10 to 20 round, bark-covered shelters called **wigwams** were grouped around a village common. Most Algonquian tribes built their villages along the banks of rivers or streams. Some were built where two rivers or streams met. In wetland areas, villages were built on high ground to keep them safe from flooding.

The Algonquian peoples built birch-bark canoes to fish in the rivers and along the coast. They used animal bones and wood to make fishing tools, such as hooks, lines, and fishing traps. Fish was a very important food source in winter, when crops would not grow. Near the coast, many tribes also made strings of beads that were cut from seashells. These beads, which they called **wampum** (WAHM•puhm), were used to keep records and send messages to other tribes. Algonquian peoples sometimes gave belts of wampum beads as gifts or in exchange for bartered goods.

Many Algonquian tribes had leaders who governed groups of villages. These villages traded together and helped one another during times of war. Other Algonquian peoples had two chiefs. One chief ruled during times of peace. The other chief ruled during times of war. Some tribes had a third leader, who was in charge of religious ceremonies.

**REVIEW** **What were some of the uses of wampum?**

This scene (below) shows an Algonquian village. The shirt (right) was worn by an Algonquian chief.

**Iroquois Nations**

0    50    100 Miles
0    50    100 Kilometers
Albers Equal-Area Projection

N W E S

St. Lawrence River

Lake Champlain

Adirondack Mountains

Lake Ontario

Mohawk River

Lake Erie

Susquehanna River

Delaware R.

Hudson River

ATLANTIC OCEAN

■ Seneca
□ Cayuga
□ Onondaga
■ Oneida
■ Mohawk
— Present-day border

**GEOGRAPHY THEME**

**Regions** These five neighboring Iroquois nations shared a government.

◆ How did the locations of the tribes help make working together so important?

The leaders of the five Iroquois nations agreed to stop fighting and unite so that together they could defend their lands against attacks from others. They recognized that they had more to gain by working together for the common good than by continuing to fight one another. The people worked together for the good of their village. To make it easier for the village to meet its needs, the work was usually divided among different workers. Some members of the village might have worked at making pots, while others made arrow points. Like the people of the Iroquois League, people living in the United States today often work together for the common good of all the citizens.

**Analyze the Value**

**1** Why was it important for the Iroquois to work together as one?

**2** **Make It Relevant** Identify some examples of people who are working for the common good of your school. Then write a paragraph that explains why their work is important.

## The Iroquois

Like the Algonquians, the Iroquois were not one tribe but a group of tribes that lived near each other and spoke a common language. Five of the largest Iroquois tribes were the Senecas (SEN•uh•kuhz), Cayugas (ky•YOO•guhz), Onondagas (aw•nuhn•DAG•uhz), Oneidas (oh•NY•duhz), and Mohawks. These tribes, known as the Five Nations, were the most common groups in what is now upstate New York and the Lake Ontario region of Canada.

Also like the Algonquians, the Iroquois tribes farmed and lived in villages. The Iroquois lived in dwellings called longhouses. A **longhouse** was a long wooden building in which several related Iroquois families lived together. It was made of elm bark and had a large entrance at each end.

The longhouse was also a symbol for the Iroquois. Just as several families shared a longhouse, the five largest Iroquois tribes shared a government. It became known as the Iroquois League and acted as a **confederation** (kuhn•feh•duh•RAY•shuhn), or a loose group of governments working together. In *The Law of the Great Peace*, the Iroquois described the League. "Five arrows shall be bound together very strong and each arrow shall represent one nation each. As the five arrows are strongly bound this shall symbolize [represent] the complete union of the nations."

This computer-generated picture shows what an Iroquois village may have looked like.

Each tribe in the League governed itself. However, matters that were important to all of the tribes, such as war and trade, were decided by the Great Council. A **council** is a group that makes laws.

For many years before the League came into being, the Iroquois had fought with each other and with neighboring tribes. The fighting often began over land.

In one Iroquois legend, a man named Deganawida (deh•gahn•uh•WIH•duh) spoke out against the fighting. He said that the Iroquois must come together "by taking hold of each other's hands so firmly and forming a circle so strong that if a tree should fall upon it, it could not shake nor break it . . ."

A Mohawk leader named Hiawatha (hy•uh•WAH•thuh) shared Deganawida's hopes for peace. Hiawatha visited each of the Iroquois tribes, asking for an end to the fighting. The tribes finally agreed to work together in the Iroquois League.

**REVIEW** What was the Iroquois League?

## LESSON 6 REVIEW

❶ **MAIN IDEA** What ways of life did the peoples of the Eastern Woodlands share?

❷ **WHY IT MATTERS** What are some ways of life that people of the United States share today?

❸ **VOCABULARY** Use the terms **confederation** and **council** in a report about the Iroquois.

❹ **READING SKILL—Compare and Contrast** In what ways were the Algonquians and the Iroquois different?

❺ **GEOGRAPHY** Why was fish an important food source in winter for the Algonquian peoples?

❻ **CULTURE** Why did the Iroquois form the Iroquois League?

❼ **CRITICAL THINKING—Analyze** How was the Iroquois longhouse a symbol of the Iroquois League?

 **PERFORMANCE—Deliver a Speech** Write and deliver a speech to persuade Iroquois leaders to join the Iroquois League. Be sure to include the benefits of working together.

# ·SKILLS·
## CITIZENSHIP

# Resolve Conflict

**VOCABULARY**
compromise
resolve

### ▶ WHY IT MATTERS

The Iroquois resolved the conflicts over land by forming the Iroquois League. In forming the Iroquois League, it is likely that the different tribes had to compromise to reach an agreement. You **compromise** when you give up some of what you want in order to reach an agreement. Knowing how to compromise gives you another way to **resolve**, or settle, conflicts.

### ▶ WHAT YOU NEED TO KNOW

Here are some steps that can help you resolve conflicts through compromise.

**Step 1** Tell the other person clearly what you want.

**Step 2** Decide which of the things you want are most important to you.

**Step 3** Present a plan for a possible compromise, and listen to the other person's plan.

**Step 4** Talk about any differences in the two plans.

**Step 5** Present another plan, this time giving up one of the things that is important to you.

**Step 6** Continue talking until the two of you agree on a plan. If either of you becomes angry, take a break and calm down.

**Step 7** Plan a compromise so that it will work for a long time.

### ▶ PRACTICE THE SKILL

Think of a disagreement that your class or your community might be facing. Form groups to discuss it. Using the steps listed in this skill, vote on a compromise plan.

### ▶ APPLY WHAT YOU LEARNED

With your classmates, choose an issue that you do not all agree on. Form sides and discuss the issue, using the steps in What You Need to Know.

This staff was used to list the members of the Iroquois League. The pegs in the staff stood for each tribe's representatives.

**CITIZENSHIP SKILLS**

# 2 Review and Test Preparation

## USE YOUR READING SKILLS

Complete this graphic organizer to compare and contrast the Indians of the Plains and the Indians of the Northwest Coast. A copy of this graphic organizer appears on page 24 of the Activity Book.

## Compare and Contrast

**The Plains Indians**

**The Northwest Coast Indians**

DIFFERENCES

1. _____
   _____
   _____

2. _____
   _____
   _____

3. _____
   _____
   _____

SIMILARITIES

**Both groups used natural resources to meet their needs.**

DIFFERENCES

1. _____
   _____
   _____

2. _____
   _____
   _____

3. _____
   _____
   _____

## THINK & WRITE

**Write an Article**   Imagine that you are one of the archaeologists that uncovered artifacts at the Meadowcroft Rock Shelter in Pennsylvania. Write an article that explains why this evidence supports the early arrival theory.

**Write a Journal Entry**   Suppose that you are an early traveler on the Columbia River. Write a journal entry about your journey as you travel to The Dalles. Describe your experiences as you travel the river and at the trading center.

Use each of the following terms in a sentence that will help explain its meaning.

archaeologist (p. 57)

technology (p. 63)

civilization (p. 65)

adapt (p. 70)

barter (p. 77)

travois (p. 85)

confederation (p. 89)

## Recall Facts

Answer these questions.

1 What connected the continents of Asia and North America long ago?

2 Why were the ancient Indians nomads?

3 How did changes in the environment affect the way of life of the ancient Indians?

4 How were the Olmecs and the Maya divided?

5 What was the purpose of Navajo sand-paintings?

Write the letter of the best choice.

6 **TEST PREP** The Pueblo peoples modified their environment by—
A traveling long distances to gather wood.
B irrigating land for farming.
C storing food in containers.
D making kachinas.

7 **TEST PREP** One of the most important resources for the Plains Indians was—
F the forest.
G the buffalo.
H the river.
J the whale.

8 **TEST PREP** The Iroquois tried to make peace by—
A forming a confederation.
B leaving the Eastern Woodlands.
C building a longhouse.
D building palisades around the villages.

## Think Critically

9 How did the environment affect the ways of life of people across North America?

10 How is North America a place of great diversity today?

## Apply Skills

**Read Time Lines**
Use the time lines on pages 60–61 to answer the following questions.

11 Between which years did the fourteenth century take place?

12 Which year was earlier, 200 B.C. or A.D. 2000?

**Use a Cultural Map**
Use the map on page 69 to answer the following questions.

13 What is the largest cultural region in North America?

14 Do you think more people relied on fishing in the Northwest Coast or in the Plains?

**Resolve Conflict**

15 Think of an issue that you and a friend disagree about. Make a list of the steps that you might follow to resolve the conflict. Include a compromise that could resolve the conflict.

# VISIT

# THE HOPI NATION

## GET READY

## WHAT TO SEE

The Hopi Nation is made up of 12 villages. The villages are located at the tops and at the bases of three mesas in northeastern Arizona. Many Hopis still follow their traditional way of life. They perform Kachina ceremonies, produce traditional craft work, and farm the land as they have done for hundreds of years. On a visit to the Hopi Nation, you can learn about Hopi culture and see examples of how Hopis keep their traditions alive.

Visitors to the Hopi Nation may have the chance to see a Kachina ceremony. The Kachina dances express prayers for rain, health, and bountiful harvests.

## LOCATE IT

ARIZONA

Hopi Nation

This young girl is dressed for the Butterfly Dance, which celebrates the harvest.

Hopi artists create jewelry, baskets, and pottery. They use patterns and styles that have been passed down from generation to generation.

## TAKE A FIELD TRIP

**GO ONLINE**

### A VIRTUAL TOUR
Visit The Learning Site at **www.harcourtschool.com/tours** to take virtual tours of other cultures.

**CNN Turner Le@rning.**

### A VIDEO TOUR
Check your media center or classroom library for a videotape tour of the Hopi Nation.

# 1 Review and Test Preparation

## VISUAL SUMMARY

**Write a News Story** Imagine that you are a news reporter. Your job is to review the Visual Summary below and choose one of the events to write a news story about. Tell when and where the event took place and its importance.

## USE VOCABULARY

Use the words from the list to complete the sentences below.

sea level (p. 21)

tributary (p. 30)

nonrenewable (p. 41)

❶ A resource that cannot be made again by nature or people is called ____.

❷ The land of the Coastal Plain region lies close to ____.

❸ A stream or river that flows into a larger stream or river is called a ____.

## RECALL FACTS

Answer these questions.

❹ Name the seven continents, from largest to smallest.

❺ Why are oceans, lakes, and rivers important to life in the United States?

❻ What are the similarities between the desert and tundra regions of the United States?

❼ **TEST PREP**  Which of these ancient cultures developed first?
A  Anasazi
B  Olmec
C  Mound Builder
D  Maya

❽ **TEST PREP**  Which groups of Native Americans call the Northwest Coast and the Arctic home?
F  Hopis, Zunis, Chinooks
G  Comanches, Kiowas, Cheyennes
H  Chinooks, Makahs, Inuit
J  Maya, Olmecs, Makahs

**Visual Summary**

12,000 years ago

8,000 years ago

**About 10,000 years ago**  ancient Indians hunted large animals   p. 62

**About 5,000 years ago**  ancient Indians begin farming   p. 64

**About 3,500 years ago**  the Olmec civilization lived in North America   p. 65

**9 TEST PREP**  Navajo religious ceremonies are led by a religious leader known as a—

**A** totem pole.

**B** kachina.

**C** kiva.

**D** medicine person.

## THINK CRITICALLY

**10** Why do you think there are different ideas as to how people may have come to live in North and South America?

**11** What role do you think farming had in the development of civilizations in North and South America? Explain.

**12** Do you think the Iroquois Nations could have survived without the Iroquois League? Why or why not?

## APPLY SKILLS

**Use Longitude and Latitude**
Use the map of the Great Plains region on this page to answer the following questions.

MAP AND GLOBE SKILLS

**13** Which location is farther north, 35°N, 100°W or 45°N, 95°W?

**14** What line of latitude is closest to the borders of North and South Dakota?

**15** What state capital is located closest to 40°N, 105°W?

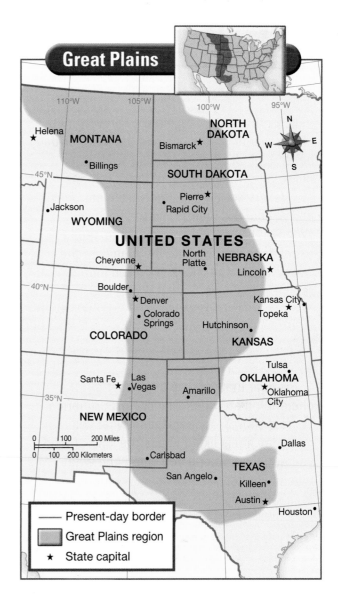

**Great Plains**

— Present-day border

▨ Great Plains region

★ State capital

4,000 years ago | PRESENT

**About 1,000 years ago**  the Navajos moved to the Southwest  p. 72

**By 800 years ago**  more than 30,000 people lived in Cahokia  p. 66

**About 700 years ago**  the Iroquois lived in the Northeast  p. 89

97

# Unit Activities

**GO ONLINE**

Visit The Learning Site at www.harcourtschool.com/socialstudies/activities for additional activities.

## Draw a Map

In a group, work together to draw a map of the United States. Include the present-day borders of all 50 states. Using a different color to represent each of these regions—the Desert Southwest, the Northwest Coast and Arctic, the Plains, and the Eastern Woodlands—divide your map into sections. Label each section with the names of the Native American tribes that lived in that region.

## Write a Short Story

Imagine that you are a member of an ancient Indian tribe living in North America. Write a short story explaining what your everyday life is like. Include the kind of food you eat, the clothing you wear, and what type of shelter you live in.

## VISIT YOUR LIBRARY

- ■ *Squish! A Wetland Walk* by Nancy Luenn. Atheneum.

- ■ *Anasazi* by Leonard Everett Fisher. Simon & Schuster.

- ■ *Earth Always Endures: Native American Poems.* Edited by Neil Philip and Edward S. Curtis. Viking.

## COMPLETE THE UNIT PROJECT

**A Multimedia Presentation** Work with a group of classmates to complete the unit project—a multimedia presentation. Decide on a topic and what information you want to include. Next, create a variety of visual and written aids to help your group present information from the unit. Invite students from other classes to see your presentation.

# Time of Encounters

A compass, 1570

Trunk Bay, United States Virgin Islands

2

# Time of Encounters

&#10077; **I saw so many islands I could not count them all . . .** &#10078;

—**Christopher Columbus, November 14, 1492**

## Preview the Content

Skim the unit. When you have finished, answer the following—
*Who* and *What* is the unit about? *Where* are the places you will
learn about? *When* did the events happen? *Why* are these events
important? Make a graphic organizer and fill in your responses.

| | |
|---|---|
| WHO → | _____ |
| WHAT → | _____ |
| WHERE → | _____ |
| WHEN → | _____ |
| WHY → | _____ |

## Preview the Vocabulary

**Related Words**   Use the Glossary to look up the vocabulary
words below. What do these words have in common?

colony      hacienda      presidio      mission

**Early European Settlements**

PACIFIC
OCEAN

NORTH
AMERICA

SEKANI
SARCEE
CREE
CARRIER
SARCEE
CREE
NOOTKA
SHUSWAP
BLACKFOOT
CHINOOK   YAKIMA   KUTENAI
CHIPPEWA
ATSINA
Columbia R.
NEZ
SIUSLAW   PERCE
MANDAN
L. Superior
MODOC
CROW
SIOUX
Mississippi R.
BANNOCK
SAUK
PAIUTE   SHOSHONI
L. Michigan
WINN
POMO
CHEYENNE
OMAHA
FOX
MIWOK
IOWA
YOKUTS
UTE
ARAPAHO   PAWNEE
ILLINOIS   MIAM
PAIUTE
MISSOURI
Colorado R.
CHUMASH
NAVAJO
KIOWA
SHAWN
MOHAVE   HOPI
OSAGE
CAHUILLA
ZUNI
WICHITA
YUMA
PUEBLOS
CHICKAS
COMANCHE
APACHE
QUAPAW
CADDO
PIMA
WACO
NATCHEZ   APP
Rio Grande
CHOCTA
YAQUI
BILOXI
ATAKAPA
CONCHO
MAYO
COAHUILTEC
TEPEHUAN
ZACATECA
NEW SPAIN
Mexico City
(1522)

ROCKY MOUNTAINS

0    250    500 Miles
0    250    500 Kilometers
Lambert Equal-Area Projection

| | French |
| | Spanish |
| ● | Settlement |
| FOX | Name of Native American tribe |
| — | Present-day border |

N
W   E
S

**Key Events**

1200 ——— 1300 ——— 1400

1275   **Marco Polo reaches China**   p. 109

1492   **Christopher Columbus lands at San Salvador**   p. 122

1498   **Vasco Da Gama reaches India by sea**   p. 118

100

## First Explorers to the Americas, 1492–1542

| COUNTRY | EXPLORER | DATES OF EXPLORATION | AREA EXPLORED |
|---------|----------|----------------------|---------------|
| Spain | Christopher Columbus | 1492 | Caribbean |
| England | Giovanni Caboto | 1497 | Newfoundland |
| Spain | Amerigo Vespucci | 1499–1501 | eastern South America |
| Portugal | Pedro Alvarez Cabral | 1500 | Brazil |
| Spain | Vasco Núñez de Balboa | 1513 | Isthmus of Panama |
| Spain | Juan Ponce de León | 1513 | Puerto Rico and Florida |
| Spain | Ferdinand Magellan | 1519–1522 | Brazil, eastern South America |
| Spain | Hernando Cortés | 1519–1536 | Mexico, California |
| France | Giovanni da Verrazano | 1524 | northeast North America |
| Spain | Panfilo de Narvaez | 1528 | Gulf of Mexico |
| Spain | Álvar Núñez Cabeza de Vaca | 1528–1536 | Texas, New Mexico, Mexico |
| Spain | Francisco Pizarro | 1531–1535 | western South America |
| France | Jacques Cartier | 1534–1541 | eastern Canada |
| Spain | Hernando de Soto | 1539–1542 | southeastern North America |
| Spain | Francisco Vásquez de Coronado | 1540–1542 | southwestern North America |
| Spain | Juan Rodriguez Cabrillo | 1542 | California |

NASKAPI

BEOTHUK

MONTAGNAIS

REE

MICMAC

Quebec (1608)

ALGONKIN

ABNAKI

MAHICAN

St. Lawrence R.

NEW FRANCE

MASSACHUSET

Ontario

IRON

IROQUOIS

PEQUOT

Plymouth (1620)

SUSQUEHANNA

DELAWARE

MTS.

POWHATAN

Jamestown (1607)

TUSCARORA

HEROKEE

ATLANTIC OCEAN

AMASEE

St. Augustine (1565)

EMINOLE

CALUSA

---

**1500** — **1600** — **1700**

**1519 Hernando Cortés arrives in Tenochtitlán** p. 129

**1607 English colonists settle Jamestown** p. 161

**1620 English colonists settle Plymouth** p. 167

101

# San Salvador

from *The World in 1492* by Jamake Highwater

San Salvador is among the many tropical islands of the Bahamas, off the coast of Florida. Before the arrival of the Europeans, who gave the island its present-day name, people known as the Tainos (TY·nohz) lived there. The Tainos grew crops in the warm climate. They hunted small animals and birds, and they fished. They also traded with the tribes living on other islands and in other coastal regions around the Caribbean Sea.

Nothing in their experience, however, prepared them for what they saw one day in the year the Europeans called 1492.

On that morning of October 12, 1492, a miraculous sight is seen by the people of a little island, now called High Cay, that lies just off the coast of San Salvador in the Caribbean Sea. There in the twilight, as they climb from their hammocks and come out of their palm-leaf-covered houses, they see three moving islands that gradually make their way across the water, coming out of the great unknown and moving ever closer to the astonished people on the shore. In the first light, the floating islands give birth to small rafts that float away from their mothers and drift toward the beach, carrying the most unbelievable creatures. They look like people made of bright colors. Their faces are covered with bushy hair, as if they are holding squirrels in their mouths.

Despite the strangeness of these creatures, the people are delighted and astounded to see them, and they run toward the water to greet them. At close range, the people realize that the strangers from the sea look like real men, except they have very pale faces covered with bunches of curly hair. They are terribly ugly and have a dreadful smell of spoiled milk. Yet they seem harmless, despite the strange gray and black weapons they carry. The people smile happily when the strangers admire their spears made of reeds and the lovely little ornaments of gold they wear on their ears and nostrils. The people cannot understand why the yellow metal is so fascinating to them. To make them happy, they bring their strange guests many gifts—green parrots and bundles of precious cotton—in return for which they are given beautiful colored beads and small bells that make a delightful sound. These strangers, who completely hide themselves behind clothing, seem ill at ease with the nakedness of the people of the island, who do not cover their handsome bodies except for lavish painted designs of black, white and red.

Then a man with a scarlet chest steps forward and tries to talk to the people, though he does not know how to speak properly and can only make strange noises and wave his arms in the air. Despite this strange behavior, the people smile at him respectfully. Hoping to teach him how to speak, they gesture across the landscape, and they tell the scarlet man that their island is called Guanahani. He seems to understand. Then the man points to himself and repeat-edly tells the people his name. At this the people of the island begin to laugh. For this stranger has a most peculiar name!

*Christopher Columbus.*

## Analyze the Literature

❶ Why do you think the Tainos were so surprised by the Europeans?

❷ Write about how Columbus may have viewed the Tainos.

## READ A BOOK

## START THE UNIT PROJECT

**An Exploration Map**  With your classmates, create a map that shows the exploration of North America. As you read, take notes about the key explorers and the routes they traveled. Your notes will help you decide which routes to show on your map.

## USE TECHNOLOGY

Visit The Learning Site at **www.harcourtschool.com/ socialstudies** for additional activities, primary sources, and other resources to use in this unit.

# 3

# A Time of Exploration

> **" *Lumbre! Tierra!* "**
> **(Light! Land!)**
> —Pedro Yzquierdo, member of Columbus's first expedition to America, midnight, October 11, 1492

## CHAPTER READING SKILL

### Sequence

A **sequence** is the order in which one event comes after another. Words like *first, then, next, before, after,* and *later* can help you recognize a sequence.

**As you read this chapter, try to put events related to exploration in the correct sequence.**

EVENT → EVENT → EVENT

**MAIN IDEA**
Read to learn how the world's cultures became connected in the 1400s.

**WHY IT MATTERS**
As people learned more about the world, they began to trade with faraway places.

**VOCABULARY**

encounter
empire
monarch
Renaissance
compass
city-state

# The World in the 1400s

1200      1475      1700

**1400–1500**

When the Tainos welcomed Christopher Columbus in 1492, almost 500 years had passed since the last **encounter**, or meeting, between Europeans and Native Americans. In about A.D. 1000 a group of people known as Vikings had come to North America from what is today the country of Norway. The Vikings did not stay long, and they met few people. The memory of their visit soon faded. As a result, Native Americans knew nothing about Europe.

In the 1400s Europeans knew nothing about the Americas and very little about the rest of the world. That was beginning to change, however, as new trade routes connected Europe with parts of Asia and Africa.

## The Americas

Long before Columbus arrived in the Americas, some groups of Native Americans had established powerful empires. An **empire** is a collection of lands ruled by the nation that conquered them. One of the largest and richest of these empires was ruled by the Incas of South America. Their empire covered about 3,000 miles (4,828 km) of the western coast of South America, including

**FAST FACT**
Legend says that the Aztecs built their capital where they saw what they believed to be a sign from the gods—an eagle with a snake in its mouth, sitting on a cactus. Today the eagle with the snake appears on the Mexican flag.

**Analyze Illustrations** The Aztecs built causeways, or land bridges, to connect the island capital of Tenochtitlán to the mainland. They also built pyramids (right).

◆ How would having water on all sides of the capital help keep it safe from attacks?

106

parts of what are now the countries of Ecuador, Peru, Bolivia, Chile, and Argentina.

The Incas expanded their empire by using force to take over other peoples' land. In time, they ruled as many as 12 million people, most of whom lived in villages along the coast, in the Andes Mountains, and in the rain forests along the Amazon River. The Incas' capital city was Cuzco (KOOS•koh), in what is now Peru.

A system of roads connected Cuzco to all areas of the Inca Empire. In fact, two major roads—one along the coast and one through the Andes Mountains—ran the length of the empire. These roads led to great cities whose grand buildings were made of stones. These stones were cut by hand to fit together. This way of building can still be seen today in the ruins of the Inca city of Machu Picchu (MAH•choo PEEK•choo).

The Incas kept records on groups of colored, knotted strings known as quipus (KEE•pooz). The different-colored knots stood for words or ideas. For example, a knot made from yellow string represented the word *gold*. A knot made from white string stood for *peace*. Although archaeologists have found many quipus, most of what is known about the Incas was written down by Spanish explorers after they arrived in the Americas.

North of the Incas lived the Mexicas, a tribe later known as the Aztecs. For many years the Aztecs moved from place to place in search of food. In about A.D. 1200 they began to settle in the Valley of Mexico, in the central part of present-day Mexico. By the late 1400s the Aztecs had taken control of much of central and southern Mexico. They ruled over a huge empire that covered about 200,000 square miles (518,000 sq km) and included more than 5 million people.

The Aztecs built their capital city, Tenochtitlán (tay•nawch•teet•LAHN), on two islands in the middle of Lake Texcoco (tays•KOH•koh). Today Mexico City, the capital of Mexico, stands on this same spot.

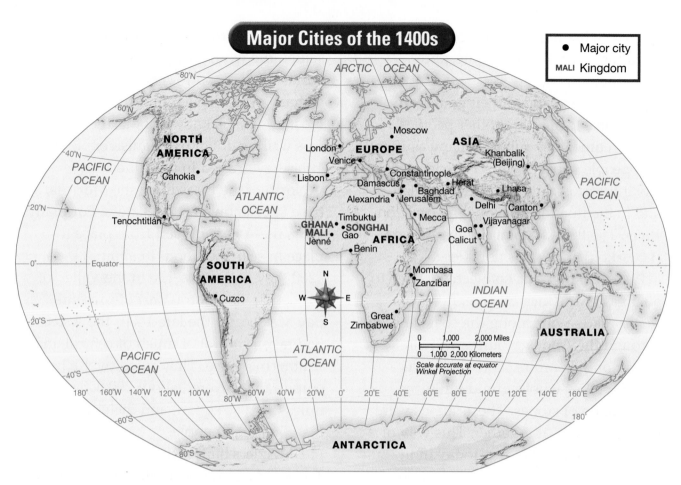

## Major Cities of the 1400s

● Major city
MALI Kingdom

ARCTIC OCEAN

80°N
60°N

NORTH
AMERICA

40°N

PACIFIC
OCEAN

Moscow
London
Venice
EUROPE
ASIA
Khanbalik
(Beijing)

Lisbon
Constantinople
Damascus
Baghdad
Herat
Lhasa
Alexandria
Jerusalem
Delhi
Canton

20°N

Cahokia

ATLANTIC
OCEAN

PACIFIC
OCEAN

Tenochtitlán

Timbuktu
Mecca
GHANA
MALI
SONGHAI
Goa
Vijayanagar
Jenné
Gao
AFRICA
Calicut

0°
Equator

SOUTH
AMERICA

Benin

Cuzco

N

Mombasa
Zanzibar

20°S

W    E

INDIAN
OCEAN

S

Great
Zimbabwe

0    1,000   2,000 Miles

AUSTRALIA

PACIFIC
OCEAN

ATLANTIC
OCEAN

0  1,000  2,000 Kilometers
Scale accurate at equator
Winkel Projection

40°S

60°S

180°  160°W  140°W  120°W  100°W   80°W   60°W   40°W   20°W   0°   20°E   40°E   60°E   80°E   100°E  120°E  140°E  160°E

180°

80°S

ANTARCTICA

GEOGRAPHY THEME

**Location**   In the early 1400s most people knew little or nothing about cities on other continents.

❓ What major cities were located in North America?

In the very center of Tenochtitlán, huge flat-topped pyramids rose toward the sky. On top of the pyramids stood the great stone temples that were built to honor the Aztecs' gods. Past the temples was a large, open area where a daily market was held.

The Aztecs recorded information by using pictures of objects and symbols to represent words and syllables. They used these pictures and symbols to make calendars and keep records. This system of communication made the Aztec Empire one of the most advanced civilizations in the Americas at that time.

**REVIEW** How did the Incas expand their empire?

## Europe

In the 1400s many changes were taking place in Europe. In earlier times, almost all of Europe had been divided into many small land areas, each owned by a different noble. Over time, some of these separate land areas had been joined to form countries. Portugal, Spain, France, England, and other European countries were now ruled by **monarchs**, or kings and queens.

Europeans at this time were making big improvements in science and technology. With this new knowledge, they entered into an age of thought, learning, art, and science. This period lasted through the 1400s and 1500s and was known as the **Renaissance** (REH•nuh•SAHNS). *Renaissance* is a French word meaning "rebirth." During this time people were eager to explore unknown lands.

Knowledge of the Renaissance spread with the help of Johannes Gutenberg. In about 1450 he invented a new way to print books that was easier and less costly. As a result, more books were printed. In addition to the Bible, one of the most popular books of the Renaissance was *The Travels of Marco Polo.* Written almost 200 years earlier, this book described what the traveler from Venice, Italy, had seen on his journey to Asia in the late 1200s. When he was just 17 years old, Marco Polo, his father, Nicolò Polo, and his uncle, Maffeo Polo, set out to explore Asia. Four years later the Polos reached Cathay, as China was then called. They also traveled to the Indies, the islands off the China coast, as well as to Myanmar (Burma), India, and Southwest Asia.

The Polos were impressed by everything they saw, especially in China. They were amazed by Chinese inventions such as gunpowder and the **compass**—an instrument for finding direction. They also held paper money for the first time and saw the palace of Kublai Khan (KOO•bluh KAHN), China's ruler.

As Europeans read Marco Polo's accounts, they became interested in the lands he had visited. They wanted to share in the great wealth he described and buy Asian goods such as silks and spices. Soon, traders from Europe were traveling the long, difficult land routes that connected Europe and Asia.

**REVIEW** **How did people react when they heard Marco Polo's stories?**

## Asia

Some Asian countries began to explore the world by sailing the oceans. The Chinese ruler Yong Le (YUHNG LEH) paid for the ocean voyages of Admiral Zheng He (JUHNG HUH). Zheng He made at least seven voyages between 1405 and 1433.

Zheng He (far right) and his crew made many ocean voyages for the Chinese emperor on junks like this one (below).

Timbuktu became a center of learning as well as a trading center.

The admiral and his crews sailed in junks, Chinese wooden boats with four-sided sails. Zheng He sailed to Southeast Asia and to present-day Sri Lanka (SREE LAHNG•kuh). He also visited several ports along the Persian Gulf, the Red Sea, and the eastern coast of Africa.

After Yong Le's death, new Chinese rulers decided to keep China apart from other civilizations. They stopped all ocean voyages and limited trading outside of China's borders. They later ordered that the records of Zheng He's voyages be destroyed.

While China moved to limit its contact with the rest of the world, other places in Asia, such as India, Korea, and Japan, continued to develop trading centers. In the southern part of India, Vijayanagar (vih•juh•yuh•NUH•ger) became an important trading center for Asian and European countries. It was also known for its art, writing, and buildings.

REVIEW How did China limit its contact with other countries?

## Africa

For centuries, groups in Africa traded with one another. In time, African trading centers grew. As early as the eighth century, Ghana in western Africa had become a great African empire. Ghana had grown from just a small town into a grand walled city with palaces and busy market centers. The capital of Ghana was Kumbi Saleh (koom•BY sah•LAY), a large market center that stood in what is now a desert region of Senegal.

In the 1100s, the powerful trading centers of Ghana began to move east to the cities of Gao (GOW), Timbuktu (tim•buhk•TOO), and Jenné (jeh•NAY). The great empire of Mali (MAH•lee) formed from these growing market cities. By the 1300s Mali had become one of the most powerful empires in Africa.

In the 1400s these market centers broke away from Mali rule. Gao became the head of a new empire known as Songhay (SAWNG•hy).

A Chinese vase traded in Africa.

Benin was known for its brass and bronze sculptures. This statue was made in the 1500s.

The Songhay Empire controlled many of the market cities. This gave the Soninkes (sawn•IN•kayz), the people of Songhay, control of much of the trade across the Sahara to the north where they traded gold for European goods.

One of the best-known leaders of the Soninkes was Sunni Ali. He ruled from 1464 to 1492. Under his rule the Songhay Empire stretched more than 1,000 miles (1,609 km). Sunni Ali also encouraged more trade, which helped Songhay remain a strong empire until the end of the 1500s.

Also in western Africa was the kingdom of Benin. Benin was located in what is now southern Nigeria, near the mouth of the Niger River. Benin was an artistic center where sculptors carved ivory and worked with brass and bronze.

On the eastern coast of Africa, groups of people called the Swahili (swah•HEE•lee) lived in several city-states. A **city-state** included a city and the surrounding area. These city-states grew from the trading centers that Arab settlers had started at ports along the coast. Trade centered around gold and ivory, which were exchanged for goods from China, India, and Southwest Asia.

**REVIEW** How did Emperor Sunni Ali keep Songhay a strong empire?

**LESSON 1 REVIEW**

**Summary Time Line**

1400 — 1450 — 1500

**1405** Zheng He makes the first of his ocean voyages

**1455** Johannes Gutenberg invents a new way to print books

**1464** Sunni Ali becomes ruler of the Soninkes

1. **MAIN IDEA** In what ways was the world changing in the 1400s?

2. **WHY IT MATTERS** How did Europeans become interested in trading with people in Asia?

3. **VOCABULARY** Use the words **monarch** and **Renaissance** in a sentence about early exploration and trade.

4. **TIME LINE** Did Gutenberg invent a new way of printing before or after Sunni Ali became ruler of the Soninkes?

5. **READING SKILL—Sequence** Whose travels led to more European interest in Asia?

6. **GEOGRAPHY** What lands did Admiral Zheng He explore?

7. **CRITICAL THINKING—Hypothesize** What do you think might have happened if China had not stopped its ocean exploration?

**PERFORMANCE—Write a Diary Entry** Imagine that you are an early trader on a journey across Africa or Asia. Write a diary entry that describes some of the civilizations you encounter. Share your diary entry with your classmates.

SKILLS·

# Follow Routes on a Map

VOCABULARY

**historical map**

## ➡ WHY IT MATTERS

Marco Polo's book *The Travels of Marco Polo* inspired other Europeans to go to Asia. You can learn more about Marco Polo, and about other people and events, by using historical maps. A **historical map** gives information about a place as it was in the past. It may show where a historical event took place. It may show where cities or towns were once located. It may also show the routes that people followed as they traveled from one place to another. Knowing how to follow a route on a historical map can help you better understand the past and gather information about it.

## ➡ WHAT YOU NEED TO KNOW

The map on page 113 shows the routes followed by Marco Polo on his journey to and around Asia. Notice on the map key that the colored arrows represent the different routes he used during his adventure. These include the route to China, the route to Pagan, and the route back to Venice. The map also shows the lands and cities he visited along these routes. The dates of his journey are included in the map title.

## ➡ PRACTICE THE SKILL

Look at the map key to learn about the routes Marco Polo used during his exploration of Asia. Use the information provided on the map to answer the following questions about Marco Polo's journey.

**1** What color shows the route Marco Polo followed to China?

Marco Polo wrote about Asia in *The Travels of Marco Polo*. This copy was printed in 1577.

**112** ■ Unit 2

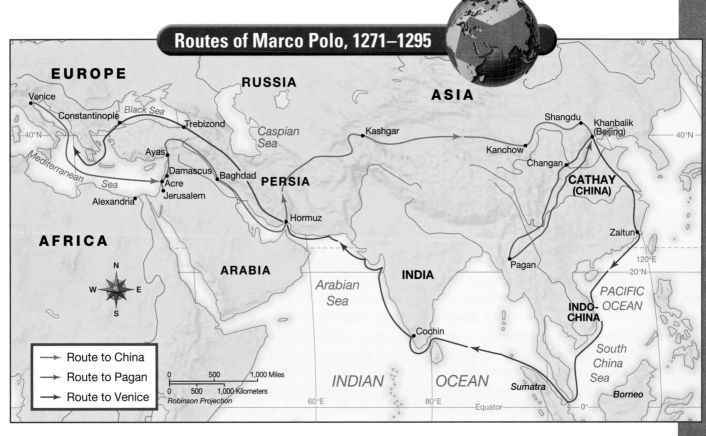

## Routes of Marco Polo, 1271–1295

EUROPE

Venice

Constantinople

Black Sea

RUSSIA

ASIA

40°N

Trebizond

Caspian Sea

Kashgar

Shangdu

Khanbalik (Beijing)

40°N

Ayas

Kanchow

Damascus

Baghdad

Changan

Acre

PERSIA

CATHAY (CHINA)

Mediterranean Sea

Jerusalem

Alexandria

Hormuz

Zaitun

AFRICA

120°E

ARABIA

Pagan

20°N

N

W E

S

INDIA

Arabian Sea

PACIFIC OCEAN

INDO-CHINA

Cochin

South China Sea

→ Route to China

→ Route to Pagan

→ Route to Venice

0      500      1,000 Miles

0   500  1,000 Kilometers

Robinson Projection

INDIAN      OCEAN

Sumatra

Borneo

60°E

80°E

Equator

0°

❷ What lands did he visit on his way to China?

❸ What lands did he visit on his way home to Venice?

❹ What geographic features did Marco Polo come across on his journey to China?

❺ What geographic features did Marco Polo come across on his journey back to Venice?

➡ **APPLY WHAT YOU LEARNED**

Imagine that the ruler of Italy has given you money to explore Asia. Like Marco Polo, you will begin your journey from Venice. Draw a map like the one on this page. Show the routes you would take on your expedition to Asia and the lands you would

visit along the way. Use a map key to explain what the symbols on your map stand for. You can use both land and sea routes to get to and from Asia.

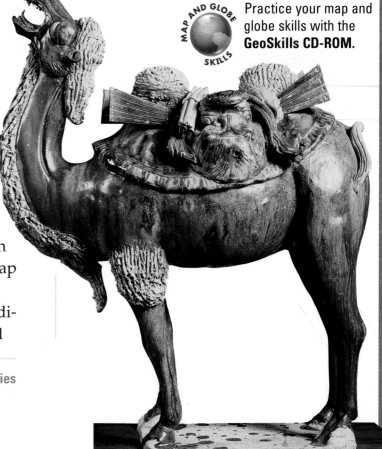

Practice your map and globe skills with the **GeoSkills CD-ROM**.

**Many travelers used camels to carry their supplies on overland journeys.**

MAP AND GLOBE SKILLS

**MAIN IDEA**
Read to learn why the Portuguese wanted to find a water route to Asia.

**WHY IT MATTERS**
Portugal's discovery of a water route to Asia led to more ocean exploration by Europeans.

**VOCABULARY**

profit
navigation
cartographer
astrolabe
caravel
expedition

# Background to European Exploration

**1450–1500**

During the Renaissance, the overland trade routes between Europe and Asia became dangerous because of fighting between religious groups in Europe and Asia. As a result, European merchants and explorers looked for less risky ways to reach Asia. This led to the development of better ways of travel and provided new opportunities for European merchants and explorers.

## An End to East-West Trade

For hundreds of years Europeans carried on a busy trade with people from Asia. To get goods from China and other places in Asia, merchants set off on the ancient Silk Road. The Silk Road, also known as the Silk Route, was not really a road, but a group of overland trade routes between China and Italy.

The Silk Road stretched over the mountains and deserts of Asia, so travel was often difficult and slow. Instead of going all the way to the Far East, as the Europeans called Asia, most European merchants traveled only part of the way. They went to trading cities in North Africa and in Southwest Asia, which the Europeans called the Middle East. The major trading cities included Alexandria (a•lig•ZAN•dree•uh) in North Africa and Baghdad (BAG•dad) and Constantinople (kahn•stant•uhn•OH•puhl) in Southwest Asia. There, European merchants exchanged their goods for goods that had been brought there from Asia.

Items such as silk (left), Chinese bank notes (center), and containers of tea leaves (right) were all traded along the Silk Road.

LOCATE IT

Pamir Plateau

TAJIKISTAN    CHINA

These people are traveling on what was once a part of the Silk Road.

The Asian goods that Europeans wanted most included gold, jewels, silks, perfumes, and spices. Spices such as pepper, cloves, cinnamon, and nutmeg were used to help add flavor to food and keep it fresh.

Asian goods were usually expensive because Europeans could not easily get them. Europeans, however, were willing to pay high prices to have them. As a result, merchants made huge profits from selling these goods. A **profit** is money left over after the goods and the costs of getting them have been paid for.

European merchants continued to enjoy these huge profits until 1453, when trade with Asia was suddenly stopped. In that year the Turks, a people from a land called the Ottoman Empire in the Middle East, captured the important trading city of Constantinople. This gave the Turks control of the Middle East, and they closed the trade routes to Asia. Now there was no way for Europeans to get Asian goods.

**REVIEW** What was the Silk Road?

## Portugal Leads the Way

By the time the city of Constantinople was captured, Portugal's monarch, King John I, had already decided to spend as much money as needed to find a new route to Asia. King John asked his son Henry to direct the country's search for a water route to Asia. Prince Henry soon set up a school for training sailors in navigation (na•vuh•GAY•shuhn). **Navigation** is the skill of controlling the course of a ship.

Prince Henry started his school at Sagres (SAH•gresh), a town on the southwestern tip of Europe. There he brought together sailors, shipbuilders, and **cartographers** (kar•TAH•gruh•ferz), or mapmakers. The cartographers drew up new, more accurate maps. Many were based on information from the journals of early travelers.

Prince Henry also hired people who helped improve two important navigation tools—the compass and the astrolabe (AS•truh•layb).

Prince Henry later became known as Henry the Navigator.

An **astrolabe** is an instrument used to calculate the positions of the sun, moon, and stars. The astrolabe helped sailors find their location by using the position of the sun or the North Star.

Sailors at Prince Henry's school learned how to sail a new kind of ship, the **caravel**. This ship used square or triangular sails to travel long distances quickly. It also was able to survive heavy seas. Since the caravel was easier to sail and could carry more cargo than older types of ships, it was the preferred ship for ocean exploration.

Prince Henry believed that the most direct way to reach Asia from Europe by sea would be to go south around Africa and then sail east across the Indian Ocean. Under his direction, dozens of Portuguese ships made their way down Africa's west coast. Altogether, Henry organized more than 50 voyages, but he did not go on any of them. For this reason he is sometimes called "the explorer who stayed at home."

## A CLOSER LOOK
### The Caravel

Many sailors in the 1400s used caravels to travel long distances.

1. side view
2. captain's cabin
3. hold
4. crow's nest
5. main mast
6. main deck
7. ship's boat

◇ Where do you think food and other supplies were kept?

## Navigational Tools

In the 1400s sailors used the compass and the astrolabe to help determine their location at sea. In the 1700s, however, they used more advanced instruments, such as the sextant and the chronometer, to help find a ship's position. The sextant was used to determine the altitude, or the height above the horizon, of the sun or stars. The chronometer (kruh•NAHM•uh•ter) kept very accurate time. It was used to measure the positions of certain stars based on the time. Today, radar and other electronic systems have replaced these tools.

**An astrolabe**

## Ahmad Ibn Majid
### 1432–1500
**Character Trait: Inventiveness**

Ahmad Ibn Majid (AH•mahd IH•bihn ma•JEED) was born in what is today the United Arab Emirates. He learned navigation skills, geography, astronomy, and Arabic literature at an early age.

In 1498, Majid helped Vasco da Gama sail around the Cape of Good Hope and on to India. He is considered by many to be a great contributor to the study of navigation.

**MULTIMEDIA BIOGRAPHIES**

Visit The Learning Site at
www.harcourtschool.com/biographies
to learn about other famous people.

As the Portuguese explored the western coast of Africa, they found new markets where they could trade European goods for nuts, fruits, and gold. They also discovered that they could trade their goods for slaves. Like Native Americans and other groups throughout history, Africans had long used prisoners of war as slaves. Traders from Portugal saw that they could make money by buying slaves in Africa and taking them to Europe to be sold as servants. By 1460 Portuguese traders were buying about 800 slaves from African traders each year.

**REVIEW** How did Prince Henry contribute to ocean exploration?

## Dias and Da Gama

After Prince Henry's death, the Portuguese continued to explore the west coast of Africa. King John II of Portugal ordered Bartolomeu Dias (DEE•ahsh) to sail to the southern tip of Africa. The king wanted to know for sure that ships could reach Asia by sailing around Africa. Earlier **expeditions**, or journeys of exploration, had failed because of the rough ocean currents along the southern coast of Africa.

Dias commanded a fleet of three ships. In 1488 the ships reached southern Africa, and a storm blew them out to sea. When the winds died down and the sky cleared, Dias realized that the storm had blown the ships around to the east coast of the continent. He and his crew had become the first Europeans to sail around the southern tip of Africa!

On their way back around the tip of Africa, Dias sighted what is now called the Cape of Good Hope. Some historians believe that Dias originally named it the Cape of Storms but that King John later renamed it the Cape of Good Hope. To King John the discovery of the cape meant that a sea route to India would soon be found.

Almost ten years later Vasco da Gama (dah GA•muh) reached India. He sailed around the Cape of Good Hope with four

FAST FACT Vasco da Gama returned to Portugal in 1499 with Indian spices and jewels. The sale of the items brought 60 times what the trip had cost!

ships. He brought back to Portugal perfumes, silks, spices, and other goods that he had traded for in India. The expedition returned to Lisbon, Portugal's capital, in September 1499. Many of da Gama's crew, however, did not survive the long voyage. Of the 170 crew members who started the voyage, only 55 lived to return home.

As a reward for his successful expedition, da Gama was given the title Admiral of the Sea of India. His voyage opened the Cape Route to India and led to the regular sailing of ships between Europe and Asia. The trade that resulted helped Portugal become wealthier and more powerful. It also spread Portuguese influence and culture to Africa and Asia. Portugal quickly became one of the most important trading powers in the Indian Ocean.

**REVIEW** What led to the regular sailing of ships from Europe to Asia?

**Routes of Dias and da Gama**

→ Dias, 1487–1488
→ da Gama, 1497–1499

**GEOGRAPHY THEME**

**Movement** Dias and da Gama were the first Europeans to sail around the Cape of Good Hope.

❓ In what direction did da Gama sail after he sailed around the Cape of Good Hope?

LESSON 2
REVIEW

**Summary Time Line**

1450 — 1475 — 1500

1453
The Turks capture Constantinople

1488
Dias sails around the tip of Africa

1498
Da Gama reaches India

**1** MAIN IDEA Why did Portugal want to find a water route to Asia?

**2** WHY IT MATTERS Why do you think a water route to Asia would lead to more ocean exploration by Europeans?

**3** VOCABULARY Use the words **navigation** and **astrolabe** in a sentence about early Portuguese exploration.

**4** TIME LINE How long after the Turks captured Constantinople did da Gama reach India?

**5** READING SKILL—Sequence How did European merchants get Asian goods before sailing to India was possible?

**6** SCIENCE AND TECHNOLOGY What instrument made it possible for sailors to calculate their position by the sun and stars?

**7** CRITICAL THINKING—Evaluate Why do you think Henry the Navigator believed European exploration was so important?

PERFORMANCE—Write a Persuasive Letter Imagine that you are a Portuguese sailor. Write a persuasive letter to King John I, explaining why he should pay for an ocean voyage you want to make to Asia. Explain why your journey would be good for the Portuguese.

# ·SKILLS· READING

# Identify Causes and Their Effects

**VOCABULARY**

cause          effect

➡ **WHY IT MATTERS**

To find the links between events in history, you need to identify cause-and-effect relationships. A **cause** is an event or action that makes something else happen. An **effect** is what happens as a result of that event or action. Knowing about causes and effects can help you predict likely outcomes so that you can make more thoughtful decisions.

➡ **WHAT YOU NEED TO KNOW**

Events in history can have more than one effect. You can use these steps to help you identify the causes and the effects of events.

**Step 1  Look for the effects.**

**Step 2  Look for the causes of those effects.**

**Step 3  Think about how the causes relate to the effects.**

➡ **PRACTICE THE SKILL**

The following cause-and-effect chart lists the effects of the Turks taking over Constantinople and closing the trade routes between Europe and Asia. Use the chart to answer these questions.

❶ The capture of what city caused Europeans to begin searching for water routes to Asia?

Causes

| In 1453 the Turks take over Constantinople. | The Turks close trade routes between Europe and Asia. |

Effects

Europeans can no longer get Asian goods, and the Portuguese search for a water route that leads to Asia.

In 1488 Bartolomeu Dias sails around the southern tip of Africa.

Vasco da Gama sails around the Cape of Good Hope and reaches India.

Vasco da Gama's voyage opens up the Cape Route to India and leads to the regular sailing of ships between Europe and the Far East.

❷ What was the immediate effect of the Turks closing these trade routes?

❸ Name an event that took place as a result of da Gama sailing around the Cape of Good Hope to India.

➡ **APPLY WHAT YOU LEARNED**

Look through pages 114–119 of your textbook, and identify at least two other cause-and-effect relationships in this lesson. Then share your findings with a classmate.

**READING SKILLS**

# Europeans Explore the World

**1200**       **1475**       **1700**

**1482–1522**

## · LESSON ·

# 3

**MAIN IDEA**
Read to learn about the European attempts to find a western route to Asia.

**WHY IT MATTERS**
The attempts to find a western route to Asia led the Europeans to the Americas.

**VOCABULARY**
claim
isthmus
demarcation
treaty

Portugal and other European countries, such as Spain, Denmark, England, Holland, and France, were determined to find new and faster water routes to Asia. These nations also hoped to **claim**, or declare they owned, new lands in the hope of building their empires and discovering new riches.

## Christopher Columbus

Born and raised in Italy, Christopher Columbus had sailed to all parts of the world that were known to Europeans, including the Mediterranean Sea, England and the European coast, the Canary Islands, and the coast of Africa. He was fascinated by the stories he had heard of the wealth in Asia, especially in China and on the islands of Southeast Asia, then a part of what was known as the Indies.

For years Columbus had worked on a plan to reach Asia by sailing west across the Ocean Sea, as the Atlantic Ocean was then known. He believed that sailing west was a more direct route to Asia than going around Africa. Columbus first took his plan to the king of Portugal in 1482. The Portuguese king turned him down. Three years later, in 1485, Columbus asked Spain's monarchs, King Ferdinand and Queen Isabella, to support his plan.

At the time, Spain's monarchs were more interested in life at home than in paying for an ocean expedition. Ferdinand and Isabella believed that Spain could be united as a nation only if all its people were Catholic. Their plan to make Spain all Catholic was called the Reconquista (ray•kohn•KEES•tah), or Reconquest.

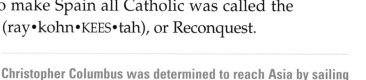

Christopher Columbus was determined to reach Asia by sailing west across the Ocean Sea.

## Voyages of Columbus

→ First voyage, 1492–1493
→ Second voyage, 1493–1496
→ Third voyage, 1498
→ Fourth voyage, 1502–1504

EUROPE
45°N
15°W
PORTUGAL SPAIN
Lisbon Palos 0°
Azores • Cádiz
30°W

ATLANTIC
OCEAN
60°W    45°W

NORTH
AMERICA    75°W
Madeira
30°N
Canary
Islands

Bahamas
Cuba    San Salvador
Hispaniola

AFRICA

Jamaica
Puerto
Rico
15°N
Caribbean Sea
75°W

Cape
Verde
Islands    15°N

N
W    E
S

60°W

0          400        800 Miles
0       400      800 Kilometers
Orthographic Projection

SOUTH
AMERICA

90°W    45°W    30°W    15°W

**Movement**    The King and Queen of Spain declared Columbus Admiral of the Ocean Sea and governor of any lands he discovered.

❓ **In which voyage did Columbus reach the islands off the coast of South America?**

By 1492 the Spanish monarchs had forced the Muslims, who would not become Catholic, out of Spain. They also forced all Jewish people to leave Spain.

When Spain was united under one religion, Columbus again asked Ferdinand and Isabella to support his expedition. He promised the monarchs great wealth and new lands. Columbus also said that he would take the Catholic religion to the people of Asia. The king and queen agreed to support his plan.

On August 3, 1492, Columbus and a crew of 90 sailors set forth on three ships—the *Niña* (NEEN•yuh), the *Pinta* (PEEN•tuh), and the *Santa María*. On October 12 they anchored off an island

that Columbus named San Salvador, which in Spanish means "Holy Savior." He claimed the island for Spain.

Columbus believed he had reached Asia and was now in the Indies. For this reason he called the people of the island Indians. The name West Indies is still used to refer to the islands Columbus visited in the Caribbean Sea.

News of Columbus's voyage stirred an excitement to explore. Columbus himself made three more voyages to the "new world." Today, his arrival in the Americas is remembered in many cities in the United States on Columbus Day.

**REVIEW** Why did King Ferdinand and Queen Isabella support Columbus's expedition?

## An Unknown Continent

Soon after Columbus's first voyage, most European monarchs wanted to send ships across the Atlantic to China and the Indies. In 1497 the king of England paid an Italian sailor named Giovanni Caboto (kah•BOH•toh) to lead an expedition.

Caboto's course across the Atlantic Ocean was far north of Columbus's course. Many believe that Caboto reached the coast of present-day Newfoundland, a part of Canada. When Caboto returned to England, he said he had found Cathay, and it was a place so rich in fish that a person could simply lower baskets into the water and draw them up filled with fish. Caboto became a hero. In England he was given the English name John Cabot.

Not everyone believed that Columbus had found the Indies or that Caboto had found Cathay. Amerigo Vespucci (veh•SPOO•chee) of Italy was one who had doubts. In 1499 Vespucci sailed to a place just south of where Columbus had landed. Two years later Vespucci sailed on an expedition down the coast of South America.

Vespucci looked for signs that he had reached Asia, but he could find none. Something else did not make sense. Years earlier he had studied the work of Ptolemy (TAH•luh•mee), an astronomer in ancient Egypt, and had learned that Earth was larger and Asia was smaller than most people had thought. If Asia were as far east as Columbus claimed, it would cover half the Earth.

Vespucci came to realize that he, Columbus, and Caboto had found an unknown continent. In 1507 a mapmaker named Martin Waldseemüller (VAHLT•zay•mool•er) published a world map that included this unknown continent. He named the new lands for Amerigo Vespucci, calling them America.

The first to prove Vespucci's idea was the Spaniard Vasco Núñez de Balboa (NOON•yays day bahl•BOH•uh), who crossed the Isthmus of Panama in 1513. An **isthmus** (IS•muhs) is a narrow strip of land that connects two larger land areas.

Many cities, like Chicago, hold parades to celebrate Columbus Day.

### • HERITAGE •

### Columbus Day

The first Columbus Day celebration was held in 1792, when New York City celebrated the three-hundredth anniversary of Columbus's landing at San Salvador. Columbus Day became a legal federal holiday in 1971. It is celebrated on the second Monday in October. Today, many cities and organizations hold parades and banquets to honor this early explorer.

## POINTS OF VIEW
### An Unknown Land?

**CHRISTOPHER COLUMBUS**, from a letter he wrote to his friend Doña Juana de Torres in 1500

❝I should be judged as a captain who went from Spain to the Indies . . . ❞

**AMERIGO VESPUCCI**, from a letter to his friend Lorenzo Medici announcing the discovery of a new continent

❝Those new regions [America] which we found and explored with the fleet . . . we may rightly call a New World . . . a continent more densely peopled and abounding in animals than our Europe or Asia, or Africa . . . ❞

### Analyze the Viewpoints

❶ What view about his discovery did each explorer hold?

❷ **Make It Relevant**  Look at the Letters to the Editor section of your newspaper. Find two letters that express different viewpoints about the same topic. Then write a paragraph that summarizes each viewpoint.

The Isthmus of Panama connects the continents known today as North America and South America. Balboa's explorers landed on the east coast of the isthmus and marched west. They eventually reached a huge, unfamiliar ocean known today as the Pacific Ocean.

**REVIEW** Why was Amerigo Vespucci's discovery important?

# First Voyage Around the World

In 1522 a Spanish expedition headed by the Portuguese explorer Ferdinand Magellan (muh•JEH•luhn) also proved Vespucci was correct. That same expedition proved that Columbus's dream was possible and that Europeans could reach Asia by sailing west. First, however, the explorers had to sail around the Americas. That proved to be a long and dangerous task.

Magellan set sail from Spain in September 1519, in command of about 250 sailors on five ships. He sailed to what is now Brazil and then south along South America's eastern coast. For many months he sailed up rivers into the middle of the continent, hoping to find a river that would lead to the ocean on the other side. However, he never did, and each time he had to sail back down the rivers, to the coast. As the ships fought their way through huge, pounding waves and against howling winds, one ship and many of its crew were lost. Finally, in the fall of 1520, the rest of Magellan's ships sailed through what is now called the Strait of Magellan, near the southern tip of South America. The sailors found themselves in the same ocean that Balboa had seen. Magellan named it Pacific, which means

When Vasco Núñez de Balboa crossed the Isthmus of Panama he proved that Vespucci was right about an unknown continent.

"peaceful," because it seemed so still and quiet compared with the Atlantic.

For more than three months, the ships sailed across the Pacific Ocean toward Asia. The voyage around the world was full of hardship—disease, shipwreck, and hunger. Four of the ships were lost. The small amount of food that was left quickly spoiled, and there was no place to stop for fresh food. Many sailors died of hunger and illness. Magellan himself was killed in the spring of 1521 during a battle with the people of one of the Philippine Islands in Southeast Asia.

Despite the terrible losses, the last of Magellan's ships, with just 18 sailors aboard, finally made it around the world.

In September 1522, the *Victoria* limped into the Spanish port of Seville.

**REVIEW** What did Ferdinand Magellan and his crew prove?

## Spain Challenges Portugal

In the early days of European exploration, explorers always claimed the lands they visited for the country they represented. Sometimes more than one country claimed the same land. Spain and Portugal often disagreed about the ownership of the lands they had been exploring. Since the monarchs of both nations were Catholic, they asked Pope Alexander VI to settle their argument.

**GEOGRAPHY THEME**

**Movement** Caboto, Vespucci, Balboa, and Magellan were among the first Europeans to sail across the Atlantic.

❖ Where did Vespucci sail in 1501–1502?

**Routes of Caboto, Vespucci, Balboa, and Magellan**

→ Caboto, 1497
→ Vespucci, 1499, 1501–1502
→ Balboa, 1501, 1513
→ Magellan, 1519–1522

0   1,000   2,000 Miles
0   1,000  2,000 Kilometers
Scale accurate at equator
Winkel Projection

The pope is the leader of the Catholic Church.

In 1493 the pope drew on a map a line of **demarcation**, or a line that marks a boundary. The line divided the world as he knew it. Portugal had the right to all lands east of the line. Spain got all lands west of the line. This included both North America and South America.

A year later, in 1494, Portugal and Spain signed the Treaty of Tordesillas (tawr•day•SEE•yahs). A **treaty** is an agreement between nations about peace, trade, or other matters. This treaty moved the Pope's line of demarcation farther west, allowing Portuguese explorer Pedro Álvares Cabral (kuh•BRAHL) to claim Brazil for Portugal when his expedition landed there in 1500. Spain claimed the rest of the Americas.

**REVIEW** What role did the pope play in settling the argument over land ownership?

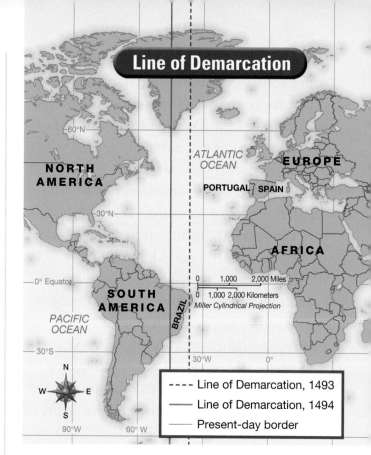

**Line of Demarcation**

- - - - Line of Demarcation, 1493
———— Line of Demarcation, 1494
———— Present-day border

**Regions** Portugal could claim lands east of the line of demarcation, and Spain could claim lands west of the line.

❷ Who would be able to claim an island off the coast of Africa?

LESSON 3
REVIEW

**Summary Time Line**

1482 ———— 1502 ———— 1522

**1492**
Columbus lands at San Salvador

**1494**
Portugal and Spain sign the Treaty of Tordesillas

**1522**
Magellan's crew sails around the world

❶ **MAIN IDEA** Why did Europeans want to find a western route to Asia?

❷ **WHY IT MATTERS** Why did Columbus and Caboto believe they had reached Asia?

❸ **VOCABULARY** Define the words **demarcation** and **treaty**.

❹ **TIME LINE** Which event took place first, Columbus's landing at San Salvador or Magellan's crew sailing around the world?

❺ **READING SKILL—Sequence** What event allowed Portuguese explorer Pedro Álvares Cabral to claim Brazil for Portugal?

❻ **CULTURE** Why do many people celebrate Columbus Day?

❼ **HISTORY** Who was the first explorer to prove Amerigo Vespucci's theory that he had landed on an unknown continent?

❽ **CRITICAL THINKING—Synthesize** Why do you think explorers became heroes?

**PERFORMANCE—Plan a Celebration**
Imagine that you are the Spanish monarch in 1522 when Magellan's crew returns home. Plan a celebration and write a speech honoring the expedition.

# The Spanish Conquerors

· LESSON ·

4

**MAIN IDEA**
Read to learn how the desire for wealth led to exploration of the Americas by Europeans.

**WHY IT MATTERS**
Further exploration of the Americas caused conflict between the European explorers and the Native Americans.

**VOCABULARY**
grant
conquistador
desertion

1200   1475   1700

1505–1545

Once Spain had claim to the Americas, explorers and soldiers from Spain soon sailed there. Some were driven by their desire to serve their country and win fame. Some dreamed of finding gold and other riches. Others wanted to change the beliefs of Native Americans, or convert them, to Christianity. To encourage the explorers, the Spanish king offered grants to those who would lead expeditions. A **grant** is a sum of money or other payment given for a particular reason.

The explorers and soldiers eventually pushed deep into North America and South America. Along the way they conquered many of the native peoples who were already living there. Among the Europeans, these explorers and soldiers came to be known as **conquistadors** (kahn•KEES•tuh•dawrz), or "conquerors."

## Juan Ponce de León

By 1508 the island of Hispaniola (ees•pah•NYOH•lah), in the Caribbean, had become the center from which the Spanish directed their conquest of the Americas. Today, Hispaniola is made up of the countries of Haiti and the Dominican Republic. From Hispaniola, the conquistadors soon conquered Puerto Rico, Jamaica, and Cuba. Eager to add to their growing empire, Spain's rulers urged the conquistadors to go farther. One of the first to do so was Juan Ponce de León (POHN•say day lay•OHN).

Ponce de León had sailed with Christopher Columbus on his second voyage and had later helped take over Puerto Rico.

Juan Ponce de León was the first conquistador known to arrive in Florida.

From the Native Americans who lived there, Ponce de León had heard about an island to the north called Bimini (BIH•muh•nee). Legend says he also may have heard about a special spring on the island. This "Fountain of Youth" was said to have water that made old people young again!

This Aztec pendant is made of gold.

In 1513 Ponce de León set out to find Bimini. Instead, he landed on the mainland of North America in what is now the state of Florida. He claimed the land for Spain and named it *La Florida*, Spanish for "flowery." To the Spanish, La Florida came to refer to all of what is now the Southeast United States. Though Ponce de León never found a fountain of youth, he was the first Spanish explorer to set foot on territory that became part of the United States.

**REVIEW** When Ponce de León discovered Florida, what was he really looking for?

## Cortés in Mexico

Ponce de León never found the great riches he was looking for, but the dramatic fight for what is today Mexico would bring Spain a great deal of wealth. Spain's fight for Mexico began in 1519 when the Spanish sent Hernando Cortés, a Spanish noble, on an expedition to find gold in the land of the Aztecs.

Cortés had heard stories about the great wealth of the Aztec Empire. Before setting out from Cuba, Cortés told his soldiers,

**66 We are waging a just and good war which will bring us fame. . . . If you do not abandon me, as I shall not abandon you, I shall make you the richest men who ever crossed the seas. 99**

In the spring of 1519, Cortés landed on the east coast of Mexico with more than

Tenochtitlan.

This painting shows the meeting of Motecuhzoma (left) and Cortés (right). Malintzin (next to Cortés) helped translate for the conquistadors.

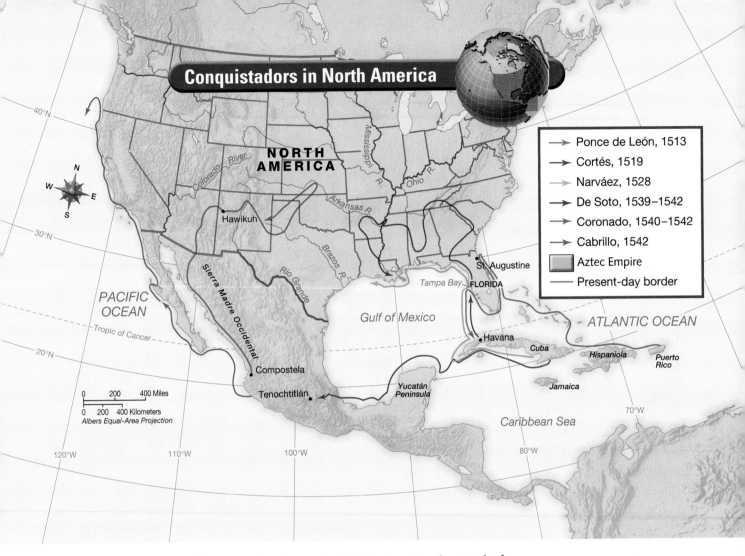

## Conquistadors in North America

**Map Legend:**
- → Ponce de León, 1513
- → Cortés, 1519
- → Narváez, 1528
- → De Soto, 1539–1542
- → Coronado, 1540–1542
- → Cabrillo, 1542
- ▨ Aztec Empire
- — Present-day border

NORTH AMERICA

Colorado River · Mississippi R. · Ohio R. · Arkansas R. · Brazos R. · Rio Grande

Hawikuh · Sierra Madre Occidental · Compostela · Tenochtitlán

PACIFIC OCEAN · Tropic of Cancer

St. Augustine · Tampa Bay · FLORIDA · Gulf of Mexico · Havana · Cuba · Hispaniola · Puerto Rico · Jamaica · Yucatán Peninsula · Caribbean Sea · ATLANTIC OCEAN

0 200 400 Miles
0 200 400 Kilometers
Albers Equal-Area Projection

40°N · 30°N · 20°N · 120°W · 110°W · 100°W · 80°W · 70°W

**GEOGRAPHY THEME**

**Movement** Many conquistadors set out to the Americas in search of gold and other riches.

❖ Which conquistador traveled through part of what is now Texas?

650 soldiers and 16 horses—the first horses in the Americas for thousands of years. Nearby he founded the settlement of Veracruz (vair•ah•KROOS). To make turning back impossible, Cortés destroyed all but the one ship he sent back to Cuba. He then led a march from the coast, over the mountains, and into the Valley of Mexico. After several months, the expedition reached the Aztec capital of Tenochtitlán. There the Spaniards saw the treasures they were seeking.

Along the way, the Spanish had been joined by groups of Indians who were unhappy with Aztec rule. They gave food to the Spanish and even agreed to help them fight the Aztecs. Yet perhaps the greatest help to Cortés came from the Aztecs' belief in a god named Quetzalcoatl (ket•zahl•KOH•ah•tuhl). According to legend, this god had sailed away years before but had promised to return. The Aztecs believed that the light-skinned Quetzalcoatl would one day return to rule his people. Thinking that Cortés might be Quetzalcoatl, Motecuhzoma (maw•tay•kwah•SOH•mah), the Aztec emperor, welcomed Cortés and offered him housing and gifts of gold.

Cortés, however, took Motecuhzoma prisoner. He hoped to rule the Aztecs by capturing their king.

When fighting broke out, Motecuhzoma tried to stop it by speaking to his people. While he was talking, someone threw a stone at him. The stone struck Motecuhzoma in the head, and the injury soon killed him. The Spanish were forced to leave Tenochtitlán, but only after heavy fighting. Half of Cortés's soldiers died.

Cortés and his expedition found safety with the Indians who had helped them earlier. The next year, in 1521, Cortés returned to Tenochtitlán to capture the Aztec treasures. With the help of the Indians, the Spanish tore down the Aztec temples and destroyed the great city. Cortés believed that only by destroying the city would he be able to break the power of the Aztecs. On the ruins of the Aztec capital, the conquistadors built Mexico City, which was officially recognized by Spain in 1522. Mexico City later became the capital of Spain's new empire in the Americas.

**REVIEW** Why did Cortés and his men try to conquer the Aztecs?

## Pánfilo de Narváez

Following the success in Mexico, Spain once again turned its attention to Florida. In 1528 Pánfilo de Narváez (PAHN•fee•loh day nar•VAH•ays) led another Spanish expedition there. The purpose of Narváez's expedition was to conquer all the lands along the Gulf of Mexico.

This ceramic figure is of an Aztec eagle warrior.

Narváez and his ships arrived near Tampa Bay, on the west coast of Florida, in April 1528. He went ashore with a landing party of 300 soldiers and 40 horses. Narváez decided that this group would travel north over land. The remaining crew and the ships, which carried most of the food and supplies, would sail north and meet the landing party at a certain harbor. This decision proved to be a terrible mistake.

Although the ships' crews searched the Gulf Coast for nearly a year, they did not find the harbor or the members of the landing party. Meanwhile, when Narváez and the landing party reached the place where they expected to find the ships, the ships were not there. Tired and hungry, the 242 survivors in the landing party decided to build small rafts and sail along the Gulf Coast until they reached Spanish lands in Mexico.

Having built their rafts by splitting pine trees into thick boards and sewing together their shirts to make sails, the survivors set sail on the Gulf of Mexico. After 31 days at sea, their rafts were wrecked in a storm off the coast of what is now Texas. The 80 men who reached shore set out to walk to Mexico City, however poor health and lack of food killed all but four of them.

**REVIEW** What was the purpose of Pánfilo de Narváez's expedition?

# Golden Cities

In 1536 the four survivors from the Narváez expedition arrived in Mexico City. They were three Spanish explorers, including Álvar Núñez Cabeza de Vaca (kah•BAY•sah day VAH•kah), and an African named Estevanico (es•tay•vahn•EE•koh), also called Esteban (es•TAY•bahn). Cabeza de Vaca told the survivors' story to Spanish leaders in Mexico City. He explained that during their long overland journey from the Texas coast to Mexico City, they had met Native Americans along the way who told them about seven cities rich in gold, silver, and jewels. The Spanish listened to the story with great interest.

In 1539 the Spanish leaders sent Esteban and a priest named Marcos de Niza (day NEE•sah) on an expedition to see if the story about the Seven Cities of Gold was in fact true. During the expedition, Esteban was killed by a group of Zuni Indians after he approached the Zuni pueblo.

De Niza, however, returned safely, saying he had seen a golden city during his travels.

After hearing about de Niza's expedition, Francisco Vásquez de Coronado (kawr•oh•NAH•doh) set out in 1540 with more than 300 Spaniards, several Africans, and more than 1,000 American Indians to find the seven cities. The expedition traveled through lands that are now parts of Arizona, New Mexico, Texas, Oklahoma, and Kansas. They marched through the Zuni town of Hawikuh (hah•we•KOO) and other Pueblo Indian towns, but they did not find any trace of the Seven Cities of Gold. Terribly disappointed, Coronado began the long journey home. The route he took would later become the Santa Fe Trail, one of the most traveled overland trade routes in North America before the time of the railroad.

Coronado arrived back in Mexico City in June 1542. Only 100 of his party returned. Many had died. Others had run away.

Cabeza de Vaca, Esteban, and two others were the only survivors of the Narváez expedition to North America.

Many historians believe that men from a scouting party of the Francisco Coronado expedition were the first Europeans to see the Grand Canyon and the Colorado River.

Although Coronado failed to find any riches, he had explored vast areas of New Spain and claimed lands in what is now the southwestern United States for Spain.

**REVIEW** Why were the Spanish leaders interested in finding the seven cities?

## De Soto in the Southeast

At about the same time that Coronado was planning his expedition, another Spanish conquistador, Hernando de Soto (day SOH•toh), was beginning one in what is now the Southeast United States. In May of 1539 de Soto and more than 600 soldiers landed near Tampa Bay. From there, they traveled north and reached what is now Georgia. Finding no gold, they moved on through parts of South Carolina and North Carolina, crossed the Smoky Mountains of Tennessee, and turned south into Alabama.

De Soto and his soldiers met many Native American peoples during this expedition. These encounters often ended in brutal battles. One of the worst took place in Alabama. There the Spanish fought the Mobile people, who were led by Tuscalusa (tuhs•kuh•LOO•suh).

A Spanish soldier who witnessed the battle wrote later that the number of Native Americans killed may have been as high as 11,000. The Spanish lost most of their supplies during the fighting. Because of this, de Soto's army was soon reduced in size by starvation and **desertions**, as soldiers ran away to save themselves.

De Soto and those who remained marched on, reaching the banks of the Mississippi River in May 1541. They were the first

De Soto brought these bells to trade for Native American goods.

## Conquest of the Incas
### Understanding Places and Regions

In 1531 Francisco Pizarro and a group of 180 soldiers explored the west coast of South America. They went in search of the riches of the Inca Empire. For months they traveled the Andes Mountains collecting gold and riches from the Native Americans they encountered. Pizarro later met with the Inca emperor, Atahuallpa (ah•tah•WAHL•pah). When Atahuallpa refused to accept Christianity and to accept the king of Spain as his ruler, Pizarro captured him and later had him killed. The Spanish then conquered the Inca Empire.

Europeans to see the great river. The Spanish built rafts to cross it and continued their search for gold on the other side of the river in what is now Arkansas and Louisiana. Then in May 1542 de Soto died of fever. The soldiers buried their leader in the Mississippi River to hide his death from the Native Americans. Then they made their way to Mexico.

Although de Soto and his soldiers found no gold, de Soto claimed for Spain much of the land his expedition had explored. The Spanish had now claimed all of what is today the Southeast United States.

**REVIEW** How did the battle against the Mobile people hurt de Soto's army?

**LESSON 4 REVIEW**

**Summary Time Line**

1505 — 1525 — 1545

**1513** Ponce de León claims Florida for Spain

**1521** Cortés conquers Tenochtitlán

**1540** Coronado sets out to find the Seven Cities of Gold

**1541** De Soto reaches the Mississippi River

1. **MAIN IDEA** How did a desire to find gold and riches affect early exploration in the Americas?

2. **WHY IT MATTERS** How were the lives of Native Americans changed by European exploration?

3. **VOCABULARY** Use the word **grant** in a sentence about Spanish exploration.

4. **TIME LINE** Which was claimed by the Spanish first, Florida or the Mississippi River?

5. **READING SKILL—Sequence** Which event happened first, the fall of Tenochtitlán or Coronado's search for the seven golden cities?

6. **HISTORY** What decision by the Narváez expedition proved to be a terrible mistake?

7. **CRITICAL THINKING—Analyze** Why did the Spanish build the settlement of Mexico City?

**PERFORMANCE—Draw a Map** Using the maps in the lesson as a guide, draw a map that shows all early Spanish expeditions in the Americas.

# PRIMARY SOURCES

# Conquistador Armor

Like most other soldiers, Spanish conquistadors wore suits of armor to protect themselves in battle. The armor, called plate armor, was made of large pieces of steel. The armor was often designed to cover and protect the entire body. Some armor-makers, or armorers, made very decorative armor that they engraved with special designs or scenes. Although the armor was a highly effective means of protection, it was very heavy, weighing up to 60 pounds (27 kg), and very hot. It was also expensive. A full suit of armor would sometimes cost as much as an entire farm!

This portrait of Hernando Cortés shows that he wore the armor of Spanish nobility.

 **FROM THE NATIONAL MUSEUM OF ARMS AND ARMOUR AND THE HIGGINS ARMORY**

Helmets were styled in various ways. Their function, however, was always the same—to protect the peoples' heads.

In the 1400s a Spanish conquistador wore this helmet.

## Analyze the Primary Source

**1** Why do you think the suit of armor included gauntlets to protect the hands?

**2** How do you think that changes in weapons affected changes in the kinds of armor worn by soldiers and conquistadors? Why do you think soldiers today no longer wear armor?

Metal helmets gave conquistadors added protection.

A suit of armor contains many connected parts, such as the collar, shoulderpiece, and elbow plates.

Gauntlets, or gloves made of steel, protected the conquistador's hands.

The breastplate protected the midsection of the conquistador. Sometimes the breastplate was adorned with decorative scenes.

### ACTIVITY

**Think Critically**

Conquistadors wore armor to avoid injury. Today, there are many activities that require the use of helmets and other protective gear. Make a list of sports and leisure activities in which the participants wear protective gear. Share your list with the class.

### RESEARCH

**GO** ONLINE Visit The Learning Site at **www.harcourtschool.com/ primarysources** to research other primary sources.

# 5

**MAIN IDEA**
Read to learn why some explorers were searching for a northern route to Asia.

**WHY IT MATTERS**
The search for a northern route to Asia led to the exploration of much of what is today Canada and the northeast United States.

**VOCABULARY**
Northwest Passage
estuary
rapid
company
mutiny

# Search for the Northwest Passage

| 1200 | 1475 | 1700 |
|---|---|---|

**1520–1610**

In the 1500s Spain became the richest nation in Europe due to its conquests. Spanish ships sailed from Mexico and South America with their treasure chests full of gold and silver. Other countries in Europe believed that if they could find a new trade route to Asia, they might also gain such wealth. The route followed by Ferdinand Magellan around South America to Asia was long and difficult. Other European explorers looked for what they called the **Northwest Passage**, a waterway along the north coast of North America connecting the Atlantic Ocean and the Pacific Ocean. The search for such a route between Europe and Asia began in the early 1500s.

## Verrazano Leads the Way

The French king Francis I was one of the many European rulers who wanted to find a Northwest Passage through North America. In 1524 he sent an Italian, Giovanni da Verrazano (ver•uh•ZAH•noh), to find it. The king gave Verrazano ships, sailors, food, and other supplies. Verrazano set sail for North America in January 1524 on his ship, the *Dauphine* (doh•FEEN). A few months later he reached what is now the Cape Fear River on the North Carolina coast.

After sailing farther north, Verrazano saw that only a narrow strip of land—perhaps a mile wide—lay between the Atlantic Ocean and another great body of water to the west.

Giovanni da Verrazano (left) sailed the *Dauphine* (right) into what is now New York Bay.

He thought that body of water might be the Pacific Ocean. It was actually what we call today the Pamlico (PAM•lih•koh) Sound. From Pamlico Sound, Verrazano sailed northward along the Atlantic coast to what is now New York Bay.

Verrazano sailed into the bay and landed the *Dauphine* on the north end of present-day Staten Island. He was given a warm welcome by the native people, who had never had contact with a European before. Verrazano developed a strong friendship with these Native Americans and described them in his report to King Francis I.

66 **These people are the most beautiful and have the most civil customs we have seen on this voyage. They are taller than we are. They are of a bronze color and some tend to whiteness, others to a tawny color. The face is clear-cut, the hair is long and black, and they take great care to decorate it . . .** 99

From New York Bay Verrazano sailed as far north as present-day Nova Scotia before returning to France. He made two more voyages to the Americas to try to find a water route to Asia. On these voyages, he searched the coastlines of North America and South America and still found no passage.

**REVIEW** Who did King Francis I send to find a Northwest Passage?

## Cartier Moves Inland

Ten years after Verrazano sailed into New York Bay, a French navigator named Jacques Cartier (ZHAHK kar•TYAY) also tried to find the Northwest Passage for France. Between 1534 and 1541, Cartier made three voyages and claimed land for France in North America.

In 1534 King Francis I sent Cartier to North America to search for gold and other valuable metals. The explorer left France with two ships to search the northern Atlantic coast. On this first voyage, he sailed up the estuary of the St. Lawrence River. An **estuary** is the wide mouth of a river where the ocean tide flows in. He landed on the Gaspé (ga•SPAY) Peninsula and claimed the land for France.

Jacques Cartier (right) wrote about his second voyage to North America in this journal (left).

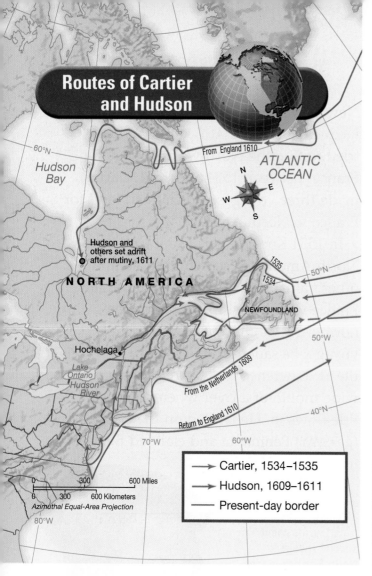

## Routes of Cartier and Hudson

From England 1610

ATLANTIC OCEAN

60°N

Hudson Bay

Hudson and others set adrift after mutiny, 1611

NORTH AMERICA

1535

1534

50°N

NEWFOUNDLAND

50°W

Hochelaga

Lake Ontario

Hudson River

From the Netherlands 1609

Return to England 1610

40°N

70°W

60°W

80°W

| | |
|---|---|
| → | Cartier, 1534–1535 |
| → | Hudson, 1609–1611 |
| — | Present-day border |

0   300   600 Miles
0   300   600 Kilometers
Azimuthal Equal-Area Projection

**Regions** Cartier and Hudson explored some of the waterways of North America.

❖ What waterways did Hudson explore?

During this expedition, Cartier was told by a group of Iroquois that jewels and metals could be found farther northwest. The French became friendly with the Iroquois and gave them gifts. When Cartier left to return to France, he carried a supply of corn that was given to him by the Iroquois. The corn was well received by northern Europeans, many of whom had never seen this vegetable before.

The following year, on his second voyage, Cartier became the first European to reach the inland of what is now Canada.

He sailed up the St. Lawrence River, hoping to find a water route through the continent. But his hopes disappeared when he came upon great **rapids**. No boat could travel through the fast-moving water. The expedition was forced to turn back. It had gone as far as what is now Montreal (mahn•tree•AWL), where a Huron Indian village called Hochelaga (hah•shuh•LA•guh) was located.

Cartier made a third journey in 1541, but he was never able to find the Northwest Passage. He sailed up the St. Lawrence near to what is now Quebec City. Some of his men remained there and built a camp while Cartier and the others searched for gold. They traveled even farther west but found nothing. Cartier returned to the camp and eventually returned to France.

**REVIEW** What stopped Cartier from searching for a water route through the North American continent?

## The Voyages of Henry Hudson

After Verrazano and Cartier, other Europeans continued to look for the Northwest Passage. Henry Hudson, an English sea captain, was one of them. In 1608, on his first expedition, he reached an island east of Greenland. He then sailed farther north by way of the Arctic Ocean but failed to find the Northwest Passage. The following year Hudson searched by way of the Barents Sea, an arm of the Arctic Ocean.

For his third voyage, Hudson had been hired by the Dutch East India Company to find the Northwest Passage. The **company**, or business, gave him a ship, the *Half Moon*, and a crew of about 20 sailors. They set sail in 1609 for the Arctic Ocean, but his crew soon **mutinied**, or rebelled. Hudson was forced to head south along the North American coast.

Hudson's journey led him to the coast of Maine, where members of the crew went ashore. They fished and traded with the Native Americans and soon went south to the Delaware and Chesapeake Bays. Hudson then sailed north to the mouth of the Hudson River. He spent a month exploring the river, which he named for himself. Hudson's voyage gave the Dutch rulers in Holland control of the whole Hudson River valley.

In 1610 Hudson set out on his final search for the Northwest Passage. This time he was sailing for an English company. On this voyage Hudson reached the bay that also carries his name—Hudson Bay.

He spent three months exploring the huge bay, located in east central Canada, north of present-day Ontario and Quebec. By November his ship was frozen in the ice, and after a cold winter and much

Henry Hudson, his son, and some of his crew were set adrift on Hudson Bay.

suffering, his crew again mutinied. They put Hudson, his son, and seven others into a small boat and left them drifting on the bay. They were never seen again.

**REVIEW** **What area of North America did Henry Hudson claim for the Dutch?**

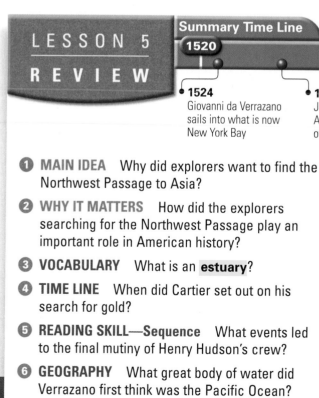

## LESSON 5 REVIEW

**Summary Time Line**

| 1520 | 1565 | 1610 |

**1524**
Giovanni da Verrazano sails into what is now New York Bay

**1534**
Jacques Cartier sails to North America in search of gold and other valuable metals

**1611**
Henry Hudson is set adrift on Hudson Bay while searching for the Northwest Passage

1. **MAIN IDEA** Why did explorers want to find the Northwest Passage to Asia?

2. **WHY IT MATTERS** How did the explorers searching for the Northwest Passage play an important role in American history?

3. **VOCABULARY** What is an **estuary**?

4. **TIME LINE** When did Cartier set out on his search for gold?

5. **READING SKILL—Sequence** What events led to the final mutiny of Henry Hudson's crew?

6. **GEOGRAPHY** What great body of water did Verrazano first think was the Pacific Ocean?

7. **CRITICAL THINKING—Evaluate** Why did explorers continue to search for the Northwest Passage?

**PERFORMANCE—Write a "Packing for a Journey" List** Imagine that you are responsible for getting the supplies for Henry Hudson's third voyage to Hudson Bay. Knowing that a crew might mutiny if they are not happy, what will you put on the list to make sure the voyage is a success? Consider where the expedition will go and that you have a limited amount of cargo space. Share your list with your classmates.

# Review and Test Preparation

**Summary Time Line**

1400

**1405**
Zheng He makes
the first of his
ocean voyages

**1453**
The Turks
capture
Constantino[

## USE YOUR READING SKILLS

Complete this graphic organizer to show that you understand the sequence of some of the key events that encouraged exploration and led to the discovery of the Americas. A copy of this graphic organizer appears on page 33 of the Activity Book.

## European Exploration

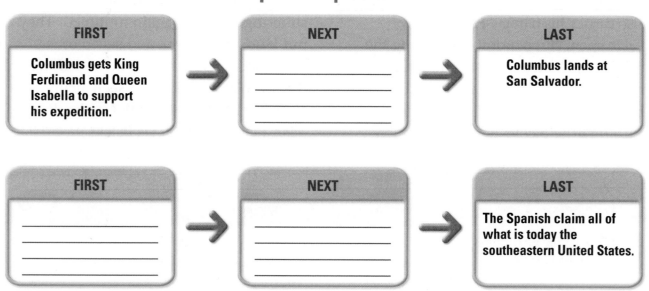

**FIRST**
Columbus gets King Ferdinand and Queen Isabella to support his expedition.

→

**NEXT**
_____
_____
_____

→

**LAST**
Columbus lands at San Salvador.

**FIRST**
_____
_____
_____

→

**NEXT**
_____
_____
_____

→

**LAST**
The Spanish claim all of what is today the southeastern United States.

## THINK & WRITE

**Write a Letter**  Imagine that you are Prince Henry of Portugal and that you have set up your navigation school in Sagres, Portugal. Write a letter to your father, King John I, describing how you are successfully training sailors to find new ocean routes to Asia.

**Write a News Story**  Suppose that you are a Spanish newspaper reporter who has been sent along with Hernando Cortés's expedition to write about the Aztec Empire. Write a short newspaper article in which you describe the Aztecs and their culture.

**1492**
Columbus lands
at San Salvador

**1498**
Da Gama
reaches India

**1541**
De Soto reaches
the Mississippi River

**1608**
Hudson sails to find
the Northwest Passage

## USE THE TIME LINE

Use the chapter summary time line to answer these questions.

**1** What happened first, the Turks' capture of Constantinople or Zheng He's voyages?

**2** How many years after Columbus landed at San Salvador did de Soto reach the Mississippi River?

## USE VOCABULARY

Identify the term that correctly matches each definition.

empire (p. 106)

astrolabe (p. 116)

claim (p. 121)

grant (p. 127)

estuary (p. 137)

**3** to declare you own

**4** a collection of lands ruled by the nation that conquered them

**5** the wide mouth of a river where the ocean tide flows in

**6** a sum of money or other payment given for a particular reason

**7** an instrument used to calculate the positions of the sun, moon, and stars

## RECALL FACTS

Answer these questions.

**8** Why did King John I of Portugal decide to spend as much money as needed on ocean exploration?

**9** How did Balboa prove Amerigo Vespucci's theory that Columbus had landed on an unknown continent?

**10** Why did the Aztecs welcome Cortés with gifts of gold?

## Write the letter of the best choice.

**11** **TEST PREP** Prince Henry helped Portugal lead the way in ocean exploration by—
  **A** giving explorers money.
  **B** encouraging people to read Marco Polo's book.
  **C** setting up a school for training sailors in navigation.
  **D** inventing the astrolabe.

**12** **TEST PREP** Hernando Cortés was sent to Mexico to—
  **F** convert the Indians to Catholicism.
  **G** make maps.
  **H** build a city.
  **J** find gold.

## THINK CRITICALLY

**13** How did trade play an important role in the growth of exploration?

**14** How might history have been different if the Turks had not captured Constantinople in 1453?

## APPLY SKILLS

**Follow Routes on a Map**
Use the map on page 113 to answer the following questions.

MAP AND GLOBE SKILLS

**15** What city did Marco Polo visit after visiting Baghdad?

**16** What two cities on the Black Sea did Polo visit on his way back to Venice?

**Identify Causes and Their Effects**

READING SKILLS

**17** Think again about the Northwest Passage. Draw a cause-and-effect chart similar to the one on page 120. Show the causes that led to the French exploration of North America.

**Chapter 3 ▪ 141**

# 4

# European Settlement

" . . . the front and vanguard of all my West Indies . . . the most important of them all—and the most coveted by my enemies. "

—King Philip IV of Spain, 1645, on the importance of Puerto Rico to Spain

## EL MORRO

El Morro, or "headland" in Spanish, was Spain's first military fort in the Americas. The fort, started in 1539, served as a base to guard the valuable port of San Juan, Puerto Rico. Much of the fort was built from sandstone that has lasted for centuries. In 1961, El Morro became part of the National Parks System.

### LOCATE IT

El Morro
San Juan
PUERTO RICO
Ponce

## CHAPTER READING SKILL

### Categorize

To **categorize** is to group information, or sort information by category. You can place people, places, and events into categories to make it easier to find facts.

**As you read this chapter, put information into the categories of key people, key settlements, and key events.**

| KEY PEOPLE | KEY SETTLEMENTS | KEY EVENTS |

Chapter 4 ■ 143

# 1

## MAIN IDEA
Read to learn about early Spanish settlements in the Americas.

## WHY IT MATTERS
A Spanish influence can still be seen in parts of the United States.

### VOCABULARY

colony

colonist

buffer zone

borderlands

presidio

permanent

hacienda

self-sufficient

missionary

mission

**FAST FACT** These irregularly shaped gold doubloons were called cobs, meaning "cut of the bar."

# New Spain

| 1200 | 1475 | 1700 |
|------|------|------|

**1500–1600**

By the 1500s several European nations had sent explorers to claim land in the Americas. Often more than one country claimed the same land because an explorer had no way of knowing that another explorer had already claimed it. In those days of exploration, people claimed the land and moved on, leaving no one to protect the claim.

Over time, Spain decided it needed to protect its claims in the Americas. To protect the land in its growing empire and govern the people there, Spain formed colonies. A **colony** is a land ruled by another country. The colony of New Spain was formed in 1535, with most of its land in Mexico and its capital at Mexico City. New Spain included mostly the Spanish lands north of the Isthmus of Panama and the many islands of the Caribbean Sea.

## Building New Spain

At first very few Spanish people settled in New Spain. Many of those who did were conquistadors. After news spread of the discovery of gold, silver, and other treasures, however, many colonists came to seek their fortunes. The people who go to live in a colony are called **colonists**.

Many of the colonists worked in the gold and silver mines. Others brought oxen and plows to work the land and horses to ride. They brought cattle and sheep, fruit trees, grain, and vegetable seeds. Over time, the Spanish began to build cities, and tens of thousands more colonists came to live in them.

The Spanish colonists needed many workers to grow their crops, to mine gold and silver, and to build and provide services in their cities. So they made slaves of the American Indian peoples they had conquered.

# Bartolomé de Las Casas   1474–1566

### Character Trait: Fairness

Bartolomé de Las Casas was one of the first Europeans to work to improve the treatment of American Indian workers. He became known as the Apostle to the Indians and wrote many essays questioning the Spanish colonists' treatment of the enslaved Indians.

Las Casas became bishop of Chiapas in Mexico in 1544. In 1547 he returned to Spain, where he continued to work for better treatment of the Indians until his death in 1566.

**MULTIMEDIA BIOGRAPHIES**
Visit The Learning Site at **www.harcourtschool.com/ biographies** to learn about other famous people.

American Indians were forced to mine gold and silver for the Spanish (left).

Thousands of Indians had already died fighting the conquistadors. Now thousands more died of hunger, overwork, and disease. The diseases the settlers unknowingly brought from Europe, such as measles, influenza, and smallpox, sometimes killed whole tribes.

In time, some colonists grew concerned about the cruel treatment of the Indians. One such colonist was Bartolomé de Las Casas (bar•toh•loh•MAY day lahs KAH•sahs). Las Casas settled on the island of Hispaniola in 1502 and became a successful plantation owner.

Las Casas used American Indians as enslaved workers, but came to believe that making the Indians slaves was wrong. In 1509 he freed his slaves and began to work to get better treatment for them. Las Casas spoke out so strongly that the king of Spain, Charles I, agreed to pass laws to protect the Indians. In 1550 the king ordered that the Spanish could no longer enslave the Indians. These orders, however, were not always carried out.

As more Indians died, the number of Indian workers fell sharply. The colonists now looked for other workers. They began to bring Africans to the colony as slaves. Even Bartolomé de Las Casas thought that Africans could be used to do the work. It was an idea he came to regret. Soon Africans were working under the same terrible conditions that the Indians had worked under.

**REVIEW** Why did the Spanish colonists need many workers?

## The Spanish Borderlands

As other European countries started colonies in North America, Spain believed it needed to protect its own. To do so, the Spanish created a buffer zone. A **buffer zone** is an area of land that serves as a barrier. The buffer zone north of New Spain came to be known as the **borderlands**. The borderlands stretched across what are today northern Mexico and the southern United States from Florida to California.

Spanish soldiers led the way into the borderlands, where they built **presidios** (pray•SEE•dee•ohz), or forts, and places for the settlers to live. In 1565 Pedro Menéndez de Avilés (may•NAYN•days day ah•vee•LAYS) and 1,500 soldiers, sailors, and settlers set sail from Spain. After several ships were lost in storms, the surviving members of the expedition reached the location of present-day St. Augustine, Florida. There they built the first **permanent**, or long-lasting, European settlement in what is now the United States.

**Analyze Diagrams** **Once the coquina was brought to St. Augustine from a nearby island, workers shaped it into blocks.**

❖ How did workers transport heavy materials?

**LOCATE IT**

Castillo de San Marcos

Tallahassee

FLORIDA

**FAST FACT**

The Castillo de San Marcos is the only early Spanish structure in Florida to survive to the present. It survived mostly because it was made from coquina.

In 1672, after years of attacks by European pirates and American Indian raiders, the queen of Spain sent money to pay for the building of a strong stone fort. Workers built the fort with coquina (koh•KEE•nuh), a type of stone formed of broken seashells. After 23 years of work, the Castillo (kah•STEE•yoh) de San Marcos, as the presidio was called, was strong enough to protect Spanish settlers from any attackers. It was one of a line of hundreds of presidios stretching from Florida to California that protected the colonists in New Spain.

**REVIEW** Why did the Spanish build the Castillo de San Marcos in St. Augustine?

## Ranches and Haciendas

The Spanish realized that gold and silver were hard to find in the borderlands. They also knew that in many places the land was so hot and dry "that even the cactus pads appeared to be toasted." But settlers moved there anyway. Most made money by raising livestock and by selling the hides to markets in the colonies and in Spain. They often traded for things they needed with Indian tribes who lived in the borderlands. In what is now the southwestern United States, for example, they traded with the Pueblos for corn, pottery, and cotton cloth.

The Spanish—and the animals they brought with them—changed life for many of the Indians living in the borderlands. Horses, long extinct in the Americas, once again roamed the land. The Plains Indians learned to tame horses and use them in hunting and in war. In what today is the southwestern United States, the Navajos learned to raise sheep. They also began weaving sheep's wool into clothing and blankets.

Some ranchers in the borderlands of northern Mexico built large estates called **haciendas** (ah•see•EN•dahs). There they raised cattle and sheep by the thousands. In what are now Texas and California, cattle were the most important kind of livestock. Ranchers who lived on the haciendas raised their own livestock, grew their own crops, and made most of what they needed to live. These **self-sufficient**, or self-supporting, communities began to grow far from the markets of Mexico City and the other large cities of New Spain.

**REVIEW** How did horses change the Indians' way of life?

# Missions

Spain's main interest in settling the borderlands was to protect its empire and to expand its economy. However, the Spanish king also said he wanted to "bring the people of that land to our Holy Catholic faith." To do this, missionaries were sent to turn the American Indians into Catholics as well as loyal Spanish subjects. A **missionary** is a person sent by a church to teach its religion.

The first successful missionaries in the borderlands were the Franciscans, members of a Catholic religious order. They built **missions**, or small religious settlements, in what are now the states of Georgia, Florida, Texas, New Mexico, Arizona, and California. Their first mission was Nombre de Dios (NOHM•bray day DEE•ohs), or "Name of God." It was built near St. Augustine as the first in a chain of missions that would eventually connect the Atlantic and Pacific coasts. On the Pacific coast of New Spain, a Franciscan priest named Junípero Serra

(hoo•NEE•pay•roh SEH•rah) later helped build a string of 9 missions in California.

When missionaries came to the borderlands, the missions they built included ranch and farm buildings as well as churches. Some of the missions were built near Indian villages. In other places, Indians settled around the missions.

The coming of the missions changed the way many Indians lived and worked. It also changed something more important to the Indians—the way they worshipped. While many Indians kept to their traditional religions, others became Catholics.

At first some of the Native Americans welcomed living at the missions. Like the missionaries, they were learning new ways. The missionaries and soldiers also protected them from enemies. Problems developed, however. Many Indians had to work on mission farms and ranches against

Father Junípero Serra (below right) founded the mission of San Carlos Borromeo del Rio Carmelo (below left) in 1770. It was the second of nine missions started by Father Serra along what is now the California coast.

LOCATE IT

Mission San Carlos Borromeo del Rio Carmelo

CALIFORNIA

their will. Some missionaries also treated the Indians cruelly.

Some Indians fought back. They destroyed churches and other mission buildings. To protect its missions, the Spanish government built roads linking them with nearby presidios. This road system was called *El Camino Real* (el kah•MEE•noh ray•AHL), or "The Royal Road." One road stretched for more than 600 miles (966 km) from San Diego to Sonoma in what is today California.

The government of New Spain, and later the Mexican government, continued to build missions in the borderlands until the 1830s. Many cities in the western and southwestern areas of the United States—such as San Antonio, Texas, and San Diego, California, began as missions.

**REVIEW** Why did the Spanish send missionaries to the borderlands?

## Major Missions of New Spain

0   300   600 Miles
0   300   600 Kilometers
Azimuthal Equal-Area Projection

New Spain
—— El Camino Real
⌂ Mission

NORTH AMERICA

San Francisco
CALIFORNIA
San Diego
Tucson
Santa Fe
El Paso del Norte
Los Adaes
Rio Grande
FLORIDA
St. Augustine
ATLANTIC OCEAN
PACIFIC OCEAN
Colorado River
Mexico City
Gulf of Mexico
CUBA
Caribbean Sea

**GEOGRAPHY THEME**

**Movement** El Camino Real connected most of the missions and presidios in New Spain.

How did this system of roads help the Spanish missionaries?

## LESSON 1 REVIEW

**Summary Time Line**

1500 — 1550 — 1600

● 1535
New Spain is formed

● 1565
Pedro Menéndez de Avilés settles St. Augustine

❶ **MAIN IDEA**  Why did colonists come to settle in New Spain?

❷ **WHY IT MATTERS**  In what parts of the United States can a Spanish influence be found today?

❸ **VOCABULARY**  Use the terms **hacienda** and **self-sufficient** in a sentence about New Spain.

❹ **TIME LINE**  How long after New Spain was formed was St. Augustine settled?

❺ **READING SKILL—Categorize**  Name some of the reasons colonists and missionaries came to New Spain.

❻ **GEOGRAPHY**  How did the location of New Spain affect the way the Spanish settled on the land?

❼ **CRITICAL THINKING—Hypothesize**  What do you think might have happened if the Spanish had not built presidios?

**PERFORMANCE—Draw a Picture**  Draw a picture of a Spanish settlement in the Spanish borderlands. Use the descriptions in the lesson to decide what kinds of structures you want to draw.

# 2

# New France

1200   1475   1700

**1600–1700**

While the Spanish were growing rich in New Spain, the French were making their own claims in what is today Canada and the northeastern United States. They found good fishing waters along the coast, and farther inland they began to trade with the Native Americans. They traded for a good that became nearly as valuable in Europe as gold—fur.

## French Settlement in North America

The fur trade between the French and the American Indians grew following Jacques Cartier's trips up the St. Lawrence River. Cartier had begun to trade with the Huron Indians. The Hurons were as eager for European goods as the French were for furs the Hurons had. Beaver fur, from which hats were made, was especially popular among the French.

By 1600, trade with the Indians was important for many Europeans, especially for French merchants. Knowing this, the French king, Henry IV, said that any merchant who wanted to trade in furs had to build a colony in North America.

French merchants jumped at the chance to get rich from the fur trade. Several of them formed a company to start a colony. In 1603 the company sent a cartographer named

Europeans (below) traded items, such as glass beads (left), for beaver furs.

## Routes of Champlain, 1603–1615

→ 1603
→ 1604–1606
→ 1608–1609
→ 1615
— Present-day border

0    150    300 Miles
0    150    300 Kilometers
Azimuthal Equal-Area Projection

NORTH AMERICA

Lake Michigan
Lake Huron
Lake St. Clair
Lake Erie
Lake Ontario
1615
Ottawa River
Saguenay River
Quebec
St. Lawrence River
Montreal
1608–1609
Lake Champlain
1604–1606
Cape Cod

Acadia
St. Croix
Port Royal
Nova Scotia
Gulf of St. Lawrence
NEWFOUNDLAND

1603
1604
ATLANTIC OCEAN

50°N
50°W
60°W

GEOGRAPHY THEME

**Movement**   **Champlain explored inland waterways in North America.**

❖ In what waterway did Champlain travel to reach Quebec?

Samuel de Champlain (sham•PLAYN) to North America to map the places where beavers were found.

Champlain explored the forests of what is now eastern Canada, which he called New France. When he returned to Europe, Champlain's reports made more people want to go there. He himself went again.

For the next five years, Champlain explored the lands along the St. Lawrence River. He also built a settlement on the St. Lawrence River at a place that the Hurons called *kebec*. In 1608 Kebec became Quebec (kwih•BEK), the first important French settlement in North America.

**REVIEW** Why were the French eager to build colonies in New France?

## The Growth of New France

The early French settlements grew very slowly. One reason for this slow growth was trouble in France. In the early 1600s, civil war kept many people from leaving France. A **civil war** is a war between two groups in the same country.

In North America, English and Dutch colonists began settling the southern coast of New France. Soon disagreements over the fur trade broke out among the French, the English, and the Dutch, as well as between the Iroquois and the Hurons. By the 1660s the French fur trade was nearly destroyed, and the French hold in North America was crumbling.

The French used birchbark canoes to explore the waterways of New France.

Hoping to rebuild the French empire in North America, King Louis XIV made New France a royal colony. A **royal colony** is ruled directly by a monarch. Louis XIV appointed leaders to live in New France to help him govern. The leader of these officials was called the governor-general.

In 1672 King Louis XIV appointed Count de Frontenac (FRAHN•tuh•nak) governor-general of New France. Frontenac encouraged exploration of the lands west of Quebec and Montreal. These lands were not easy to reach, however. Rapids and shallow waters prevented French ships from traveling very far inland. To travel the rivers, the French had to learn from their Native American trading partners how to build and use birchbark canoes. These boats could navigate in very shallow water. They also could be carried around waterfalls and rapids or overland between rivers.

The Native Americans often spoke of a great river to the west, larger than all the others. The Algonkins called it the *Mississippi*, which means "Father of Waters." Ever since the days of Jacques Cartier, the French had hoped to find the Northwest Passage through North America. Frontenac believed the Mississippi River might be that route.

**REVIEW** Why was New France made a royal colony?

## Exploring the Mississippi

In 1673 Governor-General de Frontenac sent an expedition to explore the rivers and lakes that he hoped would lead them to the Mississippi River. One member of the expedition was Jacques Marquette (mahr•KET), a Catholic missionary who spoke several Indian languages. The other members were Louis Joliet (zhohl•YAY), a fur trader and explorer, and five other adventurers.

The explorers set out from northern Lake Michigan in two birchbark canoes.

This painting by George Catlin shows La Salle and his expedition entering the Mississippi River.

They crossed the huge lake, entered the Fox River, and then traveled to the Wisconsin River. When they reached the mouth of the Wisconsin River, they saw the Mississippi River for the first time.

The explorers followed the river but soon realized that it could not be the Northwest Passage because it flowed south. As they neared the mouth of the Arkansas River, they met some Indian peoples who told them that Europeans lived farther south. The French feared that the Europeans might be Spanish soldiers so they turned back.

Marquette and Joliet had traveled about 2,500 miles (4,023 km). Their expedition opened the Mississippi River valley to French settlement and trade. In time, the French also built trading posts that later grew into towns with such names as St. Louis, Des Moines, and Louisville.

**REVIEW** How did Marquette and Joliet know the Mississippi River could not be the Northwest Passage?

## Founding Louisiana

Soon another French explorer set out, this time to find the mouth of the Mississippi River. This explorer was René-Robert Cavelier (ka•vuhl•YAY), known as Sieur de la Salle, or "Sir" La Salle. In February 1682 La Salle and an expedition of about 50 French and Indian people traveled south from the mouth of the Illinois River. Two months later the explorers reached the mouth of the Mississippi at the Gulf of Mexico. With shouts of "Long live the king!" they claimed all the Mississippi River valley for France. This claim included all the river's tributaries. It reached from the Appalachians in the east to the

**Routes of Marquette and Joliet and La Salle**

Movement **Early French explorers led expeditions down the Mississippi River.**

❖ In what waterways did La Salle travel to reach the Mississippi River?

Rockies in the west and from the Great Lakes in the north to the Gulf of Mexico in the south. La Salle named the region Louisiana in honor of King Louis XIV.

In 1684 La Salle tried to start a settlement near the mouth of the Mississippi River. However, it was difficult in the hot, swampy land. Hardships led to disagreements among the settlers, and three years later one of them killed La Salle. Without a strong leader, the settlement failed.

New France, 1760s

PACIFIC OCEAN

NORTH AMERICA

Hudson Bay

ACADIA

Quebec
Montreal

Lake Superior
Lake Huron
Lake Michigan
Lake Ontario
Detroit
Lake Erie

ROCKY MOUNTAINS

APPALACHIAN MOUNTAINS

ATLANTIC OCEAN

LOUISIANA

Missouri River
Illinois R.
Arkansas
St. Louis
Vincennes
Ohio
Tennessee R.
Mississippi River
Rio Grande

New Orleans
Gulf of Mexico

0    300    600 Miles
0    300    600 Kilometers
Azimuthal Equal-Area Projection

New France

**Location** With the claim to Louisiana, New France greatly increased in size.

❖ What mountain ranges bordered New France?

The French king then sent another expedition to Louisiana. Pierre Le Moyne (luh•MWAHN), known as Sieur d'Iberville (dee•ber•VEEL), and his brother Jean-Baptiste (ZHAHN ba•TEEST), known as Sieur de Bienville (duh bee•EN•vil), reached the northern coast of the Gulf of Mexico in 1699. Their ships entered the mouth of a great river and sailed upstream. The brothers were not sure they were traveling on the Mississippi River until they met Mongoulacha (mahn•goo•LAY•chah), a Taensa (TYN•suh) Indian. He was wearing a French-made coat and carrying a letter addressed to La Salle. Mongoulacha told the Europeans his coat was a gift from Henri de Tonti (ahn•REE duh TOHN•tee). Tonti had stayed in Louisiana after traveling with La Salle years earlier. Mongoulacha said that Tonti had asked him to give the letter to a white man who would come from the sea. The brothers then knew they had found La Salle's river.

The members of the Iberville and Bienville expedition built a settlement along the river and, in time, more settlers arrived. The settlers experienced many of the same hardships that the La Salle expedition had faced.

After claiming Louisiana for France, La Salle attempted to start a settlement.

In 1712 the king made Louisiana a **proprietary colony** (pruh•PRY•uh•ter•ee). This meant that the king gave ownership of the land to one person and allowed that person to rule it. In 1717 John Law, a Scottish banker, became Louisiana's **proprietor**, or owner. Law formed a company to build more towns and to start farms. More settlers came, and Louisiana finally started to grow. In 1718 the town of New Orleans was founded, and four years later it became Louisiana's capital.

Despite Law's efforts, the colony still needed workers—especially on the large farms called **plantations**. Many settlers began to bring in Africans to do the work as slaves.

Louisiana, like the rest of New France, failed to attract enough people for it to do well. By 1754 only

Many streets in the French Quarter have French names.

about 55,000 French colonists lived in the area that stretched from the St. Lawrence River to the Gulf of Mexico. That same year, more than 1,200,000 English colonists lived in North America.

**REVIEW** Why was it difficult to settle in Louisiana?

**Summary Time Line**

| 1600 | 1650 | 1700 |
|---|---|---|

**1608**
Quebec is founded

**1673**
Jacques Marquette and Louis Joliet explore the Mississippi River

**1682**
Sieur de la Salle claims Louisiana for the French

## LESSON 2 REVIEW

1. **MAIN IDEA** How did Henry IV get merchants to build colonies in North America?

2. **WHY IT MATTERS** What cities grew from French settlements?

3. **VOCABULARY** Explain the difference between a **royal colony** and a **proprietary colony**.

4. **TIME LINE** When was Quebec founded?

5. **READING SKILL—Categorize** Name some French explorers who helped expand New France.

6. **HISTORY** Why was the Marquette and Joliet expedition important to the French?

7. **CRITICAL THINKING—Analyze** What were the economic reasons behind the exploration and settlement of New France?

**PERFORMANCE—Make a Poster**
Suppose that you are a French citizen who is asked by the French government to get people to settle in New France. Make a poster that persuades people to move to New France. Use words and pictures in your poster to show people the benefits of moving to New France. Compare your poster with those of your classmates.

# 3

## The English in the Americas

**MAIN IDEA**
Read to learn how the English began to explore and start colonies in North America.

**WHY IT MATTERS**
Although early settlements failed, English settlers were determined to start colonies in North America.

**VOCABULARY**
sea dog
raw material
armada

| 1200 | 1475 | 1700 |
|---|---|---|

**1550–1600**

The English had been sailing to North America since John Cabot made his first voyage there in 1497. Unlike the Spanish or the French, most of the English who first came to North America did not come in search of gold or the riches of the fur trade. Instead, they came mostly for the rich fishing found at the Grand Banks, off the coast of Newfoundland. However, by the late 1500s, the English rulers began taking more of an interest in the Americas.

### England Challenges Spain

England saw that Spain had become very wealthy as a result of its colonies in the Americas. Its gold and silver mines and the sale of products from its ranches in the Americas had filled Spain's treasury. England was not as wealthy as Spain, but it did have fast ships and skilled ocean sailors. At first the English sailors went to catch fish in the Grand Banks. Then they went to capture Spanish treasure ships.

England's queen, Elizabeth I, encouraged English sea captains to attack Spanish treasure ships carrying riches to Spain. English merchants and sea captains used their own money to build ships, hoping to capture Spanish treasure. When they succeeded, they had money to build more ships. The commanders of these English warships were known as **sea dogs**. They were pirates, but Queen Elizabeth protected them

Sailing in the *Golden Hind*, Drake captured a Spanish treasure ship.

## Drake's Voyage Around the World, 1577–1580

→ Drake's route

**Movement** Before sailing back to England, Drake may have sailed as far north as Vancouver Island, Canada.

◆ Which ocean did Drake cross to reach Asia?

because they shared their wealth with the government.

England's best-known sea dog was Francis Drake. In 1577 Drake started his most famous voyage. He sailed through the Strait of Magellan at the southern tip of South America to the Pacific Ocean. Off the western coast of South America, he captured a Spanish treasure ship so loaded with riches that it took the crew four days to transfer all the gold and boxes of jewels to Drake's ship.

Worried that Spanish warships would come after him, Drake decided not to follow the same route home. Instead,

he continued north along the Pacific coast of North America. He stopped near San Francisco Bay in what is now California and claimed the land for England. Drake eventually returned to England by sailing westward. In doing so, Drake and his men became the second crew to sail around the world. Upon Drake's return, Queen Elizabeth made him a knight, and he became known as Sir Francis Drake.

**REVIEW** Why did Queen Elizabeth I protect the English pirates known as sea dogs?

When Drake returned to England, he was made a knight.

## England Starts a Colony

The treasure captured by sea dogs increased England's wealth. With that wealth, England built a strong navy and became a powerful country. At that time, Europe's most powerful countries had colonies. So in 1584 Queen Elizabeth gave Sir Walter Raleigh (RAW•lee) permission to set up England's first colony in North America.

Raleigh sent two sea captains, Philip Amadas and Arthur Barlowe, to explore the Atlantic coast to find a good place for a settlement. Upon their return, Barlowe told Raleigh that they had "found such plenty" in what is now North Carolina. The good news led Raleigh to set up his colony there. He named the area that he chose Virginia. He hoped the colony would provide lumber and other raw materials for England. A **raw material** is a resource that can be used to make a product.

Raleigh sent about 100 colonists to North America but did not go himself. In the late summer of 1585, the colonists landed on an island, which the Hatteras Indians called Roanoke (ROH•uh•nohk), just off the coast. Under the leadership of Ralph Lane, the colony's governor, the colonists built a fort and several houses, but they stayed on Roanoke Island less than a year.

The ship that had brought the colonists to Roanoke Island sailed back to England for more food and supplies. By spring, however, it had not returned. Food ran low, and the colonists wanted to go home. So when Sir Francis Drake visited the colonists, they went back to England on his ship.

**REVIEW** Why did the English set up a colony on Roanoke Island?

## The Lost Colony

In 1587 Sir Walter Raleigh sent a second group of colonists to settle a colony in Virginia. This time Raleigh chose John White to be their governor.

The English colonists reached Roanoke Island in July. They quickly rebuilt the fort

## John White's Map

**Analyze Primary Sources**

This map drawn by John White shows the eastern region of North America.

1. Florida
2. Sir Walter Raleigh's coat of arms
3. Virginia
4. a compass rose
5. measurements that may have indicated longitude
6. English ships

◆ Why do you think ships are shown along the coastline?

and repaired the old houses and built new ones. However, they arrived too late in the year to plant crops. White decided to return to England for food and other supplies.

When White reached England, he wanted to gather supplies and return quickly to his family, but he could not get a ship. England was at war with Spain and needed all of its ships for battle. Three years later, after English ships had defeated Spain's **armada**, or a fleet of warships, John White returned to Roanoke—only to find everyone gone. All that was left were some of his books with the covers torn off, maps ruined by rain, and armor covered with rust.

White did make a puzzling discovery. He found the letters *CRO* carved on a tree and the word *CROATOAN* carved on a wooden post. No trace, however, was ever found of the Roanoke Island settlers. Some people believe they went to live

When John White returned to Roanoke Island, he found that the settlers were gone and that the word *CROATOAN* had been carved into a post.

with the Croatoan Indians, who later became known as the Lumbees. Many Lumbee Indians today have the same English last names as the missing colonists from the "lost colony."

**REVIEW** Why did John White return to England?

## LESSON 3 REVIEW

**Summary Time Line**

1550 — 1575 — 1600

• **1577** Drake captures Spanish treasure and sails around the world

• **1585** Raleigh's first colonists land on Roanoke Island

• **1590** White returns to Roanoke

1. **MAIN IDEA** Why did the English begin to settle in North America?

2. **WHY IT MATTERS** Why was it difficult for the first English settlers to colonize in North America?

3. **VOCABULARY** Define the terms **sea dog** and **raw material.**

4. **TIME LINE** In what year did Raleigh's first colonists land on Roanoke Island?

5. **READING SKILL—Categorize** Who might you put into the category of "English pirate"?

6. **HISTORY** Where did the English first set up a colony?

7. **CRITICAL THINKING—Evaluate** Why do you think it would be important that the English colonists reached Roanoke Island in time to plant crops?

**PERFORMANCE—Write a Journal Entry** Imagine that you are John White. Write a journal entry describing why you decided to leave your family and go back to England to get supplies for the colonists. Then write another journal entry about returning three years later to find everyone missing. Describe what you think may have happened to them. Share your journal entries with your classmates.

# 4

# The Jamestown Colony

## MAIN IDEA

Read to learn how the English settlers overcame many hardships to make the Virginia Colony of Jamestown a success.

## WHY IT MATTERS

England's power and influence grew as more English settlers moved to North America.

## VOCABULARY

stock
prosperity
cash crop
legislature
burgess
authority

1200          1475          1700

**1600–1625**

Although English settlements at Roanoke Island had failed, the idea of settling an English colony in North America lived on. A group of English merchants decided to try again. To establish a new colony in Virginia, they needed permission from England's monarch. The English believed that the king or queen controlled all land claimed by England. With the permission of King James I, the merchants organized the Virginia Company. The aim of these merchants was to make money by starting trading posts in Virginia. Despite the company's plans, however, most of the colonists went to look for gold.

**FAST FACT** By the end of the first year at Jamestown, over half of the colonists had died.

**LOCATE IT**

James R.

VIRGINIA

Jamestown

## The Founding of Jamestown

The Virginia Company was owned by many people. Each owner had given money to organize the company. In return, each one had received **stock**, or a share of ownership, in the company. The owners hoped that over time the company would make a profit. If it did, each stock owner would make money.

In the spring of 1607, three ships sent by the Virginia Company sailed into the deep bay now called Chesapeake Bay. The 105 men and boys aboard sailed up a river that they named the James River to honor their king. They chose a spot along the shore and began to build a settlement they called Jamestown.

The location of Jamestown turned out to be a poor choice for a settlement. The land was wet and full of disease-carrying mosquitoes. The water in the wells that the colonists dug was foul, or bad.

Many of the colonists were not used to working with their hands, and they did not know how to farm or fish in this new land. They had come to Virginia to get rich, and they spent so much of their time searching for gold that no one bothered to plant or gather food for the winter. As a result, many of the colonists starved that first winter. One survivor later wrote, "Our men were destroyed with cruel diseases, . . . burning fevers, and by wars."

Jamestown might have become another lost colony, like the earlier settlement at Roanoke, if it had not had a strong leader like Captain John Smith. Smith was a soldier, an explorer, and a writer. Smith made an important rule for the colonists: Anyone who did not work did not eat. The colonists were soon very busy planting gardens and building shelters.

### A CLOSER LOOK
#### Jamestown

This drawing shows what Jamestown may have looked like in the early 1600s. The first settlers built the fort. As more settlers came, additional homes were built outside the fort.

1. pasture
2. crops
3. artillery
4. James River
5. fort
6. common
7. church

❖ Why do you think the colonists built Jamestown near the James River?

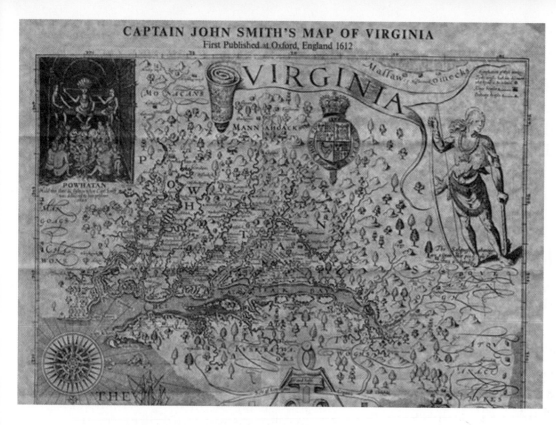

## CAPTAIN JOHN SMITH'S MAP OF VIRGINIA
First Published at Oxford, England 1612

This map, drawn by Captain John Smith, shows the locations of the Virginia Colony and the Powhatan Confederacy. The chief of the Powhatans is also shown (top left).

They also put up fences to protect the settlement from attack by Indians.

During this time, more than 30 tribes of Eastern Woodlands Indians lived in Virginia. Most were members of a confederation known as the Powhatan (pow•uh•TAN) Confederacy. Its members were united under one main chief. When the Jamestown colonists heard this, they gave the name *Powhatan* to all the member tribes, as well as to their chief. The way the colonists behaved toward the Powhatans—seizing their crops for food—put them in constant danger of attack.

One day, while in the countryside around Jamestown, Captain Smith was captured by the Powhatans. A legend says that the chief ordered

This portrait of Pocahontas shows her after she moved to England.

Captain Smith to be put to death but that the chief's daughter, Pocahontas (poh•kuh•HAHN•tuhs), saved his life. It is not known whether this story is true or not, but it is known that fighting continued between the colonists and the Powhatan Confederacy. Jamestown remained a dangerous place to live.

**REVIEW** How did Captain John Smith help the colonists at Jamestown?

## Prosperity and Growth

Despite Jamestown's troubles, the colony survived. In time, it prospered, or did well. This **prosperity**, or economic success, began when the colonists finally found the "gold" they had hoped would make them rich. Their "gold" was not a precious metal but a crop called tobacco.

A Jamestown leader named John Rolfe experimented with various kinds of tobacco and ways of drying it. By 1613 Rolfe had developed a kind of tobacco that the English liked. The colonists at Jamestown were soon growing tobacco as a **cash crop**, or a crop that people raise to sell rather than to use themselves. The Virginia Company sold its tobacco all over Europe and made huge profits.

Jamestown saw even more success when the Virginia Company began to give land to those who stayed in the colony seven years. Until then, there had been no private ownership of land. Everyone was supposed to work for the benefit of the company. After receiving land of their own, the colonists worked harder. Now individual colonists, as well as the company, enjoyed prosperity.

Most of the early colonists had planned to make money in Virginia and return to England. To encourage people to settle permanently, the company allowed the first women to become colonists in 1619.

The first Africans also arrived that year. They came as free laborers paid to work in the tobacco fields. As more workers were needed, more Africans were brought to the colony. Instead of paying these workers, however, colonial leaders enslaved them. Later, all Africans arriving in Virginia were made slaves.

By 1619 Virginia had more than 1,000 colonists. With so many people, the colony needed laws to keep order. The Virginia Company said that the English in the colony would live under English laws and have the same rights as the people living in England. One of these was the right to set up a lawmaking assembly, or legislature. A **legislature** is the branch of a government that makes laws.

Virginia's legislature, called the House of Burgesses (BUHR•juhs•iz), first met in 1619. A **burgess** is a representative who is chosen by and speaks for other people. The Virginia House of Burgesses was the first legislature in the English colonies.

**REVIEW** What was the House of Burgesses?

## DEMOCRATIC VALUES
### Representative Government

The House of Burgesses was modeled after the English Parliament. Burgesses would meet once a year with the royal governor to make local laws and decide on taxes. These representatives were wealthy landowners who were elected by the people to speak for them. Electing leaders to make decisions continues to be an important right that Americans have today.

### Analyze the Value

❶ What was the House of Burgesses modeled after?

❷ **Make It Relevant**  Identify a present-day example of representative government.

The House of Burgesses met in the Jamestown church. The tower from the original church is part of this building.

# The End of Company Control

King James I

For the Virginia Colony to continue to prosper, the settlers had to grow and sell more and more tobacco. This meant that they needed to clear more land to grow it. As a result, the Indians of the Powhatan Confederacy lost much of the land they had used for hunting and farming. In 1622 the Powhatans attacked and killed more than 340 colonists. Having lost nearly one-third of their people, the Virginia colonists fought back in an all-out war. They defeated the Powhatans and took over their remaining lands.

After the fighting ended, King James took away the charter of the Virginia Company and made Virginia a royal colony. The king, rather than business people, now held direct control over the colony.

The king knew that he ruled from too far away to look after all of Virginia's concerns and problems. As a result, he appointed a royal governor to represent him. The royal governor of Virginia shared ruling authority with the House of Burgesses. **Authority** is the right to control and make decisions. The king instructed the royal governor to meet with the burgesses "once a year or oftener."

**REVIEW** Who did King James appoint to represent him in Virginia?

## LESSON 4 REVIEW

**Summary Time Line**

1600 —————————————————————————— 1625

**1607**
English colonists land at Jamestown

**1613**
John Rolfe develops a profitable tobacco crop

**1619**
House of Burgesses meets for the first time

1. **MAIN IDEA** Why did the English continue to try to settle an English colony in North America despite the hardships?

2. **WHY IT MATTERS** How do you think the Virginia Colony's success would benefit England?

3. **VOCABULARY** Use the words **legislature** and **burgess** in a sentence about Jamestown.

4. **TIME LINE** Which happened first, John Rolfe developing a profitable tobacco crop or the House of Burgesses meeting for the first time?

5. **READING SKILL—Categorize** In what category would you put John Smith and John Rolfe?

6. **ECONOMICS** What important contribution did John Rolfe make to the Virginia Colony?

7. **CRITICAL THINKING—Evaluate** How did the success of the Virginia Colony lead to the development of the House of Burgesses?

**PERFORMANCE—Write a Letter Expressing Your Opinion** Imagine that you are a Jamestown colonist. Write a letter to Captain John Smith expressing your opinion about his leadership abilities. Do you approve or disapprove of his rule?

# ·SKILLS· Solve a Problem

## ➡ WHY IT MATTERS

People everywhere face problems at one time or another. Many people face more than one problem at the same time. Think about a problem you have faced recently. Were you able to solve it? Did you wish you could have found a better way to solve the problem? Knowing how to solve problems is a skill that you will use all your life.

## ➡ WHAT YOU NEED TO KNOW

Here are some steps you can use to help you solve a problem.

**Step 1  Identify the problem.**

**Step 2  Gather information.**

**Step 3  Think of and list possible options.**

**Step 4  Consider advantages and disadvantages of possible options.**

**Step 5  Choose the best solution.**

**Step 6  Try your solution.**

**Step 7  Think about how well your solution helps solve the problem.**

## ➡ PRACTICE THE SKILL

You have read about the problems that made life in Jamestown difficult. Colonists did not have enough food, and they were often attacked by Indians. Captain John Smith wanted to solve these problems. Think again about the problems Captain Smith saw and the way he tried to solve them.

1. What problems did Captain Smith see in Jamestown?

2. What did Captain Smith decide was a good way to solve the problems?

3. How did Captain Smith carry out his solution?

4. How did Captain Smith's solution help solve the colonists' problems?

5. Do you think Captain Smith's solution was the best way to solve these problems?

## ➡ APPLY WHAT YOU LEARNED

Identify a problem in your community or school. Use the steps shown to write a plan for solving the problem. What solution did you choose?

Why do you think that your solution will help solve the problem?

Captain John Smith

# The Plymouth Colony

**MAIN IDEA**
Read to learn how the desire for religious freedom led to the colonization of the Plymouth Colony.

**WHY IT MATTERS**
The success of Plymouth led to more English settlements in North America.

**VOCABULARY**
pilgrim
compact
self-rule
majority rule

Tobacco profits and the private ownership of land led more English settlers to North America. So did a book written by Captain John Smith after he explored the Atlantic coast in 1614. In *A Description of New England*, published in 1616, Smith mapped the coastline, described its landscape, and named the region that today includes the states of Connecticut, Maine, Massachusetts, New Hampshire, Rhode Island, and Vermont.

## The Mayflower Compact

Among those who read Smith's description of New England was a group of English people who were living in Holland. They were known as Separatists, because they had left, or separated from, the Church of England. At the time, everyone in England had to belong to the Church of England. Those who refused were not safe. In 1608 the Separatists had moved to Holland, where they could follow their own religion freely.

In Holland the Separatists had religious freedom, but they soon worried that their children would not learn English ways. So they decided to go to the Americas, where they would live among English colonists and still be able to follow their own religion. In time, these Separatists came to be known as Pilgrims. A **pilgrim** is a person who makes a journey for religious reasons.

Early in 1620 a group in England invited the Pilgrims to join them in their journey to North America. The Virginia Company agreed to pay for the colonists' voyage. In return, the colonists would send the company furs, fish, and lumber.

Items such as this beaver-fur hat and these eyeglasses were worn by settlers on the *Mayflower*.

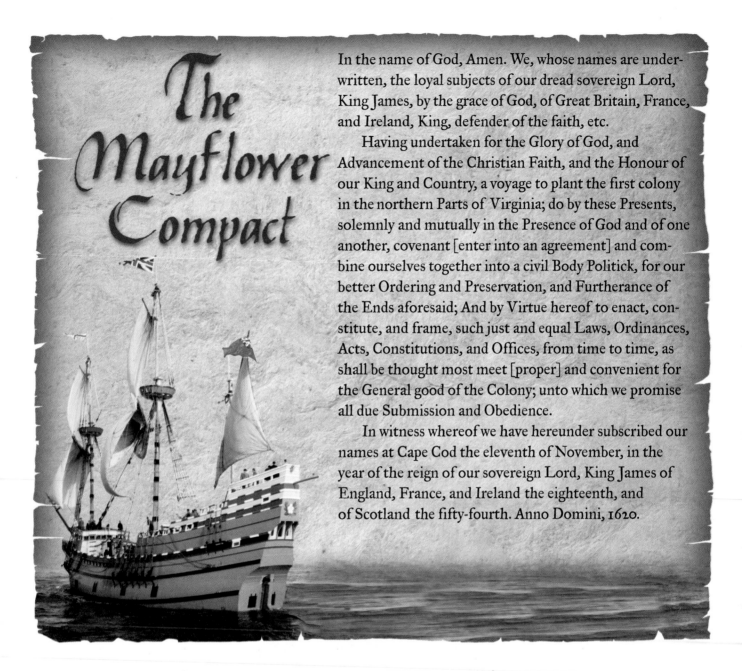

# The Mayflower Compact

In the name of God, Amen. We, whose names are underwritten, the loyal subjects of our dread sovereign Lord, King James, by the grace of God, of Great Britain, France, and Ireland, King, defender of the faith, etc.

Having undertaken for the Glory of God, and Advancement of the Christian Faith, and the Honour of our King and Country, a voyage to plant the first colony in the northern Parts of Virginia; do by these Presents, solemnly and mutually in the Presence of God and of one another, covenant [enter into an agreement] and combine ourselves together into a civil Body Politick, for our better Ordering and Preservation, and Furtherance of the Ends aforesaid; And by Virtue hereof to enact, constitute, and frame, such just and equal Laws, Ordinances, Acts, Constitutions, and Offices, from time to time, as shall be thought most meet [proper] and convenient for the General good of the Colony; unto which we promise all due Submission and Obedience.

In witness whereof we have hereunder subscribed our names at Cape Cod the eleventh of November, in the year of the reign of our sovereign Lord, King James of England, France, and Ireland the eighteenth, and of Scotland the fifty-fourth. Anno Domini, 1620.

On a cold day late in 1620, a ship called the *Mayflower* set sail for North America. It carried 101 passengers, including Captain Miles Standish, who had been hired as the new colony's military leader. Fewer than half of the passengers on the *Mayflower* were Pilgrims. Some of them were servants and workers hired by the Virginia Company to help build the new colony.

The *Mayflower* had a long and troubled journey. Violent storms drove the ship off course, and the Pilgrims ended up far north of the lands governed by the Virginia Company. They had reached Cape Cod in what is now Massachusetts.

The people had landed in a place without a government. To keep order, all the men aboard the *Mayflower* signed an agreement, or **compact**. This agreement became known as the Mayflower Compact. The signers agreed that "just and equal laws" would be made for the common good of the colony and promised to obey these laws. In other words, they would govern themselves.

At a time when monarchs ruled, **self-rule**, or governing oneself, was a very new idea. The Mayflower Compact gave everyone who signed it the right to share in the making of laws. It also recognized the right of the majority to rule. **Majority rule** means that more than half of the people have to agree for a decision to be made. The Mayflower Compact was the first example of self-rule and majority rule in the English colonies.

**REVIEW** What is self-rule?

---

· **HERITAGE** ·

## Thanksgiving Day

In the fall of 1621, the Pilgrims gathered their first harvest. William Bradford, governor of Plymouth Colony, decided they should have a celebration so that the people could "rejoice together" to give thanks to God. He invited the neighboring Wampanoag Indians to join the Pilgrims for a festival that lasted for three days.

This is what many people today think of as the first Thanksgiving. Some people think the first European Thanksgiving in the Americas took place in 1598, when Spanish settlers gave thanks for safely reaching the Rio Grande.

Thanksgiving became a national holiday in 1863, when President Abraham Lincoln declared the last Thursday in November as "a day of thanksgiving and praise to our beneficent Father."

**LOCATE IT**

Boston
MASSACHUSETTS
Plymouth Colony

## Plymouth Colony

For more than four weeks, Captain Miles Standish and the colonists explored what is now Massachusetts Bay, looking for a suitable place to settle. Finally, on December 25, 1620, they chose a place near Cape Cod with a harbor, open fields nearby, and fresh water. John Smith had called it Plymouth. William Bradford, one of the Pilgrim leaders, described the scene that day. "Being thus arrived in a good harbor, and brought safe to land, they fell upon their knees and blessed the God of Heaven, who had brought them over the vast and furious ocean, and delivered them from all the perils and miseries thereof, again to set their feet on the firm and stable earth, their proper element."

The first winter was hard for the colonists. The weather was cold, and there was not enough food. Many people became ill, and about half of them died. Help, however, came in the spring, when a Native American who spoke English walked into their settlement.

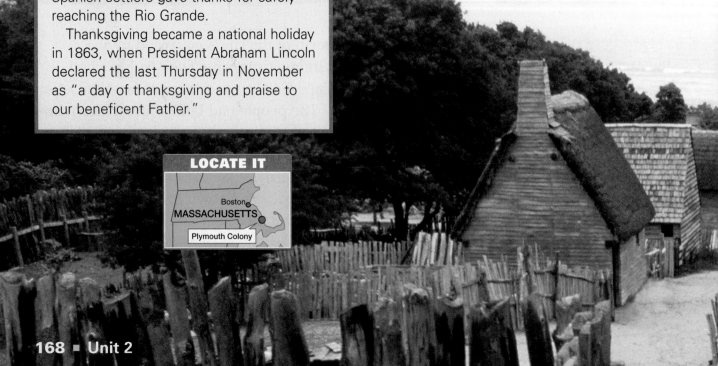

"Welcome, Englishmen," the Indian said. He was an Abenaki (AH•beh•nah•kee) Indian named Samoset who had been visiting the neighboring Wampanoags (wam•puh•NOH•agz). Samoset had learned English from sailors who fished along the Atlantic coast.

Several days later Samoset returned to Plymouth with a Wampanoag who spoke English better than he did. This was Tisquantum, or Squanto, as the English called him. Years before, Tisquantum had been taken and sold as a slave in Spain. He had escaped and spent several years in England before returning to his homeland.

Tisquantum stayed with the Plymouth colonists, showing them where to fish and how to plant squash, pumpkins, and corn. For a time the Pilgrims lived in peace with the Wampanoags, who were led by their chief, Massasoit (ma•suh•SOYT). However, as more English colonists came to settle in Massachusetts, the situation changed. Many of the new colonists were not friendly toward the Indians and settled on more and more of their lands. This caused many quarrels between the Wampanoags and the English colonists. Over time, these quarrels became fights and eventually grew into terrible wars.

**REVIEW** Who was Tisquantum?

## Plymouth Colony Prospers

When the Plymouth colonists first arrived, there was no private ownership of land. Everyone worked for the community, and the harvest was divided equally among the families. Some complained about this system because they felt they were working harder than others.

People today can visit this re-creation of the Plymouth Colony (below) in Massachusetts. Actors there take on colonial roles in which they chop wood (right), sew (far right), and plant crops (bottom right).

In 1623 the colonial leaders divided the land among the colonists. The result was the same as it had been at Jamestown—the people worked harder when they owned the land. However, the idea of community sharing remained strong. Large areas of land in Plymouth were set aside for common use.

The Plymouth colonists, including the Pilgrims, began to prosper with their fishing, farming, and fur trading. As new colonists arrived, the earlier ones had extra goods ready to sell or trade. They sold or traded milk, meat, fruit, and vegetables to the newcomers.

**William Bradford was a governor of the Plymouth Colony.**

Colonists like William Bradford provided the strong, steady leadership that kept the community alive. Bradford fought for the religious ideals of Plymouth's founders and kept the colony separate from any neighboring settlements. Bradford was so popular with the colonists that he was reelected governor of Plymouth 30 times! After a hard beginning, Plymouth continued to prosper. In 1691 Plymouth became a part of the Massachusetts Bay Colony, a larger colony that was formed later.

**REVIEW** **What helped the Plymouth colonists prosper?**

LESSON 5
REVIEW

**Summary Time Line**

1600 — 1650 — 1700

• **1620**
The *Mayflower* lands in what is today Massachusetts

• **1623**
Land is divided among Plymouth colonists

• **1691**
Plymouth becomes part of the larger Massachusetts Bay Colony

❶ **MAIN IDEA** Why did many settlers come to the Plymouth Colony?

❷ **WHY IT MATTERS** How do you think the success of Plymouth might have influenced more people to come to North America?

❸ **VOCABULARY** Describe the difference between **self-rule** and **majority rule**.

❹ **TIME LINE** When did Plymouth become part of the Massachusetts Bay Colony?

❺ **READING SKILL—Categorize** What were the names of some of the Indians who had contact with the first Plymouth colonists?

❻ **CIVICS AND GOVERNMENT** Describe the Mayflower Compact and tell why you think it would serve as a model for later documents.

❼ **CRITICAL THINKING—Hypothesize** What do you think might have happened if Tisquantum had not helped the Pilgrims?

**PERFORMANCE—Write a List of Questions** Write a list of questions you might ask people who want to join you in starting a colony. As you write the questions, think about the personal qualities and skills people need in order to start a successful colony. Compare your questions with those of your classmates.

# Compare Tables to Classify Information

### ▶ WHY IT MATTERS

Information can be easier to find if you **classify**, or group it. Knowing how to classify information can make facts easier to find.

### ▶ WHAT YOU NEED TO KNOW

When you read about European settlement in the Americas, you were given a lot of information. You learned where, when, and why the Spanish, French, and English set up colonies. This and other information can be classified by using a table.

The tables below classify information about European settlement in the Americas in two different ways. In Table A, the settlements are classified according to when they were founded. Table B gives the same information as Table A, but the information is classified according to what countries founded the settlements.

### ▶ PRACTICE THE SKILL

Use the tables below to answer the following questions.

1 Which table makes it easier to find out when the first European settlement in the Americas was founded?

2 Which table makes it easier to find out the number of settlements founded by the French?

3 When was Roanoke founded? Explain which table you used to find this information.

### ▶ APPLY WHAT YOU LEARNED

Make a table to show information about European explorers. Choose some headings under which to classify the information by topic. Then compare your table with a classmate's table.

## Table A: European Settlements in the Americas

| DATE FOUNDED | SETTLEMENT | COUNTRY |
|---|---|---|
| 1521 | Mexico City | Spain |
| 1565 | St. Augustine | Spain |
| 1585 | Fort Raleigh (Roanoke) | England |
| 1607 | Jamestown | England |
| 1608 | Quebec | France |
| 1620 | Plymouth | England |

## Table B: European Settlements in the Americas

| COUNTRY | SETTLEMENT | DATE FOUNDED |
|---|---|---|
| England | Fort Raleigh (Roanoke) | 1585 |
| England | Jamestown | 1607 |
| England | Plymouth | 1620 |
| France | Quebec | 1608 |
| Spain | Mexico City | 1521 |
| Spain | St. Augustine | 1565 |

# Review and Test Preparation

## USE YOUR READING SKILLS

Complete this graphic organizer by categorizing people and settlements with the countries they are associated with. A copy of this graphic organizer appears on page 42 of the Activity Book.

## Key Settlements in North America

| SPANISH SETTLEMENTS | FRENCH SETTLEMENTS | ENGLISH SETTLEMENTS |
|---|---|---|
|  |  |  |
| **KEY PEOPLE** | **KEY PEOPLE** | **KEY PEOPLE** |
| 1. Bartolomé de las Casas | 1. Samuel de Champlain | 1. Sir Francis Drake |
| 2. | 2. | 2. |
| 3. | 3. | 3. |
| **KEY SETTLEMENTS** | **KEY SETTLEMENTS** | **KEY SETTLEMENTS** |
| 1. Hispaniola | 1. Quebec | 1. Roanoke |
| 2. | 2. | 2. |
| 3. | 3. | 3. |

## THINK & WRITE

**Write a Classroom Compact**  The Mayflower Compact set up rules designed to help the Plymouth settlers. Write a classroom compact that lists rules for your class. Explain how this compact will benefit the members of your class.

**Write a Letter**  Imagine that the year is 1620 and you have just moved to the Plymouth Colony with your family. Write a letter to a friend in England about your new life. Describe your new environment and the challenges you and your family face.

| 1600 | 1650 | 1700 |
|------|------|------|

**1565**
St. Augustine
is settled

**1607**
Jamestown
is founded

**1608**
Quebec is
founded

**1620**
The Pilgrims
establish
the Plymouth
Colony

**1673**
Marquette
and Joliet
explore the
Mississippi
River

**1682**
La Salle
claims
Louisiana

## USE THE TIME LINE

Use the chapter summary time line to answer these questions.

**1** When was the Jamestown Colony founded?

**2** Was St. Augustine settled before Quebec?

## USE VOCABULARY

Identify the term that correctly matches each definition.

colony (p. 144)

proprietor (p. 155)

burgess (p. 163)

compact (p. 167)

**3** an owner

**4** a representative who speaks for other people

**5** a signed agreement

**6** a settlement ruled by another country

## RECALL FACTS

Answer these questions.

**7** What group of people did Bartolomé de Las Casas work to protect?

**8** What early problems did the Jamestown colonists face?

**9** How was the government of a royal colony different from that of a proprietary colony?

Write the letter of the best choice.

**10** **TEST PREP**   The forts built by Spanish soldiers were known as—

  **A** haciendas.

  **B** plantations.

  **C** presidios.

  **D** missions.

**11** **TEST PREP**   After leaders of the Plymouth Colony divided the land among the colonists—

  **F** many people starved.

  **G** people stopped immigrating to Plymouth.

  **H** people lost their sense of community.

  **J** people worked harder and the colony began to prosper.

## THINK CRITICALLY

**12** Why do you think problems developed between Native Americans and Spanish missionaries?

**13** How do you think English pirates such as Francis Drake would have been treated by Queen Elizabeth I if they had not shared their wealth?

## APPLY SKILLS

### Solve a Problem

**14** Imagine that you are a Jamestown colonist in 1622. What ideas would you offer to solve the problems between the colonists and the Powhatan Indians?

### Compare Tables to Classify Information

**15** Choose a lesson from this chapter and make a table about the explorers discussed in that lesson. Make sure to list the places the explorers visited and the dates of their travels. Compare your table to a classmate's table.

# The Mission San Diego de Alcalá

## GET READY

High on a hill overlooking the city of San Diego, California, sits the Mission San Diego de Alcalá. It was the first in a string of 21 missions that stretched across the Spanish borderlands of California. San Diego de Alcalá was founded by Father Junípero Serra on July 16, 1769. In time, the city of San Diego grew around the mission. Today, many people visit to learn about mission life hundreds of years ago. At San Diego de Alcalá, you can see artifacts that belonged to Native Americans, early Spanish settlers, soldiers, and missionaries. Experience life in another time as you walk where they once walked.

## LOCATE IT

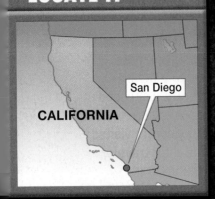

San Diego

CALIFORNIA

## WHAT TO SEE

Visitors can spend time in the mission's scenic gardens.

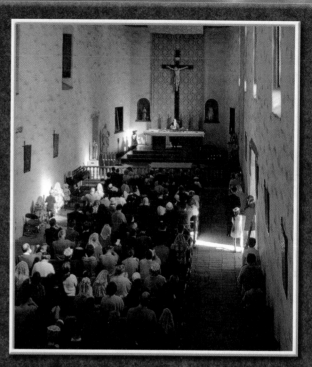

People still attend church services at the Mission San Diego de Alcalá.

This songbook, on display at the mission, was used more than 200 years ago.

A statue of Father Junípero Serra stands on the mission grounds.

## TAKE A FIELD TRIP

**A VIRTUAL TOUR**
Visit The Learning Site at www.harcourtschool.com/tours to find virtual tours of historic sites in the United States.

**A VIDEO TOUR**
Check your media center or classroom library for a videotape tour of the Mission San Diego de Alcalá.

## VISUAL SUMMARY

**Write a Journal Entry** Choose one of the events shown below. Write a journal entry from the perspective of a person present at one of the events.

## USE VOCABULARY

Use each of the following words in a sentence about exploration.

**1** **compass** (p. 109)

**2** **claim** (p. 121)

**3** **Northwest Passage** (p. 136)

**4** **missionary** (p. 148)

## RECALL FACTS

Answer these questions.

**5** Why did Prince Henry set up a school for navigators?

**6** What Native American group was one of the first to trade furs with the French?

**7** How did the Jamestown Colony finally achieve prosperity?

Write the letter of the best choice.

**8** **TEST PREP**   The Inca Empire covered thousands of miles on the western coast of—
  **A** Europe.
  **B** Asia.
  **C** South America.
  **D** Africa.

**9** **TEST PREP**   One of the first Spanish explorers to journey through what is now the state of Texas was—
  **F** Hernando Cortés.
  **G** Álvar Núñez Cabeza de Vaca.
  **H** Juan Ponce de León.
  **J** Hernando de Soto.

**10** **TEST PREP**   Sieur de la Salle set out to find—
  **A** the Northwest Passage.
  **B** the mouth of the Mississippi River.
  **C** El Dorado.
  **D** the Fountain of Youth.

**Visual Summary**

1200 — 1300 — 1400

1275 **Marco Polo reaches China** p. 109

1492 **Christopher Columbus lands at San Salvador** p. 122

1498 **Vasco da Gama reaches India by sea** p. 118

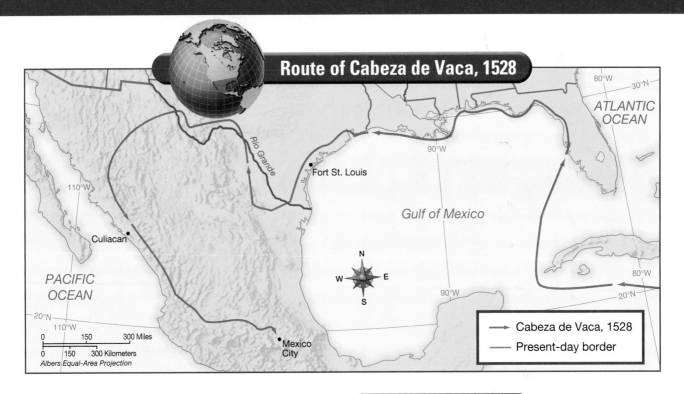

## Route of Cabeza de Vaca, 1528

ATLANTIC OCEAN

Rio Grande

Fort St. Louis

Gulf of Mexico

Culiacan

PACIFIC OCEAN

Mexico City

0   150   300 Miles
0   150   300 Kilometers
Albers Equal-Area Projection

→ Cabeza de Vaca, 1528
— Present-day border

**11** **TEST PREP**  The Mayflower Compact allowed the colonists to—

**F** govern themselves.
**G** trade.
**H** grow tobacco.
**J** join the Virginia Company.

## THINK CRITICALLY

**12** Why do you think *The Travels of Marco Polo* was such a popular book?

**13** Do you think Francisco Vasquez de Coronado's 1540 expedition was a success or a failure? Explain.

## APPLY SKILLS

### Follow Routes on a Map

Use the map on this page to answer the following questions.

**14** For the most part, did Cabeza de Vaca travel east or west on his expedition?

**15** Where did Cabeza de Vaca end his expedition?

**16** How many times did Cabeza de Vaca cross the Rio Grande on his way to Mexico City?

1500          1600          1700

**1519  Hernando Cortés arrives in Tenochtitlán**  p. 129

**1607  English colonists settle Jamestown**  p. 161

**1620  English colonists settle Plymouth**  p. 167

177

# Unit Activities

## Conduct an Interview

Work with a classmate to select an explorer from the unit and research information about the explorer. Write a list of questions to ask the explorer during an interview. Then take turns role-playing the explorer and the interviewer.

## Make a Display

Work in a group to create a chart titled *Daily Life in America*. Your chart should feature Spanish missions, French settlements, and the Jamestown and Plymouth Colonies. For each settlement or colony, list the location, climate, foods available, and buildings. To illustrate the chart, draw pictures, cut them out of magazines, or print them out from the Internet.

 **GO ONLINE** Visit The Learning Site at **www.harcourtschool.com/ socialstudies/activities** for additional activities.

## VISIT YOUR LIBRARY

■ *If you Were There in 1492* by Barbara Brenner. Macmillan.

■ *The Silk Route: 7,000 Miles of History* by John S. Major. HarperCollins.

■ *The History News: Explorers* by Michael Johnstone. Candlewick.

## COMPLETE THE UNIT PROJECT

**An Exploration Map**  Work with a group of your classmates to complete the unit project— a map that shows exploration of North America. Decide which key explorers' routes you want to include on your map. Start by drawing a map of North America on posterboard. Then draw the routes of the explorers you have chosen. Use a different color for each route. Also label each route with the correct explorer's name and the dates of the exploration.

# The English Colonies

Quaker gift to a
Native American

The home of William Penn, Pennsbury Manor, Pennsylvania

# The English Colonies

> ❝ Any government is free to the people under it where the laws rule and the people are a party to the laws. ❞

—William Penn, Frame of Government of Pennsylvania, 1682

## Preview the Content

Scan the unit. Then make a K-W-L chart. First, write what you have learned about the 13 colonies. Next, write what you would like to know about them. As you read, fill in details.

## Preview the Vocabulary

**Synonyms**   Synonyms are words with similar meanings. Look in the unit to find vocabulary words you can match to the synonyms below. Then use each word in a sentence.

| SYNONYM | VOCABULARY WORD | SENTENCE |
|---|---|---|
| 1. setting up <br> 2. shelter <br> 3. army | charter | |

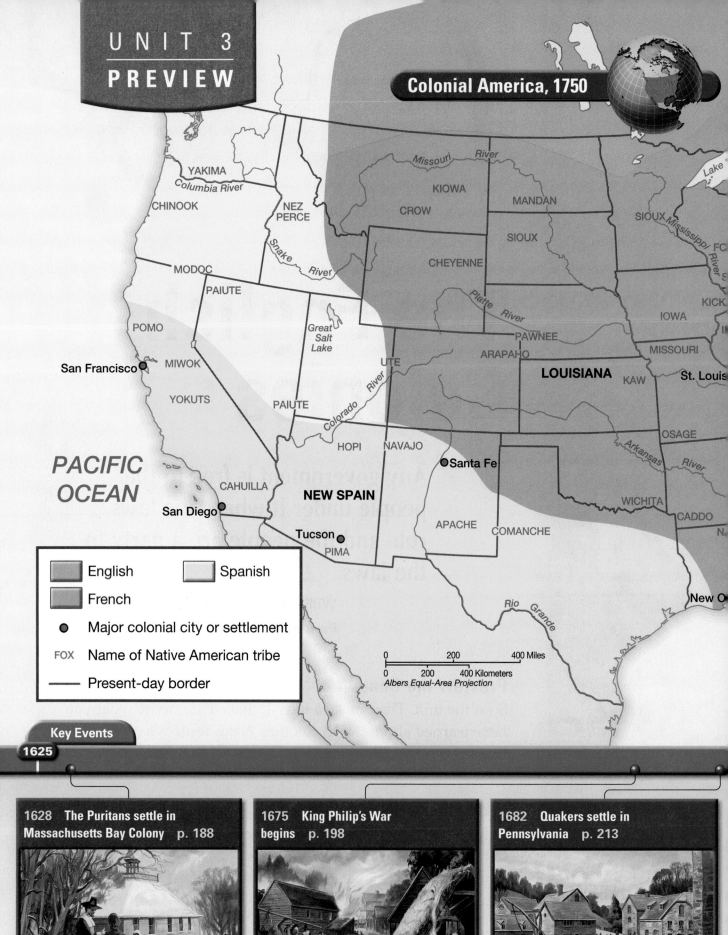

# UNIT 3
## PREVIEW

## Colonial America, 1750

YAKIMA
Columbia River
CHINOOK
NEZ PERCE
MODOC
PAIUTE
POMO
San Francisco
MIWOK
YOKUTS
PAIUTE
CAHUILLA
San Diego
Tucson
PIMA
HOPI
NAVAJO
NEW SPAIN
APACHE
COMANCHE

Snake River
Great Salt Lake
UTE
Colorado River

Missouri River
KIOWA
CROW
MANDAN
SIOUX
CHEYENNE
Platte River
PAWNEE
ARAPAHO
LOUISIANA
KAW

SIOUX
Mississippi River
FO
KICK
IOWA
MISSOURI
St. Louis
OSAGE
Arkansas River
WICHITA
CADDO
N.

Lake

PACIFIC OCEAN

Santa Fe

Rio Grande
New O

**Legend:**
- English
- French
- Spanish
- ● Major colonial city or settlement
- FOX Name of Native American tribe
- — Present-day border

0    200    400 Miles
0    200    400 Kilometers
Albers Equal-Area Projection

## Key Events

1625

1628   The Puritans settle in Massachusetts Bay Colony   p. 188

1675   King Philip's War begins   p. 198

1682   Quakers settle in Pennsylvania   p. 213

180

## The 13 Colonies

| COLONY | LOCATION | DATE FOUNDED |
|---|---|---|
| Massachusetts | New England Colony | 1630 |
| Connecticut | New England Colony | 1636 |
| Rhode Island | New England Colony | 1647 |
| New Hampshire | New England Colony | 1680 |
| Delaware | Middle Atlantic Colony | 1638 |
| New Jersey | Middle Atlantic Colony | 1664 |
| New York | Middle Atlantic Colony | 1664 |
| Pennsylvania | Middle Atlantic Colony | 1681 |
| Virginia | Southern Colony | 1607 |
| Maryland | Southern Colony | 1632 |
| North Carolina | Southern Colony | 1663 |
| South Carolina | Southern Colony | 1712 |
| Georgia | Southern Colony | 1733 |

*ATLANTIC OCEAN*

*Gulf of Mexico*

1750

1730s  The Great Awakening spreads throughout the colonies  p. 215

1733  James Oglethorpe settles the Georgia Colony  p. 236

1750s  Williamsburg, Virginia becomes a large city  p. 238

# Stranded at Plimoth Plantation
## —1626—

## words and woodcuts by Gary Bowen

On October 12, 1626, a ship bound for the Jamestown colony set sail from England. The actual name of the ship is unknown, but the Pilgrims called it the *Sparrowhawk*. On November 6, the ship crashed in the fog along the New England coast near the Pilgrim colony at Plimoth Plantation, known today as Plymouth, Massachusetts. Rescued by the colonists, the ship's passengers remained stranded there for nine months until another ship arrived to take them to Jamestown. The following is a fictional journal based on the wreck of the *Sparrowhawk*. The writer is one of the passengers, 13-year-old Christopher Sears. After being rescued, Sears stayed with the family of William Brewster, a Pilgrim church leader. Also living with the Brewsters at that time was another boy, Richard More, whose parents had died during the first years of the Pilgrim colony. The entries from Sears's fictional journal, accompanied by woodcut engravings, tell what life was like in the early New England colonies. Read now about Christopher Sears's experiences at Plimoth Plantation.

## November 24, 1626

His worship the Governor [William Bradford] met at the fort this afternoon with all of us who crossed on the *Sparrowhawk*. He told us that 21 other ships have arrived in Plimoth in six years, and said it may be months before another anchors again.

We are to earn our board by working for the families with whom we reside. Our labors are to be reported weekly to Captain Sibsey or Master Fells.

I am happy that Richard lives and works here, too. When he was six years old, he came over on the *Mayflower* with two brothers and a sister who did not survive their first year here. Richard says they had been told their mother and father died, but he does not remember their illnesses or any funeral service. He says his parents did not like each other.

My knee aches and I am cold because my garments are not warm enough for this climate.

# December 23, 1626

Governor Bradford talked with me today and showed me the notes that he has been keeping since he arrived in 1620. He commended me for recording my experiences here and said that I am participating in a "great event, which is the founding of God's community."

His Worship suggested that I make larger woodcuts and consider using color. The physician gave me these mixtures.

# December 30, 1626

I was measured for new woolen breeches as my old ones are too small. The Mistress plans to sew them from fabric that once was her skirt. She will re-dye the cloth with agrimony roots and nutshells because all textiles are imported and are difficult to come by here.

It is surprising that I have seen no spinning wheels or looms in Plimoth since they are so common in England.

# January 23, 1627

Master Brewster will include me in his tutoring of Richard, Oceanus Hopkins (who was born aboard the *Mayflower*), and Peregrine White, who Master Brewster says is the first Anglo-Saxon born in New England.

We had cold eel pie in a <u>coffin</u> for dinner.

<u>coffin</u> a pastry crust

# February 3, 1627

I am happy that my schooling continues.

Each evening Master Brewster works with me on herb lore, farming, reading, and scriptures. He says the Plimoth people are more learned than in most English villages, as all parents must educate their children, even if that requires tutoring in another home.

# March 3, 1627

I was with a group of men organized by the Governor, cutting timbers in the forest.

Indians approached us, wanting to trade some furs, three turkeys, and a deer for grain. His Worship agreed to the barter, and the Indians will receive a bushel of corn.

# April 5, 1627

I carried in 24 buckets of springwater to heat. Each member of the Brewster household had a bath today. It felt good to wash.

Love [the Brewster's son] cautioned me that it is unhealthy to have more than three or four baths a year because, if done too often, all the body's natural protection against disease is washed away.

Tomorrow we will be fishing for herring, which is plentiful this month and next.

## June 1, 1627

Because Master Brewster predicts rainy weather is coming, we worked doubly hard to sow our seeds for peas, beans, wheat, rye, barley, and turkey corn. Not all families have planted their crops yet.

Mistress Priscilla Alden gave birth to baby John. Master John Alden, her husband, was very pleased.

Love prepared mussels again.

## July 1, 1627

The weather has been hot and dry and our garden has suffered. Richard and I carried buckets of water to give the crops a drink.

Since there is no rain in sight, we plan to cut a field of grain tomorrow. After it is turned over to dry thoroughly in the sun, we will stack the barley in the shape of cones.

I boiled seawater to replenish the Brewsters' salt supply.

Love says I am growing like a weed!

## August 18, 1627

Today when we returned from the Indian settlement, I learned that two barks had arrived from Jamestown to transport the *Sparrowhawk* passengers to Virginia. For me it was not a welcome sight.

## August 22, 1627

Since the ship will depart Thursday at sunrise, tomorrow will be my last full day here.

I feel very sad.

### Analyze the Literature

1. How did people at Plimoth Plantation get goods that they needed?

2. Compare Christopher Sears's daily activities with your own. How are they alike and how are they different?

## READ A BOOK

## START THE UNIT PROJECT

**A Book on Colonial America** With your classmates, create a book on the 13 colonies. As you read, take notes about why different colonies were started, key people, economic practices, and how the colonies were governed. These notes will help you decide what to include in your book.

## USE TECHNOLOGY

Visit The Learning Site at **www.harcourtschool.com/socialstudies** for additional activities, primary sources, and other resources to use in this unit.

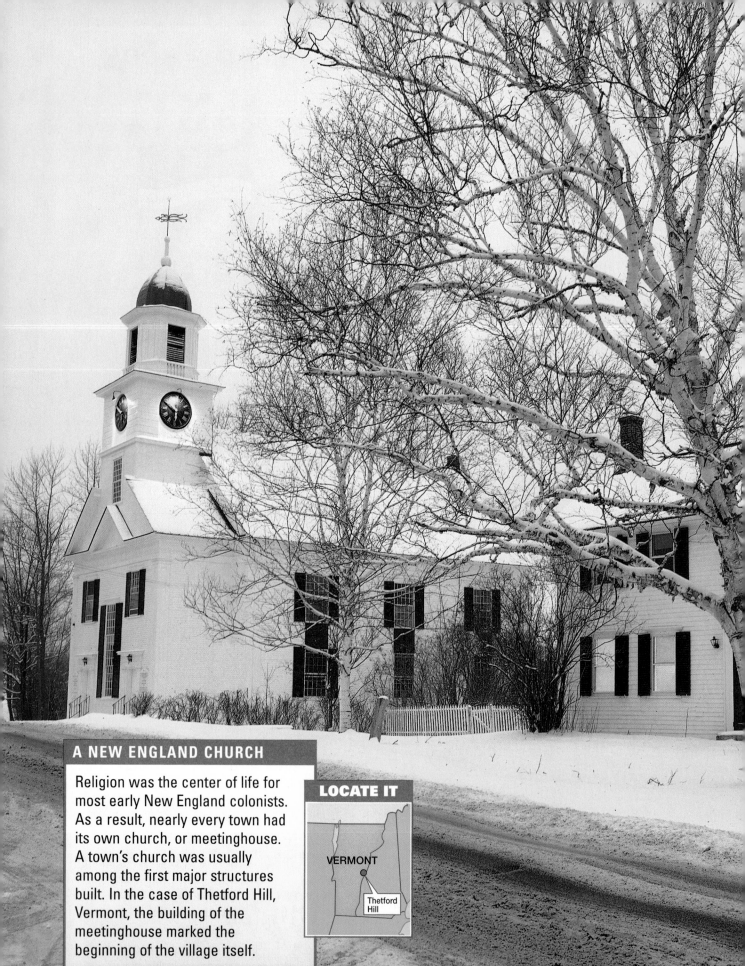

## A NEW ENGLAND CHURCH

Religion was the center of life for most early New England colonists. As a result, nearly every town had its own church, or meetinghouse. A town's church was usually among the first major structures built. In the case of Thetford Hill, Vermont, the building of the meetinghouse marked the beginning of the village itself.

**LOCATE IT**

VERMONT

Thetford
Hill

# The New England Colonies

" The New Englanders are a people of God. . . . "
—Cotton Mather,
*Wonders of the Invisible World,* 1693

---

## CHAPTER READING SKILL

### Summarize

When you **summarize,** you tell a shortened version of what you have just read.

**As you read this chapter, summarize the sections within each lesson.**

FACTS  SUMMARY

---

# The Massachusetts Bay Colony

**MAIN IDEA**
Read to find out why a group of English colonists founded the Massachusetts Bay Colony.

**WHY IT MATTERS**
The Massachusetts Bay colonists' thoughts about government and education helped shape our present-day systems of government and education.

**VOCABULARY**
Puritan
charter
common
specialize
town meeting
public office

1625       1750

**1625–1645**

Less than ten years after the Pilgrims founded Plymouth, another group of religious settlers founded an English colony in North America. Like the Pilgrims, these settlers disagreed with many practices of the Church of England. Unlike the Pilgrims, however, they did not want to separate from the church. They wanted to change some religious practices in order to make the Church of England more "pure." For this reason, they were called **Puritans**. The Puritans set up a community in North America so they could make money, freely practice their beliefs, and live by their Christian ideas.

## A City on a Hill

In 1628 a group of Puritans joined other people in England to form the New England Company. That year King Charles I granted the company a charter. A **charter** is an official paper in which certain rights are given by a government to a person or business. The king's charter allowed the Puritans to settle in the region Captain John Smith had named New England.

In 1628 John Endecott led the first group of Puritans to sail to New England. There they built a settlement named Salem on a bay they called Massachusetts Bay. The word *Massachusetts* means "at the big hill" in the Algonquian language. The following year the company became the Massachusetts Bay Company, and the king granted a new charter.

**FAST FACT**
Salem was the Puritans' first settlement in the Massachusetts Bay area. Its name comes from the Hebrew word *shalom*, which means "peace."

King Charles I is shown in the top left corner of the Massachusetts Bay Company Charter.

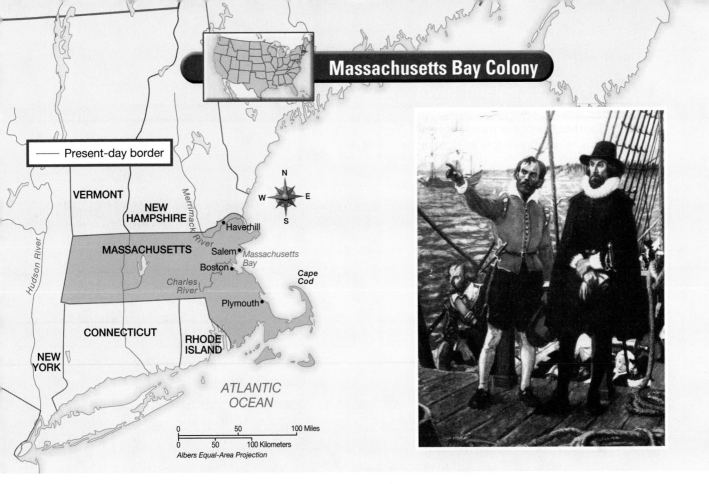

Massachusetts Bay Colony

- Present-day border

VERMONT

NEW HAMPSHIRE

Merrimack River

Haverhill

MASSACHUSETTS

Salem

Massachusetts Bay

Boston

Charles River

Cape Cod

Plymouth

Hudson River

CONNECTICUT

RHODE ISLAND

NEW YORK

ATLANTIC OCEAN

0    50    100 Miles
0    50    100 Kilometers
Albers Equal-Area Projection

**GEOGRAPHY THEME**

**Location** In 1630 John Winthrop (far right) led more than 700 Puritans to Massachusetts Bay. They soon settled on the Massachusetts coast north of Plymouth.

❖ Why do you think most of the settlements in Massachusetts were located near the coast?

In 1630 John Winthrop brought a second and much larger group of Puritans from England to settle along Massachusetts Bay. Winthrop served as the governor of the Massachusetts Bay Colony. In fact, he would serve as governor of the colony several times during the next 20 years. In that time more than 20,000 newcomers, mostly Puritans, settled in the colony.

Winthrop said that Puritan cities should be models for Christian living.

❝For we must consider that we shall be as a city upon a hill. The eyes of all people are upon us. . . .❞

The Puritans hoped that all their communities would become models for good living. They built new villages, many of which were near Boston.

In 1637 Winthrop worked at forming a confederation among the people of New England. He believed a confederation would help them better defend themselves in case they were attacked by nearby Indian groups or by the Dutch, who had started settlements to the south of New England. Winthrop became the first president of the confederation when it was formed in 1643.

**REVIEW** What did John Winthrop accomplish as leader of the Puritans?

## A CLOSER LOOK
### A New England Town

Most New England towns were self-sufficient communities in which the people grew or made most of what they needed.

1. houses
2. general store
3. mill
4. fields
5. cooper
6. blacksmith
7. common
8. well
9. cobbler
10. minister's house
11. meetinghouse
12. school
13. minister

❖ Why do you think the common was in the center of the town?

## A Puritan Village

At the center of each Puritan village was the **common**, or village green. This was a parklike area shared by all the villagers and used for grazing their animals. At one end of the common was the church, called the meetinghouse. Houses and other buildings lined the other sides of the common.

In time, other buildings that might be found around the common were a general store, a sawmill, and a blacksmith shop. Blacksmithing is one particular craft in which a person in a village may have specialized. To **specialize** is to become skilled at one kind of job.

A blacksmith might make nails for a neighbor. In exchange, the neighbor might make barrels for the blacksmith. In the early days of the Massachusetts Bay Colony, the Puritans bartered for goods and did not spend money very often.

Another building that might be found near the common was a school. Schools were important because the Puritans wanted every person to be able to read the Bible. At first, Puritan children went to schools that were run by women in their homes. Later, villagers began to build schools after the Puritans passed a law stating that every village of 50 families or more must have a school.

Puritan schools were the first community schools in the English colonies. Some of these schools still exist. They include Boston Latin School, which was founded in 1635, and Harvard College, now Harvard University, which was founded in 1636. Harvard was the first college in England's North American colonies.

The small size of a Puritan village made people feel they belonged to a community and made it easier for them to help each other. Village life also made it easier for church ministers to keep their authority in the village. The duty of the minister was to make sure people lived

their lives in ways that the Puritan leaders thought were right.

**REVIEW** How did the small size of villages help the Puritans?

## The Meetinghouse

The meetinghouse was at the center of village life because it was where church services were held. The most important part of the Puritan church service was the minister's sermon, or his explanation of the Bible's teachings. The sermon often lasted for several hours. The whole service lasted for most of the day, with a break for a meal at noon.

The meetinghouse was also where the Puritans conducted all town business. Everyone in the town could attend a **town meeting**, but only men who owned property could vote. They voted on laws and on matters that affected the whole community. At first, a man had to be a member of the Puritan church to vote. By the end of the 1600s, however, any man who owned property could vote.

Each year at a town meeting, some people were elected to **public offices**, or jobs for the community. Offices in a Puritan town included constable, town crier, digger of graves, drummer, sweeper of the meetinghouse, and fence viewer. The constable was in charge of maintaining order and keeping the peace. The town crier walked around and called out important news and other announcements. The fence viewer made sure that the fences around the crops were kept in good repair.

A town meeting held in Haverhill, Massachusetts, once elected a man to run a ferry across the Merrimack River. He could not charge passengers any price he wanted, however. The town meeting set the charges.

**REVIEW** What were some of the public offices that the Puritans could be elected to?

## Home and Farm Life

The main room of a Puritan home contained a large fireplace, where a fire was always kept burning. All cooking was done in the fireplace. Baking was done in a small oven inside the fireplace. Most food was roasted over the fire or simmered in large iron kettles hung in the fireplace. Kettles were also used to heat water for cooking and washing.

Women and girls spent many hours preparing food for the rest of the family. They used churns to turn cream into butter. They dried and preserved fruits. They pickled cabbages and other vegetables grown in the gardens they tended. Pickled vegetables could be eaten throughout the cold, hard winter.

The women and girls also made all the clothing for the family. Sometimes pieces of worn-out clothing were used to make

This reenactment shows how Puritan women prepared meals.

This scene shows a New England farm.

new clothing and patchwork quilts for bedding. Nothing useful went to waste.

The men and boys spent many hours each day working in the nearby fields. Despite the rocky soil, Puritan farmers were able to grow corn, rye, barley, and wheat. They traded some of these crops for sugar from English colonists on the Caribbean islands. Farmers also grew pumpkins and other kinds of squash among the corn. This method of farming was first used by the Wampanoag Indians.

The Puritans also raised livestock as sources of food, leather, and wool. Cattle, hogs, and sheep often grazed on the town common. The Puritans used pig bristles, or hair, to make brushes. They turned animal fat into soap and candles. The Puritans made their own tools from wood and their own shoes from leather. They also wore warm clothing from sheep's wool.

**REVIEW** What kinds of crops were grown on New England farms?

## LESSON 1 REVIEW

### Summary Time Line

1625 — 1635 — 1645

**1628** John Endecott leads the first group of Puritans to New England

**1630** John Winthrop brings Puritans to Massachusetts Bay

**1636** Harvard College is founded

1. **MAIN IDEA** Why did the Puritans settle in the Massachusetts Bay Colony?

2. **WHY IT MATTERS** How were the Puritans' thoughts about government and education similar to ours today?

3. **VOCABULARY** Use the term **specialize** in a sentence about the Puritans.

4. **TIME LINE** In what year did John Endecott lead the first Puritans to New England?

5. **READING SKILL—Summarize** What were the main activities that took place in a Puritan meetinghouse?

6. **ECONOMICS** In what ways were the people of the Massachusetts Bay Colony able to get the goods they needed?

7. **CRITICAL THINKING—Analyze** How was a Puritan town like the town in which you live? How was it different?

**PERFORMANCE—Write a Newspaper Article** Imagine you have been asked to write a newspaper article about the Puritans of the Massachusetts Bay Colony. Tell about the reasons why they settled there and the kinds of communities they started.

# New Ideas, New Colonies

**MAIN IDEA**
Read to find out what led some Massachusetts Bay colonists to form new colonies nearby.

**WHY IT MATTERS**
As the English colonies attracted even more settlers, their people expanded the ideas of freedom of speech and freedom of religion.

**VOCABULARY**
expel
consent
sedition
fundamental
frontier

1625 ━━━━━━━━━━━━━━━━━━━━━ 1750

**1630–1680**

The lives of the Puritans in the Massachusetts Bay Colony centered around religion. In fact, religion was so important to the Puritans that they expected all newcomers to follow the Puritans' beliefs. They did not welcome people whose ideas were different from theirs. When the Puritan leaders disapproved of someone's ideas, they sent that person back to England or to another English colony. Some colonists who left the Massachusetts Bay Colony started new colonies nearby.

## Roger Williams and Rhode Island

In 1631 Roger Williams and his family arrived in the Massachusetts Bay Colony from England. They settled in the village of Salem, where Roger Williams became a minister.

Roger Williams lived with the Narragansett Indians before starting a settlement he called Providence.

ROGER WILLIAMS

Williams was a popular minister because he and many people in Salem shared the same beliefs. They believed that their church should be separate from the colonial government and free from the rule of the Church of England. They also believed that people should not be punished if their beliefs were different from those of the Puritan leaders.

Roger Williams often stated his beliefs in his sermons and in letters that he wrote to Governor John Winthrop. Before long his ideas became unpopular with other ministers and with Winthrop. In 1635 the Puritan leaders voted to **expel** him, or to force him to leave. This meant that he was no longer allowed to live in the Massachusetts Bay Colony.

From Salem, Williams and his family fled beyond the border of the colony south to Narragansett (nar•uh•GAN•suht) Bay. There they received food and protection from the Narragansett Indians. In 1636 many of Williams' followers also left Salem and joined him. He bought land from the Narragansetts and founded a settlement he called Providence. It later became the capital of the present-day state of Rhode Island.

Williams set up a government based on the **consent**, or agreement, of the settlers. The new government of what would later become the Rhode Island Colony gave its people the freedom to follow any religion they chose.

**REVIEW** What did Roger Williams accomplish after he left the Massachusetts Bay Colony?

## Anne Hutchinson on Trial

Not long after the Puritan leaders expelled Roger Williams from the Massachusetts Bay Colony, they faced

Anne Hutchinson was put on trial for causing people to work against the government.

other challenges to their leadership. One such challenge came from a colonist named Anne Marbury Hutchinson.

Hutchinson and her husband, William, moved to North America in 1634. They settled in Boston and attended church services there. Hutchinson soon began to question the authority of the Puritan ministers and their teachings. Her strong and spirited personality attracted many followers. She started holding her own religious meetings at home and stated her own beliefs during these services.

The Puritan leaders said Hutchinson was "a woman not fit for our society." In 1637 they brought her to trial.

This painting by Fredric Edwin Church shows Thomas Hooker and his followers arriving in what became Hartford.

She stood trial before a Puritan court on charges of **sedition**, or the use of speech or behavior that causes people to work against a government. She was found guilty, and the Puritan leaders ordered her to leave the colony. A year later they also expelled her from the Puritan church.

With her family and many followers, Anne Hutchinson moved to Narragansett Bay. There they founded a settlement on an island near Providence. Hutchinson's settlement later united with the one founded by Roger Williams under the charter that formed the Rhode Island Colony.

**REVIEW** What were some of Anne Hutchinson's accomplishments?

Thomas Hooker

THOMAS HOOKER
1586 – 1647
FOUNDER OF HARTFORD
PASTOR—STATESMAN

## Connecticut

Other settlers also left the Massachusetts Bay Colony, but not for religious reasons. They wanted to leave the rocky fields of Massachusetts to find better farmland. By the early 1630s people began moving into the fertile Connecticut River valley. The first permanent settlement, Windsor, was founded in the river valley in 1633. It was soon followed by the Wethersfield settlement. Most early Connecticut settlers came to find better farmland, but many also came in search of religious freedom. The best-known of these settlers was a minister named Thomas Hooker. Hooker had left the Massachusetts Bay Colony because he did not like the way the colony's Puritan leaders tried to influence the lives of the colonists. Hooker thought that a colony's government should be based on what its people wanted, not on what its leaders wanted. Many of Hooker's followers went with him to the Connecticut River valley, where they founded the settlement of Hartford. Hartford, along with Windsor and Wethersfield, united in 1636 to become the Connecticut Colony. The name *Connecticut* comes from the Mohegan (moh•HEE•guhn) Indian word *quinnitukqut*, which means "at the long tidal river."

In 1638 Hooker preached a sermon calling for a government that would be based on the consent of the people. In 1639 the Connecticut Colony adopted Hooker's idea in the form of the Fundamental Orders. The word **fundamental** means "basic." The Fundamental Orders were the first written plan of government in North America. They allowed Connecticut's voters—all landowning male colonists—to elect their leaders.

**REVIEW** Why did Thomas Hooker leave the Massachusetts Bay Colony?

## New Hampshire

The Connecticut River valley was not the only place where Massachusetts Bay colonists went in search of more fertile land and greater economic opportunity. Some settlers moved north of the Merrimack River into what is now New Hampshire in search of these things.

The earliest permanent settlements in New Hampshire were started in the

 **Location** Most towns in the New England Colonies were located near a body of water.

❖ Which two rivers ran through parts of New Hampshire and Massachusetts?

1620s. In 1623 David Thomson founded the first settlement near the mouth of the Piscataqua (pi•SKA•tuh•kwaw) River. In 1630 the settlement moved to a site near a thick growth of trees and wild berries. The settlers cut down the trees and shipped them as lumber to England. The settlement was renamed Strawberry Banke. Today it is the city of Portsmouth. In 1679 the town of Strawberry Banke and other settlements in the area were united under a charter from King Charles II as the New Hampshire Colony.

**REVIEW** Why did some settlers move north into what is now New Hampshire?

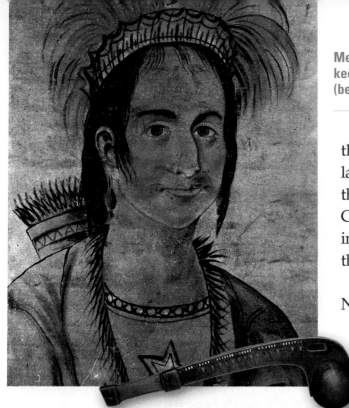

Metacomet (left) led the Wampanoags in the fight to keep their lands. Some historians believe this club (below) was Metacomet's.

## Indian Wars

As settlers moved beyond the Massachusetts Bay Colony, they tried to keep peace with the region's many Indian groups. In the Connecticut River valley, however, fighting broke out between the colonists and the Pequots (PEE•kwahts). The Pequots wanted to stop the colonists from taking over Indian lands. With the help of some soldiers from the Massachusetts Bay Colony, the Connecticut settlers defeated the Pequots in the 1630s. The conflict became known as the Pequot War.

Most of the disagreements between the Native Americans and the settlers were over land ownership. The Wampanoags, Narragansetts, Mohegans, Podunks (POH•duhnks), and Nipmucs (NIP•muhks) felt that no one could "own" land. When they "sold" land to the settlers, they thought they were agreeing to share it. The English, however, expected the Indians to leave the land when they sold it.

In 1675 bad feelings between the Indians and the settlers started an all-out war. The settlers called it King Philip's War. Metacomet, known to the English as King Philip, was the leader of the Wampanoags.

After the Indian wars settlers moved into areas like northern New Hampshire.

Metacomet was also the son of Massasoit, who years earlier had helped the Pilgrims.

The war began when the Indians attacked and destroyed the town of Swansea. To get back at the Indians, the English settlers destroyed a nearby Indian settlement and took the Indians' lands. The war quickly spread as far north as present-day Maine and as far south as Connecticut. Both sides suffered terrible losses in the fighting. At least 3,000 Indians, including Metacomet, died. Among the colonists, 1 out of every 16 men of military age died.

As a result of King Philip's War, some Native American tribes were forced off their lands and very few Indians

Buckets like this were often used by settlers who lived on the frontier.

remained along the eastern coast of New England. Because many of the Indians had left, waves of settlers began pushing farther north up the Connecticut River valley into the Berkshire Hills in what is now western Massachusetts. Others moved even farther north into areas of present-day Vermont, northern New Hampshire, and Maine. The frontier was being pushed farther west as well. A **frontier** is land that lies beyond settled areas. The New England frontier separated the land settled by Europeans from the land lived on by Native Americans.

**REVIEW** What started King Philip's War?

---

## LESSON 2 REVIEW

**Summary Time Line**

1630 — 1655 — 1680

- **1635** Roger Williams is expelled from the Massachusetts Bay Colony
- **1637** Anne Hutchinson is brought to trial
- **1639** The Connecticut Colony adopts the Fundamental Orders
- **1675** King Philip's War begins

1. **MAIN IDEA**   What led some Massachusetts Bay colonists to form new colonies nearby?

2. **WHY IT MATTERS**   How did the people of the new colonies expand the ideas of freedom of speech and freedom of religion in the English colonies?

3. **VOCABULARY**   Write a sentence about Roger Williams, using the words **expel** and **consent**.

4. **TIME LINE**   When was Anne Hutchinson brought to trial?

5. **READING SKILL—Summarize**   Why did Massachusetts Bay colonists settle Connecticut and New Hampshire?

6. **HISTORY**   What were the effects of King Philip's War?

7. **CRITICAL THINKING—Evaluate**   Do you think the beliefs of leaders such as Roger Williams, Anne Hutchinson, and Thomas Hooker helped bring positive changes to the New England Colonies? Explain your answer.

**PERFORMANCE—Write a Letter**   Imagine that you are a follower of Thomas Hooker who has just moved to the settlement of Hartford. Write a letter to a friend in England that explains why Hooker disagreed with the leaders of the Massachusetts Bay Colony.

# New England's Economy

1625 ——————————— 1750

**1700–1750**

As time passed, life in New England became less difficult. Many people, especially those who lived in the coastal towns, had to struggle less to make a living. By the 1700s the great-grandchildren of the early colonists lived much more comfortable lives. This prosperity, or economic success, was based mainly on the sea and the region's dense forests. Many colonists in New England had built successful fishing, whaling, trading, and shipbuilding industries. An **industry** includes all the businesses that make one kind of product or provide one kind of service.

## Fishing and Whaling

Many coastal towns in New England Colonies prospered because of good fishing in the ocean waters. Because New Englanders could catch more fish than they needed, they had a surplus. The surplus catch could be dried and then sold or traded to people in Europe or to other English colonists in the West Indies.

The town of New Bedford, in Massachusetts, prospered in the 1700s because some of its settlers began catching whales in addition to hunting. Colonial whalers used methods brought from England. They launched small rowboats from beaches and hunted for whales in the waters not far from the shore. Once they captured a whale, they killed it and towed it to shore. The whalers then cut up and boiled the whale's blubber, or fat, to obtain oil.

**FAST FACT**
In one year, during the peak of colonial whaling, at least 350 whale-hunting ships sailed from colonial ports.

Oil made from whale blubber was used to fuel lamps.

New Englanders fished and hunted whales in the waters of the Grand Banks, near Newfoundland, and off the Greenland coast.

Oil made from whale blubber was very popular at that time because it burned brightly without an unpleasant odor. One lamp filled with burning whale oil gave as much light as, and much less smoke than, three candles.

So many New England whalers hunted close to shore that after a while the number of whales in those waters started to decline. As a result, the New England whalers began hunting in bigger ships and sailed farther out into the ocean. As the years passed, whaling trips became longer and longer. Some whaling ships left their home ports on ocean voyages that lasted for several months or even years.

**REVIEW** What industries helped New England coastal towns prosper?

## Trading

In addition to fishing and whaling, many New England fortunes were made in trade. Ships owned by New England merchants carried trade goods to and from ports in the Caribbean, southern Europe, and England.

Many ships owned by the colonial merchants followed a direct trade route between the New England ports and England. They followed this route because the English government insisted. It wanted the colonists to send their **exports**, or goods leaving a country, only to England or to other English colonies. The English government also expected the colonists to buy only English-made **imports**, or goods brought into a country.

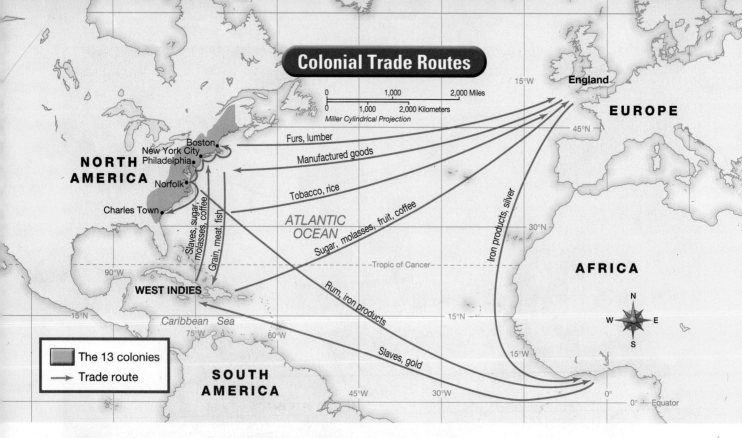

## Colonial Trade Routes

Furs, lumber

Manufactured goods

Tobacco, rice

Slaves, sugar, molasses, coffee

Grain, meat, fish

Sugar, molasses, fruit, coffee

Iron products, silver

Rum, iron products

Slaves, gold

ATLANTIC OCEAN

Caribbean Sea

Tropic of Cancer

Equator

NORTH AMERICA

SOUTH AMERICA

WEST INDIES

EUROPE

AFRICA

England

Boston
New York City
Philadelphia
Norfolk
Charles Town

0    1,000    2,000 Miles
0    1,000    2,000 Kilometers
Miller Cylindrical Projection

**Key**
- The 13 colonies
- Trade route

**Movement** England, Africa, the West Indies, and the English colonies were connected by trade routes.

❖ What goods did the colonies get from England?

Along this direct trade route, colonial ships from ports such as Boston and New Haven, in Connecticut, and Newport, in Rhode Island, carried exports of furs, lumber, and dried fish to England. The ships returned to the colonies with imports of tea and spices, as well as manufactured goods, such as buttons, cloth, and shoes.

Other New England trading ships followed what came to be known as **triangular trade routes**. These routes connected England, the English colonies in North America, and the west coast of Africa. They formed great imaginary triangles on the Atlantic Ocean. Trading ships carried goods from England and raw materials from the English colonies and the West Indies. Slave ships also carried enslaved people from central and western Africa. These people were used as workers in the English colonies. During this time, millions of enslaved Africans were forced to voyage across the Atlantic Ocean. The voyage across the Atlantic Ocean from Africa to the West Indies came to be known as the Middle Passage.

Barrels were used to ship goods.

The Africans suffered greatly on the slave ships. Many of them died during the Middle Passage. Their long voyage in overcrowded ships with cramped quarters was part of a large and cruel slave trade business. During the 1700s some of the people in the colonies became alarmed by the cruelty of the slave trade. Later, some of the New England colonists began to form groups that worked to end slavery.

**REVIEW** What were the triangular trade routes?

## Shipbuilding

Fishing, whaling, and trading encouraged the shipbuilding industry in New England. The forests of New England provided the raw materials needed for building ships in colonial times. Logs cut in inland forests were floated down rivers to the coastal towns. There, skilled craftworkers used the logs to produce **naval stores**, the products that were used to build and repair ships. Workers used oak trees to make planks, or thick boards, for shaping ships' hulls. They used tall pines to make the masts. Pine trees also provided tar and turpentine to make pitch, a coating that is used to seal the wood and to help make a ship watertight.

Workers called coopers used wood to make barrels and casks. A cooper was a regular member of a merchant ship's crew. It was the cooper's responsibility to put together and repair barrels and casks for the long ocean voyages. Merchants used barrels to store grain, dried fish, salted meats, and other foods they traded. Casks held molasses, whale oil, and other liquids.

By the late 1700s nearly one-third of all the ships sailing under the English flag were built in the New England Colonies.

This harbor scene shows the city of Portsmouth, New Hampshire in the 1700s. Portsmouth was one of the busy ports in the New England Colonies.

This painting by Ashley Bowen, a sailor, shows a newly built ship ready to be launched.

One reason was the low cost of building ships there. Ships that were built in New England cost merchants only half of what they might have to pay for them in Europe. The shipbuilding industry contributed greatly to the growth and prosperity of many coastal towns in the New England Colonies. Some of these towns became cities. By 1750 more than 15,000 people lived in Boston. It was one of the largest cities in the North American colonies.

**REVIEW** **In what ways did people in the shipbuilding industry earn a living?**

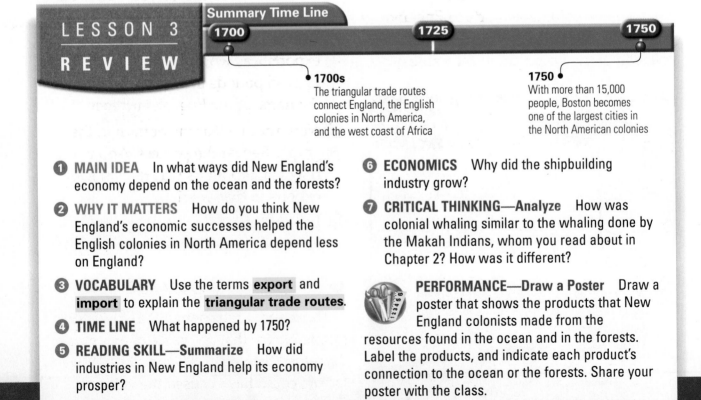

**LESSON 3 REVIEW**

**Summary Time Line**

1700     1725     1750

**1700s**
The triangular trade routes connect England, the English colonies in North America, and the west coast of Africa

**1750**
With more than 15,000 people, Boston becomes one of the largest cities in the North American colonies

1. **MAIN IDEA** In what ways did New England's economy depend on the ocean and the forests?

2. **WHY IT MATTERS** How do you think New England's economic successes helped the English colonies in North America depend less on England?

3. **VOCABULARY** Use the terms **export** and **import** to explain the **triangular trade routes**.

4. **TIME LINE** What happened by 1750?

5. **READING SKILL—Summarize** How did industries in New England help its economy prosper?

6. **ECONOMICS** Why did the shipbuilding industry grow?

7. **CRITICAL THINKING—Analyze** How was colonial whaling similar to the whaling done by the Makah Indians, whom you read about in Chapter 2? How was it different?

**PERFORMANCE—Draw a Poster** Draw a poster that shows the products that New England colonists made from the resources found in the ocean and in the forests. Label the products, and indicate each product's connection to the ocean or the forests. Share your poster with the class.

# ·SKILLS·

CHART AND GRAPH

# Use a Line Graph

**VOCABULARY**
line graph

## WHY IT MATTERS

Soon there were 13 English colonies along the Atlantic Coast. The value of exports that these colonies sent away to England changed during the years from 1700 to 1750. The numbers that show how the value of these exports changed are very large. These numbers are easier to understand if they are placed on a line graph. A **line graph** is a graph that uses a line to show changes over time.

## WHAT YOU NEED TO KNOW

This line graph shows the changes in the value of colonial exports to England from 1700 to 1750. The numbers along the left side of the graph show the value of colonial exports. Across the bottom of the graph are years. As you read the red line from left to right, you see how the value changed.

## PRACTICE THE SKILL

Use this line graph to answer the following questions.

**1** Find the year 1700 at the bottom of the graph. Move your finger up from that date until you reach the red dot. Then move your finger left to the value numbers. Your finger will be a little below 500,000, so you will need to estimate the value. To *estimate* is to make a close guess. The value of the exports was worth about 375,000 English pounds in 1700. Pounds are the name of the English currency.

**2** Now find 1740 at the bottom of the graph. Repeat the process. About how many pounds was the value of exports in that year?

**3** Look at the red line on the graph. How did the value of exports change?

## APPLY WHAT YOU LEARNED

Think about the change shown on this graph. Notice that the value of exports decreased between 1700 and 1710. What factors could have caused the value to decrease during those years?

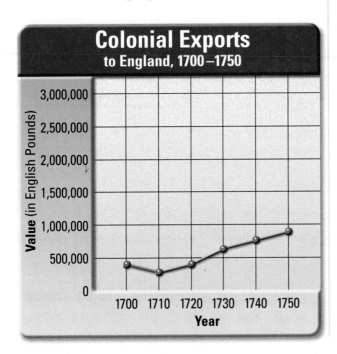

**Colonial Exports**
to England, 1700–1750

Value (in English Pounds)

3,000,000
2,500,000
2,000,000
1,500,000
1,000,000
500,000
0

1700  1710  1720  1730  1740  1750
**Year**

Summary Time Line

1625                                                    1650

1628                1635                1637
The first           Roger Williams       Anne
group of            is expelled from     Hutchinson
Puritans            the Massachusetts    is brought
arrives in          Bay Colony           to trial
New England

## USE YOUR READING SKILLS

Complete this graphic organizer by summarizing the following
facts about the Massachusetts Bay Colony. A copy of this
graphic organizer appears on page 52 of the Activity Book.

### The Massachusetts Bay Colony

FACTS → SUMMARY

1. The Puritans built many villages in North
   America.
2. The most important building in a Puritan
   village was the meetinghouse.
3. The village meetinghouse served as a
   church and a place to hold town meetings.

1. Roger Williams was forced to leave the
   Massachusetts Bay Colony.
2. Anne Hutchinson was also forced to leave
   the colony.
3. Roger Williams and Anne Hutchinson
   established their own settlements.

1. Trading goods made many people wealthy
   in New England.
2. Goods were traded between the colonies,
   England, and the west coast of Africa.
3. Trade brought the first African slaves
   to the English Colonies.

## THINK & WRITE

**Write a Folktale**  Every New England
town had several public-office jobs. These
jobs included constable, town crier, and
fence viewer. Write a folktale about a person
who held one of these jobs.

**Write a Travelogue**  New England whaling ships sometimes went on ocean voyages
that lasted for many months. Imagine that you
are a crew member on such a voyage. Write
a travelogue about your experiences.

1675　　　　　　　　1700　　　　　　　　1725　　　　　　　　1750

**1639**
The Fundamental
Orders are adopted
by the Connecticut
Colony

**1675**
King Philip's
War begins

**1750**
Boston becomes
one of the
largest cities
in North America

## USE THE TIME LINE

Use the chapter summary time line to
answer these questions.

**1** When did the first group of Puritans arrive in
New England?

**2** When did King Philip's War begin?

## USE VOCABULARY

Use a term from this
list to complete each
of the following
sentences.

town meeting
(p. 192)

consent (p. 195)

sedition (p. 196)

industry (p. 200)

naval stores
(p. 203)

**3** The government of
Providence was
based on the _____ of
the settlers.

**4** The _____ was where
public officers were
elected.

**5** Anne Hutchinson was brought to trial on
charges of _____.

**6** A major _____ in New England was shipbuilding.

**7** Logs from New England forests were used
to produce _____.

## RECALL FACTS

Answer these questions.

**8** What group of settlers set up the first community schools in the New England Colonies?

**9** What were some of the results of King
Philip's War?

**10** Why was New England a good location for
the shipbuilding industry?

Write the letter of the best choice.

**11** **TEST PREP**  Problems developed
between the New England colonists and
Native Americans because—
  **A** the colonists forced Native Americans to
  work on their farms.
  **B** Native Americans refused to trade furs
  with the colonists.
  **C** the two groups had different understand-
  ings of land ownership.
  **D** Native Americans never offered the
  colonists any help.

**12** **TEST PREP**  The New England colonists
used whale blubber to make—
  **F** tar.
  **G** turpentine.
  **H** molasses.
  **J** lamp oil.

## THINK CRITICALLY

**13** Compare the system of government of
the Connecticut Colony to that of the
Massachusetts Bay Colony.

**14** How might history have been different if
King Philip's War had not taken place?

## APPLY SKILLS

**Use a Line Graph**

**15** Look in newspapers or magazines for a line graph that shows
a trend. Cut out the graph and
tape it to a sheet of paper.
Below the graph, identify the
trend shown. How does the trend
change over time?

## LANCASTER COUNTY

Many early immigrants settled in Pennsylvania because of its rich farmland. Today, areas such as Lancaster County continue to produce a variety of crops. Among the Amish and Mennonite families who make their homes here, many live and work in the same manner as their eighteenth century ancestors.

### LOCATE IT

PENNSYLVANIA

Lancaster County

# The Middle Atlantic Colonies

" The Fields, most beautiful, yield such Crops of Wheat, And other things most excellent to eat. "

—Richard Frame, *A Short Description of Pennsylvania,* 1692

## CHAPTER READING SKILL

### Make Inferences

When you make an **inference,** you use facts and your experiences to come to a conclusion.

**As you read this chapter, make inferences about people, places, and events associated with the Middle Atlantic Colonies.**

| WHAT YOU HAVE READ |  | WHAT YOU KNOW |

| INFERENCE |

# 1

**MAIN IDEA**
Read to find out why the Middle Atlantic Colonies attracted people of many different cultures and religions.

**WHY IT MATTERS**
As in the Middle Atlantic Colonies, people from many different cultures and religions contribute to the United States today.

**VOCABULARY**
refuge
trial by jury
justice
farm produce
Great Awakening

# Breadbasket Colonies

| 1625 | | 1750 |
|---|---|---|

**1625–1700**

While the Puritans were building settlements in New England, other settlers were establishing colonies to the south. This region, which included present-day New York, New Jersey, Delaware, and Pennsylvania, came to be known as the Middle Atlantic Colonies.

The first settlers in the Middle Atlantic region discovered that when the land was cleared of trees and rocks, it was good for farming. The climate was also good for growing crops. The summers were long, and the amount of rain each year was just right for crops such as wheat, corn, and rye. In fact, the Middle Atlantic Colonies produced so many crops used in making bread that they came to be called the "breadbasket" colonies. The region's rich resources attracted people from many European countries and people of various religions.

## New Netherland

Not long after the English started colonies in North America, the Dutch began to build settlements in their own colony, called New Netherland. They settled in parts of what are today New York, New Jersey, and Delaware. The Dutch came to the

**FAST FACT** Manhattan Island was bought from the Manhattan Indians for goods worth 60 Dutch guilders, or about $24.

area because the explorer Henry Hudson had claimed it for their country, Holland, in 1609.

A few years after Hudson's visit, the New Netherland Company established several trading posts in the Hudson River valley. In 1621 the Dutch West India Company took control of trade in the area. The first Dutch settlers arrived three years later. Some were sent to a fort on the Delaware River, and others sailed to a fort on the Hudson River.

In 1626 the Dutch began building a fort and laying out a town on Manhattan Island in New York Bay. They called the settlement New Amsterdam. In that same year Peter Minuit (MIN•yuh•wuht), one of the directors of the New Netherland Colony, bought Manhattan Island from the Manhattan Indians. During the next few years, New Amsterdam grew and became the capital of New Netherland. The Dutch built other settlements that would one day become Brooklyn, Kingston,

Rensselaer (ren•suh•LIR), and Schenectady (skuh•NEK•tuh•dee), New York.

The Dutch welcomed settlers to New Amsterdam from many countries. People from Belgium, Denmark, France, Italy, and Spain all made their homes there. Among these newcomers was the first group of Jews to settle in North America. However, the Jews in New Amsterdam did not have many of the same rights as Christian colonists had. Under Dutch rule, Jews could not work at certain jobs and could not freely practice their religion.

**REVIEW** **Where did the Dutch first settle in North America?**

**GEOGRAPHY THEME**

**Place** **New Amsterdam was the capital of New Netherland. The Dutch and Swedish colonies eventually became English colonies.**

◆ **What natural resources do you think the colonists used?**

**Dutch and Swedish Colonies, 1654**

- New Netherland
- New Sweden
- Present-day border

VT
Beverwyck (Albany)
MA
Esopus (Kingston)
NY
CT
Manhattan Island
PA
Vriesendael (Tappan)
New Amsterdam (New York)
ATLANTIC OCEAN
NJ
Fort New Gothenburg (near Philadelphia)
Fort Christina (Wilmington)
MD
DE

0    40    80 Miles
0    40    80 Kilometers
Albers Equal-Area Projection

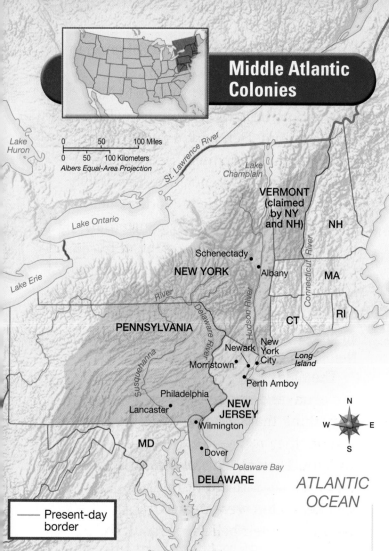

## Middle Atlantic Colonies

Lake Huron

Lake Ontario

Lake Erie

St. Lawrence River

Lake Champlain

0   50   100 Miles
0   50   100 Kilometers
Albers Equal-Area Projection

VERMONT (claimed by NY and NH)

NH

Schenectady

NEW YORK

Albany

MA

Connecticut River

CT

RI

River

Hudson River

Delaware River

PENNSYLVANIA

Susquehanna

Newark

Morristown

New York City

Long Island

Perth Amboy

Philadelphia

Lancaster

NEW JERSEY

Wilmington

MD

Dover

Delaware Bay

DELAWARE

ATLANTIC OCEAN

N
W   E
S

Present-day border

GEOGRAPHY THEME

**Regions** **Many towns in the Middle Atlantic Colonies were located near waterways.**

❓ What were some of the waterways in the Middle Atlantic Colonies?

## New Netherland Becomes New York

In 1646 the Dutch West India Company appointed Peter Stuyvesant (STY•vuh•suhnt) as director general of New Netherland. When Stuyvesant arrived in New Amsterdam the following year, he found New Netherland in trouble. The government was having problems. The settlers were fighting over land with the neighboring Delaware and Wappinger (WAHP•ihn•jer) Indians and with other European colonists. Not long after he arrived, however, Stuyvesant helped resolve the conflicts over land.

Stuyvesant's strong way of ruling helped solve some problems, but it created new problems between him and the colonists. The colonists wanted more voice in their government, which Stuyvesant would not allow.

Despite such disagreements, the colony prospered under Stuyvesant's leadership. He expanded New Netherland into what is now New Jersey. Then he pushed south into what is now Delaware, taking over the small colony of New Sweden in 1655. Swedish settlers had founded the colony in 1638. It was chiefly a group of trading posts built around Fort Christina, where today Wilmington, Delaware, stands.

Even though the population of New Netherland remained small, the English still thought that the Dutch colony prevented their own colonies from expanding. This was one reason King Charles II of England declared war on Holland. The king then told his brother, James, the Duke of York, that he could have the Dutch colonies if he could seize them.

Peter Stuyvesant

This Quaker meetinghouse was located in New Jersey. Chests (above) like this one could often be found in Quaker homes.

In 1664 English warships sailed into the harbor at New Amsterdam. Stuyvesant tried to get the Dutch settlers to fight the English, but they refused. Stuyvesant had to give up the colony. The English split up New Netherland, giving it the present-day names of New Jersey and New York. New York City grew from the Dutch capital, New Amsterdam.

**REVIEW** What were some of Peter Stuyvesant's accomplishments?

## New Jersey

Not long after the English divided New Netherland, the Duke of York gave New Jersey and part of New York to John Berkeley and George Carteret. The two offered to sell the land at low prices to anyone in England willing to settle in North America. The offer attracted many settlers to New Jersey. Among them were numerous members of the Society of Friends, a religious group also known as the Quakers. In 1674 a group of Quakers led by Edward Byllinge bought Berkeley's share of New Jersey. They started the first colony in North America founded by Quakers.

The Quakers believe that all people are equal and basically good. Because they think that violence is always wrong, they refuse to carry guns or to fight. They also believe in solving all problems peacefully. In England, Quakers often were treated poorly because of their beliefs, particularly their refusal to fight for the king. In New Jersey, they hoped to find a **refuge**, or safe place, where they could live and worship as they pleased.

**REVIEW** Why did many Quakers want to settle in New Jersey?

## Pennsylvania and Delaware

While New Jersey was being sold to groups of Quakers, King Charles II gave a charter to William Penn, who had become a Quaker. The charter made Penn the proprietor, or owner, of what is now Pennsylvania. The English king granted him the region because the king owed a debt to Penn's father. Penn wanted to call his new colony *Sylvania*, which means "woods." King Charles asked that the land be named Pennsylvania.

# DEMOCRATIC VALUES
## Justice

In his Frame of Government of Pennsylvania, William Penn included the idea that all citizens of the Pennsylvania Colony were to be treated equally by the law.

Penn's Frame of Government guaranteed everyone the right to a trial by jury. This right was important because it allowed a group of citizens, instead of a single judge, to decide whether or not someone had broken the law. This method is a more democratic way of making this kind of decision. It gives decision-making control to the people. In most countries there was no right to trial by jury.

Today the United States government upholds the idea of equal justice for all. All people in the United States have the right to a fair trial and to equal treatment under the law.

William Penn with Indian leaders

### Analyze the Value

❶ How did Penn make sure people in the colony would be treated equally under the law?

❷ **Make It Relevant** Imagine that a student in your school has been accused of breaking a school rule. With some classmates, decide whether one person or a group should determine whether the student really broke the rule.

---

The new name, which means "Penn's woods," honored William's father.

Before coming to Pennsylvania, William Penn planned his colony's government. In 1682 he wrote a document called the Frame of Government of Pennsylvania. It provided for a legislature called the General Assembly to make the laws for the colony. Penn's Frame of Government also provided for the citizens of Pennsylvania to have freedom of speech, freedom of worship, and trial by jury. **Trial by jury** guarantees a person accused of breaking the law the right to be tried by a jury of fellow citizens.

When Penn arrived in Pennsylvania, he met with many of the leaders of the local Delaware Indian tribes. He paid them for most of the land King Charles II had given him. A legend says that Penn and Tamenend (TAM•uh•nehnd), a chief of the Delaware people, exchanged wampum belts as a sign of friendship. Indian leaders came to respect Penn and believed he was their friend. Penn had said, "Let them have justice, and you win them." Penn also ensured that his colonists were ruled with **justice**, or fairness.

Penn also became the owner of what is now Delaware. When colonists in Delaware asked for their own general assembly, Penn granted it to them. The first Delaware General Assembly met in 1704.

**REVIEW** What did the right of trial by jury guarantee a person?

## Market Towns

Most people in the Middle Atlantic Colonies made their living by farming. Because the soil was fertile and the land was not too mountainous, many were able to develop large farms. On these farms they were able to grow enough food to feed their families and also have a surplus.

Farmers depended on market towns as places to trade their livestock and their surplus **farm produce**—grains, fruits, and vegetables—for goods and services. Market towns became a common sight throughout the Middle Atlantic Colonies.

In most market towns a general store sold goods, such as tools, cloth, shoes, stockings, and buttons. Near the general store there was often the shop of a cobbler, who made and repaired

Wheat was traded in market towns.

shoes. Nearby there was also a gristmill, where grain was ground into flour and meal, and a sawmill, where logs were sawed into lumber.

Unlike the New England Colonies, the Middle Atlantic Colonies welcomed people of different religions. Towns in these colonies often had more than one kind of church. A Presbyterian church, for example, might be only a block away from a Methodist church and a Quaker meetinghouse.

Interest in religion led to the **Great Awakening**, a movement that called for a rebirth of religious ways of life. This way of thinking quickly spread through other English colonies during the 1730s and 1740s.

**REVIEW** **What kinds of goods were bought and sold in market towns?**

**LESSON 1 REVIEW**

**Summary Time Line**

| 1625 | 1650 | 1675 | 1700 |

**1626** The Dutch build New Amsterdam

**1664** The English take over New Netherland

**1682** William Penn writes the Frame of Government of Pennsylvania

1. **MAIN IDEA** Why did people of many different cultures and religions settle the Middle Atlantic Colonies?

2. **WHY IT MATTERS** In what ways do people of different cultures and religions contribute to the United States today?

3. **VOCABULARY** Use the term **refuge** in a sentence.

4. **TIME LINE** In what year did the English take over New Netherland?

5. **READING SKILL—Make Inferences** Why do you think the Dutch settlers refused to fight when the English arrived to take over New Netherland?

6. **GEOGRAPHY** Where was the first Quaker colony in North America located?

7. **CRITICAL THINKING—Hypothesize** What might New York City be like today if the Dutch had kept control of New Amsterdam?

**PERFORMANCE—Draw a Picture** On a large piece of paper, draw a picture of a scene showing life in one of the Middle Atlantic Colonies. Make sure your scene includes examples of things that attracted people to these colonies.

# Great Awakening Sermons

In the 1730s and 1740s, The Great Awakening swept the English-speaking world. The Great Awakening was a revival, or rebirth, of the importance of religion in people's lives. In the colonies of North America, it was led at first by a minister named George Whitefield. He traveled from Maine to Georgia preaching sermons. Whitefield and The Great Awakening were not popular with all people. In the end, however, The Great Awakening contributed to a new sense of unity among all the English colonists.

 FROM THE LIBRARY OF CONGRESS ONLINE EXHIBIT "RELIGION AND FOUNDING OF THE AMERICAN REPUBLIC"

George Whitefield

George Whitefield used this collapsible field pulpit for open-air preaching.

Many sermons delivered by the preachers of the Great Awakening were later published as books.

THE
DANGER
OF
An Unconverted
MINISTRY,
Considered in a
SERMON
ON MARK VI. 34.

Preached at *Nottingham*, in *Pennsylvania*,
March 8. ANNO 1739,40.

By *GILBERT TENNENT*, A.M.
And Minister of the Gospel in *New-Brunswick*,
*New-Jersey*.

Jerem. V. 30, 31. *A wonderful and horrible Thing
is committed in the Land: The Prophets prophesy
falsely, and the Priests bear Rule by their Means,
and my People love to have it so; and what will
they do in the End thereof?*

*PHILADELPHIA:*
Printed by BENJAMIN FRANKLIN,
In *Market-street*, 1740.

Gilbert
Tennent

## Analyze the Primary Source

❶ In which colonies did Gilbert Tennent and Jonathan Edwards live?

❷ When and where were the original sermons delivered?

❸ When and where were the sermons published as books?

❹ Who printed Tennent's sermon?

## ACTIVITY

**Write to Explain** Make a list of the kinds of things that people might learn from sermons. Then use your list to help you write a paragraph about why you think sermons were important to the people in the colonies.

Jonathan
Edwards

A Faithful
NARRATIVE
OF THE
Surprizing Work of GOD
IN THE
CONVERSION
OF
Many HUNDRED SOULS in *Northampton,*
and the Neighbouring Towns and
Villages of *New-Hampshire* in *New-
England.*

In a LETTER to the Revᵈ. Dr. BENJAMIN
COLMAN of *Boston.*

Written by the Revᵈ. Mr. EDWARDS, Minister of
*Northampton,* on *Nov.* 6. 1736.

And Published,
With a Large PREFACE,
By Dr. WATTS and Dr. GUYSE.

## RESEARCH

**GO ONLINE** Visit The Learning Site at **www.harcourtschool.com/primarysources** to research other primary sources.

**MAIN IDEA**
Read to find out why Philadelphia became the Pennsylvania Colony's main port.

**WHY IT MATTERS**
Port cities are important to the growth and prosperity of countries.

**VOCABULARY**
township
immigrant
militia
almanac

# Colonial Philadelphia

1625 — 1750

**1700–1750**

As proprietor of the Pennsylvania Colony, William Penn planned not only its government but also its settlements. One of them, Philadelphia, became the largest and wealthiest city in all the English colonies of North America. By 1770 it had more than 28,000 people—a small population by today's city standards but very large for that time.

## Early Colonial Days

William Penn named his colony's chief city Philadelphia, a word meaning "brotherly love" in Greek. Like all of Pennsylvania, Philadelphia was founded on the idea that people of diverse backgrounds could get along with each other.

That idea was reflected in the layout of most of the colony's settlements. Penn wanted to divide his colony into townships. Each **township**, or area of land, would be 5,000 acres—a space large enough for ten families. Land belonging to individual families would be carved out of the township in giant pie-like slices. Penn wanted settlers to build their homes at the tips of the slices so that every family would be within walking distance of one another and of whatever church they chose to build.

Philadelphia grew to become one of the largest cities in the English colonies.

William Penn had a different layout in mind for Philadelphia, his colony's most important town. It covered a strip of land between the Schuylkill (SKOO•kuhl) River on the west and the Delaware River on the east. Early drawings of one plan looked like a checkerboard, with straight streets laid out in great squares. Public parks added open spaces to the city that Penn called "a green country town."

Philadelphia's location near good land and waterways contributed to growth in shipping and trading. During the 1700s Philadelphia developed into one of the busiest ports in the English colonies. By 1710 it had become the largest city in the colonies. Chief among its exports were farm products such as wheat, corn, rye, hemp, and flax. Imports consisted mostly of manufactured goods from England, which were then sent all over the Middle Atlantic Colonies.

**REVIEW** What did William Penn accomplish as leader of the Pennsylvania Colony?

## The People of Philadelphia

Philadelphia soon became the main port in Pennsylvania for receiving not only imports but also immigrants. An **immigrant** is a person who comes into a country to make a new home there. According to Reverend William Smith, Philadelphians in the 1700s were "a people, thrown together from various quarters of the world, differing in all things—language, manners and sentiment [attitude]."

The largest group in Philadelphia was made up of English and Welsh Quakers.

**GEOGRAPHY THEME**

**Place** As shown on this present-day map of Center City (right), the checkerboard pattern of William Penn's city plan can still be seen.

◆ What rivers form the east and west boundaries of Center City?

This drawing by William Penn shows his plan for Philadelphia.

Center City, Philadelphia

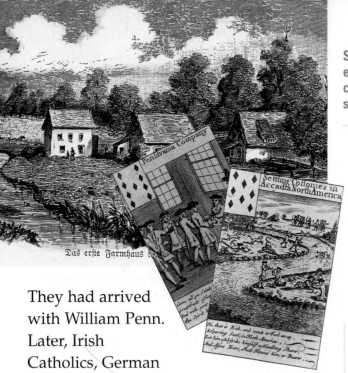

Some advertisements (below) on playing cards encouraged settlers to move to the colonies. The two cards below show people buying and settling land. The scene (left) shows a farm in Pennsylvania.

They had arrived with William Penn. Later, Irish Catholics, German Lutherans, and Jews from many countries arrived. Free Africans came, too.

Some immigrants came to Philadelphia to find refuge from war and famine, or shortage of food, in their homelands. Many sought religious freedom. Others came because Philadelphia quickly gained a reputation for offering economic opportunity. Immigrants arriving in the city included farmers and skilled workers, such as bakers, blacksmiths, butchers, carpenters, shoemakers, and tailors. They set up their own shops, selling goods and services in Philadelphia and in other Pennsylvania settlements nearby.

One of the largest groups of immigrants to arrive in Philadelphia came from what is now Germany. The Germans brought with them many

of their customs and traditions, including barn raising. First, a farmer dug his barn's foundation and prepared a frame made of lumber. He then invited his friends and neighbors and their families to help raise the frame into place. To feed all the people, the families prepared huge meals.

German immigrant gunmakers developed the long-barrel gun called the Pennsylvania rifle. In the 1700s it was the most accurate rifle in the world. It was particularly valued on the frontier, where accurate weapons were needed for hunting. German craftworkers also designed a deep-bellied wagon known as the Conestoga. Conestoga wagons were larger than regular wagons and were first used mainly by farmers to carry produce to market.

Scotch-Irish settlers also came to Pennsylvania. These were people from Scotland who had settled in northern Ireland in the 1600s.

When a visitor from England first saw Conestogas, he called them "huge moving houses."

The Union Fire Company was, according to Benjamin Franklin (left), the first group of firefighters he organized. After Franklin raised money to build a hospital, others were soon built (right).

Many of them and their descendants came to the English colonies. Like other immigrants to Pennsylvania, they entered the colony through the port of Philadelphia. Then they moved into the hilly frontier areas located near the Appalachian Mountains.

**REVIEW** For what reasons did immigrants come to Philadelphia?

## Benjamin Franklin and His City

The story of Benjamin Franklin's rise to wealth and fame matches colonial Philadelphia's rise to become one of the most prosperous cities in the English colonies. As a citizen, Franklin left a strong mark on the growing city. He organized the first trained firefighting company in the 13 colonies and the first fire insurance company. He worked to have Philadelphia's streets paved and lit at night. He raised money to help build the first hospital in Philadelphia. He also organized a **militia**, or volunteer army, to protect Philadelphia and the frontier settlements.

As a scientist, Franklin is best known for his experiments with electricity. It is believed that he proved that lightning is a form of electricity by tying a metal key to the string on his childhood kite and flying the kite in a thunderstorm. Using what he learned from his experiments, Franklin invented the lightning rod. A lightning rod is a straight, thin bar of metal attached to the top of a house or barn. It conducts, or guides, lightning into the ground. As a result, the building will not be damaged if it is struck. Until the invention of the lightning rod, buildings struck by lightning were likely to burst into flames.

Benjamin Franklin's interest in learning included the education of others. He even helped establish the first library in the colonies which people could subscribe to.

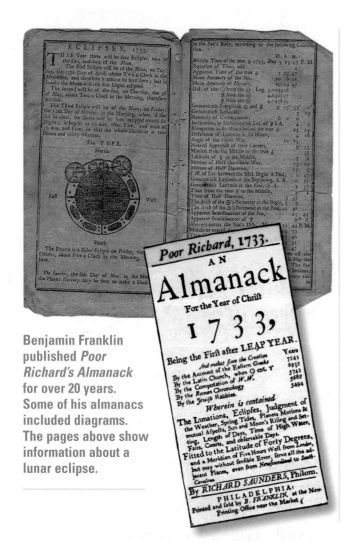

Benjamin Franklin published *Poor Richard's Almanack* for over 20 years. Some of his almanacs included diagrams. The pages above show information about a lunar eclipse.

Colonists could borrow books after paying a small fee to become a member of the library. As a result, people seeking knowledge did not have to pay much money. Franklin's opinions on education were used, too, when a school called the Philadelphia Academy was founded.

As a printer, Benjamin Franklin helped make Philadelphia a major publishing center in the English colonies. In 1729 he started printing a newspaper, the *Pennsylvania Gazette*. In 1732 he began publishing *Poor Richard's Almanack*. An **almanac** is a book issued only once each year. Franklin's had a calendar and a yearly weather forecast, which helped farmers know the best time to plant crops. It also had stories, jokes, and witty sayings, such as "Early to bed and early to rise, makes a man healthy, wealthy, and wise."

**REVIEW** What were some of Benjamin Franklin's contributions as a scientist and inventor?

## LESSON 2 REVIEW

**Summary Time Line**

1700 — 1725 — 1750

**1710**
Philadelphia becomes the largest city in the English colonies

**1732**
Benjamin Franklin begins publishing *Poor Richard's Almanack*

1. **MAIN IDEA** Why did Philadelphia become the Pennsylvania Colony's main port?

2. **WHY IT MATTERS** How are port cities important to the growth and prosperity of countries?

3. **VOCABULARY** Use the term **immigrant** in a sentence to describe why some people settled in Philadelphia.

4. **TIME LINE** When did Philadelphia become the largest city in the English colonies?

5. **READING SKILL—Make Inferences** How do you think Benjamin Franklin's lightning rod might have helped with the growth of Philadelphia?

6. **ECONOMICS** What were some of Philadelphia's chief exports?

7. **CULTURE** What did German immigrants contribute to the Pennsylvania Colony?

8. **CRITICAL THINKING—Analyze** In what ways did William Penn lead his colony most like a leader in the United States today?

**PERFORMANCE—Plan a Community** Work with a group of classmates to draw a plan for a community. Then, write a paragraph describing the plan and display it in the classroom.

# Use a Circle Graph

**VOCABULARY**

circle graph

## ▶ WHY IT MATTERS

Suppose you want to show in a simple, clear way how the population of the 13 colonies was divided between the New England, Middle Atlantic, and Southern Colonies. One way to show the information is by making a **circle graph**. A circle graph is sometimes called a pie graph because it is round and is divided into pieces, or parts, like a pie is.

## ▶ WHAT YOU NEED TO KNOW

The circle graph below shows the population of the 13 English colonies in the year 1750. The graph's parts are the colonial regions that made up the population.

**Population of the 13 Colonies,**
1750

44% Southern Colonies

31% New England Colonies

25% Middle Atlantic Colonies

A percent, shown by the symbol % in the graph, is given to each part of the graph. A percent is one-hundredth of something. For example, if you cut a pie into 100 pieces, those 100 pieces together equal the whole pie, or 100 percent (100%) of it. Fifty pieces would be one-half of the pie, or 50% of it. Ten pieces would be one-tenth of the pie, or 10% of it. Each piece would be one-hundredth, or 1%, of the pie.

## ▶ PRACTICE THE SKILL

Use the circle graph to answer the following questions.

1 In which region did the largest part of the population in the 13 colonies live in 1750?

2 What percent of the total population did the region with the largest population make up?

3 What percent of the total population did the Middle Atlantic Colonies make up?

4 What percent was made up by the New England Colonies?

## ▶ APPLY WHAT YOU LEARNED

Use information from the circle graph to write a paragraph about the different colonial regions in the 13 colonies. Compare the population sizes of the regions.

**CHART AND GRAPH SKILLS**

# 3

**MAIN IDEA**
Read to find out the many challenges colonists faced as they settled on lands farther west.

**WHY IT MATTERS**
People today often meet challenges when they move to new places.

**VOCABULARY**
backcountry
loft

This forested land in Virginia was once a part of the backcountry.

# Moving West

Settlers from Pennsylvania, especially the Germans and the Scotch-Irish, were among the first to settle farther inland, away from the Atlantic coast. There they claimed what they saw as open land, even though American Indians lived there. They hoped to make a piece of the frontier into a farm, where they could build a house and raise a family. They felt that moving to the frontier would give them a chance for a better life.

## The Great Wagon Road

In the early 1700s most cities, towns, farms, and plantations in the 13 English colonies were located near the coast, in the Coastal Plain region. At that time, few colonists had settled in the Piedmont—the land between the Coastal Plain and the Appalachian Mountains. Settlers called this frontier region the **backcountry** because it was beyond, or "in back of," the area settled by Europeans.

The waterfalls in the rivers along the Fall Line and the lack of roads made travel to the backcountry difficult. To get around the waterfalls, settlers had to portage, or carry overland, their boats and supplies. This kind of travel was so difficult that it discouraged many settlers from moving inland.

By the mid-1700s many settlers in the 13 colonies began to settle in areas west of the Coastal Plain. From Pennsylvania large numbers of German and Scotch-Irish immigrants had begun moving into the backcountry of western Virginia, North Carolina, and South Carolina. To get there, the settlers followed an old Indian trail. As more and more settlers used the trail, it became wider and wider. Finally, wagons could travel on it, and it became known as the Great Wagon Road.

From Pennsylvania the Great Wagon Road passed through the Shenandoah Valley of Virginia and along the eastern side of the Blue Ridge Mountains. The land there was hilly, and travel on the road was difficult. "[In places] it was so slippery the horses could not keep their footing but fell . . . to their knees," wrote one early traveler. However, the Great Wagon Road was the only way to get wagons loaded with household goods to the backcountry.

Thousands of people followed the Great Wagon Road to move inland from Pennsylvania. Among them was a young man named Daniel Boone. When Boone was 16 years old, his family followed the Great Wagon Road to settle in the Yadkin Valley in North Carolina. The journey took more than a year. Later, Boone would become a well-known explorer who made new trails that took settlers even farther west.

**REVIEW** Why was the Great Wagon Road important to the settlement of the frontier?

**GEOGRAPHY THEME**

**Movement** **Thousands of settlers moved to the backcountry to start farms.**

❓ By what year had settlers moved the farthest west?

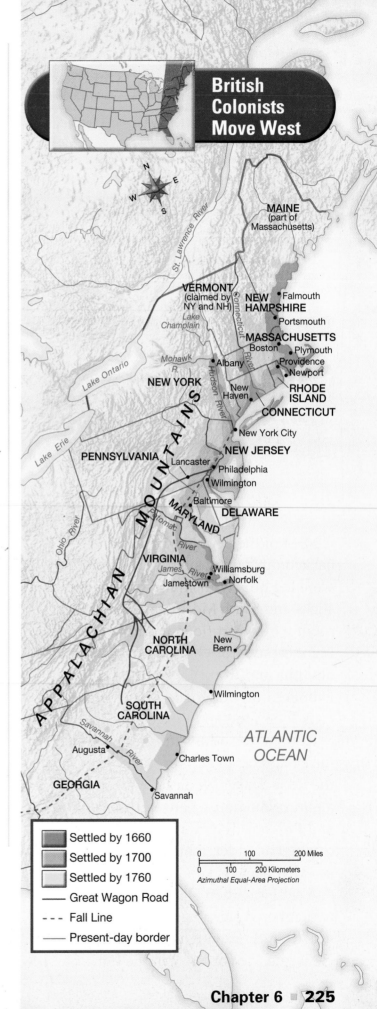

British Colonists Move West

Settled by 1660
Settled by 1700
Settled by 1760
—— Great Wagon Road
- - - Fall Line
—— Present-day border

0   100   200 Miles
0   100   200 Kilometers
Azimuthal Equal-Area Projection

## A CLOSER LOOK
### Frontier Life

Life was hard and often lonely for early settlers in the backcountry. Family members had to work together to provide all the items they might need.

1. chopping wood
2. farming
3. cleared land
4. candle making
5. churning butter
6. fire used for cooking and warmth
7. children's loft
8. mud between logs

❖ In what ways is this frontier family self-sufficient?

## Life in the Backcountry

Most of the people who settled the backcountry lived simply. Their homes were log huts with chimneys made of sticks and mud. Most homes had one room with a dirt floor and no windows. Light came through the open door in the daytime and from the fireplace at night. Families burned wood in the fireplace to cook their food and to keep warm.

At night the adults in a family spread their blankets over piles of dry leaves on the floor. The children slept in the **loft**, a part of the house between the ceiling and the roof. To get up to the loft, they climbed a ladder, which was often just wooden pegs driven into the wall.

A settler named Oliver Johnson remembered sleeping in a loft when he was a child growing up on the frontier. He wrote, "If you slept in the loft, you pulled your head under the covers during a storm. When you got up in the mornin[g], you [would] shake the snow off the covers, grab your shirt and britches [pants] and hop down the ladder to the fireplace, where it was good and warm."

People on the frontier worked hard to get food, hunting in the forests and farming in the clearings. They farmed in the Indian way. They planted corn, beans, and squash all in the same mound of soil. The cornstalks provided a stake for the beans to climb. The squash vines spread out on the ground between the mounds.

As families had done in early New England, frontier families made almost everything they needed. They churned their own butter, dyed their own cloth, and made their own soap and candles. Those who could not do things for themselves, a frontier minister observed in 1711, would "have but a bad time of it; for help is not to be had at any rate."

Life on the frontier was full of dangers. Families had to protect themselves not only from wild animals but also from possible attacks from Indians or other settlers. Despite these dangers, people still moved farther and farther west. By the mid-1700s, English settlers had crossed the Appalachian Mountains into the Ohio Valley. The land that they moved into was also claimed by France.

**REVIEW** How did frontier families get the food and goods they needed?

## LESSON 3
## REVIEW

1. **MAIN IDEA** How did settlers meet the challenges of living on the frontier?

2. **WHY IT MATTERS** What challenges do people today face when they move to a new place?

3. **VOCABULARY** Write a sentence about frontier life, using the terms **backcountry** and **loft**.

4. **READING SKILL—Make Inferences** What do you think life was like for English settlers in the Ohio Valley if the land they lived on was also being claimed by France?

5. **HISTORY** Why did settlers move west?

6. **CRITICAL THINKING—Synthesize** Why do you think settlers of the backcountry were willing to face the hardships there?

 **PERFORMANCE—Write a Journal Entry** Imagine that you are a settler who has moved to the frontier in the early 1700s. Write a journal entry in which you describe your journey to the backcountry and the building of your new home.

# Review and Test Preparation

Summary Time Line

1625                                              1650

• 1624
The first Dutch
settlers arrive in
New Netherland

## USE YOUR READING SKILLS

Complete this graphic organizer by using information you
have learned from the chapter to make inferences about the
Middle Atlantic Colonies and the backcountry. A copy of this
graphic organizer appears on page 62 of the Activity Book.

### Breadbasket Colonies

| WHAT YOU HAVE READ | WHAT YOU KNOW |
|---|---|
| The Middle Atlantic Colonies attracted people from many different backgrounds. | _____ _____ _____ _____ |

_____
_____
_____

### Moving West

| WHAT YOU HAVE READ | WHAT YOU KNOW |
|---|---|
| Colonists who settled land farther west faced many challenges. | _____ _____ _____ _____ |

_____
_____
_____

## THINK & WRITE

**Write a Wise Saying**  Benjamin
Franklin's *Poor Richard's Almanack* included
many wise sayings such as, "If you have
time, don't wait for time." Many of these
sayings suggested that good behavior is
often rewarded. Write a wise saying about
the benefits of behaving well.

**Write a Song**  Imagine the year is 1750
and your family is moving to the backcountry.
Write a song about your family's journey
along the Great Wagon Road. Be sure to
describe the changing environment and the
difficulties your family must overcome on the
journey.

**1664**
The English take
over New Amsterdam

**1682**
William Penn
writes the Frame
of Government
of Pennsylvania

**1710**
Philadelphia
becomes the
largest city
in the Middle
Atlantic Colonies

**1732**
Benjamin Franklin
begins publishing
*Poor Richard's Almanack*

## USE THE TIME LINE

Use the chapter summary time line to answer these questions.

**1** When did the first Dutch settlers arrive in New Netherland?

**2** When did William Penn write the Frame of Government of Pennsylvania?

## USE VOCABULARY

For each pair of terms, write a sentence that explains how the terms are related.

**3** **trial by jury** (p. 214), **justice** (p. 214)

**4** **township** (p. 218), **militia** (p. 221)

**5** **backcountry** (p. 224), **loft** (p. 226)

## RECALL FACTS

Answer these questions.

**6** Why did King Charles II grant William Penn the charter to Pennsylvania?

**7** How did German immigrant craftworkers contribute to western settlement?

**8** What was the name of the trail followed by settlers moving west from Pennsylvania?

Write the letter of the best choice.

**9** **TEST PREP** The Middle Atlantic Colonies included New York, New Jersey, Pennsylvania, and—
   **A** Connecticut.
   **B** Delaware.
   **C** Massachusetts.
   **D** Virginia.

**10** **TEST PREP** Farmers in the Middle Atlantic Colonies depended on market towns as places to—
   **F** meet with local Native American tribes.
   **G** sell their furs to European merchants.
   **H** trade their surplus farm produce for goods and services.
   **J** purchase naval stores.

**11** **TEST PREP** Benjamin Franklin contributed to the education of others by—
   **A** helping start the Great Awakening.
   **B** designing the layout for the city of Philadelphia.
   **C** establishing the first subscription library in the colonies.
   **D** printing playing cards.

## THINK CRITICALLY

**12** What do you think was William Penn's greatest accomplishment as proprietor of Pennsylvania?

**13** Why do you think Benjamin Franklin took such an active part in community life?

**14** What do you think backcountry families did when a family member became sick?

## APPLY SKILLS

**Use a Circle Graph**

**15** Look in newspapers, magazines, or on the Internet to find an example of a circle graph. Cut out or print out the graph, and tape it to a sheet of paper. Then write a paragraph about what the graph represents.

## CHESAPEAKE BAY

For hundreds of years the Chesapeake Bay has shaped the history, culture, and economy of Virginia and Maryland. The bay takes its name from the Native American word *Chesepiooc,* meaning "Great Shellfish Bay." Today, more than 15 million people live along its shores.

### LOCATE IT

MARYLAND

Hooper Island

# The Southern Colonies

66 Heaven and earth never agreed to frame a better place for man's habitation. 99

—John Smith, on Chesapeake Bay, 1607

**CHAPTER READING SKILL**

### Generalize

When you **generalize,** you summarize a group of facts and show the relationship between them.

**As you read this chapter, identify important facts. Then use those facts to make generalizations about the Southern Colonies.**

# Settlement of the South

1625 ——————————————————— 1750

**1633–1733**

In 1606 the king of England granted the Virginia Company a charter allowing settlement of the Chesapeake Bay region. In 1607 Virginia became the first permanent English colony in North America. By the 1730s the English had settled the remaining colonies in the South—Maryland, North Carolina, South Carolina, and Georgia. With its 13 colonies, the English claimed much of the Atlantic coast of North America from present-day Maine to present-day Georgia.

## Maryland

Maryland was founded by the Calverts, a family of wealthy English landowners. The Calverts, who were Catholic, wanted to build a colony in North America that not only made money but also provided a refuge for Catholics. Like English Quakers, Catholics in England could not worship as they wanted.

George Calvert, the first Lord Baltimore, had been a member of the Virginia Company. He had purchased a large amount of land on the large island of Newfoundland, in what is now Canada. His goal had been to establish a colony there, but he found the climate too cold and the soil too rocky. In 1628, with Lady Baltimore,

**FAST FACT** The people who today live on Tangier (tan•JIR) Island in Chesapeake Bay are descendants of English colonists, who may have settled there as early as 1686. Their language and way of life have changed very little since the first settlers arrived. They speak the way people speak in parts of western England, from which most of the island's original settlers came.

George Calvert, the first Lord Baltimore

# St. Marys City

## Understanding Places and Regions

St. Marys City, Maryland, is located near the mouth of the Potomac River. For most of the 1600s the town served as Maryland's first capital. Then the capital was moved to Annapolis, and the town was abandoned. Later the area was used as a tobacco plantation. In the 1970s historians and archaeologists dug up the area on which they thought the town once stood. What they discovered was a town designed in the shape of two triangles that met at a central square.

**This painting by Walter Crowe shows St. Marys City in 1685.**

he traveled south to the Chesapeake Bay region. There they found a site where the climate was mild and the soil was rich. King Charles I signed the final colonial charter two months after George Calvert died in 1632. The king gave the grant to Cecilius Calvert, George Calvert's oldest son and the second Lord Baltimore. As proprietor, Cecilius Calvert named the new colony Maryland in honor of Queen Henrietta Maria, wife of Charles I.

In 1633 Cecilius Calvert's first group of colonists left England. "I have sent a hopeful colony to Maryland," he wrote.

The colonists established Saint Marys, later known as Saint Marys City, not far from the mouth of the Potomac River.

Cecilius Calvert appointed his brother Leonard Calvert as the governor of Maryland. Leonard Calvert had learned about the unfortunate experiences of earlier English colonists, such as those who settled early Roanoke and Jamestown. As a result, he planned ahead and prevented the Maryland colonists from suffering a period of starvation. Calvert also knew that Jamestown was nearby in case the new settlement needed supplies or help.

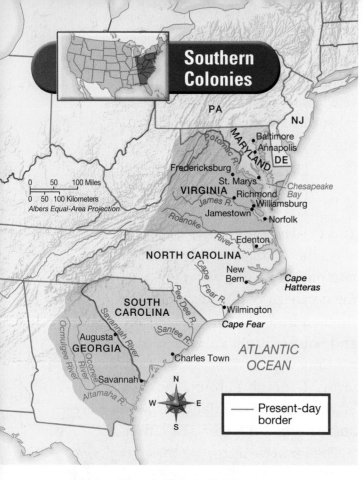

Southern Colonies

PA
NJ
MARYLAND
Baltimore
Annapolis
DE
Potomac R.
Fredericksburg
St. Marys
Chesapeake Bay
VIRGINIA
Richmond
Williamsburg
James R.
Jamestown
Norfolk
Roanoke
Roanoke River
Edenton
NORTH CAROLINA
New Bern
Cape Fear R.
Cape Hatteras
SOUTH CAROLINA
Pee Dee R.
Wilmington
Cape Fear
Savannah River
Augusta
Santee R.
GEORGIA
Ocmulgee River
Oconee River
Charles Town
ATLANTIC OCEAN
Savannah
Altamaha R.

0 50 100 Miles
0 50 100 Kilometers
Albers Equal-Area Projection

N W E S

—— Present-day border

**GEOGRAPHY THEME**

**Place** Many colonists in the Southern Colonies started plantations.

❖ Why do you think most of the settlements in the Southern Colonies were located in Virginia?

The Calverts granted some colonists large pieces of land, and these colonists used the land to start tobacco plantations. However, most of the colonists going to Maryland went as indentured servants. An **indentured servant** was a person who agreed to work for another person without pay for a certain length of time in exchange for passage to North America. Most indentured servants were men between the ages of 18 and 22. Many indentured servants were Europeans who wanted to move to the colonies but had little or no money to pay for their travel.

The indentured servants in Maryland fared better than some who went to other colonies to live and work. When their time of service was finished, they were legally free. In addition, colonial leaders helped them start their own farms. They received 50 acres of land, a suit of clothes, an ax, two hoes, and three barrels of corn.

From the beginning Maryland's leaders welcomed settlers of many religions. In 1649 the Maryland assembly, a group that made laws for the colony, passed the Toleration Act. It was the first law in North America to allow all Christians to worship as they pleased. Maryland became known throughout the English colonies for its religious freedom.

**REVIEW** Why did the Calverts want to build a colony in North America?

## The Carolinas

The Southern Colonies of Virginia and Maryland continued to grow during the 1600s. Then in 1663 King Charles II, the son of King Charles I, granted land for another colony, located between Virginia and Spanish Florida. The charter divided the colony, known as Carolina, among eight English nobles, known as the Lords Proprietors.

The Toleration Act allowed all Christians in Maryland to worship as they pleased.

Even before the charter was granted, colonists from Virginia had been building villages and were farming in the northern part of the area that became the Carolina Colony. After 1663, colonists from England and the Caribbean, as well as Huguenots (HYOO•guh•nahts) from France, came to settle there. The Huguenots were Protestants forced to leave their country by the French king because of their different religious beliefs.

One of the first actions the Lords Proprietors took was to set up a government for the colony. They chose a Virginian, William Drummond, to be governor. Then in 1669 the Lords Proprietors wrote a **constitution**, or written plan of government, for the colony. Their plan was called the Fundamental Constitution of Carolina. The plan allowed the colonists to make some laws for themselves, but it kept most of the authority in the hands of the king in England.

The Carolina colonists tried raising different cash crops. The climate was good for agriculture, and the soil was fertile. At first, they planted tobacco, grapes, and cotton, but these crops did not do as well as expected. They had more success in raising cattle and trapping animals for their fur, but they still searched for a cash crop. Only when they "found out the true way of raising and husking rice" did Carolina begin to prosper. The colonists also produced naval stores.

As the population grew, Carolina became more difficult to govern. In 1712 the northern two-thirds of the colony was divided into two colonies, North Carolina and South Carolina. Hilly North Carolina continued to develop as a colony of small farms. In South Carolina, however, landowners on the flat Coastal Plain created larger and larger plantations.

The main cash crop on many of South Carolina's plantations was rice. On drier land, where rice would not grow, landowners found they could grow indigo plants. From these plants they made **indigo**, which is a blue dye. The dye was widely used in the clothmaking process common in the 1700s.

Rice (left) was an important cash crop in the Carolinas. The drawing (below) shows workers in a Carolina rice field.

Indigo became an important cash crop after Eliza Lucas Pinckney, the 17-year-old daughter of a plantation owner, experimented with the plant. Using seeds from the Caribbean, Pinckney spent several years growing different kinds of indigo. By 1744 samples of the dye made from her plants were of excellent quality. Pinckney gave her indigo seeds to neighbors and friends. Within a few years South Carolina plantation owners were selling a million pounds of indigo a year to cloth makers in Europe.

The plantations of South Carolina required many workers, and since there were not enough workers available, many landowners bought enslaved Africans. The coastal settlement of Charles Town, later renamed Charleston, became the most important seaport, social center, and slave market in the Southern Colonies.

REVIEW What allowed the Carolina colonists to make some laws for themselves?

## Georgia

The southern one-third of what had originally been Carolina was not settled by English colonists until 1733. A year earlier King George II had given James Oglethorpe and 19 partners a charter to settle Georgia, a colony they named for the king. Oglethorpe was an English general and lawmaker. The charter gave Oglethorpe and his partners the right to settle the region between the Savannah and Altamaha Rivers for 21 years.

Many plantations in South Carolina prospered by growing indigo plants.

Oglethorpe and his partners hoped an English colony in Georgia would strengthen England's claim to the land. At the time Spain, France, and England all claimed what became the Georgia Colony.

Oglethorpe also had the idea of bringing over **debtors**—people who were in prison for owing money—to settle the colony. In the 1700s most debtors were imprisoned as punishment for not paying back money. Oglethorpe offered each settler 50 acres of land plus a bonus of 50 acres for every debtor that the settler brought along to help with the work of starting a colony. Those who paid their own way might get up to 500 acres. Oglethorpe hoped that once the debtors were out of prison, they would better themselves through hard work. Settling them in Georgia, he thought, was the answer to this social problem.

In 1733 Oglethorpe and a group of more than 100 settlers established Savannah near the mouth of the Savannah River. During the first year, to keep the colony fairly small, Oglethorpe limited the amount of land a person could own. To avoid conflicts with the Native Americans, he forbade trading with them. He also did not allow slave traders to bring enslaved Africans to the colony. As a result, there were no plantations in Georgia, only small farms.

In 1752 control of Georgia passed from Oglethorpe and his partners back to the king, making it a royal colony. With this change in ownership also came a change to allow slavery. As a result, plantations growing cash crops quickly began to develop, and Georgia landowners began to prosper. Their way of life became similar to that in the other Southern Colonies.

Rice became the most profitable cash crop in the Georgia Colony. Some Georgia planters became so wealthy from growing rice that they were able to own a house in a nearby town in addition to the one they had on the plantation.

**REVIEW** What did James Oglethorpe accomplish as the leader of the Georgia Colony?

• **BIOGRAPHY** •

## James Oglethorpe
### 1696–1785
**Character Trait: Compassion**

While working as a law-maker in England, James Oglethorpe found a special cause. He heard that a good friend of his had been sent to prison for not paying his debts. Oglethorpe hurried to the prison but arrived too late. His friend had died of smallpox from the terrible conditions in the prison. Oglethorpe made up his mind then and there to help debtors.

This 1734 engraving (below) of Savannah was used to attract settlers to the Georgia Colony.

**MULTIMEDIA BIOGRAPHIES**
Visit The Learning Site at
**www.harcourtschool.com/biographies**
to learn about other famous people.

**GO ONLINE**

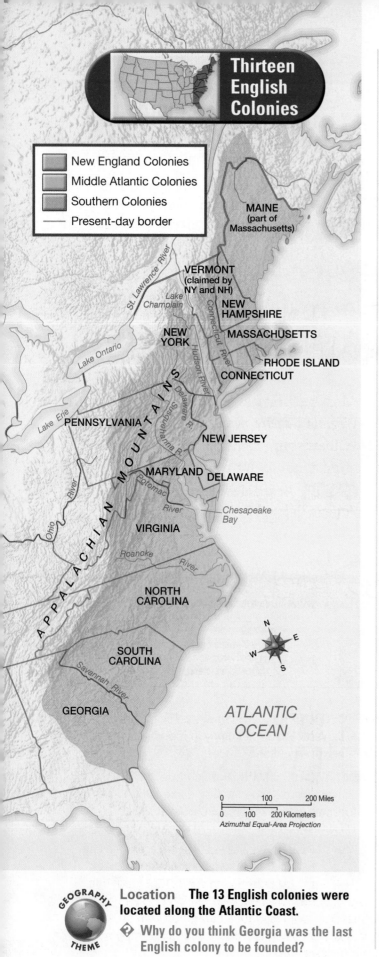

## Thirteen English Colonies

- New England Colonies
- Middle Atlantic Colonies
- Southern Colonies
- Present-day border

St. Lawrence River

MAINE
(part of Massachusetts)

VERMONT
(claimed by NY and NH)

Lake Champlain

NEW HAMPSHIRE

NEW YORK

MASSACHUSETTS

Connecticut River

RHODE ISLAND

Lake Ontario

Hudson River

CONNECTICUT

A P P A L A C H I A N   M O U N T A I N S

Lake Erie

PENNSYLVANIA

Delaware R.

Susquehanna R.

NEW JERSEY

MARYLAND

DELAWARE

Potomac River

Chesapeake Bay

Ohio River

VIRGINIA

Roanoke River

NORTH CAROLINA

SOUTH CAROLINA

Savannah River

GEORGIA

ATLANTIC OCEAN

N E S W

0    100    200 Miles
0    100    200 Kilometers
Azimuthal Equal-Area Projection

**GEOGRAPHY THEME**

**Location**   The 13 English colonies were located along the Atlantic Coast.

◆ Why do you think Georgia was the last English colony to be founded?

# Virginia Grows and Changes

By the 1730s, after all of the other Southern Colonies had been founded, the Virginia Colony continued to grow and change. By 1700 Virginia had become the largest English colony in North America. Because the population continued to grow, more and more settlers moved from the coastal areas of Virginia into the Piedmont, the Great Valley, and the mountains of western Virginia. Settlers from Pennsylvania also continued to move into these areas.

In the 1700s transportation improved throughout the Virginia Colony. It became easier to travel between the coastal areas and the western part of the colony. Indian trails became small roads, over which pack horses carried supplies. These roads soon widened and became wagon roads. Soon there were ferry boats that crossed rivers to transport passengers, livestock, tobacco, and other goods. When the ferries became very busy, the Virginia General Assembly voted to build bridges across some of the rivers. The General Assembly was made up of Virginia's governor, the Governor's Council, and the members of the House of Burgesses.

While more people in Virginia were moving west, changes were also happening along the coast. In 1699, because of fires and other problems in Jamestown, the House of Burgesses moved to the nearby village of Williamsburg, which became the colony's new capital. By the mid-1700s Williamsburg was a large, well-planned city. The city was soon being compared to other important cities of the 13 colonies, such as Boston, New York City, and Philadelphia.

The Governor's House in Williamsburg soon became known as the Governor's Palace.

Williamsburg became the political, social, and cultural center of the Virginia Colony. It was the home of many firsts for the colony. Virginia's first theater was built there in 1716. The colony's first successful printing press was set up there in 1728.

Also, the first newspaper in the colony, the *Virginia Gazette*, was started there in 1736. Williamsburg remained Virginia's most important city for much of the 1700s.

**REVIEW** How did transportation change in the Virginia Colony?

# LESSON 1
## REVIEW

**Summary Time Line**

1633 — 1683 — 1733

**1633**
Cecilius Calvert's first group of colonists leave England

**1712**
The Carolina colony is divided into two colonies—North Carolina and South Carolina

**1733**
Colonists settle Georgia

1. **MAIN IDEA** Why was selling crops for a profit important to the success of the Southern Colonies?

2. **WHY IT MATTERS** How might a crop or a product be important to a state or country today?

3. **VOCABULARY** Use **indigo** in a sentence to describe the accomplishments of Eliza Lucas Pinckney.

4. **TIME LINE** In what year was the Carolina Colony divided into two colonies?

5. **READING SKILL—Generalize** How do you think most people in the Southern Colonies made a living?

6. **GEOGRAPHY** What geographic factors led the Calverts to start a colony in Maryland instead of in Newfoundland?

7. **CRITICAL THINKING—Hypothesize** What might have happened if rice and indigo had not grown well in the South Carolina Colony?

**PERFORMANCE—Write a Paragraph**
Find out what kinds of cash crops are grown today in the states that were once the Southern Colonies. Use the Internet and other research tools to write a paragraph about the cash crops in those states. Share your paragraph with your classmates.

## · SKILLS ·

# Tell Fact from Opinion

**VOCABULARY**

fact
opinion

### ➡ WHY IT MATTERS

Knowing how to tell a fact from an opinion can help you better understand what you hear and read. A **fact** is a statement that can be checked and proved. An **opinion** is a statement that tells what a person thinks or believes.

### ➡ WHAT YOU NEED TO KNOW

You have read that the Maryland Colony was founded by the Calverts. You could check whether this is a fact by looking in an encyclopedia, in other books, or on the Internet.

Facts often give dates, numbers, and other pieces of information. To tell whether a statement is a fact, ask yourself the following questions.

- Do I know this idea to be true from my own experience?
- Can the idea be proved by testing or other checking?

Other statements in this chapter give opinions. You have read John Smith's opinion about Chesapeake Bay: "Heaven and earth never agreed to frame a better place for man's habitation." There is no way to prove that Chesapeake Bay is a better place than any other place.

An opinion is what a speaker or writer believes. The following clues can help you decide whether a statement is an opinion.

- Look or listen for phrases such as *I think, I feel,* and *in my opinion.*
- Watch for words such as *best, worst, wonderful,* and *terrible.*

Historians can use facts to help them form opinions about the past.

### ➡ PRACTICE THE SKILL

Decide whether the following statements are facts or opinions.

**1** In 1628 George Calvert traveled to the Chesapeake Bay region.

**2** Saint Marys was the best settlement in the English colonies.

### ➡ APPLY WHAT YOU LEARNED

Many people rely on newspapers for information. Look at a recent newspaper. Underline three facts and circle three opinions. Explain how you were able to tell the facts from the opinions.

**READING SKILLS**

**240** ▪ **Unit 3**

# Southern Plantations

As towns and cities in the 13 English colonies grew, plantations also grew—especially in the Southern Colonies. Plantations became prosperous because plantation owners, known as **planters**, were able to grow large amounts of cash crops, more than on small farms. Planters acquired as much land as they could in order to grow more and more crops to sell.

## The Plantation Economy

From the time that the first English colonists settled Jamestown, plantations became important to the economy of the Southern Colonies. As planters learned to grow more cash crops well, such as tobacco, rice, and indigo, they started even more plantations.

The earliest plantations were usually built in the rich soil of the southern tidewater. **Tidewater** is low-lying land along a coast. Waterways in the area made it easy for boats to get crops to market. Crop buyers from England traveled the waterways with English-made goods—shoes, lace, thread, farm tools, and dishes. The planters bartered, or traded, crops for these goods.

Owners of the largest plantations most often sold their cash crops through a broker. A **broker** is a person who is paid to buy and sell for someone else. Planters sent their crops to England together with a list of things they wanted the broker to buy there for them.

**MAIN IDEA**
Read about how southern plantations changed as plantation owners added more and more workers.

**WHY IT MATTERS**
Many plantation owners became important leaders in the 13 colonies.

**VOCABULARY**

planter
tidewater
broker
auction
overseer
spiritual
public service

Goods like these buttons (left and below) and this tea caddy (right) were brought to the colonies from England.

## A CLOSER LOOK
### A Southern Plantation

Many plantations in the Southern Colonies were self-sufficient. Planters grew food and skilled workers produced many needed goods.

1. cattle pen
2. slave cabins
3. overseer's house
4. stable
5. tobacco barn
6. tobacco fields
7. kitchen
8. main house
9. office
10. carpenter shop
11. smokehouse
12. laundry
13. warehouse
14. dock

❖ How were plantations self-sufficient?

The broker sold the crops in England, bought what the planter wanted, and sent the goods back to the colonies.

To raise more crops, planters had to keep clearing new land. Crops such as tobacco ruined the fertile soil in only a few years. As land wore out near the coast, planters began to move up the rivers to higher land. There they built even larger plantations.

**REVIEW** Why were the earliest plantations usually built in the southern tidewater?

## Plantation Workers

On small farms every member of the family worked long hours. They worked hard, making sure that the crops were planted, harvested, stored, and shipped to market. The same was true for small plantations. As plantations grew in size,

however, planters added more workers to do the hard labor. In time, the main job of the planter's family was to watch over the work of others.

Many of the earliest plantation workers came to the colonies in the South as indentured servants. However, not all indentured servants came willingly to the English colonies. Some were sent there by the English courts to work in the colonies to pay for their crimes as a form of punishment. Other indentured servants were people who had been kidnapped and then sold in the colonies against their will.

Among the first indentured servants to be sold in the English colonies were kidnapped Africans. After the mid-1600s, however, traders were bringing thousands of Africans to the English colonies not as indentured servants but as slaves. Slaves in the colonies were sold like property at an **auction**, or public sale. Unlike indentured servants, slaves were not given their freedom after a certain length of time. They were enslaved for life. Before long, laws were passed in the colonies with a ruling that said that the children of enslaved people were also slaves.

REVIEW **Why did some people come to the colonies as indentured servants?**

## A Slave's Life

There were generally two kinds of slaves—field slaves and house slaves. Field slaves worked hard in the fields, raising cash crops for the planters to sell. Some slave owners hired **overseers** to watch the field slaves as they worked and to punish them if they did not work hard.

## Olaudah Equiano  1750?–1797

### Character Trait: Courage

Olaudah Equiano (OHL•uh•dah ek•wee•AHN•oh) was 11 years old when he and his sister were kidnapped by slave traders. Later Equiano was separated from his sister when they were sold into slavery to different owners. Equiano's owner showed him some kindness and gave him some education. When Equiano was freed from slavery, he wrote a book about his life. In the book he told about his life in Africa and spoke out against slavery. A group of English people working against slavery used Equiano's book to help with the cause to end slavery.

Olaudah Equiano's book was published in 1789.

**MULTIMEDIA BIOGRAPHIES**
Visit The Learning Site at
**www.harcourtschool.com/biographies**
to learn about other famous people.

House slaves had more contact with the planter and the planter's family. House slaves often were clothed, fed, and housed better than field slaves. Women who were house slaves did the washing, cooking, cleaning, and sewing for the household. Male house slaves drove carriages, took care of horses, and practiced skills such as carpentry. Children of house slaves were often playmates of the planters' children, at least when they were young.

Slaves were treated well or cruelly depending on their owners. Some planters took pride in being fair and kind to their slaves. There was little protection, however, for slaves who had cruel masters. Slave owners were free to beat, whip, or insult any slave as often as they chose to do so. These slaves looked only

to escape or to resist their cruel treatment. "No day ever dawns for the slave, nor is it looked for," one enslaved African later wrote. "For the slave it is all night—all night, forever."

Laws in the colonies forbade slaves to learn to read and write. By the age of 10, most enslaved children were working alongside the adults.

Enslaved people spent very long days working. At night slaves often told stories and sang songs about their homeland. Later, the Christian religion became a source of strength for slaves as they tried to deal with the hardships of slave life. Some slaves expressed their belief in the Christian religion by singing spirituals. **Spirituals** (SPIR•ih•chuh•wuhlz) are religious songs based on Bible stories.

**REVIEW** What did some slaves do when their work was finished?

## A Planter's Life

Plantations in the South were often far from one another and far from any towns. Weeks or months could go by without visitors and without news about the latest happenings. For this reason, visitors were always welcome.

Because people lived so far apart, there were few schools. Nevertheless, southern planters were among the best-educated people in the 13 English colonies. Some plantations had their own schools for the planters' children, and some hired teachers from Europe. Later, the planters' sons might go to Europe to complete their education. Girls stopped going to school by the age of 12 or 13 because planters' daughters were supposed to learn only basic skills and "to read and sew with their needle."

A planter and his wife were responsible for running a business and for taking care

Girls made samplers, like this one from 1675, to practice their sewing skills.

of all the people on the plantation. They had to clothe, feed, and provide medical care not only for their family but for all the members of their household. By the 1740s a large plantation household—family, servants, and slaves—often numbered in the hundreds.

Besides taking care of a plantation, a planter's duties also included public service. **Public service** is doing a job to help the community or society as a whole. Public service for a planter could mean serving as a judge or as a representative in the colonial assembly. Some planters served as advisers to the governor. Some performed all these duties. This tradition of public service may explain why so many planters became leaders in the 13 English colonies.

**REVIEW** How were children of planters educated?

## LESSON 2 REVIEW

**1** MAIN IDEA  How did southern plantations change as planters added more workers?

**2** WHY IT MATTERS  Why did many planters become important leaders in the 13 colonies?

**3** VOCABULARY  Use the terms **planter** and **tidewater** to describe the plantation economy.

**4** READING SKILL—Generalize  What was the life of a planter like?

**5** CULTURE  Why were spirituals important to enslaved people?

**6** CRITICAL THINKING—Analyze  What were the consequences of modifying the land to grow tobacco?

PERFORMANCE—Write a Diary Entry  Suppose that you are living on a plantation in colonial times. Take on a role, and write an entry in a diary to show what a day on the plantation is like. Share your entry with a classmate.

## ·SKILLS·
MAP AND GLOBE

# Read a Resource and Product Map

### ➡ WHY IT MATTERS

A resource and product map can help you make a generalization about a place's economy. A generalization is a statement based on facts. It is used to summarize groups of facts and to show relationships between them. Symbols for resources and products, shown in the map key, tell you where they are found, made, or grown. These symbols can help you make generalizations about the areas shown on a resource and product map.

### ➡ WHAT YOU NEED TO KNOW

In the map key on the next page, pictures stand for resources found in the 13 colonies and goods produced there. These goods were important not only because they were sold in the 13 colonies but also because they were exported for sale in England. The map shows only some of the most important goods and resources in the colonies.

### ➡ PRACTICE THE SKILL

Now that you know more about the symbols in the map key, you can use these questions as a guide for making generalizations about the economy of the 13 colonies.

1. What products appear most often on the map in the New England Colonies?
2. What generalization can you make about the kinds of work most people did in the Middle Atlantic Colonies?
3. What generalization can you make about the economy of the Southern Colonies?

### ➡ APPLY WHAT YOU LEARNED

Look through encyclopedias, atlases, and almanacs to find an example of a resource and product map. Work with a partner to make some generalizations about the economy of the place or places shown on the map.

Learn more about maps with the **GeoSkills CD-ROM.**

Iron was melted in furnaces like this one (left). Lumber was cut (right) and tobacco was dried (far right) before it was sent to England.

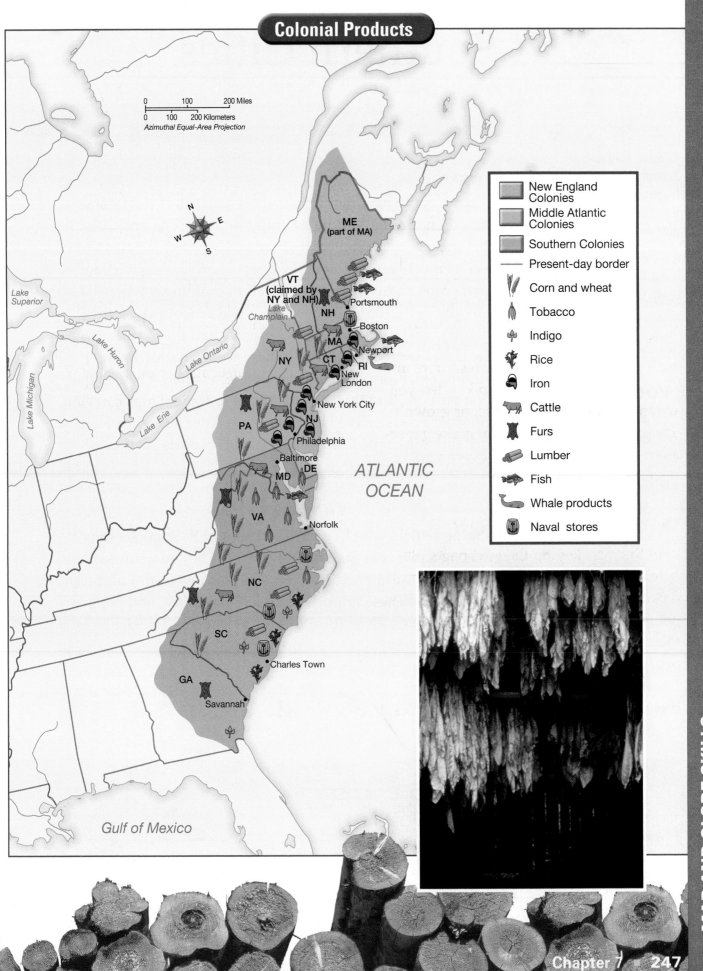

# Colonial Products

Azimuthal Equal-Area Projection

0   100   200 Miles
0   100   200 Kilometers

**Legend:**
- New England Colonies
- Middle Atlantic Colonies
- Southern Colonies
- Present-day border
- Corn and wheat
- Tobacco
- Indigo
- Rice
- Iron
- Cattle
- Furs
- Lumber
- Fish
- Whale products
- Naval stores

ME (part of MA)

VT (claimed by NY and NH)

NH

Portsmouth

Boston

MA

Newport

CT    RI

New London

NY

New York City

NJ

PA

Philadelphia

Baltimore

DE

MD

ATLANTIC OCEAN

VA

Norfolk

NC

SC

Charles Town

GA

Savannah

Gulf of Mexico

Lake Superior

Lake Michigan

Lake Huron

Lake Ontario

Lake Erie

Lake Champlain

**MAIN IDEA**
Read to learn how cities helped the Southern Colonies grow and prosper.

**WHY IT MATTERS**
Cities became important gathering places for people to share new ideas and new ways of doing things.

**VOCABULARY**
apprentice
county seat
county

# Southern Cities

1605    1655    1705    1755

1670–1730

The Southern Colonies generally had fewer towns and cities than did the Middle Atlantic and New England Colonies. This was because planters and farmers wanted to spread out over as much land as possible. They wanted to use the land to grow crops and were not interested in building towns.

By the mid-1700s, however, some settlements along the Atlantic coast of the Southern Colonies had grown into large towns and even cities. Among these were Charles Town, Wilmington, Norfolk, Baltimore, and Savannah. They all had good harbors, and they grew because of trade. Ships carrying imported goods arrived at these cities. After a few weeks in port, the ships sailed away loaded with exports such as tobacco, rice, and indigo.

## Trade Ports

Some settlers who lived inland brought their goods to port cities, where it was easy to find buyers. They sometimes traded their goods for imports that came in on ships from Europe and other places. These imports included tea, coffee, and pepper. Luxury items such as furniture, silverware, and medicine also were imported.

FAST FACT By 1760 Charles Town had become the fourth-largest city in the 13 colonies.

Many people in southern cities worked in the trade business, which helped the cities grow. Other people in the cities worked in other kinds of businesses. Some were fishers, hatmakers, tailors, and printers. Young people learned such jobs by becoming **apprentices**. A child would move in as an apprentice with the family of a skilled worker and help in the family's business for several years. In this way, a young person learned a skill.

**REVIEW** How did people make a living in southern cities?

## Charles Town

Charles Town, South Carolina, became the largest city in the Southern Colonies. In 1688 there were only about 300 people living there. Only 20 years later, in 1708, Charles Town's population had grown to about 6,000 people. An early visitor to the port at Charles Town predicted the city would grow when he said, "There were sixteen ships which had come to trade. The great number of ships will soon make this a busy town."

From 1670 to the mid-1700s, Charles Town was the center of life in South Carolina. During this time most of the people in South Carolina lived in Charles Town or in the area around it. Many residents of Charles Town enjoyed a social life that included dancing, seeing plays, and attending races and concerts.

Merchants and planters had the most power in Charles Town's society. Many wealthy planters in South Carolina lived in Charles Town during the months when insects infested the wetlands on the plantations where rice was grown.

**REVIEW** Where did most people in South Carolina live between the late 1600s and mid-1700s?

· **GEOGRAPHY** ·

### Charles Town
**Understanding Places and Regions**

Charles Town was located along the middle of South Carolina's coast where the Ashley and Cooper Rivers joined to form Charles Town Harbor. Until the settling of Georgia in 1733, South Carolina served as a buffer, or shield, between the Spanish in Florida and the other English colonies in North America.

## Other Southern Ports

The port city of Wilmington, North Carolina, was started in the 1720s after colonists from South Carolina began moving north along the Atlantic coast to the Cape Fear River. They were looking for fertile soil for establishing plantations. Instead, they found lots of trees. They brought in workers to cut the trees and to build sawmills. They also produced naval stores. From the port at Wilmington, the settlers shipped naval stores and lumber to England as exports.

Wilmington's location on the Cape Fear River helped it prosper. The river is deep enough to be used by large ships, and it flows directly into the Atlantic Ocean. Immigrants also helped Wilmington grow and prosper. They came from other colonies and from many parts of Europe. Some of the town's earliest settlers came from northern Scotland. The first Africans to come to Wilmington were brought as slaves. Eventually, free Africans also lived there. Some were farmers. Others worked as painters, tailors, carpenters, and blacksmiths.

Other coastal towns in the South grew quickly, too. Savannah became the Georgia Colony's chief port. It also served as the capital city of Georgia until the late 1700s. Norfolk, Virginia, grew because it served as a port where tobacco and naval stores were shipped to England. Lumber from North Carolina was also sent to Norfolk to be shipped out to England.

Items like this silver gravy boat could be purchased at a general store.

Baltimore's location near Chesapeake Bay helped it become a busy port city.

Baltimore, Maryland, was founded in 1729 on the Patapsco River, which flows into Chesapeake Bay. It prospered because a port was needed for the growing amounts of grain and tobacco being produced in Maryland and other nearby colonies. It quickly became a major port and a center for shipbuilding. Baltimore's shipyards later became well known for improving the way ships were built.

**REVIEW** How did immigrants affect the port city of Wilmington, North Carolina?

## County Seats

As more people in Southern Colonies moved inland in search of more farmland, some inland towns developed and grew. Most of these towns were county seats. A **county seat** was the main town for a **county**, a large part of a colony. Over time, planters and farmers who once used brokers or brought their crops to trade in coastal cities began to depend more and more on county seats as places to trade.

Several times a year plantation and farm families would pack their bags, dress in their finest clothes, and travel to the county seat. People went to church, held dances, and traded crops for goods there. Some plantation owners bought and sold slaves there. Most county seats had a general store, a courthouse, and a jail. White men who owned land and other property met at the county seat to make laws and to vote for leaders.

**REVIEW** Why were county seats important to people living on farms and plantations?

**LESSON 3 REVIEW**

**Summary Time Line**

1670 — 1700 — 1730

**1670**
Charles Town becomes the center of life in South Carolina

**1729**
The city of Baltimore is founded in Maryland

❶ **MAIN IDEA** How did cities help the Southern Colonies grow and prosper?

❷ **WHY IT MATTERS** In what ways have cities become important gathering places for people to share new ideas and new ways of doing things?

❸ **VOCABULARY** Use the term **apprentice** in a sentence to describe how some young people learned jobs in the Southern Colonies.

❹ **TIME LINE** What happened in 1670?

❺ **READING SKILL—Generalize** What was life like for people who lived in cities in the Southern Colonies?

❻ **ECONOMICS** What was the economic reason for colonists to settle Wilmington, North Carolina?

❼ **CRITICAL THINKING—Evaluate** What were the advantages and disadvantages of building more towns in the Southern Colonies?

**PERFORMANCE—Make a Map** Using maps in your textbook and other sources, draw a map showing the location of the southern towns and cities that you read about in the lesson. Near each city draw pictures of products that helped that city grow and prosper.

## USE YOUR READING SKILLS

Complete this graphic organizer by using facts you have learned from the chapter to make generalizations about the Southern Colonies. A copy of this graphic organizer appears on page 71 of the Activity Book.

### The Southern Colonies

**1. Settlement Of The South**

| FACTS | | | | GENERALIZATION |
|---|---|---|---|---|
| By 1700 Virginia is the largest English colony in North America. | | | → | |

**2. Southern Plantations**

| FACTS | | | | GENERALIZATION |
|---|---|---|---|---|
| Planters grow cash crops. | | | → | |

**3. Southern Cities**

| FACTS | | | | GENERALIZATION |
|---|---|---|---|---|
| In 20 years, Charles Town's population grows from 300 to 6,000 people. | | | → | |

## THINK  WRITE

**Write an Advertisement**   When a colony was first established, colonial leaders sometimes found it difficult to attract settlers. Write an advertisement for the Georgia Colony, describing the benefits of moving there.

**Write a Story**   During colonial times, young people who wanted to learn a special skill, such as hatmaking or printing, became apprentices. Write a story about a young person who moves in with a skilled worker's family in order to learn a skill.

1675     1700     1725     1750

**1663**
The colony of
Carolina is
established

**1712**
North and
South Carolina
are formed

**1729**
The city of
Baltimore
is founded

**1733**
The settlement
of Savannah is
established

## USE THE TIME LINE

Use the chapter summary time line to answer these questions.

**1** When was the Carolina Colony established?

**2** Was Baltimore founded before or after Savannah?

## USE VOCABULARY

Use a term from this list to complete each of the sentences that follow.

> indentured servants (p. 234)
>
> constitution (p. 235)
>
> broker (p. 241)
>
> spirituals (p. 244)
>
> county seat (p. 250)

**3** Southern plantation owners often sold their cash crops through a ____.

**4** A ____ is a written plan of government.

**5** When ____ finished their time of service, they were legally free.

**6** Several times a year southern farm families would travel to their local ____.

**7** Slaves often sang ____ when they gathered together at night.

## RECALL FACTS

Answer these questions.

**8** What was the most profitable cash crop produced by the Georgia Colony?

**9** Why were there few community schools in the Southern Colonies?

**10** How did the location of the city of Wilmington, North Carolina, help it prosper?

Write the letter of the best choice.

**11** **TEST PREP** Planters had to start building their plantations farther up the rivers because—
  **A** floods often destroyed their homes.
  **B** their homes were sometimes attacked.
  **C** crops like tobacco ruined the soil.
  **D** the English government required it.

**12** **TEST PREP** The largest southern cities were Charles Town, Wilmington, Norfolk and—
  **F** Boston.
  **G** Baltimore.
  **H** Philadelphia.
  **J** Providence.

## THINK CRITICALLY

**13** How do you think the demand for indigo affected South Carolina plantation owners?

**14** Why were southern waterways important?

## APPLY SKILLS

### Tell Fact from Opinion

**15** Write a news story that includes both facts and opinions. Then exchange stories with a classmate. Find three facts and three opinions in your classmate's story.

### Read a Resource and Product Map

Use the map on page 247 to answer these questions.

**16** What products appear most often on the map in the Middle Atlantic Colonies?

**17** What generalization can you make about the kinds of work most people did in the New England Colonies?

# *Colonial* Williamsburg

## GET READY

Colonial Williamsburg is the restored and rebuilt capital of eighteenth-century Virginia. The town is a living-history museum where you can experience the sights, sounds, and smells of colonial life. You can talk with people in historical costumes who stroll the streets or tend their shops. Guides bring history to life by portraying actual citizens who lived in Williamsburg in the 1700s. In Colonial Williamsburg, history is more than just names and dates. It is the story of people just like you who lived in another time.

## WHAT TO SEE

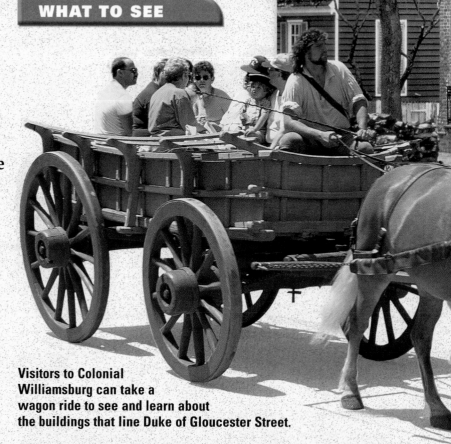

Visitors to Colonial Williamsburg can take a wagon ride to see and learn about the buildings that line Duke of Gloucester Street.

Near the James Geddy House, You can take turns at hoop-rolling, stilt-walking, ninepins, and other colonial children's games.

## LOCATE IT

VIRGINIA

Colonial Williamsburg

In this shop a violin-maker uses traditional tools to create an instrument.

Milliners (MIH•luh•nehrz) were busy in a time when women's hats were an important part of their outfits. The millinery shop displayed the latest styles in bonnets.

The Capitol is where the Virginia House of Burgesses met to pass laws and debate important issues of the day.

## TAKE A FIELD TRIP

**GO ONLINE**

**A VIRTUAL TOUR**
Visit The Learning Site at **www.harcourtschool.com/tours** to take virtual tours of other historic sites.

**CNN Turner Le@rning®**

**A VIDEO TOUR**
Check your media center or classroom library for a videotape tour of Colonial Williamsburg.

JAMES CRAIG JEWELLER

# 3 Review and Test Preparation

## USE VOCABULARY

Identify the term that correctly matches each definition.

public office (p. 192)

militia (p. 221)

debtor (p. 236)

planter (p. 241)

**1** a person who was in prison for owing money

**2** a person who grew large amounts of cash crops

**3** a job for the community

**4** a volunteer army

## RECALL FACTS

Answer these questions.

**5** What kinds of goods did the New England colonists produce from livestock?

**6** Why were the Middle Atlantic Colonies also known as the "breadbasket" colonies?

Write the letter of the best choice.

**7** **TEST PREP**   Roger Williams received help from—
A Governor John Winthrop.
B French fur traders.
C Dutch merchants.
D the Narragansett Indians.

**8** **TEST PREP**   The triangular trade routes connected England, the English colonies in North America, and the—
F east coast of South America.
G west coast of Spain.
H west coast of Africa.
J east coast of Mexico.

**Visual Summary**

1625

1628   **The Puritans settle in Massachusetts Bay Colony**   p. 188

1675   **King Philip's War begins**   p. 198

1682   **Quakers settle in Pennsylvania**   p. 213

**⑨ TEST PREP** Most people in the Middle Atlantic Colonies earned a living by—

**A** producing naval stores.

**B** farming.

**C** fur trading.

**D** building ships.

## THINK CRITICALLY

**⑩** Why do you think England wanted its colonists to buy only English-made imports?

**⑪** Why do you think the Dutch settlers in New Netherland did not try to fight the English who took over the colony in 1664?

**⑫** Why do you think Virginia was the most important of the 13 colonies to England?

**⑬** How would living on a plantation have been different from living in or near a town?

## APPLY SKILLS

### Read a Resource and Product Map

Use the map on this page to answer the following questions.

MAP AND GLOBE SKILLS

**⑭** What products appear most often on the map in the Middle Atlantic Colonies?

**⑮** Which two colonies produced iron?

**⑯** Which two colonies produced lumber?

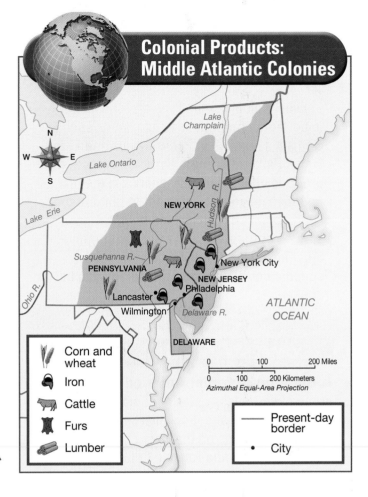

**Colonial Products: Middle Atlantic Colonies**

Lake Champlain

Lake Ontario

Lake Erie

Hudson R.

NEW YORK

Susquehanna R.

PENNSYLVANIA

Ohio R.

New York City

NEW JERSEY

Philadelphia

Lancaster

Wilmington

Delaware R.

ATLANTIC OCEAN

DELAWARE

*Legend:*
- Corn and wheat
- Iron
- Cattle
- Furs
- Lumber

0   100   200 Miles
0   100   200 Kilometers
*Azimuthal Equal-Area Projection*

— Present-day border
• City

**⑰** What generalization can you make about the colonies that produced corn and wheat?

**⑱** What generalization can you make about the economy of the Middle Atlantic Colonies?

1750

**1730s** The Great Awakening spreads throughout the colonies   p. 215

**1733** James Oglethorpe settles the Georgia Colony   p. 236

**1750s** Williamsburg, Virginia becomes a large city   p. 238

# Unit Activities

**GO ONLINE** Visit The Learning Site at www.harcourtschool.com/socialstudies/activities for additional activities.

## Design a Monument

Every colony had individuals who made important contributions to its history, such as Benjamin Franklin in Pennsylvania and Eliza Lucas Pickney in South Carolina. Work in a group to choose an individual from the unit and then design a monument to that person. Your monument can include such things as statues or gardens. Make sure your monument includes something that shows the specific contributions of the person you have chosen.

## COMPLETE THE UNIT PROJECT

**A Book on Colonial America** Work with a group of your classmates to complete the unit project—a book about colonial America. Review your notes on the New England Colonies, the Middle Atlantic Colonies, and the Southern Colonies. Then write a description of each region. Work together to illustrate your book with both drawings and pictures either cut out of magazines or printed from the Internet. Write captions describing the illustrations and give your book a title. Share your completed book with the rest of the class.

## VISIT YOUR LIBRARY

■ *Finding Providence: The Story of Roger Williams* by Avi. HarperCollins.

■ *The Story of William Penn* by Aliki. Simon & Schuster.

■ *James Printer: A Novel of Rebellion* by Paul Samuel Jacobs. Scholastic.

# The American Revolution

The Liberty Bell

Valley Forge National Historical Park, Pennsylvania

# The American Revolution

❝ **By uniting we stand,
by dividing we fall.** ❞

—John Dickinson, "The Liberty Song," 1768

## Preview the Content

Scan the chapter and lesson titles. Use them to make an outline of the unit. Write down any questions that occur to you about the American Revolution.

## Preview the Vocabulary

**Multiple Meanings**  A word can often have several meanings. You may know one meaning but not another. Use the Glossary to look up each of the terms listed below. Then use each term in a sentence.

FORK ⇒ _____  OLIVE BRANCH ⇒ _____

GAP ⇒ _____  PIONEER ⇒ _____

MONOPOLY ⇒ _____  QUARTER ⇒ _____

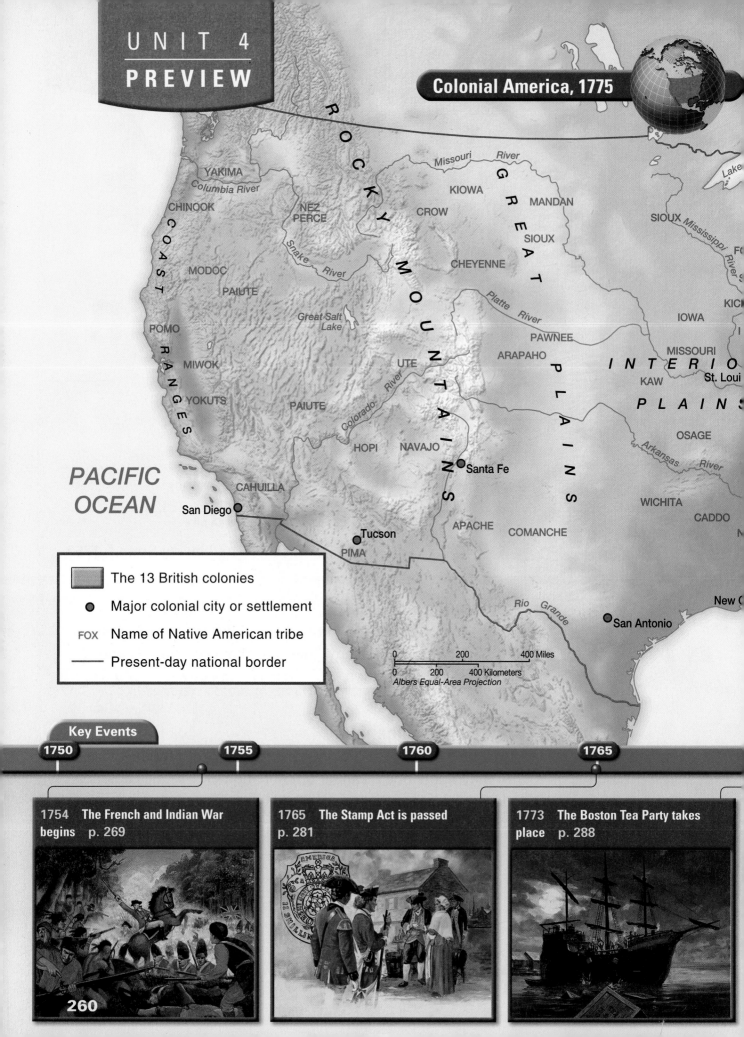

## Colonial America, 1775

ROCKY MOUNTAINS

GREAT PLAINS

COAST RANGES

INTERIOR PLAINS

Columbia River

Missouri River

Snake River

Platte River

Colorado River

Great Salt Lake

Arkansas River

Mississippi River

Rio Grande

YAKIMA

CHINOOK

NEZ PERCE

KIOWA

CROW

MANDAN

SIOUX

SIOUX

CHEYENNE

MODOC

PAIUTE

POMO

MIWOK

YOKUTS

PAIUTE

UTE

PAWNEE

ARAPAHO

KAW

OSAGE

IOWA

MISSOURI

KICK

HOPI

NAVAJO

Santa Fe

APACHE

COMANCHE

WICHITA

CADDO

CAHUILLA

San Diego

Tucson

PIMA

San Antonio

St. Loui

New

**PACIFIC OCEAN**

### Legend

- The 13 British colonies
- ● Major colonial city or settlement
- FOX  Name of Native American tribe
- —  Present-day national border

0    200    400 Miles
0    200    400 Kilometers
Albers Equal-Area Projection

## Key Events

**1750**   **1755**   **1760**   **1765**

**1754** The French and Indian War begins p. 269

**1765** The Stamp Act is passed p. 281

**1773** The Boston Tea Party takes place p. 288

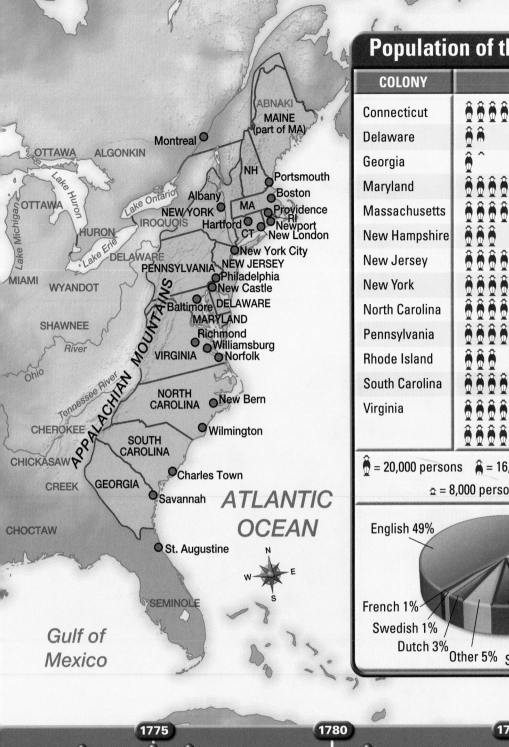

Map of the 13 Colonies region, showing Native American groups (OTTAWA, ALGONKIN, ABNAKI, HURON, IROQUOIS, MIAMI, WYANDOT, SHAWNEE, CHEROKEE, CHICKASAW, CREEK, CHOCTAW, SEMINOLE), the Great Lakes (Lake Michigan, Lake Huron, Lake Erie, Lake Ontario), rivers (Ohio River, Tennessee River), and the APPALACHIAN MOUNTAINS.

Cities and places labeled: Montreal, Portsmouth, Boston, Albany, Providence, Hartford, Newport, New London, New York City, Philadelphia, New Castle, Baltimore, Richmond, Williamsburg, Norfolk, New Bern, Wilmington, Charles Town, Savannah, St. Augustine.

Colonies labeled: MAINE (part of MA), NH, MA, CT, RI, NEW YORK, NEW JERSEY, PENNSYLVANIA, DELAWARE, MARYLAND, VIRGINIA, NORTH CAROLINA, SOUTH CAROLINA, GEORGIA.

ATLANTIC OCEAN, Gulf of Mexico.

Compass rose: N, E, S, W.

## Population of the 13 Colonies, 1750

| COLONY | POPULATION |
| --- | --- |
| Connecticut | 🧍🧍🧍🧍🧍🧍🧍🧍🧍^ |
| Delaware | 🧍🧍 |
| Georgia | 🧍^ |
| Maryland | 🧍🧍🧍🧍🧍🧍🧍 |
| Massachusetts | 🧍🧍🧍🧍🧍🧍🧍🧍🧍🧍🧍☿ |
| New Hampshire | 🧍🧍🧍 |
| New Jersey | 🧍🧍🧍🧍🧍🧍 |
| New York | 🧍🧍🧍🧍🧍🧍🧍🧍 |
| North Carolina | 🧍🧍🧍🧍🧍🧍🧍 |
| Pennsylvania | 🧍🧍🧍🧍🧍🧍🧍🧍🧍🧍🧍 |
| Rhode Island | 🧍🧍🧍 |
| South Carolina | 🧍🧍🧍🧍🧍^ |
| Virginia | 🧍🧍🧍🧍🧍🧍🧍🧍🧍🧍🧍🧍🧍🧍🧍🧍🧍☿ |

🧍 = 20,000 persons    🧍 = 16,000 persons    🧍 = 12,000 persons

☿ = 8,000 persons    ^ = 4,000 persons

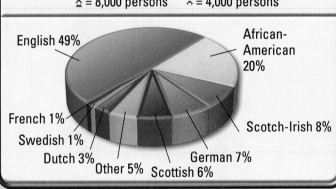

Pie chart:
- English 49%
- African-American 20%
- Scotch-Irish 8%
- German 7%
- Scottish 6%
- Other 5%
- Dutch 3%
- Swedish 1%
- French 1%

Timeline: 1775 — 1780 — 1785 — 1790

1775   **The American Revolution begins**   p. 291

1776   **The Declaration of Independence is signed**   p. 306

1781   **The British surrender at Yorktown, in Virginia**   p. 326

261

# YANKEE DOODLE

People have been singing some version of "Yankee Doodle" since the 1700s. The melody is an old English tune, but no one knows for certain who wrote its original words. Some historians credit Richard Shuckburgh, a British army doctor during the French and Indian War. His words poked fun at soldiers from New England. New Englanders were sometimes called Yankees, and *doodle* means "a foolish person."

During the American Revolution, American freedom fighters sang other words to "Yankee Doodle" and often whistled the tune in battle. Their words often poked fun at the British soldiers.

In time "Yankee Doodle" became an important symbol of the United States and of what Americans believed. Read now to discover the words to a version of "Yankee Doodle" that Americans sang.

Yankee doodle went to town,
　　Riding on a pony;
Stuck a feather in his hat
　　And called it Macaroni.

Chorus:
Yankee Doodle keep it up,
　　Yankee Doodle dandy,
Mind the Music and the step,
　　And with the girls be handy.

> Macaroni  fancy trimming, like gold braid
> dandy  a fancy young man

Father and I went down to camp,
   Along with Captain Good'in,
And there we saw the men and boys
   As thick as has-ty pud-din'.

And there we saw a thousand men,
   As rich as Squire David;
And what they wasted ev'ry day,
   I wish it could be sav'ed.

And there I saw a little keg,
   Its head all made of leather,
They knocked on it with little sticks,
   To call the folks together.

> **hasty puddin'** a thick cornmeal mush
> **keg** small barrel

And there was Captain Washington
   Upon a slapping stallion,
A-giving orders to his men;
   I guess there was a million.

And the ribbons on his hat,
   They looked so very fine, ah!
I wanted peskily to get
   To give to my Jemima.

And there I saw a swamping gun,
   Large as a log of maple,
Upon a mighty little cart;
   A load for father's cattle.

> **swamping** big or heavy

And every time they fired it off,
    It took a horn of powder;
It made a noise like father's gun,
    Only a nation louder.

The troopers, too, would gallop up
    And fire right in our faces;
It scared me almost half to death
    To see them run such races.

It scared me so I hooked it off,
    Nor stopped, as I remember,
Nor turned about till I got home,
    Locked up in mother's chamber.

**hooked** to run off quickly
**chamber** bedroom

## Analyze the Literature

❶ Why do you think the British and the Americans poked fun at each other?

❷ Work with a partner to interpret the meaning of each stanza in "Yankee Doodle." Then share your interpretation with the class.

# READ A BOOK

# START THE UNIT PROJECT

**The History Show** With your classmates, plan a history show about the American Revolution. As you read this unit, take notes about the key people and events. Your notes will help you decide which people and events to use in your history show.

# USE TECHNOLOGY

Visit The Learning Site at **www.harcourtschool.com/social studies** for additional activities, primary sources, and other resources to use in this unit.

## MINUTE MAN NATIONAL HISTORIC PARK

Visitors to Minute Man National Historic Park can see part of the Battle Road. In April 1775 American colonists and British soldiers fought alongside this road which ran from Boston to Concord. In this photograph, reenactors are marching across Concord's North Bridge.

**LOCATE IT**

Boston

MASSACHUSETTS

# Uniting the Colonies

" Here once the embattled farmers stood,
And fired the shot heard round the world. "

—Ralph Waldo Emerson,
"Concord Hymn," 1837

## CHAPTER READING SKILL

### Cause and Effect

A **cause** is an event or action that makes something else happen. An **effect** is what happens as a result of that event or action.

**As you read this chapter, list the causes and effects of key events.**

| What Caused the Event | → | Event |
|---|---|---|
| CAUSE | → | EFFECT |

**MAIN IDEA**
Read to find out why conflict over land in North America led to a war between Britain and France.

**WHY IT MATTERS**
The war between Britain and France determined who would control North America.

**VOCABULARY**
revolution
fork
ally
alliance
congress
delegate
Parliament

# The French and Indian War Begins

**1750–1755**

The events that led to the American Revolution began about 20 years before the 13 colonies cut ties with England, or Britain, as it became known. A **revolution** is a sudden, complete change, such as the overthrow of an established government. The first of the events was a war in North America between Britain and France that came to be called the French and Indian War. The war began as a competition between Britain and France for control of the Ohio Valley region.

## Rivalry in the Ohio Valley

The Ohio Valley region stretches about 1,000 miles (1,609 km) along the Ohio River from the Appalachian Mountains to the Mississippi River. Many Native Americans lived in this region before Europeans arrived, but the French and the British each believed this land belonged to them because of earlier exploration and settlement. To the French, the Ohio Valley was an important link between France's holdings in Canada and Louisiana. The British, particularly those in the colonies of Pennsylvania and Virginia, saw it as an area for trade and growth.

By about 1750 the French had moved to make their claim to the Ohio Valley stronger.

FAST FACT — When a British soldier was hit by a bullet, his bright red uniform kept nearby soldiers from knowing he was bleeding. This helped prevent the other soldiers from getting scared and running away from the battle.

They sent soldiers into the region to drive out the British traders. They also began building a line of forts near the eastern end of the valley. The British viewed this move as an act of war and took action.

In 1753 Lieutenant (loo•TEH•nuhnt) Governor Robert Dinwiddie of Virginia sent young George Washington, then 21 years old, across the Appalachians to order the French to leave. When the French replied that they intended to stay, Dinwiddie sent a small force of soldiers from Virginia. Their orders were to build a fort at the Forks of the Ohio River, where the city of Pittsburgh, Pennsylvania, now stands. A **fork** is a place where two rivers join to form a third.

The Virginians had barely finished the fort when the French attacked it. The French drove off the Virginians and built a larger fort on that site. They called it Fort Duquesne (doo•KAYN) in honor of the Marquis (mahr•KEE) de Duquesne, the newly appointed governor general of New France. Unaware of the French attack, Dinwiddie sent young George Washington to the Forks of the Ohio River to reinforce the Virginians' fort.

## North America in 1754

British
French
Spanish
Russian
Disputed
Unclaimed

**Regions** By the 1750s much of North America had been claimed by Europeans.

❖ Which two groups of Europeans claimed land east and west of the Ohio Valley?

**LOCATE IT**

PENNSYLVANIA

Fort Necessity

A re-creation of the original Fort Necessity can be seen at Fort Necessity National Battlefield near Farmington, Pennsylvania. In this photograph, reenactors take on colonial roles.

## George Washington  1732–1799

### Character Trait: Perseverance

The action at Fort Necessity was the first major event in the military career of George Washington. It was the only time he ever surrendered to an enemy. Washington returned to Williamsburg two weeks later, discouraged about the battle. Instead of blaming him for losing the battle, the colonists praised Washington and his soldiers for their bravery. The colonists would later praise Washington for even braver deeds as he led the colonial army in the Revolutionary War.

**MULTIMEDIA BIOGRAPHIES**
Visit The Learning Site at www.harcourtschool.com/biographies to learn about other famous people.

In April 1754 Washington left Williamsburg with an army of 150 Virginians. On their way to the fort, the Virginians surprised a small group of French soldiers on patrol. Thinking "we might be attacked by considerable forces," Washington later wrote, the Virginians built a makeshift fort that they called Fort Necessity.

Within days a large force of more than 600 French soldiers and 100 of their Indian **allies**, or friends in war, attacked Fort Necessity. Outnumbered, the Virginians surrendered in what turned out to be the opening battle of the French and Indian War. The French let Washington and his soldiers return to Virginia.

**REVIEW** How did the French try to strengthen their claim to the Ohio Valley?

## The Albany Plan of Union

As a result of Washington's defeat at Fort Necessity, the British government in London urged its colonial leaders to meet with the Iroquois. The British wanted to be sure of the Iroquois's loyalty in the war against the French. By the mid-1700s both Britain and France had formed alliances with many of the Native American tribes in the Ohio Valley. An **alliance** is a formal agreement among nations, states, groups, or individuals. The Iroquois had become one of Britain's most important Native American allies.

In June and July of 1754, colonial leaders met at Albany, New York, in what was called the Albany Congress. A **congress** is a formal meeting of representatives. Seven colonies sent representatives,

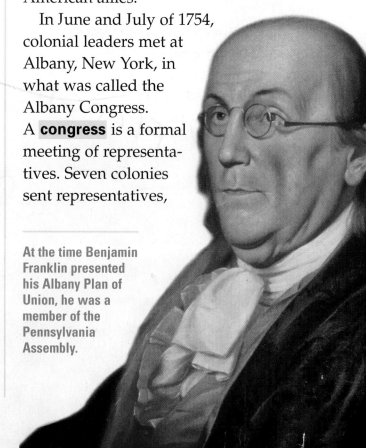

At the time Benjamin Franklin presented his Albany Plan of Union, he was a member of the Pennsylvania Assembly.

or **delegates**, including Benjamin Franklin from Pennsylvania.

Franklin and the others knew that the colonists needed more than Indian allies to defeat the French. The colonies had to be united in the fight against the French. Franklin presented his Albany Plan of Union. It was one of the first proposals for uniting all of the colonies, except for Georgia, under one government.

To get public support for his plan, Benjamin Franklin published the now famous "Join, or Die" cartoon. It first appeared in the *Pennsylvania Gazette,* one of the most widely read newspapers of that time. Franklin based the cartoon's saying on an old tale about snakes. The story said that a snake cut into pieces would come to life again if put back together before sunset.

Franklin wanted the pieces of the snake—the colonies—to come together to survive. However, in 1754, the American colonies were not yet willing to work together for a common goal.

**REVIEW** What was Benjamin Franklin's role in the Albany Congress?

## Braddock's Defeat

As the French and Indian War continued, the British colonists soon knew that they needed more help if they were to win the war. So **Parliament**, the lawmaking body of the British government in London, sent an army to the colonies to help fight the French and their Indian allies. General Edward Braddock commanded the British forces. He invited George Washington along as an adviser.

Braddock's first goal was to capture Fort Duquesne. In April 1755 he and more than 1,800 British and colonial troops began the long march to the fort. Washington later described how the soldiers looked in their bright, colorful uniforms—British red and colonial blue—marching off against the deep green of the forest.

Not far from where Washington and his men had built Fort Necessity, the British met a force of about 900 French and Indian soldiers. For two hours the French and their Indian allies fired at the British from behind trees and boulders.

Benjamin Franklin hoped this simple cartoon would help convince the colonies to approve his Albany Plan of Union. The part of the snake labeled *N.E.* represented the New England Colonies.

JOIN, or DIE.

General Braddock (above) and his troops panicked when the French and Indians fired on them from behind rocks and trees.

The British, trained to fight in open fields, had never fought an enemy this way. They "broke and ran," Washington later wrote, "as sheep before the hounds." When the battle ended, two-thirds of the British were dead or wounded. Braddock was one of those killed.

Braddock's loss left the British colonists in the Ohio Valley without protection. For the next two years, the French and their Indian allies carried out attacks against those colonists.

**REVIEW** What was a major cause of General Braddock's loss?

**LESSON 1 REVIEW**

**Summary Time Line**

1750 — 1755

1754
Fort Necessity is attacked
Albany Congress meets

1755
General Braddock is defeated

❶ **MAIN IDEA** How did conflicts over land lead to a war between Britain and France?

❷ **WHY IT MATTERS** How do you think the outcome of the French and Indian War would affect the colonization of North America?

❸ **VOCABULARY** Use the words **congress** and **delegate** in a sentence about the Albany Plan of Union.

❹ **TIME LINE** Which event took place first, General Braddock's defeat or the attack on Fort Necessity?

❺ **READING SKILL—Cause and Effect** What caused the French and Indian War?

❻ **GEOGRAPHY** Where was the opening battle fought in the French and Indian War?

❼ **HISTORY** What was George Washington's role in the French and Indian War?

❽ **CRITICAL THINKING—Analyze** Why is the Albany Plan of Union important in American history?

**PERFORMANCE—Draw a Cartoon**
Imagine that you have been asked to draw a cartoon different from the one Franklin published to show support for the Albany Plan of Union. Draw your cartoon and share it with a classmate.

# Britain Wins North America

**1750** ——————— **1770** ——————— **1790**

**1758–1763**

**MAIN IDEA**
Read to learn that the colonists were eager to settle in Britain's newly won lands.

**WHY IT MATTERS**
British leaders and the colonists began to disagree over land rights and British control of the colonies.

**VOCABULARY**
proclamation
bill of rights
pioneer
gap

For the first two years of fighting, the French and Indian War had been only a North American conflict. In 1756, however, it became a world war, known as the Seven Years War, with battles fought in Europe and Asia, as well as in North America. To win the war, William Pitt, Britain's new leader of Parliament, decided to focus on North America. He sent more troops and more supplies there and eventually turned the war in Britain's favor.

## The British Road to Victory

In 1758 the British captured three French forts—Duquesne at the Forks of the Ohio River, and Louisbourg and Frontenac, in what is now Canada. The following year they took forts at Crown Point, Niagara, and Ticonderoga in present-day New York. The British also attacked French forces near the city of Quebec in Canada. In September 1759 General James Wolfe's British troops defeated French forces under the command of the Marquis de Montcalm on the Plains of Abraham, near Quebec.

During the next year, the British closed a circle of troops and ships around French Canada.

William Pitt's leadership helped the British win many battles against the French, including the one at Fort Ticonderoga (left).

# The French and Indian War, 1754–1763

Lake Superior

NEW FRANCE

Quebec

Ft. Beauséjour

Ft. Louisbourg

MAINE
(part of Mass.)

Montreal

St. Lawrence River

Lake Huron

Lake Michigan

Lake Ontario

Ft. Frontenac

Ft. Ticonderoga

Ft. Crown Point

Ft. Halifax

NEW HAMPSHIRE

Ft. William Henry

Ft. Edward

Boston

Ft. Oswego

Ft. Niagara

NEW YORK

MASSACHUSETTS

RHODE ISLAND

CONNECTICUT

Lake Erie

Ft. Presqu' Isle

Ft. Le Boeuf

New York City

PENNSYLVANIA

Ft. Duquesne

Ft. Ligonier

Philadelphia

NEW JERSEY

Ft. Necessity

Baltimore

DELAWARE

Ft. Cumberland

MARYLAND

Ohio River

VIRGINIA

Williamsburg

Mississippi River

LOUISIANA

NORTH CAROLINA

ATLANTIC OCEAN

SOUTH CAROLINA

Wilmington

GEORGIA

Charles Town

N
W E
S

|  | 100 |  | 200 Miles |
| 0 | 100 | 200 Kilometers |

Albers Equal-Area Projection

NEW SPAIN

New Orleans

St Augustine

Gulf of Mexico

FLORIDA

60°W

45°N

60°W

40°N

35°N

65°N

30°N

75°W

70°W

85°W

25°N

80°W

| | British territory | | British fort |
| | French territory | | French fort |
| | Spanish territory | | Major battle |
| | Disputed territory | | Present-day border |

**GEOGRAPHY THEME**

**Location** Many British colonists felt threatened by the location of the French forts.

❔ At which French fort in present-day Pennsylvania was a major battle fought?

Finally, in 1760, after the British captured Montreal, another major French city, the French gave up. Fighting, however, continued in Europe.

In the closing months of the war in North America, Spain joined with France in the fight against the British. Because of its superior sea power, however, Britain defeated Spanish forces in 1762. To make up for Spain's losses in the war, France gave Spain most of Louisiana and part of what is now Florida.

The French and Indian War finally ended in Europe and in North America in 1763, when the French and the British signed a peace treaty in Paris. Under the terms of the Treaty of Paris, France gave most of its lands in present-day Canada to Britain. France also gave up claim to most of the lands between the Appalachian Mountains and the Mississippi River. Also as a result of the Treaty of Paris, Britain received Florida from Spain.

**REVIEW** **What parts of North America were given to Britain in the Treaty of Paris?**

## Pontiac's Rebellion

Now that the lands between the Appalachians and the Mississippi were under British control, many colonists began to settle there. The Native Americans who lived there, however, did not welcome these newcomers.

Chief Pontiac (PAHN•tee•ak) of the Ottawa tribe wanted to stop the loss of Indian hunting lands. So Pontiac and other Indian leaders united the tribes of the Great Lakes and Ohio Valley region to fight against the settlers.

In May 1763 Pontiac and his united tribes began attacking British forts in what is now western Pennsylvania, Ohio, Michigan, and Indiana. Most were destroyed. Two of the outposts that survived were Fort Detroit and Fort Pitt, once known as Fort Duquesne.

Pontiac and his forces attacked the forts to get guns and supplies, which in the past they had gotten from the French. However, as winter came, many Indian fighters signed peace treaties with the British and began to return to their homes. Without supplies or soldiers, Pontiac had to give up control of the British forts.

**REVIEW** What caused Pontiac's Rebellion?

After losing a battle at Bushy Run, in Pennsylvania, Chief Pontiac refused to sign a peace treaty.

## The Proclamation of 1763

Many British leaders in London blamed Pontiac's Rebellion on the back-country traders and settlers. They believed that these colonists did not have the right to claim or buy land in the region. The British government decided that stopping the westward movement of its colonists was the only way to end the fighting and prevent further trouble. To do this, the British king, George III, issued the Proclamation of 1763. A **proclamation** is an order from a country's leader to its citizens.

The Proclamation of 1763 said that British colonists could not buy land west of the Appalachians from the Indians, hunt on it, or explore it. Settlers already living there were to leave at once. George III said the lands west of the Appalachians were to be used only by the Native Americans. The king hoped the order would prevent more wars between the colonists and the Native Americans.

Indian leaders were pleased that the British king wanted to keep the colonists off their land. The colonists, however, were furious. They felt the proclamation took away their right as British citizens to travel where they wanted. As British citizens, the American colonists had the same rights as British citizens living in Britain. Those rights were listed in the English Bill of Rights which Parliament had created in 1689. A **bill of rights** is a list of rights. The English Bill of Rights said that the government could not take certain rights away from the people.

The colonists grew even more upset when the king ordered British soldiers to remain in North America to protect the newly won lands. The colonists felt this action also took away their rights. They became even angrier when the king gave his colonial governors greater authority over the colonies.

The colonists had not expected these changes. They had hoped to gain more authority to govern themselves. Instead, they now had to obey even stricter laws made by a government far away.

**REVIEW** **What changes took place in the government of the colonies after the French and Indian War?**

## Americans Continue West

The Proclamation of 1763 did not stop colonial pioneers from continuing their push west into the frontier. A **pioneer** is a person who first settles a new place. Daniel Boone was one of the earliest and best-known colonial pioneers to travel west across the Appalachian Mountains.

During the French and Indian War, Boone met John Finley, a British fur trader. Finley told Boone stories about visiting a wonderful land west of the Appalachians.

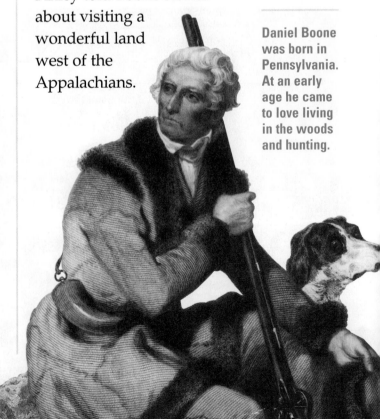

Daniel Boone was born in Pennsylvania. At an early age he came to love living in the woods and hunting.

Daniel Boone leads pioneers through the Cumberland Gap in this painting by George Caleb Bingham.

In time, colonists began to call this land Kentucky, which comes from an Indian word for "meadowland."

After the war, Boone tried to reach this land, but he could not find a way over the mountains. In 1769, with Finley's help, Boone found an Indian trail that he fol- lowed across the Appalachians through what is now the Cumberland Gap. A **gap** is an opening, or low place, between mountains. The route Boone followed was later widened for wagons and became known as the Wilderness Road.

**REVIEW** Who was Daniel Boone?

## LESSON 2 REVIEW

**Summary Time Line**

1758 — 1763

**1758**
The British capture Fort Duquesne, Fort Louisbourg, and Fort Frontenac

**1760**
The British capture Montreal

**1762**
The British Navy defeats Spanish forces

**1763**
King George III issues the Proclamation of 1763

① **MAIN IDEA** Why did many colonists settle in Britain's newly won lands?

② **WHY IT MATTERS** Why did the colonists and the British government disagree over land rights?

③ **VOCABULARY** Use the word **proclamation** in a sentence about the colonies.

④ **TIME LINE** When did the British capture Montreal?

⑤ **READING SKILL—Cause and Effect** What effect did the Treaty of Paris have on France?

⑥ **GOVERNMENT** How did the British government try to end the fighting between the Native Americans and the colonists?

⑦ **CRITICAL THINKING—Hypothesize** Why might it be difficult to govern a colony that is far away?

**PERFORMANCE—Write a Journal Entry** Imagine that you are a pioneer that is traveling through the Cumberland Gap to Kentucky. Explain in a journal entry how you think the Cumberland Gap made travel easier.

## · SKILLS ·

### MAP AND GLOBE

# Compare Historical Maps

▶ **WHY IT MATTERS**

The Treaty of Paris that officially ended the French and Indian War changed the map of North America. The historical maps on page 279 show the changes. A historical map provides information about a place at a certain time in history. Knowing how to use historical maps can help you learn how borders have changed over time.

### Flags over North America

Spain

France

Russia

▶ **WHAT YOU NEED TO KNOW**

Colors are important map symbols. Sometimes colors help you tell water from land on a map. Colors on a map can also show you the areas claimed by different cities, states, or countries.

One of the color symbols on Map B has a pattern of stripes that mapmakers call hatch lines. **Hatch lines** on historical maps often show areas claimed by two or more countries. Hatch lines may also show land that has a special purpose.

The map key on Map B tells you that the region shown by hatch lines was claimed by the British. For this reason one of the colors of the hatch lines is the color used for the British. The map key also tells you that the British reserved this land for the Native Americans.

These flags were flown over different parts of North America in the mid-1700s.

Britain

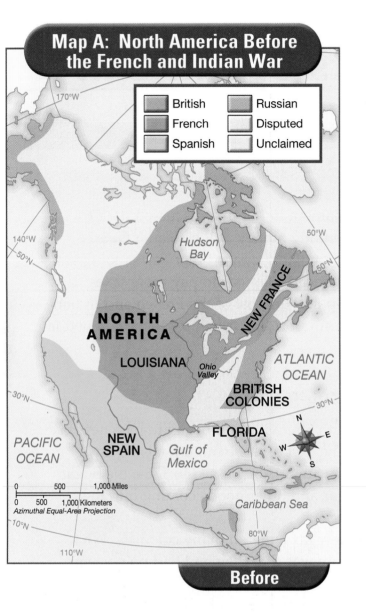

## Map A: North America Before the French and Indian War

British
French
Spanish
Russian
Disputed
Unclaimed

170°W
140°W
50°W
50°N
Hudson Bay
NORTH AMERICA
NEW FRANCE
LOUISIANA
Ohio Valley
ATLANTIC OCEAN
BRITISH COLONIES
30°N
NEW SPAIN
FLORIDA
Gulf of Mexico
PACIFIC OCEAN
N E W S
0  500  1,000 Miles
0  500  1,000 Kilometers
Azimuthal Equal-Area Projection
10°N
80°W
110°W
Caribbean Sea

**Before**

## Map B: North America After the French and Indian War

British
British (reserved for Native Americans)
French
Spanish
Russian
Disputed
Unclaimed
Proclamation Line of 1763

170°W
140°W
50°N
50°W
Hudson Bay
NORTH AMERICA
LOUISIANA
Ohio Valley
ATLANTIC OCEAN
13 COLONIES
30°N
NEW SPAIN
FLORIDA
Gulf of Mexico
PACIFIC OCEAN
N E W S
0  500  1,000 Miles
0  500  1,000 Kilometers
Azimuthal Equal-Area Projection
10°N
80°W
110°W
Caribbean Sea

**After**

### ▶ PRACTICE THE SKILL

Look at the map keys to learn what each color represents. Then use the maps to answer these questions.

**1** What color is used to show the land claimed by the French? by the British? by the Spanish?

**2** After the French and Indian War, which European country claimed the area known as Louisiana?

**3** Which European country claimed Florida before the French and Indian War? after the war?

### ▶ APPLY WHAT YOU LEARNED

Write a paragraph that describes what these historical maps show and explains why historical maps are useful. Share your paragraph with a classmate.

MAP AND GLOBE SKILLS

Practice your map and globe skills with the **GeoSkills CD-ROM.**

MAIN IDEA
Read to learn why many colonists spoke out against the new tax laws passed by the British Parliament.

WHY IT MATTERS
The colonists believed that a government should not be able to tax its citizens unless the citizens have a voice in the government. This remains a key belief of people in the United States today.

VOCABULARY
budget
representation
treason
boycott
declaration
repeal
liberty

# Colonists Speak Out

1750    1770    1790

1764–1770

As the British Parliament in London discussed its 1764 **budget**, or plan for spending money, British leader George Grenville had a suggestion. He proposed that Parliament pass new laws requiring American colonists to pay more taxes. This extra money would help pay the cost of the French and Indian War. It would also help support the British soldiers stationed in the colonies.

## The Sugar Act

Parliament agreed with Grenville and began to pass new tax laws for the colonies. The first of these money-raising laws came to be known as the Sugar Act. Passed in 1764, the Sugar Act added a tax on sugar and other goods coming into the colonies from other places.

Having to pay this new tax angered many colonists. What bothered them even more was that they had had no voice in deciding on this tax law. The king and Parliament taxed the colonists without their consent, or agreement. Many colonists believed that this action violated their rights as British citizens.

One of the first colonial leaders to speak out against the Sugar Act was James Otis of Massachusetts. He called the tax "unjust." Not all colonists agreed. Some sided with the British government. Martin Howard of Rhode Island

BROWN SUGARS
Just Imported, and to be sold cheap for Cash only, by
BENJAMIN ANDREWS, jun.
Opposite the Swing-Bridge ;
Who sells also,
New-England Rum, Philadelphia sup
fine and common Flour, Ship Bread, race and groun
ginger, copperas, allum, redwood, logwood, brimston
Lisbon salt, jar oyl, felt hats, wool cards, sheetings, crow
soap, Iron hollow ware, tar, oakham, and a parcel of
small well assorted lignum vitæ.

George Grenville urged King George III (left and on British coin) and members of the British Parliament to support new taxes on sugar and other goods.

felt that the colonists should be more grateful to the king and the Parliament than they were. Without British help, Howard reminded them, they might now be under the rule of France or Spain.

**REVIEW** **Why were many colonists angered by the Sugar Act?**

## The Stamp Act

In 1765, less than a year after the Sugar Act became law, Parliament passed a second tax law for the colonies. The Stamp Act placed a tax on newspapers, almanacs, pamphlets, all kinds of legal documents, insurance policies, licenses, and even playing cards. Each of these items had to have a special stamp on it to show that the tax had been paid. Because Parliament knew that the stamp tax might anger the colonists more than the sugar tax, it hired colonists as tax collectors.

Reaction to the Stamp Act in the colonies was the same as it had been to the Sugar Act. Once again, what really upset many of the colonists was that they had not had a voice in deciding to pass the law. They did not have a voice because they did not have any **representation** in the British Parliament.

### POINTS OF VIEW
#### Taxes

**THOMAS WHATELY,** a member of the British Parliament

❝ We are not yet recovered from a War undertaken . . .for their [the colonists'] Protection . . . and no Time was ever so seasonable for claiming their Assistance [help]. The Distribution is too unequal, of Benefits only to the colonies, and all of the Burthens [burdens] upon the Mother Country [Britain]. ❞

**SAMUEL ADAMS,** a member of the Massachusetts legislature

❝ We are told to be quiet when we see that very money which is torn from us by lawless force . . . to feed and pamper a set of infamous wretches [British soldiers and officials] who swarm like the locusts of Egypt. ❞

#### Analyze the Viewpoints

❶ What views about taxes did each person hold?

❷ **Make It Relevant** Look at the Letters to the Editor section of your newspaper. Find two letters that express different viewpoints about the same issue. Then write a paragraph that summarizes the viewpoints of each letter.

This leather box held stamps (right) that colonists had to buy to be placed on many printed items.

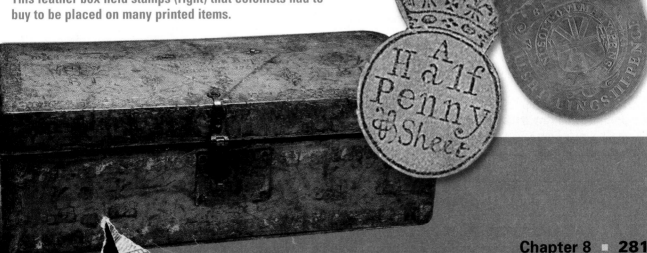

No one was acting or speaking for them in London.

James Otis again spoke out. He told a crowd in Boston that they should refuse to pay the stamp tax until they had representation in Parliament. The colonists began repeating his words,

> 66 **No taxation without representation.** 99

In Virginia, Patrick Henry told his fellow members of the House of Burgesses that they alone should decide what taxes Virginians would pay. Henry said that Parliament did not represent the colonies. The colonies had their own legislatures to represent them.

Members of the House of Burgesses who supported the British government shouted "Treason!" during Patrick Henry's speech. By accusing Henry of **treason**, they were saying that he was working against his government. Henry is said to have answered, "If this be treason, make the most of it!" Although some members protested the decision, the House of Burgesses voted against paying any new taxes Parliament passed unless the colonists gave their consent.

More and more people in the 13 colonies decided not to buy goods that had been stamped. Many colonists also began to **boycott**, or refuse to buy, any British goods. In Boston, groups of women made thread and cloth so that colonists would not have to buy cloth

*This teapot shows the colonists' unhappiness with the Stamp Act.*

## Stamp Act Protest

### Analyze Primary Sources

This 1765 drawing shows colonists in New Hampshire protesting the Stamp Act.

1. The coffin represents the colonists' wish to see the Stamp Act die.
2. The figure made of straw represents a stamp tax collector.
3. This angry protester prepares to throw a rock at the straw figure.

◈ Why do you think the protesters placed a straw figure high on a pole?

that had been made in Britain. In some colonies, people began drinking tea made from the local sassafras trees instead of buying tea from Britain.

Some colonists protested the Stamp Act in more violent ways. They attacked the homes of the stamp tax collectors, breaking windows and stealing property. They beat some tax collectors and chased several out of their cities and towns.

**REVIEW** Why did many colonists believe that Britain had no right to tax them?

## The Stamp Act Congress

Since the time of the Albany Congress, some colonial leaders such as Benjamin Franklin and James Otis had thought that the colonies should work together instead of acting separately. In 1765 Franklin, Otis, and 25 other colonial leaders met in New York City to talk about what to do about the Stamp Act. This meeting came to be called the Stamp Act Congress. Nine colonies sent representatives.

Members of the Stamp Act Congress talked about the problems the new tax laws caused. For example, people who did not obey the Stamp Act could be tried in special courts without a jury. Trial by jury had been a right of British citizens for hundreds of years. A person accused of breaking the law had the right to be tried by a jury of fellow citizens. British citizens were also considered to be innocent until proven guilty, and their property could not be taken away without just cause. The colonists felt that these basic rights and others were now being threatened.

In response, John Dickinson from Pennsylvania proposed that a "Declaration of Rights and Grievances" (GREE•vuhn•suhz) be sent to King

**Colonial Imports from Britain, 1764–1768**

Value (in British Pounds) — years 1764, 1765, 1766, 1767, 1768

**Analyze Graphs** After colonists began to boycott British goods in 1765, the value of colonial imports from Britain decreased.

By about how much did the value of colonial imports decrease from 1764 to 1766?

George III. Such a **declaration**, or official statement, was drawn up, listing the colonists' rights as British citizens. This declaration stated that the British government had no right to tax the colonists without giving them representation. Members of the Stamp Act Congress also expressed their fears that the use of the special courts took away citizens' rights.

In Britain, merchants began to worry about how the colonists' boycott would affect their businesses. Sales of British goods had decreased by almost half in several colonies, and British merchants who depended on trade with the colonies had already started to lose money. The merchants urged Parliament to **repeal**, or cancel, the Stamp Act.

After much discussion, Parliament repealed the Stamp Act in March 1766. The next year, however, it passed some new laws called the Townshend Acts.

These laws placed taxes on lead, glass, paint, paper, and tea brought into the colonies. By passing the Townshend Acts, the British government showed it believed that Parliament still had the authority to make laws for the colonists.

**REVIEW** **What did the Declaration of Rights and Grievances state?**

## · GEOGRAPHY ·

### Boston
### Understanding Places and Regions

This painting of Boston in 1770 shows the Old State House in the center. At the time it was the headquarters of His Majesty's Custom House. Taxes on trade goods were paid and collected in custom houses located in each port city in the 13 colonies. The Boston Massacre took place just east of the Boston Custom House.

## The Boston Massacre

To further show its authority over the colonists, Parliament sent more soldiers to North America. By 1770 there were more than 9,000 British soldiers in the 13 colonies. The British government said that the soldiers were there to protect the western lands won in the French and Indian War. Most of the soldiers, however, were stationed in cities along the Atlantic coast.

Having British soldiers in their cities angered many colonists. They called the soldiers "lobsters," "redcoats," and "bloody-backs," making fun of their bright red uniform jackets. Some soldiers responded to this name-calling by destroying colonial property.

As the anger between the British soldiers and the colonists grew stronger, fights broke out more and more often. Some of the worst fighting took place in Boston on March 5, 1770. In the evening a large crowd gathered near several British soldiers.

Some colonists in the crowd shouted insults at the soldiers and began to throw rocks and snowballs. As the crowd moved forward, the soldiers fired their weapons. Three colonists were killed, and two died later. Among the dead was a former slave named Crispus Attucks (A•tuhks). Many people consider Crispus Attucks the first person to be killed in the struggle for American liberty. **Liberty** means "the freedom of people to make their own laws."

Paul Revere, a Boston silversmith, made an engraving, or picture, showing the soldiers shooting at the colonists. He titled it *The Bloody Massacre*. The word *massacre* (MA•sih•ker) means "the killing

Crispus Attucks was one of the colonists killed at the Boston Massacre.

of a number of people who cannot defend themselves." The shooting in Boston was not really a massacre, but to this day the event is called the Boston Massacre.

**REVIEW** What was Crispus Attucks's role in the Boston Massacre?

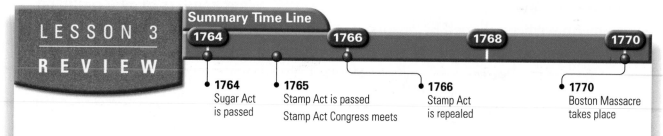

## LESSON 3 REVIEW

**Summary Time Line**

| 1764 | 1766 | 1768 | 1770 |

- **1764** Sugar Act is passed
- **1765** Stamp Act is passed / Stamp Act Congress meets
- **1766** Stamp Act is repealed
- **1770** Boston Massacre takes place

❶ **MAIN IDEA** Why did the new tax laws cause conflict between the colonists and Britain?

❷ **WHY IT MATTERS** Why do you think the idea of no taxation without representation is still important to people in the United States today?

❸ **VOCABULARY** Use the terms **representation** and **boycott** to describe the colonists' reaction to the Stamp Act.

❹ **TIME LINE** How long after the Stamp Act was passed was the law repealed?

❺ **READING SKILL—Cause and Effect** What caused the Boston Massacre?

❻ **ECONOMICS** Why did the British Parliament decide to pass new tax laws for the colonies?

❼ **CRITICAL THINKING—Evaluate** Do you think Parliament had the right to tax the colonists? Why or why not?

**PERFORMANCE—Make a Poster** Imagine that you are a colonist. Make a poster that encourages other colonists to boycott British goods. Tell why you think the tax laws are unfair, and give reasons for the boycott.

# ·SKILLS·

## READING

# Determine Point of View

VOCABULARY

**point of view**

**bias**

### ➡ WHY IT MATTERS

You can get information from many sources—television, radio, newspapers, reference books, and the Internet. Before you use this information, however, you need to decide if you can trust its reliability.

### ➡ WHAT YOU NEED TO KNOW

In the study of history, written records and pictures provide important information. They describe or show what happened. Some may show an accurate description from many points of view or from one person's point of view. A person's **point of view** is his or her set of beliefs that have been shaped by factors

such as whether that person is old or young, male or female, rich or poor. Some points of view can be supported by fact, but written records and pictures showing a single point of view may bias your thinking. You show **bias** when you favor or oppose someone or something.

To find the point of view in a picture, follow these steps.

**Step 1** **Identify who made the picture. Did that person see what happened or know about it only from the accounts of others? What appears to be a firsthand account may not be.**

This engraving by Paul Revere shows his view of the Boston Massacre.

**Step 2** Think about the audience. For whom was this picture meant? The picture's audience may have affected what was drawn and how it was drawn.

**Step 3** Check for bias. Watch for clues that show a one-sided view.

**Step 4** Compare pictures of the same event, when possible. Comparing sources can give you more balanced information and help you identify bias.

➡ **PRACTICE THE SKILL**

Drawing B is based on the Boston Massacre as it was described during the trial of the British soldiers who fired at the colonists. John Adams, a lawyer from Boston, was asked by the British government to defend the British soldiers who were arrested for murder. Adams agreed to defend them because he felt the British soldiers deserved a fair trial. He argued that the soldiers had fired their weapons in self-defense. The jury agreed. It found Captain Thomas Preston and six soldiers not guilty. Two of the soldiers were found guilty of a lesser crime.

Drawing A is the engraving of the event made by Paul Revere, a colonist who worked for colonial rights. During the massacre five colonists were killed.

**1** In what ways are the drawings alike? How are they different?

**2** Which is more likely based on first-hand information?

**3** For whom do you think Drawing A was meant? Explain.

**4** Does Drawing A show bias? What details in the picture might show Revere's feeling about the British soldiers?

**5** For whom do you think Drawing B was meant? Explain.

➡ **APPLY WHAT YOU LEARNED**

With a partner, preview the pictures in a magazine article. Follow the steps in What You Need to Know to study the pictures more closely. Describe the messages that the pictures convey.

This picture of the Boston Massacre is based on the descriptions given during the trial of the British Soldiers who fired at the colonists.

**MAIN IDEA**
Read to learn what actions the colonists took when Parliament passed more laws for the colonies.

**WHY IT MATTERS**
The colonists began to work together to find a way to respond to the growing British threat.

**VOCABULARY**

monopoly
blockade
quarter
intolerable
petition

# The Road to War

**1750** — **1770** — **1790**

**1773–1775**

The three years following the Boston Massacre were fairly quiet in the 13 colonies. Some historians have called this time "the calm before the storm." The storm came when Parliament again angered the colonists by passing more laws.

## The Boston Tea Party

In 1770 Parliament repealed all of the Townshend Acts except for the tea tax. Soon after, Parliament tried to give a monopoly on tea to the East India Company, Britain's chief tea producer. A **monopoly** is complete control of a product or service in a certain area by a single person or group. This includes control over pricing and competition.

The East India Company was able to sell tea for much cheaper. Colonial merchants could no longer make money in the tea trade. So some colonists decided to boycott tea.

In Pennsylvania, colonists did not allow ships carrying British tea to enter their ports. In Massachusetts, colonists did not want ships loaded with tea to dock at their ports either,

This painting shows one artist's idea of what happened at the Boston Tea Party. The tea leaves in the bottle on the next page are thought to be from this event.

## Samuel Adams   1722–1803

### Character Trait: Civic Virtue

Samuel Adams, a cousin of John Adams, helped plan the Boston Tea Party. He believed in the use of violence only when all else failed. Since the days of the Sugar Act in 1764, Adams had attempted to get people to work peacefully for their rights through committees and other meetings. In 1772 he set up a committee of correspondence in Boston. Then he got other colonists to do the same. These committees corresponded with, or wrote letters to, one another. In this way news of what was happening in one colony spread quickly to the others.

**GO ONLINE**

**MULTIMEDIA BIOGRAPHIES**
Visit The Learning Site at www.harcourtschool.com/biographies to learn about other famous people.

but the governor, Thomas Hutchinson, gave the order to let the ships dock.

On December 16, 1773, colonists took part in what became known as the Boston Tea Party. That night, members of a group known as the Sons of Liberty boarded the ships. Disguised as Mohawk Indians, they broke open 342 tea chests and dumped the tea into the harbor.

**REVIEW** How did the colonists respond to the East India Company's unfair advantage in the tea trade?

### Intolerable Acts

The Sons of Liberty knew that their actions would anger Parliament. After hearing about the Boston Tea Party, Parliament, now led by Lord Frederick North, passed a new series of laws to punish the colonists of Massachusetts.

The first of these laws was the Boston Port Bill, passed in March 1774. It closed the port of Boston until the colonists paid for the destroyed tea. To enforce the law,

TEA THROWN INTO BOSTON HARBOR DEC. 16. 1773.

Parliament ordered the British navy to blockade Boston Harbor. To **blockade** is to use warships to prevent other ships from entering or leaving a port.

Parliament then passed the Massachusetts Government Act. It stopped the Massachusetts legislature from making laws and banned town meetings not authorized by the governor. To further punish the colonists, the British government ordered them to **quarter** British soldiers, or to feed and provide shelter for them. Some colonists even had to take the soldiers into their homes.

In response, the colonists shouted that these laws were "intolerable acts!" The word **intolerable** means "unacceptable." The Intolerable Acts, as the new laws came to be called, led many colonists to recognize that they had a common enemy.

**REVIEW** What were some of the Intolerable Acts?

## The First Continental Congress

Many of the colonists believed that the British government would do anything, even use its army, to make them obey the British laws. So representatives of the colonies decided to meet to discuss ways they might respond to the growing British threat. The first meeting took place in September 1774 at Philadelphia's Carpenters' Hall. Because it was the first of its kind on the North American continent, the meeting was later called the First Continental Congress.

The 56 delegates at the Congress represented the wide range of thought in the colonies. Some wanted to break away from Britain. Others wanted to find a way to get along better with Britain. Following neither extreme, the Congress agreed to develop a statement of rights. The delegates stated these rights in a **petition**, or a signed request, that they sent to Parliament.

In the petition, the Congress said that the colonists had a right to "life, liberty, and property." The Congress also stated that only the colonial legislatures had the authority to make laws "in all cases of taxation and internal polity [government]." The petition concluded by issuing a warning: "We are *for the present* only resolved to pursue . . . peaceable measures."

The Congress set May 10, 1775, as the deadline for

Patrick Henry

## DEMOCRATIC VALUES
### The Right to Privacy

One of the rights listed in the English Bill of Rights prevented soldiers and other government officials from entering a person's home without the owner's permission or a warrant, or order, from a court of law. As more and more British soldiers were sent to North America, however, the British government needed more places for them to live. Some colonists' homes were seized by British soldiers. These soldiers went into the people's homes and often lived there without the owner's permission.

Today, the right of privacy remains one of the most valued rights in the United States. According to the rights of United States citizens, in most cases government officials must acquire a warrant from a court of law before they can enter a person's home without permission.

### Analyze the Value

1. Why did the American colonists believe their rights had been ignored by the British soldiers?

2. **Make It Relevant** Why do you think privacy is an important right for Americans to have?

Parliament to respond to the petition. If Parliament took no action by then, the Congress would meet again. Before ending the meeting, however, the members of the Continental Congress agreed to stop most trade with Britain.

Meanwhile, in Virginia colonial leaders such as Patrick Henry suggested that the colonists begin preparing for war. He told the House of Burgesses, "I know not what course others may take: but as for me, give me liberty or give me death!"

**REVIEW** Why did the First Continental Congress meet?

Lexington and Concord

Battle
Road
Routes:
Revere
Dawes
British

Concord
Concord River
Sudbury
River
Lincoln
Lexington
Medford
Menotomy
Mystic River
Winnisiet
Waltham
Cambridge
Charlestown
River
Charles
Watertown
Boston
Weston
Newton
Boston Harbor
Brookline
Roxbury

N W E S

0   1   2 Miles
0   1   2 Kilometers

**Movement** The battles at Lexington and Concord marked the beginning of a long war between the 13 colonies and Britain. The lantern (above, right) is one of the two lanterns that were hung in a church tower to signal that the British were coming by boat.

❖ What cities did Revere and Dawes ride through to warn of the British approach?

## Lexington and Concord

In Massachusetts the colonists responded to the Intolerable Acts by organizing special militia units. They were called Minutemen because they could be ready in a minute to defend Massachusetts.

In April 1775 General Thomas Gage heard that two leaders of the Sons of Liberty, John Hancock and Samuel Adams, were meeting in the village of Lexington. Gage also heard that the Minutemen were storing weapons in Concord, near Lexington. The general ordered 700 British soldiers to find the weapons and arrest Hancock and Adams.

Learning of the general's order, Paul Revere, a member of the Sons of Liberty, rode his horse to Lexington to warn Hancock and Adams. Revere was joined by William Dawes and Samuel Prescott.

A group of men dressed as Minutemen reenact the battle at Concord at Minute Man National Historical Park in Concord, Massachusetts.

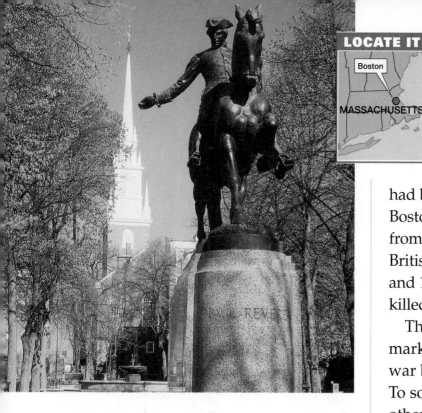

LOCATE IT

Boston

MASSACHUSETTS

This statue of Paul Revere stands near the Old North Church in Boston, Massachusetts.

From Lexington the British marched to Concord. However, the weapons they expected to find had been moved. As they marched back to Boston, the Minutemen fired at the British from the woods and fields beside the road. British losses for the day were 73 killed and 174 wounded. 93 Minutemen were killed or wounded in the fighting.

The fighting at Lexington and Concord marked the beginning of a long, bitter war between Britain and its 13 colonies. To some, it seemed a small battle, but for others it was a world event, a history-making first step in creating the United States of America. The poet Ralph Waldo Emerson would later call the shots fired at Lexington and Concord "the shot heard round the world."

**REVIEW** Why did the British go to Lexington and Concord?

They each rode off to Concord to warn the Minutemen that the British were on their way. When the British arrived at Lexington on April 19, 1775, they found that the Minutemen were waiting for them. Shots were fired, and eight of the Minutemen were killed. Several others were wounded.

## LESSON 4 REVIEW

**Summary Time Line**

1773 — 1774 — 1775

**1773**
Boston Tea Party takes place

**1774**
The Continental Congress meets

**1775**
British and colonial forces clash at Lexington and Concord

1. **MAIN IDEA** What actions did the colonists take when Parliament passed more laws for them?

2. **WHY IT MATTERS** How did colonists work together to respond to the British Parliament?

3. **VOCABULARY** Use the terms **monopoly** and **blockade** in a paragraph about the Boston Tea Party.

4. **TIME LINE** When was the fighting at Lexington and Concord?

5. **READING SKILL—Cause and Effect** What caused the Boston Tea Party?

6. **HISTORY** What was Paul Revere's role in the fighting at Lexington and Concord?

7. **CRITICAL THINKING—Analyze** Why were the shots fired at Lexington and Concord referred to as "the shot heard round the world"?

**PERFORMANCE—Make a Poster** Draw a poster that encourages people to join a colonial militia. Use words that you think will convince people to fight for liberty. Share your poster with your classmates.

# The Second Continental Congress

1750    1770    1790

1775

**MAIN IDEA**
As you read, look for ways colonial leaders prepared for war with Britain and fought the first major battle of the Revolutionary War.

**WHY IT MATTERS**
As the colonies pushed closer to a final break with Britain, more colonists began to think of themselves as Americans instead of as British citizens.

**VOCABULARY**
commander in chief
earthwork
olive branch
mercenary

**N**ews of the fighting at Lexington and Concord quickly spread throughout the 13 colonies. As a result, the Second Continental Congress was called to meet in Philadelphia on May 10, 1775. Colonial leaders gathered at the Pennsylvania State House to decide what the colonies should do. Only Georgia failed to send representatives.

## Hope for Peace, Plan for War

Once again, delegates were divided in their views, or opinions. Some called for war against the British. Others, such as John Dickinson, tried to persuade the group to avoid fighting. Dickinson believed that the "cause of liberty should not be sullied [soiled] by turbulence and tumult [commotion and uproar]." By June, however, the Congress had agreed that the colonies should at least begin to prepare for war.

The first step was for the Congress to form an army. This new "Continental Army" would have full-time, regular soldiers in addition to the part-time militia that each colony already had. The Continental Army was the first united colonial army. It would become the main army that would be assisted by the state militias.

On June 15, 1775, Congress, at the suggestion of John Adams and others, asked George Washington to lead the new Continental Army. Adams suggested Washington because of his "skill and experience as an officer, . . . great talents and universal character." Adams believed that Washington not only understood soldiers but that he knew how to fight a war.

The Second Continental Congress chose George Washington, shown here in his military uniform, to lead the Continental Army.

The next day Washington humbly accepted the role of **commander in chief**, the leader of all the military forces.

To supply the Continental Army, the Congress asked each colony to contribute money to pay for guns, bullets, food, and uniforms. The Congress also decided to print its own paper money, which came to be known as Continental currency. The Congress paid the soldiers in bills that they called continentals.

By the time George Washington left Philadelphia to take charge of the Continental Army, which was already in Massachusetts, the first major battle of the Revolutionary War had already been fought. The Battle of Bunker Hill took place near Boston on June 17, 1775.

**REVIEW** How did the Second Continental Congress prepare for war?

## The Battle of Bunker Hill

After the fighting at Lexington and Concord, angry citizens in Massachusetts started to build **earthworks**, or walls of earth and stone, near Boston. These earthworks would help the colonists defend themselves if there were another battle with the British soldiers.

Meanwhile, Boston had become the only safe place for the British. The Minutemen had taken control of the surrounding countryside. The only way the British could enter or leave Boston was by sea.

After dark on June 16, 1775, some colonists began to build new earthworks on Breed's Hill, across the Charles River from Boston. When General Gage learned of this the next morning, he ordered British ships in the harbor to open fire on the colonists. Gage also sent General William Howe and 2,400 British soldiers to capture Breed's Hill. Shortly after noon,

Bunker Hill

3

colonial forces

Breed's Hill

earthworks

lines of British soldiers marched up Breed's Hill to the roll of drums. When the British drew close to the earthworks, the 1,600 colonists inside let loose a deadly hail of shot. The fighting was so fierce that, to save bullets, colonial commander Israel Putnam said to his soldiers,

> 66 **Don't fire until you see the whites of their eyes.** 99

The colonists drove the British back twice before running out of gun powder. The British finally took the hill but at great cost. More than 1,000 of the 2,400 British soldiers were killed or wounded. About 350 colonists died or were wounded.

The battle at Breed's Hill was mis-named for nearby Bunker Hill. Although the colonists were driven from the field, they were proud of how well they had done. The British had learned that fight-ing the colonists would not be easy.

**REVIEW** What was the cause of the Battle of Bunker Hill?

## A CLOSER LOOK
### The Battle of Bunker Hill

The first major battle of the Revolutionary War, the Battle of Bunker Hill, was fought on June 17, 1775. The British won the battle, but they suffered the heaviest losses of the entire war.

1. British forces first landed near Morton's Point and formed battle lines.
2. British forces marched up Breed's Hill to attack the colonists.
3. Colonists fired on the British from behind earthworks on Breed's Hill.

? Why do you think the colonists chose to build earthworks on top of Breed's Hill?

Mystic River

Mill Pond

Bunker Hill

0   1,000   2,000 Feet
0   250   500 Meters
Transverse Mercator Projection

Breed's Hill

Morton's Point

Charlestown

Charles River

Copp's Hill

Boston

- - - Colonial forces
- - - British forces
British ship

Mystic River

Morton's Point

British ships

main landing site

1

reinforcements

2

British forces

## Phillis Wheatley    1753?–1784

### Character Trait: Patriotism

Phillis Wheatley was one of the best-known poets of her time. She was born in Africa and brought to Massachusetts as a slave. Unlike most enslaved people, however, Wheatley learned to read and write. She was later freed upon the death of her owner.

Wheatley's poetry was first published in 1770, while she was still a teenager. In October 1775 Wheatley wrote a poem honoring George Washington on his being named commander in chief of the Continental Army.

"Proceed, great chief, and with virtue on thy side,
Thy ev'ry action let the goddess guide.
A crown, a mansion, and a throne that shine,
With gold unfading, Washington! be thine."

**MULTIMEDIA BIOGRAPHIES**

Visit The Learning Site at **www.harcourtschool.com/biographies** to learn about other famous people.

## A Foreign War

Hoping to avoid more fighting, the Second Continental Congress agreed on July 5, 1775, to send another petition to King George III. This petition came to be known as the Olive Branch Petition because it expressed the colonists' desire for a peaceful end to the fighting. The **olive branch** is an ancient symbol of peace.

In London, the Battle of Bunker Hill had further angered British leaders. Lord North advised King George III to think of the fighting in the colonies as a foreign war. On August 23 the king issued a proclamation of rebellion. In it, he promised to use every measure to crush the rebellion and "bring the traitors to justice." As a result, by the time the Olive Branch Petition reached British leaders in London on August 24, it was already a lost cause.

To fight the colonists, the king called for the British army in the colonies to be enlarged. To accomplish this, he ordered the hiring of mercenaries (MER•suhn•air•eez) from Germany. A **mercenary** is a soldier who serves for pay in the military of a foreign government. Many of the German mercenaries were Hessians, from the Hesse region of Germany.

The king also called on Britain's Iroquois and other Native American allies for help. He knew that many Indian tribes hated the colonists for ignoring the Proclamation of 1763 and settling the lands west of the Appalachians. Because of this the king believed that many Native Americans would help the British fight the colonists.

Meanwhile, the Second Continental Congress also prepared for war. In October the Congress created a navy, which at first was nothing more than a few fishing boats. In November the Congress established a marine corps, or "army of the sea." It also set up a committee to seek alliances with various Native American tribes.

Earlier that fall, in September 1775, Georgia had agreed to join the Second Continental Congress and support the Revolutionary War. Many of the delegates could now agree with what Patrick Henry had told them during the First Continental Congress,

> **66 The distinctions between Virginians, Pennsylvanians, New Yorkers are no more. I am not a Virginian, but an American. 99**

Finally, the Continental Congress stood for all 13 colonies.

**REVIEW** How did the Battle of Bunker Hill change Britain's view of the fight with the colonies?

**FAST FACT**

To protect their legs, Hessian soldiers often wore thick leather boots over their regular footgear. These special boots weighed about 12 pounds (5 kg) a pair!

In addition to their leather boots (right), some German mercenaries also wore bright metal helmets like the one shown here.

## LESSON 5 REVIEW

**Summary Time Line**

| January | June | December |
|---|---|---|
| **May 1775** Second Continental Congress meets | **June 1775** Battle of Bunker Hill is fought | **July 1775** Olive Branch Petition is sent |

❶ **MAIN IDEA** How did colonial leaders prepare for war with Britain?

❷ **WHY IT MATTERS** How might the colonists' attitudes toward Britain have changed as more began to think of themselves as Americans instead of as British?

❸ **VOCABULARY** Write a letter to King George III using the terms **olive branch** and **mercenary**.

❹ **TIME LINE** Was the Battle of Bunker Hill fought before or after King George III received the Olive Branch Petition?

❺ **READING SKILL—Cause and Effect** What were the causes and effects of the Second Continental Congress?

❻ **HISTORY** What was George Washington's role in the Continental Army?

❼ **GEOGRAPHY** Where was the Battle of Bunker Hill fought?

❽ **CRITICAL THINKING—Hypothesize** What do you think might have happened if the Olive Branch Petition had reached London before King George III issued a proclamation of rebellion?

**PERFORMANCE—Write a Diary Entry** Write a diary entry from the viewpoint of either a colonist or a British soldier who fought at the Battle of Bunker Hill. Then compare your diary entry to those of classmates.

# Review and Test Preparation

Summary Time Line

1750          1755

**1754**
French and Indian
War begins

Albany Plan of
Union is proposed

## USE YOUR READING SKILLS

Complete this graphic organizer to show that you understand
the causes and effects of some of the key events that helped
unite the colonies. A copy of this graphic organizer appears on
page 82 of the Activity Book.

## Events Unite the Colonies

Cause → Effect

| Cause | Effect |
|---|---|
| The British Parliament needs extra money to pay for the French and Indian War. | _____ |
| _____ | The Boston Tea Party takes place in Boston Harbor in December 1773. |
| The British Parliament passes the Intolerable Acts to punish the colonists. | _____ |
| _____ | The Second Continental Congress is held in Philadelphia in May 1775. |
| The Battle of Bunker Hill takes place near Boston on June 17, 1775. | _____ |

## THINK & WRITE

**Write a Persuasive Letter**   Think about
how the Stamp Act Congress asked all
colonists to boycott British goods. Write a
letter to a delegate of the congress,
explaining why you do or do not support
the boycott.

**Report a News Event**   Suppose that you
are a newspaper reporter who has been asked
to write about the fighting at Lexington and
Concord. Write a short newspaper article
in which you describe the events of
April 19, 1775.

**1763**
French and Indian
War ends

**1765**
Stamp Act
Congress

**1770**
Boston
Massacre

**1773**
Boston
Tea Party

**1775**
Fighting breaks out
at Lexington and Concord
Battle of Bunker Hill

## USE THE TIME LINE

Use the chapter summary time line to answer these questions.

**1** When did the French and Indian War begin and end?

**2** How many years after the Boston Massacre did the Boston Tea Party take place?

## USE VOCABULARY

Identify the term that correctly matches each definition.

**alliance (p. 270)**

**budget (p. 280)**

**boycott (p. 282)**

**monopoly (p. 288)**

**mercenary (p. 296)**

**3** to refuse to buy

**4** a soldier who serves for pay in the military of a foreign government

**5** a formal agreement among nations, states, groups, or individuals

**6** the complete control of a product or service in a certain area by a single person or group

**7** a plan for spending money

## RECALL FACTS

Answer these questions.

**8** The French and Indian War began as a competition for control of what region?

**9** How did most colonists react to the Proclamation of 1763?

**10** Why was the Wilderness Road important to the pioneers?

Write the letter of the best choice.

**11** **TEST PREP** Colonists were upset about the Stamp Act because—
   **A** they had no representation in Parliament.
   **B** it was the second tax law.
   **C** they had to boycott British goods.
   **D** many had to work as tax collectors.

**12** **TEST PREP** The Second Continental Congress tried to make peace by—
   **F** sending a delegate to Britain.
   **G** sending the Olive Branch Petition.
   **H** uniting the 13 colonies.
   **J** refusing to fight for the British.

## THINK CRITICALLY

**13** How might history have been different if the Albany Plan of Union had been approved by the colonies?

**14** Imagine that you are a colonist. Will you speak out against the Sugar Act, or will you side with the British? Explain.

## APPLY SKILLS

**Compare Historical Maps**

**15** Use the maps on page 279 to name the countries that received land that was once claimed by the French.

**Determine Point of View**

**16** In a magazine or newspaper, find a photograph showing a recent event. Tell what the photograph shows, and describe the photographer's point of view.

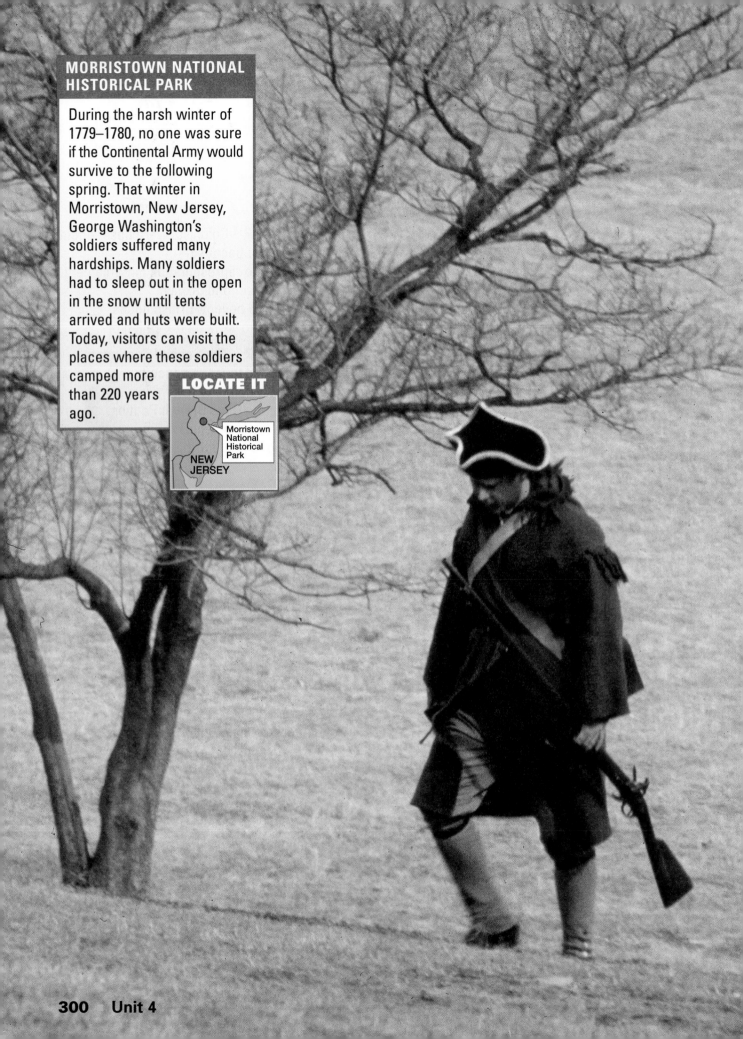

## MORRISTOWN NATIONAL HISTORICAL PARK

During the harsh winter of 1779–1780, no one was sure if the Continental Army would survive to the following spring. That winter in Morristown, New Jersey, George Washington's soldiers suffered many hardships. Many soldiers had to sleep out in the open in the snow until tents arrived and huts were built. Today, visitors can visit the places where these soldiers camped more than 220 years ago.

**LOCATE IT**

Morristown National Historical Park

NEW JERSEY

# The Revolutionary War

**"** These are the times that try men's souls. **"**

—Thomas Paine, *The American Crisis,* December 23, 1776

---

**CHAPTER READING SKILL**

### Sequence

A **sequence** is the order in which events occurred.

**As you read this chapter, put events about the American Revolution in the correct sequence.**

| FIRST | → | NEXT | → | LAST |

**MAIN IDEA**
Read to learn why the colonists cut ties with the British government and formed their own country.

**WHY IT MATTERS**
The ideas expressed about freedom in the Declaration of Independence continue to guide Americans today.

**VOCABULARY**
public opinion
independence
allegiance
resolution
preamble
grievance

Thomas Paine argued that the colonies should claim their independence.

# Independence Is Declared

1750          1770          1790

**1776–1781**

$A$lthough the colonies were already at war with Britain, many Americans still believed that their problems with the king and Parliament could be settled. They hoped the British government would change its view and allow them to take part in making laws. By 1776 that thinking began to change.

## Common Sense

One of the people who did the most to change public opinion in the colonies was Thomas Paine. **Public opinion** is the point of view held by most people. In January 1776 Paine published a pamphlet, or short book, titled *Common Sense*.

In his pamphlet Paine questioned the right of any king to rule over anyone. Paine wrote that people should rule themselves, "A government of our own is a natural right." Paine called for a revolution, and he challenged the colonists to cut their ties with the British government.

People in the 13 colonies read and talked about *Common Sense*. As a result, many began to urge **independence**. Having the

COMMON SENSE

ADDRESSED TO THE

INHABITANTS

OF

AMERICA,

On the following interesting

SUBJECTS.

I. Of the Origin and Design of Government in general, with concise Remarks on the English Constitution.

**FAST FACT**
Within a few months of being published, over 500,000 copies of *Common Sense* had been sold.

## Thomas Jefferson   1743–1826

### Character Trait: Individualism

Thomas Jefferson was a very skilled person. He is best known as the chief writer of the Declaration of Independence and later as the third President of the United States. But Jefferson did many other things in his life. He was an eager reader, an inventor, and a student of mathematics, science, agriculture, and architecture. In 1768 he designed his own house, which he called Monticello. Monticello is near Charlottesville, Virginia.

**MULTIMEDIA BIOGRAPHIES**
Visit The Learning Site at **www.harcourtschool.com/ biographies** to learn about other famous people.

freedom to govern themselves was the only way, they said, to have liberty.

Richard Henry Lee of Virginia gave a speech to the delegates of the Second Continental Congress on June 7, 1776. Lee said that the colonies no longer owed **allegiance** (uh•LEE•juhns), or loyalty, to the king. At the end, he suggested a **resolution**, a formal statement of the feelings of a group about an important topic. This resolution read, "Resolved: That these united colonies are, and of right ought to be, free and independent States."

The Congress debated the resolution for a few days, but not all the colonies were ready to vote for independence. They needed more time before taking such a dangerous action. The Congress decided to wait almost a month before calling for a vote.

**REVIEW** Why did Richard Henry Lee suggest that the colonies become independent?

## Writing the Declaration of Independence

The delegates of the Second Continental Congress hoped that the month's wait would help all 13 colonies decide to vote as one in favor of independence. In the meantime, the Congress chose a committee to write the group's view on independence. The committee consisted of Benjamin Franklin of Pennsylvania, John Adams of Massachusetts, Robert R. Livingston of New York, Roger Sherman of Connecticut, and Thomas Jefferson of Virginia.

Thomas Jefferson was a 33-year-old lawyer. He had studied government and had already written about the colonies' problems with British rule.

Jefferson's travel desk holds the first draft of the Declaration of Independence.

The Declaration of Independence includes the idea that a government gets its power from the consent of the people.

**1** date
**2** Preamble
**3** the statement of rights
**4** charges against the king
**5** statement of independence
**6** signers of Declaration

❖ What was included in the Declaration of Independence?

Two years before, Jefferson had written a pamphlet titled *A Summary View of the Rights of British America*. In it he had listed for the First Continental Congress the changes the colonies wanted in their government.

The members of the writing committee added their ideas, but Jefferson did most of the writing. Every evening for about 17 days, he wrote—and rewrote—what became the Declaration of Independence.

Thomas Jefferson planned the Declaration in several parts. In the **preamble,** the first part or introduction, he stated why the Declaration was needed. He said that sometimes a group of people finds that it has no choice but to form a new nation.

In the second part, he described the colonists' main ideas about government. These words have become some of the most famous in United States history.

“We hold these truths to be self-evident, that all men are created equal, that they are endowed [provided] by their Creator with certain unalienable Rights, that among these are Life, Liberty and the pursuit of Happiness.”

In the third and largest part of the Declaration, Jefferson listed the colonists' **grievances**, or complaints, against the British king and Parliament. He also listed the ways the colonists had tried to settle their differences peacefully. In the last part of the Declaration, Jefferson wrote that the colonies were free and independent states.

**REVIEW** What did Jefferson describe in each part of the Declaration of Independence?

## Approving the Declaration

When he finished writing the Declaration of Independence, Thomas Jefferson gave a draft of it to the whole Congress. On June 28, it was read aloud. For several days it was discussed, and changes were made. Then, on July 2, the delegates returned to vote on Richard Henry Lee's resolution to cut ties with Britain. That morning the resolution was approved. The American colonies now considered themselves free and independent states.

On July 4, 1776, the Congress voted to give its final approval for the Declaration. Delegates of only 12 colonies voted. New York's delegates had not yet received the authority to vote.

John Trumbull's painting of the signing of the Declaration of Independence shows the Second Continental Congress in what is today Independence Hall.

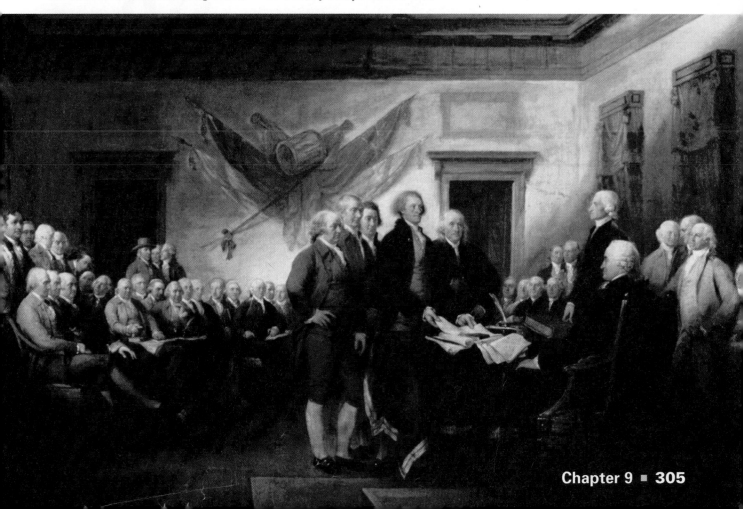

On July 8, 1776, the bell on top of Independence Hall called the citizens of Philadelphia to hear the first public reading of the Declaration of Independence. Many of the members of the Second Continental Congress stood and listened, too, as Colonel John Nixon read the document. The joy shown by the crowd so pleased John Adams that he wrote about it in a letter to his wife, Abigail. Independence Day, he said, should be celebrated "from this time forward for evermore."

By August 2, a formal copy of the Declaration of Independence was ready to be signed by members of the Second Continental Congress. The first to sign it was John Hancock, president of the Congress. He said that he wrote his name large enough so that King George could read it without his glasses. The way he signed the document became so famous that the term *John Hancock* now means "a person's signature."

**REVIEW** How did the people of Philadelphia react to the first reading of the Declaration of Independence?

## Forming a New Government

The work of the Second Continental Congress was not completed with the final approval of the Declaration of Independence. John Hancock organized a second committee to report on how to unite the former colonies into a new country. With independence, a new government had to be formed. Congress chose John Dickinson, of Pennsylvania, to

Independence Hall

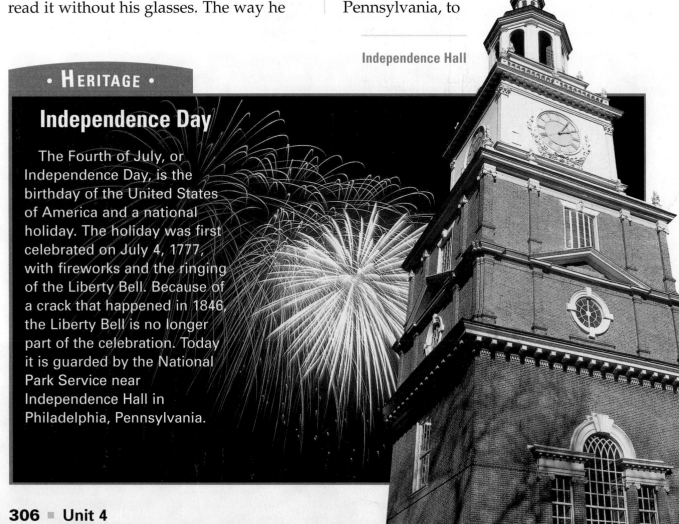

• HERITAGE •

### Independence Day

The Fourth of July, or Independence Day, is the birthday of the United States of America and a national holiday. The holiday was first celebrated on July 4, 1777, with fireworks and the ringing of the Liberty Bell. Because of a crack that happened in 1846, the Liberty Bell is no longer part of the celebration. Today it is guarded by the National Park Service near Independence Hall in Philadelphia, Pennsylvania.

head the committee to write the plan of government.

Dickinson's committee decided that the new states—the former colonies—should unite into a confederation. This Confederation of the United States of America would bring together the 13 independent states into "a firm league of friendship."

On July 12, 1776, Dickinson presented his committee's report to the Congress. The delegates discussed it off and on for more than a year. They finally approved the plan on November 15, 1777. The first constitution for the new country was called the Articles of Confederation. But the last state did not

John Dickinson helped write the Articles of Confederation.

approve this plan for a central government until March 1, 1781.

Under the Articles, voters of each state elected leaders. These leaders then chose representatives to a national legislature called the Congress of the Confederation. Each state, whether large or small, had one vote in the new Congress. Under the Articles of Confederation, this Congress served as the government of the United States. For eight years, it made laws for the new nation. It led the states during the last years of the Revolutionary War.

**REVIEW** What were the Articles of Confederation?

LESSON 1
REVIEW

**Summary Time Line**

1776 ———————————————————————————— 1781

● **1776**
The Declaration of Independence is approved

● **1781**
Congress approves the Articles of Confederation

❶ **MAIN IDEA** Why did many delegates feel that the colonies should cut their ties with Britain?

❷ **WHY IT MATTERS** What are some of the ideas listed in the second part of the Declaration of Independence that are still important today?

❸ **VOCABULARY** Use the words **preamble** and **grievance** in a letter to a friend about the Declaration of Independence.

❹ **TIME LINE** When was the Declaration of Independence approved?

❺ **READING SKILL—Sequence** Which was approved first, the Declaration of Independence or the Articles of Confederation?

❻ **HISTORY** What was the name of Thomas Paine's pamphlet?

❼ **CRITICAL THINKING—Synthesize** Why do you think the Declaration of Independence is still important today?

**PERFORMANCE— Conduct an Interview**
Imagine that you are a reporter in the late 1700s. You have been asked to interview someone who attended the first reading of the Declaration of Independence. Write a list of questions you will ask during your interview.

# Americans and the Revolution

The approval of the Declaration of Independence showed that the colonies had united against Britain. But the colonists themselves were not united. Whether to support independence or to remain loyal to the British king was a difficult decision for many Americans.

## Taking Sides

Many people in the 13 colonies supported independence. They called themselves **Patriots**. Others however, remained loyal to the king and called themselves **Loyalists**, or Tories. Friendships, neighborhoods, and families sometimes were torn apart as people chose to take either the Patriot side or the Loyalist side.

The fighting became as much a civil war, or war between people of the same country, as it was a war with the British. In her book *If You Were There in 1776*, author Barbara Brenner describes life at the time of the Revolution. "If you were part of

Thomas Hutchinson was a governor of the Massachusetts Colony and a Loyalist.

A British flag

a Patriot family, you might have been one of the children throwing garbage or stones at the British soldiers. If your family supported the king, you could have been on the receiving end of some serious violence. Your home might have been broken into. Someone you know who was a Tory [Loyalist] could have been tarred and feathered, or ridden on a rail."

Some colonists, however, chose to be **neutral** (NOO•truhl). They took neither side. Those who were neutral were willing to accept whatever the outcome of the war would be.

**REVIEW** How did colonists view the decision to declare independence from Britain?

## Churches and the War

Like other colonists, people in churches were divided on whether they supported the Patriots or the Loyalists or remained neutral. John Peter Muhlenberg, a young Lutheran minister, told his followers in a sermon, "There is a time to pray and a time to fight." Then, before their eyes, he tore off his church robes to show that he was wearing the uniform of a Patriot militia officer. His father, the colonies' Lutheran leader, was shocked. He himself was a Loyalist. The Lutherans, like the people of other church groups, were divided between Patriots and Loyalists.

Taking sides was especially hard for Anglican Church members. The British king was the head of the Anglican Church, as the Church of England was called in the colonies. Many Anglicans in the New England and Middle Atlantic Colonies were loyal to the king. Many of those in the Southern Colonies worked for independence.

Most Congregationalists, members of the largest church group in the New England Colonies, worked for independence. So, too, did many Baptists and northern Presbyterians. Many southern Presbyterians, however, were Loyalists.

Members of the Society of Friends, also called Quakers, would not fight at all.

John Peter Muhlenberg was a Patriot militia officer.

An early United States flag

Quakers are against all wars because they believe that fighting for any reason is wrong. These **pacifists**, or believers in peaceful settlement of disagreements, wrote pamphlets calling for an end to the war.

**REVIEW** Why was taking sides especially hard for members of the Anglican Church?

## African Americans, Free and Enslaved

At the start of the war, 1 out of every 5 people living in the 13 British colonies was of African descent. Most of these people lived in the Southern Colonies as slaves. African Americans everywhere in the colonies, however, viewed the Declaration of Independence with hope and excitement. It had, after all, stated that "all men are created equal."

Free African Americans were as quick to take sides as many of their white neighbors. Peter Salem was among at least five African Americans who fought at Concord as a Minuteman. A few weeks later he and other African Americans, some free and some enslaved, fought at the Battle of Bunker Hill. About 5,000 African Americans fought in the Continental Army.

Enslaved African Americans who joined the Continental Army were promised freedom after the war as a reward for their service. Many were so filled with the idea of freedom, or liberty, that they changed their names. Among the names listed in Continental Army records are Cuff Freedom, Dick Freedom, Ned Freedom, Peter Freedom, Cuff Liberty, and Pomp Liberty.

In November 1775 the royal governor of Virginia also had promised freedom to enslaved African Americans if they ran away from their owners and fought for the British. As a result, he raised a regiment of more than 300 African American soldiers. A **regiment** is a large, organized group of soldiers. These soldiers wore uniforms that had patches reading *Liberty to Slaves*.

**REVIEW** What promise caused some enslaved African Americans to take sides in the war?

As a young man James Armistead (right) spied on the British army. This proclamation (far right), issued in Virginia, promised freedom to all enslaved people who joined the British army.

Mercy Otis Warren

Sarah Franklin Bache

Abigail Adams

Martha Washington

## Women and the War

Many women in the colonies took part in the Patriots' war effort. Some ran farms and businesses. Others formed groups to raise money for the war and to collect clothing for the soldiers. Esther Reed started the Philadelphia Association in 1780 to help the Continental Army. When Reed died, Sarah Franklin Bache (BAYCH), Benjamin Franklin's daughter, took over the Association.

Hundreds of women took part in the fighting. These women, often with children, followed their husbands from battle to battle. In army camps they cooked food and washed clothes. Some nursed the sick and wounded. On the battlefield, women carried water to the soldiers. Others served as spies or messengers.

Some women used their talents to support the Patriot cause. Mercy Otis Warren wrote poems and plays. In her plays Warren often wrote about women heroes in the struggle for freedom in other countries. Later, she wrote a history of the American Revolution, the first by a woman.

Not all women were Patriots, however. There were Loyalist women in every colony. Some of them fought for the British. Many others gave the British food and other supplies.

**REVIEW** How did women on both sides take part in the war?

## People in the Western Lands

Despite the Proclamation of 1763, settlers had continued to move onto the land King George III had reserved for Native Americans. Some Indian groups grew angry about these settlers, but many came to depend on both the Americans and the British as trading partners. The Patriots and the British each hoped that the Indians would take their side or, if not, stay out of the fighting.

Most of the Native American groups had decided to stay out of the fighting.

## Thayendanegea, (Joseph Brant)
### 1742–1807

**Character Trait: Self-discipline**

Thayendanegea was born in what is now Ohio and as a young man became a friend of British General William Johnson. As a result of that friendship, Thayendanegea attended school in Connecticut, where he became a Christian and took the name Joseph Brant. Until the war Brant had been a missionary in the Ohio Valley. After the war he continued his missionary work among the Native Americans of Canada.

 **MULTIMEDIA BIOGRAPHIES**
Visit The Learning Site **www.harcourtschool.com/ biographies** to learn about other famous people.

The loyalties of others, however, were divided, just as they had been during the French and Indian War. Some Iroquois, such as the Mohawk leader Thayendanegea (thay•en•da•NEG•ah), known as Joseph Brant, fought for the British. Others fought for the Patriots.

At first, most Americans on the frontier remained neutral. They wanted to be free of any government—British or American.

After a while their feeling began to change. Although they did not support the Patriot cause, they did want to drive the British out of the western lands. They felt that if they did not help the Patriots drive out the British, the British would probably keep the western lands even if the Americans won the war.

**REVIEW** **Why did many settlers in the western lands decide to help the Patriots?**

## LESSON 2
## REVIEW

❶ **MAIN IDEA** Why did Americans have different views about independence?

❷ **WHY IT MATTERS** Why do some people refer to the American Revolution as a civil war?

❸ **VOCABULARY** What was the difference between a **Patriot** and a **Loyalist**?

❹ **READING SKILL—Sequence** Were enslaved African Americans given their freedom when they joined the Continental Army or after the war?

❺ **HISTORY** Which side did most of the Native American groups support?

❻ **GEOGRAPHY** Which side did most of the Americans living on the frontier support?

❼ **CRITICAL THINKING—Hypothesize** How might the war have been different if all Americans had supported the same side?

 **PERFORMANCE— Write a Dialogue**
Write a dialogue that might have taken place between a Patriot and a Loyalist. Be sure to include what their viewpoints on independence might have been. Share this dialogue with a classmate.

# Make a Decision

**VOCABULARY**

consequence

## WHY IT MATTERS

At the time of the Revolutionary War, colonists had to make many difficult decisions. These decisions often had lasting consequences. A **consequence** is what happens because of an action. The decisions you make can have good or bad consequences. To make a thoughtful decision, you need to think about the consequences before you act.

## WHAT YOU NEED TO KNOW

Here are some steps you can use to help you make a thoughtful decision.

**Step 1** Know that you have to make a decision.

**Step 2** Gather information.

**Step 3** Identify choices.

**Step 4** Predict consequences and weigh those consequences.

**Step 5** Make a choice and take action.

## PRACTICE THE SKILL

Imagine that you are living in one of the 13 colonies at the time of the American Revolution. You have to decide whether to join the Patriots, join the Loyalists, or stay neutral. Make thoughtful decisions based on the roles described below. Explain the steps you followed in making each decision.

1 Your family owns a plantation in North Carolina.

2 You are a merchant in Boston.

3 You are a minister in Pennsylvania.

4 You are a settler on the frontier.

## APPLY WHAT YOU LEARNED

Think about a decision you made at school this week. What steps did you follow? What choices did you have? What were the consequences of your choices? Do you think your decision was a thoughtful one? Explain.

DECISIONS FOR THE COLONISTS

★ CHOICE 1:
**Join the Patriots**
Possible Consequences
Good?   Bad?

★ CHOICE 2:
**Stay Neutral**
Possible Consequences
Good?   Bad?

★ CHOICE 3:
**Join the Loyalists**
Possible Consequences
Good?   Bad?

# 3

# Fighting the Revolutionary War

1750       1770       1790

**1775–1778**

George Washington arrived in Massachusetts to meet the Continental Army in July 1775, less than three weeks after the Battle of Bunker Hill. The 14,500 soldiers wore no uniforms—only their everyday clothes. Many had no guns, so they carried spears and axes. With little money and not much training, the Continental Army went to war against one of the most powerful armies in the world, the British army.

## Comparing Armies

The soldiers who stood before George Washington that summer day in 1775 had never fought as an army before. Some of them had fought in the French and Indian War, but most had no military experience. Washington quickly had to make rules for the soldiers and get them trained to fight against the British.

Unlike the Continental Army, the British army was made up of professional soldiers. They had the best training and the most experienced officers. But the British had problems, too. It was difficult to fight a war more than 3,000 miles (4,828 km) from home. They often had trouble delivering soldiers and supplies across the Atlantic Ocean.

In the early days of the war, the British army's greater numbers gave it an advantage over the Continental Army. The British had more than

Many soldiers in the Continental Army (left) faced shortages of food and other supplies. British soldiers (right) had plenty of supplies.

In the Battle of Saratoga, British General John Burgoyne was surrounded and had to surrender. This medal shows him surrendering to General Horatio Gates.

50,000 soldiers in the colonies. General Washington usually had no more than 15,000 soldiers in his army.

**REVIEW** How was the British army different from the Continental Army?

## The War in the North

By the spring of 1776, Washington and his ragged army had moved south from Massachusetts to New York. By the fall the British had defeated the Americans in several battles, including the Battle of Long Island. Now the British were chasing Washington and what was left of the Continental Army.

Most of the Americans **enlisted** in, or joined, the army for almost one year at a time. They might stay that long or longer, or they might not. At harvesttime, some of the Continentals went home to their farms. Washington and the Continentals who stayed with him did their best to keep moving to avoid capture by the British. By winter they had marched through New Jersey to Pennsylvania.

Most of the British army had been sent back to New York for the winter. When Washington learned that the Hessian mercenaries stationed at Trenton, New Jersey, were not prepared for an attack, he decided to move against them. On Christmas Day 1776, Washington and his army crossed the ice-choked Delaware River in boats. By night in freezing weather, the shivering soldiers silently marched toward Trenton. At daybreak the Americans made a surprise attack. More than 900 Hessians were taken as prisoners.

William B. T. Trego's painting *The March to Valley Forge* shows the hardships Washington (on white horse) and his army faced. This knapsack (right) was carried by one of the soldiers at Valley Forge.

The new year brought more good news for Washington and his army. The best news came in October 1777 with an American victory at Saratoga in New York. There the Americans defeated a British army of more than 5,000 soldiers led by British General John Burgoyne (ber•GOYN). The British plan had called for Burgoyne to move south from Canada, while British General William Howe moved north from Philadelphia. The two armies were to cut the colonies in two. Instead, Howe failed to support Burgoyne, and the British had one of their worst defeats of the war. On October 17, 1777, Burgoyne surrendered his entire army to American General Horatio Gates.

Patriots everywhere were overjoyed at the news. The Battle of Saratoga became a turning point in the war. A **turning point** is a single event that causes important and dramatic change.

**REVIEW** When was the Battle of Saratoga fought?

## Winter at Valley Forge

The Continental Army was encouraged by its victory at Saratoga. But it still faced hardships. In December 1777, General Washington set up headquarters at Valley Forge, Pennsylvania, near Philadelphia. That winter his ragtag Continental Army was almost destroyed by cold and hunger. Many men were ill, and many died.

In these hard times a German soldier named Friedrich von Steuben (vahn SHTOY•buhn) reported to Washington at Valley Forge. Von Steuben was one of many soldiers from other countries who believed in the Patriots' cause and helped them. Two Polish officers, Casimir Pulaski (puh•LAS•kee) and Thaddeus Kosciuszko (kawsh•CHUSH•koh), and the 20-year-old Marquis de Lafayette (lah•fee•ET) from France also supported the Patriots. Washington liked the young Lafayette and immediately gave him important duties.

At Valley Forge, von Steuben's job was to organize and drill the Continental Army so that it could move quickly on command. This would allow it to attack and retreat faster. Von Steuben also taught the American soldiers how to use bayonets. A bayonet is a knifelike weapon attached to a rifle. Bayonets were standard equipment for European soldiers. By the spring of 1778, Washington's soldiers were marching well.

**REVIEW** Who came to offer help to the Continental Army?

The Marquis de Lafayette, a French noble, was eager to help the Continental Army.

## Help from Other Countries

While the Continental Army was suffering the harsh, cold winter at Valley Forge, Benjamin Franklin was working in Paris, France. Franklin was there to ask the French leaders to join the war.

### · BIOGRAPHY ·

### Haym Salomon    1740–1785
#### Character Trait: Loyalty

Haym Salomon was a banker who worked for the cause of American freedom. Born in Poland, he came to New York in 1772. When the British captured the city, he stayed there and spied for the Patriots. In 1778 he fled the city with his wife and child and went into business as a banker in Philadelphia. Salomon worked to get money to pay for the Revolution.

**MULTIMEDIA BIOGRAPHIES**
Visit The Learning Site at www.harcourtschool.com/biographies
to learn about other famous people.
**GO ONLINE**

GEORGE ROGERS CLARK      FRANCIS MARION      JOHN PAUL JONES

The French wanted the Americans to win the war and weaken their longtime rival, the British. The French, however, felt that the Americans did not have much chance of winning.

Franklin talked with the French leaders for months without success. Then news of the Americans' victory at Saratoga reached France. This victory showed the French that the Americans now stood a chance of winning the war. As a result, the French sent supplies and soldiers to help the Patriots. After the victory at Saratoga, people from other places helped the Americans, too. Bernardo de Gálvez (GAHL•ves), the governor of Spanish Louisiana, sent guns, food, and money. Later, he led his own soldiers in capturing several British forts. Spanish-born Jorge Farragut (FAIR•uh•guht) fought in the Continental Army and also in the navy.

**REVIEW** Why did the French decide to help the Patriots?

Mary Ludwig Hays McCauley is shown loading a cannon at the Battle of Monmouth.

## American Heroes

During the war the Americans cheered as they heard news about the deeds of many brave people from all over the United States. Their acts of courage helped make Americans sure that they could win the war.

In the mountains of the Northeast, Ethan Allen led the Green Mountain Boys. Allen and his soldiers from what is now Vermont won one of the first American victories in the war. They captured Fort Ticonderoga in New York.

When General George Washington asked for volunteers to spy on the British in New York City, a young man named Nathan Hale from Connecticut came forward. Dressed as a Dutch schoolteacher, Hale obtained the information Washington needed. As he returned to the American side, the British captured him. According to legend, Hale told the British soldiers before they hanged him, "I only regret that I have but one life to lose for my country."

In the Ohio Valley, George Rogers Clark helped protect the frontier lands claimed by many American settlers as theirs. Leading a small army, he marched through the western lands, defending settlers from attacks by the British and their Indian allies.

From bases in the swamps of South Carolina, Francis Marion led daring raids against the British. The British called him the Swamp Fox because they could never catch

This statue of Nathan Hale was built in 1914 to honor him.

NATHAN HALE
1755-1776
CLASS OF 1773

him and his soldiers. At sea John Paul Jones, a navy commander, battled larger and better-equipped British ships. In one famous battle in the North Sea near Britain, the British asked Jones to surrender. He replied, "I have not yet begun to fight." Jones kept fighting until the British ship gave up.

Many women also won fame for their bravery during the war. Mary Slocomb joined her husband at the Battle of Moores Creek Bridge in 1776. Mary Ludwig Hays McCauley earned the name Molly Pitcher by carrying water to the troops during the Battle of Monmouth in New Jersey in 1778. When her husband was wounded, she took his place firing the cannons.

**REVIEW** Who defended settlers in the western lands?

**LESSON 3**

**REVIEW**

Summary Time Line

1775 ———————————————— 1778

1776
The Battle of Long Island

1777
The Battle of Saratoga

1. **MAIN IDEA**   How did the Continental Army turn the war in its favor?

2. **WHY IT MATTERS**   What other countries gave help to the Patriots?

3. **VOCABULARY**   Write a paragraph describing the **turning point** of the war.

4. **TIME LINE**   When did the British suffer one of their worst defeats of the war?

5. **READING SKILL—Sequence**   Which battle was fought first, Saratoga or Long Island?

6. **GEOGRAPHY**   Where did George Washington defeat the Hessian mercenaries?

7. **CRITICAL THINKING—Evaluate**   How did the military training of the Continental soldiers affect the war?

**PERFORMANCE—Write a Song**   Write a song about some of the heroes of the American Revolution. Share your song with the class.

# Washington's Mess Chest

During much of the Revolutionary War, George Washington and his troops lived in tents or other shelters. To prepare and eat his meals, Washington used this camp kitchen, or mess chest. It was equipped with all the pots, pans, and utensils he needed.

**FROM THE SMITHSONIAN INSTITUTION
NATIONAL MUSEUM OF AMERICAN HISTORY**

Glass storage jars used for storing water or tonics

Kettles used for heating food on the gridiron over an open flame

Kettles stacked inside each other to save space

One of three tin platters used for preparing and serving meals

Lift-out storage bins used for storing dry goods such as breads, flour, or grain

cork stopper

glass bottle

gridiron

collapsible legs

tin pot

detachable wooden handle

pewter tops

glass bottles

tin plate with knife and fork

## Analyze the Primary Source

1. What do you think went inside the two glass bottles with the pewter tops?

2. What do you think George Washington did with the gridiron? Why did it have collapsible legs?

3. Where might someone today use a chest like this?

### ACTIVITY

**Compare and Contrast** Make a list of items that you might include today in a mess chest. Then draw a picture showing what that mess chest might look like. Use your drawing to explain to classmates how the items you included in your mess chest are similar to and different from the ones in Washington's mess chest.

### RESEARCH

Visit The Learning Site at **www.harcourtschool.com/primarysources** to research other primary sources.

**MAIN IDEA**
Read to learn how the Americans finally won their independence.

**WHY IT MATTERS**
The United States became the first country in the history of the world to overthrow a monarchy and establish a democracy.

# Independence Is Won

1778–1783

When the British government learned that the French were helping the Americans, British army leaders shifted the fighting. The British had already captured important cities in the North—Boston, Philadelphia, and New York. They hoped now to defeat the Patriots once and for all. So they concentrated on the South, where there was greater Loyalist support.

## The War in the South

In 1778 the British captured Savannah, Georgia. In 1780, they captured the city of Charles Town, later known as Charleston, in South Carolina. From there, they attacked and defeated the Americans at Camden, also in South Carolina. This victory gave the British new hope of quickly defeating the Continental Army and winning the war.

As the British tried to stamp out the fire of independence in one place, they found that it only sprang up in another place. "We fight, get beat, rise, and fight again," General Nathanael Greene wrote. Greene commanded the Continental Army in the Southern Colonies. Under Greene's leadership General Daniel Morgan won the battle at Cowpens, South Carolina, in 1781.

The battle at Cowpens, South Carolina, was a major victory for the Americans. This photograph shows what the battlefield looks like today.

## Major Battles of the Revolution

0    100    200 Miles

0   100   200 Kilometers
Albers Equal-Area Projection

Lake Superior

Lake Huron

Lake Michigan

Lake St. Clair

Lake Erie

Lake Ontario

Lake Champlain

St. Lawrence R.

MAINE
(part of Mass.)

Mississippi River

Connecticut R.

Merrimack R.

Mohawk River

Saratoga 1777

Bennington 1777

NH

Concord 1775

Boston 1775

Lexington 1775

NEW YORK

MA

Hudson R.

River

CT

RI

Allegheny R.

West Point

40°N

New York City

NJ

Long Island 1776

Princeton 1777

PENNSYLVANIA

Delaware R.

Valley Forge

Trenton 1776

Susquehanna R.

Brandywine 1777

Germantown 1777

Philadelphia

MARYLAND

Baltimore

Potomac River

DELAWARE

70°W

Wabash River

Maumee River

VIRGINIA

ATLANTIC OCEAN

Cahokia 1778

Vincennes 1779

James River

Richmond

Kaskaskia 1778

River

Ohio

River

Roanoke R.

Yorktown 1781

Chesapeake Bay

35°N

LOUISIANA

Cumberland River

Guilford Courthouse 1781

NORTH CAROLINA

Kings Mountain 1780

Charlotte

Cape Fear R.

Tennessee River

Cowpens 1781

Camden 1780

Wilmington

Mississippi River

Savannah River

SOUTH CAROLINA

| | American colonies |
| | British |
| | Spanish |
| ⚜ | American victory |
| ⚜ | British victory |
| — | Present-day border |

GEORGIA

Ocmulgee River

Charles Town 1780

Savannah 1778

Altamaha River

N
W    E
S

80°W

Gulf of Mexico    85°W

75°W

30°N

GEOGRAPHY THEME

**Regions** This map shows the major battles of the American Revolution.

◈ In which region did most of the later battles take place?

Early in 1781 Benedict Arnold, a former Continental Army officer, led the British army's attacks on Virginia towns. Arnold was a **traitor**, or someone who acts against his or her country. Earlier, he had given the British the plans to the American fort at West Point, New York, in exchange for money and a high rank in the British army.

Then the British army in South Carolina pushed into North Carolina. There, in March 1781, the Americans suffered a terrible defeat at Guilford Courthouse. The British, however, still could not win the war, because no one city or town was the heart of America.

**REVIEW** What battle gave the British hope of winning the war?

The Battle of Yorktown was the last major battle of the Revolutionary War. American and French soldiers surrounded the British, and the fighting lasted for several weeks in September and October 1781. It was a huge victory for the Americans and it helped end the war.

1 French soldiers
2 American officers' headquarters
3 American soldiers
4 field where the British surrendered
5 British earthworks

6 British soldiers
7 Chesapeake Bay
8 French ships
9 British ships
10 York River

◆ Why were the British at a disadvantage in the Battle of Yorktown?

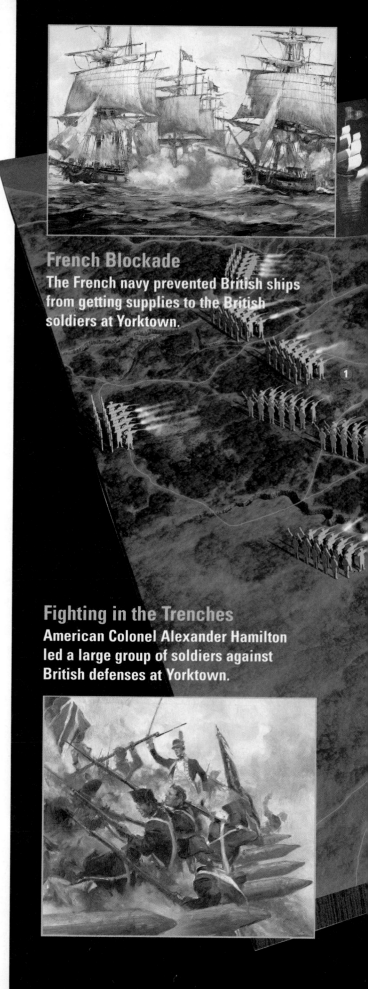

**French Blockade**
The French navy prevented British ships from getting supplies to the British soldiers at Yorktown.

**Fighting in the Trenches**
American Colonel Alexander Hamilton led a large group of soldiers against British defenses at Yorktown.

## Victory at Yorktown

By late summer of 1781, British General Charles Cornwallis had set up his headquarters at Yorktown, a small Virginia town on Chesapeake Bay. At Yorktown, it was easy for the British ships to land supplies. However, since the town was on the bay, the British could also be surrounded easily. Knowing this, the French and the Americans made a plan to defeat Cornwallis at Yorktown.

The French army joined the Continental Army near New York City and marched south to Virginia in order to surround Yorktown. At the same time, the French navy took control of Chesapeake Bay. Now the British navy could not get supplies to the British army or leave the area. Cornwallis was trapped.

In late September, Cornwallis sent word to his commander in the North. "If you cannot relieve me very soon," he said, "you must be prepared to hear the worst."

**Scuttled Ships**
Cornwallis ordered his troops to scuttle, or sink, his own ships to block the French navy from attacking Yorktown.

The painting by John Trumbull shows the British surrender at Yorktown. George Washington is shown in front of the American flag.

The worst happened. Surrounded and under attack for weeks from both land and sea, Cornwallis surrendered. A person who was there wrote, "At two o'clock in the evening Oct. 19th, 1781, the British army, led by General Charles O'Hara, marched out of its lines, with colors cased [flags folded] and drums beating a British march." When the French and American soldiers heard the drums, they stopped their fire. The British soldiers then marched out of Yorktown and laid down their weapons.

In Yorktown a British military band reportedly played a popular tune of the time. It was fittingly called "The World Turned Upside Down." When news of the surrender at Yorktown reached

The drum was used in the Battle of Yorktown.

Philadelphia, the Liberty Bell rang out the news of the American victory.

Though fighting dragged on in some places for more than two years, it was clear that the war had been decided at Yorktown in 1781. The Patriots had won after a long, hard fight.

**REVIEW** **What problem did the British face at Yorktown?**

## The Treaty of Paris

The Battle of Yorktown did not officially end the war. The Treaty of Paris did that. Work on the treaty began in April 1782, when the British and Americans sent representatives to Paris.

There the representatives stated the American terms— that is, what the Americans wanted in the treaty. They wanted the British king and Parliament to accept American independence and to remove all British soldiers from American soil. They also asked that the British pay the Americans whose property had been destroyed in the war.

The British, in turn, asked that Loyalists who chose to remain in the United States be treated fairly. Many Loyalists had fled to Nova Scotia and other parts of Canada and to the Bahamas. Some returned to Britain but were sorry they did. Most of them could not find jobs and soon became very poor. The British government ignored them.

British and American representatives **negotiated**, or talked with one another to work out an agreement. After more than a year of such talks, the representatives signed the Treaty of Paris on September 3, 1783.

The Treaty of Paris officially named the United States of America as a new coun-try and described its borders. The United States reached to Florida on the south. The northern border would be an imaginary line through the Great Lakes. The Mississippi River formed its western border. The Treaty of Paris was just as much a victory as winning at Yorktown had been. Independence was now a fact.

**REVIEW** **What were the American terms of the Treaty of Paris?**

## Washington's Farewell

Soon after the Treaty of Paris was signed, General Washington and his officers had made their headquarters in New York City. Though joyful about their victory, the American military leaders were sad to say good-bye to one another after the long war.

In early December 1783, Washington and his officers met at Fraunces Tavern in New York City for a farewell dinner.

This painting by Benjamin West shows—from left to right—John Jay, John Adams, and Benjamin Franklin negotiating a peace agreement with British representatives in Paris. The negotiations led to the signing of the Treaty of Paris.

At a meeting of Congress in Annapolis, Maryland, George Washington resigns from his position as commander in chief of the Continental Army.

Near the end of the meal, Washington stood up. "With a heart full of love and gratitude, I now take my leave of you," he said. One by one, each man at the dinner went up to say good-bye to the general. Tears streaming down his cheeks, Washington hugged each one. "Such a scene of sorrow and weeping I have never before seen," wrote one of the officers.

After saying his farewells, Washington started home to Virginia. On the way he stopped in Annapolis, Maryland, where Congress was then meeting. He told the representatives that, with peace, his work was done. "Having now finished the work assigned me, I retire from the great theater of action," Washington said. He was leaving public service forever, he thought.

**REVIEW** Why did Washington think his work was done?

## Effects of the War

Wars cause change, and the Revolutionary War was no different. The American states were no longer a source of raw materials and agricultural produce just for Britain, as they had been in colonial times. Dutch, French, Spanish, and Portuguese trading ships soon began leaving American ports loaded with American goods.

After the end of the war, more Americans moved west. From Philadelphia one person wrote, "I can scarcely walk a square without meeting [someone] . . . whose destination is principally [mainly] Ohio and Indiana." Many predicted that by the 1800s most of the people in the United States would be living in the West, which at the time was the region between the Appalachian

Mountains and the Mississippi River. Land companies were organized to sell the new lands.

To help defend the new nation's far-reaching borders, leaders later established a regular, full-time army. Since that time a regular army has been added to by the National Guard or the Reserves. To provide leaders for the military, the government established schools to train officers. On July 4, 1802, the United States Military Academy opened at West Point, New York. In 1845 the Naval School, later the United States Naval Academy, opened at Annapolis, Maryland.

The Revolutionary War was not just another war. It was a milestone in human history. The American Revolution became a model for later revolutions, including those in South America. "Government by the consent of the governed" became a guiding principle. A **principle** is a rule that is used in deciding how to act.

**REVIEW** What effect did the Revolutionary War have on the American economy?

North America in 1783

**Regions** This map shows North America in 1783, after the Treaty of Paris was signed.

❓ What were the boundaries of the United States at that time?

**LESSON 4 REVIEW**

**Summary Time Line**

1778 — 1783

1781
The Battle of Yorktown

1783
Treaty of Paris

① **MAIN IDEA** How did the United States win its independence?

② **WHY IT MATTERS** Why was the American victory in the Revolutionary War significant?

③ **VOCABULARY** Use the words **negotiate** and **principle** in a sentence about independence.

④ **TIME LINE** When was the Treaty of Paris signed?

⑤ **READING SKILL—Sequence** What battle prompted General Cornwallis to surrender his troops?

⑥ **HISTORY** Why was Benedict Arnold considered a traitor?

⑦ **CRITICAL THINKING—Evaluate** How did the war affect the American military?

**PERFORMANCE—Write a Letter**
Imagine that you are an American in 1782. Write a letter to Benjamin Franklin in Paris describing what you think the terms of the Treaty of Paris should be. Share your letter with a classmate.

# ·SKILLS·

CHART AND GRAPH

# Compare Graphs

## ▶ WHY IT MATTERS

Suppose you want to prepare a report on trade during the American Revolution. You want to show a lot of information in a brief, clear way. One way you might do this is by making graphs. Knowing how to read and make different kinds of graphs can help you compare large amounts of information.

## ▶ WHAT YOU NEED TO KNOW

Different kinds of graphs show information in different ways. A bar graph uses bars and is especially useful for quick comparisons. The bar graph on page 331 shows the chief exports of the United States in 1790. A circle graph can help you make comparisons. The circle graph on page 331 shows the main trading partners of the United States in 1790. A line graph shows change over time. The line graph shows that the amount of goods the Americans exported changed over time.

This map of the world was drawn in the mid-1700s. The exchange table (bottom) was used to compare the values of the many kinds of money that were used in the American colonies.

## ➡ PRACTICE THE SKILL

Compare the information in the bar, circle, and line graphs by answering the following questions. Think about the advantages and disadvantages of each kind of graph.

❶ Look at the circle graph. Who were the main trading partners of the United States?

❷ Who did the United States export most of its goods to?

❸ Did the United States export more goods to Spain or to Portugal?

❹ Look at the bar graph. What did the United States export?

❺ Did the United States export more corn or more wheat?

❻ How much lumber did the United States export?

❼ Look at the line graph. How did the amount of exports to Britain change over time?

❽ Why do you think the amount of exports to Britain changed over time?

## ➡ APPLY WHAT YOU LEARNED

Use the graphs on this page to write a paragraph summarizing information about trade during the late 1700s. Share your paragraph with a partner, and compare your summaries.

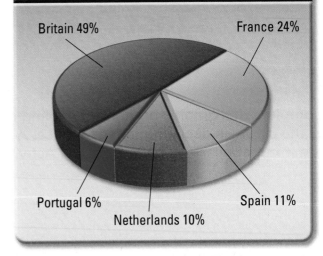

Exports to Main Trading Partners, 1790

Britain 49%   France 24%   Portugal 6%   Netherlands 10%   Spain 11%

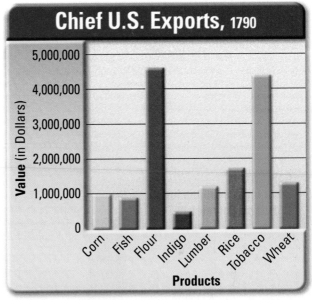

Chief U.S. Exports, 1790

Value (in Dollars): 0, 1,000,000, 2,000,000, 3,000,000, 4,000,000, 5,000,000

Products: Corn, Fish, Flour, Indigo, Lumber, Rice, Tobacco, Wheat

U.S. Exports to Britain, 1760–1790

Value (in British Pounds): 0, 200,000, 400,000, 600,000, 800,000, 1,000,000, 1,200,000

Year: 1760, 1770, 1780, 1790

# Review and Test Preparation

Summary Time Line
1775

● **1776**
Independence from the British is declared

● **1777**
The Battle of Saratoga

## USE YOUR READING SKILLS

Complete this graphic organizer by filling in the events that led to the colonies declaring independence. A copy of this graphic organizer appears on page 92 of the Activity Book.

## Independence is Declared

**FIRST**

Colonists in North America want independence for the 13 British Colonies

**NEXT**

**LAST**

## THINK & WRITE

**Write a News Story**    Imagine the year is 1776 and you are a newspaper reporter in Philadelphia. On July 8 you attend the first public reading of the Declaration of Independence. Write a news story about the event and the reactions of those present.

**Write a Speech**    One of the Continental Army's hardest tests was during the winter of 1777. That winter, soldiers who were camped at Valley Forge had to endure extreme cold and hunger. Write a speech to inspire the troops at Valley Forge.

**1781**
The British army
is defeated in
the Battle of
Yorktown

**1783**
The Treaty
of Paris is
signed

## USE THE TIME LINE

Use the chapter summary time line to answer these questions.

**1** When did the colonies declare their independence from Britain?

**2** Did the Battle of Yorktown take place before or after the Battle of Saratoga?

## USE VOCABULARY

Use these terms to write a story about the American Revolution.

**public opinion** (p. 302), **allegiance** (p. 303)

**neutral** (p. 309), **enlist** (p. 315),

**turning point** (p. 316)

## RECALL FACTS

Answer these questions.

**3** Why was the Declaration of Independence written?

**4** How did Mercy Otis Warren contribute to the Patriot cause?

**5** What schools were set up by the government to train military officers?

Write the letter of the best choice.

**6** **TEST PREP** Thomas Jefferson's greatest contribution to the American Revolution was—
  **A** commanding American forces at the Battle of Saratoga.
  **B** convincing France to support the United States.
  **C** writing the Declaration of Independence.
  **D** writing *Common Sense*.

**7** **TEST PREP** The most important effect of the Battle of Saratoga was—
  **F** France's decision to support the United States.
  **G** the defeat of more than 900 Hessian mercenaries.
  **H** the capture of Benedict Arnold.
  **J** the British army's decision to surrender.

## THINK CRITICALLY

**8** Why do you think so many people in the colonies read *Common Sense*?

**9** What do you think would have happened if American forces had lost the Battle of Saratoga?

**10** How did the military training of Continental soldiers affect the war?

**11** What do you think was George Washington's greatest contribution to the American Revolution?

## APPLY SKILLS

**Make a Decision**

**12** Imagine that the year is 1777 and a friend has asked you to allow your home to be used as a shelter for Patriot soldiers. What steps might you follow to come to a decision?

**Compare Graphs**

**13** Look in an encyclopedia or on the Internet for two population graphs of your state. Make copies of the graphs or print them out. Then write a paragraph explaining the differences between the two.

# VISIT

# THE Freedom Trail

## GET READY

The Freedom Trail is a 2½-mile (4-km) walking trail that weaves its way through the city of Boston. The trail connects landmarks that played an important role in America's struggle for independence. Along the Freedom Trail you can stop at places such as Faneuil Hall, where Bostonians protested British taxation policies. You can also visit the Old North Church, where on April 8, 1775, two lanterns were hung to warn Paul Revere and other colonists of incoming British troops. The Freedom Trail is more than just a path between places. Each stop on the trail tells a story about our nation's independence.

## LOCATE IT

Boston

MASSACHUSETTS

## WHAT TO SEE

The Freedom Trail is marked by red bricks. It gives visitors the opportunity to follow paths once walked by America's first patriots.

The Freedom Trail

A Freedom Trail Marker

Faneuil Hall

King's Chapel Burying Ground

Bunker Hill Monument

Statue of Samuel Adams at Faneuil Hall

The State House

Paul Revere's house

## TAKE A FIELD TRIP

**GO ONLINE**

**A VIRTUAL TOUR**
Visit The Learning Site at
**www.harcourtschool.com/tours**
to take virtual tours of other
historic sites in the United States.

CNN
Turner Le@rning®

**A VIDEO TOUR**
Check your media
center or classroom library
for a videotape tour of the
Freedom Trail.

# 4 Review and Test Preparation

## VISUAL SUMMARY

**Write a Paragraph** Study the pictures and captions below to help you review Unit 4. Then choose one of the events shown. Write a paragraph that describes what happened and how that event affected the American Revolution.

## USE VOCABULARY

For each pair of terms, write a sentence or two that explains how the terms are related.

1. **revolution** (p. 268), **independence** (p. 302)
2. **proclamation** (p. 276), **declaration** (p. 283)
3. **boycott** (p. 282), **blockade** (p. 289)

## RECALL FACTS

Answer these questions.

4. What was the Albany Plan of Union?

5. Why did Parliament pass new tax laws for the American colonists after the French and Indian War?

Write the letter of the best choice.

6. **TEST PREP** The Stamp Act Congress met to—
   A discuss the problems the new tax laws had caused.
   B vote on the Stamp Act.
   C form an American Parliament.
   D choose a new mayor for New York City.

7. **TEST PREP** What did the British learn from the Battle of Bunker Hill?
   F Earthworks would help them.
   G The colonists had many bullets.
   H The colonists printed their own money.
   J Fighting the colonists would not be easy.

8. **TEST PREP** Which battle of the American Revolution brought about the end of the war?
   A the Battle of Yorktown
   B the Battle of Moores Creek Bridge
   C the Battle of Saratoga
   D the Battle of Long Island

### Visual Summary

1750  1755  1760  1765

1754  The French and Indian War begins  p. 269

1765  The Stamp Act is passed  p. 281

1773  The Boston Tea Party takes place  p. 288

336

## THINK CRITICALLY

**9** Why do you think the British government believed that it had the right to make the colonists pay taxes?

**10** Do you think the British could have avoided war with the colonists? Explain.

**11** Why do you think some colonists chose to remain loyal to Britain during the American Revolution?

**12** What do you think Nathan Hale meant when he said, "I only regret that I have but one life to lose for my country"?

## APPLY SKILLS

**Compare Historical Maps**
Use the two historical maps on this page to answer the following questions.

**13** Which map would you use to determine who claimed the 13 colonies?

**14** Which map shows the land that was claimed by both Spain and the United States?

**15** What areas shown on the two maps changed very little between 1763 and 1783?

**16** Most of the British land that was reserved for Native Americans in 1763 became a part of what country by 1783?

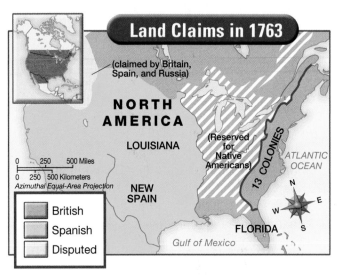

**Land Claims in 1763**

NORTH AMERICA
(claimed by Britain, Spain, and Russia)
LOUISIANA
(Reserved for Native Americans)
13 COLONIES
ATLANTIC OCEAN
NEW SPAIN
FLORIDA
Gulf of Mexico

0   250   500 Miles
0   250   500 Kilometers
Azimuthal Equal-Area Projection

British
Spanish
Disputed

**Land Claims in 1783**

CANADA
(claimed by Britain, Spain, and Russia)
(claimed by U.S. and Britain)
NORTH AMERICA
NEW SPAIN
LOUISIANA
UNITED STATES
ATLANTIC OCEAN
(claimed by U.S. and Spain)
FLORIDA
Gulf of Mexico

0   250   500 Miles
0   250   500 Kilometers
Azimuthal Equal-Area Projection

British
Spanish
Disputed

**17** Which map would you use to determine the location of the land that was reserved for Native Americans?

**18** Who claimed Florida in 1763? in 1783?

1775        1780        1785        1790

**1775  The American Revolution begins**  p. 291

**1776  The Declaration of Independence is signed**  p. 306

**1781  The British surrender at Yorktown, in Virginia**  p. 326

337

# Unit Activities

 **GO ONLINE** Visit The Learning Site at www.harcourtschool.com/ socialstudies/activities for additional activities.

## Create a Time Line

Work in a group to make a large time line to display on a classroom wall. The time line should show either the important events leading up to the American Revolution or the key events that took place during and after the war. Use the time line as you take turns describing each of the events shown.

## Honor Your Hero

Choose someone you admire from the American Revolution to be the subject of a poster for a display called Heroes of the American Revolution. Research that person's life, and write a short biography to include on the poster. To illustrate the poster, print out pictures from the Internet or draw your own. Add words or phrases around the pictures, telling what made that person a hero. Present your poster to the class.

## VISIT YOUR LIBRARY

■ *The Boston Tea Party* by Laurie A. O'Neill. Troll Associates.

■ *Thomas* by Bonnie Pryor. Morrow Junior Books.

■ *The World Turned Upside Down: George Washington and the Battle of Yorktown* by Richard Ferrie. Holiday House.

## COMPLETE THE UNIT PROJECT

**The History Show** Work with a group of classmates to finish the unit project—a history show about the American Revolution. Decide which key events and people you want to include in your show. Then write a script, create any needed illustrations or costumes, and choose the presenters. Videotape your show and invite other students to watch it, or perform the show "live" for them.

# For Your Reference

# Almanac

## Facts About the States

| State Flag | State | Year of Statehood | Population* | Area (sq. mi.) | Capital | Origin of State Name |
|---|---|---|---|---|---|---|
| | Alabama | 1819 | 4,447,100 | 50,750 | Montgomery | Choctaw, *alba ayamule*, "one who clears land and gathers food from it" |
| | Alaska | 1959 | 626,932 | 570,374 | Juneau | Aleut, *alayeska*, "great land" |
| | Arizona | 1912 | 5,130,632 | 113,642 | Phoenix | Papago, *arizonac*, "place of the small spring" |
| | Arkansas | 1836 | 2,673,400 | 52,075 | Little Rock | Quapaw, "the downstream people" |
| | California | 1850 | 33,871,648 | 155,973 | Sacramento | Spanish, a fictional island |
| | Colorado | 1876 | 4,301,261 | 103,730 | Denver | Spanish, "red land" or "red earth" |
| | Connecticut | 1788 | 3,405,565 | 4,845 | Hartford | Mohican, *quinnitukqut*, "at the long tidal river" |
| | Delaware | 1787 | 783,600 | 1,955 | Dover | Named for Lord de la Warr |
| | Florida | 1845 | 15,982,378 | 54,153 | Tallahassee | Spanish, "filled with flowers" |
| | Georgia | 1788 | 8,186,453 | 57,919 | Atlanta | Named for King George II of England |
| | Hawaii | 1959 | 1,211,537 | 6,450 | Honolulu | Polynesian, *hawaiki* or *owykee*, "homeland" |
| | Idaho | 1890 | 1,293,593 | 82,751 | Boise | Invented name with unknown meaning |

| State Flag | State | Year of Statehood | Population* | Area (sq. mi.) | Capital | Origin of State Name |
|---|---|---|---|---|---|---|
| | Illinois | 1818 | 12,419,293 | 55,593 | Springfield | Algonquin, *iliniwek*, "men" or "warriors" |
| | Indiana | 1816 | 6,080,485 | 35,870 | Indianapolis | *Indian + a*, "land of the Indians" |
| | Iowa | 1846 | 2,926,324 | 55,875 | Des Moines | Dakota, *ayuba*, "beautiful land" |
| | Kansas | 1861 | 2,688,418 | 81,823 | Topeka | Sioux, "land of the south wind people" |
| | Kentucky | 1792 | 4,041,769 | 39,732 | Frankfort | Iroquoian, *ken-tah-ten*, "land of tomorrow" |
| | Louisiana | 1812 | 4,468,976 | 43,566 | Baton Rouge | Named for King Louis XIV of France |
| | Maine | 1820 | 1,274,923 | 30,865 | Augusta | Named after a French province |
| | Maryland | 1788 | 5,296,486 | 9,775 | Annapolis | Named for Henrietta Maria, Queen Consort of Charles I of England |
| | Massachusetts | 1788 | 6,349,097 | 7,838 | Boston | Massachusett tribe of Native Americans, "at the big hill" or "place of the big hill" |
| | Michigan | 1837 | 9,938,444 | 56,809 | Lansing | Ojibwa, "large lake" |
| | Minnesota | 1858 | 4,919,479 | 79,617 | St. Paul | Dakota Sioux, "sky-blue water" |
| | Mississippi | 1817 | 2,844,658 | 46,914 | Jackson | Indian word meaning "great waters" or "father of waters" |
| | Missouri | 1821 | 5,595,211 | 68,898 | Jefferson City | Named after the Missouri Indian tribe. *Missouri* means "town of the large canoes." |

* Census 2000 figures

| State Flag | State | Year of Statehood | Population* | Area (sq. mi.) | Capital | Origin of State Name |
|---|---|---|---|---|---|---|
| | Montana | 1889 | 902,195 | 145,566 | Helena | Spanish, "mountainous" |
| | Nebraska | 1867 | 1,711,263 | 76,878 | Lincoln | From an Oto Indian word meaning "flat water" |
| | Nevada | 1864 | 1,998,257 | 109,806 | Carson City | Spanish, "snowy" or "snowed upon" |
| | New Hampshire | 1788 | 1,235,786 | 8,969 | Concord | Named for Hampshire County, England |
| | New Jersey | 1787 | 8,414,350 | 7,419 | Trenton | Named for the Isle of Jersey |
| | New Mexico | 1912 | 1,819,046 | 121,365 | Santa Fe | Named by Spanish explorers from Mexico |
| | New York | 1788 | 18,976,457 | 47,224 | Albany | Named after the Duke of York |
| | North Carolina | 1789 | 8,049,313 | 48,718 | Raleigh | Named after King Charles II of England |
| | North Dakota | 1889 | 642,200 | 70,704 | Bismarck | Sioux, *dakota*, "friend" or "ally" |
| | Ohio | 1803 | 11,353,140 | 40,953 | Columbus | Iroquois, *oheo*, "great water" |
| | Oklahoma | 1907 | 3,450,654 | 68,679 | Oklahoma City | Choctaw, "red people" |
| | Oregon | 1859 | 3,421,399 | 96,003 | Salem | Unknown; generally accepted that it was taken from the writings of Maj. Robert Rogers, an English army officer |
| | Pennsylvania | 1787 | 12,281,054 | 44,820 | Harrisburg | *Penn + sylvania*, meaning "Penn's woods" |

| State Flag | State | Year of Statehood | Population* | Area (sq. mi.) | Capital | Origin of State Name |
|---|---|---|---|---|---|---|
| | Rhode Island | 1790 | 1,048,319 | 1,045 | Providence | From the Greek island of Rhodes |
| | South Carolina | 1788 | 4,012,012 | 30,111 | Columbia | Named after King Charles II of England |
| | South Dakota | 1889 | 754,844 | 75,898 | Pierre | Sioux, *dakota*, "friend" or "ally" |
| | Tennessee | 1796 | 5,689,283 | 41,220 | Nashville | Name of a Cherokee village |
| | Texas | 1845 | 20,851,820 | 261,914 | Austin | Native American, *tejas*, "friend" or "ally" |
| | Utah | 1896 | 2,233,169 | 82,168 | Salt Lake City | From the Ute tribe, meaning "people of the mountains" |
| | Vermont | 1791 | 608,827 | 9,249 | Montpelier | French, *vert*, "green," and *mont*, "mountain" |
| | Virginia | 1788 | 7,078,515 | 39,598 | Richmond | Named after Queen Elizabeth I of England |
| | Washington | 1889 | 5,894,121 | 66,582 | Olympia | Named for George Washington |
| | West Virginia | 1863 | 1,808,344 | 24,087 | Charleston | From the English-named state of Virginia |
| | Wisconsin | 1848 | 5,363,675 | 54,314 | Madison | Possibly Algonquian, "the place where we live" |
| | Wyoming | 1890 | 493,782 | 97,105 | Cheyenne | From Delaware Indian word meaning "land of vast plains" |
| | District of Columbia | | 572,059 | 67 | | Named after Christopher Columbus |

* Census 2000 figures

# Almanac

## Facts About the Western Hemisphere

| Country | Population* | Area (sq. mi.) | Capital | Origin of Country Name |
|---|---|---|---|---|
| **North America** | | | | |
| **Antigua and Barbuda** | 66,970 | 171 | St. Johns | Named for the Church of Santa María la Antigua in Seville, Spain |
| **Bahamas** | 297,852 | 5,386 | Nassau | Spanish, *bajamar*, "shallow water" |
| **Barbados** | 275,330 | 166 | Bridgetown | Means "bearded"—probably referring to the beard like vines early explorers found on its trees |
| **Belize** | 256,062 | 8,867 | Belmopan | Mayan, "muddy water" |
| **Canada** | 31,592,805 | 3,851,809 | Ottawa | Huron-Iroquois, *kanata*, "village" or "community" |
| **Costa Rica** | 3,773,057 | 19,730 | San José | Spanish, "rich coast" |
| **Cuba** | 11,184,023 | 42,803 | Havana | Origin unknown |
| **Dominica** | 70,786 | 289 | Roseau | Latin, *dies dominica*, "Day of the Lord" |
| **Dominican Republic** | 8,581,477 | 18,815 | Santo Domingo | Named after the capital city |
| **El Salvador** | 6,237,662 | 8,124 | San Salvador | Spanish, "the Savior" |
| **Grenada** | 89,227 | 131 | St. George's | Origin unknown |
| **Guatemala** | 12,974,361 | 42,042 | Guatemala City | Indian, "land of trees" |
| **Haiti** | 6,964,549 | 10,714 | Port-au-Prince | Indian, "land of mountains" |
| **Honduras** | 6,406,052 | 43,277 | Tegucigalpa | Spanish, "profundities" —probably referring to the depth of offshore waters |
| **Jamaica** | 2,665,636 | 4,243 | Kingston | Arawak, *xamayca*, "land of wood and water" |
| **Mexico** | 101,879,171 | 761,602 | Mexico City | Aztec, *mexliapan*, "lake of the moon" |
| **Nicaragua** | 4,918,393 | 49,998 | Managua | from *Nicarao*, the name of an Indian chief |

| Country | Population* | Area (sq. mi.) | Capital | Origin of Country Name |
|---|---|---|---|---|
| Panama | 2,845,647 | 30,193 | Panama City | From an Indian village's name |
| St. Kitts-Nevis | 38,756 | 96 | Basseterre | Named by Christopher Columbus—Kitts for St. Christopher, a Catholic saint; Nevis, for a cloud-topped peak that looked like *las nieves*, "the snows" |
| St. Lucia | 158,178 | 238 | Castries | Named by Christopher Columbus for a Catholic saint |
| St. Vincent and Grenadines | 115,942 | 150 | Kingstown | May have been named by Christopher Columbus for a Catholic saint |
| Trinidad and Tobago | 1,169,682 | 1,980 | Port of Spain | Trinidad, from the Spanish word for "trinity"; Tobago, named for tobacco because the island has the shape of a person smoking a pipe |
| United States of America | 281,421,906 | 3,537,441 | Washington, D.C. | Named after the explorer Amerigo Vespucci |

## South America

| Country | Population* | Area (sq. mi.) | Capital | Origin of Country Name |
|---|---|---|---|---|
| Argentina | 37,384,816 | 1,068,296 | Buenos Aires | Latin, *argentum*, "silver" |
| Bolivia | 8,300,463 | 424,162 | La Paz/Sucre | Named after Simón Bolívar, the famed liberator |
| Brazil | 174,468,575 | 3,286,470 | Brasília | Named after a native tree that the Portuguese called "bresel wood" |
| Chile | 15,328,467 | 292,257 | Santiago | Indian, *chilli*, "where the land ends" |
| Colombia | 40,349,388 | 439,735 | Bogotá | Named after Christopher Columbus |
| Ecuador | 13,183,978 | 109,483 | Quito | From the Spanish word for *equator*, referring to the country's location |
| Guyana | 697,181 | 83,000 | Georgetown | Indian, "land of waters" |
| Paraguay | 5,734,139 | 157,043 | Asunción | Named after the Paraguay River, which flows through it |
| Peru | 27,483,864 | 496,222 | Lima | Quechua, "land of abundance" |
| Suriname | 433,998 | 63,039 | Paramaribo | From an Indian word, *surinen* |
| Uruguay | 3,360,105 | 68,039 | Montevideo | Named after the Uruguay River, which flows through it |
| Venezuela | 23,916,810 | 352,143 | Caracas | Spanish, "Little Venice" |

# Almanac

## Facts About the Presidents

### 1 George Washington

1732–1799
**Birthplace:** *Westmoreland County, VA*
**Home State:** *VA*
**Political Party:** *None*
**Age at Inauguration:** *57*
**Served:** *1789–1797*
**Vice President:**
*John Adams*

### 2 John Adams

1735–1826
**Birthplace:** *Braintree, MA*
**Home State:** *MA*
**Political Party:** *Federalist*
**Age at Inauguration:** *61*
**Served:** *1797–1801*
**Vice President:**
*Thomas Jefferson*

### 3 Thomas Jefferson

1743–1826
**Birthplace:**
*Albemarle County, VA*
**Home State:** *VA*
**Political Party:**
*Democratic-Republican*
**Age at Inauguration:** *57*
**Served:** *1801–1809*
**Vice Presidents:**
*Aaron Burr,*
*George Clinton*

### 4 James Madison

1751–1836
**Birthplace:**
*Port Conway, VA*
**Home State:** *VA*
**Political Party:**
*Democratic-Republican*
**Age at Inauguration:** *57*
**Served:** *1809–1817*
**Vice Presidents:**
*George Clinton,*
*Elbridge Gerry*

### 5 James Monroe

1758–1831
**Birthplace:**
*Westmoreland County, VA*
**Home State:** *VA*
**Political Party:**
*Democratic-Republican*
**Age at Inauguration:** *58*
**Served:** *1817–1825*
**Vice President:**
*Daniel D. Tompkins*

### 6 John Quincy Adams

1767–1848
**Birthplace:** *Braintree, MA*
**Home State:** *MA*
**Political Party:**
*Democratic-Republican*
**Age at Inauguration:** *57*
**Served:** *1825–1829*
**Vice President:**
*John C. Calhoun*

### 7 Andrew Jackson

1767–1845
**Birthplace:**
*Waxhaw settlement, SC*
**Home State:** *TN*
**Political Party:**
*Democratic*
**Age at Inauguration:** *61*
**Served:** *1829–1837*
**Vice Presidents:**
*John C. Calhoun,*
*Martin Van Buren*

### 8 Martin Van Buren

1782–1862
**Birthplace:** *Kinderhook,*
*NY*
**Home State:** *NY*
**Political Party:**
*Democratic*
**Age at Inauguration:** *54*
**Served:** *1837–1841*
**Vice President:**
*Richard M. Johnson*

### 9 William H. Harrison

1773–1841
**Birthplace:** *Berkeley, VA*
**Home State:** *VA*
**Political Party:** *Whig*
**Age at Inauguration:** *68*
**Served:** *1841*
**Vice President:**
*John Tyler*

### 10 John Tyler

1790–1862
**Birthplace:** *Greenway, VA*
**Home State:** *VA*
**Political Party:** *Whig*
**Age at Inauguration:** *51*
**Served:** *1841–1845*
**Vice President:** *none*

### 11 James K. Polk

1795–1849
**Birthplace:**
*near Pineville, NC*
**Home State:** *TN*
**Political Party:**
*Democratic*
**Age at Inauguration:** *49*
**Served:** *1845–1849*
**Vice President:**
*George M. Dallas*

### 12 Zachary Taylor

1784–1850
**Birthplace:**
*Orange County, VA*
**Home State:** *LA*
**Political Party:** *Whig*
**Age at Inauguration:** *64*
**Served:** *1849–1850*
**Vice President:**
*Millard Fillmore*

### 13 Millard Fillmore

1800–1874
**Birthplace:** *Locke, NY*
**Home State:** *NY*
**Political Party:** *Whig*
**Age at Inauguration:** *50*
**Served:** *1850–1853*
**Vice President:** *none*

Home State refers to the state of residence when elected.

## 14 Franklin Pierce

1804–1869
**Birthplace:** *Hillsboro, NH*
**Home State:** *NH*
**Political Party:**
*Democratic*
**Age at Inauguration:** *48*
**Served:** *1853–1857*
**Vice President:**
*William R. King*

## 15 James Buchanan

1791–1868
**Birthplace:**
*near Mercersburg, PA*
**Home State:** *PA*
**Political Party:**
*Democratic*
**Age at Inauguration:** *65*
**Served:** *1857–1861*
**Vice President:**
*John C. Breckinridge*

## 16 Abraham Lincoln

1809–1865
**Birthplace:**
*near Hodgenville, KY*
**Home State:** *IL*
**Political Party:**
*Republican*
**Age at Inauguration:** *52*
**Served:** *1861–1865*
**Vice Presidents:**
*Hannibal Hamlin,*
*Andrew Johnson*

## 17 Andrew Johnson

1808–1875
**Birthplace:** *Raleigh, NC*
**Home State:** *TN*
**Political Party:**
*National Union*
**Age at Inauguration:** *56*
**Served:** *1865–1869*
**Vice President:** *none*

## 18 Ulysses S. Grant

1822–1885
**Birthplace:**
*Point Pleasant, OH*
**Home State:** *IL*
**Political Party:**
*Republican*
**Age at Inauguration:** *46*
**Served:** *1869–1877*
**Vice Presidents:**
*Schuyler Colfax,*
*Henry Wilson*

## 19 Rutherford B. Hayes

1822-1893
**Birthplace:**
*near Delaware, OH*
**Home State:** *OH*
**Political Party:**
*Republican*
**Age at Inauguration:** *54*
**Served:** *1877–1881*
**Vice President:**
*William A. Wheeler*

## 20 James A. Garfield

1831–1881
**Birthplace:** *Orange, OH*
**Home State:** *OH*
**Political Party:**
*Republican*
**Age at Inauguration:** *49*
**Served:** *1881*
**Vice President:**
*Chester A. Arthur*

## 21 Chester A. Arthur

1829–1886
**Birthplace:** *Fairfield, VT*
**Home State:** *NY*
**Political Party:**
*Republican*
**Age at Inauguration:** *51*
**Served:** *1881–1885*
**Vice President:** *none*

## 22 Grover Cleveland

1837–1908
**Birthplace:** *Caldwell, NJ*
**Home State:** *NY*
**Political Party:**
*Democratic*
**Age at Inauguration:** *47*
**Served:** *1885–1889*
**Vice President:**
*Thomas A. Hendricks*

## 23 Benjamin Harrison

1833–1901
**Birthplace:** *North Bend,*
*OH*
**Home State:** *IN*
**Political Party:**
*Republican*
**Age at Inauguration:** *55*
**Served:** *1889–1893*
**Vice President:**
*Levi P. Morton*

## 24 Grover Cleveland

1837–1908
**Birthplace:** *Caldwell, NJ*
**Home State:** *NY*
**Political Party:**
*Democratic*
**Age at Inauguration:** *55*
**Served:** *1893–1897*
**Vice President:**
*Adlai E. Stevenson*

## 25 William McKinley

1843–1901
**Birthplace:** *Niles, OH*
**Home State:** *OH*
**Political Party:**
*Republican*
**Age at Inauguration:** *54*
**Served:** *1897–1901*
**Vice Presidents:**
*Garret A. Hobart,*
*Theodore Roosevelt*

## 26 Theodore Roosevelt

1858–1919
**Birthplace:** *New York, NY*
**Home State:** *NY*
**Political Party:**
*Republican*
**Age at Inauguration:** *42*
**Served:** *1901–1909*
**Vice President:**
*Charles W. Fairbanks*

## 27 William H. Taft

1857–1930
**Birthplace:** *Cincinnati, OH*
**Home State:** *OH*
**Political Party:**
*Republican*
**Age at Inauguration:** *51*
**Served:** *1909–1913*
**Vice President:**
*James S. Sherman*

## 28 Woodrow Wilson

1856–1924
**Birthplace:** *Staunton, VA*
**Home State:** *NJ*
**Political Party:**
*Democratic*
**Age at Inauguration:** *56*
**Served:** *1913–1921*
**Vice President:**
*Thomas R. Marshall*

## 29 Warren G. Harding

1865–1923
**Birthplace:** *Blooming Grove, OH*
**Home State:** *OH*
**Political Party:** *Republican*
**Age at Inauguration:** *55*
**Served:** *1921–1923*
**Vice President:** *Calvin Coolidge*

## 30 Calvin Coolidge

1872–1933
**Birthplace:** *Plymouth Notch, VT*
**Home State:** *MA*
**Political Party:** *Republican*
**Age at Inauguration:** *51*
**Served:** *1923–1929*
**Vice President:** *Charles G. Dawes*

## 31 Herbert Hoover

1874–1964
**Birthplace:** *West Branch, IA*
**Home State:** *CA*
**Political Party:** *Republican*
**Age at Inauguration:** *54*
**Served:** *1929–1933*
**Vice President:** *Charles Curtis*

## 32 Franklin D. Roosevelt

1882–1945
**Birthplace:** *Hyde Park, NY*
**Home State:** *NY*
**Political Party:** *Democratic*
**Age at Inauguration:** *51*
**Served:** *1933–1945*
**Vice Presidents:** *John N. Garner, Henry A. Wallace, Harry S. Truman*

## 33 Harry S. Truman

1884–1972
**Birthplace:** *Lamar, MO*
**Home State:** *MO*
**Political Party:** *Democratic*
**Age at Inauguration:** *60*
**Served:** *1945–1953*
**Vice President:** *Alben W. Barkley*

## 34 Dwight D. Eisenhower

1890-1969
**Birthplace:** *Denison, TX*
**Home State:** *NY*
**Political Party:** *Republican*
**Age at Inauguration:** *62*
**Served:** *1953–1961*
**Vice President:** *Richard M. Nixon*

## 35 John F. Kennedy

1917–1963
**Birthplace:** *Brookline, MA*
**Home State:** *MA*
**Political Party:** *Democratic*
**Age at Inauguration:** *43*
**Served:** *1961–1963*
**Vice President:** *Lyndon B. Johnson*

## 36 Lyndon B. Johnson

1908–1973
**Birthplace:** *near Stonewall, TX*
**Home State:** *TX*
**Political Party:** *Democratic*
**Age at Inauguration:** *55*
**Served:** *1963–1969*
**Vice President:** *Hubert H. Humphrey*

## 37 Richard M. Nixon

1913–1994
**Birthplace:** *Yorba Linda, CA*
**Home State:** *NY*
**Political Party:** *Republican*
**Age at Inauguration:** *56*
**Served:** *1969–1974*
**Vice Presidents:** *Spiro T. Agnew, Gerald R. Ford*

## 38 Gerald R. Ford

1913–
**Birthplace:** *Omaha, NE*
**Home State:** *MI*
**Political Party:** *Republican*
**Age at Inauguration:** *61*
**Served:** *1974–1977*
**Vice President:** *Nelson A. Rockefeller*

## 39 Jimmy Carter

1924–
**Birthplace:** *Plains, GA*
**Home State:** *GA*
**Political Party:** *Democratic*
**Age at Inauguration:** *52*
**Served:** *1977–1981*
**Vice President:** *Walter F. Mondale*

## 40 Ronald W. Reagan

1911–
**Birthplace:** *Tampico, IL*
**Home State:** *CA*
**Political Party:** *Republican*
**Age at Inauguration:** *69*
**Served:** *1981–1989*
**Vice President:** *George Bush*

## 41 George Bush

1924–
**Birthplace:** *Milton, MA*
**Home State:** *TX*
**Political Party:** *Republican*
**Age at Inauguration:** *64*
**Served:** *1989–1993*
**Vice President:** *Dan Quayle*

## 42 William Clinton

1946–
**Birthplace:** *Hope, AR*
**Home State:** *AR*
**Political Party:** *Democratic*
**Age at Inauguration:** *46*
**Served:** *1993–2001*
**Vice President:** *Albert Gore*

## 43 George W. Bush

1946–
**Birthplace:** *New Haven, CT*
**Home State:** *TX*
**Political Party:** *Republican*
**Age at Inauguration:** *54*
**Served:** *2001–*
**Vice President:** *Richard Cheney*

# American Documents

## THE DECLARATION OF INDEPENDENCE

**In Congress, July 4, 1776.**
**The unanimous Declaration of the**
**thirteen United States of America,**

When in the Course of human events it becomes necessary for one people to dissolve the political bands which have connected them with another, and to assume among the powers of the earth, the separate and equal station to which the Laws of Nature and of Nature's God entitle them, a decent respect to the opinions of mankind requires that they should declare the causes which impel them to the separation.

We hold these truths to be self-evident, that all men are created equal, that they are endowed by their Creator with certain unalienable Rights, that among these are Life, Liberty and the pursuit of Happiness.

That to secure these rights, Governments are instituted among Men, deriving their just powers from the consent of the governed,

That whenever any Form of Government becomes destructive of these ends, it is the Right of the People to alter or to abolish it, and to institute new Government, laying its foundation on such principles and organizing its powers in such form, as to them shall seem most likely to effect their Safety and Happiness. Prudence, indeed, will dictate that Governments long established should not be changed for light and transient causes; and accordingly all experience hath shown, that mankind are more disposed to suffer, while evils are sufferable, than to right themselves by abolishing the forms to which they are accustomed. But when a long train of abuses and usurpations, pursuing invariably the same Object evinces a design to reduce them under absolute Despotism, it is their right, it is their duty, to throw off such Government, and to provide new Guards for their future security.

Such has been the patient sufferance of these Colonies; and such is now the necessity which constrains them to alter their former Systems of Government. The history of the present King of Great Britain is a history of repeated injuries and usurpations, all having in direct object the establishment of an absolute Tyranny over these States. To prove this, let Facts be submitted to a candid world.

He has refused his Assent to Laws, the most wholesome and necessary for the public good.

He has forbidden his Governors to pass Laws of immediate and pressing importance, unless suspended in their operation till his Assent should be obtained; and when so suspended, he has utterly neglected to attend to them.

---

**Preamble**
The Preamble tells why the Declaration was written. It states that the members of the Continental Congress believed the colonies had the right to break away from Britain and become a free nation.

**A Statement of Rights**
The opening part of the Declaration tells what rights the members of the Continental Congress believed that all people have. All people are equal in having the rights to life, liberty, and the pursuit of happiness. The main purpose of a government is to protect the rights of the people who consent to be governed by it. These rights cannot be taken away. When a government tries to take these rights away from the people, the people have the right to change the government or do away with it. The people can then form a new government that respects these rights.

**Charges Against the King**
The Declaration lists more than 25 charges against the king. He was mistreating the colonists, the Declaration says, in order to gain total control over the colonies.

The king rejected many laws passed by colonial legislatures.

He has refused to pass other Laws for the accommodation of large districts of people, unless those people would relinquish the right of Representation in the Legislature, a right inestimable to them and formidable to tyrants only.

The king made the colonial legislatures meet at unusual times and places.

He has called together legislative bodies at places unusual, uncomfortable, and distant from the depository of their public Records, for the sole purpose of fatiguing them into compliance with his measures.

The king and the king's governors often dissolved colonial legislatures for disobeying their orders.

He has dissolved Representative Houses repeatedly, for opposing with manly firmness his invasions on the rights of the people.

He has refused for a long time, after such dissolutions, to cause others to be elected; whereby the Legislative powers, incapable of Annihilation, have returned to the People at large for their exercise; the State remaining in the mean time exposed to all the dangers of invasion from without, and convulsions within.

The king stopped people from moving to the colonies and into the western lands.

He has endeavored to prevent the population of these States; for that purpose obstructing the Laws for Naturalization of Foreigners; refusing to pass others to encourage their migrations hither, and raising the conditions of new Appropriations of Lands.

The king prevented the colonists from choosing their own judges. The king chose the judges, and they served only as long as the king was satisfied with them.

He has obstructed the Administration of Justice, by refusing his Assent to Laws for establishing Judiciary powers.

He has made Judges dependent on his Will alone, for the tenure of their offices, and the amount and payment of their salaries.

The king hired people to help collect taxes in the colonies.

He has erected a multitude of New Offices, and sent hither swarms of Officers to harass our people, and eat out their substance.

The king appointed General Thomas Gage, commander of Britain's military forces in the Americas, as governor of Massachusetts.

He has kept among us, in times of peace, Standing Armies without the Consent of our legislatures.

He has affected to render the Military independent of and superior to the Civil power.

He has combined with others to subject us to a jurisdiction foreign to our constitution, and unacknowledged by our laws; giving his Assent to their Acts of pretended Legislation:

For quartering large bodies of armed troops among us:

The king expected the colonists to provide housing and supplies for the British soldiers in the colonies.

For protecting them, by a mock Trial, from punishment for any Murders which they should commit on the Inhabitants of these States:

For cutting off our Trade with all parts of the world:

The king and Parliament demanded that colonists pay many taxes, even though the colonists did not agree to pay them.

For imposing Taxes on us without our Consent:

Colonists were tried by British naval courts, which had no juries.

For depriving us in many cases, of the benefits of Trial by Jury:

Colonists accused of treason were sent to Britain to be tried.

For transporting us beyond Seas to be tried for pretended offenses:

For abolishing the free System of English Laws in a neighboring Province, establishing therein an Arbitrary government, and enlarging its Boundaries so as to render it at once an example and fit instrument for introducing the same absolute rule into these Colonies:

For taking away our Charters, abolishing our most valuable Laws, and altering fundamentally the Forms of our Governments:

For suspending our own Legislatures, and declaring themselves invested with power to legislate for us in all cases whatsoever.

He has abdicated Government here, by declaring us out of his Protection and waging War against us.

He has plundered our seas, ravaged our Coasts, burnt our towns, and destroyed the lives of our people.

> The king allowed General Gage to take military action to enforce British laws in the colonies.

He is at this time transporting large Armies of foreign Mercenaries to complete the works of death, desolation and tyranny, already begun with circumstances of Cruelty & perfidy scarcely paralleled in the most barbarous ages, and totally unworthy the Head of a civilized nation.

He has constrained our fellow Citizens taken Captive on the high Seas to bear Arms against their Country, to become the executioners of their friends and Brethren, or to fall themselves by their Hands.

> The king hired Hessian mercenaries and sent them to fight the colonists.

He has excited domestic insurrections amongst us, and has endeavored to bring on the inhabitants of our frontiers, the merciless Indian Savages, whose known rule of warfare, is an undistinguished destruction of all ages, sexes and conditions.

> The king's governor in Virginia promised freedom to all enslaved people who joined the British forces. The British also planned to use Indians to fight the colonists.

In every stage of these Oppressions We have Petitioned for Redress in the most humble terms: Our repeated Petitions have been answered only by repeated injury. A Prince, whose character is thus marked by every act which may define a Tyrant, is unfit to be the ruler of a free people.

Nor have We been wanting in attentions to our British brethren. We have warned them from time to time of attempts by their legislature to extend an unwarrantable jurisdiction over us. We have reminded them of the circumstances of our emigration and settlement here. We have appealed to their native justice and magnanimity, and we have conjured them by the ties of our common kindred to disavow these usurpations, which, would inevitably interrupt our connections and correspondence. They too have been deaf to the voice of justice and of consanguinity. We must, therefore, acquiesce in the necessity, which denounces our Separation, and hold them, as we hold the rest of mankind, Enemies in War, in Peace Friends.

> The Declaration explained the efforts of the colonists to avoid separation from Britain. But the colonists said that the king had ignored their protests. Because of the many charges against the king, the writers of the Declaration concluded that he was not fit to rule free people.

We, therefore, the Representatives of the united States of America, in General Congress, Assembled, appealing to the Supreme Judge of the world for the rectitude of our intentions, do, in the Name, and by Authority of the good People of these Colonies, solemnly publish and declare, That these United Colonies are, and of Right ought to be Free and Independent States; that they are Absolved from all Allegiance to the British Crown, and that all political connection between them and the State of Great Britain, is and ought to be totally dissolved; and that as Free and Independent States, they have full Power to levy War, conclude Peace, contract Alliances, establish Commerce, and to do all other Acts and Things which Independent States may of right do.

> **A Statement of Independence** The writers declared that the colonies were now free and independent states. All ties with Britain were broken. As free and independent states, they had the right to make war and peace, to trade, and to do all the things free countries could do.

To support the Declaration, the signers promised one another their lives, their fortunes, and their honor.

And for the support of this Declaration, with a firm reliance on the protection of divine Providence, we mutually pledge to each other our Lives, our Fortunes and our sacred Honor.

John Hancock

NEW HAMPSHIRE
Josiah Bartlett
William Whipple
Matthew Thornton

MASSACHUSETTS
John Adams
Samuel Adams
Robert Treat Paine
Elbridge Gerry

NEW YORK
William Floyd
Philip Livingston
Francis Lewis
Lewis Morris

RHODE ISLAND
Stephen Hopkins
William Ellery

NEW JERSEY
Richard Stockton
John Witherspoon
Francis Hopkinson
John Hart
Abraham Clark

PENNSYLVANIA
Robert Morris
Benjamin Rush
Benjamin Franklin
John Morton
George Clymer
James Smith
George Taylor
James Wilson
George Ross

DELAWARE
Caesar Rodney
George Read
Thomas McKean

MARYLAND
Samuel Chase
William Paca
Thomas Stone
Charles Carroll of Carrollton

NORTH CAROLINA
William Hopper
Joseph Hewes
John Penn

VIRGINIA
George Wythe
Richard Henry Lee
Thomas Jefferson
Benjamin Harrison
Thomas Nelson, Jr.
Francis Lightfoot Lee
Carter Braxton

SOUTH CAROLINA
Edward Rutledge
Thomas Heyward, Jr.
Thomas Lynch, Jr.
Arthur Middleton

CONNECTICUT
Roger Sherman
Samuel Huntington
William Williams
Oliver Wolcott

GEORGIA
Button Gwinnett
Lyman Hall
George Walton

Members of the Continental Congress stated that copies of the Declaration should be sent to all Committees of Correspondence and to commanders of the troops and that it should be read in every state.

Resolved, That copies of the Declaration be sent to the several assemblies, conventions, and committees, or councils of safety, and to the several commanding officers of the continental troops; that it be proclaimed in each of the United States, at the head of the army.

# THE CONSTITUTION OF THE UNITED STATES OF AMERICA

## Preamble*

**W**e the people of the United States, in order to form a more perfect Union, establish justice, insure domestic tranquillity, provide for the common defense, promote the general welfare, and secure the blessings of liberty to ourselves and our posterity, do ordain and establish this Constitution for the United States of America.

### ARTICLE I
### THE LEGISLATIVE BRANCH
SECTION 1. CONGRESS

All legislative powers herein granted shall be vested in a Congress of the United States, which shall consist of a Senate and House of Representatives.

SECTION 2. THE HOUSE OF REPRESENTATIVES

(1) The House of Representatives shall be composed of members chosen every second year by the people of the several states, and the electors in each state shall have the qualifications requisite for electors of the most numerous branch of the state legislature.

(2) No person shall be a Representative who shall not have attained to the age of twenty-five years, and been seven years a citizen of the United States, and who shall not, when elected, be an inhabitant of that state in which he shall be chosen.

(3) Representatives [*and direct taxes*]** shall be apportioned among the several states which may be included within this Union, according to their respective numbers [*which shall be determined by adding to the whole number of free persons, including those bound to service for a term of years, and excluding Indians not taxed, three-fifths of all other persons*]. The actual enumeration shall be made within three years after the first meeting of the Congress of the United States, and within every subsequent term of ten years, in such manner as they shall by law direct. The number of Representatives shall not exceed one for every 30,000, but each state shall have at least one Representative [; *and until such enumeration shall be made, the State of New Hampshire shall be entitled to choose three; Massachusetts eight; Rhode Island and Providence Plantations one; Connecticut five; New York six; New Jersey four; Pennsylvania eight; Delaware one; Maryland six; Virginia ten; North Carolina five; South Carolina five; and Georgia three*].

*Titles have been added to make the Constitution easier to read. They did not appear in the original document.

**The parts of the Constitution that no longer apply are printed in italics within brackets [ ]. These portions have been changed or set aside by later amendments.

**Preamble**
The introduction to the Constitution states the purposes and principles for writing it. The writers wanted to set up a fairer form of government and to secure peace and freedom for themselves and for future generations.

**Congress**
Congress has the authority to make laws. Congress is made up of two groups of lawmakers: the Senate and the House of Representatives.

**(1) Election and Term of Members**
Qualified voters are to elect members of the House of Representatives every two years. Each member of the House of Representatives must meet certain requirements.

**(2) Qualifications**
Members of the House of Representatives must be at least 25 years old. They must have been citizens of the United States for at least seven years. They must live in the state that they will represent.

**(3) Determining Apportionment**
The number of representatives a state may have depends on the number of people living in each state. Every ten years the federal government must take a census, or count, of the population in every state. Every state will have at least one representative.

**(4) Filling Vacancies**
If there is a vacancy in representation in Congress, the governor of the state involved must call a special election to fill it.

**(5) Special Authority**
The House of Representatives chooses a Speaker as its presiding officer. It also chooses other officers as appropriate. The House is the only government branch that may impeach, or charge, an official in the executive branch or a judge of the federal courts for failing to carry out his or her duties. These cases are tried in the Senate.

**(1) Number, Term, and Selection of Members**
Each state is represented by two senators. Until Amendment 17 was passed, state legislatures chose the senators for their states. Each senator serves a six-year term and has one vote in Congress.

**(2) Overlapping Terms and Filling Vacancies**
One-third of the senators are elected every two years for a six-year term. This grouping allows at least two-thirds of the experienced senators to remain in the Senate after each election. Amendment 17 permits state governors to appoint a replacement to fill a vacancy until the next election is held.

**(3) Qualifications**
Senators must be at least 30 years old. They must have been citizens of the United States for at least nine years. They must live in the state that they will represent.

**(4) President of the Senate**
The Vice President acts as chief officer of the Senate but does not vote unless there is a tie.

**(5) Other Officers**
The Senate chooses its other officers and a president pro tempore, who serves if the Vice President is not present or if the Vice President becomes President. *Pro tempore* is a Latin term meaning "for the time being."

(4) When vacancies happen in the representation from any state, the executive authority thereof shall issue writs of election to fill such vacancies.

(5) The House of Representatives shall choose their Speaker and other officers; and shall have the sole power of impeachment.

SECTION 3. THE SENATE
(1) The Senate of the United States shall be composed of two Senators from each state [*chosen by the legislature thereof*], for six years, and each Senator shall have one vote.

(2) [*Immediately after they shall be assembled in consequence of the first election, they shall be divided as equally as may be into three classes. The seats of the Senators of the first class shall be vacated at the expiration of the second year, of the second class at the expiration of the fourth year, and of the third class at the expiration of the sixth year, so that one-third may be chosen every second year; and if vacancies happen by resignation, or otherwise, during the recess of the legislature of any state, the executive thereof may make temporary appointments until the next meeting of the legislature, which shall then fill such vacancies.*]

(3) No person shall be a Senator who shall not have attained to the age of thirty years, and been nine years a citizen of the United States, and who shall not, when elected, be an inhabitant of that state for which he shall be chosen.

(4) The Vice President of the United States shall be President of the Senate, but shall have no vote, unless they be equally divided.

(5) The Senate shall choose their other officers, and also a President *pro tempore*, in the absence of the Vice President, or when he shall exercise the office of the President of the United States.

(6) The Senate shall have the sole power to try all impeachments. When sitting for that purpose, they shall be on oath or affirmation. When the President of the United States is tried, the Chief Justice shall preside; and no person shall be convicted without the concurrence of two-thirds of the members present.

(7) Judgment in cases of impeachment shall not extend further than to removal from office, and disqualification to hold and enjoy any office of honor, trust, or profit under the United States; but the party convicted shall nevertheless be liable and subject to indictment, trial, judgment and punishment, according to law.

## SECTION 4. ELECTIONS AND MEETINGS

(1) The times, places, and manner of holding elections for Senators and Representatives shall be prescribed in each state by the legislature thereof; but the Congress may at any time by law make or alter such regulations, [*except as to the places of choosing Senators*].

(2) The Congress shall assemble at least once in every year, [*and such meeting shall be on the first Monday in December, unless they shall by law appoint a different day*].

## SECTION 5. RULES OF PROCEDURE

(1) Each house shall be the judge of the elections, returns and qualifications of its own members, and a majority of each shall constitute a quorum to do business; but a smaller number may adjourn from day to day, and may be authorized to compel the attendance of absent members, in such manner and under such penalties as each house may provide.

(2) Each house may determine the rules of its proceedings, punish its members for disorderly behavior, and, with the concurrence of two-thirds, expel a member.

(3) Each house shall keep a journal of its proceedings, and from time to time publish the same, excepting such parts as may in their judgment require secrecy; and the yeas and nays of the members of either house on any question shall, at the desire of one-fifth of those present, be entered on the journal.

**(6) Impeachment Trials**
If the House of Representatives votes articles of impeachment, the Senate holds a trial. A two-thirds vote is required to convict a person who has been impeached.

**(7) Penalty for Conviction**
If convicted in an impeachment case, an official is removed from office and may never hold office in the United States government again. The convicted person may also be tried in a regular court of law for any crimes.

**(1) Holding Elections**
Each state makes its own rules about electing senators and representatives. However, Congress may change these rules at any time. Today congressional elections are held on the Tuesday after the first Monday in November, in even-numbered years.

**(2) Meetings**
The Constitution requires Congress to meet at least once a year. That day is the first Monday in December, unless Congress sets a different day. Amendment 20 changed this date to January 3.

**(1) Organization**
Each house of Congress may decide if its members have been elected fairly and are able to hold office. Each house may do business only when a quorum—a majority of its members—is present. By less than a majority vote, each house may compel absent members to attend.

**(2) Rules**
Each house may decide its own rules for doing business, punish its members, and expel a member from office if two-thirds of the members agree.

**(3) Journal**
The Constitution requires each house to keep records of its activities and to publish these records from time to time. The House Journal and the Senate Journal are published at the end of each session. How each member voted must be recorded if one-fifth of the members ask for this to be done.

**(4) Adjournment**
When Congress is in session, neither house may take a recess for more than three days without the consent of the other.

**(1) Pay and Privileges**
Members of Congress set their own salaries, which are to be paid by the federal government. Members cannot be arrested or sued for anything they say while Congress is in session. This privilege is called congressional immunity. Members of Congress may be arrested while Congress is in session only if they commit a crime.

**(2) Restrictions**
Members of Congress may not hold any other federal office while serving in Congress. A member may not resign from office and then take a government position created during that member's term of office or for which the pay has been increased during that member's term of office.

**(1) Money-Raising Bills**
All money-raising bills must be introduced first in the House of Representatives, but the Senate may suggest changes.

**(2) How a Bill Becomes a Law**
After a bill has been passed by both the House of Representatives and the Senate, it must be sent to the President. If the President approves and signs the bill, it becomes law. The President can also veto, or refuse to sign, the bill. Congress can override a veto by passing the bill again by a two-thirds majority. If the President does not act within ten days, two things may happen. If Congress is still in session, the bill becomes a law. If Congress ends its session within that same ten-day period, the bill does not become a law.

**(3) Orders and Resolutions**
Congress can pass orders and resolutions, some of which have the same effect as a law. Congress may decide on its own when to end the session. Other such acts must be signed or vetoed by the President.

(4) Neither house, during the session of Congress, shall, without the consent of the other, adjourn for more than three days, nor to any other place than that in which the two houses shall be sitting.

SECTION 6. PRIVILEGES AND RESTRICTIONS
(1) The Senators and Representatives shall receive a compensation for their services, to be ascertained by law and paid out of the Treasury of the United States. They shall in all cases, except treason, felony, and breach of the peace, be privileged from arrest during their attendance at the session of their respective houses, and in going to and returning from the same; and for any speech or debate in either house, they shall not be questioned in any other place.

(2) No Senator or Representative shall, during the time for which he was elected, be appointed to any civil office under the authority of the United States, which shall have been created, or the emoluments whereof shall have been increased, during such time; and no person holding any office under the United States shall be a member of either house during his continuance in office.

SECTION 7. MAKING LAWS
(1) All bills for raising revenue shall originate in the House of Representatives; but the Senate may propose or concur with amendments as on other bills.

(2) Every bill which shall have passed the House of Representatives and the Senate shall, before it become a law, be presented to the President of the United States; if he approve, he shall sign it, but if not, he shall return it, with his objections, to that house in which it shall have originated, who shall enter the objections at large on their journal, and proceed to reconsider it. If after such reconsideration two-thirds of that house shall agree to pass the bill, it shall be sent, together with the objections, to the other house, by which it shall likewise be reconsidered, and, if approved by two-thirds of that house, it shall become a law. But in all such cases the votes of both houses shall be determined by yeas and nays, and the names of the persons voting for and against the bill shall be entered on the journal of each house respectively. If any bill shall not be returned by the President within ten days (Sundays excepted) after it shall have been presented to him, the same bill shall be a law, in like manner as if he had signed it, unless the Congress by their adjournment prevent its return, in which case it shall not be a law.

(3) Every order, resolution, or vote to which the concurrence of the Senate and House of Representatives may be necessary (except on a question of adjournment) shall be presented to the President of the United States; and before the same shall take effect, shall be approved by him, or being disapproved by him, shall be repassed by two-thirds of the Senate and House of Representatives, according to the rules and limitations prescribed in the case of a bill.

## SECTION 8. POWERS DELEGATED TO CONGRESS

The Congress shall have power

(1) To lay and collect taxes, duties, imposts and excises, to pay the debts and provide for the common defense and general welfare of the United States; but all duties, imposts and excises shall be uniform throughout the United States;

(2) To borrow money on the credit of the United States;

(3) To regulate commerce with foreign nations, and among the several states and with the Indian tribes;

(4) To establish an uniform rule of naturalization, and uniform laws on the subject of bankruptcies throughout the United States;

(5) To coin money, regulate the value thereof, and of foreign coin, and fix the standard of weights and measures;

(6) To provide for the punishment of counterfeiting the securities and current coin of the United States;

(7) To establish post offices and post roads;

(8) To promote the progress of science and useful arts by securing for limited times to authors and inventors the exclusive right to their respective writings and discoveries;

(9) To constitute tribunals inferior to the Supreme Court;

(10) To define and punish piracies and felonies committed on the high seas and offenses against the law of nations;

**(1) Taxation**
Only Congress has the authority to raise money to pay debts, defend the United States, and provide services for its people by collecting taxes or tariffs on foreign goods. All taxes must be applied equally in all states.

**(2) Borrowing Money**
Congress may borrow money for national use. This is usually done by selling government bonds.

**(3) Commerce**
Congress can control trade with other countries and between states.

**(4) Naturalization and Bankruptcy**
Congress decides what requirements people from other countries must meet to become United States citizens. Congress can also pass laws to protect people who are bankrupt, or cannot pay their debts.

**(5) Coins, Weights, and Measures**
Congress can coin money and decide its value. Congress also decides on the system of weights and measures to be used throughout the nation.

**(6) Counterfeiting**
Congress may pass laws to punish people who make fake money, bonds, or stamps.

**(7) Postal Service**
Congress can build post offices and make rules about the postal system and the roads used for mail delivery.

**(8) Copyrights and Patents**
Congress can issue patents and copyrights to inventors and authors to protect the ownership of their works.

**(9) Federal Courts**
Congress can establish a system of federal courts under the Supreme Court.

**(10) Crimes at Sea**
Congress can pass laws to punish people for crimes committed at sea. Congress may also punish United States citizens for breaking international law.

**(11) Declaring War**
Only Congress can declare war.

**(12) The Army**
Congress can establish an army, but it cannot vote enough money to support it for more than two years. This part of the Constitution was written to keep the army under civilian control.

**(13) The Navy**
Congress can establish a navy and vote enough money to support it for as long as necessary. No time limit was set because people thought the navy was less of a threat to people's liberty than the army was.

**(14) Military Regulations**
Congress makes the rules that guide and govern all the armed forces.

**(15) The Militia**
Each state has its own militia, now known as the National Guard. The National Guard can be called into federal service by the President, as authorized by Congress, to enforce laws, to stop uprisings against the government, or to protect the people in case of floods, earthquakes, and other disasters.

**(16) Control of the Militia**
Congress helps each state support the National Guard. Each state may appoint its own officers and train its own guard according to rules set by Congress.

**(17) National Capital and Other Property**
Congress may pass laws to govern the nation's capital (Washington, D.C.) and any land owned by the government.

**(18) Other Necessary Laws**
The Constitution allows Congress to make laws that are necessary to enforce the powers listed in Article I. This clause has two conflicting interpretations. One is that Congress can only do what is absolutely necessary to carry out the powers listed in Article I. The other is that Congress may stretch its authority in order to carry out these powers, but not beyond limits established by the Constitution.

(11) To declare war, grant letters of marque and reprisal, and make rules concerning captures on land and water;

(12) To raise and support armies, but no appropriation of money to that use shall be for a longer term than two years;

(13) To provide and maintain a navy;

(14) To make rules for the government and regulation of the land and naval forces;

(15) To provide for calling forth the militia to execute the laws of the Union, suppress insurrections and repel invasions;

(16) To provide for organizing, arming, and disciplining the militia, and for governing such part of them as may be employed in the service of the United States, reserving to the states, respectively, the appointment of the officers, and the authority of training the militia according to the discipline prescribed by Congress;

(17) To exercise exclusive legislation in all cases whatsoever, over such district (not exceeding ten miles square) as may, by cession of particular states, and the acceptance of Congress, become the seat of government of the United States, and to exercise like authority over all places purchased by the consent of the legislature of the state in which the same shall be, for the erection of forts, magazines, arsenals, dock-yards, and other needful buildings; —and

(18) To make all laws which shall be necessary and proper for carrying into execution the foregoing powers, and all other powers vested by this Constitution in the government of the United States, or in any department or officer thereof.

## SECTION 9. POWERS DENIED TO CONGRESS

(1) [*The migration or importation of such persons as any of the states now existing shall think proper to admit shall not be prohibited by the Congress prior to the year 1808; but a tax or duty may be imposed on such importation, not exceeding 10 dollars for each person.*]

(2) The privilege of the writ of habeas corpus shall not be suspended, unless when in cases of rebellion or invasion the public safety may require it.

(3) No bill of attainder or ex post facto law shall be passed.

(4) [*No capitation or other direct tax shall be laid, unless in proportion to the census or enumeration herein before directed to be taken.*]

(5) No tax or duty shall be laid on articles exported from any state.

(6) No preference shall be given by any regulation of commerce or revenue to the ports of one state over those of another; nor shall vessels bound to, or from, one state, be obliged to enter, clear, or pay duties in another.

(7) No money shall be drawn from the Treasury, but in consequence of appropriations made by law; and a regular statement and account of the receipts and expenditures of all public money shall be published from time to time.

---

**(1) Slave Trade**
Some authority is not given to Congress. Congress could not prevent the slave trade until 1808, but it could put a tax of ten dollars on each slave brought into the United States. After 1808, when a law was passed to stop slaves from being brought into the United States, this section no longer applied.

**(2) Habeas Corpus**
A writ of habeas corpus is a privilege that entitles a person to a hearing before a judge. The judge must then decide if there is good reason for that person to have been arrested. If not, that person must be released. The government is not allowed to take this privilege away except during a national emergency, such as an invasion or a rebellion.

**(3) Special Laws**
Congress cannot pass laws that impose punishment on a named individual or group, except in cases of treason. Article III sets limits to punishments for treason. Congress also cannot pass laws that punish a person for an action that was legal when it was done.

**(4) Direct Taxes**
Congress cannot set a direct tax on people, unless it is in proportion to the total population. Amendment 16, which provides for the income tax, is an exception.

**(5) Export Taxes**
Congress cannot tax goods sent from one state to another or from a state to another country.

**(6) Ports**
When making trade laws, Congress cannot favor one state over another. Congress cannot require ships from one state to pay a duty to enter another state.

**(7) Public Money**
The government cannot spend money from the treasury unless Congress passes a law allowing it to do so. A written record must be kept of all money spent by the government.

**(8) Titles of Nobility and Gifts**
The United States government cannot grant titles of nobility. Government officials cannot accept gifts from other countries without the permission of Congress. This clause was intended to prevent government officials from being bribed by other nations.

**(1) Complete Restrictions**
The Constitution does not allow states to act as if they were individual countries. No state government may make a treaty with other countries. No state can print its own money.

**(2) Partial Restrictions**
No state government can tax imported goods or exported goods without the consent of Congress. States may charge a fee to inspect these goods, but profits must be given to the United States Treasury.

**(3) Other Restrictions**
No state government may tax ships entering its ports unless Congress approves. No state may keep an army or navy during times of peace other than the National Guard. No state can enter into agreements called compacts with other states without the consent of Congress.

**(1) Term of Office**
The President has the authority to carry out our nation's laws. The term of office for both the President and the Vice President is four years.

**(2) The Electoral College**
This group of people is to be chosen by the voters of each state to elect the President and Vice President. The number of electors in each state is equal to the number of senators and representatives that state has in Congress.

**(3) Election Process**
This clause describes in detail how the electors were to choose the President and Vice President. In 1804 Amendment 12 changed the process for electing the President and the Vice President.

(8) No title of nobility shall be granted by the United States; and no person holding any office of profit or trust under them, shall, without the consent of the Congress, accept of any present, emolument, office, or title, of any kind whatever, from any king, prince, or foreign state.

### SECTION 10. POWERS DENIED TO THE STATES

(1) No state shall enter into any treaty, alliance, or confederation; grant letters of marque and reprisal; coin money; emit bills of credit; make anything but gold and silver coin a tender in payment of debts; pass any bill of attainder, ex post facto law, or law impairing the obligation of contracts, or grant any title of nobility.

(2) No state shall, without the consent of the Congress, lay any imposts or duties on imports or exports, except what may be absolutely necessary for executing its inspection laws; and the net produce of all duties and imposts, laid by any state on imports or exports, shall be for the use of the Treasury of the United States; and all such laws shall be subject to the revision and control of the Congress.

(3) No state shall, without the consent of Congress, lay any duty of tonnage, keep troops, or ships of war in time of peace, enter into any agreement or compact with another state, or with a foreign power, or engage in war, unless actually invaded, or in such imminent danger as will not admit of delay.

### ARTICLE II
### THE EXECUTIVE BRANCH
SECTION 1. PRESIDENT AND VICE PRESIDENT

(1) The executive power shall be vested in a President of the United States of America. He shall hold his office during the term of four years, and together with the Vice President, chosen for the same term, be elected as follows:

(2) Each state shall appoint, in such manner as the legislature thereof may direct, a number of electors, equal to the whole number of Senators and Representatives to which the state may be entitled in the Congress; but no Senator or Representative, or person holding an office of trust or profit under the United States, shall be appointed an elector.

(3) [*The electors shall meet in their respective states, and vote by ballot for two persons, of whom one at least shall not be an inhabitant of the same state with themselves. And they shall make a list of all the persons voted for, and of the number of votes for each; which list they shall sign and certify, and transmit sealed to the seat of the government of the United States, directed to the president of the Senate. The president of the Senate shall, in the presence of the Senate and House of Representatives, open all the certificates, and the votes shall then be counted. The person having the greatest number of votes shall be the President, if such number be a majority of the whole number of electors appointed; and if there be more than one who have such majority, and have an equal number of votes, then the House of Representatives shall immediately choose by ballot one of them for President; and if no person have*

a majority, then from the five highest on the list the said House shall in like manner choose the President. But in choosing the President the votes shall be taken by states, the representation from each state having one vote: A quorum for this purpose shall consist of a member or members from two-thirds of the states, and a majority of all the states shall be necessary to a choice. In every case, after the choice of the President, the person having the greatest number of votes of the electors shall be the Vice President. But if there should remain two or more who have equal votes, the Senate shall choose from them by ballot the Vice President.]

(4) The Congress may determine the time of choosing the electors, and the day on which they shall give their votes; which day shall be the same throughout the United States.

(5) No person except a natural-born citizen [*or a citizen of the United States, at the time of the adoption of this Constitution,*] shall be eligible to the office of the President; neither shall any person be eligible to that office who shall not have attained to the age of thirty-five years, and been fourteen years a resident within the United States.

(6) [*In case of the removal of the President from office, or of his death, resignation, or inability to discharge the powers and duties of the said office, the same shall devolve on the Vice President, and the Congress may by law provide for the case of removal, death, resignation or inability, both of the President and Vice President, declaring what officer shall then act as President, and such officer shall act accordingly, until the disability be removed, or a President shall be elected.*]

(7) The President shall, at stated times, receive for his services, a compensation, which shall neither be increased nor diminished during the period for which he shall have been elected, and he shall not receive within that period any other emolument from the United States, or any of them.

(8) Before he enter on the execution of his office, he shall take the following oath or affirmation:—"I do solemnly swear (or affirm) that I will faithfully execute the office of President of the United States, and will to the best of my ability, preserve, protect, and defend the Constitution of the United States."

SECTION 2. POWERS OF THE PRESIDENT
(1) The President shall be Commander in Chief of the Army and Navy of the United States, and of the militia of the several states, when called into the actual service of the United States; he may require the opinion, in writing, of the principal officer in each of the executive departments, upon any subject relating to the duties of their respective offices, and he shall have power to grant reprieves and pardons for offenses against the United States, except in cases of impeachment.

**(4) Time of Elections**
Congress decides the day the electors are to be elected and the day they are to vote.

**(5) Qualifications**
The President must be at least 35 years old, be a citizen of the United States by birth, and have been living in the United States for 14 years or more.

**(6) Vacancies**
If the President dies, resigns, or is removed from office, the Vice President becomes President.

**(7) Salary**
The President receives a salary that cannot be raised or lowered during a term of office. The President may not be paid any additional salary by the federal government or any state or local government. Today the President's salary is $400,000 a year, plus expenses for things such as housing, travel, and entertainment.

**(8) Oath of Office**
Before taking office, the President must promise to perform the duties faithfully and to protect the country's form of government. Usually the Chief Justice of the Supreme Court administers the oath of office.

**(1) The President's Leadership**
The President is the commander of the nation's armed forces and of the National Guard when it is in service of the nation. All government officials of the executive branch must report their actions to the President when asked. The President can excuse people from punishment for crimes committed.

**(2) Treaties and Appointments**
The President has the authority to make treaties, but they must be approved by a two-thirds vote of the Senate. The President nominates justices to the Supreme Court, ambassadors to other countries, and other federal officials with the Senate's approval.

**(3) Filling Vacancies**
If a government official's position becomes vacant when Congress is not in session, the President can make a temporary appointment.

**Duties**
The President must report to Congress on the condition of the country. This report is now presented in the annual State of the Union message.

**Impeachment**
The President, the Vice President, or any government official will be removed from office if impeached, or accused, and then found guilty of treason, bribery, or other serious crimes. The Constitution protects government officials from being impeached for unimportant reasons.

**Federal Courts**
The authority to decide legal cases is granted to a Supreme Court and to a system of lower courts established by Congress. The Supreme Court is the highest court in the land. Justices and judges are in their offices for life, subject to good behavior.

**(1) General Authority**
Federal courts have the authority to decide cases that arise under the Constitution, laws, and treaties of the United States. They also have the authority to settle disagreements among states and among citizens of different states.

(2) He shall have power, by and with the advice and consent of the Senate, to make treaties, provided two-thirds of the senators present concur; and he shall nominate, and by and with the advice and consent of the Senate, shall appoint ambassadors, other public ministers and consuls, judges of the Supreme Court, and all other officers of the United States, whose appointments are not herein otherwise provided for, and which shall be established by law; but the Congress may by law vest the appointment of such inferior officers, as they think proper, in the President alone, in the courts of law, or in the heads of departments.

(3) The President shall have power to fill up all vacancies that may happen during the recess of the Senate, by granting commissions which shall expire at the end of their next session.

### SECTION 3. DUTIES OF THE PRESIDENT

He shall from time to time give to the Congress information of the state of the Union, and recommend to their consideration such measures as he shall judge necessary and expedient; he may, on extraordinary occasions, convene both houses, or either of them, and in case of disagreement between them, with respect to the time of adjournment, he may adjourn them to such time as he shall think proper; he shall receive ambassadors and other public ministers; he shall take care that the laws be faithfully executed, and shall commission all the officers of the United States.

### SECTION 4. IMPEACHMENT

The President, Vice President and all civil officers of the United States, shall be removed from office on impeachment for, and conviction of, treason, bribery, or other high crimes and misdemeanors.

### ARTICLE III
### THE JUDICIAL BRANCH
### SECTION 1. FEDERAL COURTS

The judicial power of the United States shall be vested in one Supreme Court, and in such inferior courts as the Congress may from time to time ordain and establish. The judges, both of the supreme and inferior courts, shall hold their offices during good behavior, and shall, at stated times, receive for their services a compensation, which shall not be diminished during their continuance in office.

### SECTION 2. AUTHORITY OF THE FEDERAL COURTS

(1) The judicial power shall extend to all cases, in law and equity, arising under this Constitution, the laws of the United States, and treaties made or which shall be made, under their authority; to all cases affecting ambassadors, other public ministers and consuls; to all cases of admiralty and maritime jurisdiction; to controversies to which the United States shall be a party; to controversies between two or more states; [*between a state and citizens of another state;*] between citizens of different states; —between citizens of the same state claiming lands under grants of different states, [*and between a state or the citizens thereof, and foreign states, citizens, or subjects.*]

(2) In all cases affecting ambassadors, other public ministers and consuls, and those in which a state shall be party, the Supreme Court shall have original jurisdiction. In all the other cases before mentioned, the Supreme Court shall have appellate jurisdiction, both as to law and fact, with such exceptions, and under such regulations as the Congress shall make.

(3) The trial of all crimes, except in cases of impeachment, shall be by jury; and such trial shall be held in the state where the said crimes shall have been committed; but when not committed within any state, the trial shall be at such place or places as the Congress may by law have directed.

## SECTION 3. TREASON

(1) Treason against the United States shall consist only in levying war against them, or in adhering to their enemies, giving them aid and comfort. No person shall be convicted of treason unless on the testimony of two witnesses to the same overt act, or on confession in open court.

(2) The Congress shall have power to declare the punishment of treason, but no attainder of treason shall work corruption of blood, or forfeiture except during the life of the person attainted.

## ARTICLE IV
## RELATIONS AMONG STATES

### SECTION 1. OFFICIAL RECORDS

Full faith and credit shall be given in each state to the public acts, records, and judicial proceedings of every other state. And the Congress may by general laws prescribe the manner in which such acts, records, and proceedings shall be proved, and the effect thereof.

### SECTION 2. PRIVILEGES OF THE CITIZENS

(1) The citizens of each state shall be entitled to all privileges and immunities of citizens in the several states.

(2) A person charged in any state with treason, felony, or other crime, who shall flee from justice, and be found in another state, shall on demand of the executive authority of the state from which he fled, be delivered up, to be removed to the state having jurisdiction of the crime.

(3) [*No person held to service or labor in one state, under the laws thereof, escaping into another, shall in consequence of any law or regulation therein, be discharged from such service or labor, but shall be delivered up on claim of the party to whom such service or labor may be due.*]

---

**AMERICAN DOCUMENTS**

**(2) Supreme Court**
The Supreme Court can decide certain cases being tried for the first time. It can review cases that have already been tried in a lower court if the decision has been appealed, or questioned, by one side.

**(3) Trial by Jury**
The Constitution guarantees a trial by jury for every person charged with a federal crime. Amendments 5, 6, and 7 extend and clarify a person's right to a trial by jury.

**(1) Definition of Treason**
Acts that may be considered treason are making war against the United States or helping its enemies. A person cannot be convicted of attempting to overthrow the government unless there are two witnesses to the act or the person confesses in court to treason.

**(2) Punishment for Treason**
Congress can decide the punishment for treason, within certain limits.

**Official Records**
Each state must honor the official records and judicial decisions of other states.

**(1) Privileges**
A citizen moving from one state to another has the same rights as other citizens living in that person's new state of residence. In some cases, such as voting, people may be required to live in their new state for a certain length of time before obtaining the same privileges as citizens there.

**(2) Extradition**
At the governor's request, a person who is charged with a crime and who tries to escape justice by crossing into another state may be returned to the state in which the crime was committed.

**(3) Fugitive Slaves**
The original Constitution required that runaway slaves be returned to their owners. Amendment 13 abolished slavery, eliminating the need for this clause.

**(1) Admission of New States**
Congress has the authority to admit new states to the Union. All new states have the same rights as existing states.

**(2) Federal Property**
The Constitution allows Congress to make or change laws governing federal property. This applies to territories and federally owned land within states, such as national parks.

**Guarantees to the States**
The federal government guarantees that every state have a republican form of government. The United States must also protect the states against invasion and help the states deal with rebellion or local violence.

**Amending the Constitution**
Changes to the Constitution may be proposed by a two-thirds vote of both the House of Representatives and the Senate or by a national convention called by Congress when asked by two-thirds of the states. For an amendment to become law, the legislatures or conventions in three-fourths of the states must approve it.

**(1) Public Debt**
Any debt owed by the United States before the Constitution went into effect was to be honored.

**(2) Federal Supremacy**
This clause declares that the Constitution and federal laws are the highest in the nation. Whenever a state law and a federal law are found to disagree, the federal law must be obeyed so long as it is constitutional.

**(3) Oaths of Office**
All federal and state officials must promise to follow and enforce the Constitution. These officials, however, cannot be required to follow a particular religion or satisfy any religious test.

## SECTION 3. NEW STATES AND TERRITORIES

(1) New states may be admitted by the Congress into this Union; but no new state shall be formed or erected within the jurisdiction of any other state; nor any state be formed by the junction of two or more states, or parts of states, without the consent of the legislatures of the states concerned as well as of the Congress.

(2) The Congress shall have power to dispose of and make all needful rules and regulations respecting the territory or other property belonging to the United States; and nothing in this Constitution shall be so construed as to prejudice any claims of the United States, or of any particular state.

## SECTION 4. GUARANTEES TO THE STATES

The United States shall guarantee to every state in this Union a republican form of government, and shall protect each of them against invasion; and on application of the legislature, or of the executive (when the legislature cannot be convened) against domestic violence.

## ARTICLE V
## AMENDING THE CONSTITUTION

The Congress, whenever two-thirds of both houses shall deem it necessary, shall propose amendments to this Constitution, or, on the application of the legislatures of two-thirds of the several states, shall call a convention for proposing amendments, which, in either case, shall be valid to all intents and purposes, as part of this Constitution, when ratified by the legislatures of three-fourths of the several states, or by conventions in three-fourths thereof, as the one or the other mode of ratification may be proposed by the Congress; provided that [*no amendment which may be made prior to the year 1808 shall in any manner affect the first and fourth clauses in the Ninth Section of the First Article; and that*] no state, without its consent, shall be deprived of its equal suffrage in the Senate.

## ARTICLE VI
## GENERAL PROVISIONS

(1) All debts contracted and engagements entered into, before the adoption of this Constitution, shall be as valid against the United States under this Constitution, as under the Confederation.

(2) This Constitution, and the laws of the United States which shall be made in pursuance thereof, and all treaties made, or which shall be made, under the authority of the United States, shall be the supreme law of the land; and the judges in every state shall be bound thereby, anything in the Constitution or laws of any state to the contrary notwithstanding.

(3) The Senators and Representatives before mentioned, and the members of the several state legislatures, and all executive and judicial officers, both of the United States and of the several states, shall be bound by oath or affirmation, to support this Constitution; but no religious test shall ever be required as a qualification to any office or public trust under the United States.

## ARTICLE VII
## RATIFICATION

The ratification of the conventions of nine states, shall be sufficient for the establishment of this Constitution between the states so ratifying the same.

Done in convention by the unanimous consent of the states present the seventeenth day of September in the year of our Lord one thousand seven hundred and eighty seven and of the independence of the United States of America the Twelfth. In witness whereof we have hereunto subscribed our names.

George Washington—President and deputy from Virginia

**DELAWARE**
George Read
Gunning Bedford, Jr.
John Dickinson
Richard Bassett
Jacob Broom

**MARYLAND**
James McHenry
Daniel of St. Thomas Jenifer
Daniel Carroll

**VIRGINIA**
John Blair
James Madison, Jr.

**NORTH CAROLINA**
William Blount
Richard Dobbs Spaight
Hugh Williamson

**SOUTH CAROLINA**
John Rutledge
Charles Cotesworth Pinckney
Charles Pinckney
Pierce Butler

**GEORGIA**
William Few
Abraham Baldwin

**NEW HAMPSHIRE**
John Langdon
Nicholas Gilman

**MASSACHUSETTS**
Nathaniel Gorham
Rufus King

**CONNECTICUT**
William Samuel Johnson
Roger Sherman

**NEW YORK**
Alexander Hamilton

**NEW JERSEY**
William Livingston
David Brearley
William Paterson
Jonathan Dayton

**PENNSYLVANIA**
Benjamin Franklin
Thomas Mifflin
Robert Morris
George Clymer
Thomas FitzSimons
Jared Ingersoll
James Wilson
Gouverneur Morris

ATTEST: William Jackson, secretary

**Ratification**
In order for the Constitution to become law, 9 of the 13 states had to approve it. Special conventions were held for this purpose. The process took 9 months to complete.

**Basic Freedoms**

The Constitution guarantees our five basic freedoms of expression. It provides for the freedoms of religion, speech, the press, peaceable assembly, and petition for redress of grievances.

**Weapons and the Militia**

This amendment protects the right of the state governments and the people to maintain militias to guard against threats to their public order, safety, and liberty. In connection with that state right, the federal government may not take away the right of the people to have and use weapons.

**Housing Soldiers**

The federal government cannot force people to house soldiers in their homes during peacetime. However, Congress may pass laws allowing this during wartime.

**Searches and Seizures**

This amendment protects people's privacy and safety. Subject to certain exceptions, a law officer cannot search a person or a person's home and belongings unless a judge has issued a valid search warrant. There must be good reason for the search. The warrant must describe the place to be searched and the people or things to be seized, or taken.

**Rights of Accused Persons**

If a person is accused of a crime that is punishable by death or of any other crime that is very serious, a grand jury must decide if there is enough evidence to hold a trial. People cannot be tried twice for the same crime, nor can they be forced to testify against themselves. No person shall be fined, jailed, or executed by the government unless the person has been given a fair trial. The government cannot take a person's property for public use unless fair payment is made.

## AMENDMENT 1 (1791)***
### BASIC FREEDOMS

Congress shall make no law respecting an establishment of religion, or prohibiting the free exercise thereof; or abridging the freedom of speech, or of the press; or the right of the people peaceably to assemble, and to petition the government for a redress of grievances.

## AMENDMENT 2 (1791)
### WEAPONS AND THE MILITIA

A well-regulated militia, being necessary to the security of a free state, the right of the people to keep and bear arms shall not be infringed.

## AMENDMENT 3 (1791)
### HOUSING SOLDIERS

No soldier shall, in time of peace, be quartered in any house, without the consent of the owner; nor in time of war, but in a manner to be prescribed by law.

## AMENDMENT 4 (1791)
### SEARCHES AND SEIZURES

The right of the people to be secure in their persons, houses, papers, and effects, against unreasonable searches and seizures, shall not be violated; and no warrants shall issue but upon probable cause, supported by oath or affirmation, and particularly describing the place to be searched, and the persons or things to be seized.

## AMENDMENT 5 (1791)
### RIGHTS OF ACCUSED PERSONS

No person shall be held to answer for a capital, or otherwise infamous crime, unless on a presentment or indictment of a grand jury, except in cases arising in the land or naval forces, or in the militia, when in actual service in time of war or public danger; nor shall any person be subject for the same offense to be twice put in jeopardy of life or limb; nor shall be compelled in any criminal case to be a witness against himself; nor be deprived of life, liberty, or property, without due process of law; nor shall private property be taken for public use without just compensation.

*** The date beside each amendment is the year that the amendment was ratified and became part of the Constitution.

## AMENDMENT 6 (1791)
### RIGHT TO A FAIR TRIAL

In all criminal prosecutions, the accused shall enjoy the right to a speedy and public trial, by an impartial jury of the state and district wherein the crime shall have been committed, which district shall have been previously ascertained by law, and to be informed of the nature and cause of the accusation; to be confronted with the witnesses against him; to have compulsory process for obtaining witnesses in his favor, and to have the assistance of counsel for his defense.

## AMENDMENT 7 (1791)
### JURY TRIAL IN CIVIL CASES

In suits at common law, where the value in controversy shall exceed 20 dollars, the right of trial by jury shall be preserved, and no fact tried by a jury shall be otherwise re-examined in any court of the United States, than according to the rules of the common law.

## AMENDMENT 8 (1791)
### BAIL AND PUNISHMENT

Excessive bail shall not be required, nor excessive fines imposed, nor cruel and unusual punishments inflicted.

## AMENDMENT 9 (1791)
### RIGHTS OF THE PEOPLE

The enumeration in the Constitution, of certain rights, shall not be construed to deny or disparage others retained by the people.

## AMENDMENT 10 (1791)
### POWERS OF THE STATES AND THE PEOPLE

The powers not delegated to the United States by the Constitution, nor prohibited by it to the states, are reserved to the states respectively, or to the people.

## AMENDMENT 11 (1798)
### SUITS AGAINST STATES

The judicial power of the United States shall not be construed to extend to any suit in law or equity, commenced or prosecuted against one of the United States or citizens of another state, or by citizens or subjects of any foreign state.

**Right to a Fair Trial**
A person accused of a crime has the right to a public trial by an impartial jury, locally chosen. The trial must be held within a reasonable amount of time. The accused person must be told of all charges and has the right to see, hear, and question any witnesses. The federal government must provide a lawyer free of charge to a person who is accused of a serious crime and who is unable to pay for legal services.

**Jury Trial in Civil Cases**
In most federal civil cases involving more than 20 dollars, a jury trial is guaranteed. Civil cases are those disputes between two or more people over money, property, personal injury, or legal rights. Usually civil cases are not tried in federal courts unless much larger sums of money are involved or unless federal courts are given the authority to decide a certain type of case.

**Bail and Punishment**
Courts cannot treat harshly people accused of crimes or punish them in unusual or cruel ways. Bail is money put up as a guarantee that an accused person will appear for trial. In certain cases bail can be denied altogether.

**Rights of the People**
The federal government must respect all natural rights, whether or not they are listed in the Constitution.

**Powers of the States and the People**
Any powers not clearly given to the federal government or denied to the states belong to the states or to the people.

**Suits Against States**
A citizen of one state cannot sue another state in federal court.

**Election of President and Vice President**
This amendment replaces the part of Article II, Section 1, that originally explained the process of electing the President and Vice President. Amendment 12 was an important step in the development of the two-party system. It allows a party to nominate its own candidates for both President and Vice President.

## AMENDMENT 12 (1804)
## ELECTION OF PRESIDENT AND VICE PRESIDENT

The electors shall meet in their respective states, and vote by ballot for President and Vice President, one of whom, at least, shall not be an inhabitant of the same state with themselves; they shall name in their ballots the person voted for as President, and in distinct ballots the person voted for as Vice President, and they shall make distinct lists of all persons voted for as President, and of all persons voted for as Vice President, and of the number of votes for each, which lists they shall sign and certify, and transmit, sealed, to the seat of government of the United States, directed to the President of the Senate; the President of the Senate shall, in the presence of the Senate and House of Representatives, open all the certificates, and the votes shall then be counted; the person having the greatest number of votes for President shall be the President, if such a number be a majority of the whole number of electors appointed; and if no person have such majority; then from the persons having the highest numbers not exceeding three on the list of those voted for as President, the House of Representatives shall choose immediately, by ballot, the President. But in choosing the President, the votes shall be taken by states, the representation from each state having one vote; a quorum for this purpose shall consist of a member or members from two thirds of the states, and a majority of all the states shall be necessary to a choice. [And *if the House of Representatives shall not choose a President whenever the right of choice shall devolve upon them, before the fourth day of March next following, then the Vice President shall act as President, as in the case of the death or other constitutional disability of the President.*] The person having the greatest number of votes as Vice President, shall be the Vice President, if such number be a majority of the whole number of electors appointed, and if no person have a majority, then, from the two highest numbers on the list the Senate shall choose the Vice President; a quorum for the purpose shall consist of two thirds of the whole number of Senators, and a majority of the whole number shall be necessary to a choice. But no person constitutionally ineligible to the office of President shall be eligible to that of Vice President of the United States.

**End of Slavery**
People cannot be forced to work against their will unless they have been tried for and convicted of a crime for which this means of punishment is ordered. Congress may enforce this by law.

## AMENDMENT 13 (1865)
## END OF SLAVERY

### SECTION 1. ABOLITION

Neither slavery nor involuntary servitude, except as a punishment for crime whereof the party shall have been duly convicted, shall exist within the United States, or any place subject to their jurisdiction.

### SECTION 2. ENFORCEMENT

Congress shall have power to enforce this article by appropriate legislation.

**Citizenship**
All persons born or naturalized in the United States are citizens of the United States and of the state in which they live. State governments may not deny any citizen the full rights of citizenship. This amendment also guarantees due process of law. According to due process of law, no state may take away the rights of a citizen. All citizens must be protected equally under law.

## AMENDMENT 14 (1868)
## RIGHTS OF CITIZENS

### SECTION 1. CITIZENSHIP

All persons born or naturalized in the United States and subject to the jurisdiction thereof, are citizens of the United States and of the state wherein they reside. No state shall make or enforce any law which shall abridge the privileges or immunities of citizens of the United States, nor shall any state deprive any person of life, liberty, or property, without due process of law; nor deny to any person within its jurisdiction the equal protection of the laws.

## SECTION 2. NUMBER OF REPRESENTATIVES

Representatives shall be apportioned among the several states according to their respective numbers, counting the whole number of persons in each state, [*excluding Indians not taxed*]. But when the right to vote at any election for the choice of electors for President and Vice President of the United States, representatives in Congress, the executive and judicial officers of a state, or the members of the legislature thereof, is denied to any of the [*male*] inhabitants of such state, being [*twenty-one years of age and*] citizens of the United States, or in any way abridged, except for participation in rebellion or other crime, the basis of representation therein shall be reduced in the proportion which the number of such [*male*] citizens shall bear to the whole number of [*male*] citizens [*twenty-one years of age*] in such state.

## SECTION 3. PENALTY FOR REBELLION

No person shall be a Senator or Representative in Congress, or elector of President and Vice President, or hold any office, civil or military, under the United States, or under any state, who, having previously taken an oath, as a member of Congress, or as an officer of the United States, or as a member of any state legislature, or as an executive or judicial officer of any state, to support the Constitution of the United States, shall have engaged in insurrection or rebellion against the same, or given aid or comfort to the enemies thereof. But Congress may, by a vote of two thirds of each house, remove such disability.

## SECTION 4. GOVERNMENT DEBT

The validity of the public debt of the United States, authorized by law, including debts incurred for payment of pensions and bounties for services in suppressing insurrection or rebellion, shall not be questioned. But neither the United States nor any state shall assume or pay any debt or obligation incurred in aid of insurrection or rebellion against the United States, [*or any claim for the loss or emancipation of any slave;*] but all such debts, obligations, and claims shall be held illegal and void.

## SECTION 5. ENFORCEMENT

The Congress shall have power to enforce, by appropriate legislation, the provisions of this article.

## AMENDMENT 15 (1870)
## VOTING RIGHTS
### SECTION 1. RIGHT TO VOTE

The right of citizens of the United States to vote shall not be denied or abridged by the United States or by any state on account of race, color, or previous condition of servitude.
### SECTION 2. ENFORCEMENT
The Congress shall have power to enforce this article by appropriate legislation.

## AMENDMENT 16 (1913)
## INCOME TAX

The Congress shall have power to lay and collect taxes on incomes, from whatever source derived, without apportionment among the several states, and without regard to any census or enumeration.

---

**Number of Representatives**
Each state's representation in Congress is based on its total population. Any state denying eligible citizens the right to vote will have its representation in Congress decreased. This clause abolished the Three-fifths Compromise in Article I, Section 2. Later amendments granted women the right to vote and lowered the voting age to 18.

**Penalty for Rebellion**
No person who has rebelled against the United States may hold federal office. This clause was originally added to punish the leaders of the Confederacy for failing to support the Constitution of the United States.

**Government Debt**
The federal government is responsible for all public debts. It is not responsible, however, for Confederate debts or for debts that result from any rebellion against the United States.

**Enforcement**
Congress may enforce these provisions by law.

**Right to Vote**
No state may prevent a citizen from voting simply because of race or color or condition of previous servitude. This amendment was designed to extend voting rights to enforce this by law.

**Income Tax**
Congress has the power to collect taxes on its citizens, based on their personal incomes rather than on the number of people living in a state.

AMERICAN DOCUMENTS

AMERICAN DOCUMENTS

**Direct Election of Senators**
Originally, state legislatures elected senators. This amendment allows the people of each state to elect their own senators directly. The idea is to make senators more responsible to the people they represent.

**Prohibition**
This amendment made it illegal to make, sell, or transport liquor within the United States or to transport it out of the United States or its territories. Amendment 18 was the first to include a time limit for approval. If not ratified within seven years, it would be repealed, or canceled. Many later amendments have included similar time limits.

**Women's Voting Rights**
This amendment protected the right of women throughout the United States to vote.

**Terms of Office**
The terms of the President and the Vice President begin on January 20, in the year following their election. Members of Congress take office on January 3. Before this amendment newly elected members of Congress did not begin their terms until March 4. This meant that those who had run for reelection and been defeated remained in office for four months.

## AMENDMENT 17 (1913)
### DIRECT ELECTION OF SENATORS
#### SECTION 1. METHOD OF ELECTION
The Senate of the United States shall be composed of two Senators from each state, elected by the people thereof, for six years; and each Senator shall have one vote. The electors in each state shall have the qualifications requisite for electors of the most numerous branch of the state legislatures.
#### SECTION 2. VACANCIES
When vacancies happen in the representation of any state in the Senate, the executive authority of such state shall issue writs of election to fill such vacancies: *Provided*, that the legislature of any state may empower the executive thereof to make temporary appointments until the people fill the vacancies by election as the legislature may direct.
#### SECTION 3. EXCEPTION
[*This amendment shall not be so construed as to affect the election or term of any Senator chosen before it becomes valid as part of the Constitution.*]

## AMENDMENT 18 (1919)
### BAN ON ALCOHOLIC DRINKS
#### SECTION 1. PROHIBITION
[*After one year from the ratification of this article the manufacture, sale, or transportation of intoxicating liquors within, the importation thereof into, or the exportation thereof from the United States and all territory subject to the jurisdiction thereof for beverage purposes is hereby prohibited.*]
#### SECTION 2. ENFORCEMENT
[*The Congress and the several states shall have concurrent power to enforce this article by appropriate legislation.*]
#### SECTION 3. RATIFICATION
[*This article shall be inoperative unless it shall have been ratified as an amendment to the Constitution by the legislatures of the several states as provided in the Constitution, within seven years from the date of the submission hereof to the states by the Congress.*]

## AMENDMENT 19 (1920)
### WOMEN'S VOTING RIGHTS
#### SECTION 1. RIGHT TO VOTE
The right of citizens of the United States to vote shall not be denied or abridged by the United States or by any state on account of sex.
#### SECTION 2. ENFORCEMENT
Congress shall have power to enforce this article by appropriate legislation.

## AMENDMENT 20 (1933)
### TERMS OF OFFICE
#### SECTION 1. BEGINNING OF TERMS
The terms of the President and Vice President shall end at noon on the 20th day of January, and the terms of Senators and Representatives at noon on the 3rd day of January, of the years in which such terms would have ended if this article had not been ratified; and the terms of their successors shall then begin.

## SECTION 2. SESSIONS OF CONGRESS

The Congress shall assemble at least once in every year, and such meeting shall begin at noon on the 3rd day of January, unless they shall by law appoint a different day.

## SECTION 3. PRESIDENTIAL SUCCESSION

If, at the time fixed for the beginning of the term of the President, the President-elect shall have died, the Vice President-elect shall become President. If a President shall not have been chosen before the time fixed for the beginning of his term, or if the President-elect shall have failed to qualify, then the Vice President-elect shall act as President until a President shall have qualified; and the Congress may by law provide for the case wherein neither a President-elect nor a Vice President-elect shall have qualified, declaring who shall then act as President, or the manner in which one who is to act shall be selected and such person shall act accordingly until a President or Vice President shall be qualified.

## SECTION 4. ELECTIONS DECIDED BY CONGRESS

The Congress may by law provide for the case of the death of any of the persons from whom the House of Representatives may choose a President whenever the right of choice shall have devolved upon them, and for the case of the death of any of the persons from whom the Senate may choose a Vice President whenever the right of choice shall have devolved upon them.

## SECTION 5. EFFECTIVE DATE

[*Sections 1 and 2 shall take effect on the 15th day of October following the ratification of this article.*]

## SECTION 6. RATIFICATION

[*This article shall be inoperative unless it shall have been ratified as an amendment to the Constitution by the legislatures of three fourths of the several states within seven years from the date of its submission.*]

## AMENDMENT 21 (1933)
## END OF PROHIBITION

### SECTION 1. REPEAL OF AMENDMENT 18

The eighteenth article of amendment to the Constitution of the United States is hereby repealed.

### SECTION 2. STATE LAWS

The transportation or importation into any state, territory, or possession of the United States for delivery or use therein of intoxicating liquors, in violation of the laws thereof, is hereby prohibited.

### SECTION 3. RATIFICATION

[*This article shall be inoperative unless it shall have been ratified as an amendment to the Constitution by conventions in the several states, as provided in the Constitution within seven years from the date of the submission hereof to the states by Congress.*]

**Sessions of Congress**
Congress meets at least once a year, beginning at noon on January 3. Congress had previously met at least once a year beginning on the first Monday of December.

**Presidential Succession**
If the newly elected President dies before January 20, the newly elected Vice President becomes President on that date. If a President has not been chosen by January 20 or does not meet the requirements for being President, the newly elected Vice President becomes President. If neither the newly elected President nor the newly elected Vice President meets the requirements for office, Congress decides who will serve as President until a qualified President or Vice President is chosen.

**End of Prohibition**
This amendment repealed Amendment 18. This is the only amendment to be ratified by state conventions instead of by state legislatures. Congress felt that this would give people's opinions about prohibition a better chance to be heard.

**Two-Term limit for Presidents**
A President may not serve more than two full terms in office. Any President who serves less than two years of a previous President's term may be elected for two more terms.

## AMENDMENT 22 (1951)
## TWO-TERM LIMIT FOR PRESIDENTS
### SECTION 1. TWO-TERM LIMIT

No person shall be elected to the office of the President more than twice, and no person who has held the office of President, or acted as President, for more than two years of a term to which some other person was elected President shall be elected to the office of the President more than once. [*But this article shall not apply to any person holding the office of President when this article was proposed by the Congress, and shall not prevent any person who may be holding the office of President, or acting as President, during the term within which this article becomes operative from holding the office of President, or acting as President, during the remainder of such term.*]

### SECTION 2. RATIFICATION

[*This article shall be inoperative unless it shall have been ratified as an amendment to the Constitution by the legislatures of three-fourths of the several states within seven years from the date of its submission to the states by the Congress.*]

**Presidential Electors for District of Columbia**
This amendment grants three electoral votes to the national capital.

## AMENDMENT 23 (1961)
## PRESIDENTIAL ELECTORS FOR DISTRICT OF COLUMBIA
### SECTION 1. NUMBER OF ELECTORS

The District constituting the seat of Government of the United States shall appoint in such manner as Congress may direct:

A number of electors of President and Vice President equal to the whole number of Senators and Representatives in Congress to which the District would be entitled if it were a state, but in no event more than the least populous state; they shall be in addition to those appointed by the states, but they shall be considered, for the purposes of the election of President and Vice President, to be electors appointed by a state, and they shall meet in the District and perform such duties as provided by the twelfth article of amendment.

### SECTION 2. ENFORCEMENT

The Congress shall have power to enforce this article by appropriate legislation.

**Ban on Poll Taxes**
No United States citizen may be prevented from voting in a federal election because of failing to pay a tax to vote. Poll taxes had been used in some states to prevent African Americans from voting.

## AMENDMENT 24 (1964)
## BAN ON POLL TAXES
### SECTION 1. POLL TAX ILLEGAL

The right of citizens of the United States to vote in any primary or other election for President or Vice President, for electors for President or Vice President, or for Senator or Representative in Congress, shall not be denied or abridged by the United States or any state by reason of failure to pay any poll tax or other tax.

### SECTION 2. ENFORCEMENT

The Congress shall have power to enforce this article by appropriate legislation.

**Presidential Vacancy**
If the President is removed from office or resigns from or dies while in office, the Vice President becomes President.

## AMENDMENT 25 (1967)
## PRESIDENTIAL SUCCESSION
### SECTION 1. PRESIDENTIAL VACANCY

In case of the removal of the President from office or of his death or resignation, the Vice President shall become President.

## SECTION 2. VICE PRESIDENTIAL VACANCY

Whenever there is a vacancy in the office of the Vice President, the President shall nominate a Vice President who shall take the office upon confirmation by a majority vote of both houses of Congress.

## SECTION 3. PRESIDENTIAL DISABILITY

Whenever the President transmits to the President pro tempore of the Senate and the Speaker of the House of Representatives his written declaration that he is unable to discharge the powers and duties of his office, and until he transmits to them a written declaration to the contrary, such powers and duties shall be discharged by the Vice President as Acting President.

## SECTION 4. DETERMINING PRESIDENTIAL DISABILITY

Whenever the Vice President and a majority of either the principal officers of the executive departments or of such other body as Congress may by law provide, transmit to the President pro tempore of the Senate and the Speaker of the House of Representatives their written declaration that the President is unable to discharge the powers and duties of his office, the Vice President shall immediately assume the powers and duties of the office as Acting President.

Thereafter, when the President transmits to the President pro tempore of the Senate and the Speaker of the House of Representatives his written declaration that no inability exists, he shall resume the powers and duties of his office unless the Vice President and a majority of either the principal officers of the executive department or of such other body as Congress may by law provide, transmit within four days to the President pro tempore of the Senate and the Speaker of the House of Representatives their written declaration that the President is unable to discharge the powers and duties of his office. Thereupon Congress shall decide the issue, assembling within 48 hours for that purpose if not in session. If the Congress, within 21 days after receipt of the latter written declaration, or, if Congress is not in session, within 21 days after Congress is required to assemble, determines by two-thirds vote of both houses that the President is unable to discharge the powers and duties of his office, the Vice President shall continue to discharge the same as Acting President; otherwise the President shall resume the powers and duties of his office.

## AMENDMENT 26 (1971)
## VOTING AGE

### SECTION 1. RIGHT TO VOTE

The right of citizens of the United States, who are 18 years of age or older, to vote shall not be denied or abridged by the United States or any state on account of age.

### SECTION 2. ENFORCEMENT

The Congress shall have the power to enforce this article by appropriate legislation.

## AMENDMENT 27 (1992)
## CONGRESSIONAL PAY

No law, varying the compensation for the services of the Senators and Representatives, shall take effect, until an election of Representatives shall have intervened.

---

**Vice Presidential Vacancy**
If the office of the Vice President becomes open, the President names someone to assume that office and that person becomes Vice President if both houses of Congress approve by a majority vote.

**Presidential Disability**
This section explains in detail what happens if the President cannot continue in office because of sickness or any other reason. The Vice President takes over as acting President until the President is able to resume office.

**Determining Presidential Disability**
If the Vice President and a majority of the Cabinet inform the Speaker of the House and the president pro tempore of the Senate that the President cannot carry out his or her duties, the Vice President then serves as acting President. To regain the office, the President has to inform the Speaker and the president pro tempore in writing that he or she is again able to serve. But, if the Vice President and a majority of the Cabinet disagree with the President and inform the Speaker and the president pro tempore that the President is still unable to serve, then Congress decides who will hold the office of President.

**Voting Age**
All citizens 18 years or older have the right to vote. Formerly, the voting age was 21 in most states.

**Congressional Pay**
A law raising or lowering the salaries for members of Congress cannot be passed for that session of Congress.

"The Star-Spangled Banner" was written by Francis Scott Key in September 1814 and adopted as the national anthem in March 1931. The army and navy had recognized it as such long before Congress approved it.

During the War of 1812, Francis Scott Key spent a night aboard a British warship in the Chesapeake Bay while trying to arrange for the release of an American prisoner. The battle raged throughout the night, while the Americans were held on the ship. The next morning, when the smoke from the cannons finally cleared, Francis Scott Key was thrilled to see the American flag still waving proudly above Fort McHenry. It symbolized the victory of the Americans.

There are four verses to the national anthem. In these four verses, Key wrote about how he felt when he saw the flag still waving over Fort McHenry. He wrote that the flag was a symbol of the freedom for which the people had fought so hard. Key also told about the pride he had in his country and the great hopes he had for the future of the United States.

# THE NATIONAL ANTHEM

## The Star-Spangled Banner

(1)

Oh, say can you see by the dawn's early light
What so proudly we hail'd at the twilight's last gleaming,
Whose broad stripes and bright stars through the perilous fight
O'er the ramparts we watch'd were so gallantly streaming?
And the rockets' red glare, the bombs bursting in air,
Gave proof through the night that our flag was still there.
Oh, say does that star-spangled banner yet wave
O'er the land of the free and the home of the brave?

(2)

On the shore dimly seen through the mists of the deep,
Where the foe's haughty host in dread silence reposes,
What is that which the breeze, o'er the towering steep,
As it fitfully blows, half conceals, half discloses?
Now it catches the gleam of the morning's first beam,
In full glory reflected now shines in the stream.
'Tis the star-spangled banner, oh, long may it wave
O'er the land of the free and the home of the brave!

(3)

And where is that band who so vauntingly swore
That the havoc of war and the battle's confusion
A home and a country should leave us no more?
Their blood has wash'd out their foul footstep's pollution.
No refuge could save the hireling and slave
From the terror of flight or the gloom of the grave,
And the star-spangled banner in triumph doth wave
O'er the land of the free and the home of the brave.

(4)

Oh, thus be it ever when freemen shall stand
Between their lov'd home and the war's desolation!
Blest with vict'ry and peace may the heav'n-rescued land
Praise the power that hath made and preserv'd us a nation!
Then conquer we must, when our cause it is just,
And this be our motto, "In God is our Trust,"
And the star-spangled banner in triumph shall wave
O'er the land of the free and the home of the brave.

# THE PLEDGE OF ALLEGIANCE

I pledge allegiance to the Flag

of the United States of America,

and to the Republic

for which it stands,

one Nation under God, indivisible,

with liberty and justice for all.

The flag is a symbol of the United States of America. The Pledge of Allegiance says that the people of the United States promise to stand up for the flag, their country, and the basic beliefs of freedom and fairness upon which the country was established.

# Biographical Dictionary

The Biographical Dictionary lists many of the important people introduced in this book. The page number tells where the main discussion of each person starts. See the Index for other page references.

BIOGRAPHICAL DICTIONARY

## A

**Adams, Abigail** *1744–1818* Patriot who wrote about women's rights in letters to John Adams, her husband. p. 311

**Adams, John** *1735–1826* 2nd U.S. President and one of the writers of the Declaration of Independence. pp. 303, 306, 353, 377, 379

**Adams, Samuel** *1722–1803* American Revolutionary leader who set up a Committee of Correspondence in Boston and helped form the Sons of Liberty. pp. 281, 289, 353, 369

**Addams, Jane** *1860–1935* American reformer who brought the idea of settlement houses from Britain to the United States. With Ellen Gates Starr, she founded Hull House in Chicago. p. 534

**Aldrin, Edwin, Jr.** *1930–* American astronaut who was one of the first people to set foot on the moon. p. 583

**Ali, Sunni** *1400s* Ruler of African empire of Songhay from 1464 to 1492. p. 111

**Allen, Ethan** *1738–1789* American Patriot from Vermont who led the Green Mountain Boys. p. 318

**Anderson, Robert** *1805–1871* Union commander of Fort Sumter who was forced to surrender to the Confederacy. p. 454

**Aristide, Jean-Bertrand** (air•ih•STEED, ZHAHN bair•TRAHN) *1953–* Freely elected president of Haiti who was overthrown in 1991 but was returned to office in 1994. p. 661

**Armstrong, Louis** *1901–1971* Noted jazz trumpeter who helped make jazz popular in the 1920s. p. 543

**Armstrong, Neil** *1930–* American astronaut who was the first person to set foot on the moon. p. 583

**Arnold, Benedict** *1741–1801* Continental Army officer who became a traitor and worked for the British army. p. 323

**Atahuallpa** (ah•tah•WAHL•pah) *1502?–1533* Inca ruler who was killed in the Spanish conquest of the Incas. p. 133

**Attucks, Crispus** (A•tuhks) *1723?–1770* Patriot and former slave who was killed during the Boston Massacre. p. 285

**Austin, Moses** *1761–1821* American pioneer who wanted to start an American colony in Texas. p. 402

**Austin, Stephen F.** *1793–1836* Moses Austin's son. He carried out his father's dream of starting an American colony in Texas. p. 402

## B

**Bache, Sarah Franklin** *1700s* Daughter of Benjamin Franklin; took over Philadelphia Association when Esther Reed died. p. 311

**Balboa, Vasco Núñez de** (bahl•BOH•uh, NOON•yays day) *1475–1519* Spanish explorer who, in 1513, became the first European to reach the western coast of the Americas—proving to Europeans that the Americas were separate from Asia. p. 123

**Banneker, Benjamin** *1731–1806* African American who helped survey the land for the new capital of the United States. p. 376

**Barrett, Janie Porter** *1865–1948* African American teacher who founded a settlement house in Hampton, Virginia. p. 535

**Barton, Clara** *1821–1912* Civil War nurse and founder of the American Red Cross. p. 463

**Bates, Katharine Lee** *1859–1929* American educator and poet. p. 17

**Becknell, William** *1796?–1865* American pioneer from Missouri who opened the Santa Fe Trail. p. 404

**Bellamy, Francis** *1800s* Writer of patriotic oath that came to be called the Pledge of Allegiance. p. 643

**Berlin, Irving** *1888–1989* American songwriter who moved to New York City from Russia in 1893. p. 503

**Bessemer, Henry** *1813–1898* British inventor of a way to produce steel more easily and cheaply than before. p. 495

**Bienville, Jean-Baptiste Le Moyne, Sieur de** (bee•EN•vil, ZHAHN ba•TEEST luh•MWAHN) *1680–1747* French explorer who—with his brother, Pierre Le Moyne, Sieur d'Iberville—started an early settlement at the mouth of the Mississippi River. p. 154

**Birdseye, Clarence** *1886–1956* American scientist who developed methods of quick-freezing foods to preserve freshness. p. 546

**Black Hawk** *1767–1838* Leader of Sauk and Fox Indians; led fight against U.S. troops and Illinois militia. p. 398

**Bolívar, Simón** (boh•LEE•var, see•MOHN) *1783–1830* Leader of independence movements in Bolivia, Colombia, Ecuador, Peru, and Venezuela. p. 666

**Bonaparte, Napoleon** (BOH•nuh•part, nuh•POH•lee•uhn) *1769–1821* French leader who sold all of the Louisiana region to the United States. p. 385

**Boone, Daniel** *1734–1820* American who was one of the first pioneers to cross the Appalachians. pp. 225, 276

**Booth, John Wilkes** *1838–1865* Actor who assassinated President Abraham Lincoln. p. 477

**Bowie, James** *1796–1836* American soldier killed at the Alamo. p. 403

**Braddock, Edward** *1695–1755* Commander in chief of British forces in French and Indian War; defeated in surprise attack. p. 271

**Bradford, William** *1590–1657* Governor of Plymouth Colony. p. 168

**Breckinridge, John** *1821–1875* Democrat from Kentucky who ran against Abraham Lincoln in the 1860 presidential election. p. 453

**Brezhnev, Leonid** (BREZH•nef) *1906–1982* Leader of the Communist Party of the Soviet Union from 1964 until his death in 1982. President Nixon's 1972 visit with him in the Soviet Union led to arms control and began a period of détente. p. 592

**Brown, John** *1800–1859* American abolitionist who seized a weapons storehouse to help slaves rebel. He was caught and hanged. p. 449

**Brown, Linda** *1943–* African American student whose family was among a group that challenged public-school segregation. p. 585

**Brown, Moses** *1738–1836* Textile pioneer who built the first textile mill in the United States, using Samuel Slater's plans. p. 416

**Bruce, Blanche K.** *1841–1898* Former slave who became U.S. senator from Mississippi. p. 479

**Bruchac, Joseph** Author of Native American folktales and legends. p. 14

**Burgoyne, John** (ber•GOYN) *1722–1792* British general who lost a battle to the Continental Army on October 17, 1777, at Saratoga, New York. p. 316

**Burnet, David G.** *1788–1870* First president of the Republic of Texas, when it was formed in 1836. p. 403

**Bush, George** *1924–* 41st U.S. President. He was President at the end of the Cold War and during Operation Desert Storm. pp. 598–599

**Bush, George W.** *1946–* 43rd U.S. President; son of George Bush, he won the closest election in history. pp. 600, 641, 651

## C

**Cabeza de Vaca, Álvar Núñez** (kah•BAY•sah day VAH•kah) *1490?–1560?* Spanish explorer who went to Mexico City and told stories of the Seven Cities of Gold. p. 131

**Caboto, Giovanni** (kah•BOH•toh) *1450?–1499?* Italian explorer who in 1497 sailed from England and landed in what is now Newfoundland, though he thought he had landed in Asia. The English gave him the name John Cabot. p. 123

**Calhoun, John C.** *1782–1850* Vice President under John Quincy Adams and Andrew Jackson. He was a strong believer in states' rights. pp. 437, 453

**Calvert, Cecilius** *1605–1675* First proprietor of the Maryland colony; appointed his brother Leonard Calvert as governor of Maryland. p. 233

**Calvert, George** *1580?–1632* Member of Virginia Company and the first Lord Baltimore; bought land in Newfoundland, but found it too cold; moved to Chesapeake Bay area; father of Cecilius Calvert. p. 232

**Cardozo, Francis L.** *1800s* African American who became secretary of state and state treasurer in South Carolina. p. 479

**Carnegie, Andrew** *1835–1919* Entrepreneur who helped the steel industry grow in the United States. pp. 495, 496

**Carter, Jimmy** *1924–* 39th U.S. President. He brought about a peace agreement between Israel and Egypt. p. 596

**Carteret, Sir George** *c.1610–1680* Proprietor with Lord John Berkeley of territory between the Hudson and Delaware Rivers; named the state of New Jersey for his birthplace. p. 213

**Cartier, Jacques** (kar•TYAY, ZHAHK) *1491–1557* French explorer who sailed up the St. Lawrence River and began a fur-trading business with the Hurons. p. 137

**Carver, George Washington** *c.1864–1943* African American scientist who developed hundreds of new uses for peanuts, sweet potatoes, and soybeans. p. 545

**Castro, Fidel** *1926–* Leader who took over Cuba in 1959 and made it a communist nation. pp. 584, 660

**Catt, Carrie Chapman** *1859–1947* President of National American Woman Suffrage Association. pp. 535–536

**Cavelier, René-Robert** (ka•vuhl•YAY) *See* La Salle.

**Champlain, Samuel de** (sham•PLAYN) *1567?–1635* French explorer who founded the first settlement at Quebec. p. 151

**Charles I** *1500–1558* King of Spain. p. 145

**Charles I** *1600–1649* British king who chartered the colonies of Massachusetts and Maryland. pp. 188, 233

**Charles II** *1630–1685* British king who granted charters for the New Hampshire Colony and the Carolina Colony. Son of Charles I and Henrietta Maria. pp. 197, 234

**Chavez, Cesar** *1927–1993* Labor leader and organizer of the United Farm Workers. p. 588

**Clark, George Rogers** *1752–1818* American Revolutionary frontiersman who helped protect western lands and settlers. p. 319

**Clark, William** *1770–1838* American explorer who aided Meriwether Lewis in an expedition through the Louisiana Purchase. p. 386

**Clay, Henry** *1777–1852* Representative from Kentucky who worked for compromises on the slavery issue. pp. 390, 438

**Clemens, Samuel Langhorne** *1835–1910* American writer and steamboat pilot; he wrote under the pen name Mark Twain. p. 30

**Clinton, DeWitt** *1769–1828* Governor of New York who found European investors to pay for building of Erie Canal. p. 414

**Clinton, George** *1739–1812* American politician who helped form the Democratic-Republican party. p. 367

**Clinton, Hillary Rodham** *1947–* Wife of William Clinton; senator of New York. p. 640

**Clinton, William** *1946–* 42nd U.S. President. pp. 599–600

**Collins, Michael** *1930–* American astronaut who remained in the lunar orbiter during the *Apollo 11* moon landing. p. 583

**Columbus, Christopher** *1451–1506* Italian-born Spanish explorer who in 1492 sailed west from Spain and thought he had reached Asia but had actually reached islands near the Americas, lands that were unknown to Europeans. pp. 106, 121

**Cooper, Peter** *1791–1883* American manufacturer who built *Tom Thumb*, one of the first locomotives made in the United States. p. 415

**Cornish, Samuel** *1795–1858* African American who in 1827 helped John Russwurm found an abolitionist newspaper called *Freedom's Journal*. p. 448

**Cornwallis, Charles** *1738–1805* British general who surrendered at the Battle of Yorktown, resulting in victory for the Americans in the Revolutionary War. p. 324

**Coronado, Francisco Vásquez de** (kawr•oh•NAH•doh) *1510?–1554* Spanish explorer who led an expedition from Mexico City into what is now the southwestern United States in search of the Seven Cities of Gold. p. 131

**Cortés, Hernando** (kawr•TEZ) *1485–1547* Spanish conquistador who conquered the Aztec Empire. pp. 128, 652

**Crazy Horse** *1842?–1877* Sioux leader who fought against General George Custer. p. 491

**Crockett, Davy** *1786–1836* American pioneer who was killed at the Alamo. pp. 395, 403

**Custer, George** *1839–1876* U.S. Army general who led an attack against Sioux and Cheyenne Indians. Custer and all of his men were killed in the battle. p. 491

## D

**da Gama, Vasco** (dah GA•muh) *1460?–1524* Portuguese navigator who sailed from Europe, around the southern tip of Africa, and on to Asia between 1497 and 1499. p. 118

**Davis, Jefferson** *1808–1889* United States senator from Mississippi who became president of the Confederacy. p. 453

**Dawes, William** *1745–1799* American who, along with Paul Revere, warned the Patriots that the British were marching toward Concord. p. 291

**Deere, John** *1804–1886* American industrialist who created steel plows for use on the Great Plains. p. 419

**Deganawida** (deh•gahn•uh•WIH•duh) *1500s* Legendary Iroquois holy man who called for an end to the fighting among the Iroquois, a view that led to the formation of the Iroquois League. p. 90

**de Narváez, Pánfilo** *1500s* Spanish explorer who hoped to conquer lands along the Gulf of Mexico but failed. p. 130

**de Soto, Hernando** (day SOH•toh) *1496?–1542* Spanish explorer who led an expedition into what is today the southeastern United States. p. 132

**Dewey, George** *1837–1917* American naval commander who destroyed the Spanish fleet and captured Manila Bay in the Spanish-American War. p. 527

**Dias, Bartolomeu** (DEE•ahsh) *1450?–1500* Portuguese navigator who in 1488 became the first European to sail around the southern tip of Africa. p. 118

**Díaz, Porfirio** *1830–1915* Mexican dictator. p. 654

**Dickinson, John** *1732–1808* Member of the Continental Congress who wrote most of the Articles of Confederation, adopted in 1781. pp. 283, 293, 306

**Dinwiddie, Robert** *1693–1770* British Lieutenant Governor of Virginia; sent George Washington to defend Ohio Valley from seizure by the French. p. 269

**Douglas, Stephen A.** *1813–1861* American legislator who wrote the Kansas-Nebraska Act and debated Abraham Lincoln in a race for a Senate seat from Illinois. p. 452

**Douglass, Frederick** *1817–1895* Abolitionist speaker and writer who had escaped from slavery. p. 449

**Drake, Edwin** *1819–1880* American pioneer in oil industry; became first to tap petroleum at its source. p. 497

**Drake, Francis** *1543–1596* English explorer who sailed around the world. p. 157

**Drew, Charles** *1904–1950* American physician who developed an efficient way to store blood plasma in blood banks. p. 562

**Du Bois, W. E. B.** (doo•BOYS) *1868–1963* African American teacher, writer, and leader who helped form the National Association for the Advancement of Colored People (NAACP). p. 535

## E

**Edison, Thomas** *1847–1931* American who invented the phonograph and the electric lightbulb; he also built the first power station to supply electricity to New York City. pp. 498–499, 500–501

**Eisenhower, Dwight D.** *1890–1969* 34th U.S. President and, earlier, American general who led the D day invasion. pp. 565–566, 582

**Elizabeth I** *1533–1603* Queen of England from 1558 to 1603. p. 156

**Ellington, Edward Kennedy (Duke)** *1899–1974* Band leader who became well-known playing jazz during the 1920s. p. 543

**Emerson, Ralph Waldo** *1803–1882* American poet who wrote "Concord Hymn." pp. 267, 292

**Endecott, John** *1588–1665* Member of New England Company who sailed to New England in 1628 and settled at Salem. p. 188

**Equiano, Olaudah** (ek•wee•AHN•oh, OHL•uh•dah) *1750?–1797* African who was kidnapped from his village and sold into slavery. He later wrote a book describing his experiences. p. 244

**Esteban** (ehs•TAY•bahn) *1500–1539* African explorer who went with Cabeza de Vaca to Mexico City and told stories of the Seven Cities of Gold. Esteban was killed on a later expedition, the purpose of which was to find out whether the stories were true. p. 131

## F

**Farragut, Jorge** (FAIR•uh•guht, HAWR•hay) *1755–1817* Spanish-born man who fought in the Continental Army and the navy. p. 318

**Ferdinand II** *1452–1516* King of Spain who—with Queen Isabella, his wife—sent Christopher Columbus on his voyage to find a western route to Asia. p. 121

**Ferraro, Geraldine** *1935–* First woman to be nominated as a major party's candidate for Vice President of the United States. p. 589

**Finley, John** Fur trader who helped Daniel Boone find the way across the Appalachian Mountains to Kentucky. p. 277

**Fong, Hiram L.** *1906–* Chinese immigrant who settled in Hawaii; became first Chinese American senator. p. 505

**Ford, Gerald** *1913–* 38th U.S. President. The Vietnam War ended during his term. p. 593

**Ford, Henry** *1863–1947* American automobile manufacturer who mass-produced cars at low cost by using assembly lines. p. 544

**Fox, Vicente** *1942–* Elected president of Mexico in 2000. p. 655

**Frame, Richard** *1600s* Colonist and writer. p. 209

**Franco, Francisco** *1892–1975* Spanish dictator. p. 555

**Franklin, Benjamin** *1706–1790* American leader who was sent to Britain to ask Parliament for representation. He was a writer of the Declaration of Independence, a delegate to the Constitutional Convention, and a respected scientist and business leader. pp. 221, 271, 283, 303, 318, 352, 366

**Frontenac, Louis de Buade, Count de** (FRAHN•tuh•nak) *1622–1698* French leader who was appointed governor-general of New France. p. 152

**Fulton, Robert** *1765–1815* American engineer and inventor who created the first commercial steamboat. p. 415

## G

**Gadsden, James** *1788–1858* U.S. minister to Mexico who arranged to buy parts of present-day New Mexico and Arizona from Mexico—known as the Gadsden Purchase. p. 407

**Gage, Thomas** *1721–1787* Head of the British army in North America and colonial governor. pp. 291, 294

**Gálvez, Bernardo de** (GAHL•ves) *1746–1786* Spanish governor of Louisiana who sent supplies to the Patriots in the Revolutionary War and led his own soldiers in taking a British fort in Florida. p. 318

**Garrison, William Lloyd** *1805–1879* American abolitionist who started a newspaper called *The Liberator*. p. 448

**Gates, Horatio** *1728–1806* American general who defeated the British in 1777 at Saratoga, New York. p. 316

**George II** *1683–1760* British king who chartered the Georgia Colony. p. 236

**George III** *1738–1820* King of England during the Revolutionary War. pp. 276, 296

**Gerry, Elbridge** *1744–1814* Massachusetts delegate to the Constitutional Convention. p. 366

**Gibbs, Jonathan C.** *1800s* African American who became secretary of state in Florida; helped set up public school system. p. 479

**Glenn, John H., Jr.** *1921–* American astronaut who was the first American to orbit the Earth. Former U.S. senator. p. 583

**Gorbachev, Mikhail** (gawr•buh•CHAWF, mee•kuh•EEL) *1931–* Leader of the Soviet Union from 1985 to 1991. He improved relations with the United States and expanded freedom in the Soviet Union. pp. 597-598

**Gordon, William E.** *1918–* American scientist who established the Arecibo Observatory in Puerto Rico. p. 660

**Gore, Albert** *1948–* Vice President under President Bill Clinton. Defeated by George W. Bush in the 2000 election—the closest election in history. pp. 600, 641

**Granger, Gordon** Union general who read the order declaring all slaves in Texas to be free. p. 482

**Grant, Ulysses S.** *1822–1885* 18th U.S. President and, earlier, commander of the Union army in the Civil War. pp. 465, 468, 469, 471, 475

**Greeley, Horace** *1811–1872* American journalist and political leader; publisher of a newspaper called the *New York Tribune*. p. 461

**Greene, Nathanael** *1742–1786* Commander of the Continental Army in the Southern Colonies; forced British out of Georgia and the Carolinas. p. 322

**Grenville, George** *1712–1770* British prime minister who passed the Stamp Act in 1765. p. 280

**Gutenberg, Johannes** *1390–1468* German inventor; invented movable type. p. 109

## H

**Hale, Nathan** *1755–1776* American Revolutionary hero who was hanged by the British for spying for the Patriots. p. 319

**Hamilton, Alexander** *1755–1804* American leader in calling for the Constitutional Convention and winning support for it. He favored a strong national government. pp. 368, 375, 377

**Hammond, James Henry** *1807–1864* Senator from South Carolina. p. 442

**Hancock, John** *1737–1793* Leader of the Sons of Liberty in the Massachusetts Colony. pp. 306, 353, 369

**Harrison, William Henry** *1773–1841* 9th U.S. President. Earlier he directed U.S. forces against the Indians at the Battle of Tippecanoe and was a commander in the War of 1812. p. 390

**He, Zheng** *1400s* Chinese admiral who made seven voyages between 1405 and 1433. p. 109

**Henrietta Maria** *1609–1669* Queen of Charles I of England. The Maryland Colony was named in her honor. p. 233

**Henry** *1394–1460* Henry the Navigator, prince of Portugal, who set up the first European school for training sailors in navigation. p. 115

**Henry IV** *1553–1610* King of France. p. 150

**Henry, Patrick** *1736–1799* American colonist who spoke out in the Virginia legislature against paying British taxes. His views became widely known, and Loyalists accused him of treason. pp. 282, 290, 350, 353, 367, 378

**Hiawatha** (hy•uh•WAH•thuh) *1500s* Onondaga chief who persuaded other Iroquois tribes to form the Iroquois League. p. 90

**Hidalgo, Miguel** *1753–1811* Mexican priest who called for a revolution against Spain in 1810. p. 653

**Hirohito** *1901–1989* Emperor of Japan from 1926 until his death. p. 555

**Hitler, Adolf** *1889–1945* Nazi dictator of Germany. His actions led to World War II and the killing of millions of people. p. 555

**Hooker, Thomas** *1586?–1647* Minister who helped form the Connecticut Colony. His democratic ideas were adopted in the Fundamental Orders. p. 196

**Hoover, Herbert** *1874–1964* 31st U.S. President. When the depression began, he thought that the economy was healthy and conditions would improve. p. 548

**Houston, Sam** *1793–1863* President of the Republic of Texas and, later, governor of the state of Texas. pp. 403, 453

**Howard, Martin** *1700s* Rhode Island colonist who defended Britain's right to tax the colonists. p. 280

**Hudson, Henry** *?–1611* Explorer who sailed up the Hudson River, giving the Dutch a claim to the area. p. 138

**Huerta, Dolores** *1900s* Labor leader and organizer, along with Cesar Chavez, of the United Farm Workers. p. 588

**Hughes, Langston** *1902–1967* African American poet and one of the best-known Harlem writers. p. 543

**Hurston, Zora Neale** *1903–1960* African American novelist and one of the best-known Harlem writers. p. 543

**Hussein, Saddam** *1937–* Leader of Iraq. p. 598

**Hutchinson, Anne Marbury** *1591–1643* English-born woman who left Massachusetts because of her religious beliefs. She settled near Providence, which joined with other settlements to form the Rhode Island Colony. p. 195

**Iberville, Pierre Le Moyne, Sieur d'** (ee•ber•VEEL) *1661–1706* French explorer who—with his brother, Jean-Baptiste Le Moyne, Sieur de Bienville—started an early settlement at the mouth of the Mississippi River. p. 154

**Ibn Majid, Ahmad** *1432–1500* Great contributor to study of navigation; born in what is today United Arab Emirates. p. 118

**Isabella I** *1451–1504* Queen of Spain who—with King Ferdinand, her husband—sent Columbus on his voyage to find a western route to Asia. p. 121

**Jackson, Andrew** *1767–1845* 7th U.S. President and, earlier, commander who won the final battle in the War of 1812. As President he favored a strong Union and ordered the removal of Native Americans from their lands. pp. 393, 396, 437

**Jackson, Thomas (Stonewall)** *1824–1863* Confederate general. pp. 458, 466

**James I** *1566–1625* King of England in the early 1600s. The James River and Jamestown were named after him. pp. 160, 164

**Jay, John** *1745–1829* American leader who wrote letters to newspapers, defending the Constitution. He became the first chief justice of the Supreme Court. pp. 368, 375

**Jefferson, Thomas** *1743–1826* 3rd U.S. President and the main writer of the Declaration of Independence. pp. 303, 353, 368, 371, 375, 376, 377, 384

**Jenney, William** *1832–1907* American engineer who developed the use of steel frames to build tall buildings. p. 496

**John I** *1357–1433* King of Portugal during a time of great exploration. Father of Prince Henry, who set up a school of navigation. p. 115

**Johnson, Andrew** *1808–1875* 17th U.S. President. Differences with Congress about Reconstruction led to his being impeached, though he was found not guilty. pp. 477, 479

**Johnson, Lyndon B.** *1908–1973* 36th U.S. President. He started Great Society programs and expanded U.S. involvement in the Vietnam War. pp. 584, 588, 590, 591

**Joliet, Louis** (zhohl•YAY, loo•EE) *1645–1700* French fur trader who explored lakes and rivers for France, with Jacques Marquette and five others. p. 152

**Jones, John Paul** *1747–1792* American naval officer who defeated bigger and better-equipped British ships during Revolutionary War. p. 319

**Joseph** *1840?–1904* Nez Perce chief who tried to lead his people to Canada after they were told to move onto a reservation. p. 491

**Josephy, Alvin M., Jr.** *1915–* Historian and author of books about Native Americans and the United States westward movement. p. 55

**Juárez, Benito** *1806–1872* Served twice as president of Mexico; made many reforms. p. 654

**K**

**Kalakaua** (kah•lah•KAH•ooh•ah) *1836–1891* Hawaiian king who tried but failed to keep Americans from taking over the Hawaiian Islands. p. 525

**Kennedy, John F.** *1917–1963* 35th U.S. President. He helped propose the Civil Rights Act. pp. 583–584

**Key, Francis Scott** *1779–1843* American lawyer and poet who wrote the words to "The Star-Spangled Banner." p. 392

**King, Martin Luther, Jr.** *1929–1968* African American civil rights leader who worked for integration in nonviolent ways. King won the Nobel Peace Prize in 1964. pp. 586, 587

**Knox, Henry** *1750–1806* Secretary of war in the first government under the Constitution. pp. 375, 377

**Kosciuszko, Thaddeus** (kawsh•CHUSH•koh) *1746–1817* Polish officer who helped the Patriots in the Revolutionary War. He later returned to Poland and led a revolution there. p. 317

**Kublai Khan** (KOO•bluh KAHN) *1215–1294* Ruler of China who was visited by Marco Polo. p. 109

**L**

**La Follette, Robert** *1855–1925* Wisconsin governor who began many reforms in his state, including a merit system for government jobs. p. 533

**La Salle, René-Robert Cavelier, Sieur de** (luh•SAL) *1643–1687* French explorer who found the mouth of the Mississippi River and claimed the whole Mississippi Valley for France. p. 153

**Lafayette, Marquis de** (lah•fee•ET) *1757–1834* French noble who fought alongside the Americans in the Revolutionary War. p. 317

**Las Casas, Bartolomé de** (lahs KAH•sahs, bar•toh•loh•MAY day) *1474–1566* Spanish missionary who spent much of his life trying to help Native Americans. p. 145

**Law, John** *1671–1729* Scottish banker who was appointed proprietor of the Louisiana region in 1717. p. 155

**Lawrence, Jacob** *1900s* African American artist; his parents took part in the Great Migration. p. 507

Le Moyne, Jean-Baptiste *See* Bienville.

Le Moyne, Pierre *See* Iberville.

Lee, Richard Henry *1732–1794* American Revolutionary leader who said to the Continental Congress that the colonies should become independent from Britain. p. 303

Lee, Robert E. *1807–1870* United States army colonel who gave up his post to become commander of the Confederate army in the Civil War. pp. 461, 466, 471

L'Enfant, Pierre Charles *1754–1825* French-born American engineer who planned the buildings and streets of the new capital of the United States. p. 377

Lewis, Meriwether *1774–1809* American explorer chosen by Thomas Jefferson to be a pathfinder in the territory of the Louisiana Purchase. p. 386

Liliuokalani, Lydia (lih•lee•uh•woh•kuh•LAH•nee) *1838–1917* Hawaiian queen who tried but failed to bring back the Hawaiian monarchy's authority. p. 525

Lincoln, Abraham *1809–1865* 16th U.S. President, leader of the Union in the Civil War, and signer of the Emancipation Proclamation. pp. 100, 450-455, 461, 462, 468, 476-477

Lincoln, Mary Todd *1818–1882* Wife of Abraham Lincoln. p. 477

Lindbergh, Charles *1902–1974* Airplane pilot who was the first to fly solo between the United States and Europe. p. 545

Livingston, Robert R. *1746–1813* One of the writers of the Declaration of Independence. p. 303

Longstreet, James *1821–1904* Former Confederate general who wanted the South to build more factories; considered a scalawag. p. 484

Louis XIV *1638–1715* King of France. pp. 152, 153

Lowell, Francis Cabot *1775–1817* Textile pioneer who set up an American mill in which several processes were completed under one roof. p. 416

## M

MacArthur, Douglas *1880–1964* Commanded Allied forces in the Pacific during World War II. p. 567

Madison, Dolley *1768–1849* James Madison's wife and First Lady during the War of 1812. p. 392

Madison, James *1751–1836* 4th U.S. President. He was a leader in calling for the Constitutional Convention, writing the Constitution, and winning support for it. pp. 350, 352, 360, 368, 371, 378, 390

Magellan, Ferdinand (muh•JEH•luhn) *1480?–1521* Portuguese explorer who in 1519 led a fleet of ships from Spain westward to Asia. He died on the voyage, but one of the ships made it back to Spain, completing the first trip around the world. p. 124

Maguire, Matthew *1800s* Machine worker who, along with Peter McGuire, came up with the idea for Labor Day. p. 533

Mahan, Alfred T. *1840–1914* American naval officer and historian. p. 523

Malcolm X *1925–1965* African American leader who disagreed with the views of Martin Luther King, Jr., on nonviolence and integration. p. 587

Malintzin (mah•LINT•suhn) *1501?–1550* Aztec princess who interpreted for Hernando Cortés and helped him in other ways to conquer Mexico. p. 128

Mao Zedong (MOW zeh•DOONG) *1893–1976* Leader of China from 1949 until his death. President Nixon's 1972 visit with him in China led to trade and cultural exchange with the United States. p. 592

Marion, Francis *1732?–1795* Known as the Swamp Fox, he led Continental soldiers through the swamps of South Carolina on daring raids against the British. p. 319

Marquette, Jacques (mar•KET, ZHAHK) *1637–1675* Catholic missionary who knew several American Indian languages. With Louis Joliet, he explored lakes and rivers for France. p. 152

Marshall, George C. *1880–1959* U.S. Secretary of State who developed the European Recovery Program, also known as the Marshall Plan, after World War II. p. 575

Marshall, James *1810–1885* Carpenter who found gold at John Sutter's sawmill near Sacramento, California, leading to the California gold rush of 1849. p. 408

Marshall, John *1755–1835* Chief Justice of the Supreme Court in 1832; Marshall ruled that the United States should protect the Cherokees and their lands in Georgia. p. 398

Marshall, Thurgood *1908–1993* NAACP lawyer who argued the school segregation case that the Supreme Court ruled on in 1954 and, later, was the first African American to serve on the Supreme Court. p. 585

Mason, George *1725–1792* Virginia delegate to the Constitutional Convention who argued for an end to the slave trade. pp. 366, 370

Massasoit (ma•suh•SOYT) *?–1661* Chief of the Wampanoags, who lived in peace with the Pilgrims. p. 169

Mather, Cotton *1663–1728* Member of well-known family of American Congregational clergymen; published over 400 works on religious, historical, scientific, and moral subjects. p. 187

McCauley, Mary Ludwig Hays *1754?–1832* Known as Molly Pitcher, she carried water to American soldiers during the Battle of Monmouth; when her husband fell during the battle, she began firing his cannon. p. 319

McCormick, Cyrus *1809–1884* Inventor of a reaping machine for harvesting wheat. p. 419

McGuire, Peter *1800s* Carpenter who, along with Matthew Maguire, came up with the idea for Labor Day. p. 533

McKinley, William *1843–1901* 25th U.S. President. The Spanish-American War was fought during his term. pp. 526, 528

Menéndez de Avilés, Pedro (may•NAYN•days day ah•vee•LAYS) *1519–1574* Spanish leader of settlers in St. Augustine, Florida, the first permanent European settlement in what is now the United States. p. 146

Metacomet *1639?–1676* Called King Philip by the English. Son of Massasoit; leader of Wampanoags; made war upon New England settlers—called King Philip's War. p. 198

Minuit, Peter *1580–1638* A director of the New Netherland Colony who purchased Manhattan Island from the Manhattan Indians for $24. p. 211

Mongoulacha (mahn•goo•LAY•chah) *1700s* Indian leader who helped Bienville and Iberville. p. 154

BIOGRAPHICAL DICTIONARY

**Monroe, James** *1758–1831* 5th U.S. President. He established the Monroe Doctrine, which said that the United States would stop any European nation from expanding its American empire. p. 394

**Morgan, Daniel** *1736–1802* American general who defeated the British at Cowpens in the Revolutionary War. p. 322

**Morris, Gouverneur** (guh•ver•NIR) *1752–1816* American leader who was in charge of the final wording of the United States Constitution. pp. 358-359

**Motecuhzoma** (maw•tay•kwah•SOH•mah) *1466–1520* Emperor of the Aztecs when they were conquered by the Spanish. He is also known as Montezuma. p. 129

**Muhlenberg, John Peter** *1746–1807* Young minister, son of the colonies' Lutheran leader, who became a Patriot militia officer. p. 309

**Mussolini, Benito** (moo•suh•LEE•nee, buh•NEE•toh) *1883–1945* Ruler of Italy from 1922 until 1943, most of that time as dictator. p. 555

**N**

**Nast, Thomas** *1840–1902* American cartoonist who created the "Uncle Sam" character. p. 640

**Newcomen, Thomas** *1663–1729* English blacksmith and inventor who invented the steam engine. p. 414

**Nimitz, Chester W.** *1885–1966* Commander of U.S. Pacific fleet during World War II. p. 567

**Nixon, Richard M.** *1913–1994* 37th U.S. President. He tried to end the Vietnam War, he reduced tensions with communist nations, and he resigned the presidency because of the Watergate scandal. pp. 591–593

**Niza, Marcos de** (day NEE•sah) *1495–1558* Spanish priest who was sent with Esteban to confirm stories of the Seven Cities of Gold. When he returned to Mexico City, he said he had seen a golden city. p. 131

**O**

**O'Connor, Sandra Day** *1930–* First woman to be appointed to the United States Supreme Court. pp. 589, 640

**Oglethorpe, James** *1696–1785* English settler who was given a charter to settle Georgia. He wanted to bring in debtors from England to help settle it. p. 236

**O'Keeffe, Georgia** *1887–1986* American painter who developed her own style showing abstract studies of color and light. p. 543

**Osceola** *1804–1838* Leader of the Seminoles in Florida. p. 398

**Otis, James** *1725–1783* Massachusetts colonist who spoke out against British taxes and called for "no taxation without representation." pp. 280, 282, 283

**P**

**Paine, Thomas** *1737–1809* Author of a widely read pamphlet called *Common Sense*, in which he attacked King George III and called for a revolution to make the colonies independent. pp. 301, 302

**Parks, Rosa** *1913–* African American woman whose refusal to give up her seat on a Montgomery, Alabama, bus started a year-long bus boycott. p. 586

**Paterson, William** *1745–1806* Constitutional delegate from New Jersey who submitted the New Jersey Plan, under which each state would have one vote, regardless of population. p. 355

**Penn, William** *1644–1718* Proprietor of Pennsylvania under a charter from King Charles II of Britain. Penn was a Quaker who made Pennsylvania a refuge for settlers who wanted religious freedom. p. 213

**Perry, Oliver Hazard** *1785–1819* American naval commander who won an important battle in the War of 1812. p. 390

**Philip IV** *1605–1665* King of Spain from 1621 to 1665. p. 143

**Pickett, George** *1825–1875* Confederate general who led the charge against Gettysburg; forced to retreat. p. 466

**Pike, Zebulon** *1779–1813* American who led an expedition down the Arkansas River to explore the southwestern part of the Louisiana Purchase. pp. 19, 388

**Pinckney, Eliza Lucas** *1722?–1793* South Carolina settler who experimented with indigo plants. She gave away seeds, and indigo then became an important cash crop in the colonies. p. 236

**Pitt, William** *1708–1778* British leader of Parliament who helped Britain win battles against the French. p. 273

**Pizarro, Francisco** (pee•ZAR•oh) *1475?–1541* Spanish conquistador who conquered the Inca Empire. p. 133

**Plunkitt, George** *1800–1900s* Political boss in New York City. p. 534

**Pocahontas** (poh•kuh•HAHN•tuhs) *1595–1617* Indian chief Powhatan's daughter. p. 162

**Polk, James K.** *1795–1849* 11th U.S. President. He gained land for the United States by setting a northern boundary in 1846 and winning a war with Mexico in 1848. pp. 405, 407

**Polo, Maffeo** Trader from Venice; uncle of Marco Polo. p. 109

**Polo, Marco** *1254–1324* Explorer from Venice who spent many years in Asia in the late 1200s. He wrote a book about his travels that gave Europeans information about Asia. pp. 109, 112

**Polo, Nicolò** Trader from Venice; father of Marco Polo. p. 109

**Ponce de León, Juan** (POHN•say day lay•OHN) *1460–1521* Spanish explorer who landed on the North American mainland in 1513, near what is now St. Augustine, Florida. p. 127

**Pontiac** *c.1720–1769* Ottawa Indian chief who led a rebellion against the British to stop the loss of Indian hunting lands. p. 275

**Powell, Colin L.** *1937–* Chairman of the Joint Chiefs of Staff during the Gulf War; became U.S. secretary of state in 2001. p. 599

**Powhatan** (pow•uh•TAN) *1550?–1618* Chief of a federation of Indian tribes that lived in the Virginia territory. Pocahontas was his daughter. p. 162

**Prescott, Samuel** *1751–1777?* American who, along with Paul Revere, warned the Patriots that the British were marching toward Concord. p. 291

**Ptolemy, Claudius** (TAH•luh•mee) *100s* Astronomer in ancient Egypt. p. 123

**Pulaski, Casimir** (puh•LAS•kee) *1747–1779* Polish noble who came to the British colonies to help the Patriots in the Revolutionary War. p. 317

**Putnam, Israel** *1718–1790* American Revolutionary commander who fought at the Battle of Bunker Hill. p. 295

## R

**Raleigh, Sir Walter** (RAH•lee) *1554–1618* English explorer who used his own money to set up England's first colony in North America, on Roanoke Island near North Carolina. p. 158

**Randolph, Edmund** *1753–1813* Virginia delegate to the Constitutional Convention who wrote the Virginia Plan, which stated that the number of representatives a state would have in Congress should be based on the population of the state. pp. 355, 366, 375

**Read, George** *1733–1798* Delaware delegate to the Constitutional Convention who thought the states should be done away with in favor of a strong national government. p. 354

**Reagan, Ronald** *1911–* 40th U.S. President. His meetings with Soviet leader Mikhail Gorbachev led to a thaw in the Cold War, including advances in arms control. pp. 579, 597–598

**Reed, Esther** *1700s* American who, in 1780, started the Philadelphia Association to help the Continental Army. p. 311

**Revels, Hiram R.** *1822–1901* First African American elected to U.S. Senate. p. 479

**Revere, Paul** *1735–1818* American who warned the Patriots that the British were marching toward Concord, where Patriot weapons were stored. pp. 285, 291

**Rockefeller, John D.** *1839–1937* American oil entrepreneur who joined many refineries into one business, called the Standard Oil Company. pp. 497-498

**Roebling, John** *1806–1869* Engineer and industrialist who designed suspension bridges. p. 496

**Rolfe, John** *1585–1622* English colonist of the Jamestown colony whose discovery of a method of drying tobacco led to great profits. p. 163

**Roosevelt, Franklin Delano** *1882–1945* 32nd U.S. President. He began New Deal programs to help the nation out of the depression, and he was the nation's leader during World War II. pp. 548-549, 553, 556, 558, 568

**Roosevelt, Theodore** *1858–1919* 26th U.S. President. He showed the world America's strength, made it possible to build the Panama Canal, and worked for progressive reforms and conservation. pp. 527–528, 532–533

**Root, George Frederick** *1820–1895* American composer and teacher. p. 435

**Ross, Edmund G.** *1826–1907* Senator from Kansas who voted to acquit President Johnson. p. 479

**Ross, John** *1790–1866* Chief of the Cherokee nation. He fought in United States courts to prevent the loss of the Cherokees' lands in Georgia. Though he won the legal battle, he still had to lead his people along the Trail of Tears to what is now Oklahoma. p. 398

**Russwurm, John** *1799–1851* Helped Samuel Cornish found an abolitionist newspaper called *Freedom's Journal* in 1827. p. 448

## S

**Sacagawea** (sa•kuh•juh•WEE•uh) *1786?–1812?* Shoshone woman who acted as an interpreter for the Lewis and Clark expedition. p. 386

**Sagan, Carl** *1934–1996* American astronomer who worked to find life on other planets and helped NASA plan missions to explore the solar system. p. 583

**Salem, Peter** *1750?–1816* African who fought with the Minutemen at Concord and at the Battle of Bunker Hill. p. 310

**Salomon, Haym** *1740–1785* Polish banker who spied for the Patriots and helped fund the Revolution. p. 317

**Samoset** *1590?–1653?* Native American chief who spoke English and who helped the settlers at Plymouth. p. 169

**San Martín, José de** (sahn mar•TEEN) *1778–1850* Leader of an independence movement in Argentina. p. 666

**Santa Anna, Antonio López de** *1794–1876* Dictator of Mexico; defeated Texans at the Alamo. p. 402

**Scott, Dred** *1795?–1858* Enslaved African who took his case for freedom to the Supreme Court and lost. p. 440

**Scott, Winfield** *1786–1866* American general in the war with Mexico. p. 407

**Serra, Junípero** *1713–1784* Spanish missionary who helped build a string of missions in California. pp. 148, 174

**Seward, William H.** *1801–1872* Secretary of state in the cabinet of Abraham Lincoln. p. 443

**Shays, Daniel** *1747?–1825* Leader of Shays's Rebellion, which showed the weakness of the government under the Articles of Confederation. pp. 347, 352

**Sherman, Roger** *1721–1793* One of the writers of the Declaration of Independence. Connecticut delegate to the Constitutional Convention who worked out the compromise in which Congress would have two houses—one based on state population and one with two members from each state. pp. 303, 356

**Sherman, William Tecumseh** *1820–1891* Union general who, after defeating Confederate forces in Atlanta, led the March to the Sea, on which his troops caused great destruction. p. 468

**Sitting Bull** *1831–1890* Sioux leader who fought against General George Custer. p. 491

**Slater, Samuel** *1768–1835* Textile pioneer who helped bring the Industrial Revolution to the United States by providing plans for a new spinning machine. p. 416

**Slocomb, Mary** *1700s* North Carolina colonist who fought in the Revolutionary War. p. 319

**Smalls, Robert** *1839–1915* African American who delivered a Confederate steamer to the Union forces. p. 463

**Smith, John** *1580–1631* English explorer who, as leader of the Jamestown settlement, saved its people from starvation. pp. 161, 231

**Smith, Joseph** *1805–1844* Mormon leader who settled his people in Illinois and was killed there. p. 406

**Soule, John B. L.** *1815–1891* Editor of the Terre Haute (Indiana) *Express* in the mid-1800s. p. 383

**Spalding, Eliza** *1807–1851* American missionary and pioneer in the Oregon Country. p. 404

**Spalding, Henry** *1801–1874* American missionary and pioneer in the Oregon Country. p. 404

**Squanto** *See* Tisquantum.

**Stalin, Joseph** *1879–1953* Dictator of the Soviet Union from 1924 until his death. p. 555

**Standish, Miles** *1584?–1656* Captain who sailed with Pilgrims to America aboard the *Mayflower*. p. 167

**Stanton, Elizabeth Cady** *1815–1902* American reformer who organized the first convention for women's rights. p. 447

**Starr, Ellen Gates** *1860–1940* Reformer who, with Jane Addams, founded Hull House in Chicago. p. 534

**Steuben, Friedrich, Baron von** (vahn SHTOY•buhn) *1730–1794* German soldier who helped train Patriot troops in the Revolutionary War. p. 317

**Stowe, Harriet Beecher** *1811–1896* American abolitionist who in 1852 wrote the book *Uncle Tom's Cabin*. p. 448

**Stuyvesant, Peter** (STY•vuh•suhnt) *1610?–1672* Last governor of the Dutch colony of New Netherland. p. 212

**Sutter, John** *1803–1880* American pioneer who owned the sawmill where gold was discovered, leading to the California gold rush. p. 408

**T**

**Taney, Roger B.** (TAH•nee) *1777–1864* Supreme Court chief justice who wrote the ruling against Dred Scott. p. 441

**Tapahonso, Luci** *1953–* Navajo poet and author. p. 72

**Tecumseh** (tuh•KUHM•suh) *1768–1813* Shawnee leader of Indians in the Northwest Territory. He wanted to stop Americans from settling on Indian lands. p. 390

**Thayendanegea** (thay•en•da•NEG•ah) *1742–1807* Known as Joseph Brant; Mohawk leader who befriended a British general, became a Christian, and worked as a missionary. p. 312

**Tisquantum** *1585?–1622* Native American who spoke English and who helped the Plymouth Colony. p. 169

**Tompkins, Sally** *1833–1916* Civil War nurse who eventually ran her own private hospital in Richmond, Virginia. She was a captain in the Confederate army, the only woman to achieve such an honor. p. 463

**Tonti, Henri de** (TOHN•tee, ahn•REE duh) *1650–1704* French explorer with La Salle. p. 154

**Travis, William B.** *1809–1836* Commander of the Texas force at the Alamo, where he was killed. p. 403

**Truman, Harry S.** *1884–1972* 33rd U.S. President. He ordered the atom bomb to be dropped on Japan to end World War II; he later sent American soldiers to support South Korea in 1950. pp. 568, 575, 582

**Truth, Sojourner** *1797?–1883* Abolitionist and former slave who became a leading preacher against slavery. p. 449

**Tubman, Harriet** *1820–1913* Abolitionist and former slave who became a conductor on the Underground Railroad. She led about 300 slaves to freedom. p. 447

**Turner, Nat** *1800–1831* Enslaved African who led a rebellion against slavery. p. 445

**Tuscalusa** (tuhs•kuh•LOO•suh) *1500s* Leader of the Mobile people when they battled with Spanish troops led by Hernando de Soto. p. 132

**V**

**Verrazano, Giovanni da** (ver•uh•ZAH•noh) *1485?–1528?* Italian navigator who discovered New York Bay while searching for a water route linking the Atlantic and Pacific Oceans. p. 136

**Vespucci, Amerigo** (veh•SPOO•chee, uh•MAIR•ih•goh) *1454–1512* Italian explorer who made several voyages from Europe to what many people thought was Asia. He determined that he had landed on another continent, which was later called America in his honor. p. 123

**W**

**Wald, Lillian** *1867–1940* Reformer who started the Henry Street Settlement in New York City. p. 535

**Waldseemüller, Martin** (VAHLT•zay•mool•er) *1470–1518?* German cartographer who published a map in 1507 that first showed a continent named America. p. 123

**Warren, Earl** *1891–1974* Chief justice of the Supreme Court who wrote the 1954 decision against school segregation. p. 586

**Warren, Mercy Otis** *1728–1814* Massachusetts colonist who wrote poems and plays supporting the Patriot cause. p. 311

**Washington, Booker T.** *1856–1915* African American who founded Tuskegee Institute in Alabama. p. 535

**Washington, George** *1732–1799* 1st U.S. President, leader of the Continental army during the Revolutionary War, and president of the Constitutional Convention. pp. 269, 293, 314, 327, 352, 374

**Westinghouse, George** *1846–1914* American inventor who designed an air brake for stopping trains. p. 495

**Wheatley, Phillis** *1753?–1784* American poet who wrote poems that praised the Revolution. p. 296

**White, John** *?–1593?* English painter and cartographer who led the second group that settled on Roanoke Island. p. 158

**Whitman, Marcus** *1802–1847* American missionary and pioneer in the Oregon Country. p. 404

**Whitman, Narcissa** *1808–1847* American missionary and pioneer in the Oregon Country. p. 404

BIOGRAPHICAL DICTIONARY

**Whitney, Eli** *1765–1825* American inventor who was most famous for his invention of the cotton gin and his idea of interchangeable parts, which made mass production possible. p. 418

**Williams, Roger** *1603?–1683* Founder of Providence in what is now Rhode Island. He had been forced to leave Massachusetts because of his views. p. 194

**Wilson, Samuel** *1766–1854* American meat packer who inspired the "Uncle Sam" national symbol. p. 640

**Wilson, Woodrow** *1856–1924* 28th U.S. President. He brought the country into World War I after trying to stay neutral. He favored the League of Nations, but the Senate rejected U.S. membership in the league. pp. 538, 541

**Winthrop, John** *1588–1649* Puritan leader who served several times as governor of the Massachusetts Bay Colony. Helped form confederation among people of New England and served as its first president. p. 189

**Woods, Granville T.** *1856–1910* African American who improved the air brake and developed a telegraph system for trains. p. 495

**Wright, Frank Lloyd** *1867–1959* American architect known for producing unusual buildings. p. 543

**Wright, Orville** *1871–1948* Pioneer in American aviation who—with his brother, Wilbur—made and flew the first successful airplane, at Kitty Hawk, North Carolina. p. 545

**Wright, Wilbur** *1867–1912* Pioneer in American aviation who—with his brother, Orville—made and flew the first successful airplane, at Kitty Hawk, North Carolina. p. 545

**York** *1800s* Enslaved African whose hunting and fishing skills contributed to the Lewis and Clark expedition. p. 386

**Young, Brigham** *1801–1877* Mormon leader who came after Joseph Smith. He moved his people west to the Great Salt Lake valley. p. 406

**Yzquierdo, Pedro** *1400s* Member of Columbus's first expedition to America. p. 105

# Gazetteer

The Gazetteer is a geographical dictionary that will help you locate places discussed in this book. The page number tells where each place appears on a map.

GAZETTEER

## A

**Abilene** A city in central Kansas on the Smoky Hill River; a major railroad town. (39°N, 97°W) p. 488

**Adena** (uh•DEE•nuh) An ancient settlement of the Mound Builders; located in southern Ohio. (40°N, 81°W) p. 65

**Adirondack Mountains** (a•duh•RAHN•dak) A mountain range in northeastern New York. p. 89

**Africa** Second-largest continent on Earth. p. 27

**Alamo** A mission in San Antonio, Texas; located in the southeastern part of the state; used as a fort during the Texas Revolution. (29°N, 98°W) p. 404

**Alaska Range** A mountain range in central Alaska. p. 20

**Albany** The capital of New York; located in the eastern part of the state, on the Hudson River. (43°N, 74°W) p. 212

**Alberta** One of Canada's ten provinces; located in western Canada. p. 670

**Aleutian Islands** (uh•LOO•shuhn) A chain of volcanic islands; located between the North Pacific Ocean and the Bering Sea, extending west from the Alaska Peninsula. pp. 20, 526

**Alexandria** Seaport on the northern coast of Egypt. (31°N, 29°E) p. 108

**Allegheny River** (a•luh•GAY•nee) A river in the northeastern United States; flows southwest to join the Monongahela River in Pennsylvania, forming the Ohio River. p. 341

**Altamaha River** (AWL•tuh•muh•haw) A river that begins in southeastern Georgia and flows into the Atlantic Ocean. p. 234

**Amazon River** The longest river in South America, flowing from the Andes Mountains across Brazil and into the Atlantic Ocean. p. 665

**American Samoa** (suh•MOH•uh) A United States territory in the Pacific Ocean. p. 526

**Andes Mountains** (AN•deez) The longest chain of mountains in the world; located along the entire western coast of South America. p. 665

**Annapolis** (uh•NA•puh•luhs) The capital of Maryland; located on Chesapeake Bay; home of the United States Naval Academy. (39°N, 76°W) p. 234

**Antarctica** One of Earth's seven continents. p. 27

**Antietam** (an•TEE•tuhm) A creek near Sharpsburg in north central Maryland; site of a Civil War battle in 1862. (39°N, 78°W) p. 470

**Antigua** An island in the eastern part of the Leeward Islands, in the eastern West Indies. p. 658

**Appalachian Mountains** (a•puh•LAY•chuhn) A mountain system of eastern North America; extends from southeastern Quebec, Canada, to central Alabama. pp. 20, 225

**Appomattox** (a•puh•MA•tuhks) A village in central Virginia; site of the battle that ended the Civil War in 1865; once known as Appomattox Courthouse. (37°N, 79°W) p. 470

**Arctic Ocean** One of Earth's four oceans; located north of the Arctic Circle. p. 27

**Arkansas River** A tributary of the Mississippi River, beginning in central Colorado and ending in southeastern Arkansas. pp. 29, 153

**Asia** Largest continent on Earth. p. 27

**Atlanta** Georgia's capital and largest city; located in the northwest central part of the state; site of a Civil War battle in 1864. (33°N, 84°W) pp. 470, 621

**Atlantic Ocean** Second-largest ocean; separates North and South America from Europe and Africa. p. 27

**Austin** Capital of Texas; located in south central Texas. (30°N, 97°W) p. 621

**Australia** A country; smallest continent on Earth. p. 27

## B

**Baghdad** Capital of Iraq; located on the Tigris River in central Iraq. (33°N, 44°E) p. 108

**Bahamas** An island group in the North Atlantic Ocean; located southeast of Florida and north of Cuba. p. 658

**Baja California** A peninsula in northwestern Mexico extending south-southeast between the Pacific Ocean and the Gulf of California. p. 653

**Baltimore** A major seaport in Maryland; located on the upper end of Chesapeake Bay. (39°N, 77°W) pp. 47, 234

**Barbados** An island in the Lesser Antilles, West Indies; located east of the central Windward Islands. p. 658

**Barbuda** A flat coral island in the eastern West Indies. p. 658

**Baxter Springs** A city in the southeastern corner of Kansas. (37°N, 94°W) p. 488

**Beaufort Sea** (BOH•fert) That part of the Arctic Ocean between northeastern Alaska and the Canadian Arctic Islands. p. 20

**Beijing** (bay•JING) The capital of China; located on a large plain in northeastern China; once known as Khanbalik. (40°N, 116°E) p. 108

**Belmopan** A town in Central America; capital of Belize. (17°N, 88°W) p. 658

**Benin** (buh•NEEN) A former kingdom in West Africa; located along the Gulf of Guinea; present-day southern Nigeria. p. 108

**Bennington** A town in the southwestern corner of Vermont; site of a major Revolutionary War battle in 1777. (43°N, 73°W) p. 323

**Bering Strait** A narrow strip of water; separates Asia from North America. p. 57

**Beringia** (buh•RIN•gee•uh) An ancient land bridge that once connected Asia and North America. p. 57

**Black Sea** A large inland sea between Europe and Asia. p. 113

**Bogotá** A city in South America located on the plateau of the Andes; capital of Colombia. (4°N, 74°W) p. 665

**Boise** (BOY•zee) Idaho's capital and largest city; located in the southwestern part of the state. (44°N, 116°W) p. 621

**Bonampak** An ancient settlement of the Mayan civilization; located in present-day southeastern Mexico. (16°N, 91°W) p. 65

**Boston** The capital and largest city of Massachusetts; a port city located on Massachusetts Bay. (42°N, 71°W) p. 291

**Boston Harbor** The western section of Massachusetts Bay; located in eastern Massachusetts; the city of Boston is located at its western end. p. 291

**Brandywine** A battlefield on Brandywine Creek in southeastern Pennsylvania; site of a major Revolutionary War battle in 1777. (40°N, 76°W) p. 323

**Brasília** A city in South America on the Tocantins River; capital of Brazil. (15°S, 48°W) p. 665

**Brazos River** (BRAH•zuhs) A river in central Texas; flows southeast into the Gulf of Mexico. p. 404

**British Columbia** One of Canada's ten provinces; located on the west coast of Canada and bordered by the Yukon Territory, the Northwest Territories, Alberta, the United States, and the Pacific Ocean. p. 670

**Brookline** A town in eastern Massachusetts; west-southwest of Boston. (42°N, 71°W) p. 291

**Brooks Range** A mountain range crossing northern Alaska; forms the northwestern end of the Rocky Mountains. p. 20

**Buenos Aires** A city in South America; the capital of Argentina. (34°S, 58°W) p. 665

**Bull Run** A stream in northeastern Virginia; flows toward the Potomac River; site of Civil War battles in 1861 and in 1862. p. 470

## C

**Cahokia** (kuh•HOH•kee•uh) A village in southwestern Illinois; site of an ancient settlement of the Mound Builders. (39°N, 90°W) pp. 65, 108

**Calgary** A city in southern Alberta, Canada; located on the Bow River. (51°N, 114°W) p. 670

**Calicut** (KA•lih•kuht) A city in southwestern India; located on the Malabar Coast. (11°N, 76°E) p. 108

**Cambridge** A city in northeastern Massachusetts; located near Boston. (42°N, 71°W) p. 291

**Camden** A city in north central South Carolina, near the Wateree River; site of a major Revolutionary War battle in 1780. (34°N, 81°W) p. 323

**Canal Zone** A strip of territory in Panama. p. 528

**Canary Islands** An island group in the Atlantic Ocean off the northwest coast of Africa. (28°N, 16°W) p. 122

**Canton** A port city in southeastern China; located on the Canton River; known in China as Guangzhou. (23°N, 113°E) p. 108

**Canyon de Chelly** An ancient settlement of the Anasazi; located in present-day northeastern Arizona. p. 65

**Cape Cod** A peninsula of southeastern Massachusetts, extending into the Atlantic Ocean and enclosing Cape Cod Bay. (42°N, 70°W) p. 197

**Cape Fear** A cape at the southern end of Smith Island; located off the coast of North Carolina, at the mouth of the Cape Fear River. (34°N, 78°W) p. 234

**Cape Fear River** A river in central and southeastern North Carolina; formed by the Deep and Haw Rivers; flows southeast into the Atlantic Ocean. p. 234

**Cape Hatteras** (HA•tuh•ruhs) A cape on southeastern Hatteras Island; located off the coast of North Carolina. (35°N, 75°W) p. 234

**Cape of Good Hope** A cape located on the southernmost tip of Africa. (34°S, 18°E) p. 119

**Cape Verde Islands** (verd) A group of volcanic islands off the western coast of Africa. (16°N, 24°W) p. 119

**Caracas** A city in northern Venezuela; capital of Venezuela. (10°N, 67°W) p. 665

**Caribbean Sea** A part of the Atlantic Ocean between the West Indies and Central and South America. p. 658

**Cascade Range** A mountain range in the western United States; a continuation of the Sierra Nevada; extends north from California to Washington. p. 20

**Cayenne** A city on the northwestern coast of Cayenne Island, in northern South America; capital of French Guiana. (5°N, 52°W) p. 665

**Chaco Canyon** (CHAH•koh) An ancient settlement of the Anasazi; located in present-day northwestern New Mexico. (37°N, 108°W) p. 65

**Chancellorsville** (CHAN•suh•lerz•vil) A location in northeastern Virginia, just west of Fredericksburg; site of a Civil War battle in 1863. (38°N, 78°W) p. 470

**Charles River** A river in eastern Massachusetts; separates Boston from Cambridge; flows into Boston Bay. p. 291

**Charleston** A city in southeastern South Carolina; a major port on the Atlantic Ocean; once known as Charles Towne. (33°N, 80°W) pp. 234, 249, 323, 470

**Charlestown** A city in Massachusetts; located on Boston Harbor between the mouths of the Charles and Mystic Rivers. p. 291

**Charlotte** The largest city in North Carolina; located in the south central part of the state. (35°N, 81°W) p. 621

**Charlottetown** The capital of Prince Edward Island, Canada; located in the central part of the island. (46°N, 63°W) p. 670

**Chattanooga** (cha•tuh•NOO•guh) A city in southeastern Tennessee; located on the Tennessee River; site of a Civil War battle in 1863. (35°N, 85°W) p. 470

**Cherokee Nation** (CHAIR•uh•kee) A Native American nation located in present-day northern Georgia, eastern Alabama, southern Tennessee, and western North Carolina. p. 398

**Chesapeake Bay** An inlet of the Atlantic Ocean; surrounded by Virginia and Maryland. pp. 29, 233

**Cheyenne** (shy•AN) The capital of Wyoming; located in the southeastern part of the state. (41°N, 105°W) p. 488

**Chicago** A city in Illinois; located on Lake Michigan; the third-largest city in the United States. (42°N, 88°W) p. 488

**Chickamauga** (chik•uh•MAW•guh) A city in northwestern Georgia; site of a Civil War battle in 1863. (35°N, 85°W) p. 470

**Chihuahua** A city and state in northern Mexico. (28°N, 85°W) p. 653

**Cincinnati** (sin•suh•NA•tee) A large city in southwestern Ohio; located on the Ohio River. (39°N, 84°W) p. 47

**Coast Mountains** A mountain range in western British Columbia and southern Alaska; a continuation of the Cascade Range. p. 20

**Coast Ranges** Mountains along the Pacific coast of North America, extending from Alaska to Baja California. p. 20

**Coastal Plain** Low, mostly flat land that stretches inland from the Atlantic Ocean and the Gulf of Mexico. p. 20

**Cold Harbor** A location in east central Virginia, north of the Chickahominy River; site of Civil War battles in 1862 and in 1864. (38°N, 77°W) p. 470

**Colorado River** A river in the southwestern United States; its basin extends from the Rocky Mountains to the Sierra Nevada; flows into the Gulf of California. p. 29

**Columbia River** A river that begins in the Rocky Mountains in southwestern Canada, forms the Washington–Oregon border, and empties into the Pacific Ocean below Portland; supplies much of that area's hydroelectricity. pp. 29, 385

**Compostela** (kahm•poh•STEH•lah) A city in west central Mexico. (21°N, 105°W) p. 129

**Concord** A town in northeastern Massachusetts, near Boston; site of a major Revolutionary War battle in 1775. (42°N, 71°W) pp. 291, 323

**Concord River** A river in northeastern Massachusetts; formed by the junction of the Sudbury and Assabet Rivers; flows north into the Merrimack River at Lowell. p. 291

**Connecticut River** The longest river in New England; begins in New Hampshire, and empties into Long Island Sound, New York. p. 197

**Constantinople** (kahn•stant•uhn•OH•puhl) A port city in northwestern Turkey. (41°N, 29°E) p. 108

**Copán** (koh•PAHN) An ancient settlement of the Mayan civilization; located in present-day Honduras, in northern Central America. (15°N, 89°W) p. 65

**Cowpens** A town in northwestern South Carolina; located near the site of a major Revolutionary War battle in 1781. (35°N, 82°W) p. 323

**Crab Orchard** An ancient settlement of the Mound Builders; located in present-day southern Illinois. (38°N, 89°W) p. 65

**Cuba** An island country in the Caribbean; the largest island of the West Indies. (22°N, 79°W) pp. 129, 526, 658

**Cuzco** (KOOS•koh) The ancient capital of the Inca Empire; a city located in present-day Peru, in western South America. (14°S, 72°W) pp. 108, 133

**D**

**Dallas** A city in northeastern Texas; located on the Trinity River. (33°N, 97°W) p. 621

**Damascus** (duh•MAS•kuhs) The capital of Syria; located in southwest Syria. p. 108

**Deerfield** A town in northwestern Massachusetts. (43°N, 73°W) p. 197

**Delaware Bay** An inlet of the Atlantic Ocean; located between southern New Jersey and Delaware. p. 212

**Delaware River** A river in the northeastern United States; begins in southern New York and flows into the Atlantic Ocean at Delaware Bay. p. 89

**Denver** Colorado's capital and largest city. (40°N, 105°W) pp. 488, 621

**Des Moines** (dih•MOYN) Iowa's capital and largest city. (42°N, 94°W) p. A3

**Dickson** An ancient settlement of the Mound Builders; located in present-day central Illinois. p. 65

**Dodge City** A city in southern Kansas; located on the Arkansas River; once a major railroad center on the Santa Fe Trail. (38°N, 100°W) p. 488

**Dominica** (dah•muh•NEE•kuh) An island and a republic in the West Indies; located in the center of the Lesser Antilles between Guadeloupe and Martinique. p. 658

**Dominican Republic** A country in the West Indies, occupying the eastern part of Hispaniola. p. 658

**Dover** (DE) The capital of Delaware; located in the central part of the state. (39°N, 76°W) p. 212

**Dover** (NH) A city in southeastern New Hampshire. (43°N, 71°W) p. 197

**Durango** A city and state in northwestern central Mexico. (24°N, 104°W) p. 653

**E**

**Edenton** (EE•duhn•tuhn) A town in northeastern North Carolina; located on Albemarle Sound, near the mouth of the Chowan River. (36°N, 77°W) p. 234

**Edmonton** The capital of Alberta, Canada; located in the south central part of the province on both banks of the North Saskatchewan River. (53°N, 113°W) p. 670

**El Paso** A city at the western tip of Texas; located on the Rio Grande. (32°N, 106°W) p. 621

**Ellsworth** A city in central Kansas. p. 488

**Emerald Mound** An ancient settlement of the Mound Builders; located in present-day southwestern Mississippi. (32°N, 91°W) p. 65

**Equator** Great circle of Earth that is equal distance from the North and South Poles and divides the surface into Northern and Southern Hemispheres. p. 50

**Erie Canal** The longest canal in the world; located in New York; connects Buffalo (on Lake Erie) with Troy (on the Hudson River). p. 415

**Europe** One of Earth's seven continents. p. 27

**F**

**Falkland Islands** A British colony in the Atlantic Ocean; located east of the Strait of Magellan. p. 665

**Falmouth** (FAL•muhth) A town in southwestern Maine. (44°N, 70°W) p. 197

**Fort Atkinson** A fort in southern Kansas; located on the Sante Fe Trail. (43°N, 89°W) p. 406

**Fort Boise** (BOY•zee) A fort in eastern Oregon; located on the Snake River and on the Oregon Trail. p. 406

**Fort Bridger** A present-day village in southwestern Wyoming; once an important station on the Oregon Trail. (41°N, 110°W) p. 406

**GAZETTEER**

**Fort Christina**  A Swedish fort; located in present-day Wilmington, Delaware. p. 211

**Fort Crèvecoeur** (KREEV•ker)  A fort in central Illinois; located on the Illinois River; built by La Salle in 1680. (41°N, 90°W) p. 153

**Fort Crown Point**  A French fort; located in northeastern New York, on the shore of Lake Champlain. p. 274

**Fort Cumberland**  A British fort located in northeastern West Virginia, on its border with Maryland. p. 274

**Fort Dearborn**  A fort in northeastern Illinois; built in 1803; eventually became part of Chicago; site of a major battle in the War of 1812. (42°N, 88°W) p. 391

**Fort Donelson**  A fort located in northwestern Tennessee; site of a major Civil War battle in 1862. p. 470

**Fort Duquesne** (doo•KAYN)  A French fort in present-day Pittsburgh, Pennsylvania; captured by the British and new fort built and named Fort Pitt. (40°N, 80°W) p. 274

**Fort Edward**  A British fort in New York, on the Hudson River; a present-day village. (43°N, 74°W) p. 274

**Fort Frontenac** (FRAHN•tuh•nak)  A French fort once located on the site of present-day Kingston, Ontario, in southeastern Canada; destroyed by the British in 1758. (44°N, 76°W) pp. 153, 274

**Fort Gibson**  A fort in eastern Oklahoma; end of the Trail of Tears. (36°N, 95°W) p. 398

**Fort Hall**  A fort in southeastern Idaho; located on the Snake River, at a junction on the Oregon Trail. p. 406

**Fort Laramie**  A fort in southeastern Wyoming; located on the Oregon Trail. (42°N, 105°W) p. 406

**Fort Lauderdale**  A city in southeast Florida along the Atlantic coast. p. 621

**Fort Ligonier** (lig•uh•NIR)  A British fort; located in southern Pennsylvania near the Ohio River. p. 274

**Fort Louisbourg** (LOO•is•berg)  A French fort; located in eastern Canada on the coast of the Atlantic Ocean. (46°N, 60°W) p. 274

**Fort Mackinac**  A fort located on the tip of present-day northern Michigan; site of a major battle in the War of 1812. (46°N, 85°W) p. 391

**Fort Mandan**  A fort in present-day central North Dakota, on the Missouri River; site of a winter camp for the Lewis and Clark expedition. (48°N, 104°W) p. 385

**Fort McHenry**  A fort in central Maryland; located on the harbor in Baltimore; site of a major battle in the War of 1812. (39°N, 77°W) p. 391

**Fort Miamis**  A French fort located on the southern shore of Lake Michigan, in present-day southwestern Michigan. p. 153

**Fort Necessity**  A British fort located in southwestern Pennsylvania; located in present-day Great Meadows. (38°N, 80°W) p. 274

**Fort Niagara**  A fort located in western New York, at the mouth of the Niagara River. (43°N, 79°W) p. 274

**Fort Oswego**  A British fort; located in western New York, on the coast of Lake Ontario. (43°N, 77°W) p. 274

**Fort Sumter**  A fort on a human-made island, off the coast of South Carolina, in Charleston Harbor; site of the first Civil War battle in 1861. (33°N, 80°W) p. 470

**Fort Ticonderoga** (ty•kahn•der•OH•gah)  A historic fort on Lake Champlain, in northeastern New York. (44°N, 73°W) p. 274

**Fort Vancouver**  A fort in southwestern Washington, on the Columbia River; the western end of the Oregon Trail; present-day Vancouver. (45°N, 123°W) p. 406

**Fort Wagner**  A fort near Charleston, South Carolina; site of a Civil War battle in 1863. p. 470

**Fort Walla Walla**  A fort in southeastern Washington; located on the Oregon Trail. (46°N, 118°W) p. 406

**Fort William Henry**  A British fort located in eastern New York. (43°N, 74°W) p. 274

**Fort Worth**  A city in northern Texas; located on the Trinity River. (33°N, 97°W) p. 621

**Fox River**  Located in southeast central Wisconsin; flows southwest toward the Wisconsin River, and then flows northeast and empties into Green Bay. p. 153

**Franklin**  A city in central Tennessee; site of a major Civil War battle in 1864. (36°N, 87°W) p. 470

**Fredericksburg**  A city in northeastern Virginia; located on the Rappahannock River; site of a Civil War battle in 1862. (38°N, 77°W) p. 470

**Fredericton**  The capital of New Brunswick, Canada; located in the southwestern part of the province. (46°N, 66°W) p. 670

**Frenchtown**  A town in present-day eastern Michigan; site of a major battle in the War of 1812. (42°N, 83°W) p. 391

## G

**Galápagos Islands**  Nineteen islands off the coast of Ecuador; home to many unique bird and animal species. p. 667

**Gatun Lake** (gah•TOON)  A lake in Panama; part of the Panama Canal system. p. 528

**Georgetown**  A city in South America; located at the mouth of the Demerara River; capital of Guyana. (6°N, 58°W) p. 665

**Germantown**  A residential section of present-day Philadelphia, on Wissahickon Creek, in southeastern Pennsylvania; site of a major Revolutionary War battle in 1777. (40°N, 75°W) p. 323

**Gettysburg**  A town in southern Pennsylvania; site of a Civil War battle in 1863. (40°N, 77°W) pp. 470, 510

**Golconda** (gahl•KAHN•duh)  A city in the southeastern corner of Illinois; a point on the Trail of Tears. (37°N, 88°W) p. 398

**Gonzales** (gohn•ZAH•lays)  A city in south central Texas; site of the first battle of the Texas Revolution. (30°N, 97°W) p. 404

**Great Basin**  One of the driest parts of the United States; located in Nevada, Utah, California, Idaho, Wyoming, and Oregon; includes the Great Salt Lake Desert, the Mojave Desert, and Death Valley. pp. 20, 406

**Great Lakes**  A chain of five lakes; located in central North America; the largest group of freshwater lakes in the world. p. 29

**Great Plains**  A continental slope in western North America; borders the eastern base of the Rocky Mountains from Canada to New Mexico and Texas. pp. 20, 406

**Great Salt Lake**  The largest lake in the Great Basin; located in northwestern Utah. pp. 29, 406

**Great Wagon Road** A former route used in the mid-1700s by colonists moving to settle in the backcountry. p. 225

**Greenland** The largest island on Earth; located in the northern Atlantic Ocean, east of Canada. p. 20

**Grenada** (grah•NAY•duh) An island in the West Indies; the southernmost of the Windward Islands. p. 658

**Groton** (GRAH•tuhn) A town in southeastern Connecticut; located on Long Island Sound. (41°N, 72°W) p. 197

**Guadalajara** A city in western central Mexico; capital of Jalisco state. (20°N, 103°W) p. 653

**Guam** (GWAHM) United States territory in the Pacific Ocean; largest of the Mariana Islands. p. 526

**Guatemala City** Capital of Guatemala; largest city in Central America. (14°N, 90°W) p. 658

**Guiana Highlands** Highland area in northern South America. p. 665

**Guilford Courthouse** (GIL•ferd) A location in north central North Carolina, near Greensboro; site of a major Revolutionary War battle in 1781. (36°N, 80°W) p. 323

**Gulf of Alaska** A northern inlet of the Pacific Ocean; located between the Alaska Peninsula and the southwestern coast of Canada. p. 29

**Gulf of California** An inlet of the Pacific Ocean; located between Baja California and the northwestern coast of Mexico. p. 20

**Gulf of Mexico** An inlet of the Atlantic Ocean; located on the southeastern coast of North America; surrounded by the United States, Cuba, and Mexico. pp. 29, 153

**Gulf of Panama** A large inlet of the Pacific Ocean; located on the southern coast of Panama. p. 528

**Haiti** A country in the West Indies; occupies the western part of the island of Hispaniola. p. 658

**Halifax** The capital of the province of Nova Scotia, Canada; a major port on the Atlantic Ocean; remains free of ice all year. (44°N, 63°W) p. 670

**Hampton Roads** A channel in southeastern Virginia that flows into Chesapeake Bay; site of a Civil War naval battle in 1862 between two ironclad ships, the *Monitor* and the *Merrimack*. p. 470

**Hartford** The capital of Connecticut. (42°N, 73°W) p. 197

**Havana** The capital of Cuba; located on the northwestern coast of the country. (23°N, 82°W) p. 129

**Hawaiian Islands** A state; a chain of volcanic and coral islands; located in the north central Pacific Ocean. p. 526

**Hawikuh** (hah•wee•KOO) A former village in southwestern North America; located on the route of the Spanish explorer Coronado in present-day northwestern New Mexico. p. 129

**Hiroshima** Japanese city upon which first atom bomb was dropped in World War II. p. 568

**Hispaniola** (ees•pah•NYOH•lah) An island in the West Indies made up of Haiti and the Dominican Republic; located in the Caribbean Sea between Cuba and Puerto Rico. pp. 129, 658

**Honolulu** (hahn•nuh•LOO•loo) Hawaii's capital and largest city; located on Oahu. (21°N, 158°W) p. A2

**Hopewell** An ancient settlement of the Mound Builders; located in present-day southern Ohio. (39°N, 83°W) p. 65

**Horseshoe Bend** A location in eastern Alabama; site of a battle in the War of 1812; a present-day national military park. p. 391

**Houston** A city in southeastern Texas; third-largest port in the United States; leading industrial center in Texas. (30°N, 95°W) p. 621

**Hudson Bay** An inland sea in east central Canada surrounded by the Northwest Territories, Manitoba, Ontario, and Quebec. p. 138

**Hudson River** A river in the northeastern United States beginning in upper New York and flowing into the Atlantic Ocean; named for the explorer Henry Hudson. p. 89

**Iceland** An island country in the northern Atlantic Ocean; between Greenland and Norway. p. 569

**Illinois River** A river in western and central Illinois; flows southwest into the Mississippi River. pp. 29, 153

**Independence** A city in western Missouri; the starting point of the Oregon and Santa Fe Trails. (39°N, 94°W) p. 406

**Indian Ocean** One of Earth's four oceans; located east of Africa, south of Asia, west of Australia, and north of Antarctica. p. 27

**Iqaluit** The capital of Nunavut Territory, Canada; located on the eastern coast. p. 670

**Isthmus of Panama** (IS•muhs) A narrow strip of land that connects North America and South America. p. 125

**Iwo Jima** Japanese island; site of major battles during World War II. p. 568

**Jacksonville** A city in northeastern Florida; located near the mouth of the St. Johns River. (30°N, 82°W) p. 621

**Jamaica** (juh•MAY•kuh) An island country in the West Indies; south of Cuba. pp. 129, 658

**Jamestown** The first permanent English settlement in the Americas; located in eastern Virginia, on the shore of the James River. (37°N, 76°W) p. 234

**Jerusalem** The capital of Israel; located in the central part of the country. (32°N, 35°E) p. 108

**Kahoolawe** (kah•hoh•uh•LAY•vay) One of the eight main islands of Hawaii; located west of Maui. p. A14

**Kaskaskia** (ka•SKAS•kee•uh) A village in southwestern Illinois; site of a major Revolutionary War battle in 1778. (38°N, 90°W) p. 323

**Kauai** (kah•WAH•ee)  The fourth-largest of the eight main islands of Hawaii. p. A14

**Kennebec River** (KEN•uh•bek)  A river in west central and southern Maine; flows south from Moosehead Lake to the Atlantic Ocean. p. 197

**Kennesaw Mountain** (KEN•uh•saw)  An isolated peak in northwestern Georgia, near Atlanta; site of a Civil War battle in 1864. p. 470

**Kings Mountain**  A ridge in northern South Carolina and southern North Carolina; site of a Revolutionary War battle in 1780. p. 323

**Kingston**  A commercial seaport in the West Indies; capital of Jamaica. (18°N, 76°W) p. 658

## L

**La Paz**  A city in South America; capital of Bolivia. (16°S, 68°W) p. 665

**La Venta**  An ancient settlement of the Olmecs; located in present-day southern Mexico, on an island near the Tonalá River. (18°N, 94°W) p. 65

**Labrador**  A peninsula in northeastern North America; once known as Markland. p. 20

**Labrador Sea**  Located south of Greenland and northeast of North America. p. 20

**Lake Champlain** (sham•PLAYN)  A lake between New York and Vermont. p. 89

**Lake Erie**  The fourth-largest of the Great Lakes; borders Canada and the United States. p. 29

**Lake Huron**  The second-largest of the Great Lakes; borders Canada and the United States. p. 29

**Lake Michigan**  The third-largest of the Great Lakes; borders Michigan, Illinois, Indiana, and Wisconsin. pp. 29, 153

**Lake Okeechobee** (oh•kuh•CHOH•bee)  A large lake in south Florida. p. 29

**Lake Ontario**  The smallest of the Great Lakes; borders Canada and the United States. pp. 29, 89

**Lake Superior**  The largest of the Great Lakes; borders Canada and the United States. p. 29

**Lake Tahoe**  A lake on the California-Nevada border. p. 29

**Lanai** (luh•NY)  One of the eight main islands of Hawaii. p. A14

**Lancaster**  A city in southeastern Pennsylvania. (40°N, 76°W) p. 212

**Las Vegas** (lahs VAY•guhs)  A city in southeastern Nevada. (36°N, 115°W) p. 621

**Lexington**  A town in northeastern Massachusetts; site of the first battle of the Revolutionary War in 1775. (42°N, 71°W) pp. 291, 323

**Lima** (LEE•mah)  The capital of Peru; located on the Rímac River. (12°S, 77°W) p. 665

**Lisbon**  The capital of Portugal; a port city located in the western part of the country. (39°N, 9°W) pp. 108, 119

**Little Bighorn**  A location near the Little Bighorn River in southern Montana; site of a fierce battle in 1876 between Sioux and Cheyenne Indians and United States Army soldiers led by General George Armstrong Custer. p. 490

**London**  A city located in the southern part of England; capital of present-day Britain. (52°N, 0°) p. 108

**Long Island**  An island located east of New York City and south of Connecticut; lies between Long Island Sound and the Atlantic Ocean. p. 323

**Los Adaes**  Site of a mission of New Spain; located in present-day eastern Texas. p. 149

**Los Angeles**  The largest city in California; second-largest city in the United States; located in the southern part of the state. (34°N, 118°W) p. 621

**Louisiana Purchase**  A territory in the west central United States; it doubled the size of the nation when it was purchased from France in 1803; extended from the Mississippi River to the Rocky Mountains, and from the Gulf of Mexico to Canada. p. 385

## M

**Machu Picchu** (MAH•choo PEEK•choo)  The site of an ancient Inca city on a mountain in the Andes, northwest of Cuzco, Peru. (13°S, 73°W) p. 133

**Macon** (MAY•kuhn)  A city in central Georgia; located on the Ocmulgee River. (33°N, 84°W) p. 415

**Madeira** (mah•DAIR•uh)  An island group in the eastern Atlantic Ocean, off the coast of Morocco. p. 122

**Managua**  A city in Central America; capital of Nicaragua; located on the south shore of Lake Managua. (12°N, 86°W) p. 658

**Manitoba** (ma•nuh•TOH•buh)  A province in central Canada; bordered by the territory of Nunavut, Hudson Bay, Ontario, the United States, and Saskatchewan; located on the Interior Plains of Canada. p. 670

**Marshall Gold Discovery State Historic Park**  A historical park in eastern California located at the site where James Marshall discovered gold in 1848; setting of the California gold rush of 1849. p. 408

**Massachusetts Bay**  An inlet of the Atlantic Ocean; on the eastern coast of Massachusetts; extends from Cape Ann to Cape Cod. p. 189

**Maui** (MOW•ee)  The second-largest island in Hawaii. p. A14

**Mecca**  A city in western Saudi Arabia; a holy city and chief pilgrimage destination of Islam. p. 108

**Medford**  A city in northeastern Massachusetts, north of Boston. (42°N, 71°W) p. 291

**Mediterranean Sea** (meh•duh•tuh•RAY•nee•uhn)  An inland sea, enclosed by Europe on the west and north, Asia on the east, and Africa on the south. p. 113

**Menotomy**  Located in northeastern Massachusetts. p. 291

**Mérida**  A city in southeastern Mexico; capital of Yucatán state. (21°N, 89°W) p. 653

**Merrimack River**  A river in southern New Hampshire and northeastern Massachusetts; empties into the Atlantic Ocean. p. 197

**Mesa Verde** (MAY•suh VAIR•day)  An ancient settlement of the Anasazi; located in present-day southwestern Colorado. (37°N, 108°W) p. 65

**Mexico City**  A city on the southern edge of the Central Plateau of Mexico; the present-day capital of Mexico. (19°N, 99°W) pp. 149, 653

GAZETTEER

**Midway Islands** A United States territory in the central Pacific Ocean. p. 526

**Minneapolis** The largest city in Minnesota; located in the southeast central part of the state, on the Mississippi River; twin city with St. Paul. (45°N, 93°W) p. 498

**Mississippi River** The longest river in the United States; located centrally, its source is Lake Itasca in Minnesota; flows south into the Gulf of Mexico. pp. 29, 153

**Missouri River** A tributary of the Mississippi River; located centrally, it begins in Montana and ends at St. Louis, Missouri. pp. 29, 385

**Mobile Bay** An inlet of the Gulf of Mexico; located off the coast of southern Alabama; the site of a Civil War naval battle in 1864. p. 470

**Mohawk River** A river in central New York that flows east to the Hudson River. p. 89

**Molokai** (mah•luh•KY) One of the eight main islands of Hawaii. p. A14

**Monterrey** A city in northeastern Mexico; capital of Nuevo León state. (25°N, 100°W) p. 653

**Montevideo** A seaport city located in the southern part of the north shore of La Plata estuary; capital of Uruguay. (35°S, 56°W) p. 665

**Montreal** The second-largest city in present-day Canada; located in southern Quebec, on Montreal Island on the north bank of the St. Lawrence River. (46°N, 73°W) p. 274

**Morristown** A town in northern New Jersey; located west-northwest of Newark. (41°N, 74°W) p. 212

**Moscow** The capital and largest city of Russia; located in the western part of the country. (56°N, 38°E) p. 108

**Moundville** An ancient settlement of the Mound Builders; located in present-day central Alabama. (33°N, 88°W) p. 65

**Murfreesboro** A city in central Tennessee; located on the west fork of the Stones River; a site on the Trail of Tears. (36°N, 86°W) p. 398

**Mystic River** A short river rising in the Mystic Lakes; located in northeastern Massachusetts; flows southeast into Boston Harbor north of Charlestown. p. 291

## N

**Nagasaki** Japanese city upon which the second atom bomb was dropped, resulting in an end to World War II. p. 568

**Narragansett Bay** An inlet of the Atlantic Ocean in southeastern Rhode Island. (41°N, 71°W) p. 197

**Nashville** The capital of Tennessee; site of a Civil War battle in 1864. (36°N, 87°W) pp. 470, 621

**Nassau** A city on the northeastern coast of New Providence Island; capital of the Bahamas. (25°N, 77°W) p. 658

**Natchitoches** (NAH•kuh•tuhsh) The first settlement in present-day Louisiana; located in the northwest central part of the state. (32°N, 93°W) p. 385

**Nauvoo** (naw•VOO) A city in western Illinois; located on the Mississippi River; beginning of the Mormon Trail. (41°N, 91°W) p. 406

**New Amsterdam** A Dutch city on Manhattan Island; later became New York City. (41°N, 74°W) p. 211

**New Bern** A city and port in southeastern North Carolina. (35°N, 77°W) p. 234

**New Brunswick** One of Canada's ten provinces; bordered by Quebec, the Gulf of St. Lawrence, Northumberland Strait, the Bay of Fundy, the United States, and Nova Scotia. p. 670

**New Echota** (ih•KOHT•uh) A Native American town in northwestern Georgia; chosen as the capital of the Cherokee Nation in 1819. (34°N, 85°W) p. 398

**New France** The possessions of France in North America from 1534 to 1763; included Canada, the Great Lakes region, and Louisiana. p. 269

**New Guinea** (GIH•nee) An island of the eastern Malay Archipelago; located in the western Pacific Ocean, north of Australia. p. 568

**New Haven** A city in southern Connecticut; located on New Haven Harbor. (41°N, 73°W) p. 197

**New London** A city in southeastern Connecticut; located on Long Island Sound at the mouth of the Thames River. (41°N, 72°W) p. 247

**New Orleans** The largest city in Louisiana; a major port located between the Mississippi River and Lake Pontchartrain. (30°N, 90°W) pp. 391, 470

**New Spain** The former Spanish possessions from 1535 to 1821; included the southwestern United States, Mexico, Central America north of Panama, the West Indies, and the Philippines. p. 269

**New York City** The largest city in the United States; located in southeastern New York at the mouth of the Hudson River. (41°N, 74°W) p. 603

**Newark** A port in northeastern New Jersey; located on the Passaic River and Newark Bay. (41°N, 74°W) p. 212

**Newfoundland** (NOO•fuhn•luhnd) One of Canada's ten provinces; bordered by Quebec and the Atlantic Ocean. p. 670

**Newport** A city on the southern end of Rhode Island; located at the mouth of Narragansett Bay. (41°N, 71°W) p. 197

**Newton** A city in south central Kansas. (38°N, 97°W) p. 488

**Niihau** (NEE•how) One of the eight main islands of Hawaii. p. A14

**Norfolk** (NAWR•fawk) A city in southeastern Virginia; located on the Elizabeth River. (37°N, 76°W) p. 234

**Normandy** Region of northwest France; site of Allied D day invasion on June 6, 1944. p. 569

**North America** One of Earth's seven continents. p. 27

**North Pole** The northernmost point on Earth. p. 50

**Northwest Territories** One of Canada's three territories; located in northern Canada. p. 670

**Nova Scotia** (NOH•vuh SKOH•shuh) A province of Canada; located in eastern Canada on a peninsula. pp. 151, 670

**Nueces River** (noo•AY•says) A river in southern Texas; flows into Nueces Bay, at the head of Corpus Christi Bay. p. 404

**Nunavut** One of Canada's three territories; formed in 1999 and inhabited mostly by Inuit peoples. p. 670

GAZETTEER

## O

**Oahu** (oh•AH•hoo) The third-largest of the eight main islands of Hawaii; Honolulu is located there. p. A14

**Oaxaca** (wuh•HAH•kuh) A city and state in southern Mexico. (17°N, 96°W) p. 653

**Ocmulgee** (ohk•MUHL•gee) An ancient settlement of the Mound Builders; located in present-day central Georgia. p. 65

**Ocmulgee River** (ohk•MUHL•gee) A river in central Georgia; formed by the junction of the Yellow and South Rivers; flows south to join the Altamaha River. p. 234

**Oconee River** (oh•KOH•nee) A river in central Georgia; flows south and southeast to join the Ocmulgee and form the Altamaha River. p. 234

**Ogallala** (oh•guh•LAHL•uh) A city in western Nebraska on the South Platte River. (41°N, 102°W) p. 488

**Ohio River** A tributary of the Mississippi River, beginning in Pittsburgh, Pennsylvania, and ending at Cairo, Illinois. p. 29

**Old Spanish Trail** Part of the Santa Fe Trail that linked Santa Fe to Los Angeles. p. 406

**Omaha** (OH•muh•hah) The largest city in Nebraska; located in the eastern part of the state, on the Missouri River. (41°N, 96°W) p. 406

**Ontario** (ahn•TAIR•ee•oh) One of Canada's ten provinces; located between Quebec and Manitoba. p. 670

**Oregon Country** A former region in western North America; located between the Pacific coast and the Rocky Mountains, from the northern border of California to Alaska. p. 385

**Oregon Trail** A former route to the Oregon Country; extended from the Missouri River northwest to the Columbia River in Oregon. p. 406

**Orinoco River** A river in Venezuela in northern South America. p. 665

**Orlando** A city in central Florida. (28°N, 81°W) p. 621

**Ottawa** (AH•tuh•wuh) The capital of Canada; located in Ontario on the St. Lawrence Lowlands. (45°N, 75°W) p. 670

## P

**Pacific Ocean** Largest body of water on Earth; extends from Arctic Circle to Antarctic Regions, separating North and South America from Australia and Asia. p. 27

**Pagan** Ruined Asian town; capital of a powerful dynasty during the 11th–13th centuries. p. 113

**Palenque** (pah•LENG•kay) An ancient settlement of the Mayan civilization; located in present-day Chiapas, in southern Mexico. (18°N, 92°W) p. 65

**Palmyra Island** (pal•MY•ruh) One of the northernmost of the Line Islands; located in the central Pacific Ocean. p. 526

**Pampas** Plains of South America; located in southern part of the continent, extending for nearly 1,000 miles. p. 665

**Panama Canal** A canal across the Isthmus of Panama; extends from the Caribbean Sea to the Gulf of Panama. p. 528

**Panama City** The capital of Panama; located in Central America. (9°N, 80°W) p. 658

**Paramaribo** A seaport city located on the Suriname River; capital of Suriname. (5°N, 55°W) p. 665

**Paraná River** A river in southeast central South America; formed by the joining of the Rio Grande and the Paranaíba River in south central Brazil. p. 665

**Patagonia** A barren tableland in South America between the Andes and the Atlantic Ocean. p. 665

**Pearl Harbor** An inlet on the southern coast of Oahu, Hawaii; the Japanese attacked an American naval base there on December 7, 1941. p. 557

**Pecos River** (PAY•kohs) A river in eastern New Mexico and western Texas; empties into the Rio Grande. p. 488

**Pee Dee River** A river in North Carolina and South Carolina; forms where the Yadkin and Uharie Rivers meet; empties into Winyah Bay. p. 234

**Perryville** A city in east central Kentucky; site of a major Civil War battle in 1862. (38°N, 90°W) p. 470

**Perth Amboy** A port city in central New Jersey; located on Raritan Bay. (40°N, 74°W) p. 212

**Petersburg** A port city in southeastern Virginia; located on the Appomattox River; site of a series of Civil War battles from 1864 to 1865. (37°N, 77°W) p. 470

**Philadelphia** A city in southeastern Pennsylvania, on the Delaware River; a major United States port. (40°N, 75°W) p. 219

**Philippine Islands** A group of more than 7,000 islands off the coast of southeastern Asia, making up the country of the Philippines. pp. 125, 526

**Phoenix** Capital and largest city of Arizona; located in south central Arizona. p. 621

**Piedmont** Area of high land on the eastern side of the Appalachian Mountains. p. 20

**Pikes Peak** A mountain in east central Colorado; part of the Rocky Mountains. p. 385

**Pittsburgh** The second-largest city in Pennsylvania; located in the southwestern part of the state, on the Ohio River. (40°N, 80°W) p. 47

**Platte River** (PLAT) A river in central Nebraska; flows east into the Missouri River below Omaha. p. 406

**Plattsburgh** A city in northeastern New York; located on the western shore of Lake Champlain; site of a major battle in the War of 1812. (45°N, 73°W) p. 391

**Plymouth** A town in southeastern Massachusetts, on Plymouth Bay; site of the first settlement built by the Pilgrims, who sailed on the *Mayflower*. (42°N, 71°W) p. 189

**Port Royal** A town in western Nova Scotia, Canada; name changed to Annapolis Royal in honor of Queen Anne; capital of Nova Scotia until 1749. (45°N, 66°W) p. 151

**Port-au-Prince** A seaport located on Hispaniola Island, in the West Indies, on the southeastern shore of the Gulf of Gonâve; capital of Haiti. (18°N, 72°W) p. 658

**Portland** (ME) A port city in southwestern Maine; located on Casco Bay. (44°N, 70°W) p. 353

**Portland** (OR) Oregon's largest city and principal port; located in the northwestern part of the state on the Willamette River. (46°N, 123°W) p. 621

**Port of Spain** A seaport in the northwestern part of the island of Trinidad; capital of Trinidad and Tobago. (10°N, 61°W) p. 658

**Portsmouth** (NH) (PAWRT•smuhth) A port city in southeastern New Hampshire; located at the mouth of the Piscataqua River. (43°N, 71°W) p. 197

**Portsmouth** (RI) A town in southeastern Rhode Island; located on the Sakonnet River. (42°N, 71°W) p. 197

**Potomac River** (puh•TOH•muhk) A river on the Coastal Plain of the United States; begins in West Virginia and flows into Chesapeake Bay; Washington, D.C., is located on this river. p. 233

**Prince Edward Island** One of Canada's ten provinces; located in the Gulf of St. Lawrence. p. 670

**Princeton** A borough in west central New Jersey; site of a major Revolutionary War battle. (40°N, 75°W) p. 323

**Providence** Rhode Island's capital and largest city; located in the northern part of the state, at the head of the Providence River. (42°N, 71°W) p. 197

**Puebla** A city and state in southeastern central Mexico. (19°N, 98°W) p. 653

**Pueblo** (PWEH•bloh) A city in Colorado. p. 488

**Pueblo Bonito** (PWEH•bloh boh•NEE•toh) Largest of the prehistoric pueblo ruins; located in Chaco Canyon National Monument, New Mexico. p. 65

**Puerto Rico** An island of the West Indies; located southeast of Florida; a commonwealth of the United States. pp. 129, 526

**Put-in-Bay** A bay on South Bass Island, north of Ohio in Lake Erie; site of a major battle in the War of 1812. (42°N, 83°W) p. 391

**Q**

**Quebec** (kwih•BEK) The capital of the province of Quebec, Canada; located on the northern side of the St. Lawrence River; the first successful French settlement in the Americas; established in 1608. (47°N, 71°W) pp. 151, 670

**R**

**Raleigh** (RAW•lee) The capital of North Carolina; located in the east central part of the state. (36°N, 79°W) p. 621

**Red River** A tributary of the Mississippi River; rises in eastern New Mexico, flows across Louisiana and into the Mississippi River; forms much of the Texas–Oklahoma border. pp. 29, 385

**Regina** (rih•JY•nuh) The capital of Saskatchewan, Canada; located in the southern part of the province. (50°N, 104°W) p. 670

**Richmond** The capital of Virginia; a port city located in the east central part of the state, on the James River; capital of the Confederacy. (38°N, 77°W) p. 470

**Rio de Janeiro** A commercial seaport in southeastern Brazil on the southwestern shore of Guanabara Bay. (23°S, 43°W) p. 665

**Río de la Plata** A river on the southeastern coast of South America. p. 665

**Rio Grande** A river in southwestern North America; it begins in Colorado and flows into the Gulf of Mexico; forms the border between Texas and Mexico. pp. 29, 385

**Roanoke River** A river in southern Virginia and northeastern North Carolina; flows east and southeast across the North Carolina border and into Albemarle Sound. p. 234

**Rocky Mountains** A range of mountains in the western United States and Canada, extending from Alaska to New Mexico; these mountains divide rivers that flow east from those that flow west. pp. 20, 385

**Roxbury** A residential district in southern Boston, Massachusetts; formerly a city, but became part of Boston in 1868; founded in 1630. (42°N, 71°W) p. 291

**S**

**Sabine River** (suh•BEEN) A river in eastern Texas and western Louisiana; flows southeast to the Gulf of Mexico. p. 404

**Sacramento** The capital of California; located in the north central part of the state, on the Sacramento River. (39°N, 121°W) p. 621

**Sacramento River** A river in northwestern California; rises near Mt. Shasta and flows south into Suisun Bay. p. 406

**Salem** A city on the northeastern coast of Massachusetts. (43°N, 71°W) p. 189

**Salt Lake City** Utah's capital and largest city; located in the northern part of the state, on the Jordan River. (41°N, 112°W) pp. 406, 621

**San Antonio** A city in south central Texas; located on the San Antonio River; site of the Alamo. (29°N, 98°W) pp. 404, 621

**San Antonio River** A river in southern Texas; flows southeast and empties into San Antonio Bay. p. 404

**San Diego** A large port city in southern California; located on San Diego Bay. (33°N, 117°W) pp. 149, 174, 621

**San Francisco** The second-largest city in California; located in the northern part of the state, on San Francisco Bay. (38°N, 123°W) pp. 149, 621

**San Jacinto** (hah•SEEN•toh) A location in southeastern Texas; site of a battle in the Texas Revolution in 1836. (31°N, 95°W) p. 404

**San José** A city in Central America; capital of Costa Rica. (10°N, 84°W) p. 658

**San Juan** (san WAHN) Puerto Rico's capital and largest city. (18°N, 66°W) p. 658

**San Lorenzo** An ancient settlement of the Olmecs; located in present-day southern Mexico. (29°N, 113°W) p. 65

**San Salvador** One of the islands in the southern Bahamas; Christopher Columbus landed there in 1492. p. 122

**Santa Fe** (SAN•tah FAY) The capital of New Mexico; located in the north central part of the state. (36°N, 106°W) pp. 149, 406, 621

**Santa Fe Trail** A former commercial route to the western United States; extended from western Missouri to Santa Fe, in central New Mexico. p. 406

**Santee River** A river in southeast central South Carolina; formed by the junction of the Congaree and Wateree Rivers; flows southeast into the Atlantic Ocean. p. 234

**Santo Domingo** The capital of the Dominican Republic. (18°N, 70°W) p. 658

**São Francisco River** A river in eastern Brazil; flows north, northeast, and east into the Atlantic Ocean. p. 665

**São Paulo** A city in southeastern Brazil; capital of São Paulo state. p. 665

**Saratoga** A village on the western bank of the Hudson River in eastern New York; site of a major Revolutionary War battle in 1777; present-day Schuylerville. (43°N, 74°W) p. 323

**Saskatchewan** (suh•SKA•chuh•wahn) One of Canada's ten provinces; located between Alberta and Manitoba. p. 670

**Savannah** The oldest city and a principal seaport in southeast Georgia; located in the southeastern part of the state, at the mouth of the Savannah River. (32°N, 81°W) pp. 234, 470

**Savannah River** A river that forms the border between Georgia and South Carolina; flows into the Atlantic Ocean at Savannah, Georgia. p. 234

**Schenectady** (skuh•NEK•tuh•dee) A city in eastern New York; located on the Mohawk River. (43°N, 74°W) p. 212

**Seattle** The largest city in Washington; a port city located in the west central part of the state, on Puget Sound. (48°N, 122°W) p. 621

**Sedalia** (suh•DAYL•yuh) A city in west central Missouri. (39°N, 93°W) p. 488

**Serpent Mound** An ancient settlement of the Mound Builders; located in present-day southern Ohio. (39°N, 83°W) p. 65

**Shiloh** (SHY•loh) A location in southwestern Tennessee; site of a major Civil War battle in 1862; also known as Pittsburg Landing. (35°N, 88°W) p. 470

**Sierra Madre Occidental** (see•AIR•ah MAH•dray ahk•sih•den•TAHL) A mountain range in western Mexico, running parallel to the Pacific coast. p. 20

**Sierra Madre Oriental** (awr•ee•en•TAHL) A mountain range in eastern Mexico, running parallel to the coast along the Gulf of Mexico. p. 20

**Sierra Nevada** A mountain range in eastern California that runs parallel to the Coast Ranges. p. 20

**Snake River** A river that begins in the Rocky Mountains and flows west into the Pacific Ocean; part of the Oregon Trail ran along this river. p. 385

**South America** One of Earth's seven continents. p. 27

**South Pass** A pass in southwestern Wyoming; crosses the Continental Divide; part of the Oregon Trail. p. 406

**South Pole** The southernmost point on Earth. p. 50

**Spiro** An ancient settlement of the Mound Builders; located in eastern Oklahoma. (35°N, 95°W) p. 65

**Springfield** (MA) A city in southwestern Massachusetts; located on the Connecticut River. (42°N, 73°W) p. 197

**Springfield** (MO) A city in southwestern Missouri; a point on the Trail of Tears. (37°N, 93°W) p. 398

**St. Augustine** (AW•guh•steen) A city on the coast of northeastern Florida; the oldest city founded by Europeans in the United States. (30°N, 81°W) pp. 129, 149

**St. Croix** (KROY) A city on the border of Maine and New Brunswick, Canada. (45°N, 67°W) p. 151

**St. Ignace** (IG•nuhs) A city in Michigan; located on the southeastern side of Michigan's upper peninsula. (46°N, 85°W) p. 153

**St. John's** A city on the southeastern coast of Canada, on the Atlantic Ocean; the capital of Newfoundland. (47°N, 52°W) p. 670

**St. Joseph** A city in northwestern Missouri on the Missouri River. (40°N, 95°W) p. 488

**St. Lawrence River** A river in northeastern North America; begins at Lake Ontario and flows into the Atlantic Ocean; forms part of the border between the United States and Canada. p. 151

**St. Louis** A major port city in east central Missouri; known as the Gateway to the West. (38°N, 90°W) pp. 47, 385

**St. Lucia** An island and an independent state of the Windward Islands; located in the eastern West Indies, south of Martinique and north of St. Vincent. p. 658

**St. Marys** A village in southern Maryland; the capital until 1694; present-day St. Marys City. (38°N, 76°W) p. 233

**St. Paul** The capital of Minnesota; located in the eastern part of the state, on the Mississippi River. (45°N, 93°W) p. 498

**Strait of Magellan** (muh•JEH•luhn) The narrow waterway between the southern tip of South America and Tierra del Fuego; links the Atlantic Ocean with the Pacific Ocean. p. 125

**Sucre** A city in Bolivia, South America. (19°S, 65°W) p. 665

**Sudbury River** A river in western Massachusetts; connects with the Concord River. p. 291

**Suriname** A country in north central South America. p. 665

**Susquehanna River** (suhs•kwuh•HA•nuh) A river in Maryland, Pennsylvania, and central New York; rises in Otsego Lake, New York, and empties into northern Chesapeake Bay. p. 89

**T**

**Tallahassee** Capital of Florida; located in the state's panhandle. (34°N, 84°W) p. 621

**Tegucigalpa** A city in Central America; capital of Honduras. (14°N, 87°W) p. 658

**Tenochtitlán** (tay•nohch•teet•LAHN) The ancient capital of the Aztec Empire, on the islands of Lake Texcoco; location of present-day Mexico City, in southern Mexico. (19°N, 99°W) p. 108

**Tikal** (tih•KAHL) An ancient settlement of the Mayan civilization; located in present-day Guatemala, in Central America. (17°N, 89°W) p. 65

**Timbuktu** A town in Mali; located in western Africa, near the Niger River. (17°N, 3°W) p. 108

GAZETTEER

**Toledo** (tuh•LEE•doh)  A port city in northwestern Ohio located at the southwestern corner of Lake Erie. (42°N, 84°W) p. 498

**Toronto**  The capital of the province of Ontario, Canada; located near the northwestern end of Lake Ontario; largest city in Canada. (43°N, 79°W) p. 670

**Trail of Tears**  A trail that was the result of the Indian Removal Act of 1830; extended from the Cherokee Nation to Fort Gibson, in the Indian Territory. p. 398

**Trenton**  The capital of New Jersey; located in the west central part of the state; site of a major Revolutionary War battle in 1776. (40°N, 75°W) p. 323

**Tres Zapotes** (TRAYS sah•POH•tays)  An ancient settlement of the Olmecs; located in southern Mexico. (18°N, 95°W) p. 65

**Trinidad and Tobago**  An independent republic made up of the islands of Trinidad and Tobago; located in the Atlantic Ocean off the northeastern coast of Venezuela. p. 658

**Tucson** (TOO•sahn)  A city in southern Arizona; located on the Santa Cruz River. (32°N, 111°W) p. 621

**Turtle Mound**  An ancient settlement of the Mound Builders; located on the present-day east central coast of Florida. (29°N, 81°W) p. 65

**Valley Forge**  A location in southeastern Pennsylvania, on the Schuylkill River; site of General George Washington's winter headquarters during the Revolutionary War. (40°N, 77°W) p. 323

**Vancouver**  Canada's eighth-largest city; located where the northern arm of the Fraser River empties into the Pacific Ocean. (49°N, 123°W) p. 670

**Vandalia** (van•DAYL•yuh)  A city in south central Illinois. (39°N, 89°W) p. 415

**Venice**  A port city in northeastern Italy; located on 118 islands in the Lagoon of Venice. (45°N, 12°E) pp. 108, 113

**Veracruz** (veh•rah•KROOZ)  A state in Mexico; located in the eastern part of the country, on the Gulf of Mexico. (19°N, 96°W) p. 653

**Vicksburg**  A city in western Mississippi; located on the Mississippi River; site of a major Civil War battle in 1863. (32°N, 91°W) p. 470

**Victoria**  The capital of British Columbia, Canada; located on Vancouver Island. (48°N, 123°W) p. 670

**Vincennes** (vihn•SENZ)  A town in southwestern Indiana; site of a Revolutionary War battle in 1779. (39°N, 88°W) p. 323

**Wabash River** (WAW•bash)  A river in western Ohio and Indiana; flows west and south to the Ohio River, to form part of the Indiana–Illinois border. p. 323

**Wake Island**  A United States territory in the Pacific Ocean. p. 526

**Washington, D.C.**  The capital of the United States; located between Maryland and Virginia, on the Potomac River in a special district that is not part of any state. (39°N, 77°W) pp. 25, 391

**West Indies**  The islands enclosing the Caribbean Sea, stretching from Florida in North America to Venezuela in South America. p. 202

**West Point**  A United States military post since the Revolutionary War; located in southeastern New York on the western bank of the Hudson River. p. 323

**Whitehorse**  The capital of the Yukon Territory, Canada; located on the southern bank of the Yukon River. (60°N, 135°W) p. 670

**Whitman Mission**  Site of a Native American mission, established in 1836 by Marcus and Narcissa Whitman; located in present-day southeastern Washington. p. 406

**Williamsburg**  A city in southeastern Virginia; located on a peninsula between the James and York Rivers; capital of the Virginia Colony. pp. 234, 254

**Wilmington**  A coastal city in southeastern North Carolina; located along the Cape Fear River. p. 234

**Winchester**  A city in northern Virginia; located in the Shenandoah Valley. (39°N, 78°W)  p. 353

**Winnipeg**  The capital of the province of Manitoba, Canada; located on the Red River. (50°N, 97°W) p. 670

**Wisconsin River**  A river located in central Wisconsin that flows south and southeast to the Mississippi River. p. 153

**Yellowknife**  Capital of the Northwest Territories in Canada; located on the northwestern shore of Great Slave Lake at the mouth of the Yellowknife River. (62°N, 114°W)  p. 670

**Yellowstone River**  A river in northwestern Wyoming, southeastern Montana, and northwestern North Dakota; flows northeast to the Missouri River. p. 385

**York**  Former name of Toronto, Canada; located near the northwestern end of Lake Ontario; site of a major battle in the War of 1812. p. 391

**Yorktown**  A small town in southeastern Virginia; located on Chesapeake Bay; site of the last major Revolutionary War battle in 1781. (37°N, 76°W) p. 323

**Yucatán Peninsula** (yoo•kah•TAN)  A peninsula in southeastern Mexico and northeastern Central America. p. 20

**Yukon Territory**  One of Canada's three territories; bordered by the Arctic Ocean, the Northwest Territories, British Columbia, and Alaska. p. 670

GAZETTEER

# Glossary

The Glossary contains important social studies words and their definitions. Each word is respelled as it would be in a dictionary. When you see this mark ´ after a syllable, pronounce that syllable with more force than the other syllables. The page number at the end of the definition tells where to find the word in your book.

add, āce, câre, pälm; end, ēqual; it, īce; odd, ōpen, ôrder; tŏŏk, pŏŏl; up, bûrn; yŏŏ as *u* in *fuse*; oil; pout; ə as *a* in *above*, *e* in *sicken*, *i* in *possible*, *o* in *melon*, *u* in *circus*; check; ring; thin; this; zh as in *vision*

## A

**abolitionist** (a•bə•li´shən•ist) A person who wanted to end slavery. p. 448

**absolute location** (ab´sə•lŏŏt lō•kā´shən) The exact location of a place on Earth, either a postal location or its lines of latitude and longitude. p. 50

**acquittal** (ə•kwi´təl) A verdict of not guilty. p. 479

**adapt** (ə•dapt´) To adjust ways of living to land and resources. pp. 6, 70

**address** (ə•dres´) A formal speech. p. 467

**advertisement** (ad•vər•tīz´mənt) A public announcement that tells people about a product or an opportunity. p. 503

**agriculture** (a´grə•kul•chər) Farming. p. 64

**airlift** (âr´lift) A system of moving supplies by airplane. p. 581

**allegiance** (ə•lē´jəns) Loyalty. p. 303

**alliance** (ə•lī´əns) A formal agreement among nations, states, or individuals to cooperate. p. 270

**ally** (a´lī) A partner in an alliance; a friend, especially in times of war. p. 270

**almanac** (ôl´mə•nak) A yearly calendar and weather forecast that helps farmers know when to plant crops. p. 222

**amendment** (ə•mend´mənt) An addition or change to the Constitution. p. 370

**analyze** (a´nəl•īz) To look closely at how the parts of an event connect with one another and how the event is connected to other events. p. 3

**ancestor** (an´ses•tər) An early family member. p. 59

**annex** (ə•neks´) To add on. p. 394

**Anti-Federalist** (an´tī•fe´də•rə•list) A citizen who was against ratification of the Constitution. p. 368

**apprentice** (ə•pren´təs) A person who learns a trade by living with the family of a skilled worker and training for several years. p. 249

**archaeologist** (är•kē•o´lə•jist) A scientist who studies the culture of people who lived long ago. p. 57

**arid** (ar´əd) Dry. p. 36

**armada** (är•mä´də) A Spanish fleet of warships. p. 159

**armistice** (är´mə•stəs) An agreement to stop fighting a war. p. 527

**arms control** (ärmz kən•trōl´) A limiting of the number of weapons that each nation may have. p. 592

**arms race** (ärmz rās) A situation in which two or more countries build weapons to protect themselves against each other. p. 582

**arsenal** (är´sə•nəl) A place used for storing weapons. p. 348

**artifact** (är´tə•fakt) An object made by early people. p. 58

**assassinate** (ə•sa´sən•āt) To murder a leader by sudden or secret attack. p. 477

**assembly line** (ə•sem´blē līn) A system of mass production in which parts of a product, such as a car, are put together as they move past a line of workers. p. 544

**astrolabe** (as´tra•lāb) An instrument formerly used to calculate one's position compared to the sun, moon, and stars. p. 116

**auction** (ôk´shən) A public sale. p. 243

**authority** (ə•thôr´ə•tē) The right to control and make decisions. p. 164

## B

**backcountry** (bak´kən•trē) The land between the Coastal Plain and the Appalachian Mountains. p. 224

**barter** (bär´tər) To exchange goods usually without using money. p. 77

**basin** (bā´sən) Low, bowl-shaped land with higher ground all around it. p. 22

**bias** (bī´əs) An opinion or feeling for or against someone or something. p. 286

**bill** (bil) An idea for a new law. p. 356

**bill of rights** (bil uv rīts) A list of freedoms. p. 276

**black codes** (blak kōdz) Laws limiting the rights of former slaves in the South. p. 478

**blockade** (blä•kād´) To use warships to prevent other ships from entering or leaving a harbor. p. 289

**boom** (bŏŏm) A time of fast economic growth. p. 486

**border state** (bôr´dər stāt) During the Civil War, a state—Delaware, Kentucky, Maryland, or Missouri—between the North and the South that was unsure of which side to support. p. 459

**borderlands** (bôr´dər•landz) Areas of land on or near the borders between countries, colonies, or regions that serve as barriers. p. 146

**boycott** (boi´kät) To refuse to buy or use goods or services. p. 282

**broker** (brō´kər) A person who is paid to buy and sell for someone else. p. 241

**budget** (bu´jət) A plan for spending money. p. 280

**buffer zone** (bu´fər zōn) An area of land that serves as a barrier. p. 146

**bureaucracy** (byo͞o•ra´krə•sē) A system of organizing the many workers and groups that are needed to run government programs. p. 549

**burgess** (bûr´jəs) A representative in the legislature of colonial Virginia or Maryland. p. 163

**bust** (bust) A time of quick economic decline. p. 487

**C**

**Cabinet** (kab´ə•nit) A group of the President's most important advisers. p. 375

**candidate** (kan´də•dāt) A person running for office. p. 378

**capital** (ka´pə•təl) The money needed to set up or improve a business. p. 497

**caravel** (kâr´ə•vel) A ship that used square or triangular sails to travel long distances swiftly. p. 116

**cardinal direction** (kärd´nal də•rek´shən) One of the main directions: north, south, east, or west. p. A3

**carpetbagger** (kär´pət•ba•gər) A Northerner who moved to the South to take part in Reconstruction governments. p. 483

**cartogram** (kär´tə•gram) A diagram that gives information about places based on the size shown for each place. p. 626

**cartographer** (kär•tä´grə•fər) A person who makes maps. p. 115

**cash crop** (kash krop) A crop that people raise to sell rather than to use themselves. p. 163

**casualty** (ka´zhəl•tē) A person who has been killed or wounded in a war. p. 461

**cause** (kôz) An event or action that makes something else happen. p. 120

**cease-fire** (sēs•fīr´) A temporary end to a conflict. p. 582

**census** (sen´səs) An official population count. p. 359

**century** (sen´chə•rē) A period of 100 years. p. 60

**ceremony** (ser´ə•mō•nē) A series of actions performed during a special event. p. 72

**cession** (se´shən) Something given up, such as land. p. 407

**charter** (chär´tər) An official paper in which certain rights are given by a government to a person, group, or business. p. 188

**checks and balances** (cheks and ba´lən•səz) A system that gives each branch of government different powers so that each branch can watch over the authority of the others. p. 363

**chronology** (krə•nä´lə•jē) Time order. p. 2

**circle graph** (sûr´kəl graf) A round chart that can be divided into pieces, or parts; often referred to as a pie graph. p. 223

**city-state** (si´tē•stāt) A city and the surrounding area that stands as an independent state. p. 111

**civic participation** (si´vik pär•ti•sə•pā´shən) Being concerned with and involved in issues related to the community, state, country, or world. p. 9

**civics** (si´viks) The study of citizenship. p. 9

**civil rights** (si´vəl rīts) Rights guaranteed to all citizens by the Constitution. p. 535

**civil war** (si´vəl wôr) A war between two groups in the same country. p. 151

**civilian** (sə•vil´yən) A person who is not in the military. p. 557

**civilization** (si•və•lə•zā´shən) A culture that usually has cities with well-developed forms of government, religion, and learning. p. 65

**claim** (klām) To declare that a person or a country owns something. p. 121

**clan** (klan) A group of families that are related to one another. p. 78

**class** (klas) A group of people who are alike in some way. Classes are treated with different amounts of respect in a society. p. 65

**classify** (kla´sə•fī) To group. p. 171

**climate** (klī´mət) The kind of weather a place has most often, year after year. p. 33

**climograph** (klī´mə•graf) A chart that shows the average monthly temperature and the average monthly precipitation for a place. p. 492

**code** (kōd) A set of laws. p. 445

**cold war** (kōld wôr) Hostilities in which opposing nations attack each other by using propaganda and money rather than soldiers and weapons. p. 575

**colonist** (kä´lə•nist) A person who lives in a land ruled by a distant country. p. 144

**colony** (kä´lə•nē) A land ruled by a distant country. p. 144

**commander in chief** (kə•man´dər in chēf´) A person who is in control of all the armed forces of a nation. p. 294

**commerce** (kä´mərs) Trade. p. 351

**commission** (kə•mi´shən) A special committee that is set up to study something. p. 532

**common** (kä´mən) An open area where sheep and cattle graze; village green. p. 190

**commonwealth** (kä´mən•welth) A nation that governs itself but is a territory of another country. p. 660

**communism** (käm´yə•ni•zəm) A social and economic system in which all land and industries are owned by the government, and individuals have few rights and little freedom. p. 574

**compact** (käm´pakt) An agreement. p. 167

**company** (kum´pə•nē) A business. p. 138

**compass** (kum´pəs) An instrument used to find direction. p. 109

**compass rose** (kum´pəs rōz) A circular direction marker on a map. p. A3

**compromise** (käm´prə•mīz) An agreement in which each side in a conflict gives up some of what it wants in order to get some of what it wants. p. 91

**concentration camp** (kon•sən•trā´shən kamp) A guarded camp built by the German National Socialist party, or Nazis, where prisoners were held. p. 555

**Confederacy** (kən•fe´də•rə•sē) The group of eleven states that left the Union, also called the Confederate States of America. p. 453

**confederation** (kən•fe•də•rā´shən) A loosely united group of governments working together. p. 89

**congress** (käŋ´grəs) A formal meeting of government representatives who have the authority to make laws. p. 270

**conquistador** (kän•kēs´tə•dôr) Any of the Spanish conquerors in the Americas during the early 1500s. p. 127

**consent** (kən•sent´) Agreement. p. 195

**consequence** (kän´sə•kwens) Something that happens because of an action. p. 313

**conservation** (kän•sər•vā´shən) The protection and wise use of natural resources. p. 533

**constitution** (kän•stə•tōō´shən) A written plan of government. p. 235

**consumer good** (kən•sōō´mər good) A product made for personal use. p. 544

**contour line** (kän´tōōr līn) A line on a drawing or map that connects all points of equal elevation. p. 24

**convention** (kən•ven´shən) An important meeting. p. 351

**cotton gin** (kä´tən jin) A machine that removed seeds and hulls from cotton fibers much more quickly than workers could by hand. p. 418

**council** (koun´səl) A group that makes laws. p. 90

**county** (koun´tē) The large part of a colony or a state. p. 250

**county seat** (koun´tē sēt) The main town of a county. p. 250

**crossroads** (krôs´rōdz) A place that connects people, goods, and ideas. p. 46

**cultural region** (kul´chə•rəl rē´jən) An area in which people share some ways of life. p. 45

**culture** (kul´chər) A way of life. p. 10

**current** (kûr´ənt) The part of a body of water flowing in a certain direction. p. 26

**decade** (de´kād) A period of ten years. p. 60

**declaration** (de•klə•rā´shən) An official statement. p. 283

**deficit** (de´fə•sət) A shortage. p. 597

**deforestation** (dē•fôr•ə•stā´shən) The cutting down of most or all trees in an area. p. 668

**delegate** (de´li•gət) A representative. p. 271

**demand** (di•mand´) The need or want for a product or service by people who are willing to pay for it. p. 418

**demarcation** (dē•mär•kā´shən) A line that marks a boundary. p. 126

**democracy** (di•mä´krə•sē) A form of government in which the people have power to make choices about their lives and government, either directly or through representation. p. 395

**depression** (di•pre´shən) A time of little economic growth when there are few jobs and people have little money. p. 547

**descendant** (di•sen´dənt) A person's child, grand-child, and so on. p. 58

**desertion** (di•zûr´shən) Leaving one's duties, such as military service, without permission. p. 132

**détente** (dā•tänt´) An easing of tensions, especially between countries. p. 592

**dictator** (dik´tā•tər) A leader who has complete control of the government. p. 402

**dictatorship** (dik´tā•tər•ship) A form of government where a leader has complete control of the government. p. 555

**distortion** (di•stôr´shən) An area that is not accurate on a map. p. 530

**diverse economy** (də•vûrs´ i•kä´nə•mē) An economy that is based on many kinds of industries. p. 632

**division of labor** (də•vi´zhən uv lā´bər) Work that is divided so that each worker does a small part of a larger job. p. 544

**doctrine** (däk´trən) A government plan of action. p. 394

**drainage basin** (drā´nij bā´sən) Land drained by a river system. p. 31

**drought** (drout) A long period with little or no rain. p. 36

**due process of law** (dōō prä´ses uv lô) The principle that guarantees the right to a fair public trial. p. 372

**dugout** (dug´out) A boat made from a large, hollowed-out log. p. 76

## D

**D day** (dē dā) June 6, 1944, a day on which Allied forces during World War II worked together in the largest water-to-land invasion in history. p. 565

**debtor** (de´tər) A person who was put in prison for owning money. p. 236

## E

**earthwork** (ûrth´wərk) A wall made of dirt or stone. p. 294

**e-commerce** (ē•kä´mərs) The buying and selling of goods and services through computer connections. p. 634

**economic region** (e•kə•nä´mik rē´jən) An area defined by the kind of work people do or the products they produce. p. 45

**economics** (e•kə•nä´miks) The study of how people use resources to meet their needs. p. 8

**economy** (i•kä´nə•mē) The way people of a state, region, or country use resources to meet their needs. p. 8

**effect** (i•fekt´) The result of an event or action. p. 120

**electoral college** (i•lek´tə•rəl kä´lij) A group of officials chosen by citizens to vote for the President and Vice President. p. 360

**elevation** (e•lə•vā´shən) The height of land in relation to sea level. p. 24

**emancipation** (i•man•sə•pā´shən) The freeing of enslaved peoples. p. 445

**embargo** (im•bär´gō) The refusal of one nation to trade goods and services with another. p. 660

**empire** (em´pīr) The conquered lands of many people and places governed by one ruler. p. 106

**encounter** (in•koun´tər) A meeting. p. 106

**enlist** (in•list´) To join. p. 315

**entrepreneur** (än•trə•prə•nûr´) A person who sets up and runs a business. p. 495

**equality** (i•kwä´lə•tē) Equal rights. p. 448

**erosion** (i•rō´zhən) The wearing down of Earth's surface, usually by wind or water. p. 42

**estuary** (es´chə•wer•ē) The wide mouth of a river where ocean tides flow in. p. 137

**ethnic group** (eth´nik grōōp) A group of people from the same country, of the same race, or with a shared way of life. p. 622

**expedition** (ek•spə•di´shən) A journey. p. 118

**expel** (ik•spel´) To force to leave. p. 195

**export** (ek´spôrt) A product that leaves a country. p. 201

**extinct** (ik•stingt´) No longer in existence. p. 64

## F

**fact** (fakt) A statement that can be checked and proved to be true. p. 240

**fall line** (fôl līn) A place where the elevation of the land drops sharply, causing rivers to form waterfalls or rapids. p. 31

**farm produce** (färm prō´dōōs) Grains, fruits, and vegetables for sale. p. 215

**federal system** (fe´də•rəl sis´təm) A system of government in which the authority to govern is shared by the central and state governments. p. 354

**Federalist** (fe´də•rə•list) After the American Revolution, a citizen who wanted a strong national government and was in favor of ratifying the Constitution. p. 368

**fertilizer** (fûr´təl•ī•zər) Matter added to the soil to make it produce more crops. p. 41

**flow chart** (flō chärt) A diagram that shows the order in which things happen. p. 364

**fork** (fôrk) A place in which a river divides. p. 269

**forty-niner** (fôr•tē•nī´nər) A gold seeker who arrived in California in 1849. p. 409

**frame of reference** (frām uv ref´rəns) A set of ideas that determine how a person understands something. pp. 3, 442

**free election** (frē i•lek´shən) An election that offers a choice of candidates. p. 661

**free enterprise** (frē en´tər•prīz) An economic system in which people are able to start and run their own businesses with little control by the government. p. 494

**free state** (frē´ stāt) A state that did not allow slavery before the Civil War. p. 437

**free world** (frē wûrld´) The United States and its allies. p. 575

**freedmen** (frēd´mən) Men, women, and children who had once been slaves. p. 481

**free-trade agreement** (frē•trād´ ə•grē´mənt) A treaty in which countries agree to charge no tariffs, or taxes, on goods they buy from and sell to each other. p. 636

**front** (frənt) A battle line. p. 565

**frontier** (frən•tir´) The land that lies beyond settled areas. p. 199

**fugitive** (fyōō´jə•tiv) A person who is running away from something. p. 445

**fundamental** (fən•də•men´təl) Basic. p. 197

## G

**gap** (gap) An opening or a low place between mountains. p. 277

**generalization** (jen•ə•rə•lə•zā´shən) A statement based on facts, used to summarize groups of facts and to show relationships between them. p. 68

**geography** (jē•ä´grə•fē) The study of Earth's surface and the way people use it. p. 6

**glacier** (glā´shər) A huge, slow-moving mass of ice covering land. p. 56

**global economy** (glō´bəl i•kä´nə•mē) The world market in which companies from different countries buy and sell goods and services. p. 636

**gold rush** (gōld´ rush) A sudden rush of new people to an area where gold has been found. p. 409

**government** (gu´vərn•mənt) A system by which people of a community, state, or nation use leaders and laws to help people live together. p. 9

**grant** (grant) A sum of money or other payment given for a particular purpose. p. 127

**Great Awakening** (grāt ə•wā´kən•ing) A religious movement started by a Dutch minister in the Middle Atlantic Colonies that called for greater freedom of choice in religion. p. 215

**grid system** (grid sis′təm) An arrangement of lines that divide something, such as a map, into squares. p. A3

**grievance** (grē′vəns) A complaint. p. 305

**hacienda** (ä•sē•en′dä) A large estate where cattle and sheep are raised. p. 147

**harpoon** (här•pōōn′) A long spear with a sharp shell point. p. 79

**hatch lines** (hach līnz) A pattern of stripes used on historical maps to show areas claimed by two or more countries. p. 278

**heritage** (her′ə•tij) Culture that has come from the past and continues today. p. 10

**high-tech** (hī•tek′) The term used to describe industries that invent, build, or use computers and other kinds of electronic equipment. p. 633

**hijack** (hī jak′) A person who illegally takes control of something. p. 600

**historical empathy** (hi•stôr′i•kəl em′pə•thē) An understanding of the thoughts and feelings people of the past had about events in their time. p. 3

**historical map** (hi•stôr′i•kəl map) A map that provides information about a place as it was in the past. p. 112

**history** (hi′stə•rē) Events of the past. p. 2

**hogan** (hō′gän) A cone-shaped Navajo shelter built by covering a log frame with bark and mud. p. 72

**Holocaust** (hō′lə•kôst) The mass murder of European Jews, during World War II. p. 573

**homesteader** (hōm′sted•ər) A person living on land granted by the government. p. 488

**human feature** (hyōō′mən fē′chər) Something created by humans, such as a building or road, that alters the land. p. 6

**human resource** (hyōō′mən rē′sôrs) A worker who brings his or her own ideas and skills to a job. p. 499

**humidity** (hyōō•mi′də•tē) The amount of moisture in the air. p. 36

**immigrant** (i′mi•grənt) A person who comes into a country to make a new home. p. 219

**impeach** (im•pēch′) To accuse a government official, such as the President, of "treason, bribery, or other high crimes and misdemeanors." p. 361

**imperialism** (im•pir′ē•ə•liz•əm) Empire building. p. 526

**import** (im′pôrt) A product brought into a country. p. 201

**impressment** (im•pres′mənt) The taking of workers against their will. p. 389

**inauguration** (i•nô•gyə•rā′shən) A ceremony in which a leader takes office. p. 384

**indentured servant** (in•den′chərd sûr′vənt) A person who agreed to work for another person without pay for a certain length of time in exchange for passage to North America. p. 234

**independence** (in•də•pen′dəns) The freedom to govern on one's own. p. 302

**indigo** (in′di•gō) A plant from which a blue dye can be made. p. 235

**industrial revolution** (in•dus′trē•əl re•və•lōō′shən) The period of time during the 1700s and 1800s in which machines took the place of hand tools to manufacture goods. p. 412

**industrialization** (in•dəs•trē•ə•lə•zā′shən) The growth of industry. p. 545

**industry** (in′dəs•trē) All the businesses that make one kind of product or provide one kind of service. p. 200

**inflation** (in•flā′shən) An economic condition in which more money is needed to buy goods and services than was needed earlier. p. 347

**Information Age** (in•fər•mā′shən āj) The period in history that began in the second half of the twentieth century and is marked by the growing amount of information people can get. p. 633

**informed citizen** (in•fôrmd′ si′tə•zən) A citizen who knows what is happening in the community, the state, the nation, and the world. p. 641

**inlet** (in′let) An area of water extending into the land from a larger body of water. p. 27

**inset map** (in′set map) A smaller map within a larger one. p. A3

**integration** (in•tə•grā′shən) The bringing together of people of all races in education, jobs, and housing. p. 587

**interchangeable parts** (in•tər•chān′jə•bəl pärts) Identical copies of parts made by machines so that if one part breaks, an identical one can be installed. p. 418

**interdependent** (in•tər•di•pen′dənt) Depending on each other. p. 635

**interest** (in′trəst) The fee a borrower pays for the use of money. p. 562

**interest rate** (in′trəst rāt) The amount a bank charges to lend money. p. 656

**intermediate direction** (in•tər•mē′dē•it də•rek′shən) One of the in-between directions: northeast, northwest, southeast, southwest. p. A3

**international trade** (in•tər•na′shə•nəl trād) Trade among nations. p. 635

**Internet** (in′tər•net) The system that joins computers around the world for the exchange of information. p. 624

**intolerable** (in•täl′ər•ə•bəl) Unacceptable. p. 289

**investor** (in•ves′tər) A person who uses money to buy or make something that will yield a profit. p. 414

GLOSSARY

**irrigation** (i•rə•gā´shən) The use of canals, ditches, or pipes to move water to dry areas. p. 41

**island-hopping** (ī´lənd•hä´ping) The process of the Allies capturing island after island as they advanced toward Japan during World War II. p. 567

**isolation** (ī•sə•lā´shən) The policy of remaining separate from other countries. p. 541

**isthmus** (is´məs) A narrow strip of land that connects two larger land areas. p. 123

**J**

**jury** (jûr´ē) A group of citizens who decide a case in court. p. 641

**justice** (jus´təs) A Supreme Court judge. p. 361

**justice** (jus´təs) Fairness. p. 214

**L**

**land use** (land yo͞os) The way in which most of the land in a place is used. p. 43

**landform** (land´fôrm) A physical feature, such as a plain, mountain, hill, valley, or plateau, on the Earth's surface. p. 18

**legislature** (le´jəs•lā•chər) The lawmaking branch of government. p. 163

**liberate** (li´bə•rāt) To set free. p. 666

**liberty** (li´bər•tē) The freedom of people to make their own laws. p. 285

**life expectancy** (līf ik•spek´tən•sē) The average number of years a person can expect to live. p. 662

**line graph** (līn graf) A chart that uses one or more lines to show changes over time. p. 205

**lines of latitude** (līnz uv la´tə•to͞od) Lines on a map or globe that run east and west; also called parallels. p. 50

**lines of longitude** (līnz uv lon´jə•to͞od) Lines on a map or globe that run north and south; also called meridians. p. 50

**location** (lō•kā´shən) The place where something can be found. p. 6

**locator** (lō´kā•tər) A small map or picture of a globe that shows where an area on the main map is found in a state, on a continent, or in the world. p. A3

**lodge** (läj) A circular house of the Plains Indians. p. 82

**loft** (lôft) The part of a house located between the ceiling and the roof. p. 226

**long drive** (lông drīv) A trip made by ranchers to lead cattle to the market or the railroads. p. 487

**longhouse** (lông´hous) A long wooden building in which several related Iroquois families lived together. p. 89

**Loyalist** (loi´ə•list) A person who supported the British government during the American Revolution. p. 308

**M**

**Magna Carta** (mag´nə kär´tə) The English charter granted in 1215 by King John. It lists the rights of the royal class and limits the rights of the king. p. 370

**majority rule** (mə•jôr´ə•tē ro͞ol) The political idea that the majority of an organized group should have the power to make decisions for the whole group. p. 168

**manifest destiny** (ma´nə•fest des´tə•nē) The belief, shared by many Americans, that the United States should one day stretch from the Atlantic Ocean to the Pacific Ocean. p. 402

**map key** (map kē) A part of a map that explains what the symbols on a map stand for. p. A2

**map scale** (map skā l) A part of a map that compares a distance on the map to a distance in the real world. p. A3

**map title** (map tī´təl) Words on a map that tell the subject of the map. p. A2

**mass production** (mas prə•duk´shən) A system of producing large amounts of goods at one time. p. 418

**mechanization of agriculture** (me•kə•nə•zā´shən uv a´grə•kul•chər) The use of machines to plant and harvest crops. p. 546

**median age** (mē´dē•ən āj) The average age of all the people in a country. p. 662

**mercenary** (mûr´sən•er•ē) A soldier who serves for pay in the military of a foreign nation. p. 296

**meridian** (mə•ri´dē•ən) A line of longitude that runs from the North Pole to the South Pole. p. 50

**merit system** (mer´ət sis´təm) A way of making sure that the most qualified people get government jobs. p. 533

**metropolitan area** (me•trə•pä´lə•tən ar´ē•ə) A large city and the suburbs that surround it. p. 47

**middle class** (mi´dəl klas) The group of people who are economically between the rich and the poor. p. 656

**migrant worker** (mī´grənt wûr´kər) Someone who moves from place to place with the seasons to harvest crops. p. 588

**migration** (mī•grā´shən) The movement of people. p. 57

**military draft** (mil´ə•ter•ē draft) A way to bring people into military service. p. 538

**militia** (mə•li´shə) A volunteer army. p. 221

**millennium** (mə•le´nē•əm) A period of 1,000 years. p. 60

**mission** (mi´shən) A small religious settlement. p. 148

**missionary** (mi´shə•ner•ē) A person sent out by a church to spread its religion. p. 148

**modify** (mä´də•fī) To change. pp. 6, 40

**monarch** (mä´närk) A king or queen. p. 108

**monopoly** (mə•no´pə•lē) The complete control of a product or service. p. 288

**mountain range** (moun´tən rānj) A group of connected mountains. p. 19

**mutiny** (myōō´tə•nē) Rebellion against the leader of one's group. p. 138

**national anthem** (na´shə•nəl an´thəm) A song of praise for a country that is recognized as the official song of that country. p. 393

**nationalism** (na´shə•nəl•i•zəm) Pride in one's country. p. 394

**natural resource** (na´chə•rəl rē´sôrs) Something found in nature that people can use. p. 40

**natural vegetation** (na´chə•rəl ve•jə•tā´shən) The plant life that grows naturally in a place. p. 33

**naval store** (nā´vəl stōr) A product that is used to build and repair a ship. p. 203

**navigation** (na•və•gā´shən) The method of planning and controlling the course of a ship. p. 115

**negotiate** (ni•gō´shē•āt) To talk with another to work out an agreement. p. 327

**neutral** (nōō´trəl) Not taking a side in a disagreement. p. 309

**new immigration** (nōō i•mə•grā´shən) After 1890, the large group of people who came from southern and central Europe and other parts of the world to settle in North America. p. 503

**nomad** (nō´mad) A wanderer who has no settled home. p. 63

**no-man's-land** (nō´manz•land) In a war, land that is not held by either side but is filled with obstacles such as barbed wire and land mines. p. 539

**nonrenewable** (nän•ri•nōō´ə•bəl) Not able to be made again quickly by nature or people. p. 41

**nonviolence** (nän•vī´ə•ləns) The use of peaceful ways to bring about change. p. 587

**Northwest Passage** (nôrth´west pa´sij) A waterway in North America thought to connect the Atlantic Ocean and the Pacific Ocean. p. 136

**old immigration** (ōld i•mə•grā´shən) Before 1890, people who came from northern and western Europe to settle in North America. p. 502

**olive branch** (ä´liv branch) An ancient symbol of peace. p. 296

**open range** (ō´pən rānj) Land on which animals can graze freely. p. 489

**opinion** (ə•pin´yən) A statement that tells what a person thinks or believes. p. 240

**opportunity cost** (ä•pər•tōō´nə•tē kôst) the value of the thing a person gives up in order to get something else. p. 564

**oral history** (ôr´əl his´tə•rē) Stories, events, or experiences told aloud by a person who did not have a written language or who did not write down what happened. p. 2

**ordinance** (ôr´dən•əns) A law or set of laws. p. 349

**origin story** (ôr´ə•jən stōr´ē) A story or set of stories by Native American people that tell about their beginnings and how the world came to be. p. 59

**overseer** (ō´vər•sē•ər) A hired person who watched field slaves as they worked. p. 243

**pacifist** (pa´sə•fist) A believer in the peaceful settlement of differences. p. 310

**palisade** (pa•lə•sād´) A wall made of sharpened tree trunks to protect a village from enemies or wild animals. p. 87

**parallel** (par´ə•lel) A line of latitude. It is called this because parallels are always the same distance from one another. p. 50

**parallel time line** (par´ə•lel tīm līn) Two or more time lines that show the same period of time. p. 570

**Parliament** (pär´lə•mənt) The lawmaking body of the British government. p. 271

**patent** (pa´tənt) A license to make, use, or sell a new invention. p. 419

**pathfinder** (path´fīn•dər) Someone who finds a way through an unknown region. p. 387

**Patriot** (pā´trē•ət) A colonist who was against British rule and supported the rebel cause in the American Colonies. p. 308

**patriotism** (pā´trē•ə•ti•zəm) Love of one's country. p. 643

**permanent** (pûr´mə•nənt) Long-lasting. p. 144

**petition** (pə•ti´shən) A signed request made to an official person or organization. p. 290

**petroleum** (pə•trō´lē•əm) Oil. p. 497

**physical feature** (fi´zi•kəl fē´chər) A land feature that has been made by nature. p. 6

**piedmont** (pēd´mänt) An area at or near the foot of a mountain. p. 19

**pilgrim** (pil´grəm) A person who makes a journey for religious reasons. p. 166

**pioneer** (pī•ə•nir´) A person who is first to settle a new place. p. 276

**pit house** (pit hous) A house that was partially built over a hole in the earth so some rooms could be underground. p. 78

**plantation** (plan•tā´shən) A huge farm. p. 155

**planter** (plan´tər) A plantation owner. p. 241

**plateau** (pla•tō´) A broad area of high, mostly flat land. p. 21

**point of view** (point uv vyōō) A person's perspective. pp. 3, 286

**political boss** (pə•li´ti•kəl bôs) A powerful, often corrupt leader who has many dishonest employees and who is able to control the government. p. 534

**political party** (pə•li´ti•kəl pär´tē) A group whose members seek to elect government officials who share the group's points of view about many issues. p. 377

**political region** (pə•li´ti•kəl rē´jən) An area that shares a government and leaders. p. 45

**population density** (po•pyə•lā´shən den´sə•tē) The number of people who live within 1 square mile or 1 square kilometer of land. p. 602

**population pyramid** (po•pyə•lā´shən pir´ə•mid) A graph that shows the division of a country's population by age. p. 662

**population region** (po•pyə•lā´shən rē´jən) An area based on where people live. p. 45

**potlatch** (pät´lach) A special Native American gathering or celebration with feasting and dancing. p. 78

**prairie** (prer´ē) An area of flat or rolling land covered mostly by grasses and wildflowers. p. 38

**preamble** (prē´am•bəl) An introduction; first part. p. 304

**prediction** (pri•dik´shən) A decision about what may happen next, based on the way things are. p. 559

**prejudice** (pre´jə•dəs) An unfair feeling of hate or dislike for members of a certain group because of their background, race, or religion. p. 504

**presidio** (prā•sē´dē•ō) A Spanish fort. p. 146

**primary source** (prī´mer•ē sôrs) A record of an event made by a person who saw or took part in it. p. 4

**prime meridian** (prīm mə•ri´dē•ən) The meridian marked 0 degrees and that runs north and south through Greenwich, England. p. 50

**principle** (prin´sə•pəl) A rule that is used in deciding how to behave. p. 329

**proclamation** (prä•klə•mā´shən) An order from a leader to the citizens. p. 276

**profit** (prä´fət) The money left over after all expenses have been paid. p. 115

**progressive** (prə•gre´siv) A person who wants to improve government and make life better. p. 532

**projection** (prə•jek´shən) A way of showing Earth on flat paper. p. 530

**proprietary colony** (prə•prī´ə•tər•e kä´lə•nē) A colony owned and ruled by one person who was chosen by a king or queen. p. 155

**proprietor** (prə•prī´ə•tər) An owner. p. 155

**prospector** (präs´pek•tər) A person who searches for silver, gold, and other mineral resources. p. 487

**prosperity** (präs•per´ə•tē) Economic success. p. 162

**province** (prä´vəns) A political region, similar to a state. p. 670

**public office** (pub´lik ô´fəs) A job a person is elected to do. p. 192

**public opinion** (pub´lik ə•pin´yən) The point of view held by the majority of people. p. 302

**public service** (pub´lik sûr´vəs) A job someone does to help the community or society as a whole. p. 245

**pueblo** (pwe´blō) A Spanish word for *village*. p. 66

**Puritan** (pyûr´ə•tən) A member of the Church of England who settled in North America to follow Christian beliefs in a more "pure" way. p. 188

**quarter** (kwôr´tər) To provide or pay for housing at no cost to another person. p. 289

**R**

**rain shadow** (rān sha´dō) The driest side of a mountain. p. 35

**rapid** (ra´pəd) The fast-moving, dangerous place in a river caused by a sudden drop in elevation. p. 138

**rapid-transit system** (ra´pəd tran´sət sis´təm) A passenger transportation system that uses elevated or underground trains or both. p. 629

**ratify** (ra´tə•fī) To approve. p. 366

**rationing** (rash´ən•ing) The limiting of a supply of something. p. 561

**raw material** (rô mə•tir´ē•əl) A resource that can be used to make a product. p. 158

**Reconstruction** (rē•kən•struk´shən) The time during which the South was rebuilt after the Civil War. p. 476

**recycle** (rē•sī´kəl) To reuse. p. 562

**refinery** (ri•fī´nə•rē) A factory in which materials, especially fuels, are cleaned and made into usable products. p. 487

**reform** (ri•fôrm´) To change for the better. p. 532

**refuge** (re´fyōōj) A safe place. p. 213

**refugee** (ref´yōō•jē) A person who leaves home to seek shelter and safety elsewhere. p. 573

**regiment** (re´jə•mənt) A large, organized group of soldiers. p. 310

**region** (rē´jən) An area of Earth in which many features are similar. p. 6

**register** (rej´ə•stər) To enroll as a voter. p. 641

**regulation** (re•gyə•lā´shən) A rule or an order. p. 505

**relative location** (re´lə•tiv lō•kā´shən) The position of one place in relation to another. p. 44

**relocation camp** (rē•lō•kā´shən kamp) A temporary settlement in which Japanese Americans were forced to live during World War II. p. 563

**Renaissance** (re´nə•säns) A French word meaning "rebirth," used to name a time of advances in thought, learning, art, and science. p. 109

**renewable** (ri•nōō´ə•bəl) Able to be made or grown again by nature or people. p. 42

**repeal** (ri•pēl´) To cancel, or undo, a law. p. 283

**GLOSSARY**

**representation** (re•pri•zen•tā´shən) The act of speaking on behalf of someone else. p. 281

**republic** (ri•pub´lik) A form of government in which people elect representatives to govern the country. p. 346

**reservation** (re•zər•vā´shən) An area of land set aside by the government for use only by Native Americans. p. 490

**reserved powers** (ri•zûrvd´ pou´ərz) Authority that belongs to the states or to the people, not to the national government. p. 372

**resist** (ri•zist´) To act against. p. 445

**resolution** (re•zə•lōō´shən) A formal statement of the feelings of a group of people about an important topic. p. 303

**resolve** (ri•zälv´) To settle. p. 91

**responsibility** (ri•spän•sə•bil´ə•tē) A duty. p. 640

**retreat** (ri•trēt´) To fall back. p. 458

**revolution** (re•və•lōō´shən) A sudden, great change, such as the overthrow of an established government. p. 268

**royal colony** (roi´əl kä´lə•nē) A colony ruled directly by a monarch. p. 152

**ruling** (rōō´ling) A decision. p. 398

**rural** (rûr´əl) Like or having to do with a place away from a city. p. 46

**S**

**satellite** (sa´tə•līt) An object in orbit around Earth. p. 583

**savanna** (sə•va´nə) A kind of grassland that has areas with a few scattered trees. p. 39

**scalawag** (ska´li•wag) A rascal; someone who supports something for his or her own gain. p. 484

**scandal** (skan´dəl) An action that brings disgrace. p. 593

**sea dog** (sē dôg) A commander of English warships that attacked Spanish ships carrying treasure. p. 156

**sea level** (sē le´vəl) The level of the surface of the ocean. p. 21

**secede** (si•sēd´) To leave. p. 453

**secondary source** (se´kən•der•ē sôrs) A record of an event written by someone who was not there at the time. p. 5

**secret ballot** (sē´kret ba´lət) A voting method in which no one knows how anyone else voted. p. 484

**sectionalism** (sek´shən•ə•li•zəm) Regional loyalty. p. 436

**sedition** (si•di´shən) Speech or behavior that causes other people to work against a government. p. 196

**segregation** (se•gri•gā´shən) The practice of keeping people in separate groups based on their race or culture. p. 484

**self-rule** (self•rōōl´) Control of one's own government. p. 168

**self-sufficient** (self•sə•fi´shənt) Able to provide for one's own needs without help. p. 147

**separatist** (se´pə•rə•tist) A citizen of Quebec who wants Quebec to be independent. p. 672

**settlement house** (se´təl•mənt hous) A community center. p. 535

**sharecropping** (sher´kräp•ing) A system of working the land in which the worker was paid with a "share" of the crop. p. 483

**siege** (sēj) A long-lasting attack. p. 393

**slash-and-burn** (slash•and•bûrn) A method of clearing land for farming that includes cutting and burning of trees. p. 87

**slave state** (slāv stāt) A state that allowed slavery before the Civil War. p. 437

**slavery** (slā´və•rē) The practice of holding people against their will and making them carry out orders. p. 66

**society** (sə•sī´ə•tē) A human group. p. 10

**sod** (sod) Earth cut into blocks or mats, held together by grass and its roots. p. 82

**sound** (sound) A long inlet often parallel to the coast. p. 28

**specialize** (spe´shə•līz) To work at one kind of job and do it well. p. 190

**spiritual** (spir´i•chə•wəl) A religious song based on Bible stories. p. 244

**standard of living** (stan´dərd uv li´ving) A measure of how well people in a country live. p. 664

**staple** (stā´pəl) Something, such as milk or bread, that is always needed and used. p. 71

**states' rights** (stāts rīts) The idea that the states, rather than the federal government, should have the final authority over their own affairs. p. 436

**stock** (stäk) A share of ownership in a business. p. 161

**stock market** (stäk mär´kət) A place where people can buy and sell shares of a business. p. 547

**strategy** (stra´tə•jē) A long-range plan. p. 459

**suburban** (sə•bûr´bən) Of or like the area of smaller cities or towns around a large city. p. 46

**suffrage** (su´frij) The right to vote. p. 535

**Sun Belt** (sun belt) A wide area of the southern United States that reaches from the Atlantic coast to the Pacific coast. p. 621

**superpower** (sōō´pər•pou•ər) A nation that is one of the most powerful in the world. p. 580

**supply** (sə•plī´) The amount of a product or service that is available. p. 418

**surplus** (sûr´pləs) An amount that is more than what is needed. p. 71

**T**

**tariff** (tar´əf) A tax on goods brought into a country. p. 436

**technology** (tek•nä´lə•jē) The use of scientific knowledge and tools to make or do something. p. 63

**teleconference** (te´li•kän•frəns) A conference, or meeting, that uses electronic equipment to connect people. p. 625

**tenement** (te´nə•mənt) A poorly built apartment building. p. 503

**tepee** (tē´pē) A cone-shaped tent made from wooden poles and buffalo skins. p. 84

**territory** (ter´ə•tôr•ē) Land that belongs to a national government but is not a state. p. 349

**terrorism** (ter´ər•i•zəm) The use of violence to promote a cause. p. 596

**textile** (tek´stīl) Cloth. p. 416

**theory** (thē´ə•rē) A possible explanation. p. 57

**tide** (tīd) The regular rise and fall of the ocean and of the bodies of water connected to it. p. 27

**tidewater** (tīd´wô•tər) Low-lying land along a coast. p. 241

**time line** (tīm līn) A diagram that shows events that took place during a certain period of time. p. 60

**time zone** (tīm zōn) A geographic region in which the same time is used. p. 674

**totem pole** (tō´təm pōl) A tall wooden post carved with shapes of animals and people and representing a family's history and importance. p. 79

**town meeting** (toun mē´ting) An assembly in the New England Colonies in which male landowners could take part in government. p. 192

**township** (toun´ship) An area of land. p. 218

**trade-off** (trād´ôf) The giving up of one thing to get another. p. 564

**traitor** (trā´tər) One who works against one's own government. p. 323

**transcontinental railroad** (trans•kän•tə•nen´təl rāl´rōd) The railway line that crossed North America. p. 494

**travois** (trə•voi´) A device made of two poles fastened to a dog's harness, used to carry possessions. p. 85

**treason** (trē´zən) The act of working against one's own government. p. 282

**treaty** (trē´tē) An agreement between nations about peace, trade, or other matters. p. 126

**trespass** (tres´pas) To go onto someone else's property without asking permission. p. 388

**trial by jury** (trī´əl bī jûr´ē) The right of a person accused of a crime to be tried by a jury, or group, of fellow citizens. p. 214

**triangular trade route** (trī•ang´gyə•lər trād rōōt) A shipping route that linked England, the English colonies in North America, and the west coast of Africa, forming an imaginary triangle in the Atlantic Ocean. p. 202

**tribe** (trīb) A group of people who share the same language, land, and leaders. p. 64

**tributary** (tri´byōō•ter•ē) A stream or river that flows into a larger stream or river. p. 30

**tundra** (tun´drə) A cold, dry region where trees cannot grow. p. 37

**turning point** (tûr´ning point) A single event that causes important and dramatic change. p. 316

**underground** (un´dûr•ground) Done in secret. p. 446

**unemployment** (un•im•ploi´mənt) The number of people without jobs. p. 549

**urban** (ûr´bən) Of or like a city. p. 45

**urbanization** (ûr•bə•nə•zā´shən) The movement of people into cities. p. 546

**veto** (vē´tō) To reject. p. 361

**volcano** (väl•kā´nō) An opening in Earth, often on a hill or mountain, through which hot lava, gases, ash, and rocks may pour out. p. 23

**volunteer** (vä•lən•tir´) A person who works without pay. p. 642

**wampum** (wäm´pəm) Beads made from cut and polished seashells used to keep records, send messages to other tribes, barter for goods, or give as gifts. p. 88

**war hawk** (wôr hôk) A member of Congress who wanted war with Britain before the War of 1812. p. 390

**wigwam** (wig´wäm) A round, bark-covered Native American shelter. p. 88

GLOSSARY

# Index

Page references for illustrations are set in italic type. An italic *m* indicates
a map. Page references set in boldface type indicate the pages on which
vocabulary terms are defined.

La Salle, Sieur de, 153–154
Marquette, Jacques, 152–153
Polo, Marco, 109, 112, *112,*
   *m113*
Ponce de León, Juan,
   127–128
Verrazano, Giovanni da,
   136–137
Vespucci, Amerigo, 123–124
Zheng He, 109–110
**Exports, 201,** 205, 219, 246, 248,
   250, *331*
**Extinct, 64**

## F

**Fact, 240**
**Fact and opinion, 240**
**Factories, 416**
**Fairness, 145**
**Fall line, 31**
**Family heritage, 79**
**Faneuil Hall,** *335*
**Far East, 114**
**Farm produce, 215**
**Farmland, 43**
**Farragut, Jorge, 318**
**Father of the Constitution, 352**
**Federal**
   court system, 361–362
   formation of government,
      351–357, 638–640
   judges, 640
   reforms, 532–533
   and state government,
      354–355
   system, **354**
   System of Government, *354*
*Federalist, The,* 368
**Federalist party,** 377–378
**Federalists, 368**
**Ferdinand, archduke, 537**
**Ferdinand, king of Spain,**
   121–122
**Ferraro, Geraldine, 589**
**Ferry boats, 238**
**Fertilizer, 41**
*Fiestas Patrias,* 654
**Fifteenth Amendment,** 480,
   *480*
**Finley, John, 277**
**First Bank of the United**
   **States, 397**
**First Continental Congress,**
   290, 304
**First Nation peoples, 671**
**Fishing and whaling,** 76–79,
   200–201
**Five Nations, 89**
**Flags over North America in**
   **mid-1700s,** *278*
**Fleming, Sandford, 674**
**Florida,** 128, 148, 275, 394, 453,
   621
**Flow chart,** 364–365
**Fong, Hiram L.,** 505, *505*
**Ford, Gerald, 593**
**Ford, Henry, 544**
**Ford's Factory,** *544–545*

**Forest region,** 37–38
**Forests,** 41–42, 43, *86*
**Fork, 269**
**Fort**
   Christina, 212
   Duquesne, 269, 271
   Mandan, 386
   McHenry, 392
   Necessity, *268–269,* 270
   at New Orleans, *384*
   Sumter, 454–455, *454–455,*
      *m456, m457*
   Ticonderoga, *273,* 318
   at West Point, 323
**Forty-niners, 409**
**Fountain of Youth, 128**
**Four Corners, 72**
**Fourteenth Amendment, 479**
**Fox Indians, 398**
**Frame, Richard, 209**
**Frame of Government of**
   **Pennsylvania, 214**
**Frame of reference,** 3, **442–443,**
   473
**France,** 108, 211
**Francis I, king of France,** 136,
   137
**Franciscans, 148**
**Franco, Francisco, 555**
**Franklin, Benjamin,** 221–222,
   *270,* 271, 283, 303, 317–318,
   327, 352, 353, 366
**Free elections, 661**
**Free enterprise, 494**
**Free enterprise economy,**
   512, 636–637, 649
**Free state, 437**
**Free-trade agreement, 636**
**Free world, 575**
**Freedmen, 481**
**Freedmen's Bureau,** 481–482
**Freedmen's Bureau school,** *481*
**Freedom**
   of the press, 371
   of religion. *See* Religion,
      freedom of
   search for, 621
   of speech, 214, 371
   of worship, 214, 370–371
**Freedom Trail,** 334–335,
   *334–335*
**Freedom Trail marker,** *335*
*Freedom's Journal,* 448
**French and Indian War,**
   268–272, 273, *m274,* 275, 276
**French blockade, 324**
**French colonies,** 268–272
**French heritage, 672**
**French Quarter, The,** 155
**Fritz, Jean,** 342–343
**Frontenac, de, count of New**
   **France,** 152
**Frontier, 199**
   *See also* Backcountry
**Frontier, last,** 486–491
**Frontier life,** 226–227
**Fronts, 565**
**Fugitive, 445**
**Fugitive Slave Act,** 445
**Fulton, Robert, 415**

**Fundamental, 197**
**Fundamental Orders, 197**
**Furnace, colonial,** *246*

## G

**Gadsden, James, 407**
**Gadsden Purchase, 407**
**Gage, Thomas** (general), 291,
   294
**Galápagos Islands,** 667, *667*
**Gálvez, Bernardo de, 318**
**Gao, 110**
**Gap, 277**
**Garrison, William Lloyd, 448**
**Gaspé Peninsula, 137**
**Gates, Horatio,** 315, 316
**Gateway to the West,** *405*
*Gemini 4, 678*
**General Assembly, 214**
**Generalization, 68,** 246
**Generalize, 231**
**Geographic factors, 46**
**Geographic tools.** *See* Map and
   globe skills
**Geography**
   environment and society,
      548
   essential elements of, 7
   five themes of, 6
   human systems, 47
   importance of, 6
   places and regions, 133, 233,
      249, 408, 490, 667
**George II, king of England,**
   236
**George III, king of England,**
   276, *280,* 283, 296
**Georgia,** 148, 236–237, *237,* 250,
   453, 621
**Georgia Colony,** 236–237
**German invasions, 556**
**German soldiers,** *556*
**Germano, Eddie,** 594–595, *595*
**Germany,** 220, 554–555, 556,
   *m581*
**Germany divided, 574**
**Gesner, Abraham, 497**
**Gettysburg, Pennsylvania,**
   466–467, 510–511
**Gettysburg Address,** 467–468
**Gettysburg National**
   **Cemetery,** *510*
**Gettysburg National Military**
   **Park,** 510–511
**Ghana, 110**
**Ghost town,** *486–487*
**Gibbs, Jonathan C., 479**
**Glaciers, 56,** *669*
**Glenn, John,** 518, 583
**Global economy,** 635–**636**
**Global Positioning System**
   **(GPS), 625**
*God Bless America,* 503
**Gods,** 71–72, 73, 79, 106, 108,
   129
**Gold**
   coins, *144*
   discovery of, 398, 491

mines, 144, 156
nugget, *409*
rush, 408–409, **409,** 486–487,
   525
search for, 144–145, 160, 525
Seven Cities of, 131–132
*Golden Hind,* 156
**Goods,** 385, 412, 414–415
   wartime, 560–561
**Goods and services,** 220, 347,
   418, 634, 635–636, 636–637
**Gorbachev, Mikhail,** 597–598
**Gordon, William E., 660**
**Gore, Al, 600**
**Government**
   constitution, **235**
   foreign, 276, 654–655,
      660–661, 672
   formation of, 306–307
   Frame of Government of
      Pennsylvania, 214
   Fundamental Orders, 197
   local. *See* Local govern-
      ments
   Mayflower Compact,
      166–168, *167*
   national. *See* National gov-
      ernment
   Native American, 89–90
   purpose of, **9**
   reconstruction, 479–480, 483
   regulation, 505, 532–534,
      562
   representative, 163
   self-rule, **168**
   state. *See* State governments
**Governor's Palace,** *239*
**Grand Canyon, 22**
**Grand Teton Mountain Range,**
   *16–17*
**Granger, Gordon, 482**
**Grant, 127**
**Grant, Ulysses S.,** 465–466,
   *465,* 468–469, *469,* 475
**Graph activities,** 493, 656
**Graph analysis,** 397, 445, 448,
   459, 496, 497, 545, 547, 561,
   589, 591
**Graphs**
   analysis of, *283*
   bar, 330–331
   circle, **223,** 229, 330–331
   climograph, **492–493**
   line, **205,** 207, 331
   pie. *See* Graphs, circle
   population pyramid,
      662–663
**Grassland region, 38**
**Great Auk,** *401*
**Great Awakening, 215,**
   216–217
**Great Basin,** 22, 29, 406
**Great Compromise,** 355–356
**Great Compromiser, 439**
**Great Council, 90**
**Great Depression, The,** 547–548
**Great Lakes,** 28, 670
**Great Migration,** 506–507, *506*
**Great Plains,** 21, 488–489, *492,*
   548

INDEX

For permission to reprint copyrighted material, grateful acknowledgment is made to the following sources:

*Atheneum Books for Young Readers, an imprint of Simon & Schuster Children's Publishing Division:* Cover illustration from *Anasazi* by Leonard Everett Fisher. Copyright © 1997 by Leonard Everett Fisher. Cover illustration by Ronald Himler from *Squish! A Wetland Walk* by Nancy Luenn. Illustration copyright © 1994 by Ronald Himler. Cover illustration by Jerry Pinkney from *Goin' Someplace Special* by Patricia McKissack. Illustration copyright © 2001 by Jerry Pinkney.

*Candlewick Press Inc., Cambridge, MA:* Cover illustration by P. J. Lynch from *When Jessie Came Across the Sea* by Amy Hest. Illustration copyright © 1997 by P. J. Lynch.

*Candlewick Press Inc., Cambridge, MA, on behalf of Walker Books Ltd., London:* Cover illustration by Kevin Tweddell from *The History News: Explorers* by Michael Johnstone. Illustration copyright © 1997 by Walker Books Ltd.

*Dutton Children's Books, an imprint of Penguin Books for Young Readers, a division of Penguin Putnam Inc:* Cover photograph by Art Wolfe from *Journey Through the Northern Rainforest* by Karen Pandell. Photograph copyright © 1999 by Art Wolfe.

*Jane Feder, on behalf of Julie Downing:* Cover illustration by Julie Downing from *If You Were There in 1492* by Barbara Brenner. Illustration copyright © 1991 by Julie Downing.

*Harcourt, Inc.:* "If We Should Travel" from *Between Earth & Sky* by Joseph Bruchac. Text copyright © 1996 by Joseph Bruchac.

*HarperCollins Publishers:* Cover illustration by James Watling from *Finding Providence: The Story of Roger Williams* by Avi. Illustration copyright © 1997 by James Watling. From *Stranded at Plimoth Plantation 1626* by Gary Bowen. Copyright © 1994 by Gary Bowen. Cover illustration by Stephen Fieser from *The Silk Route: 7,000 Miles of History* by John S. Major. Illustration copyright © 1995 by Stephen Fieser. Cover illustration by Bert Dodson from *American Adventures: Thomas* by Bonnie Pryor. Illustration copyright © 1998 by Bert Dodson.

*David Higham Associates Limited:* Cover illustration by Martin Jordan from *Angel Falls: A South American Journey* by Martin and Tanis Jordan. Illustration copyright © 1995 by Martin Jordan. Published by Larousse Kingfisher Chambers Inc.

*Holiday House, Inc.:* Cover illustration by Peter Fiore from *The Boston Tea Party* by Steven Kroll. Illustration copyright 1998 by Peter Fiore.

*Henry Holt and Company, LLC:* From "San Salvador" by Jamake Highwater in *The World in 1492* by Jean Fritz, Katherine Paterson, Patricia and Fredrick McKissack, Margaret Mahy, and Jamake Highwater, cover illustration by Stefano Vitale. Text copyright © 1992 by The Native Land Foundation; cover illustration copyright © 1992 by Stefano Vitale.

*Lee & Low Books, Inc., 95 Madison Avenue, New York, NY 10016:* From *Dia's Story Cloth: The Hmong People's Journey to Freedom* by Dia Cha, illustrated by Chue and Nhia Thao Cha. Copyright © 1996 by Denver Museum of Natural History.

*Robin Moore and BookStop Literary Agency:* Cover illustration by Robin Moore from *Across the Lines* by Carolyn Reeder. Illustration copyright © 1997 by Robin Moore.

*Northland Publishing Company:* Cover illustration by Julia Miner from *The Unbreakable Code* by Sara Hoagland Hunter. Illustration copyright © 1996 by Julia Miner.

*Orion Books, a division of Random House, Inc.:* From *All for the Union* by Robert Hunt Rhodes. Text and photograph copyright © 1985 by Robert Hunt Rhodes.

*G. P. Putnam's Sons, an imprint of Penguin Putnam Books for Young Readers, a division of Penguin Putnam Inc.:* From *Shh! We're Writing the Constitution* by Jean Fritz, illustrated by Tomie dePaola. Text copyright © 1987 by Jean Fritz; illustrations copyright © 1987 by Whitebird, Inc. Cover illustration by F. John Sierra from *My Mexico—México mío* by Tony Johnston. Illustration copyright © 1996 by F. John Sierra.

*Scholastic Inc.:* Cover illustration by Mark Summers from *James Printer: A Novel of Rebellion* by Paul Samuel Jacobs. Illustration © 1997 by Mark Summers. Published by Scholastic Press, a division of Scholastic Inc. Cover illustration by Dan Andreasen from *By the Dawn's Early Light: The Story of the Star-Spangled Banner* by Steven Kroll. Illustration copyright © 1994 by Dan Andreasen.

*Simon & Schuster Books for Young Readers, an imprint of Simon & Schuster Children's Publishing Division:* Cover illustration from *The Story of William Penn* by Aliki. Copyright © 1964 by Aliki Brandenberg; copyright renewed © 1992 by Aliki Brandenberg. From "The *Eagle* Has Landed" in *The Children's Book of America*, edited by William J. Bennett, illustrated by Michael Hague. Text copyright © 1998 by William J. Bennett; illustrations copyright © 1998 by Michael Hague.

*Steck-Vaughn Company:* Cover illustration by Debbe Heller from *Tales from the Underground Railroad* by Kate Connell. Illustration copyright © 1993 by Dialogue Systems, Inc.

## ILLUSTRATION CREDITS

Pages 12-13, Angus McBride; 13, Steve Weston; 14-15, Leland Klanderman; 28, 34, 35, Sebastian Quigley; 56-57, Tom McNeely; 62-63, Dennis Lyall; 71, Luigi Galante; 77, Inklink; 100-101, Uldis Klavins; 102-103, Dave Hendersch; 107, Steve Weston; 106-107, Studio Liddell; 116-117, Dennis Lyall; 160-161, Mike Lamble; 167, Bill Smith Studio; 180-181, Andrew Wheatcroft; 182-185, Nina Martin; 190-191, George Gaadt; 220, 226-227, Yuan Lee; 260-261, George Gaadt; 308-309, Vincent Wakerley; 324, Dennis Lyall; 324-325, Sebastian Quigley; 325, Dennis Lyall; 340-341, Gino D'Achille; 355, Vincent Wakerley; 376-377, Chuck Carter; 393, Bill Smith Studio; 412-413, Don Foley; 428-429, Cliff Spohn; 430-433, George Gaadt; 454-455, Luigi Galante; 468, Bill Smith Studio; 494-495, Dennis Lyall; 516-517, Bill Maughan; 544-545, Chuck Carter; 566-567, Dennis Lyall; 612-613, Rick Johnson; 638-639, Studio Liddell; 643, Bill Smith Studio; 644-645, Vincent Wakerley.

**All maps by MapQuest.com**

## PHOTO CREDITS

Cover: Stephen Krasemann/DRK Photo (eagle); Roger Ressmeyer/Corbis (shuttle); The Image Bank (Mt. Rushmore); G. George Diebold/Corbis Stock Market (waves).

**PLACEMENT KEY:** (t) top; (b) bottom; (l) left; (c) center; (r) right; (bg) background; (i) inset

**POSTER INSERT**

Flag: Don Mason/Corbis Stock Market, eagle: Minden Pictures.

**TITLE PAGE AND TABLE OF CONTENTS**

(fg) Andria/Hendrickson; (bg) Doug Armand/Stone; iv, The Detroit Institute of Arts; v, National Maritime Museum Picture Library; vi, Historical Society of Pennsylvania, Silver Gorget, c. 1757 Artist: Joseph Richardson, Sr., S-8-120; vii, Lester Lefkowitz/Corbis Stock Market; viii, Independence National Historical Park; ix, Smithsonian Institution; x, NASA.

**INTRODUCTION**

1 (t) Andria/Hendrickson, (l) Doug Armand/Stone; 2 (t) Bob Daemmrich/Stock, Boston/PictureQuest; 2 (b) ChromoSohm/Sohm/Visions of America; 3 (t) Christie Parker/Houserstock, Inc.; 3 (b) Underwood & Underwood/Corbis; 4 National Park Service; 4 National Park Service; 4 National Park Service; 5 (br) John McGrail; 5 (tl) The Granger Collection, New York; 5 (inset) National Park Service; 7 (tl) Mattew Borkoski/Stock, Boston Inc./PictureQuest; 7 (tr) Andre Jenny/Focus Group/PictureQuest; 7 (cl) Peter Pearson/Stone; 7 (cr) Jeffrey Muir Hamilton/Stock, Boston Inc./PictureQuest; 7 (bl) Robert Hildebrand; 7 (br) David Young-Wolff/PhotoEdit/PictureQuest; 8 (l) Jeff Lepore/Panoramic Images; 8 (r) David Young-Wolff/PhotoEdit; 9 (bl) Joseph Sohm/Stock, Boston Inc./PictureQuest; 9 (br) Bill Bachman/PhotoEdit; 10 (t) David Young-Wolff/PhotoEdit/PictureQuest; 10 (b) Calumet Regional Archives, Indiana University Northwest.

**UNIT 1**
**UNIT OPENER,** (fg) The Detroit Institute of Arts; (bg) Tom & Susan Bean, Inc.; 11 (t) The Detroit Institute of Arts; (l) Tom & Susan Bean, Inc; 16-17 Robert Hildebrand Photography; 18-19 (b) Russ Finley; 19 (t) David Muench/Corbis; 21 (b) Dave G. Houser; 22 (b) Marc Muench/David Muench Photography, Inc.; 23 (t) David Muench; 26 (b) Stocktrek/Corbis Stock Market; 30 (t) Greg Ryan/Sally Beyer/Positive Reflections; 30 (inset) Bettmann/Corbis; 31 (br) Stock Barrow; 32 (t) David Muench; 33 (b) Mark E. Gibson Photography; 37 California Stock Photography; 39 Tom & Susan Bean; 40 Ted Streshinsky/Corbis; 41 Mark E. Gibson Photography; 43 (t) Charles Gupton/Corbis Stock Market; 44 Henry T. Kaiser/Stock Connection/PictureQuest; 46-47 (b) Mark E. Gibson Photography;  48 Place Stock Photo; 54-55 David Muench Photography; 58 (b) John Maier, Jr./JB Pictures; 58 (inset) Mercyhurst Archaeological Institute; 59 Lawrence Migdale; 63 (t) Courtesy of Arizona State Museum, AZ/Jerry Jacka Photography; 64 (tl) Harald Sund/The Image Bank; 64 (tr) Zion National Park; 65 (br) Werner Forman/Art Resource; 66-67 (t) Michael Hampshire/Cahokia Mounds Historic Site; 67 (tr) Richard A. Cooke/Corbis; 68 American Hurrah; 70 Place Stock Photo; 72-73 (b) James Cowlin/Adstock; 72 (inset) Monty Roessel; 73 (t) Fifth Generation Traders, Farmington, N.M./Jerry Jacka Photography; 74 (t) Stephen Trimble; 74 (b) Smithsonian Institution; 75 (t) Aldo Tutino/ Art Resource, NY; 75 (c) John Bigelow Taylor/Art Resource, NY; 75 (b) Gift of

Clark Field, The Philbrook Museum of Art, Tulsa, Oklahoma. Photo by Don Wheeler; 76 (b) Canadian Museum of Civilization; 77 (t) Mark E. Gibson; 79 (b) Kevin Fleming/Corbis; 79 (inset) The Heard Museum, Phoenix, AZ./Jerry Jacka Photography; 80 (t) Michael Evan Sewell/Peter Arnold, Inc.; 81 (b) Smithsonian American Art Museum, Gift of Mrs. Joseph Harrison, Jr./Art Resource; 82 (b) Tom & Susan Bean; 82 (inset, l)) Mandan Dress, 1805; Peabody Museum, Harvard; 82 (inset, r) R. Webber/The Bata Shoe Museum; 83 (l) Gift of Enron Art Foundation/Joslyn Art Museum, Omaha, NE; 84 (t) Museum of South Dakota State Historical Society; 84-85 (b) Thomas Gilcrease Museum, Tulsa, 86 (b) Robert Hildebrand Photography; 87 (tl) National Museum of the American Indian/Smithsonian Institution; 87 (tr) New York State Museum; 88 (bl) Granger; 88 (br) Ashmolean Museum, Oxford; 90 (t) CGI, Pathways Productions; 91 (b) Cranbrook Institute of Science; 94 (c) Jerry Jacka Photography; 94-95 (bg) Jerry Jacka Photography; 95 (bl) Russ Finley/Finley-Holiday Film Corp.; 95 (tl) Russ Finley/Finley-Holiday Film Corp.; 95 (tr) Tom Bean/Corbis; 95 (br) Bob Rowan, Progressive Image/Corbis.

**UNIT 2**
**UNIT OPENER;** (fg) National Maritime Museum Picture Library; (bg) Superstock; 99 (t) National Maritime Museum Picture Library; (l) Superstock; 104-105 Heather R. Davidson; 109 (b) The Art Archive/Eileen Tweedy; 109 (inset) China Stock Photo Library; 110 (t) The Art Archive; 110 (bc) Werner Forman Archive/Tanzania National Museum, Dar es Salaam/Art Resource; 111 (b) Gift of Mrs. Walter B. Ford/Detroit Institute of Arts; 112 (bl) Giraudon/Art Resource; 112 (bc) Erich Lessing Culture and Fine Arts Archives/Art Resource; 113 (b) Genius of China Expedition/The Art Archive; 114 (bc) Werner Forman Archive/Art Resource; 114 (inset) The Art Archive; 114 (bg) Genius of Chinese Expedition/The Art Archive; 115 (t) Michael Yamashita; 115 (b) Bibliotheque Nationale, Paris; 117 (b) National Maritime Museum; 118 The Bridgeman Art Library International, Ltd.; 121 Museo Navale de Pegli, Genoa; 123 (b) Kevin Fleming/Corbis; 124 (bc) The Art Archive; 127 (b) Timothy O'Keefe/PictureQuest; 128 (b) American Museum of Natural History; 128 (tc) National Museum of Anthropology, Mexico City/Werner Forman Archive/Art Resource; 130 (tc) John Bigelow Taylor/Art Resource; 131 (b) Hulton Archive; 132 (t) Private Collection/The Bridgeman Art Library; 132 (br) The Granger Collection; 132 (inset) Jeffery M. Mitchem; 134 (t) Giraudon/Art Resource, NY; 134 (bl) Don Eaton/Higgins Armory Museum; 134 (br) Don Eaton/Higgins Armory Museum; 135 Half Armour, North Italian, c. 1560. 80 (11.47; IV.129) © Board of Trusties of the Armouries. 136 (b) Culver Pictures; 136 (inset) Bettmann/Corbis; 137 (b) National Archives of Canada; 137 (inset) Virtual Museum of New France; 139 Tate Gallery, London/Art Resource, NY; 142-143 Robert Frerck/Odyssey/Chicago; 144 (bc) Jeffrey L. Rotman/Corbis; 145 (tl) Courtesy of the Hispanic Society of America, New York; 145 (tr) Archivo Fotographico Seville; 146 (c) Victor Boswell/National Geographic Society; 146-147 (b) Morton Kunstler/National Geographic Image Collection; 148 (b) Lowell Georgia/Corbis; 148 (inset) The Santa Barbara Mission; 150 (b) Head of Pechaunigum (Rabbit) Rapids Nipigon River, Lake Superior by William Armstrong 1911/Public

Archives of Canada C-114494; 150 (inset) Minnesota Historical Society; 152 (t) James Swedberg/The Adirondack Museum; 152 (b) National Gallery of Art, Washington D.C.; 154 Texas Department of Transportation; 155 (c) Bob Daemmrich/Stock, Boston; 156 (b) The Art Archive; 157 (bc) Jean-Leon Huens/NGS Image Collection; 158 (b) The Bridgeman Art Library International, Ltd.; 159 (t) The Granger Collection, New York; 162 (t) Crandall Shifflett; 162 (b) National Portrait Gallery, Smithsonian Institute/Art Resource; 163 (b) The Association for the Preservation of Virginia Antiquities; 164 (t) Gianni Dagli Orti/Corbis; 165 (b) The Granger Collection, New York; 166 (b) Courtesy of The Pilgrim Society, Plymouth, Massachusetts; 166 (b) Walter Meayers Edsards/National Geographic Image Collection; 167 (cl) Bettmann/Corbis; 168-169 (b) Kevin Fleming/Corbis; 169 (c) Cary Wolinsky/Stock, Boston/PictureQuest; 169 (r, inset) Catherine Karnow/Corbis; 169 (b, inset) Lee Snider/Corbis; 170 Hulton Archive/Getty Images; 174-175 (bg) David Olsen/Stone; 174 (inset) Richard Cummins/Corbis; 175 (t) James L. Amos/Corbis; 175 (c, inset) Lowell Georgia/Corbis; 175 (bl) John Elk III/Stock, Boston.

**UNIT 3**
**UNIT OPENER;** (fg) Historical Society of Pennsylvania, Silver Gorget, c. 1757 Artist: Joseph Richardson, Sr., S-8-120; (bg) John McGrail Photography; 179 (t) Historical Society of Pennsylvania, Silver Gorget, c. 1757 Artist: Joseph Richardson, Sr., S-8-120; (r) John McGrail Photography; 186-187 Henryk Kaiser/Leo De Wys, Inc.; 188 The Commonwealth of Massachusetts, Archives Division; 189 Bettmann/Corbis; 192 Todd Gipstein/National Geographic Society; 193 Collection of the New-York Historical Society; 194 (bl) Architect of the Capitol; 194 (br) The Granger Collection; 195 The Granger Collection; 196 (t) Burstein Collection/Corbis; 196 (b) Old State House, Hartford, CT; 198 (t) © Shelbourne Museum, Shelbourne, Vermont; 198 (c) Fruitlands Museums; 198-199 (b) Phil Schermeister/Corbis; 199 (t) Smithsonian Institution, Domestic Life Division, Neg. #LIA-83-30016-9; 200 Smithsonian; 201 Kendall Whaling Museum; 202 (t) Peabody Essex Museum, Salem, MA. Photo by Mark Sexton; 203 Claire White-Peterson Photo/Mystic Seaport, Mystic, CT; 204 Photo Courtesy of Marblehead Historical Society, Marblehead, MA; 208-209 H. Mark Weidman; 210-211 (b) Museum of the City of New York; 212 Hulton Archive; 213 (tl) Haverford College Library Quaker Collection; 213 (tr) The Newark Museum/Art Resource, NY; 214 Francis G. Mayer/Corbis; 215 Mary Steinbacher/PhotoEdit; 216 (t) American tract Society; 216 (b) Library of Congress; 217 (tl) Library of Congress; 217 (tc) Princeton University, gift of the Reverend R.J. Nevin, in 1904; 217 (bc) Princeton University. Presented in 1860 by the great grandsons of President Edwards: Photo Credit: Bruce M. White; 217 (br) Library of Congress; 218 (b) Independence National Historical Park; 219 (bl) Historical Society of Pennsylvania; 220 (tl) Stock Montage; 220 (inset) The Provost and Fellows of Worcester College Oxford; 220 (inset) The Provost and Fellows of Worcester College Oxford; 221 (r) Courtesy Henry Francis du Pont Winterthur Museum, Joseph Downs Manuscript Collection, NO. 62 x 33; 221 (inset) CIGNA Museum and Art Collection; 222 (t) Gettysburg College; 222 (inset) Bettmann/Corbis; 224 Jeff Greenberg/Photo

Researchers; 230-231 Tyler Campbell/Mira; 232 Bettmann/Corbis; 233 (t) Courtesy of Historic St. Marys City; 234 Maryland State Archives; 235 (b) North Wind Picture Archives; 235 (inset) PhotoEdit; 236 (t) Alan & Linda Detrick/Photo Researchers; 237 (t) Hulton Archive; 237 (b) Archives and History Center of the United Methodist Church, Madison, New Jersey; 239 Scott Barrow; 240 Gift of Mrs. Robert Bogle/Maryland Historical Society; 241 (bl) Collection of Tender Buttons/BlackStar; 241 (bc) Collection of Tender Buttons/Black Star; 241 (br) Historical Society of Pennsylvania; 244 (tl) EX17082 Negro portrait: Olaudah Equiano by English School, (18th Century) Royal Albert Memorial Museum, Exeter/Bridgeman Art Library, London; 244 (inset) Crandall Shifflett; 245 Peabody Essex Museum; 246 (b) Lee Snider/Corbis; 247 (c) PhotoEdit; 247 (b) John Mead/Science Photo Library/Photo Researchers; 248-249 (b) Colonial Williamsburg Foundation; 250 (b) Dorothy Mills (English), George II sauce-boat, 1748, Silver, 4 3/4 x 5 1/4 x 3 7/8 in., The National Museum of Women in the Arts, Silver collection assembled by Nancy Valentine, purchased with funds; 250-251 (t) Maryland Historical Society; 254-255 (bg) Colonial Williamsburg Foundation; 254-255 (c) Dave G. Houser/Houserstock; 254 (b) Mary Ann Hemphill; 255 (c) David Hiser/PictureQuest; 255 (cr) Colonial Williamsburg; 255 (bl) Mary Ann Hemphill.

**UNIT 4**
**UNIT OPENER;** (fg) Lester Lefkowitz/Corbis Stock Market; (bg) John McGrail Photography; 259 (t) Lester Lefkowitz/Corbis Stock Market; 259 (l) John McGrail Photography; 266-267 Joanne Pearson/Fair Haven Photographs; 268-269 Larry Olsen Photography; 270 (t) Washington-Custis-Lee Collection, Washington and Lee University, Lexington, Va.; 270 (b) Historical Society of Pennsylvania/Bridgeman Art Library International, Ltd., The; 271 (b) The Granger Collection, New York; 272 (tl) State Historical Society of Wisconsin Museum Collections; 272 (tr) The Granger Collection; 273 (b) Phil E. Degginger/Mira; 273 (inset) Hulton/Archive; 275 (bl) Hulton Archive/Getty Images; 275 (inset) Fort Wayne Historical; 276 Hulton/Archive; 277 George Caleb Bingham, Daniel Boone Escorting Settlers Through The Cumberland Gap, 1851-52, detail. Oil on canvas, 35 1/2 x 50 1/4. Washington University Gallery of Art, St. Louis; 280 (bl) Bettmann Archive/Corbis; 280 (bc) Collection of the Boston Athenaeum; 280 (br) Larry Stevens/Nawrocki Stock Photo, Inc. All Rights Reserved; 281 (bl) Smithsonian Institution; 281 (b) Massachusetts Historical Society; 282 (t) Colonial Williamsburg Foundation; 282 (b) The Metropolitan Museum of Art, Bequest of Charles Allen Munn, 1924; 284 (b) Courtesy of the Massachusetts Historical Society; 285 (tr) The Granger Collection, New York; 285 (inset) Stock Montage; 286 The Granger Collection; 287 Hulton/Archive; 288 Bettmann/Archive/Corbis; 289 (t) Deposited by the City of Boston. Courtesy of The Museum of Fine Arts, Boston; 289 (bc) American Antiquarian Society; 290 (c) NYPL; 290 (b) The Carnegie Institute/Bridgeman Art Library International, Ltd.; 291 (t) Concord Museum, Concord MA; 291 (b) Stanley L. Rowin/Mira; 292 (tl) Eliot Cohen/Janelco Photographers; 293 (b) Yale University Art Gallery, Gift of the Associates in Fine Arts and Mrs. Henry B. Loomis in Memory of Henry B. Loomis, B.A. 1875.; 296 (t) Courtesy

of the Massachusetts Historical Society; 297 (c) Peabody Essex Museum, Salem, MA. Photo by Mark Sexton; 297 (tr) Jamestown-Yorktown Foundation; 300-301 Morristown National Park; 302 (bc) Hulton/Archive; 302 The Granger Collection; 303 (b) Smithsonian Institution; 303 (tr) Independence National Historical Park; 305 Francis G. Mayer/Corbis; 306 (br) Lee Snider Photo Images; 306 (bkgd) Scott Barrow; 307 Historical Society of Pennsylvania; 308 (bl) Courtesy of the Massachusetts Historical Society; 309 (br) Martin Art Gallery, Muhlenberg College, Allentown, Pennsylvania; 310 (b) Valentine Museum, Richmond History Center; 310 (inset) Tracey W. McGregor Library/University of Virginia; 311 (tl) Bequest of Winslow Warren/Courtesy, Museum of Fine Arts, Boston; 311 (tr) Bettmann/Corbis; 311 (tlc) Detroit Publishing Co. Photograph Collection/Library of Congress; 311 (trc) Richard Walker/New York Historical Association, Cooperstown; 312 Independence National Historical Park; 314 (br) Eliot Cohen/Janelco Photographers; 314 (bl) Russ Finley; 315 (t) Fort Ticonderoga Museum; 315 (bl) Russ Finley; 315 (inset) The Granger Collection; 316 (t) The Valley Forge Historical Society; 317 (t) Bettmann/Corbis; 317 (b) Jewish-American Hall of Fame; 318 (b) Bettmann/Corbis; 318 (tl) Hulton/Archive Photos; 318 (tc) Hulton/Archive Photos; 318 (tr) Independence National Historical Park Collection; 319 Edifice/Corbis; 320-321 American Museum of American History/Smithsonian Institution. Trans. no. 76-3259; 322 (b) David Muench Photography; 325 (br) Roy Andersen/National Geographic Society; 326 (b) Yorktown Victory Center; 326 (t) a detail, John Trumbull "The Surrender of Lord Cornwallis at Yorktown, 19 October 1781", Yale University Art Gallery, Trumbull Collection; 327 (b) Courtesy, Winterthur Museum; 328 (t) Hulton/Archive Photos; 330 (b) Royal Geographical Society, London/The Bridgeman Art Library International; 330 (inset) American Antiquarian Society; 334 (t) Peter Southwick/Stock, Boston; 334 (bc) Michael Dwyer/Stock Boston; 334 (bg) Gibson Stock Photography; 335 (br) Danilo G. Donadoni/Bruce Coleman; 335 (tr) Tibor Bognar/Corbis Stock Market; 335 (tc) Susan Cole Kelly; 335 (cl) Dave G. Houser/Corbis; 335 (tl) Ed Young/Corbis; 335 (bl) Richard Cummins/Corbis; 335 ( cr) Dave G. Houser/Corbis.

## UNIT 5
UNIT OPENER; (fg) Independence National Historical Park; (bg) Independence National Historical Park; 339 (t) Independence National Historical Park; (l) Independence National Historical Park; 344-345 Johnathan Wallen Photography; 346 Roman Soumar/Corbis; 347 (tc) From the Robert H. Gore Jr. Numismatic Collection; 347 (tr) American Antiquarian Society; 348 (bl) The Granger Collection; 348 (br) The New-York Historical Society; 350 Library of Congress; 351 (bl) The Granger Collection; 351 (br) The Granger Collection; 352 Bettmann/Corbis; 355 (tl) The Library of Virginia; 355 (tc) Ralph Earl Roger Sherman (1721-1793) M. G. (Hon.) 1786 Yale University Art Gallery/Gift of Roger Sherman White, BA. 1899, L. L. B. 1902; 355 (tr) Princeton University; 356 Emmet Collection, Rare Books and Manuscripts Division, The New York Public Library, Astor, Lennox, and Tilden Foundations; 357 (t) 'Residences and Slave Quarters of Mulbery

Plantation' by Thomas Coram, The Gibbes Museum of Art, Charleston, SC; 358 (b) Joseph Sohm/Stock, Boston/PictureQuest; 358 (inset) Northwind Picture Archives; 359 O and J Heaton/Stock, Boston; 360 (b) Dave G. Houser/Houserstock, Inc.; 361 Lee Snider Photo Images; 362 (bl) Dennis Brack/Black Star Publishing/PictureQuest; 362 (br) Richard W. Strauss/Smithsonian Institute/Supreme Court Historical Society; 363 Independence National Historical Park, Phil; 365 (l) James Foote/Photo Researchers; 365 (cr) James Foote/Photo Researchers; 366 Independence National Historical Park; 367 Virginia Museum of Fine Arts, Richmond. Gift of Edgar William and Bernice Chrysler Garbisich. Photo: Ron Jennings@Virginia Museum of Fine Arts.; 368 (bl) New York Historical/The Bridgeman Art Library International; 368 (br) Colonial Williamsburg Foundation; 370 National Archives and Records Administration; 371 (c) Culver Pictures; 371 (bl) Franklin Institute; 371 (br) The Granger Collection, New York; 372 Dover Publications; 373 (b) Courtesy, Winterthur Museum; 374 (b) LM Cooks Salute to General Washington in NY Harbor, Gift of Edgar Williams & Bernice Chrysler Garbisch Board of Trustees/National Gallery of Art, Washington; 374 (inset) Museum of the City of New York, Bequest of Mrs. J. Insley Blair in Memory of Mr. and Mrs. J. Insley Blair; 375 Courtesy of the John Carter Brown Library at Brown University; 376 (b) Maryland Historical Society; 378 White House Historical Assoc.; 379 The New-York Historical Society; 382-383 David Muench Photography; 384 C. Jean/Reunion des Musees Nationaux/Art Resource, NY; 386 (t) National Park Service; 386-387 (b) Amon Carter Museum; 386 (bl) Courtesy Independence National Historical Park; 387 (br) Courtesy Independence National Historical Park; 389 Bettmann/Corbis; 390 Bettmann/Corbis; 392 (t) Library of Congress; 392 (b) Collection of the New York Historical Society; 393 (br) Corbis; 394 Bettmann/Corbis; 395 (b) Burstein Collection/Corbis; 395 (inset) Lawrence County Historical Society; 396 (t) The Granger Collection, NY; 396 (b) Library of Congress; 397 Collection of The New York Historical Society; 399 Troy Anderson; 400 (bl) National Portrait Gallery/Smithsonian Institution/Art Resource, NY; 400 (br) Academy of Natural Sciences of Philadelphia/Corbis; 401 (t) Academy of Natural Sciences of Philadelphia/Corbis; 401 (c) North Carolina Museum; 401 (br) Academy of Natural Sciences of Philadelphia/Corbis; 401 (cl) Academy of Natural Sciences of Philadelphia/Corbis, Inc.; 402 The State Preservation Board, Austin Texas; 403 (b) Friends of the Governor's Mansion, Austin, Texas; 404 H. K. Barnett/Star of the Republic Museum, Jefferson, Texas; 405 (t) The Saint Louis Art Museum; 405 Whitman Mission National Historic Society; 406 Bettmann/Corbis; 407 The Granger Collection; 408 Smithsonian American Art Museum, Washington DC/Art Resource, NY; 409 Gill C. Kenny/The Image Bank; 410 National Archives; 412 Russ Poole Photography; 414 (t) Cooper Hewitt Museum; 414 B & O Railroad Museum; 418 (tl) Art Resource, NY; 418 (bl) Bettmann/Corbis; 419 (tr) Courtesy of the John Deere Company; 419 (inset) John Deere.

## UNIT 6
UNIT OPENER; (fg) Smithsonian Institution; (bg) Peter Gridley/FPG International; 427 (t) Smithsonian Institution; (l) Peter Gridley/FPG International; 430 All for the Union; 434-435

David Muench Photography; 436 The American Clock and Watch Museum; 437 Stock Montage/Hulton Archive/Getty Images; 438 Bettmann/Corbis; 441 Missouri Historical Society; 442 (bl) Courtesy of the South Carolina Library; 442 (br) Courtesy of the South Carolina Library; 443 (br) Hulton-Deutsch Collection/Corbis; 443 (br) Bettmann/Corbis; 444 (br) Scala/Art Resource, NY; 444 (cl) The Charleston Museum; 446 Library of Congress; 447 (t) Hulton/Archive Photos; 447 (b) National Museum of American Art, Washington DC/Art Resource, NY; 448 (bl) National Portrait Gallery, Smithsonian Institution/Art Resource, NY; 448 (inset) Book cover slide of "Uncle Tom's Cabin" by Harriet Beecher Stowe. Courtesy of the Charles L. Blockson Afro-American Collection, Temple University; 449 (t) National Portrait Gallery, Smithsonian Institution/Art Resource, NY; 450 (b) Morton Beebe, S.F./Corbis; 451 Courtesy of the Illinois State Historical Library; 452 (bl) National Portrait Gallery, Smithsonian Institution/Art Resource, NY; 452 (bc) Corbis; 453 (t) National Portrait Gallery, Smithsonian Institution/Art Resource, NY; 453 (b) The Granger Collection; 458 (b) Brown Military Collection, Brown University; 458 (bl) National Portrait Gallery, Smithsonian Institution/Art Resource, NY; 460 James P. Rowan Photography; 461 Library of Congress; 462 (t) National Portrait Gallery; 462 (b) Library of Congress; 463 (b) Bettmann/Corbis; 464 Chicago Historical Society; 465 (bc) Salamander Books; 465 (br) National Portrait Gallery, Smithsonian Institution, Washington, D.C.; 466 (t) Courtesy of General Dynamics Corp., Electric Boat Div.; 466 (cl) Richmond, Virginia/Katherine Wetzel; 467 (b) New Hampshire Historical Society; 469 (b) Tom Lovell©National Geographic; 471 Tom Prettyman/PhotoEdit/PictureQuest; 476 (bl) Corbis; 476 (bc) Library of Congress; 477 (t) Hulton Archive/Getty Images; 477 (inset) Library of Congress; 478 Corbis; 479 (c) Library of Congress; 479 (tl) The Granger Collection, New York; 480 (tl) American Treasures of the Library of Congress; 480 (tr) Library of Congress; 481 (bl) Corbis; 481 (br) Southern Historical Collection; 482 (br) Bob Daemmrich Photography; 482 (cl) Bob Daemmrich Photography; 483 (t) The Metropolitan Museum of Art, Morris K. Jessup Fund; 483 (inset) Smithsonian Institution, Division of Agriculture; 484 (t) Hulton/Archive/Getty Images; 484 (b) Smithsonian Institute; 485 The Granger Collection; 486 (inset) The Bancroft Library; 486-487 Joseph Sohm/Visions of America/PictureQuest; 488 (b) Jeff Greenberg/PhotoEdit; 488 (tc) William Manns Photo/Zon International Publishing; 489 Solomon D. Butcher Collection, Nebraska State Historical Society; 490 Corbis; 491 Corbis; 492 Michael Forsberg; 496 Corbis; 497 Corbis; 499 From the Collections of Henry Ford Museum & Greenfield Village; 500 (t) Transfer from the National Museum of American Art; Gift of Dr. Eleanor A. Campbell to the Smithsonian Institution, 1942.; 500 (bl) Henry Ford Museum & Greenfield Village; 500 (br) History of Technology Division, National Museum of American History, photographed by John Tsantes/Smithsonian Institution; 501 (t) Henry Ford Museum & Greenfield Village; 501 (c) Science Museum, London, UK/The Bridgeman Art Library International; 501 (br) Alfred Harrell/Smithsonian Institution; 502 (inset) "By Courtesy of the Statue of Liberty National Monument"; 503 (tl) Corbis; 504-505 (b) Corbis;